W9-AVE-580

theatre

a history of the art

THEATRE

A HISTORY OF THE ART

JERRY V. PICKERING
CALIFORNIA STATE UNIVERSITY, FULLERTON

WEST PUBLISHING COMPANY
ST. PAUL NEW YORK LOS ANGELES SAN FRANCISCO

50 West Kellogg Boulevard
P.O. Box 3526
St. Paul, Minnesota 55165

Printed in the United States of America

Library of Congress Cataloging in Publication Data

Pickering, Jerry V., 1931-
Theatre : a history of the art.

Includes index.
1. Drama—History and criticism. 2. Theatre—History. I. Title.
PN1721.P5 792'.09 77-28058
ISBN 0-8299-0200-7

Preface

When I began this book, nearly five years ago, I had hopes of doing something totally original—that is, treating theatre not in terms of concepts and things but rather by concentrating on those great theatricians who themselves created the concepts and things. It was to be a book about theatre by way of its great critics, philosophers, and practitioners. However, during a long series of reviews by many of my coworkers in the fields of theatre criticism, history, and literature, it became apparent that such an approach was not entirely satisfactory. It tended to cause spotty coverage of the field, leaving out the gradual development that was the result of more minor contributions by many dedicated theatre people whose names have been lost in time. Also, because theatre is so much a reflection of its age, a need was perceived to place theatre in the social-economic-political milieu of the major periods in history. Thus, this final work has become a combination that attempts a general, overall view of theatre history, within the context of the times, while still maintaining an emphasis on the great creative geniuses who so much influenced the course that theatre would follow.

No book on a subject so vast can be the work of only one person; numerous teachers, colleagues, and students have, along the way, contributed greatly. There are far too many of these people to credit them individually, but I would like at this point to acknowledge several major contributors. For their comments and suggestions on the original proposal I would like to thank Professors Robert K. Sarlos and Robert A. Fahrner, both of the University of California, Davis. For reading and commenting on the first manuscript of the book I would like to thank Professors Paul S. Hostetler, University of Washington; Michael McPherson, California State University, Fullerton; Jon Mezz, University of North Carolina at Chapel Hill; Carl R. Mueller, University of California, Los Angeles; Robert Rence, California State University, Fullerton; and Sanford Sternlicht, State University of New York at Oswego. For their comments and suggestions on both the original manuscript and its revision I especially wish to thank Professors John W. Brokaw, University of Texas, Austin; and Alan Stambusky, University of California, Davis.

California State University, Fullerton, must be acknowledged for allowing me a sabbatical leave to do much of the writing. Associate Dean Donald R. Henry, California State University, Fullerton, School of the Arts, graciously opened up to me his extensive theatrical library. Jane Dibbell, graduate student in Theatre Arts, was kind enough to provide me with some fine material on the Irish Theatre Movement.

Finally, I would like to thank Mrs. Gladys Stetler for her faithful support of so many projects over the years; my wife, Eve, whose work on every aspect of the manuscript was invaluable and whose support and encouragement were often badly needed and always generously given; and last and most importantly my brother George, to whose memory this book is lovingly dedicated.

Contents

1

The Beginnings—Myth, Ritual, Magic

1

The Beginnings—Myth, Ritual, Magic

Theatricality—the urge to mimic, the need to act out some aspect of life and the concomitant belief that this acting out in some mysterious way affects the natural world—has been with humanity from its earliest beginnings. When the first primitive tribesman mimed before his fellows some important aspect of daily life such as the hunt, a conflict with a neighboring tribe, the coming of summer, or the end of winter death, it was certainly theatrical in the sense that it was done in dramatic terms. However, it was not theatre as we regularly define it. Even after several participants had joined in the dramatic action, and after that action had been carefully determined in advance, it remained dramatic in essence but still was more of a rite or ritual than it was theatre. *Theatre*, as we use the term, is a sophisticated art form that requires two or more performers, acting and reacting, using their voices and bodies in planned sequences of oral and physical action, in a setting that is to varying degrees predetermined, acting out *before an audience* some aspect of life.

The primary difference between these early dramatic activities and theatre as we know and define it seems largely to be a matter of intent. For primitive man dramatic activities were always purposeful. That is, they existed to accomplish some specific end result. The result might vary from communicating an idea or emotion too complex for a primitive vocabulary to encompass to creating sympathetic magic urging the growth of crops or herds, demonstrating the myths that composed the history and science of the tribe, or fulfilling the conditions of religious ritual. Theatrical activity extended the learning process. Anyone who has ever watched a developing child learn through imitating, by undertaking what are essentially a series of dramatic roles—playing mother or father, for example—has witnessed this process. Such activity may take place before an audience, but it does not require a human audience as a condition of performance, as does theatre. In fact, many primitive dramatic ceremonies were specifically performed by initiates in the ceremony, without a human audience, under the watchful eye of a tutelary god who, it was believed, would react well or badly depending on the skills of the actors performing the ritual—on how faithfully they recited the sacred words and how accurately they performed the traditional movements.

In *The Golden Bough* (2 vols. 1890, expanded to 12 vols. 1911-15), Sir James George Frazer advanced the concept that much of this primitive dramatic activity was designed to produce sympathetic magic, under the assumption that like produces like. That is, if water is ritually poured over the body of an actor representing by way of his leafy costume the growing crops, this mimetic action will create a magic causing the rain to fall. Such a belief operates on the assumption that what is done mimetically will somehow set up a sympathetic response in the natural order, and this response will cause the desired things to actually come about. Theodor H. Gaster, in the introduction to his own abridgement of Frazer's work, warned against accepting this idea as a true primitive belief. To Gaster the rituals that Frazer cites were probably dramatized prayer and not a form of magical procedure. Thus, in such dramatic presentations the performers were merely showing the gods or spirits what they wanted done. What Gaster misses is that for primitive man there was very little if any substantive difference between prayer and magical incantation. Magic existed through the aid or connivance of the gods or spirits, and thus magic and prayer were both remarkably similar methods of changing in some way the physical or spiritual order of the real world through supernatural intervention, and both were made clear to the gods through dramatic activity.

For the primitive tribe the making of sympathetic magic or the dramatizing of prayers through dramatic rite or ritual was purposeful in that it was always designed to promote something in the physical world surrounding them.

Sketch of an old Stone Age cave painting from southern France, showing the primitive dancer dressed in animal costume. In this case the animal is a stag and the performer is likely costumed for a hunting dance.

Thus, the dramatic activity that aided in making this magic or transmitting these prayers incorporated in itself the body of tribal wisdom and was, in fact, the most fundamental of sciences in that through it the environment could, primitive man hoped, be controlled. That is, the necessary rain could be induced to fall on the crops, the winds could be prevented from blowing excessively, storms at sea could be abated so that they would not endanger the fishermen, the hunt could be assured of success, and victory over an enemy could be guaranteed. If the dramatic action was performed properly it either created magic or induced the gods to make these things happen.

GATHERING FOOD AND CELEBRATING THE HARVEST

For the primitive tribe the most immediate physical necessity was assuring the food supply. Therefore, most of the early rituals which we have been able to collect in late, degenerate forms, or learn from more contemporary primitive tribes, were in some way related to the food-gathering process. They were designed to impell the herds to thrive and bear, or to urge the changing of the seasons from winter death to summer fruitfulness. Most such rituals were primarily related to vegetation and the growth of crops. Thus, they were mostly spring ceremonies, beginning at that point in the seasons when the ground was ready for initial plowing and continuing through the planting and sprouting of the seed. The May Day celebrations that still take place in parts of western Europe and America are the residue of such spring ceremonies.

And just as it was necessary to produce magic or in some way induce the gods to make the crops grow, so was it necessary to thank these same gods for their aid. Therefore, the autumn also had its share of dramatic ceremonies, usually featuring some characterization such as the Straw Bear, dressed in the residue of the harvest, who mimed gratitude to the gods for a successful harvest and invoked their aid during the coming winter. The shards of these dramatic ceremonies still exist in such autumn festivals as the Oktoberfesten, which can be found all over Europe and in those parts of America that carry on old-country traditions.

DANCE AND MUSIC

In most cases the earliest of these dramatic activities combined words, music, and dance, with the dance aspect having primacy. Thus, these performances were called dances even when the words seemingly made the point of the performance. Some scholars suspect that the words which accompanied these rituals were, in fact, late additions to what were originally nonverbal dance-dramas. Examples of these early rituals can be seen in the surviving dances of tribes that are (or were in the recent past) still close in time to their period of hunting and simple agriculture—for example, the Buffalo Dance of the Mandan Indians of the American Great Plains. Other such dances, either because of their spectacle or innate appeal to the ceremonial instinct that seems to be part of human nature, have managed to survive even into this cen-

The Buffalo Dance of the Mandan Indians, in this painting by Charles Bodmer, was performed to assure a successful hunt.

tury as pleasurable though no longer meaningful remnants of the past. Such ceremonies as the Abbot's Bromley Horn Dance (an English hunting dance-drama) or the Sword Dance (a battle dance with variants that can be found all over Europe) can occasionally be seen in performances that still reflect some part of their primitive origins.

The music that accompanied these dances is quite difficult to determine. In their earliest manifestations the dances probably received only rhythmic accompaniment beaten out on a hollow log or skin drum. At a later time instruments were added, with bagpipes becoming standard for the Sword Dances and flute or pipe (plus drum) becoming popular for most other dances. In the beginning the music that accompanied these events was probably as rigidly standardized as the words and movements, but as the potential for musical instrumentation increased, a variety of folk melodies were fitted to the dance patterns.

COSTUMES

Costume was one of the most important aspects of these primitive dramatic rituals. Masks, or occasionally some special form of facial makeup, were the dominant aspect of this costuming. In a sense the masks served three functions. First, they allowed the performer to take on in a clear, recognizable way the specific identity of the character or creature he was impersonating. Second, they aided the performer in actually becoming that character or creature. In costume the actor could be possessed by the spirit of that which he represented. Third, the mask disguised the performer so that he was no longer a recognizable member of the tribe and could act out with impunity any aspect of tribal life.

The styles and materials of the masks varied greatly, from the absolutely realistic to stylized representations. In the hunting dances those performers taking the part of the hunted beasts often wore the actual head of their specific animal. When the animal-head mask was not used, or in dances other than the hunting dance, the performers used such materials as animal teeth, skins, feathers, antlers, and paint to create masks resembling the creatures they mimed.

And costume was not restricted to the mask or headdress. Usually some form of dramatic adornment covered the entire body. Again, for the hunting dance the skins of the animals being portrayed were the most common costume, usually worn along with some highly decorative elements that operated to raise the characterization above the level of reality to ritual. Brightly colored cloth, beads, feathers, paint, and freshly picked greenery all were used to costume the performers.

PLAYING AREAS, SETTINGS, PROPS

In their earliest manifestations these dance-dramas almost certainly had no special playing areas. The nomadic aspect of most tribal life, and the occasional nature of such productions, would effectively preclude a formalized playing space. Thus, the area could vary from the ceremonial open space usually found at the center of the camp to the bank of the nearest lake or stream for a ritual invoking rain. However, as the rituals took on ever greater significance in terms of tribal well-being, it is likely that certain specific areas within or close to the camp area were set aside and consecrated to dramatic-religious use. These areas were probably circular in shape, except when bounded by a lake or stream, for this is the natural way in which people group themselves to watch an event. Also, most of the dance-dramas that have survived are the round dances common to primitive tribes rather than the processional dances that tend to develop in more sophisticated societies. Therefore, the form of the playing area would likely have developed to fit the shape of the performance.

Eventually, as certain of the tribes deserted their nomadic ways for agriculture, and as they developed societies that went far beyond a state that could accurately be described as primitive, more permanent playing areas were developed. The Aztecs were one of the first groups to build permanent

Vegetation ceremonies were common to most primitive tribes. In this Hopi corn drama (*The Great Serpent Play*) the puppet snakes symbolize floods and try to destroy the corn crop. Ultimately the snakes are defeated in their design. (From Charles Bodmer's 1832-34 *Atlas*)

theatres, but many peoples used the architecture of their existing buildings to present their dance-dramas. In some cases temporary scene buildings were erected; in others the land was graded so that it encompassed and enhanced the theatrical event. This well may have been the case in Cornwall, where some scholars have indicated that early dramas were performed in a dish-shaped playing area surrounded by a moat.

In addition to specific playing areas, limited scenic effects were introduced. For the vegetation ceremonies fresh-cut trees were often brought to the playing areas, eventually developing into the Maypoles of a later period. Fire pits were common features of such settings, as fire was necessary to so many purification ceremonies. Many other objects such as rocks (menhirs), various types of vegetation (such as constalks or wheat) in addition to the trees, carved animal representations, totem poles, and even paintings (on sand or wood or cloth) became common parts of these settings.

Props, although used in most such dramas, were rarely entrusted to "prop men" but were either the personal possession of the performer or (if especially consecrated) the shaman. Such objects as the bow and arrow of the hunting dance, the spear or sword of the battle dance, and the many sacred talismans of those dances designed to control nature were all common to the dance-drama.

RITUAL TO DRAMA

Exactly what the condition (or more probably combination of conditions) is that allowed or provoked the leap from ritual to drama is unknown. Some of these early rituals did go on to become legitimate folk drama, with their ritual significance lost in the remote past. Other equally dramatic rituals quietly died out at an early period. A number of suggestions may be advanced as to why rituals in some geographic areas made the leap to drama and rituals in other geographic areas failed to do so.

Tribal well-being certainly played a large part in dramatic development. As long as a tribe remained poor and nomadic, following the seasons and the animal migrations for their food supply, ritual remained important and true drama was too cumbersome and ephemeral to demand even minimal consideration. However, when a tribe attained some security—when the nomadic period ended and crops were planted and harvested, when animals were raised rather than hunted, and when permanent dwellings replaced temporary shelters—the drama achieved one of the conditions necessary for its development.

Nationalism, seemingly an outgrowth of tribal well-being, has seemed to play a significant role in drama. In later times the great periods of drama—for example, fifth century Athens, Golden Age Spain, Elizabethan England, and seventeenth century France—all were periods of strong nationalistic sentiment. That is, the people of these cultures were proud of their civilization and institutions and wanted to see them reflected in the arts.

A lessening of religious controls also seems to have been a necessity for the development of secular drama. The ritual that caused desired things to happen was sacred and could not be tampered with or its virtue would be destroyed. However, once tribal security was achieved and religious control relaxed, the dramatic elements inherent in the sacred ritual could be applied to the secular art of drama.

The presence of one or more great creative artists also seems to have been a necessity in the development of drama. The ritual provided the elemental form and some of the techniques, but it remained for the great artists to shape these materials into something that goes beyond religious ritual—that becomes, in fact, drama in its truest sense.

Ancient Egyptian Drama

The Egyptians quite early developed a highly sophisticated civilization, far in advance of the Greek or any other society in the Western world. However, the dramatic activities that took place in this early civilization (the advanced Egyptian Old Kingdom that produced the pyramids dates from about 2980 B.C.) seem not to have kept up with other aspects of Egyptian society, never developing much beyond mortuary and fertility rituals.

Most of the surviving Egyptian plays are contained in the fifty-five Pyramid Texts, which date from the beginning of the Old Kingdom. These texts, written on the walls of *mastabas* (a special form of Egyptian tomb with sloping walls and a flat roof), tombs, and of course pyramids, all concentrate in some way on the process of passing successfully from this life to the next. Apparently these texts were designed to help the deceased achieve the transition, and they did this by fulfilling two separate functions—pointing out the proper process which must be followed to gain admittance to the afterlife and becoming, in their production, an important part of the process they described. Whether these texts were, in fact, dramas or merely recordings of appropriate myths has long been debated. However, their inclusion of dialogue and what seem clearly to be stage directions has swung the balance of opinion to the belief that these were indeed plays and, importantly, plays that were actually produced.

A photo of a Ptolemaic relief depicting what seems to be a play about Horus and his revenge upon Set, brother and murderer of Osiris. The play was probably written and staged by Imhotep, vizier of King Zoser, about 2980 B.C.

In terms of dramatic rituals other than the mortuary dramas, two examples of what seem to be annual fertility rites are of great importance. The first, at least as far as chronological order is concerned, is probably the *Mephite Play*, which dates from approximately 2500 B.C. This play resembles the spring rites that would later be found all over northern Europe, and very likely was performed each year at a similar date in the spring. It tells the traditional story of the death and resurrection of Osiris and the resulting coronation of Horus.

The second ritual fertility drama, and easily the most important in terms of popularity, size, and complexity, is the *Abydos Passion Play*. Again the subject matter is the death of Osiris at the hands of his brother Set, who dismembers his victim, burying parts of Osiris all over Egypt in an attempt to prevent his powerful brother's resurrection. This seasonal death and dismemberment is remarkably like the death that is later undergone by the Greek god Dionysus—who has been referred to as a later Greek version of Osiris—and the probable relationship of both these gods to the drama of their time is strikingly similar. The play relates how Isis, the sister-wife of Osiris, recovered the pieces and put them back together, thus allowing the dead god passage to the underworld. Isis' son, Horus, then goes on to contend with Set and wins back the kingdom of his father, Osiris.

This myth is certainly very old, and the play may date from as early a period as the *Mephite Play*. However, its length and complexity would seem to indicate a somewhat later dramatic origin. Unfortunately, no part of the text of this important work has survived, and what we know of it comes primarily from an account by Ikhernofret (I-kher-nefert) who at some time between 1887 B.C. and 1849 B.C. was commissioned to produce the play and act the leading role. He then wrote down what he did and observed. Ikhernofret's account is backed up by some wall illustrations and inscriptions, but it is difficult to tell whether these are depictions of the play in production or artistic interpretations of the myth alone. It must also be pointed out that according to some scholars the dramatization of the myth is seen less as a traditional spring fertility rite than as a sophisticated mortuary drama that portrays the current pharaoh and all past pharaohs as resurrected in the character of Osiris.

The civilization achieved by Egypt remains one of the early wonders of the world, not only for its sophistication and its complex system of government, but also because of its ability to sustain itself—it lasted nearly three thousand years. The fact that it failed to produce a large body of significant drama during this extended period of time is both unfortunate and surprising, especially when one looks forward to the theatres of Classical Greece and the Medieval European societies that were as yet to develop. Egypt certainly achieved two of the four major considerations listed earlier as necessary for the development of ritual into drama. It was a great, secure nation and it was a highly nationalistic one, even demanding tribute from the less developed states surrounding it. Perhaps Egyptian theatre never fully developed because it remained sacred. Unlike the drama in ancient Greece and Medieval Europe, the Egyptian drama never went on to become profane. From beginning to end it remained a purposive part of the religious ceremonies, and when the Egyptian gods died out as meaningful deities, their drama died with them.

2

The Drama in Ancient Greece

2

The Drama in Ancient Greece

Classical Greek drama, unlike the Western drama of any other time or place, was one of the primary functions of the government—of the Athenian democracy. As such its form and function, its content, its rapid growth and equally rapid decline, were all part of and thus largely determined by the political-social complex to which it belonged. Other types or styles or modes of drama have grown up under a specific form of government or social condition, and have managed to survive the death of that government or social condition and even to flourish under subsequent social organizations. Not so the Classical Greek drama, which was unable to exist outside that social organism of which it was such an important and integral part.

THE AEGEAN WORLD

Surrounded by the shores of the Greek peninsula, Asia Minor, and southern Europe, and peppered with numerous islands many of which are too small even to show on an ordinary map, is the Aegean Sea. Behind the sea is the Greek peninsula and the Aegean Basin, with an irregular seacoast providing many ports and bays. This basin is surrounded by numerous short mountain ranges. Because the whole of this area is thus arbitrarily divided by such geographical features into small units of mountain, valley, and island, any centralization of government was impossible for the ancient peoples who inhabited this area. Social and political groupings tended to remain not only physically separate but autonomous. Therefore, with geographical expansion limited and population remaining relatively constant, each social system in the Greek city-states was soon developed to its own particular peak. In Athens, enriched by the materials from its own immediate past, which was still very much alive because of the city's extraordinarily swift development, and surrounded by states which the Athenians considered to be almost barbarous, the institution of democracy brought about a particular turn of mind. The Athenians had an abiding interest in exploring their own roots to determine exactly what had brought about their present circumstances.

In terms of the rest of western Europe, civilization came early to the Aegean area. The islands, especially Crete, were occupied by a reasonably sophisticated people who were not yet Greeks as we know them, but who may legitimately be referred to as Aegeans. They could make and work bronze, and they had mastered such crafts as pottery and the making of stone bowls and jars. They developed a system of phonetic writing and, as might be expected of the inhabitants of a number of small, autonomous communities living in close conjunction with each other, they had developed a high level of military skills, both offensive and defensive. Between 1600 and 1500 B.C. the city of Cnossus on the island of Crete became the dominant center of this island civilization, taking the lead in commerce and military might. However, its wealth soon attracted Egyptian attention. Subsequently Egypt asserted both political and military control over the island, and thus its period of glory was soon over.

The city of Mycenae, located on the Plain of Argos in southern Greece, succeeded Cnossus as the Aegean center of advanced civilization—along with the city of Troy on the coast of Asia Minor. By the year 1200 B.C., however, the influence of Mycenae and Troy had waned, primarily because of the influence of the Hittites. This large tribe, which dwelt in the heart of Asia Minor, in a series of migrations penetrated western Asia and moved into the Aegean world. They influenced the Aegeans in every aspect of life, from commerce to religion and architecture. Their scribes introduced and spread a system of rather awkward cuneiform or wedge-shaped writing, and their armies, well mounted on horses and in chariots, revolutionized military tactics, conquering a large portion of Asia Minor. The Hittite capital, the walled city of Khatti, became a center of trade and learning, a position of prominence it held for nearly two hundred years.

While the Aegeans were interacting with each other and with the Egyptians and Hittites, the collection of pastoral, nomadic tribes that, together with the Aegean peoples would eventually become the Greeks, was beginning to move down from the grasslands of south-central Europe to the Greek peninsula. The first of these groups, the Achaeans, arrived about 2000 B.C. They were followed about five hundred years later by the Dorians, who conquered the Achaeans and the Aegeans, occupying the Greek peninsula, the islands including Crete, and the coast of Asia Minor. Sparta became their leading city. Meanwhile, the Ionians arrived to settle in the area north of Athens and the Aeolians arrived to settle the northern portion of the peninsula. The conquests of these tribes were made secure by two successive invasions of Asia Minor by the Armenians and Phrygians, who conquered the Hittites and thereby destroyed the only potential challenge to the rule of the northern conquerors.

The invaders retained their own language and most of their religious beliefs, but they did adopt some aspects of the civilization of their defeated foes, the Aegean peoples, with whom they eventually intermarried to produce the Greeks. The cuneiform writing introduced by the Hittites was soon lost, a fact that may be fortunate in that it cleared the way for the later, more practical writing style derived from the North Semitic peoples by way of the Phoenicians. At first the invaders clung to their tribal form of government based on the clan (families related by blood), with a number of clans making up a tribe. At the head of each tribe was a chief who held his position by virtue of his victories in war. The chief was aided in his tasks by a Council of Warriors who advised on military matters and a Council of Elders who advised on the day-to-day problems inherent in governing the tribe. Influenced by the civilization of the Aegeans, the northerners began crowning their chiefs as kings and gave up their nomadic ways, settling down to agriculture and seagoing. Eventually the Greeks, this new combination of northern nomad and Aegean, developed substantial cities and initiated the city-state form of government.

THE BEGINNINGS OF CLASSICAL TRAGEDY

The origins of Classical tragedy are lost in Greek prehistory. What we know certainly tends to come fairly late in the development of the form, and is based primarily on civic records after the state embraced the art of tragic drama as part of its political-social responsibility. Thus, our earliest mention of tragedy comes in 534 B.C. when the state established a prize to be awarded to the best tragedy presented at the City Dionysia. However, in spite of this late mention, a reasonably formalized drama, although primitive, must certainly have existed long before this date.

Currently there are two explanations for the development of the great Classical drama in ancient Greece. One is the traditional explanation, compounded out of Classical studies, anthropology, and religion, that sees the Greek drama as a continuing development, beginning with a primitive, ritualistic drama similar to those discussed in Chapter 1 and ending with the great works of Aeschylus, Sophocles, and Euripides. The second, more recent explanation, based primarily on the work of Professor Gerald F. Else, sees the

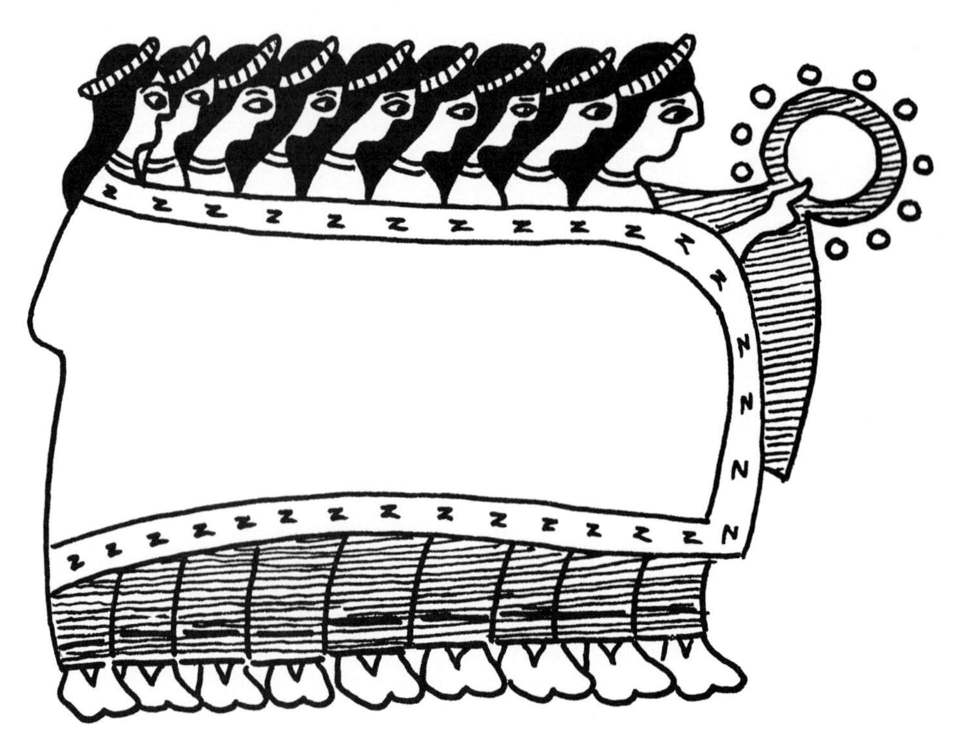

Female dancers from pre-Classical Greece. (Drawn from an early Attic vase.)

great Greek drama not as a matter of development, but as the result of successive "creative acts" by those two geniuses of the theatre, Thespis and Aeschylus. Because each of these theories is quite distinct, they must be examined separately.

The Developmental Theory of the Origin of Tragedy

One of the primary assumptions of the "developmental" theory of the origin of Greek tragedy is that the basic form grew out of the primitive drama that must have existed in Greece, with parallels all over western Europe and Asia. These little plays, discussed in Chapter 1, almost certainly were present in Greece long before the more sophisticated later works with which we are familiar. Surviving examples of such primitive folk dramas were observed in the Greek rural areas at the beginning of the twentieth century by two young Englishmen who were attending the British School at Athens. In the season between New Year's Day and May, while traveling through Thessaly and Macedonia, they saw performed numerous examples of "winter-summer-combat" plays—that is, plays designed to urge the fruitfulness of spring. In almost every case the plays featured a combat, a "death," and a resurrection. These features, in a fossilized form, seem to exist in the later, far more sophisticated myths, and in the dramas based on these myths.

Aristotle, and most critics and historians since his time, have called the dithyramb the forerunner of tragedy. Originally the dithyramb was a narrative Dorian lyric chanted by a chorus. In its earliest period the lyric was always in honor of Dionysus, but in later periods the form was adapted to do honor to other gods and heroes. The chorus of fifty men who chanted these dithyrambs was usually costumed in goatskins, after the sacred animal of the god, to represent the satyr companions of Dionysus. This probably accounts for the term *tragôedia*, translated by developmental theorists as "goat song," from which the word *tragedy* is thought to be derived. According to Herodotus, the Greek historian, Arion of Lesbos (c. 625-c. 585 B.C.) began the process of turning the dithyramb into tragic drama by inserting spoken lines into the lyrics. Thus, the leader of the chorus who spoke the lines became a solo performer who probably told the traditional stories of the god to lyric accompaniment. It is undoubtedly this semidramatic aspect of the post-Arion dithyramb, and the fact that Arion lived at Corinth on the Peloponnesian peninsula, home of the Dorian Greeks, that later led the Dorians to claim the honor of having invented tragedy. It is certainly the reason that many of the ancient writers did not consider Thespis of Attica (c. 550-c. 500 B.C.) to be the "father of tragedy."

Even if the ancient writers are correct in their comments on Arion, to consider him as the creator of drama is to disregard the fundamental requirement of drama—reaction. This, then, brings us to Thespis, who has long been regarded as the founding father of Classical tragedy. Little is known of Thespis' life, and even the major contributions to drama that have been credited to him have little historical evidence to back up such an attribution. In terms of legend he created the first actor (*hypokrites* or "answerer") who performed between the dances of the chorus, playing several roles and speaking at times

A contemporary scene from Sophocles' *Oedipus the King* at California State University, Sacramento. Directed by Gerard A. Larson.

with the leader of the chorus. That Thespis did perform in and even write plays seems reasonably certain. Horace, the Roman poet, wrote that Thespis traveled about the countryside on a wagon presenting his plays, four titles of which have come down to us: *Phorbas, The Priests, The Youths,* and *Pentheus.* Whether such legends regarding the part Thespis played in creating the tragic drama are true is impossible to prove. He certainly did, however, popularize the form, and for that we must always be in his debt.

Dionysus and the City Dionysia

The myths that comprised the Greek religion form a pathway from the tribal prehistoric period to the great Golden Age. Exactly when the first stories of the gods began we have no way of knowing, for those we have are not the ritualistic materials of the folk but the creation of the great poets. The earliest history of Greece is, in fact, the *Illiad*, and thus Greek mythology and history both begin with Homer, who probably lived no more than a thousand years before Christ. By this time the myths, passed on from generation to generation in an oral tradition of literature and history, had become the complex and often contradictory materials that we now possess, and their primary unifying quality, linking them with the past and with each other, was the residue of ritual.

Dionysus, as far as can be determined, was the last of the gods to enter Olympus. There are no early mentions of his story—Homer did not touch on him and Hesiod in the eighth or ninth century B.C. only mentions him briefly. In fact, a large part of what is known about Dionysus is contained in a late fourth or fifth century B.C. hymn and in the last play of Euripides (*The Bacchae*, c. 405 B.C.).

Dionysus, so the myth goes, was born in Thebes, the son of Zeus and the Theban princess Semele. Zeus, more in love with Semele than he had ever before been with a mortal woman, swore by the river Styx that he would do anything that she asked. Hera, Zeus' perpetually and justifiably jealous wife, then put into Semele's mind the wish to see Zeus in all his splendor as King of Heaven and Lord of the Thunderbolts. When Semele asked this of Zeus he knew that it would kill her, for no mortal could see him in this form and live, but he had sworn an oath by the Styx, which even the gods could not break. He appeared before her as she had requested and she died in the awful glory of his burning light. Semele was pregnant by him, and Zeus managed to save her unborn child, hiding it in his own side until it was ready to be born, at which time he gave the baby into the care of the nymphs in the wet, fertile valley of Nysa. Later, in gratitude, Zeus placed the numphs in the sky as stars, who bring rain when they are near the horizon. Thus, Dionysus, the god of the vine, was born in fire and nursed by water, like the fruit he represents which is born in the sun's blazing heat and nourished by the rain.

The full story of Dionysus' life has little to do with his position at the center of Classical tragedy, but certain aspects of his being must be understood in order to gain a full understanding of the art form devoted to him. On one hand Dionysus stood for total freedom and ecstatic joy, and on the other for madness resulting in savagery and bestiality. Both of these seemingly contradictory qualities grew out of the Greek understanding that the ultimate fruit of the vine is wine, which makes men happy and cheerful, but which also maddens them. This understanding is represented by the cult most associated with Dionysus, the Maenads (or Bacchantes). The Maenads were women who, in their worship, left the cities to return to nature for their religious observance, roaming the hills and woodlands amidst the growing things of their god. There Dionysus ministered to them, providing nuts and berries for their food, milk from the wild goat for their drink and, of course, the wine that was sacred to him. The

A fifth century B.C. cup painting showing a Maenad and a satyr.

wine provoked the other aspect of this woodland freedom and ecstacy. The Maenads, crazed with the wine of their tutelary god, raced through the woods uttering sharp cries, waving pinecone-tipped wands, tearing to bits the wild creatures (and by most accounts the men) they met along the way, and then devouring the bloody flesh. It is this dual nature of Dionysus that, in part, made him so perfect as the god for whom the tragedies were performed.

A second aspect of Dionysus that made him appropriate to theatre generally and to the tragic spirit particularly was the unique aspect of his situation as a dying and reviving god. Other, older gods had fulfilled this function of symbolically dying to represent the dead winter season and then undergoing revival to urge and explain the coming of summer, and certainly this was a major aspect of the folk plays that antedated Classical tragedy. Dionysus, however, unlike such gods as Demeter and Persephone, did not die comfortably. Like the vine that dies with winter and is cut into pieces—pruned back to the stump—Dionysus died each year in bloody and horrible fashion. In some versions of the myth he was torn apart by the Titans; in other versions he was dismembered by Hera, who still resented the fact that Dionysus was the illegitimate son of her philandering husband, Zeus. In both versions, however, the death suffered by the god was the same terrible death inflicted by his Maenads on all other living things and, more importantly, the deaths and savage punishments regularly inflicted on the heroes of Classical tragedy.

Eventually the god of the vine, who freed men from care and woe through wine, also became a god of light who freed men not through drink but through artistic elevation and inspiration. Exactly when this second aspect was added to his character is not known. However, Dionysus developed groups of followers who did not drink as part of his ceremony, but instead presented poetry to the god and to their fellow Greeks. The result of this was that the greatest of the four festivals of Dionysus—the City (Great) Dionysia—became foremost among all festivals in Greece. It took place in the spring, with the annual resurrection of the god when the vine began to put forth its branches, during five days in March/April. These were days devoted to peace and the total enjoyment of life. Even prisoners were granted leaves during the festival so that they too might attain fulfillment and share in the joy and merrymaking. On the first day of the festival a procession in honor of the god took place, involving the entire citizenry. On the second day ten dithyrambs of high seriousness were dedicated to the god. On each of the third, fourth, and fifth days were presented groupings of three tragedies followed by a satyr play and, eventually, one comedy.

These plays constituted a large part of the greatest poetry in all Greece. The poets who wrote the plays, the actors who performed them, and even the audiences who attended them were all involved in a sacred act of worship. Thus, the worship of Dionysus as a god who could inspire men not merely to ecstasy with his wine but also to sublime creation with his spirit became the predominant version of the religious ceremony. The festival of Dionysus, unlike

Dionysus visits a dramatic poet. (A Roman copy of a Greek original.)

the closed mysteries of certain other gods, was open to the world and became the foremost vehicle of all time for artistic expression.

The Creative Act Theory of the Origin of Tragedy

There are five basic concepts involved in the "creative act" theory of the origin of tragedy: (1) Everything that happened outside Athens is insignificant in terms of the origin of tragedy—it is Athens alone that is meaningful; (2) Tragedy did not "develop" in a gradual, measured sense, but had its origin in two "creative leaps," the first of which was made by Thespis and the second by Aeschylus; (3) These leaps were separated by a reasonably lengthy period of time, but the second is in direct line with the first and the intervening years thus have no real effect on what happened; (4) Tragedy was never Dionysiac in origin or intent and its only connection with Dionysus is that it happened to be presented during the City Dionysia in Athens; and (5) There is no evidence to support the theory that tragedy grew out of any type of "possession" or "ecstasy," including the possession or ecstasy usually attributed to the followers of Dionysus.

At the base of this theory is Thespis, a man who, if he did not exist, it would be necessary to invent. The relationship of Thespis to tragedy is perhaps contained in his name, which seems to be a diminutive of either *Thespesios* ("divinely speaking") or *Thespiôidos* ("divinely singing"), both names that a parent would be unlikely to give a child, and therefore one that was possibly awarded to Thespis as a result of his dramatic contributions.

Our biographical information regarding Thespis is scanty at best. He is, in some sources, identified with Icaria in northern Attica near Marathon, but this is called into question by another source that refers to him as Athenian. These two references may not be as exclusive as they seem. Certainly Thespis could have been born in Icaria but received Athenian citizenship as a result of his dramatic contributions made in that city. In any case, establishing Thespis' relationship with Athens provides a kind of secondary proof of the significance of both Thespis and Athens in the development of tragedy, but it does not answer the question of what Thespis actually did.

Thespis is not mentioned in the parts of the *Poetics* that survived, but Themistius has stated that (presumably in the last dialogue "On Poets") "Aristotle says that first the chorus as it came in used to sing to the gods, but Thespis invented a prologue and a [set] speech." Second, and last, Aristophanes has a character in the *Wasps* refer to "those old-fashioned dances with which Thespis used to compete." All other references to Thespis are so far removed from him in time that their accuracy must be highly questionable.

Based on the statement attributed to Aristotle, scholars in the past have decided that Thespis' creation of the first actor meant that he merely developed the character of the *exarchon* ("leader off") or the *coryphaeus* ("chorus leader") into an actor by separating him from the chorus. However, Thespis may well have done much more than this. If the term *tragôidia* does not translate as "goat song," from *tragos* ("goat") and *ôidia* ("song"), but is a secondary compound work meaning "goatsinger," then the goatsinger referred to must be the poet-actor and not the song of the chorus. Since Thespis was, by general acclamation, the first tragic poet to appear at the City Dionysia, then he was the first *tragôidos* and *tragôidia* was what he invented.

If Thespis invented the first actor, and he had only one actor —himself—then what did he do? The simple answer would be that the chorus acted as a second actor to which Thespis could respond, and which could respond to him, but the collective quality of the chorus, and its generally low social station, makes that seem unlikely. Thespis' first actor or goatsinger was most likely alone and it is for this reason that Thespis created the *prologue,*which was probably introductory and spoken by the *tragôidos*.

The other innovation that Aristotle apparently ascribed to Thespis is the *rhêseis* or set speech. The set speech generally is circular in composition, with the opening thought restated at the end, logical rather than lyrical in quality, and it exists to introduce the material that follows.

Perhaps the greatest contribution made by Thespis, in terms of the creative act theory, is not the provision of the first actor, or the prologue, or the *rhêseis*, but the development of the Chorus as commentator on the great passions of the tragic hero. In Thespis' chorus the characterization is always (with only two extant exceptions) at one with the common people, which thus allows the audience to be drawn into the play, linking the spectator with the tragic fate of the hero. Exactly what this chorus did is open to speculation. What it did not do was to sing dithyrambs, which is the only lyric genre that has left little or no residue in the fifth century.

At the center of Thespis' drama he put *pathos*. What most interested him was not the hero's life but his death. The hero's failure, not his success, attracted Thespis' interest. Along with those attributes that made the character a hero, Thespis presented those traits that linked the hero to the ordinary mortals that peopled Athens, and it was this, viewed and commented on by the chorus, that drew the audience into touch with the hero's *pathos*.

Ultimately, the dramatic contribution of Thespis was not only technical—that is, setting up the form of tragedy—but philosophical and social. This new form provided, for the new age in Athens, the necessary access to the old Homeric vision on which all the Greek institutions had been founded. The *Illiad* had dealt with heroes in a narrative way, leaving the common or average person removed from the action, a bystander to a story that took place long ago and far away. Tragedy provided an immediate contact with that age. Through the person of the actor, who was the hero, and the chorus, which represented men like himself, the ordinary Athenian was able to participate in the heroic spirit.

The second step in this theory of the origin of tragedy was taken by Aeschylus, a playwright whose enormous contribution to the history of drama has rarely been recognized. Essentially, Aeschylus took the *pathos* which Thespis placed at the core of his drama, and made it more believable by making it grow logically out of the events of the plot or situation in which the hero found himself. This necessity to seek cause and effect in what had been, heretofore, a world in which the hero defied logic, led Aeschylus to examine all aspects of man's relationships—to the natural world, to his fellow men, and to

God. And this examination of relationships in turn led Aeschylus to expand the whole of tragedy, from its resources in the epic tradition, to its poetry, and even to what may be called theatre technology.

All this led to at least eight major developments in tragedy. Tradition has it that Aeschylus introduced the second actor, and a number of scholars (including Professor Else) have, in recent years, decided that he undoubtedly introduced the third actor late in his career. He developed the artistic means for providing contrast and conflict between individuals and even between the actor and chorus. Aeschylus also developed a structure for organizing the episodes, so that the hero's *pathos* grew logically from the material presented. He also created the concept of *choice*, where the hero stands at a crossroads recognized by the audience but not by him, and his choice seals his tragic doom.

Perhaps as an outgrowth of this complex organizing of the tragic materials, and a resultant intuition about life itself, Aeschylus also developed an optimism that problems can ultimately be resolved. This is perhaps what led him to develop the connected trilogy, for in the *Oresteia*, the only extant example, the plays move from *pathos* to resolution. Aeschylus also began the practice of reinterpreting the myths, perhaps in the necessity of providing *pathos* and resolution. He also worked to increase the effectiveness of the stage picture

FIFTH CENTURY TRAGEDY

The fifth century was, clearly, the peak of Greek drama, both comic and tragic. Unfortunately, what we know of the tragedy produced in this century is based almost completely on the few surviving works of three major playwrights: Aeschylus, Sophocles, and Euripides. To assume that their few plays (only thirty-one tragedies have survived) are, in fact, representative of the more than one thousand plays that we know were written is dangerous indeed. Their basic format is probably typical of most such tragedies, but many of the plays that failed to survive might differ in some substantial way from anything that we have. For example, all of the surviving texts deal with characters and legends drawn from Greek mythology; that is, with materials familiar to a Greek audience. However, such was not always the case. We know that toward the end of the fifth century B.C. the poet Agathon in his tragedies created original characters and stories different from anything his audience knew. His example apparently never attracted many followers, but it illustrates the possibility that the plays we have may not in every aspect be representative of the Greek tragic drama.

What we can assume about the plays we have, and feel some security in our assumption, is that in the critical judgment of succeeding generations these plays were considered the best of the Greek tragic dramas and their authors were considered the best of the playwrights. If one play (or even two) by these authors had survived and all the other plays by other playwrights had been lost, then we might attribute such survival to mere chance. But when several plays by each author survive then it means that many people over the years went to great lengths to preserve manuscripts by these specific playwrights.

In any case, whatever their relationship to the other plays of the time, these few plays are all we have left from one of the greatest and most prolific periods in dramatic history, and so it is on their evidence that we must base our judgments.

While the plays we possess may not be totally representative of the drama of that time, there are enough similarities from play to play to support the concept of a standard, recurring play structure. That is, most of the plays we have begin with a *prologue*, although two extant plays by Aeschylus (*The Persians* and *The Suppliant Maidens*) do not have a *prologue*. The *prologue* outlines in iambic verse, often spoken by a single actor, what is essentially past action; it is usually exposition designed to let the audience know the material necessary for a full understanding of the action that is to come. Following the *prologue* comes the *parados* or entry of the chorus, usually chanted in anapestic meter. In the two cases where there is no *prologue*,the *parados* begins the action of the play. The function of the *parados* is to introduce the chorus, establish the fundamentals of the action, and create the proper mood, often one of foreboding because of the tragic action that follows. Especially in those cases where the *parados* begins the play, it also provides a certain amount of exposition. After the *parados* comes a series of *episodes* (scenes of action) separated by *stasima* (lyric songs) sung by the chorus. The *episodes*

Contemporary representation of an ancient Greek drama at the Odeon of Herode Atticus in Athens.

and *stasima* are followed by the *exodos*, which is the action following the chorus' final *stasimon*. This concluding action ends with the departure of the characters and the chorus chanting in anapestic meter.

This strict formal structure of tragedy was accompanied by an equivalently strict formalization of the language. While comedy made use of everyday speech, the language of tragedy was, from first to (nearly) last, elevated, reserved, and formal. In the later plays of Sophocles there is what seems to be a tentative attempt at natural language, and Euripides moved so far from the formal tragic speech that Aristophanes bitterly and often accused him of destroying the tragic art. However, for the largest part of the greatest period of tragedy the language was appropriate to the lofty, mytho-historical subject matter.

In a society that passed both its history and its religious mythology along in an oral tradition, there was very little real separation between the mythic and the factual/historical. Thus, the subjects of tragedy were drawn from the myths of the gods and heroes, and from historically based legend. This would seem, at first consideration, to make the subject matter of tragedy as restrictive as form and language. However, for the Greeks the myths were essentially archetypes or models illuminating universal aspects of human behavior. Thus, as long as the basic pattern of mythic action was followed, the poet was free to deal with the material in his own way and from his own point of view, extracting from the myth his own particular interpretation of its meaning.

AESCHYLUS: Even though he was the first of the great Greek tragic playwrights, little information about the life of Aeschylus has come down to us that is not in some way suspect. The only full treatment, the anonymous *Life of Aeschylus*, is a mixture of what seems to be historical fact and the legendary material that was already springing up about this outstanding poet. Thus, the only totally reliable facts we have are those which are directly concerned with his productions, for these come from the archives of Athens. However, some of the material about major, public aspects of his life is available in enough sources so that it can be cross-checked. Such checking indicates that it is probably reliable and that the following outline is reasonably accurate.

Aeschylus was born in 525/24 B.C., the son of an Athenian nobleman named Euphorion. His clan name has been lost to time, but the family belonged to the Eupatridai, which means that it was an old family indeed, extending back in time to the clan society of primitive Attica. Aeschylus may have been born in Eleusis, and in any case he certainly spent a large part of his childhood in that city famous for its mysteries. His first entry in the contest for tragedies at the City Dionysia was in 499 B.C., but it was not until 484 B.C. that he was awarded the first prize.

By the time that his dramatic genius was recognized with the prize for tragedy, Aeschylus had also made his mark on Athenian civic and military history. He fought the Persians, apparently with distinction, as an infantryman at Marathon in 490 B.C., and when the Persians invaded a second time in 480 B.C. he served with the Athenian navy and was present at the victory of Salamis, which largely destroyed Persian power and helped put an end to this external threat. In fact, the earliest of his tragedies that we now possess (*The Persians*, 472 B.C.) is based on that victory. The play was such a success that Aeschylus was invited by the Sicilian tyrant Hiero I to stage it in Syracuse, where again it scored a major triumph. There is no record of how long Aeschylus remained in Syracuse, but by 468 B.C. he was again in Athens where he was beaten in the tragic competition by Sophocles. The following year, however, Aeschylus was awarded the prize for the tetralogy which contained *The Seven Against Thebes*, and just a few years later his tetralogy containing *The Suppliant Maidens* gave him the prize over Sophocles. In 458 B.C. he produced his final great trilogy, the *Oresteia*. After this production he left Athens for Sicily, where he died at Gela in 456/55 B.C., leaving one son, Euphorion.

This bare-bones outline, while seemingly telling us very little, in fact makes clear a great deal about the poet and his plays, and the extant comments by his contemporaries adds to this picture. The dates of Aeschylus' birth and death tell us something about the man in terms of what he witnessed. He was born during the rise of democratic government in Athens, near the end of the age of Solon, which means that he was in the first generation to enjoy that great statesman's reforms. He lived in a state which had abolished land mortgages and slavery for debt, that provided a jury of citizens to hear appeals, and that made all citizens members of the public assembly. Such democratic reforms, carried on well into Aeschylus' own lifetime by Cleisthenes, were a part of the atmosphere in which the poet reached maturity. That he remained close to the leaders of this growing democracy is made clear by the fact that for his production of *The Persians* his *choregus* was Pericles of Alkmaionidai, who would become the outstanding political-social leader and finest orator of Greece's Golden Age. Also during his lifetime Aeschylus witnessed the rise of Sparta as a major military power and the resulting Spartan League, which would later oppose Athens. As well, he witnessed the formation of the Delian League, a grouping of the Ionian states with Athens at its head, designed to ward off future Persian invasions. Finally, as an old man he saw the beginnings of the Peloponnesian War, and in a spiritual sense it is probably best that he died before he could realize what was happening or witness the eventual outcome.

Little is known about Aeschylus' personal life. In *Frogs* (405 B.C.) Aristophanes has provided us with a caricature that may have some validity. If it is accurate in general outline, then Aeschylus was a kind, thoughtful, and generous man who was, however, capable of a fiery passion. These are aspects of the poet which, according to most critics, are common to his poetry and therefore probably accurate. Other contemporary anecdotes seem to support this view of his personality. In addition, several Greek writers who were his contemporaries (or near contemporaries) claim that Aeschylus wrote his plays while drunk, and this is supported by Gorgias' comment that the plays of Aeschylus are "packed with Dionysus" and Aristophanes' crowning of this great tragic poet as the "Bacchic King." Whether these comments are accurate regarding Aeschylus' personal life, or whether they are merely a way of pointing out the intoxicated, ecstatic, visionary quality of his poetry is open to debate.

The fact that Aeschylus spent a number of his youthful years at Eleusis is also important to his plays, for he was deeply affected by the mystical traditions of this city. For example, at the beginning of the *Oresteia* the Watchman alludes to such mysteries in the line, "The rest I leave to silence; for an ox stands huge upon my tongue." From that early line on, several of the most famous mysteries are referred to—in the tale of how Orestes sought to cleanse himself, and especially in Clytemnestra's worship of Mother Dia, which relates to the most famous of the Eleusian mysteries. His contemporaries obviously were impressed by Aeschylus' reference to the mysteries and, according to some nearly contemporary legends, Aeschylus was prosecuted for revealing in his plays some of the secrets of these religious ceremonies. He was found innocent of ill-intent, the legend goes, when he pointed out in his plea that he was unaware that these were secrets. There is also a tradition that some of the costumes he designed for staging tragedies were taken over by the priests at Eleusis for use in the mysteries.

The line of the Watchman, along with Cicero's comment that Aeschylus was a "Pythagorean as well as a poet," makes clear another aspect of Aeschylus' plays. The patron god of the Pythagoreans was Apollo, the god who speaks for Zeus in the *Oresteia*, and Pythagorean beliefs in one way or another are all inherent in this trilogy. The Pythagoreans believed in reincarnation, which they objectified as the "wheel of necessity," and this reincarnation was symbolically depicted by the rebirth of the individual at major points in his life, just as Orestes is reborn (by achieving new understanding) at several points in his lifetime. The Pythagoreans were ascetic, much given to meditation, and they placed great ethical significance on a concept of balance in life. It is this emphasis on achieving balance in a judicial and religious sense that gives the *Oresteia* so much of its force and meaning. Also, they believed that the

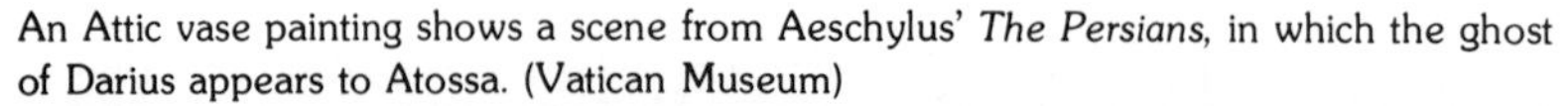

An Attic vase painting shows a scene from Aeschylus' *The Persians*, in which the ghost of Darius appears to Atossa. (Vatican Museum)

individual was morally responsible for his actions, and it is this moral responsibility that Orestes (and the play itself) must resolve.

It is generally accepted that Aeschylus wrote some ninety plays, seven of which are extant. Of the rest, seventy are known to us by their titles or, in some few cases, by short fragments which have allowed us to reconstruct the subject matter and to some degree the style of the plays. The thirteen plus remaining plays are totally unknown. The earliest of the extant plays is probably *The Persians*, which was produced in 472 B.C. This play, dealing with the Persian defeat at Salamis, was the second play of a tetralogy. The first play of this grouping was *Phineus* and the third was *Glaukos Potnieus*, followed by a satyr play titled *Prometheus Pyrkaeus*. These titles indicate that there was no continuity of plot, making this the earliest example of a disconnected trilogy and indicating that the contemporary belief in the requirement of a connected plot structure for the early trilogies may be somewhat unfounded.

The second play which can be dated exactly is *The Seven Against Thebes* (467 B.C.) and the third, fourth, and fifth are the plays that comprise the *Oresteia* (*Agamemnon, Choephorae, Eumenides*), which was produced in 458 B.C. *The Suppliant Maidens* was at one time dated c. 490 B.C., but recent evidence (it is part of the Danaid tetralogy which won Aeschylus the prize over Sophocles) indicates that it was probably produced sometime after 467 B.C. The last of the seven extant plays, *Prometheus Bound*, is undated. It is known that Aeschylus' son, Euphorion, following his father's death, won four victories with tetralogies that his father had written but not produced. Some critics speculate that *Prometheus Bound* was very possibly one of those plays.

Traditionally, Aeschylus has been given credit for being the real creator of Greek tragedy as we know it. It is said that he was the first to use tragedy to deal with great moral and religious problems, and that his magnificent poetry was the foundation of the later tragic style. Certainly there must be some truth to this, for Sophocles, who is often called the greatest of the tragic dramatists, pointed out that he learned to write tragedies from Aeschylus. Additionally, Aeschylus is given credit for adding the second actor, increasing the dialogue, and thus proportionally reducing the importance of the chorus.

What can finally be said about Aeschylus is that he was a bold, independent philosopher who wrestled with the grand religious, moral, and political problems of his day. He created spectacular effects, magnificent poetry, and some of the most compelling tragic dramas in the history of the form.

SOPHOCLES: Sophocles, considered by many to be the finest of the three great writers of Greek Classical tragedy, was born in 497/96 B.C. in Colonus, a village outside Athens, and subsequently lived for ninety years. A short work on his life, written by an anonymous scholar some two hundred years after the great poet's death, provides a picture of his life that is probably accurate in basic fact and spirit, even though some of the material is clearly legendary. This memoir tells of an almost idyllic childhood spent in a prosperous and intellectually sophisticated home; a youth devoted to achieving intellectual, physical, and social polish and grace; a manhood enhanced by service to the state in civic, military, and artistic affairs; and an old age rich with honors and popular affection.

Of the three great tragic dramatists, Sophocles more than the other two epitomizes the spirit of Classicial Greece in fifth century Athens. Born just as Athens began its climb to power and glory in the Persian Wars, Sophocles witnessed as a boy the Persian invasion of Greece and the defeat of the Persian army at Marathon by a small force of Athenians. As a young man he took part in the festival celebrating the second and final Persian defeat at Salamis. This was the victory that resulted in the formation of the Delian League and thus launched Athens on the road to empire. He saw the establishment of this empire and watched the resulting birth of the Golden Age under the guidance of the great statesman, Pericles. By the time of Sophocles' death in 406 B.C., Athens was already badly strained, materially and morally, by the demands of the Peloponnesian War, and only two years after he died Athens surrendered and the Golden Age and Greek democracy were no more.

Throughout the approximately fifty years during which Athens enjoyed an almost unparalleled civic and artistic growth and prosperity, Sophocles contributed in a major way to the richness and breadth of this extraordinarily free social life and culture, holding high civil and military offices. He was treasurer of the Athenian Naval League and fought as a general under Pericles during the war that was undertaken to put down the revolt of Samos. Later in his life he was probably a member of the *Probouloi*, the committee appointed to guide Athens after the disaster in Sicily, and he was selected several times to act as ambassador to foreign states.

As is true of Aeschylus, we know very little about Sophocles' private life. His legitimate son, Iophon, went on to become a tragic poet of some distinction. Of Ariston, Sophocles' son by another woman, we know almost nothing. Sophocles was, as a private citizen, a devoutly religious man. He was a priest serving the god Halon, a relatively minor god of the healing arts, and legend has it that when the worship of Asclepius was introduced into Athens from Epidaurus, Sophocles received the god in his own home because the shrine of Asclepius was not yet ready. This legend probably has some basis in fact, and the god that he received into his house was probably the sacred snake. That Sophocles' personal life was one of probity and good nature seems evident in the fact that he remained always on good terms with the great and near-great who surrounded him. His relationship with Pericles was friendly and close enough so that Pericles could gently tease Sophocles about being a better poet than he was a general. He remained on the best of terms with the historian Herodotus, and even the contentious philosopher Socrates warmly mentions hearing Sophocles speak during the poet's old age. His relationship with his fellow dramatist, Euripides, is demonstrated by the fact that when Euripides' death was announced in Athens in 406 B.C., Sophocles made public his sorrow by having his chorus come onstage dressed in mourning. A year after Sophocles' death, Arisophanes, in his play *Frogs*, has Dionysus in Hades say of him, "He is a good tempered person here, as he was there."

Whatever his civil, military, and religious contributions were, however, Sophocles' greatest contribution to his own age and to succeeding ages was made in the theatre—Athens' prime temple. By all accounts he wrote nearly one hundred twenty-five plays, winning the first prize twenty-four times and never finishing lower then second place. Of his total output eight plays are extant. Of these, seven are tragedies and one, *The Trackers*, is a satyr play. Like Aeschylus he acted in his own plays, at least the early ones, but eventually he gave up performing, which provided a welcome precedent for Euripides, who apparently was not comfortable acting and who seems never to have appeared onstage.

Sophocles first entered the contest for tragedies in 468 B.C. and won the prize on this maiden voyage, probably with *Triptolemos*, fragments of which are still extant. The little we have of the play shows a strong influence by Aeschylus, which accords with Sophocles' own statement that Aeschylus was his mentor in playwriting. We may assume also that the music of this early play was derivative of Lampros, his music teacher, for like all of the Greek poets, Sophocles composed both the words and music for his plays.

One of the great dramatic innovators, Sophocles is generally given credit for adding the third actor, which allowed for a greater number of major characters on a speaking level and also provided the opportunity for far more interesting dramatic situations in that instead of using only two character confrontations, it was now possible for triangular scenes to be played as well. In addition to increasing the number of actors, Sophocles is also credited with increasing the number of chorus members from twelve (the number which Aeschylus supposedly had determined) to fifteen. Exactly why this was done is not certain; one can assume that he explained his reasoning in the lost prose

A contemporary production of the Classic Greek drama can be seen in this production of *Oedipus the King* by the Guthrie Theatre Company, Minneapolis-St. Paul. Translation and adaptation by Anthony Burgess; directed by Michael Langham.

work, *On the Chorus*. However, there is at least one practical reason for having a chorus with an uneven number of members—it allows the chorus to be evenly divided onstage with a chorus leader mediating between the two groups or conducting both halves.

Based on the testimony of Aristotle, Sophocles is often given credit for the introduction of scene painting. Whether this means that he in fact introduced painted scenery by way of *periaktoi* or painted flats, or whether he merely made greater and better use of existing painting techniques is unclear. It should also be noted, in this regard, that Vitruvius gave credit to Aeschylus for inventing scene painting. In any case, however, Sophocles' involvement with scene painting implies a movement toward greater theatrical realism. This move toward realism is also inherent in his dialogue—at least when it is compared with the dialogue of Aeschylus.

In addition to the above, Sophocles is usually credited with breaking the pattern traditionally ascribed to Aeschylus of making the three tragic plays of the tetralogy part of a continuous whole. According to most scholars it was Sophocles who established the concept of presenting three separate plays that were each an organic whole, with no attempt at thematic unity. Again, this seems to be somewhat questionable. The earliest example of such a disconnected trilogy is one by Aeschylus, and what thus seems most likely is that the popularity of Sophocles as a dramatist firmly established a pattern that was already making its appearance.

The plays that Sophocles produced, if we may judge by the seven extant tragedies, have a number of outstanding characteristics that indicate a significant shift in emphasis from the earlier works of Aeschylus. Sophocles' plays keep the dramatic focus always on the masked actor and not just on the problem that confronts the city or state. Also, his plots are highly complex, with enough foreshadowing and dramatic irony to keep an audience on the edge of their seats even though they already know the inevitable outcome of the story they see and hear unfolding. And the characters of these plays are subtly delineated and fully drawn, so that at the end of *Oedipus the King*, for example, we feel that we "know" Oedipus, Jocasta, Creon, and Teiresias. Earlier tragedy—that is, Aeschylean—deals with houses or cities or states, but Sophoclean tragedy deals with individuals.

Sophocles, as is clear from what we know of his personal life and his priesthood, held to what might be defined as the orthodox religious view. Indeed, in all his plays the position of the gods is one of absolute supremacy whenever the purposes of the gods come into conflict with the desires of man. However, unlike the gods in the plays of Aeschylus, with ideals and motivations that are clear-cut and just, at least by their own lights, the gods in the plays of Sophocles are almost unknown and essentially unknowable. The gods that walk the earth and clearly state their positions in the plays of Aeschylus are, in the plays of Sophocles, reduced to enigmatic riddles. Thus, the focus of his plays, insofar as it includes the gods, tends not to be on the gods but on the daring men who challenge them in some way and go striving to their inevitable doom.

As is the case with all great dramatists, Sophocles' themes are numerous and varied, but some general statements may be made with security. He deals with the heroic dignity of man, not so much in spite of man's imperfections, but because of them. In his plays the sins of arrogance and pride lead men to disaster because divine retribution is inevitable. Everyone suffers; even the innocent suffer, but out of that suffering comes wisdom, which teaches humility and the limitations of man.

Of the approximately one hundred twenty-five plays that Sophocles wrote, we have titles of one hundred nine, eight of which are complete, with several of the remaining works existing in fragments. The eight complete plays are, with approximate dates: *Ajax* (c. 447 B.C.), *Antigone* (c. 441 B.C.), *The Trackers* (c. 440 B.C., a satyr play), *Oedipus the King* (c. 430/29 B.C.), *Electra* (c. 418/14 B.C.), *The Maidens of Trachis* (c. 413 B.C.), *Philoctetes* (409 B.C.), and *Oedipus at Colonus* (c. 406/05 B.C., produced posthumously in 401 B.C.).

EURIPIDES: The third and last of the great Greek tragic dramatists whose plays have managed to survive, Euripides presents a real enigma to the historian. The sources of material are few; the *scholia* or marginal notes written by ancient scholars in the manuscripts of his works, the oldest of which date from nearly two hundred years after his death; the comments about him that the comic writers, especially Aristophanes, made in their plays; an anonymous work titled *The Life and Race of Euripides*, probably written near the end of the third century B.C.; a few comments by his contemporaries; and the *Attic Chronicle* of Philochorus, probably written in the early third century B.C., slightly more than one hundred years after Euripides died. It is likely that none of these sources is entirely accurate, and some of them, especially the comedies, may be highly inaccurate. However, by comparing them all certain facts do emerge.

Tradition has it that Euripides was born the son of Mnesarchus in 480 B.C. in Salamis, on the very day and location of the great victory over the Persians. This is probably a bit of fabulous legendry, and a more likely date is 484 B.C., the date specified in an ancient chronicle titled *Parian Marble*. A more accurate place for his birth is the town of Phyla, near the center of Attica. This location is important because at that time Phyla was renowned for its mysteries, and it contained temples of Demeter Anesidora, Dionysus, and Eros, as well as temples to most of the traditional Homeric gods. That young Euripides was influenced by this, especially by the women's mysteries of Demeter and the mysteries of Eros, is evident in his plays.

As a young man, Euripides saw the growth of the Athenian empire and the birth of the Golden Age. Athens represented Hellenism, and Hellenism was equated with wisdom and the arts. He was still a young man during the age of Phrynichus, the first of the great tragic writers, and he was part of a society that stressed not only the dramatic arts, but also poetry, music, sculpture, and painting. In fact, legend has it that he was himself a painter of some ability.

By the age of eighteen, Euripides officially became a "youth," and as such must have put in two years of military service, which consisted primarily of garrison duty and war games. Along with this there is some indication that he emphasized athletics. There is nothing unusual in this, for most boys in Greece became reasonably proficient at running, boxing, and wrestling. However, we are told there were records indicating that Euripides won athletic contests at both Athens and Eleusis.

But there was more going on in Athens than the arts, the military, and athletics. It was the philosophers who, perhaps more than any other group, helped to shape the growing Euripides. Such men as Anaxagoras, Protagoras, Diogenes, and possibly even Socrates (a verse in an ancient comedy has come down to us saying that "Socrates piles the faggots for Euripides' fire") exerted a great influence on the budding playwright.

Euripides' first play, *The Daughters of Pelias* (which did not survive), was produced in 455 B.C., the year following the death of Aeschylus, but he did not win his first victory until 442 B.C. The middle years of Euripides' life were his great years of play production—he is reputed to have written some ninety plays—and then he moved to Macedonia in the north of Greece where, according to legend, he lived a hermitlike existence in a cave on the island of Salamis, refusing to see most visitors and all women. It was here, in the year 406 B.C., that he died.

In his own time Euripides was hardly one of the most popular playwrights, and to some degree this dislike lasted for more than two thousand years, through most of the nineteenth century. However, in this century attitudes have greatly changed and he is now considered to be the most modern of the great tragic dramatists. In part the attitude toward his plays is based on his insistence on dramatic realism, which in his own time was recognized for what it was, but still was not widely admired. When Sophocles said, as reported by Aristotle, that his own characters represented men as they ought to be and Euripides' characters represented men as they were, he was merely commenting on a fact that all of his contemporaries recognized and that few of them approved, at least in terms of Euripides. By insisting on dramatic and even psychological reality in his characterizations, Euripides was drawing a line between the drama of Aeschylus and Sophocles on one hand and himself on the other, and his contemporaries felt that this would lead to the downfall of tragic drama.

This emphasis on realism, however, aided Euripides in creating some of the most memorable characters in the history of the dramatic arts—characters such as Electra, Medea, Phaedra, and Theseus. In part these characters are memorable because the realism gave them a breadth of characterization that was often lacking in the more conventional dramatic form. In Euripides' plays there are very few heroes or villains. Instead there are people who manage to combine within themselves both good and evil, and one is never quite sure at the beginning of a Euripidean drama whether the attitudes and reactions provoked by the early part of the play will hold up at the end. For example, at the beginning of *Medea* the audience is quite sympathetic to the deserted wife and wholly antagonistic toward Jason because of his cold materialism and total lack of human understanding. However, by the end of the play the sympathy has turned to disgust with the witch who has murdered her children to achieve revenge on her roving husband. In the same way an audience feels sympathy for Phaedra, in spite of her unnatural passion, because it grows out of a curse in her blood and is therefore not really her fault. However, by the time she falsely involves the innocent Hippolytus in her sins the sympathy has turned to loathing.

This realism also carried over to Euripides' treatment of the gods, and it is here, especially, that he fell afoul of certain of his contemporaries. In the plays of Aeschylus the gods walk the earth, clearly stating (and illustrating by their actions) that the will of the gods, the patriarchal, Hellenic gods at least, must be honored and carried out by men, with wisdom and salvation the reward for such obedience. In the plays of Sophocles the gods may not as often walk the earth, and their presence may often be limited to obscure riddles, but the idea that men must honor and obey the gods is still present. In the plays of Euripides, on the other hand, the gods walk the earth in human form, but their will—their desires, lusts, and whims—does not always bring wisdom and salvation. Just as often the will of the gods causes suffering to no discernible end, and blind obedience to these deities—more personifications of elemental forces than the anthropomorphic gods of Aeschylus—brings neither wisdom nor salvation. In spite of his attitudes, Euripides made great use of the gods. Twelve of his extant plays are resolved by supernatural intervention, with the gods appearing from on high to resolve the complex problems which the playwright has set up. In fact, however, in Euripides' plays the gods seldom resolve anything. Instead their purpose seems to be to predict the way in which the future will be affected by the current action. This complements the *prologue*, which links the coming action of the play to past history. This linking of the plays to both past and future gives Euripides' works a timeless quality which may well explain why his plays seem so contemporary, even to an age nearly twenty-five hundred years after the dates of their composition.

For contemporary times the fact that Euripides created some of the greatest female roles in the history of dramatic literature is of great interest. It is especially interesting in terms of the legends about his deep-seated misogyny. Whether the legends are true and his dramatic fascination with women sprang from his hatred of them, or whether the early influence of the mysteries of Demeter Anesidora at Phyla is responsible for his interest, the fact remains that such characterizations as Medea, Electra, and Phaedra provide some of the greatest female acting roles of all time.

The dramatic technique and style of Euripides has been thoroughly examined, especially in recent years. However, in brief it may be said that he dealt with plots far more complex in nature than did Aeschylus or Sophocles, and that his dramatic interest in terms of those plots was always on the individual in the real world and rarely on the grand design. These plots are occasionally episodic or fragmented, as for example in his *Hippolytus*, where Hippolytus never quite becomes the protagonist of what Euripides clearly believed was Hippolytus' play. Instead, the first half of the play belongs to Phaedra and the second half (after Phaedra's death) belongs to Theseus. Because of this lack of organic unification, and because he made use of a number of highly dramatic suspense elements, Euripides has sometimes been characterized as the father of melodrama.

Euripides' plays are psychological dramas or problem plays. Like the plays of Aeschylus and Sophocles, his works comment on such grand topics as fate and divine power, but from the point of view of the individuals directly concerned rather than from the point of view of specific political or religious groups. Largely this is because in his plays the primary aspects that interested the author seem to be the conflicts of human emotions, sometimes between two or more characters (Hippolytus-Phaedra-Theseus) and sometimes within one character (Medea or Electra).

In terms of style, Euripides uses a simple, lucid, everyday form of dialogue, at least when compared to the dialogue written by his predecessors, and yet he manages to capture a lyric beauty that by today's standards seems almost exquisite when compared to the majestic organ tones of Aeschylus.

Euripides was not popular in his own day, and this lack of critical acclaim did last up to our own century, but those few who admired his work did so wholeheartedly. As a result, more of his plays have survived than have plays by Aeschylus and Sophocles. We have some fifty-six titles of lost plays, and eighteen works have survived intact, along with an anonymous play (*Rhesus*) which was long attributed to Euripides because of a final scene that seems to be Euripidean in nature, with a mother weeping over the body of her dead son while an embarrassed soldiery looks on. The extant plays, with the dates usually attributed to them, are *Alcestis* (438 B.C., written to take the place of the satyr play); *Medea* (431 B.C.); *Hippolytus* (428 B.C.); *The Children of Heracles* (c. 427 B.C.); *Andromache* (c. 426 B.C.); *Hecuba* (c. 425 B.C.); *Cyclops* (c. 423 B.C., a satyr play); *Mad Heracles* (c. 422 B.C.); *The Suppliants* (c. 421 B.C.); *Ion* (c. 417 B.C.); *The Trojan Women* (415 B.C.); *Iphigenia in Tauris* (414/12 B.C.); *Electra* (413 B.C.); *Helen* (412 B.C.); *The Phoenician Women* (c. 410 B.C.); *Orestes* (408 B.C.); *Iphigenia at Aulis* (405 B.C.); and *The Bacchae* (405 B.C.).

THE SATYR PLAY

The writers of tragedies were required by tradition to perfect at least one form of comic writing, for along with their tragic trilogies they were required to submit one satyr play. We know little about this dramatic form as only one complete text (Euripides' *Cyclops*, c. 423 B.C.) and one nearly complete text (Sophocles' *The Trackers*, c. 440 B.C.) have survived—this in spite of the fact that Aeschylus was held to be the finest writer in this particular dramatic form.

Indeed, we are not even sure of why the satyr play existed. Perhaps because it was produced in the final position, after the tragedies, we should look on it as a last bow to that other, less terrible aspect of Dionysus—the woodland god who was both vegetation and fertility symbol. Also, it may have been the result of psychological insight on the part of the Greeks—an attempt to fill the void left by the purgative effect of the earlier three tragedies with the lusty good humor of the satyr play.

The satyr play was named for its chorus, which in both of the plays that have survived (and apparently in most of those which did not) is composed of satyrs, the mythical, goatish, half-human companions of Dionysus. The chorus leader was the aged patriarch of the satyrs, Silenus. In both of the surviving texts (and apparently in most such works) the setting is bucolic—for *Cyclops*

Vase painting showing Dionysus and Ariadne surrounded by actors from the satyr play. (Museo Nazionale)

the island of Sicily near Mt. Aetna, and for *The Trackers* the slope of Mt. Cyllene in Arcadia—and the action fast and furious, providing opportunities for lively dance and farcical stage business. The themes were sometimes related to the subjects of the preceding tragedies, and were often burlesques of traditional myths in which heroes (Odysseus in *Cyclops*) and gods (Apollo in *The Trackers*) were held up to ridicule. In a sense this burlesquing of apparently serious figures within the religious ceremony of the theatre, especially following the serious treatments of such figures in the preceding three tragedies, is similar in nature to the later Medieval Feast of Fools, which consisted of usually good-natured mockery of Christian tradition.

The structure of the satyr play apparently followed that of traditional tragedy, consisting of a *prologue, parados*, a series of *episodes* separated by *stasima* or choral songs, followed by an *exodos*. The language and meter, however, were closer to everyday speech than the elevated language of the tragedies and, indeed, the satyr plays were filled with obscene language and indecent gesture.

COMEDY

The origins of Greek comedy are perhaps even more obscure than the origins of Greek tragedy. The source of the name given to this form of drama hints that comedy grew out of the traditional fertility festivals—"comedy" is derived from *kōmos*, which means "song of revelry"—but such derivation is far from conclusive evidence. The choral element of Old Comedy, which is the comedy of Aristophanes that held the Greek stage from approximately 487 B.C., when it was absorbed into the state cult of Athens, to 400 B.C., probably comes from the phallic choruses and processions held at the festivals of Dionysus, along with a number of other influences. These phallic choruses and proces-

A scene taken from a Greek vase painting of an Old Comedy. "Cheiron goes upstairs."

sions were essentially fertility rites in which the revelers, dressed in the skins of animals and carrying phalluses, danced through the streets and carried on obscene badinage with each other and with those they met along the route of the procession. In addition to the choruses there is reason to give at least some credit to the Doric farces, which now exist only in terms of commentary, but which apparently included dialogue between as many as three performers, tragic burlesques, and much farcical action. Old Comedy may also have been affected by Megarian farce and Sicilian mime.

The Greeks themselves often attributed the development of comedy to Chionides, winner of the prize for comedy at the first official competition at Athens in 486 B.C. Other sources attribute the development to Magnes, who won the prize thirteen years later, and even to Susarion, another early comic playwright. This is all very hard to prove, however, so relying on the testimony of Aristotle, as scholars are so often forced to do, most historians credit Epicharmus of Syracuse for taking the decisive step that united the early influences into something that resembles the Old Comic form. Little is known about Epicharmus except that he lived a long life, probably from the middle of the sixth century well into the fifth, and that he was certainly writing plays between 486 and 467 B.C. A few fragments of his works (we have thirty-seven titles, most of which did not survive even in part) are extant, and these indicate a form featuring three actors and containing burlesque, parody, and apparently some limited farcical action. Epicharmus also created comic characters, such as the cook, braggart, courtesan, and parasite, that would later become the stock characters of New Comedy. References to the plays of Epicharmus indicate a dramatic form that was not yet quite Old Comedy, partly because in the fragments there is no indication of a chorus, except in the title of his play *The Dancers*. Also, the fragments depend more on the witty lines and aphorisms for which he was contemporarily admired than on the wild farce and burlesque of Old Comedy.

Given its ancestors it is easy to see why Old Comedy, from its earliest beginnings, was farcical and bawdy. In terms of its basic format the comedy soon developed a structure (both external and internal) that was as strict as that which developed around the tragic form. On one level Old Comedy has a faint similarity to contemporary musical comedy—that is to say, it is comic in intent and uses music to further and enhance the action. In terms of subject matter, Old Comedy tends toward the fantastic (establishing a Utopia in the land of the birds, or following the adventures of a dim-witted and cowardly god on a trip to Hades to bring back Euripides) or toward an exaggerated, heightened reality (the women of Athens putting an end to war by refusing their husbands' sexual demands until the husbands refrain from doing battle). In most cases the plays are satiric, pointedly and correctively concentrating on contemporary foibles, issues, and excesses, and holding up to ridicule a number of well-known personages of the time.

In comedy as in tragedy there are a number of variations on what is essentially a basic format. First there is a *prologue* in which the leading character conceives the "happy idea." This happy idea is the comic basis of everything that follows. The *prologue* is often quite long, rather elaborate, and generally contains more characterization than is common to the *prologue* of tragedy. Usually the happy idea contained in the *prologue* is fantastic in concept and comic in its absurd lack of traditional logic. Following the *prologue* comes the *parados*—the entry of the chorus. Upon occasion the chorus supports the happy idea, but most often it opposes the idea. The chorus members are, sometimes, parodies of human types or conditions (such as old men and old women), but most often they are costumed as animals. After the *parados* comes the *agon*, a dramatized debate (occasionally with some form of physical contest) between the proponents of the happy idea and its opponents. In the *agon* the comic hero eventually overcomes all opposition to his idea and readies himself to put it into effect. Before this can happen, however, the action is interrupted by the *parabasis*—the "coming forward" of the chorus—in which the chorus members at least partially put aside their characterization to address the audience directly as mouthpiece of the playwright. Choral comment in the *parabasis* is usually directed at subjects relating in some way to the action of the play, but there is no real restriction on subject matter and so, in fact, comments are aired on any and all subjects, ranging from light humorous fantasy to venomous personal attacks on contemporary personages. The *parabasis* consists of seven parts, two of which are lyrical with the remaining five being prosaic. Most of the choral passages are pointed toward comedy or satire and do not strive for great lyric qualities, but upon occasion there are choral odes of great beauty. Following completion of the *parabasis* the action is resumed in a series of *episodes* in which the hero attempts to implement his happy idea. Each of these *episodes* builds to a greater degree of absurdity and then, sometimes, may come a second though shorter *parabasis*. The finale of the comedy consists of a feast, though not necessarily a marriage feast, and male and female union (*gamos*).

ARISTOPHANES: That Aristophanes of Athens was the greatest writer of Attic Old Comedy can be surmised from the fact that he is the only playwright in this genre whose plays have survived. This testifies to the esteem in which he was held, not only in his own lifetime but also in the thousands of years since his death. However, the interest that his own and succeeding generations showed in his plays seems never to have carried over to his personal life, and little is known of him. He was born in about 445 B.C., the son of Philippus, whose business is not known but who seems to have been a wealthy man. Aristophanes maintained this wealth and is usually identified in attitude and interests with the "knights," a conservative and reasonably wealthy group that existed somewhere between the very rich aristocracy and the working level of Greek society. If the biographical hints in his plays may be accepted as fact, then he was in some way connected with the island of Aegina, possibly by way of family estates, and he was a political activist, at least in terms of his comedies. In *Acharnians* he mentions that he has offended Cleon, a powerful political leader and one of the prime movers in the war against Sparta. In *Clouds, Wasps,* and *Peace* he repeats this mention of the enmity that has continued to fester between himself and Cleon, and given Aristophanes' early penchant for personal invective it is probably accurate in general outline.

The Banqueters, Aristophanes' first known play, though unfortunately one that did not survive, was produced in 427 B.C. It was a satire on contemporary educational methodology and it was awarded the second prize in a comic contest, probably (though not certainly) the Lenaea. During the following year he produced *The Babylonians*, which like his first play did not survive, and then in 425 B.C. he produced *Acharnians*, the earliest of his plays that has come down to us intact. The play is essentially a plea for peace with Sparta during the Peloponnesian War, but along the way it presents a burlesque of the Athenian Assembly, a sharp satiric attack on the gullibility of the Athenian people, and holds Euripides up to ridicule as an inept, slovenly writer of bad tragedies.

In 424 B.C., the year following the *Acharnians*, Aristophanes produced *Knights*. The play contains specifically a bitter, biting attack on his old enemy, Cleon, and generally a sharp satire on all such demagogues. Also, it presents an impassioned plea for a return to the limited democracy that existed during the early years of the fifth century. In *Clouds*, presented in 423 B.C., Aristophanes returned to the concerns of his first recorded play, satirizing the "new" education of the Sophists. In addition he attacks science as destructive of morality and religion; characterizes intellectuals as bad citizens in much the same sense that Plato found poets to be bad citizens; and presents a devastating picture of the philosopher Socrates suspended in a basket from the roof of his "thinkery," unable to think unless he is in a rarefied atmosphere, removed from the often unpleasant realities of everyday life. This play was, apparently, Aristophanes' first failure, winning third prize at the City Dionysia. The extant edition is not the one which failed but a later, rewritten version in which the poet severely criticizes the audience for not appreciating the original version. He also castigates his fellow playwrights for lack of high seriousness, accusing them of writing only for coarse laughs and of stealing his plots.

Wasps, produced in 422 B.C., continued Aristophanes' unrelenting attack on Cleon and his war party, pointing out how such demagogues use the law and the courts to deceive the people and attain their own unjust ends. Again, however, the citizens of Athens themselves do not escape unscathed, and the play ridicules the Athenian love for litigation and the excesses and abuses to which they subject the judicial system. *Peace*, which Aristophanes produced in 421 B.C., is the last of the extant plays which mounts a frontal assualt on specific persons and politicians in Athens. In it Aristophanes continues his assault on the war parties, both in Athens and Sparta. Also, by including groups from outside of Athens as being worthy of Athenian consideration, this play becomes the first shot in the playwright's crusade for Pan-Hellenism, which reaches its peak in *Lysistrata*.

Following *Peace* there is a seven-year gap between extant plays, and when we meet Aristophanes again in *Birds* (414 B.C.) a change has taken place. This play, which Classics scholars have long held up as Aristophanes' finest work, contains less of his earlier, biting invective and fewer direct attacks on identifiable contemporary personages, leading to the speculation that perhaps the politicians won out in the end. On the other hand, *Birds* contains some of the playwright's finest poetry and is a brilliant, utopian fantasy. It takes sharp, satiric aim at all those aspects of Athenian life that have restricted personal freedom and destroyed democracy. Also, it attains a universality by pointing out that humans are by nature too corrupt to attain Utopia—that the ideal state is doomed before it even begins.

If Classics scholars would likely select *Birds* as Aristophanes' best play, theatre scholars would almost certainly select *Lysistrata* as the most playable and certainly as the most comic to contemporary audiences. The play was written in 411 B.C., a year during which Athenian fortunes had sunk to a very low ebb indeed. The city had suffered a nearly disastrous defeat in Sicily in 413 B.C., the empire was on the verge of collapse, and the city was balanced on the brink of revolution. In this context *Lysistrata* can be seen as pleading for peace between Athens and Sparta, urging an end to the Peloponnesian War, and postulating Pan-Hellenism as the best solution to the problems confronting the city and the empire.

Thesmophoriazusae (*Ladies' Day*) is also dated 411 B.C., and in it Aristophanes leaves off his antiwar crusade and goes back to his literary tilt with Euripides. In the play the women of Athens meet at the Thesmophorion and vote to put Euripides to death because his tragedies have so deeply insulted their sex. The effeminate poet Agathon refuses to help his fellow playwright, and though Euripides finally manages, rather ingloriously, to escape the clutches of the women, both he and Agathon come off as completely ridiculous figures.

In many respects Aristophanes' next extant play, *Frogs*, which he presented in 405 B.C., is his most ambitious undertaking. It is a fantasy dealing with literary criticism in which he not only attacks his old foe Euripides but also finds fault with Aeschylus. The play also comments on the destruction that the trend toward dramatic realism is wreaking on the traditional tragic form and on various aspects of public morality. And he does not neglect his usual political theme, though again the central idea is the necessity for national unity and the need for recalling those conservative political leaders who, for espousing ideas very much like Aristophanes' own, have been driven into exile. This last indicates the growing power of the war parties and probably explains why the bombastic political invective that characterized so many of his earlier plays is deserted in the later works.

After *Frogs* there is another long break between the extant plays, and when we again meet Aristophanes it is in the year 392/91 B.C. with his production of *Ecclesiazusae* (*Women in Parliament*). This is a transitional play that contains many of the aspects of Old Comedy while introducing some of the characteristics of Middle Comedy. Basically the play ridicules the social and economic programs being stressed in the fourth century as panaceas for the many ills besetting Athens. It also satirizes the democracy that Aristophanes once championed, finding it a breeding ground for demagogues.

Aristophanes' last extant comedy, *Plutus* (388 B.C.), is also the only extant Middle Comedy, as the characteristics that made their appearance in *Ecclesiazusae* have now taken over. In it the playwright deals purely in utopian fantasy where the good life is achieved through the elimination of economic injustice. It should be noted that political and social injustice are not really touched upon, and that the grand, obscene, biting, bitter satire is no more.

Altogether Aristophanes (c. 445/385 B.C.) wrote some forty plays and successfully spanned two distinct periods and styles of comedy. He displayed an unparalleled comic imagination, managing to combine exquisite lyric poetry with obscenity and farce, and high seriousness with low comedy. His primary concern was always the welfare of Athens and thus, in a sense, the welfare of all mankind. He may have given in to the demagogues near the end of his career, at least in terms of political satire, but he never gave up his attempt to better the conditions surrounding humanity.

DRAMA IN THE FOURTH CENTURY

The Peloponnesian War, which lasted from 431 to 404 B.C., ended in chaotic political and social conditions in Athens, the loss of the entire Athenian navy, the disintegration of the Athenian empire, and ultimately the surrender of Athens. Athens never recovered from this loss of human life, loss of material wealth, and the bitterness that such a long-running war provokes. There was a growing political, social, and economic crisis. Runaway inflation exaggerated the gulf between the increasing number of poor and the very rich, and this precipitated a fierce internal class struggle in most of the city-states. Democracy had broken down with the death of Pericles in 429 B.C., and there was a resulting increase in militarism, often resulting in tyrants supported in their rule by professional armies.

Beginning in approximately 358 B.C., Philip of Macedon (382-36 B.C.) and his son, Alexander the Great (356-23 B.C.), conquered the Greek states, Asia Minor, and the north coast of Africa. This resulted in the spread of Hellenism

A fourth century vase painting shows a burlesque of a mythological love scene.

over the area under their control and a racial and cultural fusion of the native peoples with the Greek (Macedonian) conquerors. In this environment of military conquest and its resulting economic and social unrest, tragedy gradually ceased to be the dominant form of drama. A growing individualism and a resultant interest in things of immediate significance ruled out a type of drama that dealt with things past and what an older, more unified civilization had deemed to be the eternal verities. A new audience was evident in the theatres. People from all walks of life and all economic stations no longer thronged to the plays. Instead, theatregoers more and more became an intellectual and economic elite.

In the Old Comedy, Aristophanes had carped incessantly at Euripides, accusing him of destroying the very fabric of tragedy—and Aristophanes may not have been far wrong. Certainly the impact of Euripides tended to alter the basic form of drama in the fourth century. Through his growing realism he tended to bring the exalted aspects of tragedy down to earth. This realism also militated against the use of myth as the basic subject matter for the drama.

Euripides often concentrated on the results of romantic love, and this became the primary interest of theatre for a later time. As well, Euripides' deemphasis of choral aspects of tragedy tended toward a growing disregard of the chorus as a dramatic element.

Tragedy continued to be written, but gradually the emphasis came to be on acting rather than writing, leading to a kind of literary hackwork. We have the names of several of these writers, but only one manuscript, *Rhesus*, which probably survived because it was included in the manuscripts of Euripides and for many years was ascribed to him. This play departs a bit from the traditional mythology, retelling an incident from the tenth book of Homer's *Iliad*. Fictional plots, such as those of Agathon, or plots based on historical incident, became commonplace for tragedy, replacing plots based on the old mythology. In some cases, apparently, the great plays of the previous century were exhumed for production, but often in a revised and degraded form. Apparently formulaic utterance replaced the grand search for universal truth, provoking Aristotle's comment that "the older poets made their characters speak like citizens; the poets of the present day make them speak like rhetoricians."

For many of the same reasons, Old Comedy also died along with Greek democracy and the Golden Age. Comedy itself, however, did not die. The comic drama maintained and even increased its popularity, though by the year 400 B.C. it was no longer Old Comedy.

Following Old Comedy came the form known as Middle Comedy, which became the primary dramatic form between the years 400 and 338 B.C. We have the names of more than forty authors and six hundred plays representing this form, but the only Middle Comedies extant are two by Aristophanes (*Ecclesiazusae* and *Plutus*), who managed to span both periods. These comedies are far less bawdy and obscene than Old Comedy. The burlesquing of myth is still common to the plot, but now the emphasis is on comic situations and the

Menander (a Roman copy of a Greek original).

pleasures of food and sex. Political, social, and even personal abuse had died out under regimes with strong police powers and no gift for laughing at themselves. The language tends toward the realistic, and the chorus is present merely to do unrelated material and interlude dances.

In 323 B.C. Alexander the Great died and his empire was torn apart by his generals. This state of extreme unrest provoked major changes in all the arts and especially in comedy, where Middle Comedy gave way to the form called New Comedy. Essentially, New Comedy is represented only by the playwright Menander of Athens (c. 342-c. 292 B.C.), who is usually referred to as the father of the genre. He wrote over one hundred plays, but of these only one play is extant in its entirety (*The Grouch*, 317/316 B.C.) and we have fragments of three other plays (*The Arbitration*, *The Shearing of Glycera*, and *The Girl from Samos*). Nine more of his plays survive in adaptations by the Roman dramatists Plautus and Terence.

New Comedy was the principal contribution of the Hellenistic period to dramatic literature, and it differs from Old and Middle Comedy in both structure and intent. Basically it is comedy of manners, which is to say that it is cosmopolitan, sophisticated, and polished, designed for an educated, leisure-class audience. It is reasonably realistic in plot, often dealing with the difficulties that beset young lovers, and idiomatic in dialogue. Certain stock features seem to have been inherent in this form from its beginning, such as the recognition scene, reversal of the difficulties (thanks to the recognition scene), and a resultant happy ending. In addition, there are a number of stock types, perhaps based on the characterizations of the rustic festivals, that people New Comedy. These are the parasite, the courtesan, the knavish slave, the loyal slave, the bold adventurer, the twins, the foundling, the boor, and the miser. Of the Old Comic structure, only the *prologue* is maintained, and this *prologue* is followed by five short acts. The chorus is relegated to performance of musical interludes. Ultimately, the primary value of New Comedy was to provide later writers, by way of the Romans, with the traditional stock characters and the five-act structure.

ASPECTS OF PRODUCTION
(Selection and Financing)

The Greek theatre was, from its earliest beginnings, a festival theatre, which means that it existed only periodically during the festivals of Dionysus in Athens. In the earliest periods there was the City (Great) Dionysia, the Lenaea in January/February, and the Rural Dionysia in December/January. Eventually the City Dionysia became primarily a contest for the tragic drama, and the Lenaea featured comedies. The Rural Dionysia consisted of phallic songs and dances, though late in the Classical period there is evidence that it also included the most popular of the plays from the previous year's two major festivals.

To compete in the contests that were part of these festivals, each playwright had to apply to a state official, an *archon*, for a chorus. There were twelve *archons*, two of whom had jurisdiction over play production: the *Archon Eponymous*, who was the most powerful of the city magistrates, was in charge of the City Dionysia, and the *Archon Basileus*, the primary religious official, supervised the Lenaea. The process tht the *archon* used in determining which of the applicants would be allowed to compete is unknown, though it has been suggested that the poets may have been required to read for him, or for a committee appointed by him, portions of the works they hoped to produce. In any case, three tragic playwrights and five comic playwrights were selected. Each of the tragic playwrights offered a tetralogy—a group of four plays that consisted of (in the early period of the contest) three tragic plays on one unified theme and a satyr play that often burlesqued some aspect of the tragic theme. Later the concept of the trilogy was modified so that the plays could deal with separate subjects and themes.

After the selection of the competing poets, a panel of contest judges representing each of the ten Attic tribes was carefully selected by the Athenian Council. After the contest was completed the ten judges cast their ballots and five of these ten ballots were drawn at random by the *archon*. This final drawing determined the winner of the contest. The honor of being a contest judge was great, for the competition was a serious religious business held with the backing of the state, and the conduct of the judges was reviewed after the event by the Athenian Assembly.

In the beginning the city probably funded the production costs, but starting in about 501 B.C. after the poets had been selected for the competition, each was assigned by the *archon* to a wealthy Athenian citizen, called a *choregus*. The *choregus* paid for the cost of production: the salaries of the musicians, the rehearsal costs, and the costumes. Acting as *choregus* was a duty imposed by the state on its wealthiest members, but it was not a duty that was in any way onerous or avoided. Indeed, it was considered a high honor to be chosen and the position was greatly sought after by men of affluence. In part this is because the prize for the winning play was awarded jointly to both the poet and the *choregus*.

THE CHORUS

The importance of the chorus in Greek drama cannot be overemphasized. The *parados* provided an unparalleled opportunity for exposition and foreshadowing and also for providing to the audience that material which the author felt was crucial to an understanding of his theme. In the choral interludes the author found a method of scene transition and also a technique for commenting on the action of the play and restating the theme. Also, because they were poetic and musical in nature, they provided welcome breaks from the action and allowed the playwright to display his skills in both of these adjunct areas.

For contemporary playgoers the chorus may seem intrusive, breaking the stage reality with which we are so familiar and which we seem more and more to demand of drama. However, for the Greek audience the chorus was central to the production. The basic functions of the chorus were several. They provided a special form of beauty in their inclusion of poetry, music, and dance. They used the poetry, especially, to invoke the mood and central theme of the drama, interpreting the events depicted in the *episodes* and generalizing on the meaning of the action. Also, the chorus provided a connection between the actors and the audience, allowing the audience to see the event twice by viewing it themselves and also viewing its effect on the chorus. In addition, the chorus often provided advice to the characters, especially in the *kommos*, a responsive lyric passage between the chorus and an actor.

Under no circumstances should the tragic chorus ever be understood to have been merely a mouthpiece for the author. In comedy this certainly was the case, with the chorus stepping forward in the *parabasis* to address the audience directly about any and all subjects dear to the author's heart. In tragedy, however, the chorus was always given a character—Old Men of Thebes, or Corinthian Women, or Eumenides—and they remained in character throughout the play. Thus, when they commented on or explained the action or theme it was always in terms of the characterization the author had assigned to them.

ACTING

In the earliest phase of Classical Greek drama the actor and the playwright were one and the same. Because of Aristotle, Thespis is still given credit for creating the first actor (*hypokrites* or "answerer") who performed between the dances of the dithyrambic chorus, playing several roles and speaking at times with the chorus leader. According to tradition the second actor was added by Aeschylus and the third by Sophocles; however, this seems highly speculative and an examination of Aeschylus' *Oresteia* seems to indicate that three actors were available to him. Playwrights did, however, continue to act in their own plays (we know certainly that Aeschylus acted in his plays) until the time of Sophocles, when he supposedly set a precedent by refusing to act in his later plays. By the time that the contest for tragic actors was initiated in 449 B.C. the practice of playwrights acting in their own plays had been discontinued.

Whether the convention that finally fixed the number of actors in Greek tragedy at three was ever really observed is open to debate. Certainly after 468 B.C. the number of primary actors available to each playwright in the competition was limited to three. However, these three could play any number of roles and were supplemented by supernumeraries who were allowed to play minor roles and even speak a limited number of lines. These rules never seem to have been applied strictly to comedy. Most of the comic plays that we have can, with some difficulty, be acted by three players, but one requires at least five major actors.

The art of acting was highly prized in ancient Greece, and was open to people from all walks of life. The acting companies were made up almost exclusively of men, though occasionally a few young boys were included. By the time of the Hellenistic period everyone involved in the production of plays had become united in their trade guild, the Artists of Dionysus, and in fact their employment in putting on plays was considered to be a religious function which made them in a sense an adjunct of the priesthood, even exempting them from

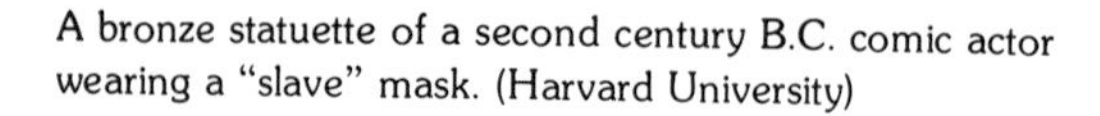

A bronze statuette of a second century B.C. comic actor wearing a "slave" mask. (Harvard University)

military service. Their guild formulated the rules that governed their employment and the working conditions under which the members performed. In many respects it was the equivalent of today's unions, and the general attitude of admiration in which the theatre artists were held was higher than it has ever been until our own time.

Members of the actor's guild were carefully selected and trained. The Greeks put a primary emphasis on vocal training, judging an actor's competence in terms of beauty of tone, ability to create mood and character, and ability to speak beautifully from any posture. The actor was also trained as a singer, since in the course of a play he was expected to deliver oral material in three ways: the iambic trimeter lines were declaimed: the recitative was intoned to musical accompaniment; and the lyrical passages were sung (sometimes solo and sometimes in duet or chorus).

Training in movement was important, especially in the later period, since the tragic masks and robes and slightly elevated footwear made facial expression of no importance at all and movement extremely difficult. Actors did have to know, however, a broad category of standardized gesture, and were required to move gracefully in costume so that they could perform in the *emmeleia*, the slow, stately tragic dances to which costume excesses restricted them. The actors specializing primarily in comic roles did not have the costume problems that limited the tragic actor, and given the lines of the comedies it is probable that the comic actor practiced a somewhat more realistic vocal pattern and broad movement tending toward the farcical or burlesque. The comic dance, the *kordax*, was fast, bawdy, and perhaps even obscene by our contemporary standards, and the dance of the satyr play, the *sikinnis*, was a fast-moving parody of the tragic dance.

COSTUME AND MAKEUP

The Greek tragic costume was dominated by the mask, and it is probably the oldest convention of their theatrical dress, coming directly from the primitive dramatic festivals. The masks were constructed of cloth, cork, or wood, or some combination of these, and covered the full face. They were larger than life size and in their late manifestations included the *onkos*, a dome above the features that had the effect of adding substantially to the height of the actor. The masks allowed the actors to double and even triple in their roles. Sometimes one character would have several masks representing that character at different stages of the play. For example, the mask of blind Oedipus must have been quite different from the mask the same character wore earlier in the play. It is likely that the tragic mask became more to the actor than a method of disguising his own features; in fact, the mask may well have become the personna, allowing the actor to take on the spiritual qualities of a character merely by donning his mask.

Unlike the masks, the rest of the Greek tragic costume changed considerably, with the early robe of the priest of Dionysus giving way to the long-sleeved, ornate dress of the later period. Eventually the colors the actors wore became standardized to represent specific characters; outer garments were added to enliven and identify the physical characterization. Thus, an overgarment of purple signified a king, a white robe trimmed in purple a queen, and olive color signified mourning. Chorus members and supernumeraries in minor roles were dressed according to their characterization.

On their feet the tragic actors wore boots, at first the traditional Asiatic leg boot, but later on, in the continued attempt to make the characters even larger than life (which was appropriate to their elevated station and which also helped the audience visually in the large theatres), the *kothurnos* was developed. This was an elevated boot featuring cork soles ranging from six to twelve inches thick. These boots, together with the dome (*onkos*) atop the tragic mask, added more than a foot to the actor's height and made him an awesome figure indeed.

The costume for comedy, which dealt with characters of somewhat less elevation, was considerably different. The comic robe was short and worn over a grotesquely padded undergarment resembling a body stocking. The male characters sported large leather phalluses, usually red in color, and which may have had cords attached so that the actors could elevate them in appropriate circumstances. By the time of Middle Comedy the wearing of the phallus had lost its popularity, and by the end of the period the tradition had been discontinued.

Because the characters of comedy were not treated with reverence, and because of the fast dancing and excessive physical action, the comic actor wore *socci* (or low, soft boots) on his feet. On his head he wore the comic mask, which lacked the *onkos* of the tragic mask and which attempted to portray in

Theatre mask decorates a frieze on the theatre at Perge.

grotesque fashion a much wider variety of characters than existed in tragedy. In some cases the masks seem to have been caricatures of existing personages—both Sophocles and Euripides were impersonated in the plays of Aristophanes. The chorus in comedy was usually costumed in some form of colorful or fantastic dress. However, in this aspect both comedy and tragedy came together because it is hard to imagine a comic chorus of birds, for example, being more imaginatively dressed than the chorus of Furies in Aeschylus' tragedy, whose appearance onstage is traditionally supposed to have caused children to die of fright and pregnant women to give birth.

THE GREEK STAGE

The ancestor of the Classical Greek theatre was very probably nothing more than a circular area of hard-packed earth—possibly a threshing floor with a low, thick post set in its center to which teams of oxen were hitched and driven about in a circle to tramp out the grain. When this threshing floor was pressed into duty as a theatrical area, probably at first for the production of dithyrambs in honor of Dionysus, it was consecrated to the god and his statue was placed on the hitching post in the center of the floor, which thus became an altar of the god. The people viewing the event probably grouped themselves about the circumference of the circle, in much the same manner that people of all times and places have grouped themselves to witness an event. Eventually this circular area became the most prominent aspect of the sophisticated Classical Greek theatre—the *orchestra* or dancing place. The earliest Greek plays, such as those by Thespis, probably took place in just such an *orchestra*.

When the plays grew longer and more complex, and the resulting crowds grew larger, the simple threshing floor or simple *orchestra* could no longer accommodate them. As a result an *orchestra* was laid out at the foot of a hill so that the audience could group itself on the slope, thereby making it easier to see and hear. To continue the existing tradition an altar (*thymele*) was placed in the center of the *orchestra* to replace the hitching post and hold the representation of the god to whom the plays were dedicated. As productions got longer and crowds grew ever larger and demanded greater comfort, wooden bleachers were set up on the hillside. Eventually the slope itself was graded, with seats cut into the hillside and faced with wood and, eventually, stone flags.

In the earliest versions the *orchestra* was a totally open area, with no real possibility for entrances and exits or for changes on the part of the players. In come cases the area immediately behind the *orchestra* may have been graded down to make the back of the *orchestra* a low wall behind which actors could change and the gods could appear and disappear. This wall may also have provided an opening to a tunnel running beneath the back of the *orchestra* to a trap near the *orchestra's* center, but there is no real evidence to support such a supposition.

At some time prior to 458 B.C. a scene house (*skene*) was built behind the *orchestra*. The word *skene* translates as "hut" or "tent," which indicates that this early structure must have been a temporary, rather flimsy building de-

The Greek theatre at Epidaurus, showing the symmetrical seating, *orchestra*, and general configuration of the scene house.

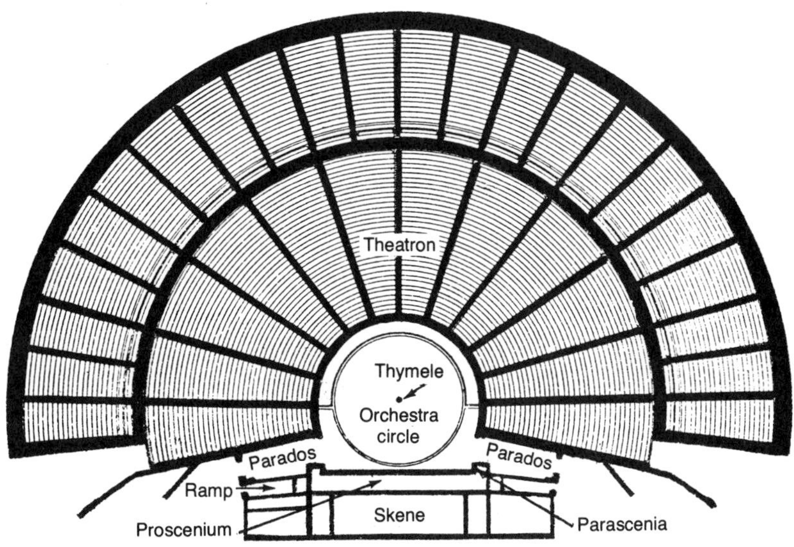

signed primarily as a changing house for the performers. Soon, however, it grew into a rather impressive edifice. The *proscenium* was the façade of the *skene*, and its architectural embellishment provided most of the scenery for the plays, especially before the middle of the fifth century. These plays, as far as can be determined, all seem to have taken place before a palace or temple, so the architecture of the *skene* would be appropriate. The roof of the *skene* was given an acting area of its own, the *theologeion*, from which the gods and heroes could speak, from which the Watchman of Aeschylus' play *Agamemnon* could address the audience, and from which Medea in Euripides' play could seem to be escaping from vengeance in her dragon-drawn chariot.

The *skene* contained two major mechanical devices—the *mechane* and the *eccyclema*. The *mechane* ("machine") was apparently a type of crane, mounted on the roof of the *skene*, for the purpose of raising or lowering flying figures (in chariots or on the backs of birds and flying animals) and to introduce and remove gods. In the tragic plays the *deus ex machina* ("god from the machine") was a common device. Essentially this allowed the writers a miraculous conclusion for their plays. The god appeared on high, suspended from the *mechane*, and resolved all the problems which the playwright had created. It should be noted that while Euripides often made use of the *mechane* to bring in the gods and resolve his plots, there is no need for the "god machine" in any of the surviving plays of Aeschylus and Sophocles. This does not mean that the *mechane* was not available to these earlier playwrights, but that the Greek playwrights made use of mechanical contrivances only when absolutely necessary. The *mechane* was also used for comedy, allowing Aristophanes to display Socrates suspended in a basket, halfway between heaven and earth, and to parody the great deeds of the heroes by having one of his characters ascend to heaven mounted not on a grand steed such as Pegasus, but on a beetle.

The *eccyclema* seems, on one hand, to be a device designed for less spectacular events than the *mechane*, but in fact may have provided audiences with highly exciting spectacles. Basically the *eccyclema* was a wheeled vehicle or platform that in its most sophisticated form ran on tracks much like a modern railway car. Its purpose was to roll out from behind the scenes or appear in the great central doorway of the *skene*, with the actors mounted on it, depicting in tableau the events (usually violent) that happened offstage or before the action began. The appearance of Clytemnestra the murderer, posed over the body of Agamemnon, must have been as exciting to the audience as the depictions of flying gods and heroes.

Perhaps the most important thing about the Greek theatre machines is that there were so few of them. This does not indicate a technological incapacity but a production emphasis placed elsewhere—probably on acting.

The *skene* was sometimes flanked on either side by *parascenia*, which were forward-projecting wings somewhat resembling the wings of contemporary theatres. Between the *parascenia* and the *theatron* ("seeing place," or audience seating area) were long passageways, *paradoi*, used for entrances and exits of the chorus, entrances and exits of wheeled vehicles such as chariots, and before and after productions for the entrance and exit of the audience. In front of the *skene* there may have been a low stage of some sort—the *logeion*. There is little agreement as to its size, although it presumably ran the full length of the scene building and was shallow enough not to encroach upon the *orchestra*. Neither is there any real evidence as to its height, though it was probably rather low, only high enough to elevate the actors three or four feet above the level of the *orchestra*. There is also no way of ascertaining when, if ever, this stage was added to the original scene building. Some scholars believe that it was not a stage area at all, in any formal sense, but rather a broad set of steps leading up to the *skene*.

The most important theatre during the fifth century—the greatest period of Greek Classical drama—was the Theatre of Dionysus at Athens, and the development previously described closely follows what must have been the pattern of that theatre, with the hillside being the Acropolis itself. Probably the most impressive aspect of that specific theatre was the seating capacity. Fourteen to seventeen thousand people could be accommodated in the *theatron*, and some scholars have raised that estimate to as much as twenty thousand. It is ironic and rather sad that the permanent stone structure of this great theatre was not fully completed until sometime around 325 B.C., when the Athenian theatre had lost its influence and the great period of drama was already over.

The period generally referred to as Hellenistic saw some significant physical changes in the structure of the Greek theatre. Exactly when these changes began to occur is still hotly debated, with some scholars opting for Hellenistic modifications beginning as early as the fourth century, while others feel that such changes could not have taken place before the beginning of the second century. In any case, the change in style from the Classic theatre to the Hellenistic must have been completed by the year 150 B.C. The theatres at

The theatre at Epidaurus today, seen from the top center of the *theatron* looking down at the *orchestra*.

Priene and Epidaurus are often used as examples of Hellenistic theatres, and certainly they work well as illustrations of two basic Hellenistic types. In the theatre at Epidaurus the *orchestra* circle remains whole, and the entire scene building and stage area remain behind the *orchestra*. The theatre at Priene, on the other hand, illustrates the pattern in which the *orchestra* circle was cut off at the back and joined to the scene building.

Perhaps the most interesting innovation of the Hellenistic theatre was the establishment of a high (compared to the *logeion* of the Classic Greek theatre) raised stage. At its lowest this stage was designed to be higher than a man standing in the *orchestra*, thus allowing simultaneous action on both levels, and averaged between eight and thirteen feet in height. This stage was shallow but long, running the width of the scene house, and the *parascenia* were eliminated, thus allowing a narrow ramp or steps to lead up to the stage. The front or audience edge of the stage was supported by the *proskenion*, the facade of the first story of the stage, and the *episkenion* (or second story) formed the back of the stage area.

In the earliest of such Hellenistic theatres the *proskenion* was formed of pillars spaced several feet apart and notched or grooved on their sides so that panels (*pinakes*) could be slid in and out. These panels probably had scenic materials painted on them and were similar in most respects to the flats of modern theatre. Their presence on the ground floor of these theatres indicates that major action was still taking place in the *orchestra*. However, in the

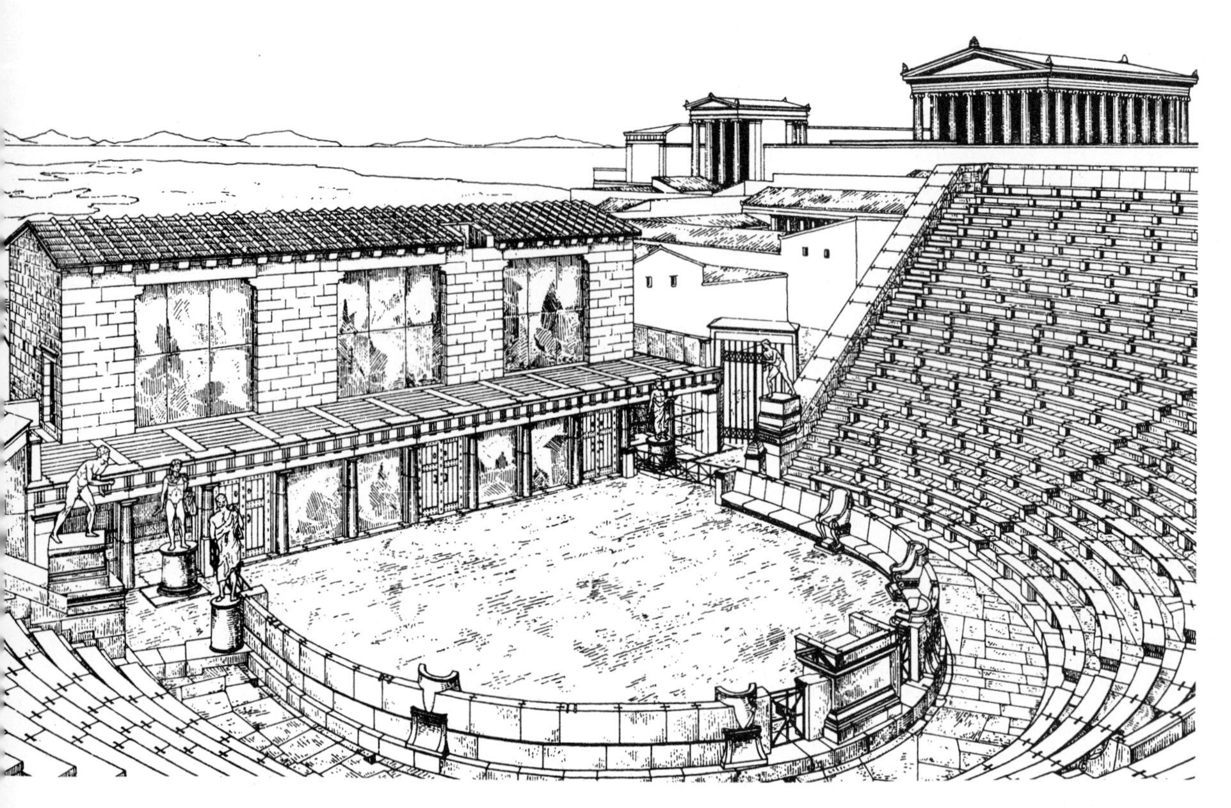

A drawing of the Greek theatre at Priene as it existed in c. 150 B.C. This represents the Hellenistic period of the theatre, in which the *orchestra* was reduced and joined to the scene house, with the actors performing primarily on an elevated stage above the lower level of the house. (From Armin von Gerkan, *Das Theatre von Priene*, Munich, 1921)

theatres that date after the second century the notches no longer appear, leading to speculation that the dramatic action had moved back out of the *orchestra*, and that the pillars had become merely an architectural scenic device.

An equivalent change was also made in the facade of the *episkenion*. In the earliest Hellenistic theatres this second-story facade had featured three doors, much in the manner of the Classic Greek theatre. However, sometime during the second century these doors became merely openings (*thyromata*) ranging from three to seven in number and separated by narrow upright supports or pillars. Thus, the second story may have provided an inner stage (the area behind the openings), though this is still widely debated, and an outer stage (the narrow forestage). Some scholars believe that this change came about as a result of the declining importance of the chorus and the resulting tendency to play the entire action on the higher level.

The Hellenistic theatre ended the line of Greek theatre buildings, for beginning in the second century the Romans began their march to power that soon saw them masters of the eastern area of the Mediterranean. Having conquered, they took over the existing Greek theatres and modified them to their own uses.

ARISTOTLE

Born in 384 B.C. in Stagira, a small village far to the north of Athens, Aristotle was the son of the court physician to the King of Macedon. In 367 B.C., at the age of seventeen, he was sent to study with the famous philosopher, Plato, in the school called the Academy. He remained at the Academy until Plato's death, some twenty years later, studying under the master and composing his own philosophical works, which at first were basically defenses of Plato's own ideas but which later began to differ in subtle ways that sometimes conflicted with the master's own teachings. Following Plato's death in 347 B.C., Aristotle left Athens, spending approximately five years in Lesbos and Asia Minor and another three years in Macedon where he was tutor to Alexander the Great. Returning to Athens in 335 B.C., he set up his own school, which he named the Lyceum after the sanctuary of Apollo Lykeios in which it was located. He remained at the school until 323 B.C., when the death of Alexander the Great allowed the city's strong anti-Macedonian elements to make their feelings known. Stating that he did not wish to be responsible for Athens' "sinning against philosophy a second time" (the first time being the execution of Socrates in 399 B.C.) he left the city to dwell on a nearby island, where he died within one year.

Aristotle is one of the most important of the Greek philosophers for a number of reasons. His interests were broad, ranging over the whole area of philosophy as he understood it from Plato's teaching. He also spent a great deal of time doing research in the biological sciences, perhaps because of the influence of his physician father. However, in terms of theatre he becomes especially important because he is the author of the earliest known philosophical study of tragedy. The work, titled *Peri poietikes* ("On Poetry") is generally known in English as the *Poetics* and it is not so much a finished

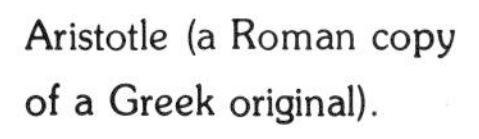
Aristotle (a Roman copy of a Greek original).

treatise as a compendium of research and lecture notes. However, from the sixteenth century to the present it has been one of the most influential works on the development of the theatrical arts.

The age of great tragic writing was nearly one hundred years past when Aristotle first arrived in Athens, and therefore when he speaks of the tragic art he is not referring to plays that were being written during his own lifetime or even offering guidance to his contemporary artists. Instead, he is examining works from the past, seeking to understand how they function by putting together a philosophical model for perfect tragedy. The model that he finally constructed was based on carefully selected examples and primarily on *Oedipus the King* (c. 430/29 B.C.) by Sophocles. He refers to Euripides as "the most tragic of poets" but gives his work short shrift, and he pays even less attention to Aeschylus.

Tragedy had been of great philosophical interest to Plato, Aristotle's teacher, and probably also to Socrates, who had been the teacher of Plato and quite probably of some influence on the late work of Euripides. This led Aristotle quite naturally to his study of tragedy, especially because his teacher had, in the course of his studies, concluded that tragedy is basically irrational in its approach to life and therefore dangerous to the state. According to Plato, tragedy is an instrument for promoting unenlightened beliefs and ideals. Thus, in a state set up to achieve the highest possible ideal of human happiness, tragedy would have to be excluded.

Probably because he had already redefined some of Plato's thought, and because Plato's concept of tragedy called some of his redefinitions into doubt, Aristotle felt compelled to justify the existence of and need for tragedy in a rational universe. Plato had indicated that tragedy is irrational because it appeals to the emotions and to the subconscious, an aspect of man that should only operate while man is asleep and that should in no way be part of his waking life. If man operates on an emotional and thus irrational level while he is awake, Plato reasoned, then he will be as compulsive, unrestrained, criminal, and even insane while awake as he is while asleep. To counter this argument, Aristotle was forced to show that the performance of tragedy (and, of course, the viewing as well) is good for man while in a waking state, since by arousing such undesirable emotions in the theatre, tragedy thus purges him of irrationality and of the potential for evil behavior. This purging (Aristotle's term was *katharsis*) probably was meant as a psychic equivalent to the medical purgation with which Aristotle was so familiar from his own studies in the biological sciences.

The other aspect of Aristotle's work which has, throughout the centuries, caused so much dissension among scholars, is his comment on *hamartia*, which has traditionally been translated as "tragic flaw." Probably the best way to understand what Aristotle presumably meant by this is to remember that he was attempting to counter the teachings of Plato on tragedy, which makes it necessary to go back to the commentary of Socrates by way of Plato. Socrates and his student believed that all good men (and *only* good men) are happy, and conversely that all bad men (and *only* bad men) are miserable. Tragedy, Plato pointed out, makes use of *mythoi* which tell of men who are represented as being good but who nevertheless undergo extreme misery.

What is worse, this misery is suffered with the consent of and often, in fact, at the behest of the gods, who should always be good and just when interfering with human destinies. This is bad, according to Plato, because *mythoi* are designed to teach, and what they teach in tragedy is a perverted view of life in which goodness is rewarded not with happiness but with suffering.

Aristotle accepts the Socratic/Platonic view of *mythoi* and of good and evil. He admits that a play in which a purely good man suffers misery through no fault of his own would be defiling, but he points out that this is never true, for in all of the successful tragedies there is a major flaw (*hamartia*) in the protagonist that brings the tragic action down upon him. Thus, tragedy does not defile the "good" spectator and, in fact, is good for him in that it rids him of the irrational by purging it away.

Because Aristotle's work was the first major examination of the great tragic dramatists, and because it has been for so long the most influential work on the subject, a brief outline of his work is necessary. This outline should not be taken as exhaustive, however, and any student of theatre should carefully consult the work either in the original or one of the better translations.

The Poetics

The subject is the poetic art and its particular species; the essential quality of each is examined. The ultimate aim is to examine the structure of the ideal poetic work.

(1)

Art is an imitation of an object in some particular medium; there is one art whose medium is language. Verse is not essential to poetry. Certain of the arts combine rhythm, melody, and verse.

(2)

The objects of artistic imitation are men in action. The men are represented as either better or worse than in real life, or as they are.

Tragedy differs from comedy in that it represents men as better than they are in real life.

(3)

The story may be told in narrative and dialogue, in narrative alone, or in action.

(4)

Poetry grows out of the impulse to imitate and the pleasure derived from the results of this imitation, even when the object imitated is repulsive. Part of the pleasure arises from recognition, part from execution.

Aeschylus increased the number of actors to two; Sophocles increased the number to three. Tragedy evolved from change in the scope of plots, the improvement of diction by the use of suitable meters, and the increase in number of episodes.

(5)

Tragedy differs from epic in meter, in form of presentation, and in length or duration of the action. Tragedy endeavors to confine itself to a single revolution of the sun.

(6)

Tragedy is an imitation of an action that is serious, complete, and of adequate magnitude. Its language is embellished in different ways in different parts. It exists in the form of action, not narration. Through pity and terror it effects the purgation of these emotions.

The six elements of tragedy are plot, character (*ethos*), diction, thought (*dianoia*), spectacle, and melody. Plot is the most important, because tragedy is the imitation of an action. In fact, plot is so important that with it tragedy can exist, even without *ethos*. The most vital features of tragedy—reversals and recognitions (discoveries)—are elements of the plot; in fact, plot is the soul of tragedy. Next in importance is character, then thought, diction, melody, and last is spectacle since it demands the lowest order of artistic skill and is least concerned with poetry.

(7)

In constructing the plot the action must be complete, that is, it must have a beginning, a middle, and an end; and it must not begin or end arbitrarily. In length the parts and the whole must each be of a length that can easily be retained in the memory. So long as the plot remains clear throughout, length is a merit. The hero should undergo a change of fortune through a series of incidents in probable or inevitable sequence.

(8)

The provision of a single hero is not enough to assure unity of plot. The *Odyssey* and the *Illiad* illustrate unity. The plot should present an organically unified action.

(9)

The poet does not represent actual fact, but what might happen. He relates what is typical or what a certain person is bound to do or say in a given situation. History deals with the particular.

Tragic poets have mostly adhered to traditional stories because these seem more credible. However, they are not restricted to these and have sometimes deviated from them.

Episodic plots are the worst kind. There is a danger of adopting this type merely to make the play long enough.

Plots affect us most strongly if the incidents have an unexpected casual relation.

(10)

Uninvolved plots are constructed of incidents forming a single, continuous action. Involved plots include reversal of fortune or recognition.

(11)

Reversal (*peripateia*) is a chain of action that produces the opposite of the effect intended, as the revelation of the Messenger in *Oedipus the King*. Discovery is the transition from ignorance to knowledge; its best form is recognition attended by reversal, as in *Oedipus*.

(12)

The divisions of Greek tragedy are *prologue, episodes, exodos,* choric songs, (*parados, stasima, kommos*).

(13)

In the ideal structure for tragedy the involved plot is best. Such an ideal plot will avoid good and just men falling into misery, evil men rising to prosperity, or excessively wicked men falling into misfortune.

The ideal situation will have a man who stands in the middle, between these two extremes, and who is brought low by some error of judgment or shortcoming (*hamartia*).

The best plot features a fall into misery, through *hamartia*, by a man who is as good as the average or better. This is supported by practice as well as by theory. Euripides justified this in his unhappy endings, for they have the greatest tragic effect.

The next best is the double plot, with a happy ending for the good people and a bad ending for the wicked. This is a concession to the public and is proper to comedy.

(14)

Pity and terror are best aroused by incidents of the plot and not by spectacular means. The most impressive tragic plots involve friends in deeds of violence or horror. Possibilities for such plots are: (a) the doer may know what he is doing to someone who knows who the doer is, (b) the doer may be ignorant, (c) the doer may discover the relationship and withdraw from the deed, and (d) the doer may be aware of what he is about to do and then refrain (this is the least tragic). In *Antigone*, Haemon refrains from killing his father. This is the best of such plots, when one refrains because he learns just in time.

(15)

Characterization must be good, true to type, true to life, consistent. Speech and action must spring from character.

The ending should arise from the previous action and not be brought about by arbitrary devices.

If there is an irrational element, it should lie outside the tragedy. The poet must ennoble the tragic hero, giving him good qualities in addition to his tragic flaw.

(16)

There are six types of recognition. The best is that which arises from the action itself.

(17)

The poet should visualize the action, to save himself from inconsistencies and blunders.

He should assume the attitudes and gestures of those he intends to depict.

He should make a brief outline of his plot and insert episodes.

(18)

The plot must include complication and resolution, separated by a turning point.

The chorus should take a share in the action, as in the plays of Sophocles.

(19)

The ideal of diction is to be clear without being vulgar.

(20)

The poet should prefer probable impossibilities to improbable possibilities.

3

The Roman Theatre

3

The Roman Theatre

The Roman theatre no longer occupies the place, either in terms of dramatic literature or production, that it held during the Renaissance. The Latin plays have become little more than the preserve of Classics scholars, and even the scholars tend to be far more concerned with the original plays of the great Greek writers than with their Latin translators and adaptors. Yet knowledge of this now neglected period is of great importance in understanding our own theatre because the influence of Roman theatre on the Renaissance was enormous and was passed on to affect even later times. Thus, it is necessary to know Plautus, Terence, and Seneca in order to know Marlowe, Jonson, and Shakespeare and those later theatricians who were so much influenced by these Renaissance giants.

THE ROMAN WORLD

At almost the same time that Greece was entering its Golden Age a new and essentially puritanical, militaristic power was making its presence felt on the Italian peninsula. From its insignificant beginning as a small town in the area of Latium, Rome grew rapidly in size and power. First it conquered its own Latin neighbors, then the whole of the peninsula. It defeated and subsequently destroyed Carthage, conquering the Near East and North Africa as far as the Strait of Gibraltar. Eventually it moved northward, annexing Gaul and Britain to its empire, and then it settled down to rule, for several hundred years, nearly the whole of the civilized world.

The early Romans were Indo-Europeans who had migrated south, as had their neighbors and near kinsmen the Greeks, but unlike the Greeks they came to a land without major harbors and that was not so divided by topographical features into small units—a land, in other words, that tended toward geographical unity. It was an area of rich valleys and pastures, and the migrating Romans quickly settled down to stock raising and agriculture, assimilating with ease the peoples they found there, so that they soon became a nation of highly mixed ethnic stock.

Because the land had such geographic unity the Romans found it easy to invade and conquer, and for the same reasons it was equally difficult for them to defend their new territory. This led to a continuing emphasis on the martial arts and toward the warlike activities that would eventually result in their conquests and the formation of their empire. Certainly it was this aspect of Roman existence that led them to crowd out the earlier Etruscans and take over the Etruscan capital of Rome, a fortified city situated atop a series of hills on the south bank of the Tiber River.

In terms of the drama, indeed of the entire civilization that the Romans eventually would develop, their subjugation of the Greeks is of the utmost importance. The Greeks had long been a power on the Italian peninsula, especially in the south and in Sicily. At one time, in fact, it appeared that the Greeks would conquer the whole of the peninsula when two consecutive victories by Pyrrhus, the Greek general and leader of Epirus, threatened to destroy the Roman colonies. However, the Romans held on and eventually defeated Pyrrhus, after which they systematically conquered the remaining Greek cities in Italy.

Rome's first major conflict with the Greeks outside Italy (214-205 B.C.), carried on with the support of her Aetolian allies, broke up the league that existed between Philip, King of Macedon, and Hannibal. The second conflict (200-196 B.C.) forced Philip to grant freedom to the Greek cities within his empire. The third conflict (190 B.C.) drove the Syrian Antiochus out of Asia Minor, and the fourth (148 B.C.) ended with the subjugation of Macedonia and Greece as Roman provinces. These wars with the Greeks and the eventual occupation of the Greek cities had a lasting effect on the whole spectrum of Roman society, especially on Roman culture. The Romans became indebted to the Greeks for the designs of their ships, coins, weights, measures, and even their religion. They adopted the Greek alphabet, though modified by the Latin language, Greek dress, Greek styles and types of literature, and most importantly they adopted the Greek drama.

EARLY ETRUSCAN DANCE AND DRAMA

Just as the Greeks found the origin of their drama in the rhythms of music, dance, and recitation, so the Romans seem to have discovered their early pre-Greek drama in the equivalent activities that took place at the rustic festivals of Etruria. In the music, dance, and dialogue of the neighboring Etruscans the Romans found a perfect vehicle for expressing all types of intellectual and emotional concepts.

This belief that the Etruscans actually began the Roman drama, or at least that they provided the earliest significant influence, depends on the authority of Horace, who states that the origin of Roman drama can be found in the "Fescennine Verses." Historians have generally decided that the Fescennine Verses refer to the planting and harvest entertainments that took place in the town of Fescennium on the Etrurian border. Whether this is an accurate understanding of the word *Fescennine*, or whether it was derived from *fascinum*, the term for the male reproductive organ (a symbol that was highly popular at the fertility festivals where it represented reproductive magic), is debatable. Both understandings have validity in terms of the rustic fertility drama, and it may well be that "Fescennine" represents an intentional ambiguity by which the Romans meant a specific type of festival (fertility) in a designated geographical area (the town of Fescennium).

In any case, the Fescennine Verses seem to have been rather primitive, crude dramatic events with obscene dialogue that was in part improvised and in part passed on in an oral tradition from performer to apprentice. In addition to the dialogue, one can assume a prominence of song and dance. The performers were masked, probably in the beginning not so much because the mask actually represented the character (as it did for the Classical Greek drama) but to protect the performer from reprisals because of the often satiric nature of the materials presented.

The circus performances, so much a part of Roman tradition, also have their roots in Etruscan history. The Circus Maximus was almost certainly built by the elder Tarquin (616-578 B.C.), the first of Rome's Etruscan kings, and not by the mythical Romulus. The early performances consisted of chariot races and boxing and wrestling matches, which the nobles watched from specially built grandstands, with the balance of the people seated on the ground. Every September, following the harvest, the Romans gathered at the Circus for the *ludi Romani*. As was the case with the early Greek drama, this was a political as well as a social function, supported and even encouraged by the state, and the whole population, including women and the slaves, was invited to attend.

The Roman historian Livy (59 B.C.-17 A.D.) recounts how, in the year 364-63 B.C., Rome was ravaged by a severe plague. This brought on a superstitious panic in which the plague was popularly believed to be the result of the wrath of the gods. To appease the angry gods, dancers and musicians were brought to Rome from Etruria. The Romans were, apparently, deeply impressed by the grace of the Etruscans in dancing to the flute (pipe), and afterward re-created this mimetic Etruscan dance in conjunction with the dialogue of the Fescennine Verses. The resulting entertainment is referred to by Livy as a *satura* or medley, and the performers as *histriones*, the Etruscan word for dancers. These *histriones* continued for many years to entertain the Romans with their *ludi scaenici*.

At the beginning of the first Punic War (264 B.C.), which would result in these early dramatic forms being almost overpowered by the sophisticated Greek drama, came the last importation from Etruria—the gladiatorial combat. That prisoners should be set to battle each other as a form of public entertainment seems somehow to be worse than the already existing Roman custom (which lasted up to the time of Julius Caesar) of sequentially executing prisoners of war as military commanders ascended Capitoline Hill. The popularity of the gladitorial contest never waned following its introduction to Rome, and the probable influence exerted by such a regular diet of bloody entertainments can be seen when one looks closely at Roman tragedy and the mimes of the Empire period.

NATIVE ROMAN FESTIVALS

In early Roman times, before the Republic began to decay (133-27 B.C.), public theatrical performances all took place during the various festivals (*ludi*). These festivals were essentially state-supported religious celebrations in honor of the derivative Roman gods, many of them also commemorating such historical events as great military victories, the birth or death of major personages, or any happening to which the government wished to attach special significance. During this early period the festivals probably took up between six and twelve days per year. It is difficult to determine the exact number of days included in the various festivals because the festivals themselves varied from year to year. And it is even more difficult to determine how many days of each festival were devoted to theatrical performance, as opposed to chariot races, gladiatorial bouts, and circus-type entertainments. However, the dramatic festival days did increase steadily, and by the time of the Augustan Age (63 B.C.-14 A.D.) the festivals accounted for approximately forty days out of each year. The Roman policy of bread and circuses was well underway.

Perhaps the oldest and certainly the most important of the festivals was the *ludi Romani*, which was a harvest festival held each September in honor of Jupiter, the Roman equivalent of Zeus and first among the gods. This festival, certainly of ancient origin, was formally established early in the sixth century B.C. and did not include theatrical entertainment as a feature until 364 B.C. with the importation of the Etruscan dancers. The more traditional dramatic forms of comedy and tragedy were not added as a regular aspect of this festival until 240 B.C.

The other major festivals, like the *ludi Romani*, were certainly late versions of ancient ceremonies that had to do with the plowing, planting, sowing, and harvesting of crops, and the dates of official recognition of such ceremonies mean little except that what had traditionally been merely folk ceremonies now had official sanction and state support for their entertainments. The *ludi Florales* was given each April in honor of Flora, the Roman goddess of flowers and, more generally, of spring vegetation. It was first supported by the state, in an irregular fashion, in 238 B.C., but did not become a regular annual event until 173 B.C. The *ludi plebeii*, a November festival honoring Jupiter, was probably a traditional slaughter festival celebrating the harvest of cattle, held each year after the herds were thinned. It was instituted as a state festival sometime before the year 220 B.C., with theatrical performances initiated about the year 200 B.C. The *ludi Apollinares*, originally a vegetation ceremony held early in the growing season, honored Apollo. It was incorporated as a state function in 212 B.C., with theatrical performances coming about thirty years later. The *ludi Megalenses* and the *ludi Cereales* were both spring vegetation festivals that took place in April. The first, *ludi Megalenses*, did honor to the Great Mother and was established in 204 B.C. The *ludi Cereales*, in honor of Ceres, goddess of the fields and the Roman equivalent of Demeter, was established sometime before 202 B.C. Both festivals began to feature theatrical performances only a few years after their formal inclusion in the state program.

ATELLAN FARCE

One of the seemingly native Italic forms predating the arrival of Greek drama was the Atellan farce. The term *fabula Atellana*, according to

A wall painting from Pompeii showing a young actor in costume to play a king in a late tragedy. (Museo Nazionale, Napoli)

Late Roman mime actor holding a mask with three faces. (Fourth century A.D.)

Diomedes, is derived from an Oscan town called Atella. Oscan was an Italic dialect, closely related to Latin, that was spoken by the Osci (a people who resided in the southern Apennines). Beginning early in the fifth century B.C. the Osci overran most of southern Italy, and as a result their popular entertainment became quite widespread.

Whether, in fact, the explanation of Diomedes (and Livy) regarding the origin of the *fabula Atellana* is accurate cannot be determined and may be little more than an educated guess. In any case, our information concerning the structure and content of Atellan farce is almost as limited and fragmentary as our information on the history of the form, and the lack of existing manuscripts indicates that as literature it had little or no importance. However, after it was discovered by the Romans (who made themselves the absolute masters of Oscan territory early in the third century B.C.) and exported to Rome, it became a staple of Roman theatrical entertainment.

Some scholars have attempted to prove that Atellan farce grew out of the Greek mimes of southern Italy, and descriptions of these farces often seem to give substance to such a supposition, indicating that the viewers thought of Atellan farce as a form of mime. Certainly it was related to the mimes in that the mimes were often improvised and the farces made common use of improvisational techniques. However, the Romans were quite able to distinguish the mimes from the farces, probably based on the fact that the farces contained certain traditional stock characters, each wearing a specific costume and mask. From titles and fragments we can identify four of these characters—Pappus, Maccus, Bucco, and Dossennus. All were apparently low, coarse, greedy clowns who amused their originally rustic audiences with scenes based on gluttony, drunkenness, sexual byplay, and obscene jest.

THE MIMES

Of all the dramatic forms that existed in Rome, the mime was probably the most primitive, the most adaptable, and certainly the most permanent. It was also the first "professional" theatrical activity in Rome and thus differed markedly from the earlier types. In its earliest forms the mime was not really drama at all, but a public entertainment, put on by male and female performers, that included juggling, acrobatics, dancing, singing, and mimicry. The performances were given in village marketplaces, at festivals, and any other place and time where the *mimi* could gather an audience that might be expected to pay for such wares. And the mime was not merely a localized form, but one that existed all over the ancient world.

Apparently from the beginning the mimes had a frank indecency impressed upon their character. Largely this was because they were never pointed toward anything but entertainment—*mimicus risus*—and so they concentrated on that which pleased their audience. Even when the entertainment tended toward mythological tales, the mimes concentrated on the sexual or the sensational. This can be seen in Xenophon's description of a performance by a boy and girl, slaves of a Syracusan mime-master, who presented for an audience the love of Dionysus and Ariadne. After the performance the girl's master mentioned that she was both his dancer and his concubine. But the principal reason that the mimes seemed indecent to the Romans is that the mimes employed both men and women, where the early Roman drama followed the Greek example of all-male casts.

The exact date when the Romans came into contact with the mimes is not certain. The popularity of farce in the Greek towns of southern Italy means that the mimes probably existed there very early, and thus the Roman contacts with Greece that grew out of the Pyrrhic War and the battle for Sicily must have introduced mime at a period when the Roman literary drama was still unborn. In any case, only two years after a literary drama was established by Livius Andronicus in 240 B.C., the mimes were apparently already popular enough to take over the *ludi Florales*.

In many ways the mimes seem to be the most obvious ancient ancestor of the later *commedia dell'arte*. They were performed by traveling players on wagons or rough, portable stages that provided little more than a curtain backdrop, perhaps painted to provide scenic effects, with a slit at the center to allow entrances and exits. In most cases the material these players performed was improvised from a scenario or plot summary, though such improvisation depended so much on set speeches and actions regularly in the repertory of each performer that improvisation may not be a completely accurate term. Also like the *commedia*, the mime troupes apparently supported themselves by collecting coins from the audience during performances. Each company had its leading performer (either actor or actress), for whom the balance of the company merely acted as supporting players.

Perhaps the most important aspect of the mime as a dramatic genre was its hardiness. Appearing early, it outlasted both comedy and tragedy, and finally, in the Roman Empire period, it became the primary dramatic form. It made itself at home in the marketplaces of country villages, in the streets of Rome, and in the courts of tyrants. It took the Christianizing of Rome, and eventually, the closing of the theatres by Justinian in the sixth century to put an end to mime—and the appearance of the *commedia* nearly a thousand years later indicates that perhaps it never came to an end but merely went underground to eventually emerge and bloom anew.

THE GOLDEN AGE OF ROMAN DRAMA

The literary drama of Rome—that is, the drama outside the farces and mimes—was largely derivative, even in its greatest period from 240 B.C., when Livius Andronicus produced a Greek tragedy in Latin, to 86 B.C., the year Lucius Accius died. Most such drama, if we can judge fairly from twenty-six extant comedies and only titles and fragments of the tragedies, were translations, imitations, and/or adaptations of original Greek plays. Specifically, Roman tragedy was a reworking of plays by the great Greek playwrights—Aeschylus, Sophocles, and especially Euripides. Roman comedy, on the other hand, tended to ignore the great Greek Old Comedy and even the lesser Middle Comedy, instead taking as its model and source the Greek New Comedy, especially the plays of Menander, Apollodorus of Carystus, Philemon of Syracuse, and Diphilus of Sinope. This slighting of Aristophanic comedy, with its emphasis on obscenity, farce, and general buffoonery, stems in part from the fact that Greek Old Comedy was full of topical and highly critical references to the existing political system and to major contemporary politicians. Such material, translated and updated with equivalent Roman references, would have brought severe reprisals down on the head of the translator/adaptor. New Comedy, on the other hand, was cosmopolitan in style, universal in subject matter, and totally uncritical of sensitive and powerful institutions and personages. Also, the Romans of the Republic were rather puritanical and did not encourage the licentiousness of Greek-style drama. Their interests were political and military, and this along with their religious conservatism, determined their lack of interest in Aristophanic-like comedy.

These Roman translations and adaptations of Greek New Comedy were referred to as *fabula palliata*—literally "comedy in Greek dress"—but in the hands of the great comic playwrights they achieved true orginality. This came about by the author adding to the Greek original such native Italian elements as music, song, dance, and the often crude physical horseplay of the mimes and farces. Also, especially in the case of Terence, the development of the double plot and the use of a technique called *contaminatio* (combining the plots ot two Greek dramas into one Latin play) helped make the reworked materials into something quite new.

During this period of greatness, Roman comedy developed a number of conventions relating primarily to stage production. Probably for reasons of pace the drop curtain (*auleum*) was discarded and the action became continuous, without act or scene divisions. Technically, such a staging concept requires at most a single set production or, very probably, no set at all, and this was the case with Roman comedy, with all the action of the play developing outdoors, in front of the houses of the major characters. Events that must take place indoors are either described by the characters involved in them or partially reenacted.

Onto this basic form certain other conventions were grafted, some the result of earlier dramatic traditions and some the result of production considerations. Thus, acting was, for certain recurring characters, conventionalized, with the players wearing recognizable masks and wigs. Public performances were given in daylight, and so there were no lighting effects, although there is some evidence that private performances put on in the homes of wealthy Romans used torches and (probably) reflectors to provide artificial lighting. Playwrights made frequent use of such stage conventions as the aside and soliloquy. Stock plots were common, featuring such characters as the miser, the braggart warrior, and the aged lover.

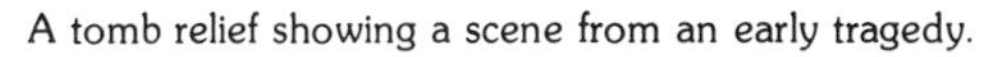
A tomb relief showing a scene from an early tragedy.

Roman tragedy, while quite popular with its contemporary audiences, has not held up as well as comedy. In spite of the fact that tragedy existed as a major dramatic form for over two hundred years, producing three writers (Ennius, Pacuvius, Accius) that the Romans considered to be great tragic dramatists, no complete play from the greatest period of Roman drama has survived. Thus, whatever opinions we form concerning the tragic drama in this period must depend on fragments of plays, opinions of ancient commentators, and titles of lost plays.

Excepting Plautus and Terence, this greatest period of Roman drama produced only six playwrights of significant stature. The earliest, and perhaps for this reason the most important, was *Livius Andronicus* (c. 284-c. 204 B.C.), a Greek who is said to have been born in Tarentum in southern Italy. Apparently an actor and teacher, certainly a poet and playwright, Livius Andronicus is generally credited with introducing the literary drama to Rome. He translated the *Odyssey*, composed lyrics from the Greek, and of his plays the titles of nine tragedies and three comedies have come down to us. His nine tragedies, all clearly adapted from Greek originals, are *Achilles, Aegisthus, Ajax the Whipbearer, Andromede, Danae, The Trojan Horse, Hermione*, and *Tereus*. Of comedies by Andronicus only three titles have survived—*Gladiolus, Ludius*, and *Virgo*. Perhaps this paucity of comic titles indicates that Andronicus wrote only a few such works, or perhaps it merely indicates that he wrote comedy badly. For whatever reason, he was not highly regarded as a comic writer, even by those Roman writers who came immediately after him. Terence, speaking of his own predecessors in the art of comic writing, fails to mention Andronicus.

Gnaeus Naevius (c. 260-c. 201 B.C.), perhaps a Campanian by birth, seems to have been the first native Roman dramatist to achieve significance, not only because of the quality of his compositions, but also because of his originality in creating a native historical drama, two titles of which (*Clastidium* and *Romulus*) have survived. Titles of seven tragedies from the Greek have survived. However, comedy seems to have been Naevius' favorite form, for we have titles of thirty-four comedies based on Greek sources. Unfortunately, Naevius' literary jibes at certain senators and their families led to his imprisonment and exile. This disgrace effectively stopped production of his works, clearing the stage for a successor.

PLAUTUS: Plautus (Titus Maccius, c. 254-184 B.C.), probably the greatest of the Roman comic playwrights, was born in Sarcina, Umbria. Little is known of his youth except that he went to Rome at an early age, where he acted on the stage. The particular roles in which he may have specialized are not known, but a few scholars believe that he probably played Maccus, the clown of the *fabula Atellana*, and that the name Maccius was bestowed on him as a result of this role. Whatever character he played, he seems to have been quite successful. In fact, one of the ancient legends—once given wide credence but recently cast into doubt—has it that Plautus made so much money in the theatre that he left acting in favor of business. Here, however, he was not so successful and lost all his money. He found a job working in a mill and, putting his stage training to work, began writing comedies in his spare time, eventually becoming even more successful as a writer than he had been as an actor. Whether or not this story is true, it is probable that his early training as a comic actor is one of the reasons that Plautus displayed, in all of his plays, such a mastery of stage technique and farcical action.

On the surface the plays of Plautus seem to be totally indebted to Greek New Comedy, both for plots and characters, but in fact he is one of the most original of comic playwrights, with a deep indebtedness to the comic scenes and characters of his own Italian heritage. His plots are usually devoted to love affairs that are seemingly thwarted by certain meddling characters, and the comedy arises from the subsequent intrigues, mistaken identities, and basic stupidities and monomanias of the characters. For some reason the breadth of comic styles that Plautus' plays encompass is rarely recognized, and as a result he has all too often been passed off as being nothing more than a writer of farces. In fact, in addition to farcical comedy he also wrote romantic comedy, broad burlesque, mythological parody, and a type of reasonably light comedy somewhat similar to the later "humor comedies" of Jonson, which Plautus possibly influenced.

A Roman mosaic from Naples shows a comic scene in which two young women visit the home of a witch. Possibly a scene from Plautus' comedy *The Casket.*

More than anything else, Plautus seemed to be interested in making his audience laugh, and as a result he employed many of the techniques he had learned from the mimes and rustic farces. His plays alternate rapidly from pratfall to comic monologue, from beating scenes to comic asides, from mistaken identities to direct address to the audience. In this sense, while his plots come primarily from Greek New Comedy, his techniques come closer to the native Italian farce and even to the practices of Greek Old Comedy. It is this ability to combine brilliant comic dialogue with sparkling physical comedy that makes Plautus so effective even today. This timeless quality can be seen in the popular 1962 musical comedy, *A Funny Thing Happened on the Way to the Forum* (by Burt Shevelove, Larry Gelbart, and Stephen Sondheim), which was based on several comedies by Plautus, primarily *Miles Gloriosus, Mostellaria*, and *Pseudolus*.

At an earlier time nearly one hundred twenty comedies were ascribed to Plautus, but fewer than half of those were probably written by the master. The more recent assumption has been that because Plautus was so popular his name on a comedy could assure its success, and that lesser writers and promoters took advantage of this popularity. Marcus Terentius Varro (c. 116-27 B.C.), a Roman scholar and admirer of Plautus, listed only twenty-one of these many plays as authentic, based on their acceptance by all earlier critics, but he felt that a number of others were probably genuine given their distinctive style and humor. Those plays of Plautus that are now extant—twenty plus one fragment—may very well be the twenty-one plays listed by Varro. They are all comedies based on Greek New Comedy originals and seem to have been written during the last twenty-five years of Plautus' life. There have been numerous attempts to find some method of dating the plays, but none are completely satisfactory. In any case, the plays, not in any chronological order, are *Amphitryon, Asinaria (Comedy of Asses), Aulularia (Pot of Gold), Bacchides (Two Bacchides), Captivi (The Captives), Casina, Cistellaria (The Casket), Curculio, Epidicus, Menaechmi (Twin Menaechmi), Mercator (The Merchant), Miles Gloriosus (The Braggart Soldier), Mostellaria (The Haunted House), Persa (The Girl from Persia), Poenulus (The Carthaginian), Pseudolus, Rudens (The Rope), Stichus, Trinummus (Three Penny Day)*, and *Truculentus*.

TERENCE: Terence (Publius Terentius Afer, c. 195-159 B.C.), the second of the two great Roman comic playwrights, was born in Carthage and brought to Rome as a slave. Here he was educated and eventually freed by his master, the senator Terentius Lucanus. His obvious philosophic and artistic interests soon gained him the friendship of Publius Cornelius Scipio Aemilianus, which in turn provided him entry into Rome's best known literary and philosophical club—the Scipionic Circle. This group, which also included such leading Roman intellectuals as the Greek philosopher Panaetius, the Roman satirist Lucilius, and the Greek historian Polybius, probably provoked Terence into dramatic production, and legend has it that he submitted his first comedy, *Andria*, to the elderly playwright Caecilius. The play was read at Caecilius' home following a dinner party, and proved highly popular with the listeners. Whether this specific legend is true or not (it seems doubtful in that Caecilius died two years before Terence's first known production), the reading of plays was a popular Roman pastime and it is probable that all of Terence's plays received their first private hearing in this manner.

Terence wrote only six comedies, all of which were produced by the famous actor-producer Ambivius Turpio, five of them with great success. (One play, *Hecyra*, was a failure in its first production because, supposedly, the audience was distracted by a rope-dancer in another show. In its second production it also failed, reportedly because of competition from a nearby gladiatorial bout.) The comedies were all based on Greek originals for which we have titles, but the Greek originals no longer survive. Terence died on a trip to Greece, and some scholars have speculated that the purpose of the trip was to collect more original plays by Menander, Terence's favorite playwright, for adaptation to the Roman stage.

Terence's plays are quite different from those of Plautus, his predecessor. Whereas Plautus' humor tends toward the farcical and exaggerated, Terence's is subtle and low-keyed. In nearly all of his plays the audience feels that the laughter the play generates is secondary to the philosophical principle the playwright is trying to illustrate. Also, Terence did away with several antiquated dramatic conventions and provided a number of theatrical innovations. His onstage characters rarely carry on conversations with characters who are indoors and thus out of sight, there is little of dramatic importance that happens offstage, and his slaves are not the traditional sly tricksters making fools of their masters, but rather they are either comic bunglers or faithful servants who manage to keep their headstrong young masters from making serious mistakes.

In terms of innovation, Terence restructured the prologue, getting rid of the plot summary. He used the prologue to defend himself from attack on such charges as plagiarism and *contaminatio*, though in a sense he was clearly guilty of both charges. Perhaps his most famous theatrical innovation is the double-plot structure, which presents two closely intertwined and essentially interdependent stories.

Because of his restrained comedy and his concentration on a philosophical ideal, eschewing the bawdiness and physically unrestrained comedy of Plautus, Terence's plays remained popular after the collapse of Classicism. Throughout the Middle Ages they were read and admired in the monasteries and, in fact, the earliest literary plays that we have from the Middle Ages are the "moral plays" of Hrotswitha, which were based on the dramatic structure and style of Terence. After the Renaissance the plays of Terence continued to maintain their popularity, exerting influence on such later playwrights as Molière and the eighteenth century English dramatists.

Terence's six plays, together with the dates generally assigned to them, are *Andria* (*The Woman of Andros,* 166 B.C.), *Hecyra* (*The Mother-in-Law,* 165 B.C.), *Heautontimorumenos* (*The Self-Tormentor,* 163 B.C.), *Eunuchus* (*The Enunuch,* 161 B.C.), *Phormio* (161 B.C.), and *Adelphoe* (*The Brothers,* 160 B.C.).

Quintus Ennius (239-c. 169 B.C.) is usually accorded full honors as the first truly great Roman poet. Born in Rudiae of Greek and Italian parents, he

From the Medieval manuscript of Terence's *The Woman of Andros*, this drawing shows the simplest form of Roman staging—a platform, a door, and one set piece. (Vatican Library)

early became a broad humanist, fired equally by the grand literature of Greece and the glorious history of Rome. Supporting himself by teaching, Ennius wrote *Saturae*, an epic on Roman history (the *Annals*), and poetic miscellanies. His dramatic composition included comedies (three titles of which have survived) and native historical plays in the manner begun by Naevius (*Ambracia, Sabine Women*). However, tragedy was his forte and titles of twenty tragedies, plus nearly four hundred lines of fragments, have come down to us. While Ennius was rated highly as a poet, his plays, both comic and tragic, were not highly regarded in his own lifetime—though it must be noted that Cicero loved his tragedies.

After Ennius the literary values of Roman drama tend to fall off quite sharply. Marcus Pacuvius (c. 220-c. 130 B.C.) apparently wrote only eleven tragedies and one native historical drama (*Paulus*). Not even fragments of his work survive, so it is difficult to evaluate his contribution, though the opening of his tragedy *Iliona* is mentioned approvingly by Roman commentators more often than any other single scene in the whole of Roman tragic drama. Following Pacuvius comes Caecilius Statius (c. 219-c. 166 B.C.), an Insubrian Gaul who, according to tradition, began his career in Rome as a slave. His known production is totally devoted to comedy, forty titles (and extensive fragments) of which have come down to us. Statius' reputation took some time to develop, and in his own lifetime he was not the most successful comic playwright on the stage. Yet, according to some contemporary critics, including Cicero, he was the greatest of the Latin comic writers. The last of the major writers produced during this greatest period of Roman dramatic literature is Lucius Accius (c. 170-86 B.C.). Tragedy was evidently Accius' primary interest (we have titles for fifty tragedies), but he also wrote several historical plays on native Roman subjects.

Finally, the most certain statement that can be made about this phase of the Roman tragic drama is that it was almost entirely derivative. The Roman writers of tragedy apparently depended totally on Greek sources, as did the comic writers, but unlike the comic writers the writers of tragedy showed little originality in dealing with the materials, keeping the basic story line and form and concentrating on the creation of a rhetorical style and sentiment that has little appeal to today's playgoer. There is some reason to believe that the tragic playwrights may have adopted the technique of *contaminatio*, but evidence that use of the technique was widespread is inconclusive at best and it seems doubtful considering the lack of originality in all other aspects of the surviving fragments. In any case the use of this technique would be in itself derivative considering the fact that it was developed by the comic playwrights.

DRAMA UNDER THE EMPIRE

Under the Empire, theatre became even more popular as mass entertainment than it had been throughout its earlier and greater period during the Republic. Theatres, both large and small, were erected in every province to house a variety of "theatrical" performances. However, when we examine the types of performances that took place in these theatres, what we find is artistically questionable and theatrically disappointing. Nearly all the commentaries available to us indicate that the largest part of these performances, whether pantomime, mime, tragedy, recitation, or gladiatorial combat, were both brutal and degrading.

The degeneracy that developed in Rome during the Empire—popularly symbolized by the two infamous emperors, Caligula and Nero—has become almost legendary, and the degeneracy that existed from the top of the political-social system to the bottom carried over to the stage. Seneca himself said that "the mimes fail in reproaching the rankness of this age. Truly they must omit much more than they put on the stage. Such a heap of incredible vices is to be found in this age of ours that the mimes may even be accused of negligence." This carryover of public degeneracy and taste for blood to the stage can be illustrated by examining the third mime of Catullus, about which an unknown scholiast left the following note:

> *In this mime they pretend to crucify Laureolus. Juvenal intends to say that Lentulus is worthy of a true cross, because his very skill in the performance makes him so much more villainous. This Lentulus was a brilliant actor, and took the part in the mime of a slave who was, in pretence, crucified on the stage.*

Josephus also mentions this particular mime, recalling that a great deal of artificial blood flowed down the cross. Josephus is corroborated by Suetonius, who remarks that "the stage ran with blood." This alone might be enough to illustrate the spectacularly gory staging the Romans were used to, but a remark by Martial, who attended the same mime (if not the same performance), leads some scholars to believe that upon occasion the crucifixion took place in reality, with a condemned felon taking the place of the actor. "Laureolus hanging on no false cross" is Martial's comment on the scene. Whether this understanding of Martial's comment is correct or not, we know certainly that in this mime the audience was at least treated to a realistic presentation of a crucifixion. In addition to the crucifixion scene in the Catullus mime, there are many other examples. If Hermann Reich's belief that an incident mentioned by Josephus corresponds to the Anubis mime mentioned by Tertullian, then we have a mime that is erotic in its material, that mocks religious convention by taking place in a temple, and that ends spectacularly in mass crucifixion.

In the first Oxyrhynchus Papyrus there is a mime fragment containing specific stage directions for a fool suffering from flatulence, much music and dance, and a boat, supposedly floating on a river, which appears at the edge of the stage. The boat is indicated as being large enough to carry off the nine persons onstage and three nude barbarian women who are bathing in the river.

Adultery themes were apparently the most popular theatrical fare among the Empire audiences, according to the comments and condemnations of onstage sexual activities made by the writers of the time. And just as with the earlier mentioned crucifixion scene, there are many suggestions that the scenes of adultery were not always pretended. Lactantius and Minucius Felix both indicate the reality of such happenings, and Aelius Lampridius, in his life of the Emperor Heliogabalus, says that the emperor specifically ordered that "in mimic adultery plays those things which should be done in fiction were to be carried out in reality."

Going beyond those subjects and scenes which the Empire audience was viewing in the mimes, at least in terms of blood and physical brutality, were the spectacles which were presented in both the theatres and arenas. It is commonly pointed out that Nero's reconstruction of the theatre at Athens provided a method whereby the whole of the *orchestra* could be flooded for scenic effects or the presentation of mimic sea battles. These sea battles were certainly part of the *spectacula* and not part of the drama as such, but the fact that they existed sheds some light on the presentation of the Oxyrhynchus mime, which requires a boat floating in the *orchestra*. We assume that these mimic sea battles, certainly in miniature, took place within the theatre. We know certainly that they took place in the *naumachia*, those large, outdoor ponds or lakes that were created to present mimic sea battles. In addition to the sea battles, the gladiatorial bouts must have been epic, for, also in the Athens theatre a marble balustrade was erected for the purpose of protecting the spectators during such events.

And so, during or shortly after the period of Seneca there was presented to the Roman audience real or pretended crucifixion, real or pretended adultery, flatulence, and the blood of real gladiators fighting real battles to real death.

SENECA: Lucius Annaeus Seneca, called Seneca the Younger (c. 4 B.C.-65 A.D.), was born in Cordoba, Spain, to a literary family that provided him in his early years with a thorough background in rhetoric and philosophy. Perhaps because of this background he was, from early adolescence onward, attracted to a philosophy of austerity, and as a result he became a strong advocate of stoicism. Through the influence of an aunt he was given the position of Quaestor, or public prosecutor, and became a member of the Roman senate. By the time that Tiberius died and Caligula ascended the throne, Seneca was already famed as a philosopher and writer. Indeed, it was probably this fame that provoked the literary Caligula's jealousy to the point where he contemplated having Seneca executed. Legend has it that Seneca was saved by Caligula's mistress, who convinced the mad emperor that the sickly philosopher would soon die of natural causes.

In 41 A.D., Claudius succeeded the murdered Caligula, but in this succession Seneca merely exchanged danger for disaster, and in that same year, at the instigation of Messalina, he was exiled to Corsica for what were probably political reasons, though the official charge was adultery. He spent eight desolate years on the island before he was permitted to return to the mainland and Rome. He owed this reprieve to Agrippina, who had succeeded Messalina as Claudius' wife. She had Seneca recalled so that he could act as tutor to her son, Domitius, later called Nero. When Nero ascended the throne he was totally under Seneca's influence, and as a result the first five years of Nero's reign were long remembered as a miniature Golden Age.

Seneca had achieved high position and influence, but again, involved in intrigues and power struggles over the Roman throne, he became the victim of a jealous emperor. Realizing that the end was near, Seneca requested that he be allowed to donate his fortune to the emperor and retire, so that he might spend the remaining years of his life with his young wife. He managed to live quietly until 65 A.D., when he was ordered by Nero to take his own life.

While most Roman writers based their plays on Greek plots and themes, the need to meet the demands of Roman popular taste required an infusion of horror, spectacle, and cruelty. Seneca based his plots primarily on the works of Euripides, but at that point departs from the Classical Greek dramatist, for little of Euripides' realism appears in his scenes. Seneca was a sensationalist, exaggerating the melodramatic qualities of plays like *Medea* and *Orestes*. His tragedies are thick with the mood of dark, gloomy, impending doom. The villains are obsessed with their evil deeds, and all the dramatic figures are overcome with the feeling that their future is terrible indeed. The tone Seneca sets in his plays is oppressive; his dialogue is bombastic, oratorical, and often for the contemporary reader rather dull, although at times he made use of *stichomythia*, or the quick exchange of staccato lines in a two-character dialogue to liven up the rhetorical exchanges. Like Terence he cast his plays in five formal acts, retained the chorus, and incorporated the prologue into the action.

It must be acknowledged that while he provided material to satisfy the tastes of his time, Seneca was not interested only in horrific themes, philosophical commonplaces, and rhetorical excesses. In addition, he attempted to un-

A contemporary production of Seneca's *Oedipus* by the Oxford Playhouse, Hollywood, California. Adapted by Ted Hughes.

derstand and illuminate his material, concentrating on the psychological motivations of his characters and thereby infusing them with a timeless, universal quality. The materials with which he dealt are indeed the materials of great tragedy, and at their best his plays succeed in arousing pity and fear, just as did those of his Greek predecessors.

At this point it must be noted that for many years a debate has raged over whether Seneca's plays were ever really produced on stage as dramas, or whether they were in fact only closet dramas, broadcast dramas, or plays designed purely for recitation. Certainly there is evidence, or at least plausible speculation, on both sides of the question. Many scholars object to the possibility of Seneca's plays having been staged on the basis of the horror and brutality they contain. This objection, however, can be put out of court by looking at what actually was being produced before the Roman public during Seneca's time. Such information as we possess suggests that the entertainment normally provided in the imperial theatres consisted of trivial, degrading, and brutal performances, whether mime, recitation, pantomime, or even gladiatorial combat.

While those who claim that Seneca's tragedies were too violent and bloody for production are easily put off, some other objections are not so easily put aside. Some critics have pointed out that no Roman under the Republic or the Empire ever wrote for the stage for any reason other than money, and as Seneca was one of the richest men in Rome, and also one who disliked contact with the common people, he was hardly likely to write plays intended to win the favor of the general public. Also, they point out, the plays contain none of the usual stage directions (i.e., techniques of bringing characters on or off stage are ignored), speeches may not even be speeches but thoughts (see *Agamemnon*, lines 108-124), and some of the physical action that is described is patently ridiculous (i.e., Hercules' attempt to shoot himself with his own bow and arrow).

Perhaps the most damning argument against the plays ever having been performed is the lack of direct evidence of staging. There is not one mention by any of Seneca's contemporaries that would indicate a fully staged production. Given Seneca's standing in Roman society, a fully staged production of even one of his plays would likely have excited at least a minimum of comment.

On the other side of the controversy, those scholars who believe that Seneca's plays were certainly produced on stage adduce to their argument two strong bits of evidence. In Palermo there is a wall painting showing a tragic scene of a hero and messenger which, from the positioning of the characters, seems to be an illustration from Seneca's *Oedipus* at that moment when the messenger from Corinth tells him of the death of his adoptive father. Another wall painting, from the Casa del Centenario, Pompei, is of Medea pointing her sword at her children. This must be a scene from the play of Seneca, where the children are killed on stage, because it depicts that scene accurately. What is particularly important about these paintings is that in both cases the characters are depicted in stage costumes. This means that they are probably not scenes merely visualized by the artists from reading the texts, but pictures of fully staged productions that the artists witnessed.

Finally, claim the proponents of production, the plays of Seneca contain such effective roles for actors that it is hard to accept the theory that the great actors of the time would allow them to pass unacted. Certainly Seneca's own emperor, Nero, did not allow such roles to escape. Suetonius tells us that Nero appeared in almost any or all major roles—as a god, a hero, or even a heroine. He sang the parts of the blind Oedipus, Hercules insane, and Orestes the matricide. He even took the role of Canace and mimicked the cries of a woman in labor. We are not sure in which plays Nero acted, or even whether they were plays as opposed to dramatic recitations; however, Suetonius refers to them as tragedies and indicates that they were performed on a stage.

There is no likelihood that this debate over production will soon be resolved. However, the physical evidence of the wall paintings makes it seem likely that some productions of Seneca's plays were staged during or close to his own lifetime.

Of the ten tragic plays once attributed to Seneca, the *Octavia*, a *fabula praetexta* (tragedy on Greek materials) regarding the first wife of the Emperor Nero, is no longer considered to have been written by him. The nine tragedies still ascribed to his pen are *Mad Hercules, The Trojan Women, The Phoenician Women, Medea, Phaedra, Oedipus, Agamemnon, Thyestes*, and *Hercules on Oeta*, which some critics feel is not Senecan, but in which Seneca surely had a hand, if only in the plotting and certain of the speeches.

Rich in dramatic devices such as asides, ghosts, soliloquies, and surprise, Seneca's plays are a reflection of his own moral philosophies and provide in-depth studies of psychological motivation in which human life is both dignified and meaningful. Superhuman forces may be at work in his plays, interfering in some way in the human condition, but Seneca's characters, even more than their Greek originals, always have freedom of choice and so are ultimately responsible for their own deeds, either good or evil.

HORACE: Horace (Quintus Horatius Flaccus, 65-8 B.C.), lyric poet and critic, was born at Venusia, a small city near the border of Apulia. His father was a former slave who had managed to purchase his freedom before the birth of his son, and it was perhaps this history of slavery that made the father determined to improve the family name. He sent his young son to school in Rome and then, when the boy became a young man, sent him on to Athens to study philosophy. With the outbreak of civil war, Horace broke off his studies to enlist in the army of Brutus, ultimately serving with distinction at Phillippi. When his term of service expired he returned to Rome to renew his studies, but the proscriptions that resulted from the civil war cost him all his property, and at the age of twenty-four he was forced to take a job as clerk in a public office. However, Horace's talent and intelligence were too great to be held back by such a minor misfortune, and he soon became acquainted with the epic poet Vergil, who introduced him to Maecenas, the statesman who was to become his patron.

With some early support from Vergil, Varius, and Maecenas, Horace quit his job to devote himself to literary endeavors, and his maiden work, the first book of *Satires*, was published in 35 B.C. Its success was such that within a year Maecenas had given him the famous Sabine Farm, which left Horace financially independent. The *Odes*, the later *Epistles*, and the *Ars poetica* (The *Art of Poetry*, "Epistle to the Pisos," Epistle II.3) were all products of his mature years at the Sabine Farm and display his mastery of phrase and poetic form. His verse, though it owes much to the Greek Archilochus, reflects an emancipated Roman cultivation of the arts and the true spirit of the Augustan Age. He was an urbane Epicurean, and the pungency, beauty, and power of his verse greatly influenced English poetry, just as his dramatic criticism influenced Renaissance English drama.

The *Art of Poetry*, generally considered to have been written sometime between 24 and 7 B.C., is the only complete work of Roman literary and dramatic criticism that has survived—and it is a reflection of the values of the period that the largest part of the work is concerned with drama. It has been determined that *Art of Poetry* is not totally original; Horace drew on an earlier work (that did not survive) by Neoptolemus of Parium. However, Horace's work clearly reflects his ideas and precepts, and whatever he drew from the earlier Alexandrian critic must have fit his own already developing ideas.

Directed at what Horace felt was the degenerate standard of Roman drama, the *Art of Poetry* is a rather rigid work in its way, with primary attention given to the more formal aspects of writing. Following is a brief outline of those portions devoted to drama, with approximate line references:

(I)

(73-118) Each type of poetry has its appropriate meter, which was established by the Greek poets. The poet must master these meters as well as the tone and style that is suitable (and that has already been established) for the particular genre in which he determines to write. In dramatic poetry, it is necessary to keep comedy and tragedy completely separate in terms of style, meter, and tone. All poetry [though this is directed primarily at dramatic poetry] must have beauty, but it must also work on the emotions of the audience. The dialogue of each of the characters must be appropriate to their own personalities and the circumstances in which they find themselves, or else they will appear ridiculous to the audience.

(II)

(119-152) The playwright [poet] may either follow the traditional myths or create a new plot. If it is determined to use one of the traditional stories, then the characters must be kept consistent with the myth. If the playwright determines to create a new plot, then the characters must be kept consistent with the material of their story. Because it is so difficult to create a full range of human characteristics in an original drama, it is best to dramatize a theme from Homer. However, even a Homeric theme should be handled with originality. The playwright should make use of certain of Homer's techniques, holding fast to his rapid, simple beginnings, and hurrying the audience *in medias res*. Nothing should be included in a drama except the essentials, and the beginning, middle, and end should be kept consistent.

(III)

(153-188) The successful playwright will study humanity, noting the characteristic behavior of man in his successive ages (childhood, youth, maturity, and old age) so that he will never confuse them. The plot can be demonstrated either through action or narrative. Narrative is the least desirable method. When presenting action, however, violence and "revolting" incidents should not be performed before the audience. When such actions are necessary they should be presented through narration.

(IV)

(189-219) Plays should be presented in five acts. The *deus ex machina* should seldom be employed. No more than three speaking characters should ever be onstage at the same time. The chorus should be part of the action and treated as if it were a single actor. This means that there should be no interruptive choral interludes that take it out of character. Instead, the chorus should give good advice, support right action, and praise moderation, law, justice, and peace. It should sympathize with the humble and avoid the proud. Plays demand musical accompaniment, but the flute should be kept simple and unembellished, as it was in the old days. Diction, too, should be kept clear and simple, without rhetorical flourishes.

(V)

(220-250) Satyr plays are, by their nature, full of pranks and good spirits, but these must be presented with restraint. The gods and heroes should not use vulgar speech and should not be presented in silly or indelicate situations. In satyr plays the language of comedy and the language of tragedy should meet.

(VI)

(251-274) In terms of meter, the poet should avoid the crude clumsiness of the early Latin writers by studying the Greek models. Judged by these models, the poetry and wit of Plautus was much overrated by earlier generations.

(VII)

(275-294) Thespis invented tragedy, but Aeschylus perfected it. Old Comedy was so licentious that it had to be restricted by the law, and its abusive language had to be silenced. Roman poets began by imitating the Greeks, but they invented a national Roman drama. They might have created a more outstanding drama had they been more demanding of themselves. Every poetic work should be painstakingly polished, and that which is not should be condemned.

THE ROMAN ACTOR

In the early local farces, Roman actors were most probably members of the community who participated only because they enjoyed performing; however, following the establishment of a serious literary drama, acting became the permanent occupation of a large number of people in all the areas under Roman domination. In these regular dramas the Romans not only made use of Greek materials, they also followed the Greek custom of barring women from the stage. However, in the mimes, and perhaps in the pantomimes and casual entertainments, women were employed in playing the female roles.

While the Romans followed Greek theatrical custom in many ways, they never accepted the Greek attitude toward actors. Some Roman actors were slaves (very few were citizens), and many earned starvation wages at best. However, the best of the Roman actors earned enormous incomes, some of them becoming independently wealthy. Roscius, a famous Roman comedian whose name passed into theatrical parlance as being synonymous with fine acting, became so well-off financially that in his later years he performed without salary. This allowed him to pick and choose his roles very carefully, and while he received no formal payment for playing these roles it is reasonable to suppose that he received rich gifts from his many admirers. This giving of gifts to favorite performers was a Roman custom, and it has been said that Sulla gave Roscius a golden ring which, in effect, raised the actor to knighthood.

While individual actors such as Roscius could win great wealth and fame, theatrical performers as a group were classed as *infami*. They could

A bronze statue of a Roman comic actor, wearing the grotesque mask of a comic servant and with his body padded to add to the effect.

claim no civil rights and, should a Roman citizen perform or in any way earn money by working in the theatre, he was stripped of the civil rights otherwise guaranteed to all citizens. Punishment was even more drastic for the military, and a Roman soldier appearing onstage faced sentence of death.

Like the Greek audience, the Romans expected a high degree of skill from their performers. However, the demands made on the Roman performer were somewhat different from those made on their Greek predecessors. The musical parts of the Roman plays were usually sung by trained singers, while the actor pantomimed the action. According to Livy this tradition began when Livius Andronicus lost his voice due to the strain of the great vocal demands faced by the actor. He asked for permission to let a singer stand before the flute player and sing the monody, while he acted it himself. Having been granted permission for this change in format, he performed with a vivacity that gained from not having to use his own voice. From that time on, Livy points out, actors used singers to accompany their pantomime, keeping only the dialogue parts for themselves.

While the Roman actors were thus relieved of the necessity to develop a high degree of skill as singers, they had to replace this with skill in pantomime. They also had to be skilled dancers, although dancing was more often found in the mimes than in the regular drama. Also, because of the Roman emphasis on rhetoric they had to be skilled speakers, able to denote vocally every nuance in their roles.

Because the Roman theatre had no restriction on the number of actors who could be used in a play, the need for doubling, at least in the major roles, was eliminated; though undoubtedly because of expense doubling was common in the minor parts. This freedom of cast size allowed the actors to specialize as tragedians, comedians, mimes, or pantomimists. Specialization also existed within these broad categories. An actor could develop his techniques to play either male or female roles, young or old, gods and princes or slaves, or any other combination of these various types.

Under the Empire, acting reached its lowest point as a profession, and by the time that Rome became Christianized acting was, for a large part of the populace, anathematized, with Christians forbidden to attend plays. Interestingly, however, some of the great performers during this period achieved wealth and fame in spite of the restrictions that faced actors, and in the sixth century the mime actress Theodora achieved what may have been the epitome of recognition for the performer, marrying Justinian, Emperor of the Eastern Empire.

THE STRUCTURE OF THE ROMAN THEATRE

Perhaps the most surprising aspect of the Roman theatre structure, at least after it became a reasonably permanent building, is that it comes at a substantial distance in time after the great period of Roman drama. In Rome proper the first recorded wooden theatre building was not erected until 179 B.C. That it was not intended as even a semipermanent architectural monument is evidenced by the fact that it was torn down in the same year. In fact, it was not until 55 B.C., nearly thirty-one years after the end of Rome's Golden Age of drama, that Pompey build a theatre of stone and Rome got its first permanent theatre building. Even at this late date, apparently, a theatre could only be build by resorting to subterfuge. Pompey placed a small temple to Venus Victrix above the last row of seats in the *cavea* (auditorium), thus pretending that the ascending rows of seats were merely steps leading to the temple and its altar to the goddess. It is unlikely that anyone was fooled by this obvious pretense, but it gave the Romans an excuse for erecting the theatre buildings they had needed for so long—Pompey's theatre was built nearly two hundred years after the beginning of serious Roman drama, and more than one hundred years after the date of the last great comedy.

The importance of Pompey's theatre cannot be overestimated. Because it was the first permanent theatre in Rome it almost certainly had great influence on the buildings that followed. The basic design for the theatre was *in conspectu dei*, no matter how ironic the necessity for such design, and the ancestry for this structure, which combined both theatre and temple, obviously goes back to Greece. The remains of Greek theatres indicate that they were never physically bound to temples, and in its late period the Greek theatre seems to have lost even its spiritual bond to the altars of the gods. At Athens, though the *orchestra* was within the precinct of Dionysus, a road was built separating temple and *orchestra*, and in later periods the stage building completely hid the temple from view. However, the close connection between Greek theatre and religion—indeed, the fact that the scene building doubled as temple—may well have influenced Pompey, (whose temple abutted the *cavea*, not the *scaena*, or stage house) for it is notable that the religious aspects of the *ludi* were not often in evidence during the course of Roman theatre.

In determining the physical aspects of the Roman theatre we are on fairly solid ground, not only in terms of what the Roman theatres were like, but also how they came about. Practically every city in Sicily where Roman troops were stationed had a theatre, and during the time of Hiero II the demand for theatrical fare was so enormous that new theatres were regularly being built. We now possess physical evidence of Hellenistic theatres in Syracuse, Tauromenium, Segesta, Tyndaris, Akrae, Catania, and Agyrion. On the evidence of these remains, plus the remains of the approximately one hundred twenty-five Roman theatres that were built in nearly every province of the Empire, from England to North Africa, it is possible to reconstruct the history of the Roman theatre structure with some accuracy.

During the two hundred years of drama that preceded the building of Pompey's theatre, a number of temporary theatres were built, none of which survive, and the information we possess regarding their shape and size is extremely limited. Most scholars, attempting to reconstruct them, come up with temporary wooden versions of the later stone theatres, departing from these late models in only small details. This may, in fact, be a quite accurate picture of the early wooden theatres, for we have no reason to believe that when the Romans finally agreed to the construction of permanent stone theatres they felt any need to depart from the basic design that had served them well for nearly two centuries.

In any case, the Roman theatres that have survived are clearly modifications of the Greek theatres of the Hellenistic period, and, generally speaking, they follow a rather rigorous pattern. Unlike their Greek ancestors, the Roman theatres were often free-standing structures. Having discovered the principle of the arch, the Romans built many of their theatre structures on level ground rather than cutting them into a hillside. In some cases, when available, a hillside was used, but in such cases corridors were dug into the hillside to match the corridors and stairways beneath the auditoriums of the free-standing structures so that, whether built on level ground or excavated into a hillside, the Roman theatre showed slight variation in its general pattern.

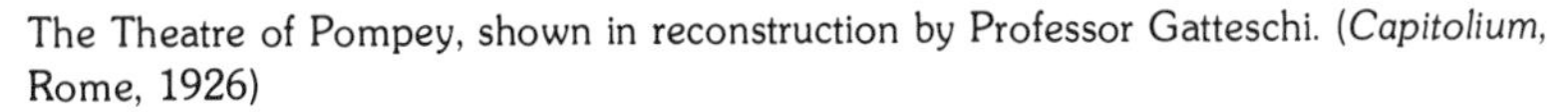
The Theatre of Pompey, shown in reconstruction by Professor Gatteschi. (*Capitolium*, Rome, 1926)

Plan of a typical Roman theatre.

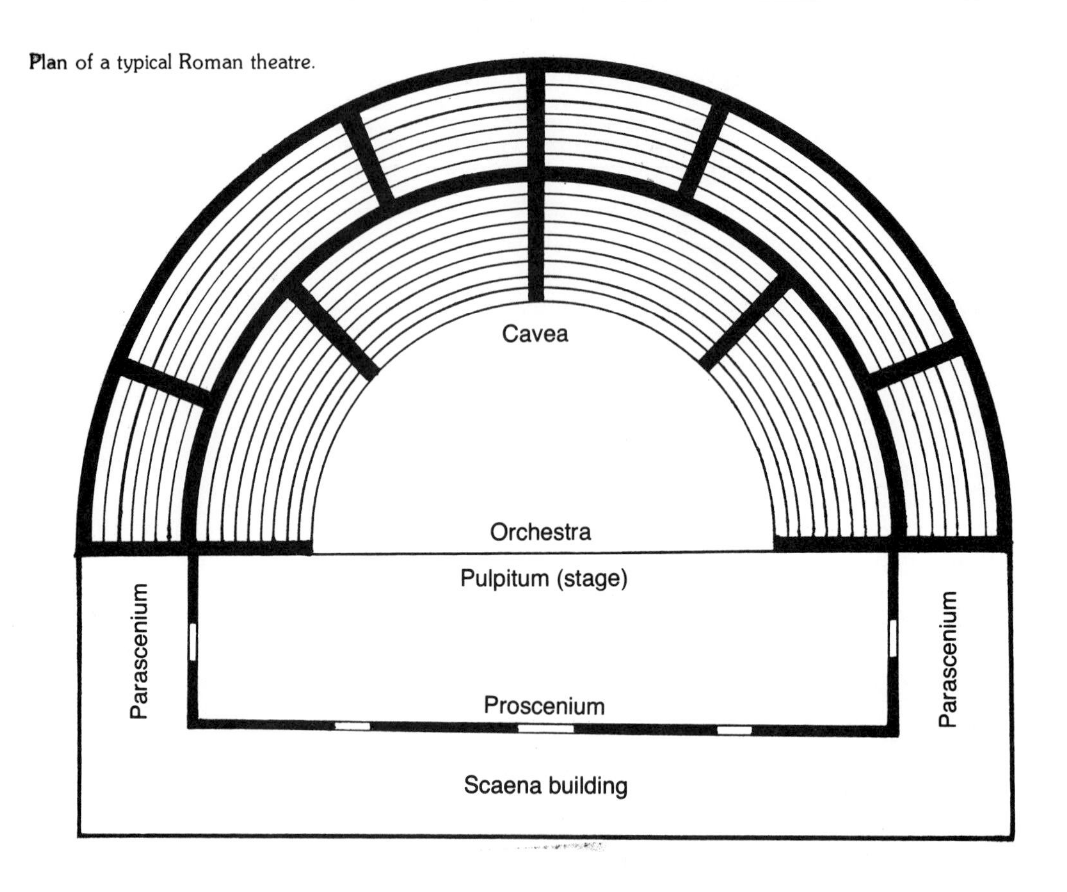

The stage house (*scaena*) was joined to the auditorium (*cavea*) to form a single structural unit. The *paradoi* of the Hellenistic theatre were roofed over to provide enclosed corridors (*vomitoria*) that emptied into the *orchestra* and the *auditorium*. The *orchestra* was reduced to a perfect half circle and was used for a variety of purposes—dignitaries were seated there, it was flooded for mimic sea battles for some of the mimes, and it was even encircled by a marble balustrade for gladiatorial bouts.

Directly in front of the *scaena* was the stage (*pulpitum*), about five feet above the level of the *orchestra*. The front of the stage was laid out along the diameter of the *orchestra*. In the early theatres a trough at the front of the stage provided a receptacle for the curtain (*auleum*), which was dropped into the trough, but in the later stages other means were developed for handling the curtain, or it was done away with entirely. The size of the stage tended to vary in terms of the size of the total structure, but even the smallest of the Roman stages (one hundred feet long by twenty feet deep) is quite large by contemporary standards, and the large Roman stage (three hundred feet long by forty feet deep), again in comparison with the modern stage, is absolutely gigantic.

The front surface of the stage house (*scaenae frons*) was a decorated architectural façade with columns, porticos, and niches that often contained statues. This was also true of the facing on the front stage elevation. In the wall of the *scaenae frons* were from three to five doors. In comedies these became the doors of houses opening onto a city street, represented by the stage itself. In tragedies the *scaenae frons* represented the exterior of a palace or temple. In both cases the architectural allure was enhanced by painting and gilding.

Concern for the comfort of the patrons led the Romans to perfect a method for cooling their theatres by blowing air over fountains of cold water, often perfumed to provide a pleasant odor along with the welcome coolness. They also managed to provide their audiences with shade by mounting huge, movable awnings, tended by sailors, along the top of the exterior walls.

The basic pattern of the Roman stage, as it developed, was away from the pattern of its Greek ancestors. In most cases the *orchestra* was little used—except for gladiatorial bouts and miniature sea battles—and so the audience, instead of rimming the action on three sides, looked almost directly into a stage that in almost every way except dimension resembled today's proscenium-arch theatres.

Scaenae frons of the Roman theatre at Aspendos, which dates from the second century A.D. Note the doors, steps, niches, remains of pillars, and general decorative aspect.

VITRUVIUS: It is difficult to know exactly how to place Marcus Vitruvius Pollio (70-15 B.C.). He was a Roman author and architect who had no significant effect on the theatre of his own time, but whose influence during and after the Renaissance was enormous. His great work was a ten-book treatise on architecture, *De architectura*, the fifth book of which deals with theatre construction. Discovered in manuscript at St. Gall in 1414 and printed in 1484, the work provides a guide for planning, laying out, and building an ideal city. The ten books include architectural principles; the evolution of building and the use of materials; Ionic temples; Doric and Corinthian temples; public buildings such as theatres, music halls, and baths; town and country houses; interior decoration; water supply; dials and clocks; and mechanical and military engineering. It is a detailed and comprehensive compendium of the available data on architecture of Vitruvius' own time.

Vitruvius lists specific requirements for the planning, design, and construction of theatres. One of the first requisites, as for all public buildings, is the choice of the healthiest possible site. He cautions that marshy neighborhoods should be avoided because such places breed pestilence. He also warns against a site that permits direct exposure to the sun, endorsing the theory that heat "removes by suction the natural virtues." As an example, he explains that iron, when exposed to fire, becomes soft and malleable, but that it hardens again when it cools. His conclusion is that heat weakens all bodies. As a result, he recommends that the walls be built high enough to provide shade for the audiences.

Regarding foundations for theatres, he suggests that a hillside site lends itself to easier construction of good foundations than do other sites. However, if a level, marshy site must be used, he stresses the importance of reinforcing the foundation by the use of piles and substructures. He states that stone or marble ought to be used to build up the stepped seats from the substructure.

Another important consideration that must be given to selection of a theatre site is acoustics. He notes that there are places which "naturally hinder the passage of the voice." He lists four classifications of such hindrances. The *dissonant place* is one in which the voice rises until it contacts solid bodies that reverse the flow of the sound so that it travels backward, colliding with and garbling the sound that follows it. The *circumsonant place* is that in which the voice circulates around until it is collected and dissipated in the center, causing loss of the terminations of words and resulting in a confusion of sounds that make the words unintelligible. The *resonant place* is one in which the voice strikes against a solid body and reverberates back against the oncoming sounds so that the terminations of words are repeated, thereby causing an echo. The *consonant place* is one in which the voice is reinforced from the ground, rises with greater fullness, and is heard "with clear and eloquent accents." It is obvious that a site compatible with consonance is the most desirable from the point of view of enhancing the quality of the actors' voices; such a site does not hinder the passage of sound as it flows in an ascending pattern from stage to theatre seats. Vitruvius describes a way in which acoustics can be improved by the use of especially designed bronze vases, installed at selected points in the seating areas in such a manner as to reverberate harmonically

Plan of a Roman theatre from Vitruvius' *Ten Books on Architecture*. This plan makes clear the use of the triangles mentioned in the text and displays the symmetry which the Romans so prized.

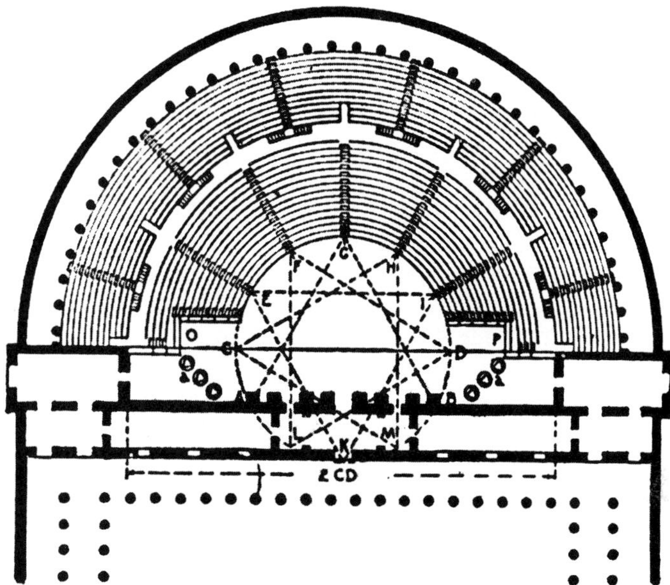

with the human voice and reinforce it. Earthenware vases can be used when economy is a factor, but they are not as effective as bronze.

In Vitruvius' plan for a Roman theatre, the *orchestra* is circumscribed by a circumference, using the center point of the allotted area. Four equilateral triangles are described within the circumscribed area so that the angles touch the circumference at equal intervals. The front of the scene is determined by the side of the triangle nearest the scene where the side of the triangle cuts the curve of the circle. The platform of the *proscenium* is divided from the *orchestra* by a parallel line equal to the diameter of the circumference; the platform is used as the stage and the *orchestra* is used to seat the senators. The stage is limited to a height of five feet so that the people seated in the *orchestra* can see all the gestures of the actors. The seats of the theatre are divided into curved upper and lower blocks by aisles leading up in ascending steps. These aisles are located at those seven points where the angles of the triangles touch the circumference of the *orchestra*. The remaining five angles of the triangles determine the arrangement of the stage. The center angle locates the palace doors; the two angles on each side of the center angle locate the two doors for strangers, and the two end angles determine the direction of the revolving scene.

The seats in the auditorium are aligned in rows at a height ranging from sixteen to eighteen inches. The width of a seat is a minimum of two feet and a maximum of two and one-half feet. The innermost seats on the wings at either side of the entrance to the *orchestra* are cut back to a perpendicular height equal to one-sixth of the *orchestra*'s diameter taken between the lowest steps. This measurement is used to determine the spring of the arch over the passages so that the vaulting will have a sufficient height.

The roof of the colonnade is level with the top of the backwall of the stage so that the voices will rise evenly from the stage to the top seats and the roof. If the roof is not level the voices will be interrupted at that height of the roof which they reach first.

The length of the stage will be twice the width of the *orchestra*. Additional details are provided for measurements and dimensions of the backwall above the level of the stage but are highly detailed and complex.

Vitruvius has retained the Greek name *periaktoi* for the three-sided rotating wing scenes used to show changes of locations. The three scenic changes are tragic, comic, and satyric.

Vitruvius warns that all theatres cannot meet the specific design features he has proposed, and he cautions that architects must adjust their plans to the "nature of the site or the magnitude of the work." He asserts that a versatile mind combined with technical skill and good taste can make the appropriate minor additions or corrections necessary so that a clumsy effect will be avoided.

By the year 1500, Vitruvius' position as an authority on architecture, especially theatre, paralleled Aristotle's in literature. During the Italian Renaissance, members of the Roman Academy, who began staging plays around 1468, adopted Vitruvius' ideas on theatrical architecture and staging, and used him as their guide. Young men from all over Europe came to Italy to study with Pomponius Laetus of the Academy, learned to reconstruct theatre in accordance with Vitruvius' plans, and to apply the results in play productions. When they returned to their homes, they took this knowledge with them, and Vitruvius' influence on theatrical architecture and staging spread throughout Europe.

STAGE SETTINGS

The basic setting for the Roman drama was, as mentioned in the section on theatre structure, the *scaenae frons*. That this wall was highly decorated we know from the remains of the ancient Roman theatres, with shallow porticoes, niches that often contained statues, columns, and bas reliefs. The *scaenae frons* had, in most cases, five doors, three in the upstage wall and one each at the wing ends. How much else the *scaenae frons* contained has been a matter of often acrimonious conjecture, especially in terms of staging Roman comedies. Was the *scaenae frons* usually rather flat, with the three-dimensional effect created by skillful stage painting? Were the niches and porticoes deep enough to contain the interior scenes? Could such scenes have been played behind one of the opened doors, surrounded by an essentially backstage set? There is no absolute way of answering these questions. What seems most likely, however, is that in the early wooden theatres the *scaenae frons* was a flat wooden wall with painted scenes and decoration. As the permanent stone theatres were built the *scaenae frons* became continuously more elaborate, primarily to satisfy the Roman taste for luxury and display.

In these permanent stone theatres the Romans used *periaktoi*, devices that they borrowed from the Greeks, as their primary method of changing scenes. Writing in approximately 15 B.C., Vitruvius describes the *scaenae frons* as having double doors in the center "decorated like those of a royal palace." To the right and left of these central doors are the smaller doors of the guest chambers, and beyond these "are the spaces provided for decoration—places that the Greeks call *periaktoi*, because in these places are triangular pieces of machinery which revolve, each having three decorated faces." In terms of what was displayed on each of these three faces, Vitruvius is quite specific, pointing out that there are three types of scenes—tragic, comic, and satyric. "Tragic scenes are delineated with columns, pediments, statues, and other objects suited to kings; comic scenes exhibit private dwellings, with balconies and views representing rows of windows, after the manner of ordinary dwellings; satyric scenes are decorated with trees, caverns, mountains, and other rustic objects delineated in landscape style."

Perhaps the most innovative aspect of the Roman stage setting was the development of the front curtain (*auleum*) to mask the scenic area until the play was ready to get underway. The curtain, usually itself highly decorated, was kept in a trough at the front edge of the stage. It was raised before the audience entered the theatre, dropped into its trough when the play began, and raised again when the play was over. The primary reason for the development of such a curtain may well have been the intrusion of the mime shows into the legitimate theatres, as well as the development of some rather spectacular settings that could not be revealed to the audience before the play began without spoiling the dramatic effect.

In addition to the front curtain there was, in cases where mime shows were being produced, a back curtain or *siparium*, with scenes painted on it and slits cut into it so that performers could enter and exit. In its earliest form the *siparium* was almost certainly the simple background curtain that backed the portable wooden stage of the traveling mime shows, with various types of scenes painted on it. However, like the *scaenae frons* (which it partially covered) the *siparium* got progressively larger and more elaborate.

There are tales of mechanical marvels performed on the Roman stage, with settings that included mountains, trees, flowing streams, herds of grazing goats, and even a fountain of wine that sprang up from the stage floor. How realistic these effects would be, if judged by a modern audience, we have no way of knowing, but they certainly impressed Apuleius, who recorded a description of the scene, pointing out that at the end of the play the whole thing sank out of sight. Given the Roman engineering genius it is not hard to believe that such scenes were very well done indeed, though they would be difficult if not impossible to achieve in any of the Roman theatres with which we are familiar. Professor Jack Brokaw has perhaps solved this seeming inconsistency by suggesting that productions like the one described by Apuleius were probably produced in the Roman ampitheatres, which could handle something of this size.

Masks for Terence's *Phormio*. (From the Ambrosianus manuscript, Vatican Library)

COSTUMES AND MASKS

Just as they followed Greek example in so many other aspects of theatre, so did the Romans turn to the Greeks for their theatrical costume. Thus, they adopted long gowns and elevated boots for tragedy and short gowns and flat sandals for comedy. Within this general practice there were, apparently, some variations, so that the tragic gown worn for the *fabula crepidata* (tragedy on Greek materials) probably was designed to follow Greek originals, wheras the long tragic gown worn in the *fabula praetexta* (tragedy on Roman materials) was apparently the Roman toga. This was also true in the comedies, so that in the *fabula palliata* (comedy on Greek materials) the Greek style was followed, and in the *fabula togata* (comedy based on Roman materials) the short Roman tunic became stage dress. By the time of the Empire this costuming, perhaps because it was merely copied rather than traditional to the Romans, became rather mixed up, with the result that both comic and tragic dress, in Greek and Roman styles, could sometimes be found on the same stage in the same production.

Outside the serious drama, costume tended to vary widely. Early mime performers generally wore the short tunic, went barefoot, and did not wear masks. They did, in most cases, wear a hood (*ricinium*) that could be pulled up over the head in certain types of roles, for example, roles calling for disguise, or thrown back. This hood became an identifying device for mime performers. Certain of the mime characters, clowns or fools with shaven heads, wore a patchwork jacket (*centunuculus*) over tights and, perhaps, a phallus. As the mimes became ever more popular this distinctive costuming underwent some changes. More and more of the characters began to dress in nontraditional costumes that were either appropriate to their role or, if they were public favorites, costumes that were lavish, striking, and designed to emphasize their "star" status. Also, as the adultery themes became ever more popular, and especially after the emperor's order that they be done in reality, the women

One of the tragic masks made of terracotta. The high dome resembles the Greek *onkos*, and the tragic expression also betrays Greek origin.

mime dancers wore progressively less and less, to the point where many apparently wore nothing at all.

Little is known of the costumes worn by the pantomimists, perhaps because the complex physical requirements of the form made lavish costuming impossible, or perhaps because the art was better served by simplicity. In the tragic pantomime, which was the only form able to maintain its popularity throughout the Roman period, the performers wore long tragic robes, probably in the same styles as those worn on the tragic stage. Over the robes the pantomimists wore loose, flowing cloaks which permitted the maximum freedom of movement.

The use of the mask in Roman theatre has long been a matter of debate, largely because of a statement by a fourth century writer that the famous actor Rosius (c. 126-62 B.C.) introduced the mask to Roman drama in an effort to hide his severe squint. The assumption has been that because Roscius was the most popular actor of his time the lesser actors all quickly followed his example in donning the mask. This statement, once widely accepted, has recently fallen into disregard and is probably false. There is no corroborating evidence to support it, it is not based on direct observation by the author or anyone to whom the author could have spoken as it was written nearly three hundred years after the event supposedly took place, and recent scholarship has unearthed numerous references to the use of masks in early Roman theatre long before the time of Roscius. Given these references and the basic influence of Greece on the developing Roman theatre, it becomes reasonable to believe that the masks were present from the beginning.

In any case the masks were similar to those used in Greek theatrical production, including such specific types as young and old men and women, peasants, and slaves. That the masks were often formed of terracotta is evidenced by the survival of casts for making the masks. However, they were also constructed of linen which, with wigs attached, covered the whole head.

The mimes used no masks, but the players apparently made extensive use of makeup. The pantomimes used masks that varied from the tragic masks of the stage in that the mouths, not needed for uttering lines, were closed. Some early writers describe the pantomime masks as being more realistic than those of regular tragedy. However, the mask described by Quintilian in the first century seems the opposite of natural, with one side of the mask cheerful and the other side serious.

4

The Medieval Theatre

4

The Medieval Theatre

In large part as a result of the anarchy and disorder that plagued the Roman provinces during the fourth and fifth centuries, and in part because of the closing of the Roman theatres in the sixth century, theatre as a reasonably sophisticated art form disappeared from view for nearly four hundred years—from the sixth to the tenth century. This is not to say that theatre ceased to exist, but that even in the most highly civilized areas it existed on a reduced and far more primitive level than had been the case during the periods of Greece and Rome. The early folk fertility rituals that had never died out in the countryside took on more prominence, even in the cities. Amusements—juggling, tumbling, singing, dancing, trained animal acts—were put on by traveling entertainers.

Some limited types of theatrical activity must have continued to exist side-by-side with the amusements, for Church records (of council, synod, and diet) between the sixth and tenth centuries constantly inveigh against actors and theatrical performances, and references in various early documents to *mimi* and *histriones* seem to indicate that some form of theatre other than folk ritual still existed. Indeed, theatre as a legitimate art form may have continued in a limited fashion throughout the period, at least in the Eastern Empire. Church documents seem to indicate some kind of theatrical performance at Constantinople as late as the year 692. In addition there is, in a document from Barcelona, a rather cryptic reference to theatre which indicates some type of performance early in the seventh century. Also, plays were written, though there is no record of their production, in Byzantium during the early Medieval period. St. John Damascene, early in the eighth century, soundly condemned theatrical performances because, he said, they became rivals to the Mass. Nearly one hundred years later a Church decree forbidding the clergy to watch actors in plays given on stages or at marriages tends to confirm the theory that theatrical performance was reasonably common.

Thus, when a major drama was finally reborn out of Christian practice, there was still in existence enough material from folk ritual and from Classical drama to nourish the infant theatre.

THE MEDIEVAL WORLD

In terms of reviewing the background material necessary to place theatre in its proper historical perspective, the enormous diversity of the Medieval world may be divided neatly (and rather simplistically) into two distinct aspects. The first is the rise of Christianity and the second is the development of feudalism and the social structure which thus came about.

The Rise of Christianity

Because of their refusal to acknowledge the absolute authority of the Roman emperors, the early Christians in Rome and other major cities in the Empire were often severely persecuted by the civil authorities with the delighted sanction of those same emperors. This began in a major way under the Emperor Nero and lasted until 313 A.D. when the Emperor Constantine, himself a convert to Christianity, issued the famous Edict of Milan in which he demanded

Churchmen not only propagated Christianity, but also kept alive the arts throughout the Medieval period.

tolerance for all religions, specifically singling out the Christian faith. During the fifth century, following the Emperor Julian's unsuccessful attempt to restore paganism to its previous position of ascendancy within the Empire, Christianity became the only legitimate religion in the areas still controlled by Rome. The emperors accepted the religion as their own and this led many of the lesser officials to accept Christianity, on a verbal if not on a spiritual level.

The ascendancy of Christianity had two major results as far as theatre was concerned. From the earliest days of the Christian period the Church fathers denounced theatre—that is to say, they reacted strongly against the bloody and licentious theatre of the Empire period in Rome. On the other hand the Church provided the materials and the occasions (both from the liturgy) for the ultimate rebirth of the drama. The Church also provided the monastic orders, which helped to keep Classical learning and thus a limited sense of the Classical drama alive during the theatre's long, dark period.

The idea of separating the individual from the world to avoid its temptations and resultant sins was surely pre-Christian in its origins, but it was quickly adopted by developing Christianity. The early Christian hermits living out their lonely lives of contemplation were soon followed by separatist groups which combined the concept of community with that of isolation, and thus the monasteries came into existence and spread quickly throughout Europe. The monasteries dispensed charity, did research in farming methodology and taught the results to the nearby communities, developed and sent out missionaries for the conversion of the heathen, and kept alight the lamp of learning during the period that was for so long referred to as the Dark Ages. Indeed, the plays of Terence were even taught in some of the monasteries, though more as models of polite Latin conversation than as plays to be performed.

The Development of Feudalism

Feudalism is the term that is generally applied to the economic, social, and political conditions that existed in Europe during the Medieval period. The seeds of feudalism were sown during the reign of Charlemagne (742-814), the Frankish king who conquered the Saxons, the Lombards in Italy, and who also acquired Aquitaine, Bavaria, Bohemia, a large part of the western Slavic territories, and northeastern Spain. This unification of most of territorial Europe created the Frankish Empire, and after the Pope proclaimed Charlemagne to be Emperor of the Romans it became known as the Holy Roman Empire. Two of Charlemagne's three sons failed to outlive their father and the Empire remained united, but his three quarreling grandsons finally divided it at the Treaty of Verdun in 843. The Empire was reunited briefly under the incompetent Charles the Fat, but he proved unable to hold even his own crown and, invaded by the Northmen along the coast, the Slavs and Hungarians from the east, and the Saracens in the south, the Empire again fell apart. It was once more reunited and, with some variations in its geographical boundaries, it lasted until Napoleon destroyed it.

Feudalism, as a social ideal, was characterized by a strong nobility, a numerous peasantry, and weak kings unable to dominate their barons. This, of course, led to much petty warfare between the powerful nobles. The kings, hoping to control the situation, attempted to purchase loyal followers by the granting of immunities and gifts of land (*beneficiums*). However, this continual breakdown of territories into ever smaller *benefices* or *fiefs* tended to make feudalism even stronger.

Feudalism depended, essentially, on the relationship that existed between the lord and his vassal, and between the vassal and his serfs. The vassal owed his lord military service, court service, and such special services as ransoming the lord's person should he be taken prisoner, providing a dowry for the lord's oldest daughter, paying the expenses of knighthood for the lord's eldest son, and providing lodging for the lord when he might be traveling. The lord, on the other hand, had only one primary obligation to his vassal, but it was an all-

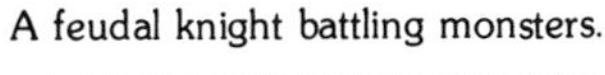
A feudal knight battling monsters.

important one—protection. The vassal, in descending order, received from his serfs (those bound to the land) such monetary and physical benefits as taxes, portions of crops, and military service. This chain of mutual obligation was the bond that held feudalism together. In theory, everyone was a vassal of another human being except for the king, who was himself the vassal of God.

The village (or manor) was the basic social and economic unit of the feudal structure. Usually developed from land gifts, from seizures of land, or even from voluntary surrender in order to gain the protection of a powerful lord, the village generally consisted of little more than a single street bordered by houses. Each village contained a church, which was not only the religious center of the community, but also the social center, and usually one large house for the lord or, if the lord controlled more than one village, for the lord's representative. The villages were inhabited by the villein, who held a virgate (thirty acres) of land and who was also responsible for working the lord's land (domain), and the cottars, who had smaller personal holdings than the villein and who sometimes worked directly for the lord but more often worked for the villein.

The Medieval town was the largest social and economic unit of the feudal state. Some of these were old Roman towns that survived because they were located on trade routes and easy to defend, some grew up around the castles of powerful barons from whom they might gain protection, some grew around traditional market places or religious shrines, and still others grew up in areas of special economic significance such as ports or sheltered locations on major waterways, mining areas, or areas with salt or mineral deposits.

Within the towns there developed merchant guilds and craft guilds. The merchants began their guilds both as fraternal organizations to unite themselves in a social brotherhood and also as quasi-political power groups dedicated to gaining trade and monopoly privileges for the members. The craft guilds, which came later, were based on the same principles as the older merchant guilds—fraternity and the gaining of economic advantage.

During the eleventh and twelfth centuries the increase in trade and industry and the increasing contact with such highly civilized areas as Saracen Spain and Sicily brought on a revival of learning throughout western Europe. The twelfth century saw the establishment of many of Europe's major universities, including those at Paris, Salerno, and Bologna. Oxford and Cambridge were soon to come. These early universities brought back the study of Roman law and emphasized the study of such great Greek philosophers as Plato and Aristotle. In fact, the Classical civilizations and their products, including theatre, became the core of the curricula (*trivium, quadrivium*) of the universities.

In western Europe, approximately between the years 1000 to 1400, much of the great Medieval literature was composed. There were metrical romances and there was lyric poetry that was often set to music. There were historical works, such as the *chronicles* and *memoires*, and epic poems represented by the Medieval High German *Nibelungenlied*, the Italian *Divine Comedy*, and the Scandinavian *Eddas*. But most important of all, there was the rebirth of the drama.

A painting in the Galleria dell'Accademia, Florence, Italy, by an unknown Florentine artist of the fourteenth century, may illustrate an early use of multiple sets. The steps on which the child Mary stands are clearly temporary and thus part of a stage setting that is somewhat "Terentian" in style.

THE CLASSICAL HERITAGE

Even before the developing liturgical drama was well underway the Classical heritage was provoking Medieval dramas. A play written in Greek and dealing with the passion of Christ and the sorrows of the Blessed Virgin was long attributed to St. Gregory Nazianzene, a writer of the fourth century. However, such internal evidence as meter, prosody, and grammar indicate quite clearly that the play dates from the early tenth century. Excepting for an absence of lyric choruses the play follows closely along the lines of traditional Greek tragedy, incorporating a few lines from the *Prometheus Bound* of Aeschylus, several hundred lines from Euripides, and lines, only tentatively identified, from plays that did not survive. Such a play has little theatrical interest—one cannot even wager with any certainty that it was ever produced—except to the theatre historian, for it preserves lines from the Greek drama that otherwise would have been lost. However, in conjunction with the six "moral" plays of Hrotswitha, the playwright nun of Gandersheim who wrote in the style of the Roman Terence, the play gives an indication of what was likely taking place in monasteries all over Europe. The Classical heritage did not keep the drama alive for the secular community of the Middle Ages, but the earlier forms were preserved and, with the development of the schools and universities the Classical forms came once more into their own.

HROTSWITHA: Hrotswitha (Hrotsvitha, Hrosvitha, Roswitha, c. 935-c. 1001), poet, playwright, and historian, was a nun in the Benedictine monastery at Gandersheim in northern Saxony. Little factual material about her life has survived, and so most historians depend on the nun's own works to provide some basis for speculation about the life of this extraordinary woman. Because Gandersheim, an important cultural center in Saxony, was administered by abbesses of noble rank, some scholars have speculated that Hrotswitha was herself of the nobility; even that she was the niece of Otto I (912-973), Emperor of the Holy Roman Empire, about whose career she wrote an historical account. Whether nobly born or not, Hrotswitha clearly was highly educated and had greater access to the world outside the monastery than the Benedictine nuns of the time would likely have had, leading some to speculate that she was, perhaps, a canoness. If true, this meant that she was living in a religious community but without the restraints imposed by vows. Instead, she would be living under a rule of order and thus not wholly set apart from the world outside.

There is no objective proof that any of Hrotswitha's six short plays (*Paphnutius*, *Sapientia*, *Gallicanus*, *Dulcitius*, *Calimachus*, and *Abraham*) were ever performed in her own day. There is no real reason, in fact, to believe that they were even intended for production. In the prefaces to her plays she points

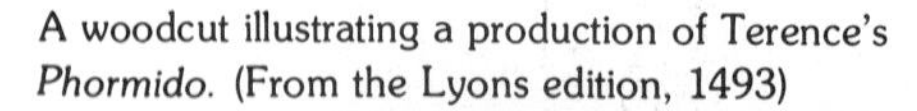

A woodcut illustrating a production of Terence's *Phormido.* (From the Lyons edition, 1493)

out that many of the pagan writers, because of their "polished elegance," are preferred above the Holy Scriptures. Indeed, even those who eschew the other pagans, she says, make an exception of the plays of Terence, because of his charming style and manner, and thus risk corruption by the wickedness of the material. So, she continues, in writing her plays she has not hesitated to imitate "a poet whose works are so widely read. . . ." The emphasis here should probably be on the word "read." The pagan writers were widely *read* in the Middle Ages, especially Terence, whose works, we are told, bore a charmed life in the monasteries. However, there is no indication that Terence's plays were ever *performed* in the monasteries, and neither is there any real reason to believe that Hrotswitha's six moral plays were produced.

Whether or not they were designed for stage performance, Hrotswitha's most recent translator, Sister Mary Marguerite Butler, has worked with the plays onstage and has found them to be eminently playable. Taking the manner of Terence as her model, but providing subjects of greater moral significance to the Medieval community (piety, chastity, martyrdom), Hrotswitha wrote didactic but interesting plays that Sister Mary Marguerite feels may well have been staged in the monastery, probably in the cloister walk with the traditional arcades providing an architectural setting.

Given the Church attitude toward drama, even the formal (Classical) drama, and given the great number of oral readings that we know were given in the monasteries, perhaps the most likely possibility for production of Hrotswitha's plays is a type of readers theatre production, with the parts read but not fully acted out.

Critics in earlier periods have not always been kind to Hrotswitha, treating her plays in a cavalier fashion that they clearly do not deserve. A. W. Pollard refers to her "supersensuous modesty" and points out that it is infinitely more offensive than the license of her original. Her language, he says, is bald, and her characters are without life or humanity. On the other hand, Sister Mary Marguerite and her contemporaries have very probably made more of Hrotswitha's work than it deserves.

Like most early playwrights, Hrotswitha went to the *Acta sanctorum*, the Apocryphal Gospels, and Christian legendry for her source materials. In every case she treats her source with respect, following her material closely rather than using is as a point of dramatic departure. The worst (or perhaps the best) that can be said of her in this regard, is that she takes characters who are merely mentioned in her sources and develops quite complete characterizations around them.

Dulcitius is perhaps the most interesting of Hrotswitha's plays, at least from a theatrical point of view, because it includes a magnificent farcical scene between the evil governor, Dulcitius, and some dirty kitchen utensils. The play deals with the martyrdom of the three virgins—Agape, Chionia, and Irena—at the command of the Emperor Diocletian. The governor, Dulcitius, is ordered to torture the virgins to obtain their denial of Christ and eventual consent to court-arranged marriages. The women refuse. Dulcitius lustfully goes to seek his prisoners in the apartment where they are imprisoned. However, before he can complete his evil plans a miracle happens and instead of raping the virgins he makes love to the kitchen pots and pans, getting himself covered

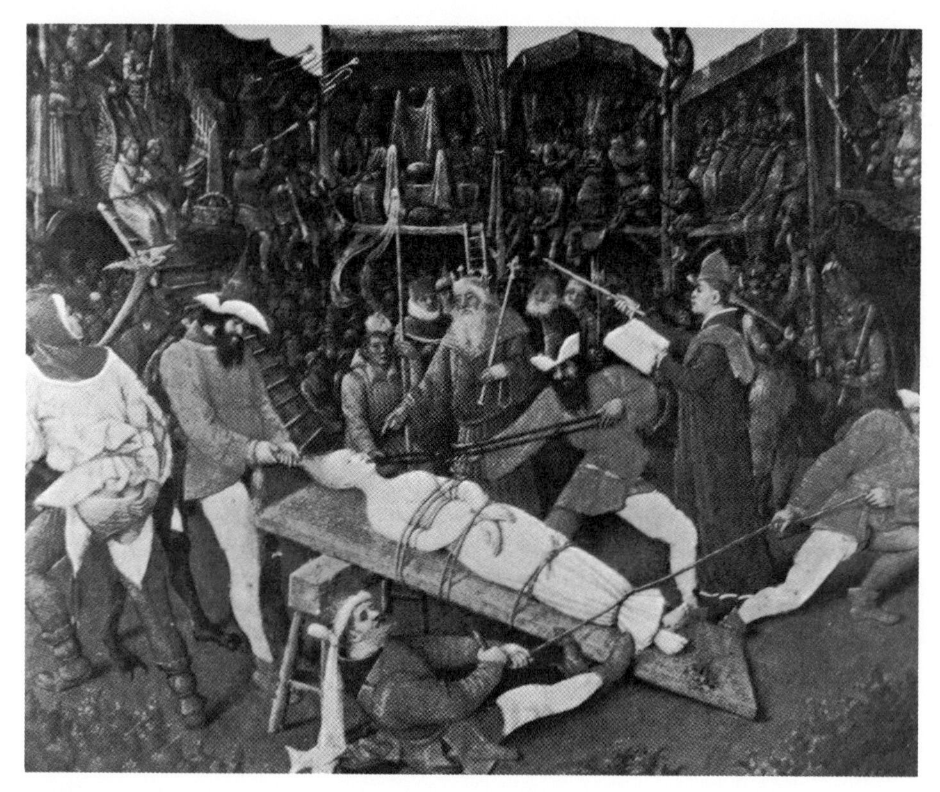

"The Martyrdom of St. Apollonia." A scene from a mystery play recorded in miniature by Jean Fouquet in 1460 for the *Book of Hours* of Etienne Chevalier.

with soot and grease for his trouble. Diocletian orders Dulcitius to turn the women over to Sisinnius for punishment. Again there is heavenly intervention, but finally Sisinnius manages to have Agape and Chionia executed. Irena is killed shorty thereafter by a soldier's arrow. Thus, all three virgins are martyred but their virtue is preserved, which greatly pleased a Medieval Christian audience.

The most important aspect of Hrotswitha's work, at least from an historical point of view, is that it provides the link between Classical and Medieval drama. Her plays are Classical in form, but they reflect Medieval Christianity in their themes and sentiments. And they all contain flashes of wit and farcical good humor that make them timeless.

THE FOLK DRAMA
Mummings and Disguisings

It is impossible to determine with any accuracy just how far the folk drama dates back in European history. Certainly most of the semidramatic rituals unearthed and collected by Sir James George Frazer are prehistoric in origin. However, the atavistic chord that these plays seemed to touch, buried deep in man's psyche, was not to be denied and, in the countryside though not in the cities, they lasted through the whole of the Medieval period as a reasonably popular dramatic form. By the late fifteenth century many aspects of the folk drama were taken over by the court group as light entertainments, but the form itself, garbled but still similar to its ritual origins, lasted into the twentieth century.

While the original purpose of these dramatic rituals had little real meaning for the Medieval European, they were easily adapted to the requirements of a developing Christianity. Thus, the early central figure of the English hero-combat play (Galatian in one of the Scottish texts) became St. George, and some of the later Christianized figures of the Robin Hood fertility myth (Maid Marion, Friar Tuck) were included in the May Games. And these little ritual dramas, repeopled by characters acceptable to Christianity, were also changed in time to adapt to the new religion. Thus, the hero-combat play, originally a spring fertility rite, was performed during the Christmas season, with a new presenter or narrator, Father Christmas, to announce the action.

Along with the Christmas mummings there were presented such ancient folk entertainments as the Sword Dance and Morris Dance. The Sword Dance, almost certainly an ancient pyrrhic or battle dance, was "Christianized" by

The Christmas mummers present the play of St. George in the great hall of a Medieval castle. Note the "leaf-covered" figure at the center of the woodcut. This is a traditional mummers' costume and indicates how these plays began as part of the spring vegetation ceremonies.

peopling it with the great saints of Christendom (see the *Shetland Sword Dance* as collected by Sir Walter Scott), giving these saints as their dramatic objective the defeat of anti-Christian enemies, and performing the dance on Ash Wednesday. Similar to the Sword Dance in some respects, the Morris Dance was perhaps brought back to northern Europe by the returning crusaders. Featuring such characters as the clown, fool, hobby horse, and Maid Marion, the Morris Dance was regularly performed during carnival season.

A number of other such dramatic seasonal entertainments remained popular with the folk (and with more than a few of the gentry) throughout the Medieval period. Semidramatic activities such as the Abbot's Bromley Horn Dance, the Furry Dance, and the "Geese" Dance provided seasonal opportunities for folk celebration and merriment. Plough plays and pace-egg plays provided somewhat more dramatic forms of entertainment.

Exactly what effect such folk-related activity had on the developing liturgical drama is uncertain. What can be stated positively is that in the liturgical dramas the vaunts of Herod, for example, or the comic, farcical activities of Mak, Gill, and the three shepherds, are directly related to the folk rituals. In any case, the dramatic activities of the ancient Celtic and Teutonic peoples, handed down in a mystical oral tradition, kept the spark of drama or at least dramatic activity alive for the folk during the largest part of the Medival period.

A fifteenth century representation of the *festum asinorum* in a French cathedral.

THE LITURGICAL DRAMA

In spite of the occasional entertainments, the traveling minstrels, the folk drama, the Classical heritage, and all the other essentially dramatic Medieval conventions, it was in the Christian Church, traditionally the arch-enemy of theatre, that the drama was reborn.

The importance of the Mass (the celebration of the Eucharist) within the Church service goes back to the earliest period of Christianity. However, by the end of the sixth century under Pope Gregory I (Gregory the Great) it had become the single most important service of the Church. The Mass was, of course, in Latin, and on one level its ritual was specific and inviolable—that is, there was a pattern of prayer, chant, and song that could not be changed. This was especially true of the second part of the Mass—the Sacrament. However, within the introductory portion, which included biblical readings, prayers, singing of psalms, and sermons, variations were not only possible but quite common given the possible selections of material. Some scholars have stoutly maintained the position that the Mass itself is a drama. Whether or not this is true, it is certainly dramatic, and while no dramatic ceremony ever attached itself permanently to the Mass because the central sacrament is too important, it was by way of the Mass that drama was finally revived.

One aspect of the Mass was the singing, at various points in the service, of the "Alleluia." Within the text of the Alleluia were areas for musical interpolation or tropes. At first these were merely extended musical passages using the final syllable of *alleluia*. However, given such a musical opportunity a number of ecclesiastical musicians apparently could not resist the challenge to elaborate at length, and the wordless sequences they developed became complex and beautiful tunes designed to complement specific feast days. Eventually words were added to the tunes, employing one syllable for each note. There is no way of determining exactly when and by whom words were first introduced. Legend has it that the famous musician Notker Balbulus (c. 840-912), at the monastery of St. Gall in what is now Switzerland, first introduced the words as a mnemonic device for remembering sequences that he had once found difficult to learn when he was a choirboy. The legend is most likely apocryphal; however, the idea proved to be highly popular and by the middle of the tenth century tropes could be found in most of the choral sections of the Mass.

Certain other aspects of Medieval religious observance, besides the Mass, contributed to the eventual development of drama. The Church calendar, because it placed so much emphasis on specific happenings from biblical history, tended to provide the Medieval playwright with ready-made, highly colorful subjects waiting to be illustrated in dramatic terms. In fact, long before drama finally made its appearance, certain mimetic elements had become traditional to major Church events. For example, during the Good Friday service precedng Easter a cross, usually that which hung behind the high altar, was taken down, wrapped in grave cloths, and mimetically buried in a representation of the sepulchre. At the Easter service the cross was removed from the grave, unwrapped, and elevated once more behind the altar as a symbolic presentation of the Resurrection. A mimetic presentation was also

A 1473 painting by Hans Multscher shows what seems to be a theatrical presentation of the birth of Christ, as the spectators looking on are all in contemporary dress.

provided at Christmas when parishioners were treated to a pantomime of Mary and the Christ Child in the manger, being visited by the shepherds and the Wise Men.

Another aspect of the Medieval Church that aided in the development of theatre was the emphasis placed on providing visual representation of major elements within the services. The vestments of the priests, the altar, the statues, the pictures, and the stations of the cross all contributed to an essentially dramatic presentation of the most important events and personages within sacred history and practice.

The liturgical drama is usually believed to have had its inception early in the tenth century. The oldest extant text, which dates from approximately 925, is the *Quem quaeritis* from the Benedictine Abbey of St. Gall. Taken from the Introit (that part of the Mass sung by the choir as the priests approach the high altar) of the Easter Mass, the *Quem quaeritis* is probably purely antiphonal; that is, it was sung by the choir with no attempt at dramatic impersonation. The original Latin text, with interlinear translation, is short enough to be reproduced below in its entirety.

INTERROGATIO: *Quem quaeritis in sepulchro, o Christicolae?*

QUESTION (BY THE ANGELS): Whom seek ye in the sepulchre, O followers of Christ?

RESPONSIO: *Jesum Nazarenum crucifixum, o caelicolae.*

ANSWER (BY THE THREE MARYS): Jesus of Nazareth, who was crucified, just as he foretold.

ANGELI: *Non est hic; surrexit, sicut praedixerat. Ite, nuntiate quia surrexit de sepulchro.*

ANGELS: He is not here; he is risen as he foretold. Go and announce that he is risen from the sepulchre.

While the *Quen quaeritis* was purely a choral element, and while the Easter Resurrection pantomime described earlier was an act without words, the combination of these two dramatic elements (action and dialogue) in the same service led directly to a truly dramatic production. This is the playlet, complete with directions for performance, found in the *Regularis Concordia*, compiled sometime around the year 970 by St. Ethelwold, Bishop of Winchester. The playlet contains stage directions for the angel seated in the tomb and for the monks playing the three Marys. It also contains instructions on costuming and directions on vocalization (the Angel is instructed to sing his lines in a "dulcet voice of medium pitch").

The popularity that the Easter play must have had is evidenced not only by the rapid proliferation of this Easter liturgical drama, but also by the way in which the basic format developed for Easter was so quickly adapted to other occasions. For example, a Christmas trope about the visit of the shepherds to the manger, already common as a pantomimed action, was given lines beginning "*Quem quaeritis in praesepe, pastores, dicite,*" ("Whom seek ye in the manger, shepherds, tell us").

The geographical spread covered by the liturgical drama was great indeed, stretching from Scandinavia in the north through Italy in the south, and from England in the west into Russia in the east. The most productive areas were France, Germany, and England, and the least productive were Italy, where papal opposition to drama limited the number of plays produced, and Spain, where the Moorish occupation of all but the northeastern part of that country limited severely the spread of Christian drama. The plays were particularly popular in areas dominated by Benedictine monasteries. Thus, we find much dramatic activity at such spots as Limoges and Fleury in France, Richenau in Germany, St. Gall in Switzerland, and Ripall in Spain.

For slightly more than three hundred years the plays remained almost exclusively the property of the clergy in that they were usually played only within the physical confines of the church. Indeed, it was not until the last quarter of the thirteenth century that the plays generally moved outdoors, and then it was to the west wall of the church, which tended to keep the dramatic activities on consecrated ground.

During their period within the confines of the Church, or at least on church grounds, the most popular subject for the plays continued to be the events surrounding the Resurrection; that is, the visit of the three Marys to the tomb and such subsequent or contiguous actions as visits by doctors, priests,

A relief from a church in Cologne, done in the late twelfth century, seems to record the scene of the three Marys at the tomb—a scene highly popular in the early tropes.

soldiers, and even by Christ himself in his heavenly form. The doctor is asked to provide an unguent to raise the dead, but his price is far too great; the Jewish high priests appear, escorting a group of Roman soldiers who are to keep watch over the tomb to prevent Christians from stealing the body and then claiming resurrection; and Christ himself appears, usually in disguise, to recount how he has forced the gates of hell and freed the imprisoned Christians. Interestingly, considering the great popularity of Resurrection drama, the Crucifixion was rarely touched upon, and only three plays treating this subject have survived.

After Easter, the season attracting the most plays was Christmas. The Christmas play described earlier, the *Praesepe*, was expanded to include scenes of the Annunciation, the birth of John the Baptist, and of Joseph displaying his doubts of Mary. The "Doubting Joseph" scene eventually became one of the most popular of Medieval dramatic subjects, along with (especially in

France) the "Miracles of Our Lady" scenes. Scenes depicting the visits of the Wise Men and the shepherds were interspersed with scenes featuring the first and greatest villain of Medieval liturgical drama—Herod. Herod's vaunting of his might and his evil deeds, and his demands to be told the whereabouts of the Child, made him one of the most popular—if not the most beloved—of characters for the Medieval audience.

One of the most important plays of the Christmas season came about when the famous *Sermon against Jews, Pagans, and Arians*, long mistakenly attributed to St. Augustine, was dramatized for presentation at the Christmas matin service. The sermon attempts to prove the errors of the Jews in their stand against Christ by calling their own prophets to testify. The prophets were called to testify, one by one, and because the material is so rhetorical one must suspect that it was the costuming and the rich presentation that made the play a success with the audiences. Indeed, the play was also quite flexible. On some occasions it was done with only two of the prophets being called, and on other occasions a full twenty-eight stood forth, along with such Classical characters as Vergil and Sybil (got up in the Medieval concept of Classical costume), and such biblical additions as Adam, Noah, and even Balaam mounted on an ass. The *Prophet's Play* soon became so large and unwieldy that it was divided into a number of smaller plays which were then staged sequentially as the *Procession of the Prophets*.

A miniature from the manuscript of the Valenciennes Passion Play, showing the healing of the paralytic and the woman with dropsy. (Gustave Cohen, *Le Théâtre en France au moyen âge*, Paris, 1228-31)

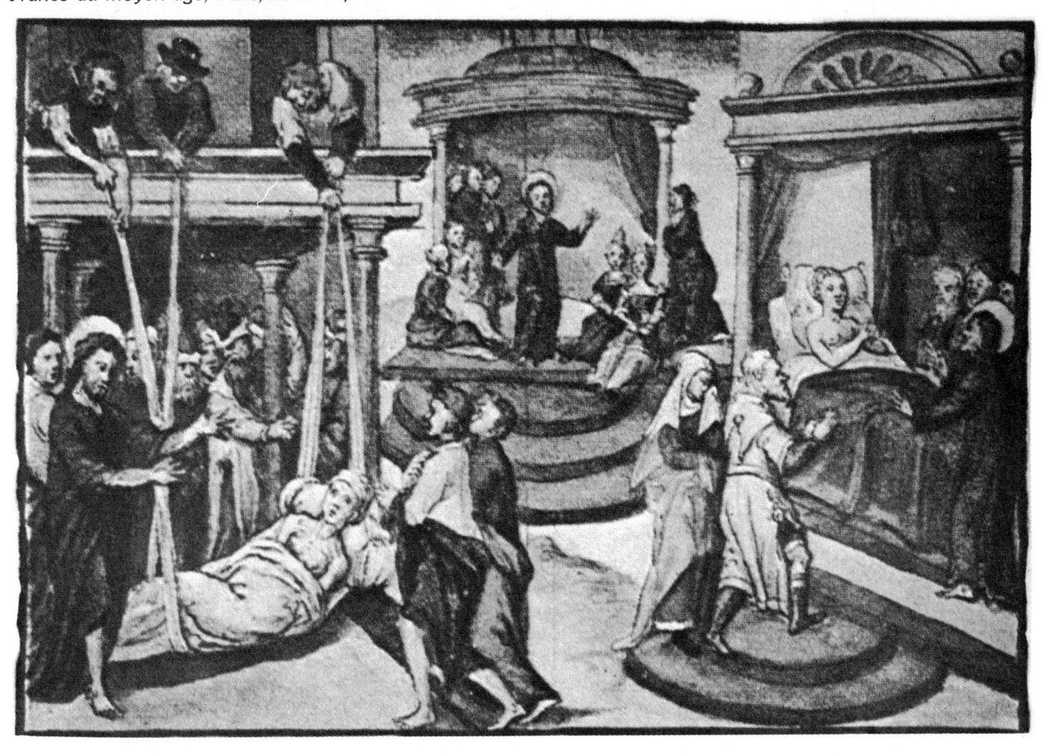

Although the seasons of Easter and Christmas had, respectively, the most plays, there were a number of other such liturgical dramas scattered throughout the year and produced on major feast days. There were plays dealing with Isaac and Rebecca, Daniel and the lion, Joseph and his brethren, the conversion of St. Paul, Lazarus risen from the dead, and many episodes from the life of the Virgin Mary. These plays, taken together, provided for an often illiterate congregation a dramatic illustration of the entire plan of salvation, from Original Sin through the birth, death, and resurrection of Christ.

Staging the Liturgical Drama

Trying to illuminate the methods of staging the liturgical dramas inside the church would seem, upon superficial consideration, not to be worth the candle. After all, the great mansion sets or the traveling wonders on pageant wagons that were developed soon after the drama moved out of the church are, quite legitimately, of primary concern to the student of theatre history. However, what happened inside the church gave direction to what happened outside, and it is possible and even necessary to see in the Church liturgical settings the scenic basis of everything that would develop outside the church during the greatest period of Medieval drama.

Originally, of course, the liturgical dramas made scenic use of little beyond the church architecture. For example, in producing the Easter pantomime the high altar and the cross provided two of the three major scenic elements for the set, and the representation of the sepulchre provided the third. In some cases such a representation was also provided as part of the architectural design; that is, a permanent model of the sepulchre was built in as a part of the church interior. However, in most cases a model had to be built that could be erected for the Good Friday and Easter services and then broken down and stored away for future use. This model was almost certainly the first "mansion" set. By the late tenth century, when the playlet in the *Regularis Concordia* was being produced, all the action took place at the sepulchre and the pantomime involving the high altar and the cross (or importantly that portion of the action that made symbolic use of the church architecture) had been separated from the drama.

Gradually, as these dramas became more complex, especially in terms of geographical and architectural requirements, a number of such mansion sets became necessary. These small scenic structures (*sedes, loci,* or *domi*) provided visual evidence regarding the scenic location and could also be used to store props or disguise mechanical equipment necessary for some rather spectacular stage effects. However, because of their necessarily reduced size they were usually too small to accommodate actors, and as a result they were surrounded by a generalized acting area usually referred to as the *platea*. For complex productions requiring changes in geographical location a number of these small mansions could be arranged about a large playing area, with the performers thus enabled to move easily from one set to the next. In the early Medieval church, before the Gothic period was well underway, this could easily be done as there was no separation between the choir and the nave. As a

The "Prologue" speaks in a fifteenth-century French mystery play. The lectern-style structure from which he is speaking indicates the beginning of multiple sets. (Manuscript 697, Bibliothèque Publique, Arras, France)

result of this availability of space, plus a continuing elaboration in the plays themselves, the mansions grew richer and more complex, often containing a curtained inner area that could be used for dramatic display. In many cases some spectacular properties were housed in the mansions and, especially for the Christmas plays, simple flying machinery was installed so that the star of Bethlehem could guide the three Kings to the manger.

Costumes during this period were, at first, little more than the traditional Church vestments. In the *Regularis Concordia* the monk playing the role of the Angel is to be dressed in an alb, and the monks playing the three Marys apparently wear their own robes, copes, and carry censers. However, as the plays became larger and more characters were added, certain symbolic items were added to the costumes, so that angels were equipped with wings of gauze and major historical figures were given equivalent identifying props to carry. For such nonclerical figures as the three Kings or Herod, rich-appearing nonclerical garments were developed.

Throughout the period that the liturgical drama remained within the church the actors were usually members of the clergy. However, as the plays expanded choirboys were drafted for acting duties, and there is evidence that late in the thirteenth century wandering theological scholars and even local schoolboys were included in the action.

THE PLAYS ARE SECULARIZED

By the beginning of the thirteenth century the liturgical plays had completed their evolution and were ready to leave the church. Some outdoor productions had probably taken place late in the twelfth century, but the first recorded instance of an outdoor production is in 1204. Because of the attitudes toward drama held by many of the higher clergy, the limited playing space within the church structure, the restrictions regarding who could perform, and especially the demands of an ever-growing audience, the liturgical drama reached a dead end. Artistic advancement required that the plays be taken out of the church and set in the marketplace. Thus, the years between 1204 and the early fourteenth century became a period of transition from a restricted liturgical drama to a complex, elaborate, and often very large outdoor drama based rather loosely on religious materials but including a heady mix of the profane with the sacred.

Because these were transition years, few records or plays have survived to indicate exactly how the transition occurred. No longer a part of the Church service, ecclesiastical records ignored the plays; not yet taken over by the cities or guilds, civic and business records paid the plays scant attention. And yet, changes were taking place. One major change that had to occur, now that the plays were being performed outdoors, especially in central and northern Europe, was a shift in their traditional playing times so that the plays could be produced during the warmer periods of the year. This shift to spring and summer production became standardized after 1264 when Pope Urban IV decreed the celebration of Corpus Christi Day on the Thursday following Trinity Sunday. This places it in time anyplace between May 23 and June 24, a period when outdoor productions could at least be viewed comfortably. The day was instituted to celebrate the doctine of transubstantiation—the decision that the bread and wine of communion actually becomes the body and blood of Christ. Because this was a late decision that related not to any particular feast but to the power of the Sacrament to redeem sinners, any and all of the plays could safely be produced without danger of conflict with existing religious ceremony.

However, this clustering of so many plays around a single day led to problems regarding not only the physical aspects of production but, even more importantly, in terms of the philosophical considerations, about the order in which the plays would be presented. A decision to produce the plays as nearly as possible in the traditional biblical order seems reasonable, and this decision almost certainly led to the development of cycles of plays which, as holes in the earlier informal structure were filled in, would demonstrate the whole of biblical history, from Creation to the Last Judgment.

Stage area for a play by Jacob Ruof, produced in Zurich in the early sixteenth century. (Max Herrmann, *Forschungen zur deutschen Theatergeschichte des Mittelalters und der Renaissance*, Berlin, 1914)

In addition to a common production date, by leaving the church confines the plays gained several advantages; they could grow larger, take longer in performance, use more actors, and become more meaningful to their audiences by speaking in the vernacular. However, the most important advantage gained by their leaving the church turned out to be their swift humanization into what was essentially a new dramatic form. The actors and authors of these expanded and sometimes new plays were now free to emphasize those dramatic elements that made for popular success. Especially enjoyed by the audience, for instance, was the comic motif that had largely been ignored while the plays remained within the church. Thus, the balkiness of Noah's wife about entering the ark became more and more farcical, emphasizing less and less the biblical materials and more and more the struggle for mastery between husband and wife that was so popular a theme in such nondramatic Medieval literature as Chaucer's "The Wife of Bath's Tale." Herod, a popular villain within the liturgical drama, extended those aspects of his character that so pleased audiences. Embarrassed by the escape of the Wise Men the secularized Herod played to his audience by roaring and ranting and tearing his beard.

In addition to the use of humor to please the audience, though usually adding greatly to the comic potential, was the inclusion in the plays of extra-religious material that had no generic relationship either to the theme or the subject of the original religious story. Thus, in *The Second Shepherd's Play* the farcical early section dealing with sheep stealing in England near "Horbury Shrogs" provides much laughter and also some gently ironic comment on the main subject of the play, which is the visit of the biblical shepherds to the manger in Bethlehem.

By the year 1350 most of these transitional developments had finally taken place and the cycle plays had displaced the liturgical drama. This allowed the Medieval drama to at last attain its ultimate development.

JEAN BODEL: Jean Bodel (c. 1165-1210) was born in Arras, capital of the northern province of Artois. Arras was a rich city, one of the many commercial and industrial centers that were beginning to spring up as Europe moved from feudal agrarianism to an urban industrial economy. Probably as a result of its growing leisure class, Arras became well known for its arts—for its crafted wares, its tapestries, its music, and its literary societies.

Not much is known regarding the details of Bodel's life. He was a writer and a member of the Confrérie de la Sainte Chandelle, the most significant literary club in Arras. This Confrérie was responsible for the care of a candle to which numerous miracles were attributed. The candle had appeared in miraculous visions to two rival minstrels early in the twelfth century, when Arras was being ravaged by sickness, and its drippings were reputed to have the power of curing the ill. Perhaps because the Confrérie had begun with the visions of two minstrels, it soon became a literary society as well as a semi-religious group and included in its membership both professional artists and rich citizens who enjoyed rubbing shoulders with the arts.

Like other, similar brotherhoods, the Confrérie de la Sainte Chandelle produced a number of artistic events, and among these were mystery and miracle plays. It also provided the occasion and the production organization to stage Bodel's *Jeu de Saint Nicholas* (*Play of Saint Nicholas*). In the year 1200 the candle was moved from its original home in the small chapel of the Saint Nicholas Hospital to a larger building in the city that could accommodate more members and more visitors. This occasion was probably celebrated by a number of artistic events strung out over the following year, one of which was almost certainly Bodel's play.

Before Bodel wrote his play there had been a number of Latin plays—five of which have survived—written on the subject of Saint Nicholas. However, Bodel's work is the earliest such play we have in the vernacular. It is also, quite clearly, the best of them all. It presents, in short space (approximately ten thousand words), a whole series of epic events based around the crusades. During Bodel's period, troops and funds were being raised for the Fourth Crusade, and even the debacles of the first three such ventures had not diminished the Christian fervor to march into the East.

The epic events in the play are the Christian invasion, the call to arms of the Saracens, the arrival of the Christian knights, and their resulting slaughter on the battlefield. All this material is "moved" so that at the end of these events a lone surviving "Good Christian" can be left standing, holding fast to his Saint Nicholas. Juxtaposed to these epic events is a group of thieves who come out of their tavern to carry on a mock epic battle, which provides a sardonic commentary on the more significant events. Saint Nicholas appears, a sophisticated *deus ex machina*, saves the Good Christian, converts the infidel king, and drives off the thieves. This not only unites the various actions of the play, providing a neat denouement, it also glorifies the saint whose hospital housed the sacred candle. As Oscar Mandel has so ably pointed out, Saint Nicholas may be considered merely legendary in our own day, but was believed to be a real historical, religious figure in Bodel's time.

Sometime around the turn of the century, perhaps right after the production of his *Saint Nicholas*, Bodel contracted leprosy. In 1202 he entered a lazar house, where he died, some say in the year 1210.

Bodel's genius was severalfold. He helped to popularized the vernacular for use in the religious drama. He had a sharp ear for realistic dialogue, which he managed to combine with a love for romantic fantasy. Had he lived and written more, French drama might not have had to wait for the seventeenth century to produce its most enduring masterpieces.

ADAM DE LA HALLE: Adam de la Halle (also called le Bossu d'Arras, c.1240-88), was, like his playwright predecessor Jean Bodel, born in Arras. Apparently young Adam showed an early academic promise and though his father, a minor civil servant, could not afford to educate him he was, with the monetary help of some well-to-do citizens, sent to a local Cistercian monastery to complete the first part of his studies. Returning to Arras he very likely joined the Confrérie de la Sainte Chandelle which, like the rest of Arras, had continued to prosper since Bodel's death. There is no record of how Adam earned his living during this period; probably he existed on the patronage of some of the richer members of Arras society.

Eventually, having fallen in love with and married a girl as poor as himself, Adam set out for Paris to begin his higher education at the Sorbonne. Before leaving Arras, however, he presented for the Confrérie a satiric play, *Le jeu de la feuillée* (*The Play of the Canopy*). This work seems less a play than a vaudeville-style revue, with a series of sketches that poke occasionally bitter fun at himself, his father, his wife, and ultimately the whole citizenry of Arras.

The studies in Paris did not last long and there is no indication that they benefited Adam by securing for him one of the traditional government sinecures often provided to educated young artists. Indeed, returning to Arras he took up a life apparently similar in every respect to the one he had led before his departure. At this point in time the wealthy citizens of the town, who had in the past supported Adam, were engaged in a protest over a special tax levied by Louis IX to support yet another crusade. By this time three more crusades had been undertaken since the one that had inspired the citizens of Arras during Bodel's time, and the Christian fervor for such endeavors had obviously fallen away. The citizenry eventually carried their resistance to the point where they were exiled from Arras to the town of Douai. Adam, who had apparently been one of their pamphleteers, went into exile with them.

In 1271, following the death of Louis IX, the Eighth Crusade came to an end and Philip III was crowned. Philip visited Arras to restore relations between the crown and the city, the exile was lifted, and Adam and his fellow protesters returned to their homes. In the following year, perhaps at the urging of his influential friends, Adam was taken into the household of the Count of Artois, who was the nephew of Louis IX the redoubtable crusader. Adam had never been a poor, wandering poet. From his youth onward he had received the patronage of the wealthiest families in Arras. However, his new position in the household of an outstanding nobleman gave him, for the first time, a fixed income, official standing, and great prestige.

In 1282 the famous Vespers Massacre occurred when the Sicilians rose up to throw off the French yoke. The King of Naples and Sicily, Charles of Anjou, was also an uncle of Adam's patron, and so the Count of Artois took his entire household—guards, retainers, *and minstrels*—off to Naples to aid his uncle. It was a futile gesture, for Sicily was already lost. However, at some time during his stay in Naples, perhaps provoked by his absence from France, Adam composed his idyllic *pastourelle, Robin and Marion*. There is no record of its production in Naples, but it probably was staged, for Charles' French court would have loved in a nostalgic sense the scenes of a distant France that never really existed except in romantic fantasy.

The tale of Robin and Marion was hardly a new one, even in Adam's time. In English-speaking countries it is likely to be confused with tales of Robin Hood and Maid Marion, a *slightly* related legend but with far different roots. In Adam's play Robin and Marion are the traditional young lovers (shepherd and shepherdess) of the *pastourelle*. They are separated when Marion is captured by a knight who is overcome with her beauty. However, Marion remains true to Robin, the knight with reasonably good grace withdraws his attentions, and the peasants celebrate the happy ending of the episode with song and dance.

Robin and Marion was Adam's last major work, and in approximately 1288 he died. His major contribution to the developing drama was his artistic use of the *pastourelle* form, which in its earlier manifestations tended toward the rustic and coarse. To this revised form he grafted a new and delicate music to replace the traditional folk melodies. As a result of these revisions, his work stands delightfully between the traditional *pastourelle* and the pseudo-classicism of such later writers as Tasso and Guarini.

MYSTERIES, MIRACLES, AND MORALITIES

The breakdown of the Medieval dramas into such subdivisions as mystery, miracle, and morality plays has often been called into question, but because the terminology is not only traditional but pervasive it is necessary to at least define the terms as they are regularly used. A mystery play is one that presents an event or series of events from the Bible; a miracle play presents an event or legend from the religious extrabiblical literature, such as the life of a saint or martyr; a morality play is an allegory designed to inculcate a useful religious or moral lesson (and later used to inculcate equivalent lessons in law, education, and science). The term *mystery play* did not originate in England, and many of the English cycle plays only fit the definition in a very loose manner. However, the cycle plays and the mystery plays are usually treated as being synonymous, with the noncycle plays including both the miracle and morality plays.

At the peak of popularity for the cycle play, most of the substantial towns in Europe produced their own cycles. There is evidence of cycles belonging to London, Worcester, Beverley, Lancaster, Leicester, and Canterbury in England, and to Rouen, Padua, Friuli, Ravenna, and many other major towns on the continent. However, in England only a few such cycles have survived: the York cycle, which contains forty-eight plays; the Chester cycle, containing twenty-five plays; the Wakefield cycle (sometimes called the Towneley cycle after the family that owned the manuscript), made up of thirty-two plays; and the Coventry cycle, of forty-two plays (usually called *Ludus Coventriae* or N——— Town Plays and recently assigned by some scholars to the City of Lincoln). A number of single plays have survived which were probably once part of cycles. The Brome *Abraham and Isaac*, for example, is thought by many to be a remnant of the London cycle.

These cycles maintained their great popularity from the last half of the thirteenth century through the fourteenth century, and though their popularity then declined a bit they lasted through the fifteenth century as major attractions and well into the sixteenth, though now more of antiquarian than public interest. New cycles were being produced throughout most of this period and new plays were replacing old or less popular ones in the already existing cycles. Some of the best known of these are the *Mysteries and Moralities*, adapted for production by the Sisters of Ste. Michel at Huy, Arnoul Greban's *Mystery of the Passion*, which according to tradition took a full forty days to perform, and the five plays in the Wakefield cycle that are generally attributed to an unknown author called the Wakefield Master.

A much larger number of cycles survived in France than in England. These vary from short works that can be produced in one day to massive plays taking twenty-five or more days to perform. Unlike the English cycles, which covered the major events throughout the whole of the Bible, the French cycles tended to be narrower in time and space, treating a single subject in depth. The most popular subject for the French plays was the central event of Christianity—the death and resurrection of Christ.

By the middle of the sixteenth century the English (and French) cycle plays had reached their end and were no longer regularly produced. The last production of the Coventry cycle was in 1591, and a revival of the Chester cycle only sixteen years later was regarded by most as being no more than a historical curiosity. The traditional reason advanced for this seemingly untimely ending of the cycle and miracle plays is that the public had become indifferent to them, switching allegiance to the secular drama that had already become a major artistic force—and there is much to say for such an opinion. By 1591, for example, traveling troupes were regularly performing plays—great plays—in most major population centers and these professional productions were undoubtedly more interesting than the largely amateur productions of the miracle

An etching of the Coventry Miracle Play, with Jesus standing before Pilate. (Thomas Sharp's *Dissertation on the Pageants or Dramatic Mysteries Anciently Performed at Coventry*, Coventry, England, 1825)

and mystery plays. Recent scholars have, however, pointed out that the religious drama had been burdened with so many repressive measures, both religious and civil, that their disappearance was more likely due to enforced cancellation than to loss of public favor.

Just as the cycle plays (mysteries) developed from the liturgical drama, so late in the twelfth century the noncycle plays (miracles) grew out of the cycle plays. These plays also depended on religious material for their sources, but they used primarily that religious material that stood outside the Bible. Thus, the lives of saints and such popular legendry as miracles performed by the saints and, especially, by the Virgin Mary, were the primary sources for such works. The most popular dramatic figure in these plays, at least in France, was the Virgin Mary, whose cult became widespread throughout the Medieval period. The *Quarante miracles de Notre-Dame* (*Forty Miracles of Our Lady*), some forty miracle plays dating from the latter part of the fourteenth century, are preserved in two manuscripts at the Bibliothèque Nationale. In these plays the Virgin becomes a *deus ex machina*, stepping in to bring about the denouement. The most common theme of these plays is the wife slandered by the vengeful lover. After the Virgin Mary, in terms of popularity, comes St. Nicholas. The Fleury Play-Book contains four St. Nicholas plays, and several more are known, including one by the playwright Hilarius. All the major saints were eventually honored by one or more plays based on their lives, as were patron saints of towns and villages.

A third type of Medieval drama, the morality play, began to develop around the middle of the fourteenth century, and perhaps because it began so late it was able to maintain its popularity well into the sixteenth century. As a dramatic form the morality play owes little to the other drama of its time. Instead, it grew out of the Medieval fondness for homilies, for cautionary tales, and especially for allegory. Many of the greatest, most influential literary works of the Medieval period, such as the French *Roman de la rose* and Dante's

The design of the playing area for *The Castle of Perseverance*, 1425. (From the Macro Morals manuscript)

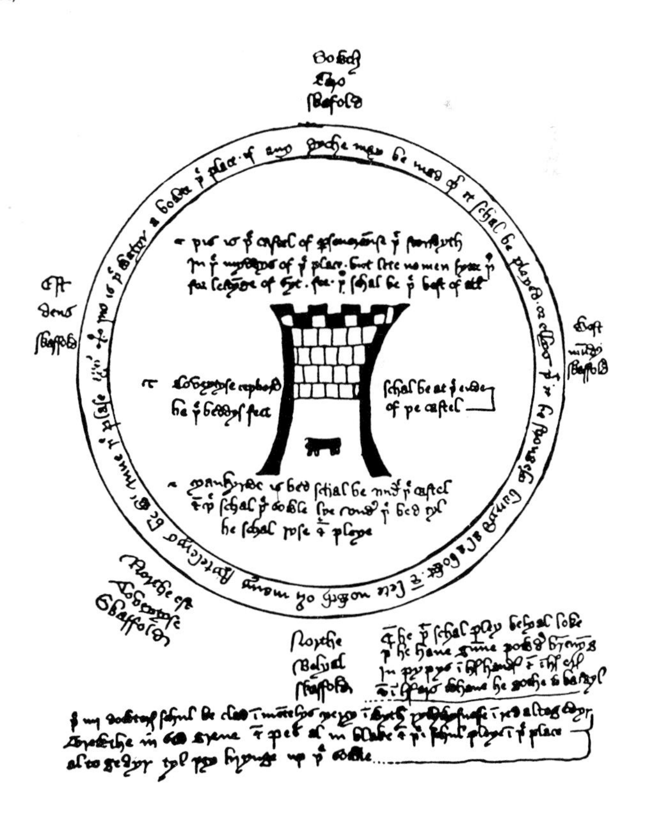

Divine Comedy, were allegories, and it was to be expected that the form would be adapted to drama. The morality play was known all over Europe, but it was especially popular in England, where it played an important role in the transition that took place from Medieval to Tudor to Elizabethan drama.

The most common explanation of the development of the morality is that, like the liturgical drama, it began in the church with presentations by the clergy, but that it achieved its ultimate development only when it left the church and was taken over by the community. The immediate ancestor was the Lord's Prayer, which the ecclesiastics had divided into seven parts, each part dedicated to combating one of the seven deadly sins. This made of the prayer a type of dramatic event called *Paternoster*, which had a protagonist (Man), an antagonist (the Seven Deadly Sins), and to aid Man in combating the Sins, the Seven Moral Virtues.

The popularity of the morality play was clearly great, but only a few of the early texts have survived. The earliest play that we have received in its entirety is *The Castle of Perseverance*, which runs to 3,600 lines and which was first produced sometime around 1425. In this play can be seen the three parts, each with its own theme, that characterized morality play structure. Part 1 displays a conflict of the sins and virtues for Man's soul; a *psychomachia* while Man is still alive. Part 2 covers the arrival of Death and the summoning of Man to judgment. Part 3 then becomes a type of courtroom scene featuring a debate, with Mercy and Peace ranged against Truth and Justice, for the soul of Man.

The greatest of these plays has come down to us only as a fragment. *Everyman*, written sometime during the late fifteenth century, is in itself a complete play, but in fact it is only the second part of an original three-part play and thus should probably be titled *The Summoning of Everyman*. A number of sources have been identified for the play. It may be a translation of a Dutch play titled *Elckerlijk*, or it may be based on the *Barlaam and Josaphat* of the eighth century writer St. John Damascene, which in turn may be based on one of the parables of Buddha.

The basic plot of *Everyman* is rather simple, designed to demonstrate those qualities necessary to cultivate in earthly life in order to achieve salvation after death. God calls upon Death and orders him to go and take Everyman. Everyman is not ready to go when Death comes and begins seeking someone to accompany him on the dread journey. He turns to Fellowship, Kindred, Cousin, and Goods, but is rejected by each. He then calls upon Knowledge, Confession, Discretion, Strength, Beauty, and Five-wits, who agree to accompany him along the pathway. However, eventually they too desert him, and only Good Deeds is prepared to enter the grave with Everyman. The moral of all this is then explained to the spectators by a doctor.

The contributions of the morality play to the history of English drama are several. It took the grotesque devil characters of the folk drama and transformed them into the character of the "Vice," a popular, mischievous imp whose history on the English stage, in later periods under the guise of Elizabethan clowns and pranksters, is quite distinguished. It created exciting, spectacular scenes, such as the parade of the Seven Deadly Sins, which entranced the Medieval audience and remained so popular for so long that Marlowe included it in his *Doctor Faustus*. Finally, it provided an exciting format

Title page from the c. 1520 John Skot edition of *Everyman.*

for what is essentially didactic drama. This format was used, eventually, to instruct on a number of subjects, by way of such plays as John Rastell's *The Nature of the Four Elements*, which urges the study of nature, and *Lusti juventus*, which propagandizes in favor of Protestantism.

Farce, and several less well-known types of Medieval comic drama, had no real place in the liturgical drama, and for this reason it is particularly difficult to trace in terms of origins. Scholars have searched for and found comic dramatic elements in such diverse sources as folk drama, the vaunting of Herod in the late liturgical drama, and the dramatic aspects and activities of the Feast of Fools, when comic presentations were acted out to mock the established order and rituals of the Church. As a dramatic activity, farce existed all over Europe and England during the Medieval period, but it reached its peak of development in France.

In 1262, when Adam de la Halle wrote his *Jeu de la feuillée*, the basic outlines of the comic drama were still a bit blurred. He perhaps composed his *Jeu* for the townspeople of Arras, his hometown, but such a conclusion is tentative at best. In any case the play is a savage satire on his own family and friends, and includes scathing comment on old men (his father), on women (his wife), and also on the priesthood and many of the intimates of the court of Bethune.

In the fourteenth century, with its emphasis on allegory and philosophical writings, the comic drama declined, only to be revived in the fifteenth century by the rise of the *confréries* or *sociétés joyeuses*. Similar in formation to the groups organized to produce religious drama, these "comic" brotherhoods were formed by students and townspeople to produce comedies primarily for their own amusement. Of these groups the most famous was the Enfants sans Souci or Sots, who apparently were aligned with the Basochiens, the corporation of clerks to the *procureurs* of the Parlement of Paris.

The plays produced by such groups fall into four basic categories: the *sermon joyeux*, which was a parody of the Sunday sermon; the *moralité*, in France as in England a usually allegorical work designed primarily for teach-

Woodcut illustration from a 1490 edition of *The Farce of Master Pierre Pathelin.*

ing; the *sottie*, a sharp satire, often taking an aspect of politics as its target; and the farce and farce-monologue of which some one hundred fifty are extant and which usually dealt with everyday people in everyday situations in a way intended merely to provoke laughter. However, as can be seen in one of the great plays of Medieval French drama, *The Farce of Master Pierre Pathelin*, the farce could and often did have sharp satirical overtones.

Pathelin has been called the "epic of an age of rogues," and that is certainly a fair characterization of the play. Roguery is indeed the play's catalyst, with the rogue of a cloth merchant cozzened by a crafty lawyer who is in turn cheated by a wily shepherd. Thus, we have a piling on of the theme of the trickster tricked, and all done with marvelous characterization, detail, and economy. Unlike most other farces, *Pathelin* is more than a play merely intended to raise laughter. It is, in fact, a witty attack on the law, with the lawyer playing shyster to the judge's fool; and both tricked by a not so simple shepherd. For these reasons it might be said that *Pathelin*, perhaps more than any other play no matter of what type, deserves the title of "masterpiece of Medieval French drama."

The best known of the farce-monologues is probably *Le franc-archer de Bagnolet*. The Franc-archer begins his monologue in a manner that reminds one of the folk drama—with the vaunt. He brags of his courage and prudence, but when he notices a scarecrow standing by the road he becomes terrified and begs for mercy. Then the wind blows down the scarecrow and, reassured, the Franc-archer recommences his vaunting. Again, there seems to be no real attempt to make the play a vehicle for social or philosophical comment, beyond that inherent in the situation; however, one is reminded of Miles Gloriosus and his many descendants.

THE WAKEFIELD MASTER: The body of the Wakefield cycle is found in the Towneley Manuscript, which was written sometime between 1440 and 1485. Once known as the "Towneley cycle" because the manuscript was in the possession of the Towneley family of Lancashire for nearly two hundred years, the cycle is now usually identified in terms of its geographical association with Wakefield. Exactly how and when the document came into the Towneley family's ownership is not known; however, it was in the family during the life of Christopher Towneley (1604-74), an antiquarian who possibly acquired it. The manuscript contains all or part of thirty-two plays. There is an indication that marginal notes once existed to show which guild was responsible for each play, but these notes were lost when, at some unknown time, the leaves were trimmed for binding. The manuscript has been edited at least once; a new play has been added; and one play was "corectyd" in red ink to meet Reformation standards.

This manuscript is apparently a "register"; that is, a master book into which each individual play was copied. From this register plans for production could be made and the correctness of performances could be monitored by the town corporation which oversaw the productions.

Of these thirty-two plays, five are quite distinctive, showing the consistent hand of a single author, a sophisticated dramatist possessing his own style and a unique sense of humor. A sixth play shows signs of having been heavily doctored by this hand. This writer is known as the "Wakefield Master." Only one historical figure has been strongly presented as the probable author of these five plays—Gilbert Pilkington, author of the *Turnament of Totenham*, but there is little substantiating evidence for this claim.

Scene from a Medieval-style farce produced during carnival season in Paris during the mid-sixteenth century. (From the Bibliothèque de l'Arsenal, Paris)

It can be assumed that the playwright was connected in some way with the Church, since he knew Latin and the Church liturgy and was highly literate. Internal evidence in the plays seems to indicate that he wrote between 1400 and 1450, but there is no indication that he is the scribe who set down the manuscript copy. What seems most likely is that he was commissioned by several individual guilds to write their plays, and that his originals were among those scripts copied when the register was compiled. The plays apparently predate (slightly) the register and are thus part of the cycle as it was performed at the time the register was made.

The plays usually attributed to the Wakefield Master and their place in the register are *Processus noe cum filiis* Wakefield (III—*Noah*), *Prima pastorum* (XII—*The First Shepherd's Play*), *Secunda pastorum* (XIII—*The Second Shepherd's Play*), *Magnus Herodes* (XVI—*Herod the Great*), and *Coliphizacio* (XXI—*The Buffeting*). The sixth partial (or questionable) play is *Mactacio Able* (II—*The Killing of Abel*).

The Wakefield Master used a distinctive stanza, a good many proverbs, allusions whose origins are buried deep in English folk history, and a very earthy wit. His best play and one of the best of all Medieval plays is the *Second Shepherd's Play*, so called because it is the second of two shepherd's plays (*pastorum*) in the cycle. The play is in two parts: the first is based on an ancient folk tale dealing with a sheep-thief; the second represents the shepherds visiting the Christ Child in Bethlehem. The first part is a farcical tale about Mak, a thief, who uses magic to keep three shepherds asleep while he steals a lamb. He then takes the lamb to his wife, Gill, and when the shepherds come looking for their lamb, he has her pretend that it is a newborn son. The shepherds at first fall for the ruse and accept the lamb as an ugly, foul-smelling child. However, when they return to bring birth gifts to the baby their goodness is rewarded and Mak is discovered and punished. Suddenly we find the shepherds back in the fields, which were Horbury Shrogs (outside of Wakefield) but which have now become the fields outside of Bethlehem, where the scene just parodied is reverently reenacted as the shepherds bring their simple gifts of cherries, a bird, and a ball to the Christ Child.

The remaining plays of the Wakefield Master seem more on a level with the plays being done in other areas. His *Noah* for example is little different than the *Noah* done at Chester, and the Chester play, in fact, has a much more humorous exchange between Noah and his wife. *The First Shepherd's Play* is very tightly written but is not nearly as original or as humorous as is *The Second Shepherd's Play*. Where the author is most consistent is not in his artistic use of the materials, but in his careful metrical construction and use of rhyme. The Wakefield stanza is the author's undisputed signature, a poetic form he created himself, used brilliantly, and which is found nowhere else, not even in other plays which seem to be related somehow to the Wakefield cycle. A similar nine-line stanza is found in some nonrelated poems written in the same geographical area, but the rhyme scheme and alliteration patterns are not the same as those used by this singular author.

The artistic use of dialect, Latin and proverbs are trademarks of this remarkable writer. In *The Second Shepherd's Play* he gives Mak a southern dialect for comic effect, and has the shepherds, on awakening, curse in Latin their exhausted, resisting limbs. In *Abel* he used slang terms for steal and armor (combined: robber or armed robber) to create a name (Pickharnes) for the unruly son of Cain. He also used Latin, slang, and dialect to improve his rhyme. Thus, Mak's southern dialect moves casually from one geographic dialectical area to another as the rhyme scheme requires, and bits of Latin are used to fill in those lines where the dialects fail to count properly.

An attempt was apparently made to "correct" at least one of the Wakefield plays, but the full annotation reads "corectyd & not playd." The register eventually found its way to the Towneley library, the guild copies vanished, and the works of the Wakefield Master became the property of a privileged few until a little over a hundred years ago. Today, *The Second Shepherd's Play* is enjoyed with some regularity and the man who was England's first great playwright, though unknown by name, still brings laughter and warmth to audiences of another age.

PLAY PRODUCTION

The process of secularization was almost completed by the last quarter of the fourteenth century, and the plays were out-of-doors and steadily growing in both size and scope. This meant that the Church gave up direct responsibility for producing the plays—though a number of individual churchmen remained personally involved with the plays for many years—and someone or something was necessary to fill the production gap. Thus, a variety of production arrangements developed.

On the continent, where a single staging area set with mansions became the primary method of production, and where the productions sometimes became monstrous in size, often taking several days and hundreds of actors to perform, the religious guilds or confraternities took over the largest part of the production responsibilities. These guilds had begun to appear at the beginning of the fourteenth century and fulfilled two distinct though related functions. They provided the opportunity for specialized religious observance, and they also provided a type of social club that could include a broad spectrum of the local populace in its membership because they were not restricted by the narrow economic considerations that existed for the trade guilds. In most cases these confraternities, each of which was devoted to a specific saint, did plays about or in honor of their own particular saint. In those cases where they did plays that did not touch on their own saint, the play was still done as a devotional exercise.

In England some equivalent fraternities, such as the Guild of St. George (founded in Norwich in 1385), also took on the production of plays. The Guild of St. George, for example, put on entertainments featuring its own patron saint. However, in most cases the city took on the responsibility of being primary producer, farming out the individual plays to appropriate trade or craft guilds. These guilds, like the confraternities, had specific religious affiliations, with each guild devoted to an appropriate saint. Thus, their production of a play was, in a sense, a religious observance. In addition to the religious significance it also provided a chance to promote their guild, an opportunity to become in-

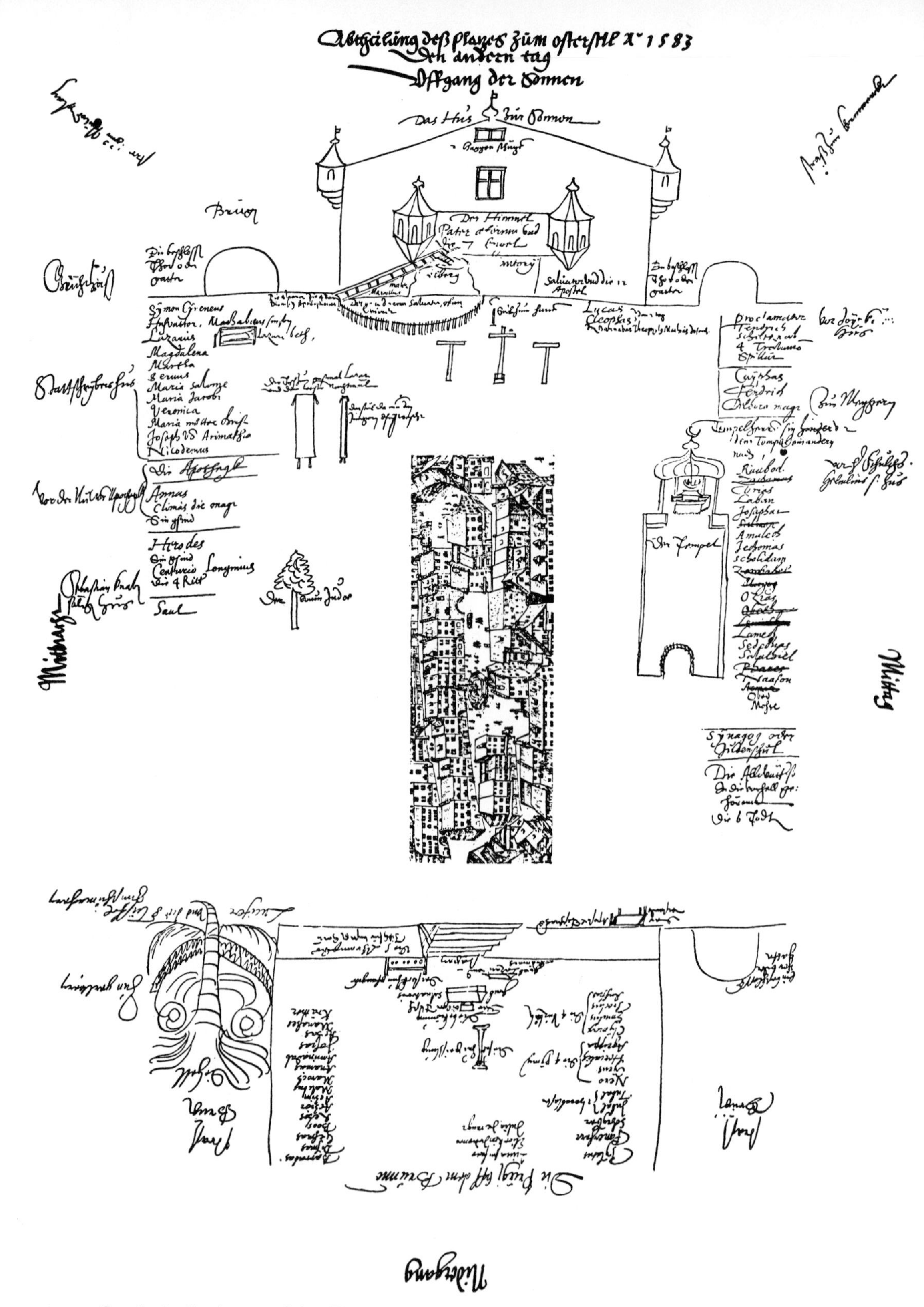

Cysat's plan for the second day. The rectangular woodcut at the center of the plan is of the same market place, published fifteen years later.

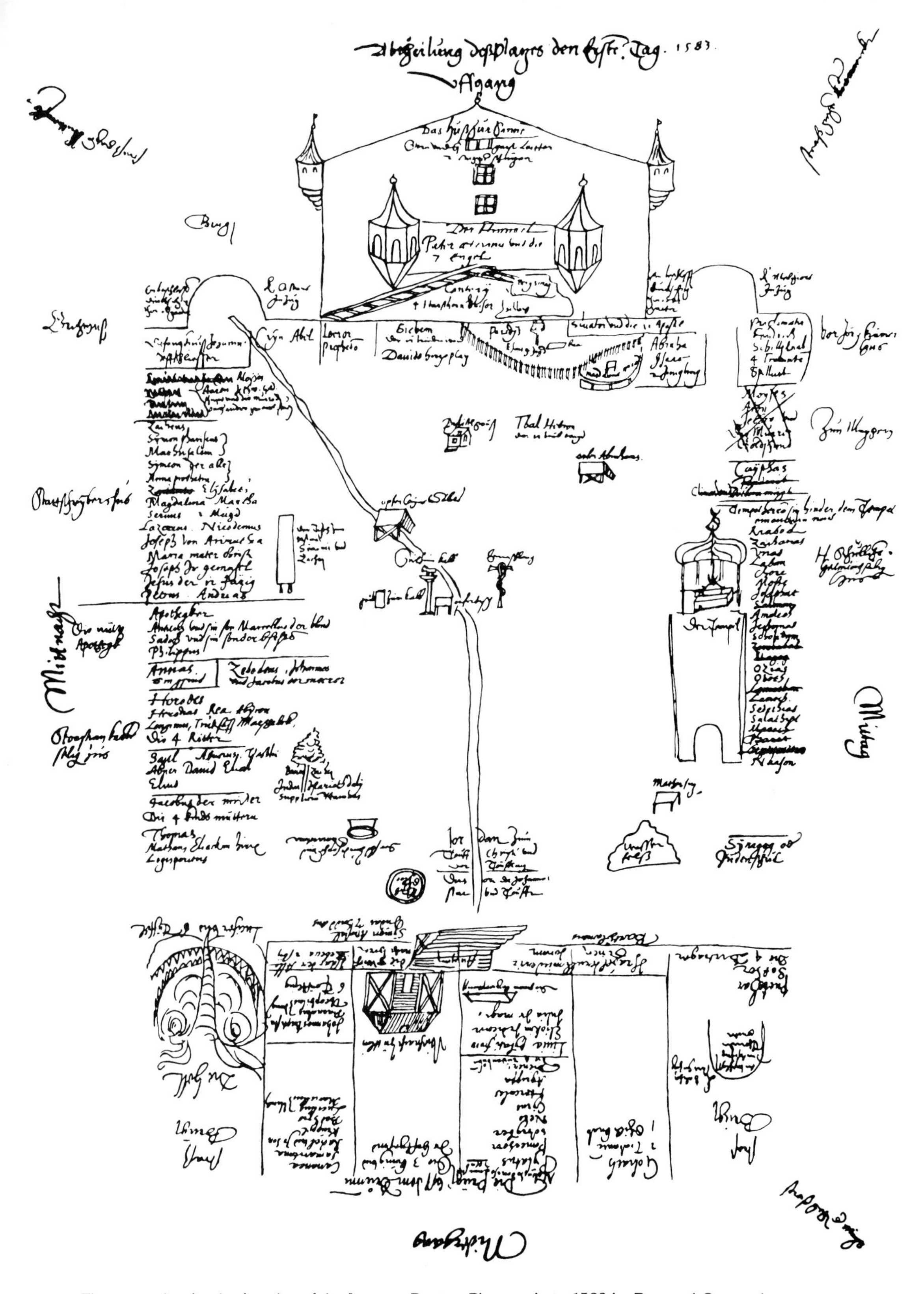

The stage plan for the first day of the Lucerne Passion Play, made in 1583 by Renward Cysat, who was twice the director of the play. The entire market place was used as a stage.

volved in the artistic excitement of play performance, and offered many possibilities for geniality and good fellowship.

The guilds were, when possible, assigned their plays on the basis of some basic relationship between the craft and the subject of the play. Thus, the shipwrights would do the material about Noah and the ark, the bakers guild would do the material relating to the fishes and loaves, and the carpenters or plasterers guild might do God creating the world. Once the plays were assigned, each guild became responsible for providing their own pageant wagon, scenery, props, costumes, actors, and anything else necessary for putting on the play. Because the plays were self-contained units done in sequence at various points along a production route, the order of production and the general supervision of the total effect was the responsibility of the city.

STAGES AND SCENERY

It was not until the drama moved outside the church grounds that significant staging practices got underway. On the continent the mansion-style staging that began in the church remained the production standard even after the plays deserted the church for the marketplace. As discussed earlier, the mansions began in the church as small structures representing such special areas as heaven and hell and some earthly spots in between. These mansions were certainly not large—they could not have been given the restricted space in which they had to be set up—and no production could have used many of them without more open space than most churches could provide. In fact, to enhance visibility the mansions were often set on platforms in the nave. However, the plays kept on growing, often spreading into the choir and sanctuary. Therefore, removal of the plays from the church and the development of a vernacular drama were necessary to major staging efforts.

The mansions were, in fact, small wood and fabric constructions somewhat like booths at a fair. Generally speaking, they were not large even after they left the church, though they were usually colorful and often highly complex. The actors, as a result of the limited space inside the mansions, performed primarily on the *platea*, the area in front of and (in a limited sense) on either side of the mansions. The practice begun in the church of putting the mansions on platforms was generally continued, but now there was enough space available to provide a variety of spatial arrangements. In some cases the mansions were mounted in a line, against an exterior church wall or down one side of a market square or even on the stage of the Hôpital de la Trinité in Paris, where the Medieval religious drama was played for more than one hundred years.

Heaven and hell, the two most common mansions and in most cases the two with the most audience appeal, were given the two end positions when the mansions were set up in a row, with heaven at stage right and hell at stage left. In some cases, in an attempt to capture the concept of "up and down" that has been attached to heaven and hell, heaven was elevated several feet above the rest of the mansions and hell lowered several feet. In addition to setting the mansions up in a row, as on a stage or platform, they were in many cases set up

The passion play of Valenciennes (1547) provides a beautiful illustration of Medieval mansion staging. The mansion at stage right is Paradise, featuring God surrounded by angels and saints. At stage left is Hellmouth, with Satan, his devils, and damned souls. In between are mansions necessary for telling the story of Christ, even including a lake for Peter the Fisherman. (Gustave Cohen, *Le Théâtre en France au moyen âge,* Paris, 1928-31)

around the perimeter of an essentially closed area, such as an inn-yard or town square. In such cases the audience was grouped in the center space and followed the action as it moved from mansion to mansion.

The mansions were colorful, highly decorated, and mechanically quite complex. The "masters of machine," mechanics responsible for developing the technical effects that were often part of the mansions, were highly skilled craftsmen who achieved results that are impressive even by today's standards. Concealed torches provided imaginative lighting effects, angels "flew" between heaven and earth, and the star of Bethlehem, sparkling and shiny, passed over the audience to hang suspended above the manger. Some mansions had interiors covered by curtains which could be drawn to reveal dramatic effects, and many were furnished with tables, chairs, benches, altars, and even lavish thrones. The richness of these mansions can best be seen by looking at heaven and hell. Heaven seems always to have impressed audiences with its magnificence. In part this magnificence may have been a result of its size in comparison with the other mansions. Because it had often to hold fairly large numbers of persons (in some cases up to at least fifteen) and some rather complex machinery, it tended to be rather large. Also, it was gilded and brightly lighted to give the effect of heavenly radiance. Hell, on the other hand, was not designed to impress the audience with its magnificence. It was as terrifying as the Medieval genius could make it. In most cases it was represented by "hellmouth"—the head of a monster with gaping jaws, out of which issued smoke and flame and devils who captured sinners and dragged them kicking and screaming back through the jaws to eternal damnation.

Along with the mansion stages, the Medieval period also saw the development of the wagon stages, especially in England and, to some degree, in Holland and Spain. Unfortunately, no definitive description of the English wagon stages—pageant wagons—has survived. Some of the most persuasive reconstructions argue that the standard pageant wagon was probably a one-story structure with a small loft. In such cases the wagon served primarily as a background, with the largest part of the action taking place on the ground in front of the wagon or on the flat bed of a second wagon, several of which were permanently drawn up at specific spots along the route of the procession. Other conjectures, such as two-story wagons with acting areas on both the upper and lower levels, have received some support. While all these theories have their proponents, it is almost certain that the wagons varied widely in their basic structure, each designed to the requirements of its own special play and then modified over the succeeding years.

While the basic structure and appearance of the wagons may be unknown and perhaps unknowable, to achieve the technical effects dictated by most of the scripts they all must have had certain types of equipment in common. For instance, most wagons probably had a machine loft with some kind of "flying" equipment, and certainly a trap or traps in the floor to allow trees to sprout up, fountains to gush, and actors to appear and disappear. In addition, some of the wagons must have had a flat, reinforced playing area on the roof to allow God to appear and speak from on high.

The variety of Medieval stages and stage arrangements was great indeed, but in nearly all cases there is an interesting similarity. The audience and actor relationship is always the same, whether a pageant wagon drawn up behind an open flat-bed wagon acting as a forestage; or a single wagon drawn up by itself and the players acting not only on the wagon but also on the ground before it; or a mansion that allowed an acting area within itself and on the ground or platform directly before it. In each case the audience is grouped

Drawing of a probable arrangement of Medieval English pageant wagon and acting area. (Based on material in Wickham's *Early English Stages*, Columbia University Press)

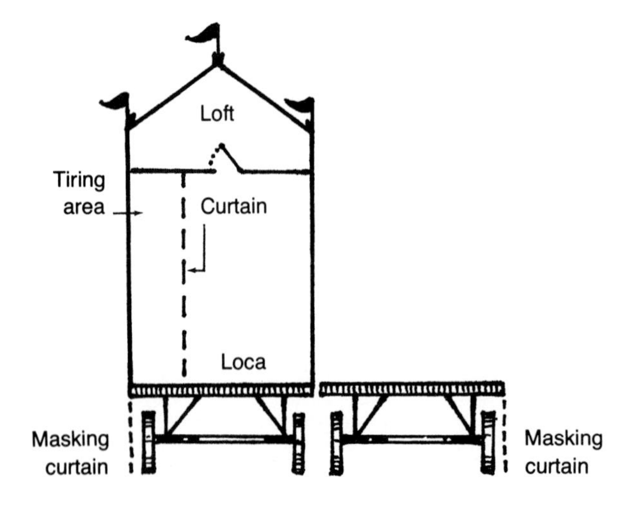

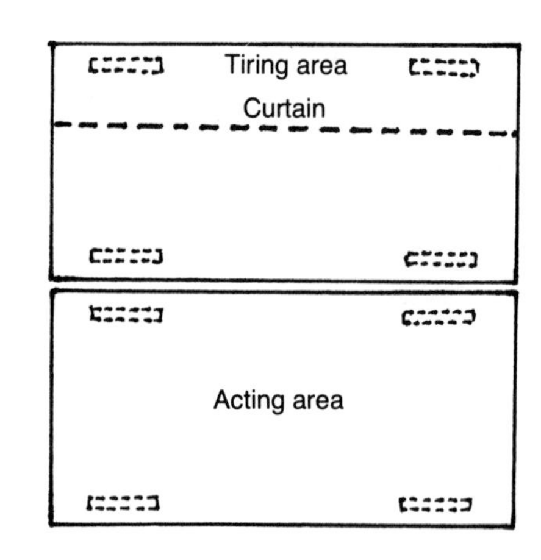

along three sides of a playing area, much like a miniature version of the audience/acting area relationship of the Classical Greek theatre.

SPECTACLE

The Medieval love of lavishly produced spectacles can be seen in the grandeur of the chivalric tournament, the pomp and circumstance of the royal processions and pageants, and the mechanical marvels of the dramatic productions. This last was particularly evident during the fifteenth and sixteenth centuries, when the developing skill of the masters of machine reached such a level that special scenes were often included in plays just to provide an opportunity for some spectacular effect.

The English drama, while it produced some spectacular effects, was limited in this area by the fact that the plays were produced on pageant wagons which were unable to carry the complex machinery necessary for producing lavish and sustained spectacles. However, in France with its stationary, simultaneous settings, the effects were lavish indeed. In Italy, during the same period that the Medieval drama was winding down in France and England, the Renaissance was already underway, and so the highly spectacular effects achieved by the Italians, with designs by such famous architects and artists as Brunelleschi, are not really Medieval at all. However, the fact that they existed and were certainly viewed by many of the producers in the Medieval north may explain in part why the Medieval religious drama in France became so technically, spectacularly elaborate.

Flying effects were especially popular, if the number of such effects can be taken as an indication. Angels flew between heaven and earth; the star of Bethlehem flew over the audience to guide the Wise Men; devils flew about the stage area; and in at least one case Lucifer flew with Christ to the top of the temple. Heavy rainfall, suddenly gushing wells of water, wine, and even blood, and lakes designed to permit Christ to walk on water or Peter to cast his nets, were just a few of the water effects.

The playbook for the 1501 performance at Mons specifies some very complicated technical effects and even indicates how these effects can be achieved. As God creates the earth, trees and flowers spring forth; Noah's vines bear grapes as soon as they are planted; the deluge falls realistically from pipes run over the nearby rooftops; hellmouth is alive with flames and thunderous sounds; Christ's crucifixion is supposed to be realistically done; and when Christ is resurrected a cloud descends to bear him off to Paradise. Productions in Vienna in 1510 and at Valenciennes in 1547 speak of similar and in some cases even greater wonders.

ACTING

While there were professional actors practicing their art during the Middle Ages, it was still, by and large, a period of primarily amateur production. In part this was because play production was not a matter of year-round operation but of occasional theatre—that is, essentially festival pro-

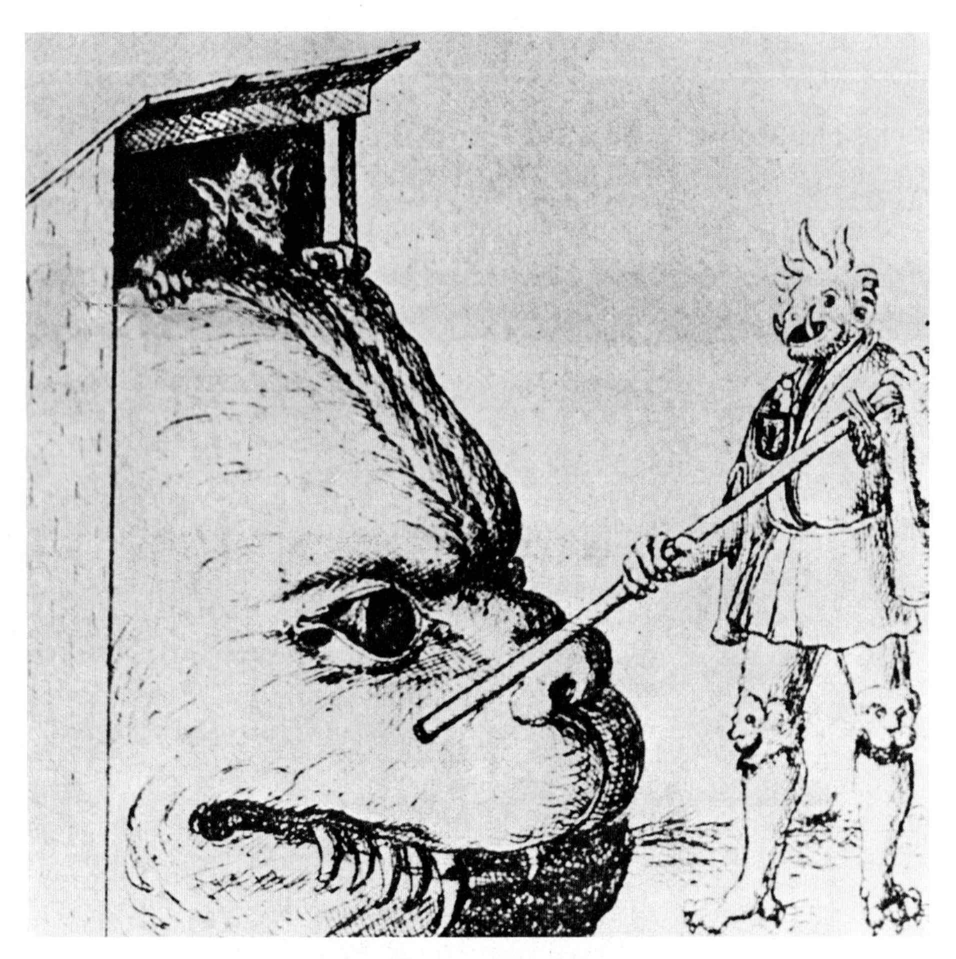

Hellmouth, with a messenger (or imp) in front and, apparently, Satan at the top. From the set for *The Vineyard of the Lord* by Jacob Ruof, staged in the Cathedral Square, Zurich, 1539. (Max Herrmann, *Forschungen zur deutschen Theatergeschichte des Mittelalters und der Renaissance*, Berlin, 1914)

ductions marking a special day or time of year—and such occasional drama could hardly support a corps of professional players. Also, especially early in the period after the plays were secularized, the casts tended to be small ones which could easily be handled by talented amateurs. Finally, as the cast sizes grew much larger (as many as 494 in a 1536 production of *The Acts of the Apostles* at Bourges) it became economically impossible to assemble a cast of professionals, even had so many been available and had the producer wished to cast them.

There were, however, some professionals working at acting during this time. That they were full-time actors is unlikely, for the reasons noted above. In most cases they were probably the wandering minstrels (or gleemen or scops) who played roles during the play-producing seasons. It is probable that they were particularly valued for such roles as God, where a trained, resonant voice would be highly desirable. In the accounts of the guilds and towns there are many references to the costs of producing the plays, and fees for professional actors are often listed among production costs. For their 1490 production of the *Trial, Condemnation, and Passion of Christ*, the Smiths of Coventry show the following item in their accounts: "Md payd to the players for corpus xisti daye." There follows a list of money payed to God, Cayphas, Heroude, Pilatt, Bedull, one of the knights, the "Devyll," Judas, and Anna.

The largest number of the actors were probably chosen from the merchant or craft groups, if only because they would better be able to afford the time necessary for production than the peasant class. In addition, some members of the clergy continued to take part in the productions, and there is evidence that a few members of the nobility were also overcome with the urge to act or produce. Most of the performers were men or boys, especially in England, but in France women are known to have occasionally taken roles on stage.

Rehearsals varied greatly according to the material. For the short English cycle plays four or five days was usually sufficient. In part this is because roles tended to be performed by the same actor, year after year, even though open tryouts were held. For some of the larger plays, especially in France, longer rehearsals were in order, and in some cases the players were

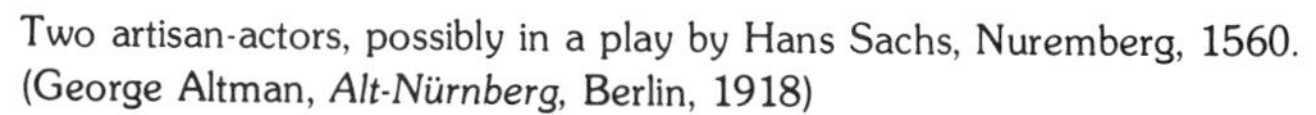

Two artisan-actors, possibly in a play by Hans Sachs, Nuremberg, 1560. (George Altman, *Alt-Nürnberg*, Berlin, 1918)

told to arrange for extra time in which they could work together outside the formal rehearsals. Because these amateur casts were apparently not quite trustworthy, attendance at rehearsals and, even more important, at productions was assured by legal means, with the entire cast required to sign notarized agreements that they would attend as required. Those that did attend, while not paid formally, were treated to an astonishing array of rewards. The accounts of the Smiths of Coventry, for example, shows expenses "for the furste reherse of our players in Ester weke" that include wine, ale, ribs of beef, dinner, supper, soup, roast goose and herring.

Acting styles (and certainly acting quality) varied considerably, and contemporary references in day books and letters both praise and condemn specific actors and performances. In most cases the praise and criticisms are leveled at the actor's vocal presentation, which was apparently valued above all else. Physically there was opportunity for great variation, from the restrained physical behavior of God to the farcical capering of the Vice. It is probable that the vocal presentation was tailored to the physical aspects of the role, so that the lines of God would be rich and restrained and, on the other hand, the vaunts of Herod would be full of roaring and bluster.

COSTUMES

In most cases, Medieval theatrical costuming was simple in the extreme. That is, the Medieval audience was not at all bothered by anachronism, so that Roman soldiers wore Medieval armor, God was dressed like the Pope or as the designer imagined an emperor would dress, angels were dressed, often, as lower churchmen, with gilded wings attached, and the Jews wore clothing common to the Medieval Jewish community. In most cases the actor supplied his own costume, unless it was so unusual that it had to be separately purchased. The total purchases for the *Play of Paradise*, produced in 1391 at Beverley, consisted of the "karre" or pageant wagon, eight hasps, eighteen staples, two visors, a pair of wings for the angel, a fir spar (to construct the Tree of Knowledge), a worm (costume for the serpent), two pair of linen breeches, two pair of shifts, and one sword. A similar play in 1565 required expenditures only for a tail for the serpent, a "face and hair" for God, hair for Adam and Eve, and a "rybbe colleryed Red."

Certain of the costumes became standardized. Judas usually was costumed in a red wig and yellow robe, though there is no indication as to how or why this specific costuming came about. Saved souls were traditionally dressed in white robes, and damned souls in black.

Probably the most imaginative costuming was reserved for Satan and the devils. Satan was horribly masked, wore a hairy jacket that covered his torso, and often carried a staff or heavy club. The devils varied greatly according to the fancy of whoever was constructing the costume, but most illustrations indicate misshapen figures with heads resembling birds of prey or carnivorous and often legendary animals. Scales, tails, horns, claws, and fangs all figured prominently in the devil costumes.

THE WANING OF MEDIEVAL DRAMA

From the tenth through the early sixteenth century (at least in most of northern and central Europe and England) the Medieval drama grew and flourished, with the simple religious tropes eventually becoming the great cycles and pageants. However, the winds of religious change were blowing across the continent, and by the sixteeth century, the Renaissance was already well underway in Italy. These two forces, in combination, swiftly put an end to what was one of the most vital dramatic flowerings in the history of the art.

The religious change was highly important. In England, following Henry VIII's break with the Roman Catholic Church in the 1530s, an increasingly powerful Protestantism frowned darkly on plays that smacked of popery and, even worse, idolatry. The degree of civil religious strife forced Elizabeth I, upon ascending the throne in 1558, to ban all religious plays. This ban was not totally effective at first, but within fifteen years of her pronouncement the great cycle plays had, essentially, been abandoned except for occasional performances undertaken for antiquarian reasons. On the continent similar religious strife led to the Catholic Church withdrawing all support for the plays, which in turn provoked the civil authorities to ban further productions as incitements to religious strife.

Even more important than the religious issue in putting an end to the cycles was the development and spread of the Renaissance. Beginning in the fourteenth century in Italy, this essentially humanistic movement with its renewed emphasis on education, and on the study of Classical learning and arts, blended with the existing Medieval culture to produce something completely new.

5

The Italian Renaissance

5

The Italian Renaissance

Almost no period in history begins and ends neatly on some particular date, because of some specific happening. In trying to mark the beginning of the Renaissance in Italy several dates immediately spring to mind—1394 and the birth of Henry the Navigator, whose voyages opened up the sea routes so important to the Renaissance; 1436 and Johann Gutenberg's invention of moveable type, which made printed material generally available for the first time; or 1453 and the fall of Constantinople, which resulted in a small part of the contents of the great library being carried by scholars north into Europe. A number of other such dates could as well be adduced. Perhaps, for drama at least, the year 1349 and the production of Petrarch's *Philologia* marks the beginning of the Renaissance. But, in any case, the concern should be less with the exact date the movement begins than with the spirit that led to this remarkable flowering called the Renaissance.

THE RENAISSANCE WORLD

During the fourteenth century in Italy, and the fifteenth and sixteenth centuries in France and Germany, people began to shed themselves of many of the beliefs and characteristics of Medieval society that had been accepted for nearly ten centuries. Suddenly they were no longer ready to accept the old curricula of the universities, they questioned the absolute temporal power of the Pope, they insisted on challenging the Mohammedans for economically important land areas about the Mediterranean, and they refused to accept the literary and artistic standards of the ages immediately past. Philosophers and merchants alike began to look about them for new ways of thought and action—and the Renaissance (or rebirth), that great cultural, social, and economic awakening, began.

In the fourteenth century Italy was, in a political sense at least, one of the most backward of European countries, with the nation divided into so many warring, petty princedoms that it would seem an unlikely area for the birthplace of the greatest flowering of the arts, sciences, and crafts since Classical Greece. However, Italy was also the home of the old Roman civilization and there, still available to those who were willing to look, were the great works of art, the still beautiful ruins of the buildings, and the old manuscripts of the

This woodcut illustrates an early Italian Renaissance production of a play by Terence. The stage, still essentially Medieval in concept, suggests a simple, modest production.

great Greek and Roman writers. Italian scholars studied the art and architecture and resurrected the manuscripts and began a revival of art and learning that would eventually spread all across Europe.

The Medieval universities had long been the primary educational influence, but their relationship with the Classical manuscripts had become something more in the nature of philological exercise than an honest attempt to study and comprehend the content of the manuscripts. As a result of this attitude, many of the most important figures of the early Renaissance were people who stood outside the universities. Dante, the last of the great Italian writers of the Middle Ages, was highly important in setting the tone of the new movement. A scientist, scholar, and poet, he advanced the cause of the vernacular, writing what well may be the greatest of the Medieval poems, *The Divine Comedy*, in his native Italian. Dante espoused some rather advanced ideas on the physical aspects of earth, heaven, and hell, and his veneration of the great Classical writers gave to them a certain respectability in spite of their paganism.

After Dante, but every bit as important to the growing humanistic movement, came Francesco Petrarch (1304-74), the first of the great Renaissance poets. Petrarch reverted to the Latin for his compositions, largely because of his admiration for the Classical poets. He traveled widely, influencing many other writers, and his sonnet sequence and his humanistic plays, beginning with *Philologia* in the middle of the fourteenth century, ushered in the Italian Renaissance.

This great rebirth of art and learning touched all areas of human existence. A skepticism unheard of throughout the Middle Ages became the touchstone of the age. Philosophers and scholars ridiculed some religious activities and openly questioned (and in some cases rejected) certain Church abuses. They made the pagan gods once more a subject for study, promoted the study of Latin for purposes other than reading Church materials or understanding the Latin services, and prompted the establishment of libraries to preserve the old manuscripts. This all led to a growing conviction that life here and now was at least as important as the life hereafter, and that certain rewards in this world were perhaps preferable to uncertain rewards in the afterlife. There was also a developing belief in the human potential. For humans, the people of the Renaissance believed, almost nothing was impossible, and it was this confidence in people's infinite capacity that, more than anything else, led to the great music, art, and literature, and the scientific geographic discoveries of the period. It was an explosive age, a diverse age, an age that could breed a Machiavelli alongside a Petrarch and feel comfortable with both of them.

Politically the Renaissance was the period in which the seeds of modern democracy were sown. Erasmus, ex-monk, Church reformer, and author of *The Praise of Folly,* and Thomas More, the author of *Utopia*, a work picturing a world where all property was held in common, were both strongly opposed to absolute monarchies. All across Europe, and especially in the Netherlands, eminent scholars wrote works in praise of popular democracy. The essence of these works was that rulers of states should not receive their offices through heredity, but should be elected and then held responsible to the electorate for their misdemeanors. Erasmus and More also favored popular education, featuring a balanced curriculum in which the Bible and the great Classical works would both receive appropriate attention.

While all this agitation for democracy was going on, the rulers of England, Spain, and particularly France continued to do everything in their power to expand the royal prerogatives. There were attempts to limit the powers of the Parliament in England, the Estates-General in France, and the Cortés in Spain. There were restrictions placed on the nobility which were designed to make them more responsible to the crown, and the municipal councils found themselves obligated to the king in myriad new ways. Even the Church found itself losing ground to the kings in their drive toward absolute power. In France, between 1485 and 1560, the Estates-General held no meetings. In the sixteenth century in England, Parliament was acknowledged by the crown as an important institution, but was totally ignored in all important matters except the levying of taxes, which only Parliament could do. Thus was the way made clear for the autocracy that would plague Europe in the seventeenth and eighteenth centuries.

It was, finally, a combination of all of this—the rediscovery of the Classics, advanced trade and the resulting intercourse between previously

The festival hall in the castle of the Duke of Urbino, as painted by Paolo Uccello, showing the semi-Medieval multiple stage that was situated against the long side of the hall.

isolated geographic areas, emphasis on the here and now and the resulting loss of Church influence, increasing urbanization, and much tough political infighting—that resulted in the unique mix that was the Renaissance.

THE RISE OF SECULAR THEATRE

The early Renaissance in Italy consisted primarily of two quite distinct secular forms: the elite and essentially literary theatre of the humanists and the popular theatre which eventually came to be called the *commedia dell'arte*. In addition to these two major forms, Italian theatre also contributed the *intermezzi*, the opera, and the pastoral.

Humanist Theatre

While the humanistic theatre in Italy can be dated with some certainty in terms of the first of Petrarch's humanistic plays, *Philologia*, the transition from the Medieval religious drama was gradual and depended in part on the study of Roman drama. The plays of Seneca had long been required reading in Italian higher education; however, they were not studied as plays but as models of rhetorical style or as cautionary moral tales. A similar fate was reserved for those other two great Roman dramatists, Plautus and Terence, who were read respectively as models for oral style and for polite conversation. Indeed, it was not until late in the fourteenth century that scholars began to look at these Classical works as plays to be produced. This new attitude is likely responsible for the first significant Renaissance tragedy, *Achilles* (c. 1390), by Antonio Laschi. The only thing that kept this play (and many later fifteenth century plays also based on Classical materials) from achieving a widespread audience was the fact that it was written in Latin. In imitating the Classical forms, and using Classical subject matter, the early humanist playwrights were led into the trap of using the Classical language as well.

And the early comedy did not fare much better. Like tragedy, humanistic comedy began appearing in the fourteenth century, though it came a few years after tragedy made its appearance. The earliest known comedy is the *Paulus* (1390) of Pier Paolo Vergerio. This comedy, like its tragic counterparts, was Latinate in both form and language, and subsequent comedies written throughout the fifteenth century retained this Classic influence.

In the early sixteenth century the Classical influence not only continued, it became stronger. In 1429 in Germany, Cusano discovered twelve previously unknown plays by Plautus. In 1473 the comedies of Terence were printed. The invention of the printing press and moveable type greatly speeded up the dissemination of Classical materials. In 1502 a Venetian printer, Aldus Manutius, published the seven extant plays of Sophocles. In the following year he published the works of Euripides, and in 1518 he put out the works of Aeschylus. At last the works of the great Classical writers were generally available.

And yet, in spite of this increased emphasis on Classicism, a healthy vernacular drama finally appeared at the beginning of the sixteenth century. The availability of printing probably provoked a determination on the part of playwrights to make their wares available to potential patrons among the nobility, and this determination increased the flow of vernacular drama. While this increased production of works in the vernacular produced few plays of lasting literary or theatrical value, it managed to influence drama in all of Europe.

LODOVICO ARIOSTO: Lodovico Ariosto (1474-1533), Italian poet and playwright, was born at Reggio in Lombardy, where his father, Niccolo Ariosto, was commander of the citadel. From his earliest years, young Ariosto showed a strong inclination toward poetry, but was forced by his father to study law as the more lucrative profession—a profession, by the way, which Ariosto despised and in which he later said he had lost the five best years of his life. Allowed at last to follow his own inclinations, he applied himself to the study of

A scene from *Il Pellegrino* of Girolamo Parabosco in the mid-sixteenth century illustrates the style of the humanistic theatre.

Classical literature under the tutelage of Gregorio de Spoleto. After a short period of study, during which he concentrated on the Latin writers, he lost his instructor, who went to France as the tutor of Francesco Sforza. Ariosto thus lost the opportunity to learn Greek, as he had fully intended. Soon after the loss of his tutor his father died and Ariosto was forced to forego his literary ambitions to undertake the management of his family's affairs, which were in unfortunate economic shape, and to provide for his nine brothers and sisters, one of whom was crippled.

While managing the family estate he found time to write some prose comedies and a few lyrical pieces which attracted the notice of Cardinal Ippolito d'Este, who took the young poet under his patronage and appointed him one of the gentlemen of his household. If Ariosto can be believed, the Cardinal merely pretended to be a patron of literature, and the only reward the poet re-

A mid-seventeenth century design by Filippo Juvara for a court masque in Windsor Castle. Juvara followed Torelli in using what we now call a unit set, with permanent arches at the sides and back, and the backdrop changed to indicate a new scene.

ceived for having dedicated to him the *Orlando Furioso* was the casual question, "Where do you find so many stories?" The Cardinal was so insensitive regarding Ariosto's literary endeavors that the poet later deplored the time spent under his patron's yoke, complaining that while he was given a niggardly pension, it was not to reward him for his poetry, which the Cardinal really despised, but to reward the poet for running like a messenger boy at the prelate's pleasure. Nor, it seems, was this pension regularly paid.

In 1518 the Cardinal went to Hungary and asked Ariosto to accompany him, but the poet pleaded ill health, the need to care for his private affairs, and even the age of his mother as reasons why he could not leave Italy. His excuses were not accepted and even an interview with the Cardinal to plead his case was denied him. Ariosto then suggested in a letter that he should be released from the Cardinal's service, thus leaving him free to seek a more generous patron, and the Cardinal was undoubtedly glad to oblige.

The Cardinal's brother, Alphonso I, Duke of Ferrara and husband of Lucrezia Borgia, took the poet into his service. Ariosto, who had demonstrated some talent as a diplomat, was sent on two missions to Rome as ambassador to Pope Julius II. The rigors and exhaustion caused by the first mission brought on a bout of consumption from which Ariosto never fully recovered. On the second mission he narrowly escaped execution at the order of the Pope, a man of legendary bad temper who at the time was furious at the Duke of Ferrara.

Asking to leave the Duke's service when his salary was not paid, Ariosto was instead appointed governor of the province of Garfagnana, high in the Apennines. His salary was restored and he held the post for three years, apparently with some distinction, which was no small feat in a province overrun by *banditti* and sharply divided by political factions. Upon leaving the governorship he returned to Ferrara where, in 1527, he married his mistress of fourteen years, Alessandra Benucci. He spent the balance of his career writing comedies, superintending their performance, helping with the construction of a theatre, and editing the *Orlando Furioso*, which was published in a final edition only a year before his death. He died of consumption on July 6, 1533.

At the court of Ferrara the romantic epic had a continuing popularity reaching back to the late Middle Ages. In Ariosto's early period as a writer the people he hoped to impress with his poetry were enthralled with Matteo Boiardo's uncompleted *Orlando Innamorato*, a romantic poem on the adventures and loves of Orlando (Roland in the French epic). In 1506, inspired by the earlier poem and determined to capitalize on its popularity, Ariosto began his continuation of the Orlando epic, *Orlando Furioso*, which was first published in 1516 and twice revised. The poem is both comic and tragic by turns, with Orlando driven mad when his love for the beautiful Angelica is not returned. Written in skillful *ottava rima*, the poem was highly influential on such later poets as Tasso, Sidney, Spenser, and Lope de Vega.

Ariosto imitated the Latin styles of Plautus and Terence in his five comedies: *La cassaria* (*The Strong Box*, 1508); *I suppositi* (*Supposes*, 1509); *Il negromante* (*The Necromancer*, 1520); *La Lena* (1528); and the unfinished *I studenti* (*The Students*). His plays had little literary merit, but they apparently played well, especially in front of a court audience, and so they helped inaugurate a vogue for Classical style comedies during the Renaissance.

Baldassare Peruzzi's design (c. 1530) for a perspective setting. (Uffizi, Florence, Italy)

After Ariosto, the most important writer of comedy was Bernardo Dovizi da Bibbiena (1470-1520), whose *La Calandria* (1513) was highly successful, influencing the course of Italian comedy and even providing the kind of material that Shakespeare would make use of in *Twelfth Night* nearly one hundred years later—that is, the errors growing up around fraternal twins of different sexes who look amazingly alike. The play centers on an elderly fool named Calandro who is in love with a beautiful young woman named Santilla, who is the twin sister of a handsome young man named Lidio, who is in turn the lover of Calandro's wife, Fulvia. The plot is full of disguisings and mistaken identities, drawn largely from Plautus' *Menaechmi* and *Casina*, and also makes use of some incidents from Giovanni Boccaccio's *Decameron*. The language is realistic; the story is one that was highly popular in the late Medieval and Renaissance periods, concerning the sexual jackassery of old men; and the tone is one of amoral, sardonic mockery.

Similar to Bibbiena's work in attitude and story, but quite different in its sources, is *La mandragola* (*The Mandrake*, 1520), written by Niccolo Machiavelli (1469-1527). The play tells how Callimaco, smitten with the beautiful and virtuous Lucrezia, arranges to have himself presented to her aged fool of a husband as a doctor who is capable of curing what the husband believes is his young wife's sterility. Through a complex plot and some disguising, and with the help of a rather disgusting priest, Callimaco ends up in Lucrezia's bed. The lady, shamed and tricked by both her husband and the priest who is her confessor, and overwhelmed by Callimaco's passion, agrees to continue the affair, and the play ends. This is the first truly great Italian comedy and it is important not only because it remains a highly playable work, but also because it represents an ideal mix of several types and styles of drama. The models are from Classical Latin; the subject is close to rustic farce; the dialogue is realistic prose; and the characterization has a depth that is sadly lacking in most plays of the period.

Joseph Furttenbach's 1655 Strassburg setting was supposed to have used *periaktoi*, but in the drawing they look more like flat wings. (Joseph Furttenbach, *Architectura Civilis*, Ulm, 1628)

Giangiorgio Trissino (1478-1550) wrote *Sofonisba* in 1515, and it stands as the first major humanist tragedy. In this play Trissino attempted to follow the model of Greek tragedy, even to the use of a fifteen-man chorus, and avoid the pervasive influence of Seneca. In this he succeeded, thereby provoking a contest between those playwrights favoring the Greek ideals and those who stood by the Roman. That the "Romans" eventually won out was due in large part to the popularity of Giovanni Battista Giraldi (1504-73), the Italian humanist known as "il Cinthio." Cinthio wrote three tragedies in the Senecan style—*Orbecche*, *Dido*, and *Cleopatra*—and then abandoned tragedy for serious plays with happy endings because, as he pointed out, they were far more pleasing to audiences. Cinthio's plays achieved the popularity he desired and exercised great influence on succeeding Italian dramatists, but they have not stood the test of time and today go largely unplayed.

From a historical point of view, perhaps the most important contribution of the Italian Renaissance humanist drama is the pastoral, popularized first by the *Aminta* (1573) of Torquatto Tasso (1544-95), and then by *Il pastor fido* (*The Faithful Shepherd*, 1590, produced in 1598) by Giovanni Battista Guarini (1538-

1612). This form, already made somewhat familiar by the Medieval *pastourelle*, swiftly spread all over Europe. Shakespeare made use of the form (albeit with tongue firmly planted in cheek) in *As You Like It*, and in the middle of the nineteenth century Leigh Hunt's translation of Tasso's *Aminta* indicated its continuing interest.

To begin to understand the tradition in which the Italian pastoral dramatists were working it is necessary to go back to Angelo Ambrogini (in English, Politian, 1454-94) and his *Favola d'Orfeo* (1480), which is an adaptation of the legend of Orpheus and Eurydice to the form of the Christian *sacra rappresentazione*, or, to put it from another point of view, an adaptation of the *sacra rappresentazione* to a type of secular and rather pagan drama in which the prologue is delivered by Mercury instead of the traditional angel, and where the last third of the play ends with the Bacchantes, who have already torn Orpheus to bits, joining in a riotous Bacchanalian *ballata*. The *Favola d'Orfeo* is particularly important because it begins that long-lived, prolific, and popular genre, the mythological pastoral.

The choruses of the *Favola d' Orfeo* are indicative of its ancestry. They are much closer to the *canti carnascialeschi* than to the Classical Greek or Roman choruses. The descent following the *Orfeo* is fairly obvious. It led to the *Arcadia* (1480-85) of Jacopo Sannazzaro which, though a romance and not a drama, was the ancestor of Agostino Beccari's *Il sacrificio* (1554). The *Arcadia*

A 1602 engraving illustrating a scene from Gianbattista Guarini's *Il Pastor Fido*.

was the first pastoral romance following Boccaccio's *Ameto*, and while there was a kind of masquerade interest in it for contemporary audiences (several members of the Pontian Academy appear in pastoral disguises), the bits drawn from Vergil, Ovid, Theocritus, and others left it little interest of its own. However, it did lead almost directly to Beccari's pastoral play *Il sacrificio*. Beccari's play was, in many ways, a better play than its immediate ancestor was a romance, but it suffered from the same problem—a few elegant imitations of Vergil and Ovid were not enough to give it interest of its own.

Following Sannazzaro and Beccari the pastoral idyll became firmly established. The Italian Renaissance man was expected to affect a love for the placid, simple, idyllic pastoral life, and this produced a plethora of eclogues by Ariosto, Trissino, Alamanni, and others that were, if not direct pilferage, certainly composed in slavish imitation of the Florentine quattrocentist idyllic poetry and Sannazzaro's *Arcadia*. It is out of this background that Tasso and Guarini created their masterpieces.

TORQUATO TASSO: Torquato Tasso (1544-95), Italian poet and playwright, born in Sorrento, was the son of Bernardo Tasso, a man of letters and a professional diplomat who received appointments from several of the larger Italian courts. Tasso spent most of his youth at the court of Urbino, where his father held a diplomatic post, and in 1560 he began work on what would eventually be his masterpiece, the epic poem *Gerusalemme liberata* (*Jerusalem Delivered*). Almost as soon as the poem was underway, Tasso began agonizing over the moral aspects of his romantic epic, and also over its religious orthodoxy. As a result, he began revising long before the poem was finished.

In 1565 Tasso entered service with the house of Este at Ferrara, first serving Cardinal Luigi d'Este and later entering the service of Duke Alfonso II. At Ferrara he continued working on his epic, alternately forging ahead and then furiously revising in an unsettling fervor that foreshadowed the madness which eventually overtook him. While working on *Gerusalemme* he also wrote sonnets to some of the ladies of the court, especially Lucrezia Bendidio. But when the Duke's powerful minister, Pigna, began his platonic wooing of the lady, Tasso cravenly quit writing his own sonnets and contented himself with editing the minister's *canzoni* to Lucrezia, the "ideal mistress."

In 1573, with *Gerusalemme* still unfinished, Tasso began his career as a dramatist with the pastoral play *Aminta*, which still stands as one of the two best plays of the genre. It was enormously successful, beginning a type of drama that swept through the courtly literature of Europe. Critics have generally been content to give the play a surface hearing, concentrating on the pastoral elements and ignoring the possibility that beneath a surface of nymphs, shepherds and satyrs, *Aminta* is a carefully constructed drama which combines the pastoral elements that were present in most areas of Italian literature with the still developing concept of courtly love.

The plot of the play is a simple one. The young Arcadian shepherd, Aminta, loves his former playmate, Silvia. She, however, does not return his love because she is one of Diana's nymphs, vowed to chastity and too deeply involved in the pleasures of the hunt. He tries to prove his love and devotion, but

A series of scenes illustrating the *Aminta* of Torquato Tasso. (F. Leclerc, Amsterdam, 1678)

to no avail. Following the suggestion of Daphne, an older and rather worldly nymph, Aminta decides to attack Silvia as she bathes naked in a woodland pool. However, when he comes near he sees his beloved about to be raped by a satyr who has tied her to a tree with her own long hair. Aminta drives the satyr away and frees Silvia who, shamed and embarrassed, flees into the woods. There she meets and takes shelter with another nymph, Nerina. They hunt together, at last pursuing a great wolf. Silvia soon outdistances her friend, and when Nerina later finds a pack of wolves feeding on bones near a bloodstained veil she had given to Silvia, she concludes that her friend has been devoured and goes to tell Aminta. He is distraught over the supposed death of his love and attempts suicide, throwing himself over a precipice. Silvia, who is in fact safe and sound, returns and hears what Aminta has done. His act stirs pity, love, and remorse in her heart, and she goes to find his dead body. When she finds him, however, he is alive and well, albeit unconscious and a bit bruised.

The plot is indeed a simple one, and to a modern reader must sound more than a bit ridiculous. However, the setting, the unrequited love of the faithful shepherd for the nymph (or shepherdess), and the eventual triumph of romantic love, all became standard in terms of the genre and helped change the course of European drama.

In 1575 Tasso finished *Gerusalemme*, complete with its many revisions. It enjoyed an immediate and lasting popularity and today stands with Ariosto's work as one of the great epic poems of the Italian Renaissance. However, by this time Tasso's bouts of madness and depression had become much worse. He continued working in the area of drama, writing a complex and uninspired prose comedy that was never finished during his lifetime, but which was completed and published posthumously as *Intrighi d'amore* (The Intrigues of Love).

In 1579 the madness became intense and Tasso was shut away in the Hospital of Sant'Anna in Ferrara. He was not released until 1586. Then, apparently still unstable, he began a series of disturbed wanderings from one city to another. During this period he found the time to write one more play, a poorly done tragedy entitled *Il re Torrismondo* (*King Torrismondo*) published in 1585. Perhaps as a result of his madness, the play is full of horrors that foreshadow the tragic dramas of the following century.

In 1595, in the monastery of Sant'Onofrio in Rome, Tasso died. A master epic poet and an important playwright, his influence on succeeding generations of writers was great indeed.

COMMEDIA DELL'ARTE

The Italian popular theatre, which originated in Italy in the mid-sixteenth century, was in its earliest form close to what we sometimes refer to as "street theatre." It was also the first theatre since the Greek that was truly developed for a mass audience. Usually referred to simply as *commedia dell'arte* (comedy of the guild, or by professional players), it also included such various forms as *commedia all'improviso* (improvised comedy) and *commedia a*

Commedia dell'arte performances on the Piazza Navona in Rome. (Detail from a 1708 engraving by Petrus Schenk, Amsterdam)

soggetto (comedy from plot or subject). Before it came to an end, the *commedia* had spread throughout western Europe, lasted nearly two hundred years, and become the single most important influence on the development of comic drama.

The origin of the *commedia* is difficult to determine, though most scholars seem to believe that it grew out of the remnants of the Atellan farce and the Roman mimes. Certainly in its robust vulgarity and its use of masked, stock characters, it seems very close to these earlier forms. Some scholars, however, on somewhat more slender evidence, argue that it grew from degenerate productions of the comedies of Plautus and Terence. There has also been some suspicion that *commedia* was an Italianate form growing out of the Byzantine mimes, which entered southern Europe after the fall of Constantinople in 1453.

Whatever its distant ancestors, the immediate precursors of *commedia* were the acting troupes like that of "il Ruzzante" (Angelo Beolco), which were busily giving semi-improvisational performances in the first quarter of the sixteenth century. At the same time, troupes of Italian musicians, dancers, acrobats, and jugglers were plying their trade not only in Italy but in many of the major urban centers of Europe. Undoubtedly, all of these influences came together about the middle of the century, and the new *commedia* troupes were formed, usually along family lines.

One of the first and greatest of these troupes was the Gelosi (the zealous to please), assembled by Francesco Andreini and his highly talented wife Isabella. Before the end of the century such troupes as the Uniti, the Confidenti, the Desiosi, and the Fideli were traveling throughout Europe. Each prominent city in Italy had a troupe, some sponsored by the city and some by the local nobility (the Duke of Mantua, for example, sponsored two such troupes), but in most cases the troupes were unsponsored examples of private enterprise, owned and operated by the actors themselves.

Most of the troupes numbered from ten to twelve players, though some numbered as many as twenty and some, usually the poorer troupes, as few as seven. They usually included seven or eight men and three or four women in fairly standard combinations—that is, a servant girl, Capitano, at least two *Zanni*, Pantalone, Dottore, and one or two sets of young lovers.

Economically the companies were arranged along profit-sharing lines. They shared expenses and drew percentages of the profits according to their position or stature in the troupe. The troupe leader, either the family patriarch or the most respected member of the troupe, who usually acted as script writer for the scenarios and, in a sense, director, certainly drew the largest share. On the other hand, some of the younger performers who were understudying major roles and performing minor supporting bits were given only salaries until they completed their apprenticeship and became full-fledged members of the company, which then entitled them to share in the profits.

About a dozen stock characters were the common property of all the companies. The most important of these, not only because they were the most popular but also because their physical antics were often so difficult to perform, were the *Zannis*. The bits of comic business (*lazzi*) performed by these

Jacques Callot's early seventeenth century etching of *commedia dell'arte* performers. The simple outdoor stage of the *commedia* can be seen in the background.

characters ranged from comic gestures, movements and vocal deliveries, through comic dance and acrobatics. The roles might vary from day to day, from production to production, with a *Zanni* on one day playing a stupid servant whose oafishness causes his master (and himself and everyone else) untold problems; on the next day the same *Zanni* might well find himself playing the sly, clever valet whose machinations are undone in a comic manner by the bumbling of his stupid master. In either case, however, the *Zannis* were, first and foremost, clowns, ready to turn every opportunity into comic action or dialogue. The popularity of these figures is testified to by the fact that their names, nearly four hundred years after they began, are still recognized, not only by theatre historians, but in some cases by people who know little or nothing about the history of the art—Arlecchino (Harlequin), Scaramuccia (Scaramouche), Brighella, Pulcinella, Pedrolino, Coviello, Scapini, and others.

Along with the *Zannis*, certain other *commedia* characters achieved special importance. Each troupe had its *Magnifico*, usually called Pantalone, who was a comic old man. Pantalone was, traditionally, a successful Venetian merchant, married to a reasonably young and often justifiably shrewish wife, who spent his time chasing young women—with great comic abandon but with only rare success. In almost every case, Pantalone was himself cuckolded as a result of his ventures. Equal in importance to the *Magnifico* was the Dottore (usually a doctor of laws, but sometimes a horse doctor or quack), usually called Gratiano, who hailed from Bologna. The Dottore, a gullible old fool who was usually a friend of Pantalone and a participant in Pantalone's schemes, was often the butt of much of the comic action. The third of these major characters was *Capitano*, a Spanish captain in the tradition of *Miles Gloriosus*—that is, a braggart warrior who constantly boasts of his valor and skill at arms, but who collapses in sniveling terror whenever he is confronted by anybody who threatens violence, even a *Zanni* with a slapstick in place of a sword. Capitano, called by such names as Coccodrillo or Matamoros, usually played the comic love interest. He was a jealous and generally unwelcome suitor, rarely successful, who contrasted nicely on one hand with the old fool Pantalone in his amorous pursuits and on the other with the traditional young lover. The young hero (*Innamorato* or *Amoroso*) and heroine (*Innamorata*) varied more than any of the other characters. Their love affair, often temporarily thwarted by the bungling of the *Zannis*, provided a norm against which the comedy could unfold.

These major characters remained relatively constant as long as the *commedia* endured, but some of the names varied from troupe to troupe. Only a few of the heroines won the fame that accrued to the *Zannis* and their ilk. Isabella Andreini became famous in her own right as one of the most beautiful and talented women in all Europe, but the heroines in which she specialized are not highly memorable. The names of Isabella, Flaminia, Silvia, Olivetta, and Valeria were all given to heroines. Colombina, the most popular of the female clown figures, was usually a large, overly amorous woman who pleased audiences. Violetta, Fioretta, and especially Smeraldina also appeared in varying connections with the *Zannis*.

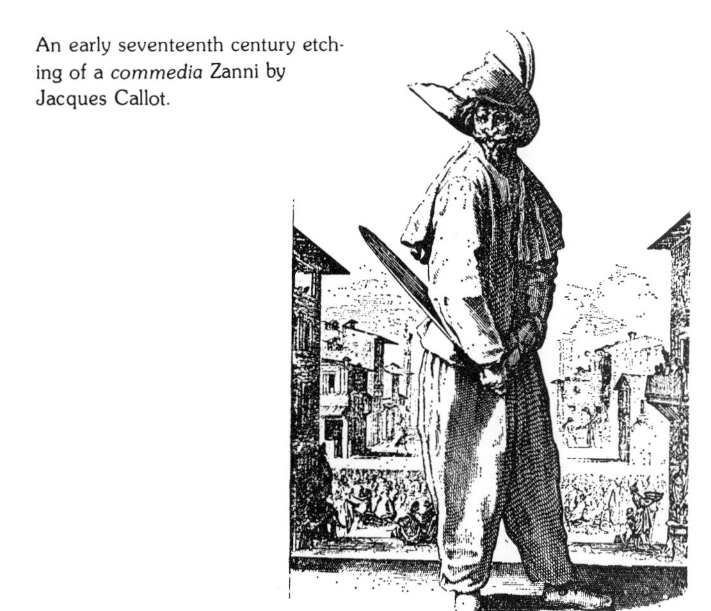

An early seventeenth century etching of a *commedia* Zanni by Jacques Callot.

The actors of the *commedia* troupes were highly specialized, usually playing the same character for many years and, sometimes, if they were among the very best of the players, achieving an identity in the role that overwhelmed their own personality. For example, Francesco Andreini was, in his own time, more often referred to as Captain Spavento (Spavento da Vall'Inferno was his Capitano's stage name) than by his own name. G. B. Biancolelli, who specialized in the role of Arlecchino, was better known by that name than by his own. Among the women, Zanetta Benozzi, in most material written about the eighteenth century French *commedia*, is usually referred to merely as Silvia, the heroine she played so well.

This specialization in a specific character had a direct bearing on the aspect of *commedia* which has provoked the greatest contemporary interest—improvisation. The actors of the *commedia* worked from a scenario or plot outline that gave them only the bare bones of a plot, without specific lines or actions. In some cases the scenario gave the complete lines of the prologue, which was considered highly important, especially when it contained the argument of the play. Also, some scenarios contained the closing lyric lines. In most cases, however, the players were free to improvise from beginning to end, restricted only by the basic progression of the plot outlined by the scenario. The degree to which this improvisation actually existed, however, is unclear. Because each actor played one specific character for so many years, it is certain that each developed set speeches, bits of dialogue, and particular physical actions that were appropriate to the character being portrayed. As a result, casts which had acted together for so long could probably predict, onstage and with some degree of certainty, what would happen in almost any case, and could themselves predictably respond with their own set materials.

More than seven hundred of the *commedia* scenarios have been preserved, and these, along with some woodcuts, paintings, and commentary by observers and in some cases by *commedia* actors themselves, give us an accurate idea of what happened on the *commedia* stage. The greatest number of these scenarios are comic; however, a few are tragic, many are melodramatic, and some of the late ones are basically operatic in nature.

The outstanding professional expertise of the *commedia* players is always commented on by the writers of the period. The actor had to be able to "read" his audience in a way that contemporary actors, hemmed in by their scripts, find to be either unnecessary or unproductive. However, the *commedia* player had choices to make in every situation, and these choices were limited only by the player's own imagination and talent, and the ability of the fellow players to follow his lead. As well, the player had to "read" the fellow actors, anticipating what they might do in any situation. In addition to this talent to read and anticipate, the *commedia* player also had to be an accomplished mimic and acrobat, and additional skills as singer, dancer, and musician were often required.

Once the *commedia* had attained its popularity in Italy it began to spread out, carrying the genre to all of Europe. Apparently, given the broad physical action of most shows and the ability of the *commedia* players to work in pantomime, language proved to be no real problem. By the end of the sixteenth century, *commedia* troupes had played in France (early 1540s), England (1546), and Spain (1574). The Andreini troupe (the Gelosi) played several times at the French court between 1571 and 1604. Italian companies played in both Windsor and Reading in 1577, and appeared before Elizabeth I in 1602. By the middle of the seventeenth century, troupes were moving into the Germanic kingdoms and the Slavic countries.

INTERMEZZI

There is some belief that the *intermezzi* represented a special theatrical form, descended from the *mascherata*, which were short dramatic works presented at the courts to mark special occasions. However, the form is too widely spread to believe that it developed out of anything more special than the universal theatrical need to entertain the audience while the sets were being changed. In England the form was called the interlude, in Spain the *entremés*, and the *entremets* in France. In England the form was adapted to a special, nontheatrical usage when John Heywood wrote interludes as dialogues to entertain the nobility between the courses of court banquets. Eventually the form would be put to an equivalent usage in Italy. In the Spanish theatre the *entreméses* were eventually developed into one-act plays. It was in the Italian theatre, however, that the *intermezzo* achieved its highest development.

In the Italian court, *intermezzi* first appeared between the acts of comedies late in the fifteenth century. This practice was carried over to the production of the pastoral dramas in the late sixteenth century, where elaborate sets required substantial time for changes and audiences were likely to grow restive. To make these brief, *entr'acte* productions as attractive as possible, spectacle was added. This growth of spectacle, coupled wih the gradual disappearance of spectacular staging in the neoclassical Italian court drama, made the *intermezzi* ever more popular.

In its early form the *intermezzo* featured dialogue or poetry around which the spectacle was designed, but as the form became more complex the spectacle itself became primary and dialogue disappeared, except to the degree that it was sometimes necessary in order to explain an overelaborate allegorical presentation.

Eventually these theatrical entertainments were taken over by the court and used to cover short breaks or intermissions in all sorts of court happenings, such as celebrations of traditional holidays, engagements, weddings, and visits of royalty or foreign dignitaries. In this last case, the *intermezzi* were used to pay extravagant compliments to the person, group, or country being honored.

When the *intermezzi* first began they consisted of short, unrelated bits of business. As they became longer, more complex, and often more popular than the drama whose acts they separated, there was a growing tendency to give all the *intermezzi* a related theme, making them essentially a series of acts. Eventually these related acts of the *intermezzi* became, in essence, a masque. It was at this point, in the middle of the seventeenth century, that the form was absorbed by the ever more popular opera.

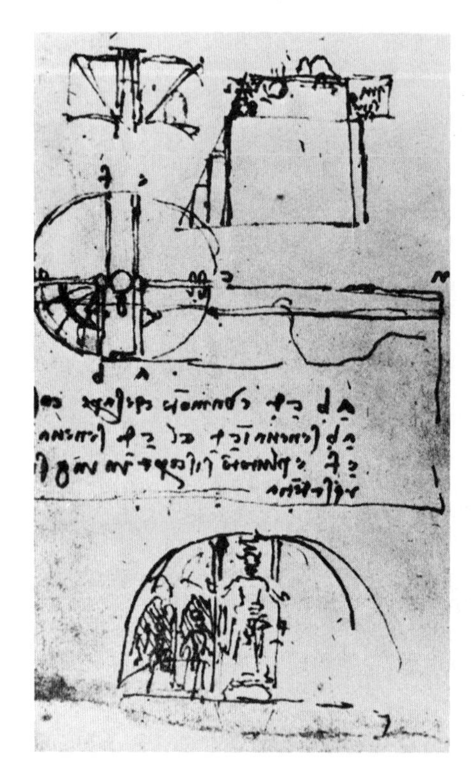

(Left) Leonardo da Vinci's 1490 plans for an allegorical spectacle, *Il Paradiso*, featured a revolving stage.
(Below) A cutaway of Leonardo da Vinci's stage plan for *Il Paradiso* detailing the machinery that appears in the main plan.

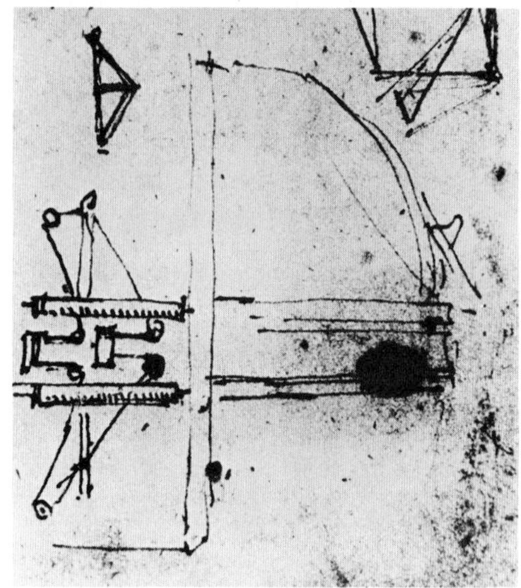

OPERA

Opera, the most distinctive and enduring theatrical form that developed in Italy during the Renaissance, began rather neatly in 1597 with the production of *Dafne*, which featured music by Jacopo Peri and book by Ottavio Rinuccini and Giulio Caccini. Unfortunately, the music for *Dafne* has not survived. However, the text indicates that it only faintly resembles opera as we know it, with choral passages that were merely chanted to musical accompaniment.

The basis of opera is, quite obviously, drama plus music, and it grew up out of the Renaissance concern with Classicism and the Classical arts. The members of one of the many Italian academies that flourished throughout the Renaissance, specifically the Camerata of Florence, were fascinated by the great Greek tragedies with their intricate combination of music and drama, and they tried to create works that were similar to though not mere imitations of the Greek. *Dafne* was the first of these, and from this work the whole art form that is opera developed.

Although its distant ancestors were, in a sense, the great Classical tragedies—the lyric theatre of ancient Greece—true opera was a creation of the baroque in Italy. The first of the major opera composers was Claudio Monteverdi (1567-1643), whose bold experiments in instrumentation contributed greatly to the development of the modern orchestra. He wrote religious music and madrigals as well, but his greatest musical accomplishment was in the field of opera. His *Orfeo* in 1607 changed the direction of the genre, which until this work had been essentially drama with background music. *Orfeo* began the emphasis on music, tied together rather simply by an uninspired story line. Monteverdi's second work, *L'incoronazione di Poppea* (*The Coronation of Poppea*), continued this trend of placing the musical values above the dramatic.

Early opera remained primarily the property of the academies and the courts, but in 1637 this elitism came to an end when the first public opera house opened in Venice. This proved so successful a venture that three more houses were soon opened and opera became the property of the whole world.

A definite opera tradition developed. The aria and the virtuoso soloist became exalted above the recitative and chorus, plots were taken from a romanticized mythology, and a great deal of bombast, irrelevant episodes, and mechanical contrivances became the rule. This last was especially true after the middle of the seventeenth century, when opera absorbed the *intermezzi*, giving it the spectacular staging that would remain the trademark of the genre. Late in the century the three-act, dramatically unified *opera seria* was developed to combat operatic excesses, but in terms of staging it was too late to do more than partially alleviate the problem. Opera continued to maintain, even into the present century, its reputation for opulent, excessive staging.

Lodovico Burnacini's scenic design for Cesti and Sbarra's opera, *Il pomo d'oro*, Vienna, 1668. This scene shows Hellmouth and Charon the ferryman. (Engraving by Mathäus Küsel)

THEATRE ARCHITECTURE

The staging in *commedia* was, of course, quite simple, and so the theatre itself was usually nonexistent. The earliest *commedia* performances were played on crude platforms backed with simple drop curtains, sometimes painted with a semblance of houses or a forest scene, and sometimes left unadorned. Onstage furnishings were equivalently simple—tables, chairs, stools, and a chest or basket. In other words, the *commedia* was primarily an actors' theatre in which the performers created "place" with words, gestures, and movements. Even when the *commedia* moved out of its street environment into real theatres, containing stage equipment, or into the great halls of the nobility, the staging remained little different than it had been when performed in the marketplace or the town square.

The almost stark simplicity of the *commedia* was balanced, on the other hand, by excessive staging demands that took place in the formal humanist theatre. The first productions were apparently given out-of-doors in formal gardens with flat, grassy areas where the actors could play and the audience could comfortably sit. This practice never really died out until late in the eighteenth century. In fact, theatres were "planted," with shrubs outlining the playing area and the viewing area and providing a particularly appropriate background to the pastoral plays that became so popular.

However, early in the sixteenth century most productions went indoors, usually into the great banqueting halls where there was room to perform. These productions depended for their staging on what the Renaissance humanists fondly believed were the staging practices of Plautus and Terence, plus their knowledge of Medieval mansions, and so the great hall that could accommodate a number of platforms with elaborately painted backdrops provided a perfect theatre.

There is some testimony that the first permanent theatre was constructed in Ferrara, but that it burned down, as so many of these early theatres did, in 1532. However, the oldest surviving Renaissance theatre is the Teatro Olimpico. In 1580 the Olympic Academy of Vicenza, which had been founded to study the Greek drama, offered a commission to one of its members, Andrea Palladio (1518-80), to build a theatre based on the best Classical ideals. Palladio, a student of Vitruvius, whose works had been rediscovered in 1414, accepted the challenge and undertook to create a truly Classical theatre inside a preexisting building. The theatre he designed had thirteen tiers of seats, arranged in a semielliptical bank around a small open floor area called the orchestra. The stage, seventy feet long and eighteen feet deep, was enclosed at the back and ends by a decorative façade, similar to the elaborate façade of the Roman theatre, and covered with pillars, niches containing statuary, and bas-reliefs. The façade had five openings, one at each end and three across the back, also in the manner of the Roman theatre, with the central or "royal door" being the largest. The tiers of seats were bounded by a series of columns, and eighty statues of the sponsoring academicians decorated the building.

Palladio died before he could bring his theatre to completion, and the task of finishing the structure was assigned to Vincenzo Scamozzi. Scamozzi apparently revised Palladio's plans for the stage area, placing behind each

The stage of the Teatro Olimpico. The growing interest in Classical theatre was furthered by the discovery in 1414 of the Latin manuscript of Vitruvius' work on architecture, and its subsequent publication seventy years later, resulting in the construction of the Teatro Olimpico. Begun by Andrea Palladio in 1580, the theatre was completed by Vincenzo Scamozzi in 1584. The stage, slightly redesigned by Scamozzi, provided diminishing street perspectives behind the three archways at the back of stage and the two at the sides. (From Giovanni Montenari, *Del Teatro Olimpico*, Padua, 1749)

stage opening a perspective vista (behind the large center opening he placed three vistas) created out of lath and plaster. According to Scamozzi, these vistas represented the seven streets of Thebes, which was appropriate as the opening production, presented on March 3, 1585, was a presentation of *Oedipus the King*. The production was touted by the Academy as being a faithful re-creation of the great Greek masterpiece.

Impressive as the Teatro Olimpico was and is, it really stands alone as a kind of sport, dreamed up by academicians in an effort to re-create past glories. More important to the development of the modern theatre is the theatre at Sabionetta, designed by Scamozzi for Duke Vespasiano Gonzago of Mantua. This small theatre (it seated only about three hundred persons) opened in 1588 and represented for the first time a totality of theatrical design. The interior was still, in essence, the design proposed by Sebastiano Serlio (1475-1554) in the second book of his *Trattato di architettura* (1545), but the stage area was significantly modified by Scamozzi. There was no proscenium arch, and angle wings provided the settings. The seating was a semicircular horseshoe arrangement, facing a stage which contained only a single vista.

Nearly thirty years later, in 1618, the Teatro Farnese opened in Parma. Designed by Aleotti the Farrarese at the behest of the Prince of Ferrara, the

The steep auditorium of the Teatro Olimpico provided good sightlines because of its extreme rake and shallow, semielliptical shape. (Giovanni Montenari, *Del Teatro Olimpico,* Padua, 1749)

building also followed Serlio's plan in some ways: the seating was the same, but unlike the theatre at Sabionetta, this structure seated nearly thirty-five hundred people. This theatre also kept the open space between the audience and the stage, which could be used for seating more spectators, for dancing, or for creating a water area for boats to be floated during the spectaculars, just as had been done in the orchestras of the Roman theatres. It had, however, in addition to its traditional features, something special—a permanent proscenium arch and flat wings for scenic changes.

Exactly how the proscenium arch came about is still a matter of speculation. Some have determined that it developed as a structural rather than an artistic change—that is, a bearing arch was inserted at the audience edge of a stage area bounded by wings similar to the *parascenium* of the basic Roman stage, and this could very possibly account for what has been considered to be a purely artistic device. Another opinion is that, as the great Renaissance artists began more and more to create scenic designs for the stage, the architects began to think of the stage set in terms of a painting and determined to put a picture frame around it. A third, highly persuasive view, is that as perspective settings became more common the design artists demanded a proscenium arch, because it is only possible to work in perspective within (or behind) a frame.

While the Teatro Farnese represented the first real step toward a modern theatre, it should be noted that it was not a popular or commercial theatre open to the general public. It was, in fact, a court theatre with limited, semicircular seating and a traditional orchestra. The greatest impetus for modern theatre was not to be the Teatro Farnese, but the Italian public theatres that began to open up in Venice in the mid-sixteenth century. The San Cassiano was the first of the Venetian public opera houses, and it set a pattern for all those buildings which would follow. The auditorium was built in five levels, the first two of which were generally occupied by the rich nobility, with the top three taken over by the middle classes. The pit or ground floor was left open, without seats, for the lower classes. This pattern would be followed many times over, for many years. There are probably a number of significant theories that explain why court auditoriums were constructed in one way and the public theatres in another. However, the primary reason is likely the practical one—the court auditoriums were built to contain a small, select audience, and the public theatres were designed to admit as many paying patrons

In Italy the evolution of the picture stage and scene-changing devices was rapid and highly successful. After the prisms of the Greeks came angled wings, nestled in grooves, which slid on and off stage. This 1620 design by Joseph Furttenbach shows how well this device worked. (From Joseph Furttenbach's *Architectura Civilis*, Ulm, 1628)

as possible. Accommodating the paying public has been a major consideration in public theatre architecture from Greek times to the present.

STAGING AND SCENIC PRACTICE

Stage design and the mechanics of realizing that design onstage became increasingly complex throughout the Renaissance period. The sets that began as imitations of the illustrations in late fifteenth century editions of the plays of Terence, or that were based on the Medieval mansion settings, grew steadily richer, with more decorations, golden drop cloths, specially created tapestries, such architectural adjuncts as columns, and artistic additions such as statuary. In addition, the demand for spectacular staging, featuring scenes with sea monsters, floating clouds, flying angels, and other such effects, began greatly to increase the machinery necessary for production. These sets evidenced the competitive attitudes of both courts and artists; by striving to provide more lavish spectacles than their rivals, the designers carried ornamentation and striking effect to considerable heights.

The systematization and rapid exploitation of perspective drawing and painting in the early fifteenth century also revolutionized theatrical design. The basic principles of perspective had long been known, but until they were organized by Filippo Brunelleschi (c. 1377-1446) and popularized by Leon Battista Alberti (1404-72) in his *Della pittura* (1435), little theatrical use had been made of these principles. This early perspective was still somewhat impractical as a theatrical device, for it required everything to be laid out parallel to the basic plane of the stage picture. However, by the time of Leonardo da Vinci (1452-1519) space had been accurately perceived as spherical, and thus reasonably accurate perspective sets could at last be designed.

In 1508 Pellegrino da San Daniele designed the first known perspective setting for a production of Ariosto's *La cassaria* at Ferrara. The technique he used, putting real houses in front of a drop painted in perspective, was too unwieldy to have much success except as an artistic curiosity. It did, however, provide a new level of reality for theatrical production. With rare exceptions, ever since the days of ancient Greece, the primary critical and audience demand on theatre has been for ever greater reality. Thus Baldassare Peruzzi, designing a set featuring palaces, temples, loggias, and cornices, took great pains to point out that he had made them "appear to be what they represented."

When Sebastiano Serlio, who had been one of Peruzzi's pupils, published in 1545 the second book of his *Architettura*, he included the principles he had developed while designing a setting at Vicenza. Taking the position that plays would usually be done in already existing halls rather than in specially designed theatres, he force-fit the seating designed by Vitruvius into the standard rectangle of the great hall, building bleachers around an orchestra space which had no real function other than the seating of dignitaries. The front of the stage, where the actors performed, was flat, but the rear of the stage where all the scenery was to be placed was raked up to enhance the forced perspective and thereby help create an illusion of depth. This design began the use of the raked stage, which had substantial popularity for nearly two hundred years, and which in a minor way has lasted even into this century.

Serlio included in his book the three basic scenes from Vitruvius (comic, tragic, and pastoral) which he felt would meet the needs of any type of production. These settings, architectural in nature, were all achieved by using three sets of angle wings placed in front of a set of flat wings, and all of this backed by a drop painted in forced perspective. For the comic plays Serlio specified houses for citizens, including a brothel, an inn, and a church. The tragic setting was to include "stately" houses, chimneys, towers, pyramids, and obelisks. The satyric or pastoral scene featured trees, rocks, herbs, hills, flowers, and some country houses. Such sets were not designed to be changed during performance.

Serlio's basic sets raise the logical question that, since Serlio was not ignorant of the means to change scenery quickly and well, why did he insist on an unchangeable set? The answer has to be that his sets were created only for the legitimate drama which, because of the theoretical unity of place, required no changes. In this connection it must be remembered that while *formal* acceptance of the concept of that unity did not come until 1570, it had been practiced in legitimate drama for quite some time. On the other hand, this unity was not applied to the *intermezzi* and opera, and these two entertainment forms created a demand for more flexible arrangements than Serlio provided in his scenic prescriptions. Also, the legitimate drama was beginning to change, with both writers and designers showing ever more interest in theatrical realism, which also caused a growing interest in methods of scenic change.

In any case, the limitation of unchangeable sets had to be overcome, and again the scenic designers went for a solution to Vitruvius, and also to Julius Pollux, a Greek sophist and grammarian of the second century A.D. In this case, what they found were *periaktoi*, the revolving three-sided prisms with different scenic materials painted on each flat side. The earliest use of *periaktoi* in the Renaissance was by Aristotile da San Gallo in 1543, but they eventually received fairly wide usage, and some were even developed with as many as six sides.

Nicola Sabbattini (c. 1574-1654), in his *Manual for Constructing Theatrical Scenes and Machines* (1638), discusses three methods for changing scenes during the course of a show: *periaktoi*; placing new wings in front of those already onstage; and having differently painted canvas hung over wings already in place. None of these solutions was quite satisfactory to him. However, he also discusses (with diagrams) "How to Make Dolphins and Other Monsters Appear to Spout Water While Swimming," "How to Produce a Constantly Flowing River," "How to Divide the Sky into Sections," "How Gradually to Cover Part of the Sky with Clouds," "How to Make a Cloud Descend Perpendicularly with Persons on It," and even how to make the same cloud descend at an angle. He also discusses stage lighting, recommending oil lamps with strong wicks, and describes how to achieve color effects by using vessels containing colored water, backed by lamps and reflectors.

As long as playwrights wrote scenes depicting only outdoor areas, the angle-wing system remained dominant, and this meant difficulty in scene changing. It was not until Giovanni Aleotti put new principles of drawing perspective to work on flat wings, at Ferrara in 1606, that perspective sets could be done entirely with flat wings. A groove system was designed to facilitate changing these flats, and though large numbers of scene shifters were required to remove and replace the flats, scene shifts could be accomplished with some swiftness.

The first significant mechanical device for shifting flats was designed by Giacomo Torelli (1608-78) working at the Teatro Novissimo. This device, called the "chariot and pole," utilized grooves cut in the stage floor, through which protruded upright poles. These poles were mounted on "chariots" below the stage, which were in turn mounted on casters and tracks. Flats were attached to the poles and then, through a complex set of ropes and pulleys, the chariots moved the flats in and out from the wings.

Serlio's comic scene.

(Right) Serlio's tragic scene. (From his *Tratto su l'architettura scenica)*

(Right and below) Serlio's rustic or satiric scene.

A winter landscape designed by Burnacini. Such painted backgrounds are no longer on one cloth but two. (From Joseph Gregor, *Monumenta Scenica,* 1924)

Joseph Furttenbach the Elder (1591-1667), a German who spent ten years in Italy studying the mechanical marvels of Italian Renaissance theatre, wrote three works describing in detail most of the lighting practices of the time. He also describes a seating arrangement featuring parallel rows of seats rather than the elliptical arrangement favored by the scenic descendants of Vitruvius. Perhaps most important of all, he describes the use of the area at the back of the stage, behind the drop, which he points out can be used not only for interior scenes (which become more and more common) but also to produce a sea area to hold some of the mechanical marvels of which the Renaissance audiences were so fond.

The Renaissance theatrical designers, building on the Classical concepts in Vitruvius and Pollux, on the Medieval wonders produced by the masters of machine, and on the Renaissance developments in the graphic arts, produced an explosion in technical theatre that would remain unmatched until the eighteenth century.

SEBASTIANO SERLIO: Sebastiano Serlio (1475-1554), architect and architectural theorist, painter, and engraver, was born in Bologna. He became involved quite early in the rapidly developing school of perspective artists and achieved wide renown for his early accomplishments at Pesaro between the years 1509 and 1514. In 1514 he left Pesaro for Rome, where he remained until 1527, working with Baldassare Peruzzi and studying Classical art. After the sack of Rome in 1527 he fled to Venice, where he published in 1537 the fourth book of his *Trattato di architettura*. He had planned a total of seven books for this work. Book three, dealing with Roman antiquities, was published in 1540. Books one and two, covering geometry and perspective drawing, were published in 1545. Book five, on church architecture and decoration, was published in 1547. The seventh book was published in 1575 after his death, and book six and the first part of an originally unplanned book eight went unpublished.

The most important aspects of the *Architettura* were, of necessity, covered earlier in the text, but it remains to be pointed out that this work is of great importance because of its influence on Italian architecture and, subsequently, on French and English architecture. In part this is because Serlio combined architectural theory with a practical, handbook approach to the art, featuring illustrations of architectural form and decoration so that, theoretically, any master mason could follow the instructions and complete the desired building.

In 1541 Serlio went to France, where he worked for a short time with Primaticcio at Fontainebleau. After the death of Francis I he moved to Lyons, where he published his *Libro extra-ordinario delle porte.*

Serlio's theories came not only from his studies of Classical architectural forms, but also from extensive study of early sixteenth century buildings. After studying the architecture in Venice, he attempted to free the Italian architectural form from its dependence on Classical styles and give it movement (light and shadow) in the sense that this had been accomplished by Sansovino, Sanmicheli, and Palladio.

Serlio tended toward the Classical models. Deciding that the theatre building was an unlikely place to house an ephemeral art form, and that most plays would thus be given in the halls of already existing buildings, he concentrated on keeping the form defined by Vitruvius. Stage machinery discussed by Serlio in his six chapters on theatre include the machines from antiquity, such as the thunder machine and lightning maker. However, he added some innovations from the late Middle Ages and from his own time, including invisible wires for "flying" actors and objects, revolving globes, colored lights created by placing light sources behind bottles of colored liquids, cutout objects, and moving mechanical figures of men and animals.

What Serlio did was hardly daring or new—it all came from Vitruvius or from the Middle Ages or from the foremost theatrical practitioners of his own time—but such was his reputation that he influenced the course of theatre for many years after his death.

PALLADIO: Andrea di Pietro (1518-80), better known as Palladio, was born in Padua. As a boy, Palladio became an apprentice to a sculptor, and then at the age of sixteen he moved to Vicenza and enrolled in the guild of bricklayers and stonemasons. Subsequently he worked as a mason, making monuments and decorative sculpture. While engaged in this work, between 1530 and 1538, Palladio came to the attention of Count Giangiorgio Trissino, the author of *Sofonisba*, a noted humanist, poet, and scholar, whose Roman-style villa housed an academy for the study of mathematics, music, philosophy, and Classical literature.

Palladio became Trissino's protege, studying with him and traveling extensively throughout Italy, meeting the leading architects, artists, literary men, and heads of the prominent families of the aristocracy. It is thought that he met Serlio, and it is certain that he was familiar with book two of Serlio's *Architettura*. Serlio's theories were based on the work of Vitruvius, which Palladio had also studied. In addition to these two sources, the design of the Tournament Arena, located between St. Peter's and the Castel Sant'Angelo in Rome, built sometime around 1565, appears to have influenced Palladio's thinking about theatre architecture, especially the semicircular arrangement of seats at the far end of the arena and their relationship to the performance area.

In 1556 Palladio became a cofounder of the Olympic Academy of Vicenza, a literary society primarily interested in the study of antiquity and in the production of Classical and pseudo-Classical drama. Palladio was an ardent Classicist and by this time had built a number of magnificent palaces, villas, and churches, all based on his studies of Vitruvius, his observations and measurements of Roman antiquities, and his scrutiny of the works of such great Renaissance artists as Bramante, Raphael, and Peruzzi. In 1565 he designed and built the Compagnia della Calza theatre in Venice. The building burned down in 1630, but a description of the building (and of a performance by a *commedia* troupe) by a traveling Englishman, Thomas Coryat, condemned it as being a wooden structure that was "beggarly and base" compared to English playhouses.

When the Olympic Academy decided to build a theatre, Palladio was commissioned to design and construct it. The result was the Teatro Olimpico, which was modeled along the lines of an ancient Roman theatre. Erection of the theatre began in 1580 under the supervision of Palladio, who died later that year. It was completed by Vincenzo Scamozzi, a student of Palladio's and later his coworker. It was a wooden structure with a stage similar to the Roman stage, backed by a decorative wall. The wall was flanked on both ends by shorter walls, each having a central doorway. The center opening or "royal door" in the back wall was designed as a Roman triumphal arch. It has been conjectured that Palladio probably planned to close off the five doors with curtains, or by placing *periaktoi* behind them in the manner of Vitruvius. Scamozzi redesigned them, however, adding a vista behind each of the four smaller doors, and three vistas behind the large, central door. Perhaps Palladio's outstanding innovation in this theatre is the contiguity of the stage and auditorium, a feature that was to become characteristic of the later baroque theatres.

Thirteen rows of spectator seats rose in an elliptical pattern in the ampitheatre to provide excellent sightlines and great intimacy; the seating capacity was approximately three thousand. The permanent architectural set was done in the style of Vitruvius, with the decorative back wall covered with niches containing statues, and with bas-reliefs. The themes of the statuary and reliefs were drawn from Classical mythology, and included generals, heroes, and philosophers, the deeds of Hercules, trials of strength, abductions, and many combats with centaurs, lions, and bulls.

A remarkable likeness to an open-air Roman theatre was achieved by painting the ceiling to look like a blue sky with clouds. The auditorium was lighted by windows, and the stage was lighted by overhead openings. Performances were clearly expected to take place primarily during the daylight hours.

In 1570, after twenty years as Italy's foremost architect, Palladio published a summary of his Classical architectural studies in four volumes under the title, *I quattro libri dell'architettura*. He included illustrations to support the principles of Roman design. In the first volume he includes studies of materials, the Classical orders, and decorative ornaments; in the second are his designs for town and country houses, together with his Classical reconstructions. In the third volume he includes designs for bridges, town planning, and basilicas; and in the fourth volume he deals with the reconstruction of Roman temples.

Many of the features of modern-day theatrical architecture and scenic design are directly traceable to Palladio. In numerous metropolitan and provincial theatres of Europe and America, especially in the first part of the twentieth century, there was evidence of almost pure Renaissance style in such items as the traditional scenes, backdrops, street drops, wings, borders, tormentors, and grand draperies. Typical permanent sets in theatres up until the time of World War II included such items as the grand drawing room set, known as the "fancy interior" with its double entrance doors in the center backwall ("center door fancy"), the humble cottage kitchen, and the woodland set.

It is almost impossible to measure the contributions and influence (and in a sense limitations) on theatre by such people as Palladio. His influence was not limited to architectural design and construction alone, but included scenic design and production practices. This influence spread throughout Europe in his lifetime, and was continued thereafter by way of his student and successor, Vincenzo Scamozzi. The Burnacini family in the seventeenth century, followed by the Bibiena family in the eighteenth, were both influenced by Palladio. The works of the noted English architect and theatrical designer, Inigo Jones, reflect his detailed study of Palladio. In turn, this European influence, especially that of England, was transmitted to the early American theatre.

NICOLA SABBATTINI: Nicola Sabbattini (c. 1574-1654), architect, engineer, and scene painter, is perhaps the least known personally of all the great theatricians of the Italian Renaissance, in spite of the fact that his *Practica di fabricar scene e machine ne' teatri* (*Manual for Constructing Theatrical*

Scenes and Machines, 1638) is the standard work on the late sixteenth and early seventeenth century Italian theatre.

The most common assumption about his birth is that he was born in Pesaro, a hotbed of the perspective movement in art. Becoming an architect, he was taken into the service of the Duke of Urbino, where he was soon awarded the title of architect to the duke. In 1598 he designed and built a chapel in the Church of the Madonna di Servi at Pesaro, the *appartamento di madama* in the ducal palace at Pesaro, and the Palazina di Sant'Angelo at Vado. And buildings were not his only interest. In 1614, in collaboration with another architect, he designed and built the Canale della Foglia. Several more buildings at the court of Pesaro are generally attributed to Sabbattini, as is the Chiesa del Suffragio (1637).

Sabbattini was obviously a man thoroughly grounded in all the technical aspects—architectural and scenic—of the theatre, and he may well have been involved in the design and building of several. However, the only one that can be identified certainly is the Teatro del Sole, which was built at Pesaro in 1637. The premiere production in this theatre was the tragedy *L'Asmondo* (with *intermezzi*), and in his final chapter of the *Practica*, Sabbattini briefly mentions this specific production.

Sabbattini was not an inventor of theatrical machinery or devices, and he had nothing to do with developing new theories of perspective drawing. His *Practica* is, clearly, a handbook on Italian stage practice, describing the machines and devices that were currently in common use. Indeed, some of the machines he mentions were already nearly obsolete by the time the *Practica* was published. The book is based on a small conceit, supposedly being a set of directions for a young architect whose task is to turn a ducal hall into a theatre. Thus, the author had an excuse to take the reader backstage and explain in detail how the magnificent stage effects are achieved. Given his construction of the Teatro del Sole in the previous year, it is likely that the architect being addressed in the *Practica* is Sabbattini himself, and the information in the work represents what he learned from the experience.

In book one of the *Practica*, Sabbattini covers the basic problems of theatrical construction, the arrangement of the audience in relation to the stage, scene building, painting, and lighting. The primary emphasis in this book is on perspective drawing and, as might be expected from a ducal architect, how best to locate the duke's chair in relationship to the vanishing point. Sabbattini's materials are not at all new; he drew most of the material on perspective from his fellow Pesarian, Guido Ubaldus (1540-1601), who had published his own handbook on the subject in 1600.

Having set up his vanishing point (and the duke's chair), Sabbattini proceeds to give the reader detailed instructions on scene painting. This is especially complex in terms of the angle wings on which doors and windows must match the mathematics of the perspective, given the angle at which the wing is placed. Light and shadow, those two major requirements for achieving an illusion of depth, are also discussed at length.

Sabbattini goes on to discuss aspects of theatrical presentation that would seem essentially outside the purview of the architect, even in the early seventeenth century. He writes about the provision of seats for spectators, the duties of the ushers, and even how to draw the stage curtain to achieve the ultimate effect of "wonder and awe." Lighting problems, from methods for dimming stage lights to the danger of hot wax dripping from candles, finish book one.

Book two of the *Practica* is concerned with the *intermezzi*; most importantly with methods for achieving swift changes of scene. Interestingly, even though Aleotti had introduced the use of flat wings, probably by 1606 at Ferrara and certainly by 1618 at Parma, Sabbattini makes no mention of them. Instead, he presents methods for changing two-sided angle wings, *periaktoi*, and shutters. Also of historical interest, he describes methods for achieving the spectacular stage effects which had become so much a part of the *intermezzi*.

Sabbattini was clearly not important as a theatre architect, scenic designer, or generally as a theatrical innovator. However, his *Practica* is the most complete statement about the technical aspects of a theatre that was, in the next one hundred years, copied all over Europe.

GIACOMO TORELLI: Giacomo Torelli (1608-78), architect and scenic designer, was above all a practical man of the theatre who left behind him a legacy of theatrical innovation almost unmatched in the history of the art.

One of Torelli's primary accomplishments was his revolutionary method of handling side wings or flats. Because of difficulties with the relatively new art of scenic perspective, and the fact that it was quite difficult to work in depth on a flat side wing, most scenic designers stayed with the Serlian angle wings until late in the seventeenth century. However, the developing complexity of the drama and the expanding demand for spectacular staging made it necessary that a method be devised by which flat wings could be used to create perspective sets, and that machinery be developed so that these flat wings could be rapidly shifted during a production. Before Torelli there had been some use of flat wings, but while they could be changed faster and more easily than angle wings, they were still awkward to use. Essentially, they were placed in grooves on the floor and slid in and out by hand at the moment of change. This required numerous stagehands—at least one for each flat—to complete the change in an acceptably short time. The groove system was radically altered (except in England) by the development of the chariot and pole system. This method of scene changing may have been developed by Torelli, or it may have been the product of Guitti at the Teatro Farnese in 1628; but in any case Torelli must receive the major credit for perfecting the system. The basic elements of the chariot and pole were described earlier in the chapter, but its importance in changing theatrical practice in Italy, France, and Germany cannot be overstated.

Perhaps because of his development of this system for making rapid scene changes, or perhaps out of an aesthetic ideal that became possible only after the system had been perfected, Torelli began to include the scene change as part of the scenic structure. Instead of attempting to distract audience attention while making the change, or trying to mask it in some way, he made the changes in full audience view. And so subtly was this done, and so carefully were the sets designed to flow, one into the other, that audiences found them-

Giacomo Torelli's design for a musical play, *The Jealous Venus*, designed in 1643, featured twelve different settings. In this one three wings represent trees. The background is painted on two drop cloths, with the back cloth visible where the front cloth is cut away.

selves suddenly viewing new scenes without knowing exactly what had happened to the earlier ones—and all this without a break in the dramatic action.

Along with moving his scenery swiftly and delicately, Torelli also experimented with the use of cut-out flats for trees instead of the traditional painted ones. This allowed the audience to see through the trees, as they would in reality, following with their own eyes a rapidly diminishing woodland pathway. Also, being able to change sets with minimum manpower and maximum speed, Torelli was able to make use of more scenic pieces than were available to most designers, thereby creating more realistic (though more complex) sets.

The scenic wonders he created can best be described in the designer's own words, in this case the description that accompanies one of the engravings of his designs for *Les noces de Pélée et de Thétis:*

The Grotto of the Centaur Cheiron is wholly created out of stones and fearsome rocks; this is vaulted over with stones and gives an impression at once of beauty and horror. Above, an aperture is seen from which the Grotto receives its light, and through which can be seen a landscape with mountain paths which lead down to the entrance of the Grotto. Two doors of rustic architecture open out on each side. There can be seen many diverse tombs of a majestic type which enclose the remains of those heroes who were worthy to die disciples of so great a master. Beneath the high opening is another which reveals the furthest part of the dwelling. By ingenious use of perspective the background seems quite distant. There a more superb tomb than the others can be seen. At the incantation of the sorcerers, led by Cheiron, a chariot bearing Peleus rises with thunder and lightning. It rises into the air amidst flame and smoke, crossing the Grotto and leaving through the aperture. The smoke vanishes into the air and the flames recede into the background.

Perhaps Torelli's greatest contribution to world theatre is the way in which he popularized the Italian scenic methods throughout Europe. Having achieved fame in his native Italy, primarily at the Teatro Farnese and later at the Teatro Novissimo in Venice, which he built in 1640, he was eagerly sought out by the greatest courts of Europe. In fact, many of his greatest designs were accomplished at the court of Louis XIV in France, where he introduced the fashion for spectacle plays, refurbishing the backstage area of Molière's theatre, the Petit Bourbon, in order to create the spectacle of Corneille's *Andromède*.

Lastly, in spite of the fact that his rival Vigarani destroyed much of his work, Torelli managed to leave behind him an unusual number of engravings that were of great influence on the development of the baroque stage.

COSTUMES

The costumes of the *commedia* were reasonably standardized, though they differed slightly from troupe to troupe. Dealing as the troupes did with the same established characters, such standardized costumes were necessary for immediate audience identification of each character. Pantalone, the Venetian merchant, at first wore a long red cloak with a red cap and long Turkish-style slippers that curled up at the toes. Eventually the red cloak was changed to black, but the red cap and slippers were retained. The Dottore wore a black academic gown and black hat. The Capitano was somewhat less standardized, wearing the Italian ideal of Spanish military costume. Pedrolino, best known in his French identity as Pierrot, wore a loose white costume and pointed white hat. Arlecchino began in a patched, ragged costume, but the patches soon evolved into the diamond-shaped check design which is so familiar.

Perhaps the most distinctive aspect of *commedia* costume was the mask. These masks are often adduced by theatre historians as proof of the *commedia's* ancestry. The dark mask of Pantalone, with its great curved nose, white hair, and beard, strikes scholars as being descended from Dossennus of

Bernardo Buontalenti's costume designs for the *intermezzi* at the 1589 Medici Theatre Festival.

the Atellan farce. The dark mask of the Dottore, with its red cheeks and short beard, and the curved nose of Pulcinella seem to be descended from the Roman mimes. So, too, does the black half-mask of Arlecchino, which may very well have as its ancestor one of the black servant masks of the mimes. Pedrolino wore no mask, but his white-powdered face became standard for clowns. Among the women only Pasquella wore a full mask to indicate her traditional character as an ugly, evil old woman. Columbina wore a half-mask similar in nature to that of Arlecchino. The *innamorata* and *innamorato* were not masked and were dressed in rich (to the degree that the troupe could afford) contemporary clothes.

The costumes of the humanist drama, as long as it remained primarily the property of the court (of the wealthy nobility), were rich and highly decorative, as much a part of the setting as any piece of the scenery. There was some little effort to costume those plays dealing with Classical materials in terms of Renaissance concepts of Classical dress, but these attempts bore little real relationship to the costumes of antiquity and, again, were primarily decorative. In most plays the costume was contemporary. Because the players were often themselves rich dilettantes, costume had also the function of disguising the players from their friends in the audience.

ACTING

As was true in every other aspect of Italian Renaissance theatre, there was a distinct break between the acting traditions of the *commedia* and the humanist theatre. The *commedia* troupes, often organized along family lines, featured actors who were used to working together in a close-knit group. Actors specialized in certain roles, usually playing one character for the largest part of their acting career. The general nature of *commedia* performance has already been discussed. The exact nature of the *commedia* acting style, however, is not so easy to define. The illustrations that have come down to us indicate a generally broad, farcical style of playing, with exaggerated gesture and movement. Because so much of the performance depended on visual effect rather than dialogue, such exaggeration is understandable and to be expected.

The humanist theatre, on the other hand, was far less professional in its approach, and very likely far less broad in its style than *commedia*. The plays were usually more serious, and the dialogue, written by the greatest of Italian poets, was far more important than the physical action. Thus, vocal delivery was highly prized and physical movement probably corresponded closely to the graceful and highly stylized types of movement specified at the courts. In contrast to the *commedia* players, who were professionals, the performers of humanist drama were often talented amateurs drawn from the courts and academies. Indeed, such notables as Cesare Borgia are known to have played roles in court productions.

Neither group of actors, *commedia* or humanist, worked toward what we today would define as a realistic style of performance. Instead, acting was stylized in terms of the materials presented—broad and primarily physical for the simple, lusty *commedia*; restrained and primarily vocal for the literary humanist drama.

6

The Spanish Renaissance

6

The Spanish Renaissance

The greatest period in the history of Spanish theatre began in the late Middle Ages, grew in quantity and quality throughout the Renaissance, and by 1650 was essentially over. Following the death of Calderón in 1681, there were no more great Spanish playwrights, at least on an international scale, until this century.

THE MEDIEVAL BACKGROUND

The early Medieval history of Spain was marked by an almost unceasing series of small and occasionally large-scale wars, sometimes between the fiercely competitive Christian princedoms, but primarily between the Moors (the Moslem tribes who had invaded Spain from North Africa in 711) and the Christians. The Moors had been successful in their invasion, establishing an Emirate (later the Western Caliphate) at Córdoba and developing a rich and powerful civilization. However, the Moors were divided among themselves and they were never able to conquer the northern areas, where the kingdom of Asturias survived as the seed of Christian (or Spanish) reconquest. Leon, Castile, and Aragon grew steadily more powerful and, in spite of continuing petty warfare among themselves that was made worse by various temporary alliances with several Moorish lords, these Spanish Christian states eventually conquered the Moors. The crucial Spanish victory was at Navas de Tolosa in 1212, but the final Moorish stronghold at Granada did not fall until 1492.

The stage was set for the final victory of Christianity over the Moorish forces when, in 1469, King Ferdinand of Aragon married Queen Isabella of Castile. After their victory at Granada, some twenty-three years after their union, the two monarchs set out to establish an absolute form of government. They took away some of the power of the Church courts, they reduced the prerogatives of the Cortés (parliaments), and they weakened the power of the nobles. Following their final conquest of the Moors they decreed that all Jews must become Christians or leave Spain, and in 1502 they published a similar decree to the Mohammedans. They greatly increased the strength of the army and this, in conjunction with a strong central government, made Spain the most powerful nation in the Western world during the first half of the sixteenth century.

Battling the Moors.

The fall of Granada in 1492 may have been that year's most important event in terms of unifying Spain, but another event during that same year shaped the new country's course for the next two centuries—the discovery of the New World by Christopher Columbus. This provided the foundation for the Spanish Empire which, by the accession of Charles I (Emperor Charles V) in 1516, extended more than halfway around the world.

The reign of Charles' son, Philip II, saw Spain centralized (Portugal was annexed in 1580 only to become free again in 1640), the power of the Inquisition greatly increased, and a great inward flow of wealth from Spanish possessions in Central America and the Philippines. Spanish art and literature flourished to the degree that the late sixteenth and seventeenth centuries are today known as the Spanish "Golden Age."

THE SPANISH DRAMA
Sacred and Secular

The usual position taken by theatre historians is that the drama in Spain developed along the same lines as it did in other western European countries;

that is, out of the liturgy of the Medieval Church. While this may be an accurate assessment of the development of Spanish drama, it is a limited one that fails to take into account the fact that such drama never gained a major foothold in Castilian Spain. For approximately three hundred years, from about 1150 to 1450, there are no extant dramatic texts in Castilian Spanish, and there are only a few vague references to what may have been dramatic productions. In the eastern area of the Iberian Peninsula, specifically the Catalan-speaking areas, there was a flurry of dramatic production, but the mystery plays (*misteris*) of that area never developed the substantial form that they found in other areas of Europe, and seem to have had no effect at all on the development of an essentially Castilian drama during the Golden Age.

What this lack of a Medieval drama means is that when Spanish theatre exploded onto the Renaissance scene it was not an extension or re-creation of an earlier form. It was, in fact, the birth of Spanish drama. That it developed so swiftly, from its origins to the great plays of Lope de Vega and Calderón de la Barca, explains the rather motley character of this great period of Spanish theatre. Along the way a number of titles were coined as the equivalent of the English word "play," which refers to the whole dramatic genre and not merely to some specific aspect of it. Eventually the Spanish settled on the term *comedia* to refer to all plays, and the result was that, like the Italian *commedia*, the art remained more comic in nature than tragic.

The types of Spanish drama that developed were several: the *autos sacramentales*; the *autos*; the pastoral or eclogue; tragicomedy or "quasi-comedy"; tragedy; farce; interlude; and a reasonably serious though romantic semihistorical drama called *comedia de capa y espada* or "play of cloak and sword." Most of these are types already well known, but the *autos sacramentales* and the *autos* were especially native to Spain and may need some explanation. Basically the *autos sacramentales* were short, one-act religious dramas dealing in a highly formalized, serious, and erudite manner with religious concerns related to the Eucharist. In comparison, the *autos* were similar one-act religious plays, but they dealt with subjects other than the Eucharist. The "cloak and sword" plays, also uniquely Spanish, were merely romantic historical plays, usually dealing with conflicts between love and honor, and that featured disguisings and sword play as a method of furthering and resolving plots.

The most sophisticated dramatic text of the early Spanish Renaissance is usually referred to as *La Celestina* and was published sometime around 1500. It contains a prose first act (by an anonymous writer) that was found by a young law student named Fernando de Rojas (?-1541), who then went on to complete the play, eventually coming up with two separate versions of the work. The first version, a sixteen-act comedy which he entitled *La comedia de Calisto y Melibea* (*The Comedy of Calisto and Melibea*), is less successful than the second version of twenty-one acts, which he retitled *La tragicomedia de Calisto y Melibea* (*The Tragicomedy of Calisto and Melibea*). The play features, perhaps unintentionally, a hag named Celestina (a procuress, witch, and seller of cosmetics), who later generations found to be far more interesting than the young lovers. As a result of audience enthusiasm, the play has since been renamed after this highly popular character.

The frontispiece from the 1538 edition of *La Celestina*, Toledo.

La Celestina began a vogue for prose dramas (most of which were unperformable) which eventually reached their peak in *La Dorotea* (1632) by Lope de Vega. However, perhaps because the prose drama never seemed to settle on a form (comedy, tragedy, tragicomedy), as the retitling of Rojas' play indicates, it remained a minor aspect of Spanish theatre. However, at the same time that *La Celestina* was being produced and imitated, another type of drama was being created by Juan del Encina (Juan de la Enzina) for production in the "great halls" of private homes throughout Castile.

Juan del Encina, a lyric poet and accomplished musician, is considered by many scholars to be the founder of Spanish drama. He started by composing pairs of what are essentially one-act plays, designed for production during the Christmas and Easter season, in the palace of the Duke of Alba. The first play of each pair is a secular prologue to the second, which is a play in the tradition of the *Officium Pastorum*, the liturgical service for Christmas Eve. Because of his apparent fascination with the pastoral form even Encina's Christmas plays are filled with shepherds. There is a certain logic in having Christmas plays filled with shepherds, but *all* of Encina's characters seem to be shepherds, though they are recast as kings, queens, or biblical characters. In fact, because of Encina's preoccupation with the *Officium Pastorum*, for better or worse, it became the basis of Spanish classical drama.

Encina was too much of an artist to be content working only in the form he pioneered. He experimented with different types of characters, even turning the courtiers of his own time into shepherds. He went from pairs of short one-acts to long one-act plays that ran to more than two thousand lines. Eventually, as a result of a trip to Italy and the influence of the Italian theatre, he composed his greatest work, the *Ecloga de Plâcida y Vitoriano* (*Eclogue of Placida and Vitoriano*, 1513).

The earliest *auto* (or "act"), a small play designed for production at the Corpus Christi festival, is Gil Vicente's *Auto de San Martinho* (1504). This was not an *auto sacramentale* in the sense that it did not glorify the subject of transubstantiation, but it was religious in subject and tone and was produced for this specific holy celebration.

Gil Vicente (c. 1470-c. 1536) was not, in fact, a Spaniard, but a Portuguese residing at the Lisbon court. Some of his plays, however, were written entirely in Spanish; others were written in a mixture of Spanish and Portuguese. Vicente, like Encina, began with little religious dramas in the "faithful shepherd" tradition, but he went on to try almost every known dramatic form except pure tragedy. He completed, as far as we know, sixteen *autos*, three comedies, ten tragicomedies, and twelve farces. His best play is usually considered to be the *Tragicomedia de Don Duardos* (*Tragicomedy of Don Duardos*), a work which is based in part on one of the chivalric legends.

At the same time that Encina was working in Spain and Vicente in Portugal, a Spanish humanist and expatriot named Bartolome Torres Naharro (?-1524) was residing in Italy and writing plays in Spanish. These plays were far more sophisticated than anything else in Spanish at that time, probably because of Naharro's involvement with Italian drama. The first edition of his collected works, the *Propalladia* (*First Fruits of Pallas*), was published at Naples in 1517. In spite of its Italian publication, its influence on the Spanish stage can be seen by the fact that at least four subsequent editions were published in Seville (in 1520, 1526, 1533, and 1545) and one in Toledo (in 1535).

These miniatures from a Medieval Spanish manuscript (c. 1100) in the British Museum portray an entertainer and St. John the Evangelist.

The Golden Age

In Spanish, *Siglo de Oro* means literally "Golden Century" and its application is usually restricted to that great period of Spanish drama in the seventeenth century. The term *Golden Age* is somewhat broader and, in a sense, more appropriate in that it can also include the first great flowering of Spanish drama during the period of Lope de Rueda.

LOPE DE RUEDA: By the middle of the seventeenth century the *autos sacramentales* were being publicly presented in the streets of most cities in Spain. The performances moved from place to place, as specified by the municipal governments, at whose behest they were given and who paid the costs of production. It is in connection with his company's production of such an *auto*, in Benevento in 1554, that we first meet Lope de Rueda (c. 1510-65), called by many the father of Spanish drama.

Lope de Rueda is the first *autor de comedias* (head of an acting troupe) of whom we have any knowledge, and his influence on the course of Spanish theatre was great indeed. Lope de Vega, probably Rueda's greatest successor, often mentions Rueda, pointing out that he was the first to put the *comedia*, as it later came to be known, on the public stage. And the term *autor* is doubly applicable to Rueda inasmuch as he was also an author of dramatic works, writing short farces and comedies for his company to perform in the city streets and town squares as they traveled about the countryside.

Little is known about Rueda's early life. He was born in Seville, and as a young man he was apparently apprenticed as a goldsmith. It is not until the 1554 production of the *auto* at Benevento (in honor of Philip II, who was passing through the town enroute to England), however, that we begin to find documented information regarding his life and art. His next documented appearance was at Segovia, where his troupe performed "a small *comedia*" as part of the dedication ceremonies for that city's new cathedral. During the following year his troupe performed two *autos* (*El hijo prodigo* and *Navalcarmelo*) at his home town of Seville. The contract for these productions still exists. In it Juan de Coronado, the supervisor of rents and properties for the city, agrees to pay to Lope de Rueda, "residing in this city, forty ducats on account of seventy ducats in payment for two representations, to be given on two wagons, with certain figures, on Corpus Christi . . . with all the costumes of silk and other things that may be necessary." Attached to the contract is a receipt, signed by Rueda, acknowledging receipt of the forty ducats.

By 1561 the court had moved from Valladolid to Madrid, and it is there that we next meet Rueda, married now to a woman from Valencia. Apparently things failed to go well professionally in the new capital, for when he departed the city of Valencia he left behind a portion of his company wardrobe as security for a debt. By 1564 he had returned to his home in Seville, for it was there that Juana Luisa, "daughter of Lope de Rueda and his wife, Rafaela Anxela" was baptized.

Perhaps the most interesting document we have regarding Rueda, certainly the one that best displays some aspects of his early theatrical career, and in a sense the careers of all entertainers of that time, is the court record of

A sketch of a production similar to Rueda's "Olives."

a 1554 lawsuit brought by Lope de Rueda and Mariana de Rueda, apparently his first wife before Rafaela, against Juan de la Cerda, heir of Don Gaston de la Cerda, Duke of Medinaceli, for services rendered by Mariana to Don Gaston. It seems that in 1546 two women, entertainers who earned their living by singing and dancing, arrived from Aragon and put on a public performance which Don Gaston attended. The Duke was so taken by one of these women, Mariana, that he took her into his service where, we are told, she took extreme solicitude in amusing him. She spent six years in the Duke's service, "dedicating herself exclusively to furnishing him with recreation, singing and dancing before him whenever he desired and giving him always great pleasure and contentment." The old Duke admitted her to his chamber, lavishing gold and silver on her, even taking her along on his hunting trips, for which reason she had her hair cut short and took to wearing male attire. Eventually the Duke died, still owing Mariana a substantial amount of money.

Mariana had entered the Duke's service in 1546 and spent six years with him. Testimony at the trial indicates that in 1554 she had already been married to Rueda for two years, so they must have married soon after the Duke's death. What eventually happened to Mariana is unknown, but Rueda married Rafaela in 1563.

In any case, testimony at the trial gives us a brief but fascinating glimpse of Rueda's troupe at that time. The first witness was Pedro de Montiel, a "silk spinner and a member of the company of Rueda." A later witness testified that "whenever Rueda presents a play, he calls him [the silk spinner] and pays him well for playing the *biguela* in the comedy." This indicates that the majority of actors in the troupes at this time were local performers who were hired temporarily to play specific roles. A musician and a dancer also testified, the latter pointing out that he was not a member of Rueda's troupe because he (the dancer) was married, implying that the roving profession of player was not quite legitimate for a married man.

In 1561 Rueda presented an *auto* on Corpus Christi Day in Toledo, and in October of that same year he was paid one hundred reals for two *comedias* acted at the request of Queen Doña Isabel de la Paz. Rueda's troupe had

A painting by Goya of a scene from *The Betwitched,* by Antonio de Zamora. The sun was setting on the Golden Age when the plays of Zamora were produced at Buen Retiro under Philip V.

arrived at the top of the profession. On March 21, 1565, he died at Cordoba. Rueda's speciality was, along with the *auto* which all traveling companies presented, the *entremés* or interlude. This was a one-act farce in prose, originally designed for presentation between the acts of a *comedia*. When the bookseller and publisher Timoneda arranged Rueda's interludes for publication he called them *pasos* or "steps." Perhaps the finest of these interludes is Rueda's *Las aceitunas* (*The Olives*), in which a peasant couple who have just planted a small olive tree exalt about how much money they can make by selling the fruit when it matures. They soon project this tree into an orchard and themselves into an olive-selling empire, whereupon they begin arguing bitterly over how they will spend the fortune this will bring.

Rueda wrote, as well as *autos* and interludes, prose pastorals and adaptations of Italian *commedia* scenarios. In every way he was truly Spain's first great theatre professional.

In the closing years of the sixteenth century, following the contributions of Rueda, a major humanistic theatre developed in Seville. In 1554 the city corporation began this movement by taking over from the guilds the costs of producing the Corpus Christi Day plays. In that same year, probably not by accident, we find recorded the first reference to the presentation of a religious play by a professional acting company, appropriately enough the company of Lope de Rueda. The growth of the city's reputation for producing drama spurred the writing of plays. Juan de Mal Lara (1524-71) was said to have composed a thousand tragedies, none of which survived. Juan de la Cueva (1560-1610), though seemingly less productive in total output, left fourteen comedies and tragedies that are still extant.

In 1565 the first public theatres—*corrales* or "yards" —were opened in Madrid. The fact of a rapidly increasing body of national drama, plus these new public facilities for performance, made the development of professional companies inevitable.

LOPE DE VEGA: Lope (Felix) de Vega (Carpio) was born on November 25, 1562, in Madrid, and he died in the same city on August 26, 1635. Born into a poor but noble family, by today's standards his life would seem to be exciting and eventful. By the standards of the day, however, his life was, for the most part, typical. Spain was still at the peak of her glory. Gold was pouring in from the New World; new territories were being conquered around the globe; and after defeating the Turks at the battle of Lepanto, Spain took control of the Mediterranean Sea, thereby becoming the most powerful nation in western Europe. It was an adventurous age in which Spanish youth from all walks of life were seeking their fame and fortune in all corners of what seemed then to be an exclusively Spanish world.

So many legends have grown up about Lope de Vega that it is difficult to separate truth from fiction. One especially persistent legend is that he was a child prodigy. At five years of age he supposedly had mastered Latin, and was writing verse; at ten he had written his first play; at fourteen he was sent to the Imperial College in Madrid. At college he excelled in the arts; that is literature, ethics, fencing, dancing, and music, finding the more practical subjects such as mathematics "unsuited to his humor." He left school for a short time, serving in the army during one of the perennial wars with Portugal. He apparently soon tired of war and, after securing the patronage of Geronimo Manrique, Bishop of Avila, he once again entered school, this time the University of Alcalá. He received his bachelor's degree and would have taken his vows for the priesthood except for "Dorothea," the first in a splendidly long line of love affairs. Leaving school and all that it represented behind, he entered into the public life of Madrid, eventually marrying the daughter of a gentleman of the court. Remarks made about her fidelity led Lope into a duel, then prison for a short time, and finally exile in Valencia. It was in this exile that Lope began to cultivate the talent for playwriting that would soon gain him national acclaim.

Second only to Madrid, Valencia was the literary capital of Spain, and it was just beginning to blossom as a theatrical center. In the two years he spent there, Lope learned much from the famous Valencian poets, Gaspar de Aguilar and Guillen de Castro; he repaid this debt by writing a series of poetic dramas that turned the infant Spanish theatre into a mature art form.

Breaking his exile, Lope returned to Madrid with his wife. In less than a year after their return she died of "complications," one of which might have been the knowledge that her husband was having another of his seemingly endless affairs. Following his wife's death, Lope made public his love for another woman, and she in turn made public her rejection of his suit. The year was 1588, and in part out of embarrassment over public reaction to his rejection, Lope decided to give up public life. Of course, this was that fateful year when every Spaniard who could carry a musket was hurrying to join the Invincible Armada for the glorious invasion (and subsequent pillaging) of England. Lope and a friend sailed on the *San Juan*, one of the few ships that would make it back to Spain after the disaster.

Lope de Vega was highly disliked by many contemporary poets. Luis de Gongora y Argote, a rather pedantic poet who insisted that all verse should be very carefully worked out, leveled many attacks against Lope's "hasty written" and admittedly careless style. Cervantes, the only writer of the day who approached Lope's literary stature, was unable to compete with the sheer bulk turned by Lope's pen, and in indignant retaliation referred to his rival as a "monster of nature."

So, just how influential was Lope de Vega in light of this criticism? The answer to that question must be that he was very influential indeed, perhaps not so much on future generations of writers as he was on the playwrights and the theatre of his own time. When Lope began writing, Madrid had only two companies of strolling players in the city; at the time of his death there were forty companies, with over one thousand actors.

Vega was in no major way an experimenter. He gave the people what they wanted, when they wanted it, and as much of it as he could write. To do this was not as difficult as it sounds, for the majority of his plays turned on two themes: the point of honor, and who will bed the lady. However, the "cloak and sword" play which he pioneered was to become the mainstay of the Spanish stage for many years, even after Lope's death—and he turned out approximately eighteen hundred of them during his career. In the case of any playwright who has written so much, it is to be expected that many of his plays will be duplications of previous work. But, duplication or not, the public loved his work and he was acclaimed, from peasant to king, as the greatest playwright not only in Spain, but in the whole world.

As far as Lope was concerned, the most important element in a play was the plot, and he was a master of plot-building. At performances he would come before the audience and warn them to pay close attention to what was being said, for if they missed even one word, they could miss the entire plot of his play. But, being a master theatrical craftsman, there was little chance of that happening, for he well knew how to keep his audience's attention, pointing out that a playwright must "keep the explanation of the story doubtful till the last scene; for, as soon as the public know how it will end, they turn their faces to the door, and their backs to the stage."

Character development was important to Lope only in so far as it aided the plot. In the rare case where a good person turns out to be bad, then that character is developed in such a way that the audience might reasonably expect the tranformation that is coming; otherwise, good characters in Lope's play display only good qualities, and bad characters only bad ones. There is little room for character study in his work, and if there was any chance that it might interfere with the plot, he did not want it. Lope was certainly not a stupid man, or an insensitive one; he understood the complexities of human behavior as well as any playwright, but he chose not to bother with them. Instead he explored the manners and morals of the day.

Lope de Vega paid as little heed to scenery as he did to character—perhaps even less. He did not like the influence the Italians were having on the

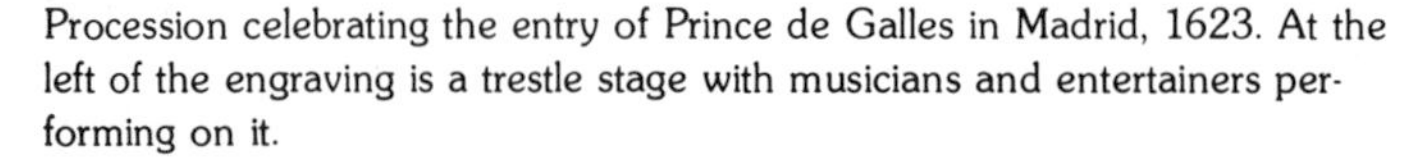
Procession celebrating the entry of Prince de Galles in Madrid, 1623. At the left of the engraving is a trestle stage with musicians and entertainers performing on it.

Spanish stage, cluttering it with unnecessary scenery and technical marvels. He believed that what the audience saw and felt should be painted for them by the playwright and not by some carpenter or graphic artist.

Vega did much to change the character of the Spanish theatre, with many of his techniques and innovations becoming the standard according to which future plays were to be written. The most important of these was the concept of the "cloak and sword" play. He also introduced the comic subplot, a concept that we are more familiar with by way of Shakespeare. These comic subplots added humor to otherwise deep and tragic happenings. He reintroduced the three-act division to his plays, but he claimed that it was his own idea. The purpose of this was more practical than artistic in that it provided a break in the action of the play which allowed both the audience and the actor to relax. He wrote most of his plays using the traditional ballad measure for his verse. However, his total works contain every meter of which the Spanish language is capable.

Lope has been called a *commedia dell'arte* unto himself, and the *commedia* technique of improvisation is perhaps the reason he was able to write so many plays. His format is basically that of the *commedia*; that is, stock characters, simple plots, and stories that deal with popular and familiar ideas.

Lope was not trying to revolutionize the theatre or promote any widespread changes. He apparently wrote for only one reason—to make money. His primary concern was to give the theatre-going public what they wanted, and he obviously did this very well indeed. The nobility showered him with favors, and admiring crowds followed him everywhere he went. Towards the end of his life, after he finally took his vows for the priesthood, the Pope awarded him the Cross of Malta and the degree, Doctor of Theology.

Lope de Vega was neither innovator nor imitator. He merely wrote the way the public wanted, and he threw all rules out of the window. "When I am going to write a play I lock up all precepts, and cast Terence and Plautus out of my study, lest they should cry out against me, as truth is wont to do even from such dumb volumes; for I write according to the art invented by those who sought the applause of the multitude, whom it is but just to humor in their folly, since it is they who pay for it."

How great a playwright was Lope de Vega? Comments from his own time testify that he was very great indeed. In 1647 the Inquisition went to great lengths to suppress a credo which began, "I believe in Lope de Vega the Almighty, the poet of heaven and earth." Mothers named their children after him; farmers named cantaloupe after him; more than one cigar carried his name. He was a sixteenth century phenomenon with more than twenty-two hundred theatrical works to his name. And yet, it is only in recent times that Vega has been widely recognized outside his own country. There are several reasons for this enduring lack of recognition. First, much of his work was unsigned and unpublished. Also, many of his plays were pirated, published under another title and crediting another author, so that only after extensive analysis of meter and content could Lope's authorship be determined. Also, in the reverse, many plays that he did not write were presented under his name in order to attract an audience. What it all finally amounts to is that nobody is totally sure what Lope de Vega did or did not write. Norris Houghton probably solved the whole problem when he said, "One reason, I suspect, why Lope de Vega is no more widely known than he is in our country is that his output was so tremendous. One does not know where to start, so one simply avoids him."

TIRSO DE MOLINA: Probably the greatest of Lope de Vega's immediate successors was a Spanish ecclesiastic named Gabriel Téllez (c. 1571-1648). Probably because he was a Mercenarian friar, Fray Téllez did his secular writing under the pseudonym of Tirso de Molina. Under this byline he wrote both novels and plays, many of which have since been lost. By his own testimony, he wrote four hundred plays, of which more than eighty are extant. Of these many are *autos sacramentales* and biblical plays that exemplify the sin of despair and the wonder of divine grace.

Much of the technique in Tirso's plays, especially the secular works, seems to have been learned from Lope de Vega, whom Fray Téllez much admired, but this is modified by his own interests in psychology and philosophy. His plays indicate an almost romantic involvement in the pastoral myth, demonstrating the superiority of innocent country morality over the immoral corruption of city life, which takes its cues from social institutions rather than from the natural world created by God. Tirso was especially adept at investigating the internal spiritual and psychological aspects of his characters—especially his women. Basically a misogynist, Tirso nevertheless managed in his comedies to create the most memorable female characters of his time, and in *La prudencia en la mujer* (*Prudence in a Woman*, c. 1622), a title which he undoubtedly intended to be taken as an hilarious paradox, he managed to create the most interesting woman in all early Spanish drama—the heroic Queen Maria.

By nearly general consensus Tirso's best play, and certainly his most famous, is *El burlador de Sevilla y convidado de piedra* (*The Deceiver of Seville and the Stone Guest*, written sometime before 1630). This is the first drama to deal with the Don Juan myth, that has since been treated by such major play-

This old Spanish print shows a scene within one of the theatres.

wrights as Moliére and Shaw. In Molina's version Don Juan seduces enormous numbers of women, delighting the hearts of liberal thinkers everywhere by refusing to discriminate between shepherdesses and the noble ladies of the court. He is at last dragged down to hell by the "stone guest," God's representative and the statue of a man Don Juan has killed, not because of his murders or seductions but because he has taken the name of the Lord in vain. Tirso also dealt with the exigencies of grace and damnation in *El condenado por desconfiado* (*Damned for Lack of Trust*, c. 1620). In this play a religious hermit named Paulo commits theological impiety by asking of God that He reveal to the hermit what his fate will be in the afterlife. The Devil, in his role of deceiver, then appears disguised as an angel and tells Paulo that his fate will be the same as that of Enrico, an infamous though colorful criminal. Crushed by this revelation, Paulo himself becomes a criminal, reasoning that if he is going to be damned anyway he might as well savor the earthly rewards of sin. Enrico, on the other hand, at the behest of his beloved father, repents. Thus, ironically, Enrico receives God's grace and is saved, while Paulo, who does not repent because of his mistaken despair, is damned.

For a contemporary audience, perhaps the most exciting aspect of Tirso de Molina's plays is his unending sense of social injustice. In *The Deceiver of Seville*, for example, Don Juan is able to get away with his outrageous and illegal behavior through the intercession of his noble family, who are themselves ministers of justice and favorites at the royal court. *Prudence in a Woman* carries this one step further in attacking the whole concept of Machiavellian statecraft in which concepts of good and evil are subordinated to the interests of the ruler or ruling group.

Other major plays by this playwright-friar are *Marta la piadosa* (*Pious Martha*, c. 1615), and *El vergon zoso en palacio* (*A Bashful Man at Court*, c. 1611), both delightful comedies.

Juan Ruiz Alarcón (c. 1581-1639), born in the Spanish colony in Mexico, wrote comedies of manners which strongly influenced the French classical comedy. In his plays the comedy grows out of the extremes created by some excessive aspect of character, a technique that later would be perfected by Molière, and out of the plots of a sly servant, which would reach its peak of development in France in the character of Figaro as created by Beaumarchais.

Guillén de Castro (1569-1631), a playwright from Valencia and the finest of a whole group of Classically oriented dramatists working in that city, had an equivalent effect on French classical tragedy. His most important work, *Las mocedads del Cid* (*The Youthful Exploits of The Cid*, published in 1621) became the source for Corneille's *Le Cid* (1637).

MIGUEL DE CERVANTES: Miguel de Cervantes (Saavedra, 1547-1616), whose novel *Don Quixote* has established him as one of the great writers of the world, was also a successful poet and playwright. However, in his plays especially he seems to be outside the mainstream of Spanish literary development during the Renaissance. Born a generation before Lope de Vega, the writer who established the *comedia* of the Renaissance, Cervantes owed his intellectual and artistic development more to the humanistic impulses of Erasmus than to the reaffirmation of Catholic orthodoxy that was imposed on Spanish art following the Council of Trent (1545-64).

Cervantes was born in Alcalá de Henares, where he received an early academic and philosophical grounding in the Academy of Lopez de Hoyos, a renowned humanist. He wrote a few rather undistinguished poems and then seemingly gave up the arts, going to Italy in the service of a cardinal. The following year, apparently dissatisfied with religious work, he enlisted in the army in time to see combat in the battle of Lepanto (1571). Here he received a serious wound that permanently maimed his left hand, but he remained in the army and, after several months in a hospital, he participated in military expeditions to Corfu and Tunis. In 1575, while on a ship returning to Spain, he was taken prisoner by the Barbary pirates and imprisoned in Algiers, where he was held for five years. During this period his conduct apparently was exemplary of militarism and honor—he never gave in to his captors and was involved in several escape attempts. Finally he was ransomed by a religious order dedicated to freeing Spanish prisoners and was returned to Spain.

His life after returning to Spain was marred by one disaster after another, both economic and civil. Without funds he began writing plays, but with little success, and this early period is distinguished only by *El cerco de Numancia* (*The Siege of Numantia*, 1580-90). In 1584 he married, and in 1585 published the pastoral romance *La Galatea*, a work that failed to win him critical acclaim but that began his flirtation with the Medieval romance genre that would one day be so integral a part of *Don Quixote*. As a result of his literary efforts and, probably more importantly, his military record, he was given a government post as purveyor of provisions to the Invincible Armada. However, even this was a mixed blessing, and because of irregularities in his accounts he was twice sent to jail, in 1597 and 1602. Moving to Valladolid in 1603, Cervantes was imprisoned once more, this time for possible complicity in a murder committed in front of his house.

Following his release from prison, Cervantes began to devote himself totally to his art, publishing works in amazingly rapid succession: *Don Quixote* (Part I, 1605; Part II, 1615); *Novelas ejemplares* (*Exemplary Stories*, 1613); *Viaje del Parnaso* (*Journey to Parnassus*, 1614); *Ocho Comedias y ocho entremeses* (*Eight Plays and Eight Interludes*, 1615); and *Persiles and Sigismunda* (published posthumously in 1617).

While Cervantes' greatest contribution to the literature of his time —indeed, of all time—was *Don Quixote*, his dramatic efforts were also important, and the most important of these were the *entreméses* or interludes. Writing primarily in prose, clearly his best medium, Cervantes used this essentially farcical form to consider some of the most important and sensitive issues of the time. He savagely attacked racism in *El retablo de las marvillas* (*The Wonder Show*), using an "Emperor's New Clothes" motif to illustrate the stupidity of the crusade against the Jews. In *El juez de los divorcios* (*The Divorce-Court Judge*) he considered what might happen if such a court were allowed to operate in Spain. This was an extremely touchy issue and even though the conclusion of the play accepts the status quo, pointing out that "the worst reconciliation is better than the best divorce," the play's enumeration of the many miseries of marriage was courageous indeed.

All of Cervantes' interludes grew out of the author's deep sensitivity to the human condition. Greed and pomposity, inhumanity and sham are all savagely dealt with, but that which is noble in the human spirit is admired and nurtured. Certainly no dramatist before or since has worked better in this form.

CALDERÓN DE LA BARCA: Pedro Calderón de la Barca (1600-81) was the last, and in the opinion of some, the greatest of the Spanish Golden Age playwrights. His output was indeed prodigious, though after Lope de Vega's amazing creativity, Calderón's over two hundred full-length plays, seventy plus *autos*, and numerous incidental plays (such as mythological drama, musicals, and librettos) seem almost painfully few.

Calderón was born in Madrid, the son of Don Diego, Secretary of the Council of the Royal Treasury, a position every bit as important and powerful as it sounds. Because of Don Diego's court appointment, the family moved to Valladolid and then back to Madrid when it became the permanent capital. In 1608 young Calderón was enrolled for his preparatory studies in a Jesuit college and, at the age of fourteen, showing great academic potential, he was en-

Scenic design for a Calderón production at Buen Retiro. The wings, sky borders, and backdrop are not disguised.

rolled at the University of Alcalá, where he studied rhetoric and logic. For six years Calderón pursued his studies, dividing his academic time between Alcalá and Salamanca, but continuing to maintain his residence in Madrid.

Exactly when Calderón's poetic activity began is uncertain, though it probably began early because the composition of poems was not only a required exercise of the time, it was also a pastime in which all well-educated young Spaniards were expected to indulge. However, by 1620 he had achieved real poetic proficiency. Entering a poetry contest held in honor of San Isidro he received excellent comment on his work from a particularly appropriate judge—Lope de Vega.

Just as we do not know when he began writing poetry, neither do we know when he began composing plays. Perhaps immediately following the poetry contest and the kind words of Lope de Vega; certainly such timing seems appropriate, for in 1623 he virtually exploded onto the scene as one of Spain's finest and most prolific playwrights. This early period of dramatic production, that began with the performance of three plays in his first year (*Amor, honor y poder—Love, Honor, and Power; The Tangled Forest;* and *Judas Maccabeus*), ended in 1637 with two volumes of his plays being edited and published by his brother José. He had, in this fourteen-year period, written sixty-six plays. Following the death of Lope de Vega in 1635, Calderón became director of court productions and in 1637 was made Knight of Santiago following his production of his own musical drama, *El mayor encanto, amor* (*Love, the Great Enchanter*), as the inaugural production at the palace in Buen Retiro.

From this peak of success, Calderón's fortunes dipped sharply. In 1638-39 the court interest in drama waned, and perhaps as a result Calderón joined the army in 1640, being sent to Catalonia to put down an insurrection. Two years later he was discharged due to illness. The closing of the public theatres drove him into service with the Duke of Alba, where he remained from 1646 to 1650. In that brief period his two brothers were killed and his mistress died, leaving him with a young son. Resigning from the Duke's service, Calderón took Holy Orders and the following year was ordained a priest. He continued his dramatic writing—by 1653 he had completed thirty-three more plays and over twenty *autos*—even after being appointed chaplain in Toledo, and in 1663 the king reappointed him to his former post. He remained at the court until his death in 1681, writing *autos.*

The subjects and styles of Calderón's plays are difficult ones with which to deal. Given only the amount of his production, it can be seen that his subjects are numerous. He was born at the peak of Spain's grandeur, but by the time he reached young manhood the nation had begun an economic and cultural degeneration from which it did not recover. As a result, his plays reflect a dying society desperately trying to maintain the status quo. Past glories are unearthed to prop up the national ego, and chivalric attitudes toward love, honor, and duty are flaunted as talismans in the face of disaster.

Structurally his late works are the most interesting. The early years had been passed—brilliantly, to be sure—in servitude to the public theatre. However, when released unwillingly from that bondage, Calderón was able to give free rein to his love for symbolic expression, and the Spanish *auto*, that compact, imagistic, symbolic drama, provided him with a perfect form.

The best of Calderón's secular plays is generally considered to be *La vida es sueño* (*Life is a Dream*, c. 1636), a romantic allegory that probes predestination, man's ability to overcome fate through the exercise of his will, and the duties of a true king. When a son, Segismundo, is born to King Basilio of Poland, all the portents of nature indicate that he will be a violent and bloody king. Therefore, King Basilio has his infant son imprisoned and brought up in a wilderness tower. Later, before crowning his nephew as king, Basilio decides to test the portents about Segismundo, the true heir. The young man is given a sleeping potion, brought into the palace, and placed on the throne. Perhaps because the portents truly revealed his character, or perhaps because of his years of imprisonment, Segismundo is every bit as bloody as foretold. Again he is drugged and this time sent back to his prison tower, where he is told that the memories of being a king are merely a dream. Finally, rebel soldiers liberate Segismundo from his prison and proclaim him the true king. This time, upon ascending the throne, he acts justly and well, as a king should, because if this too is a dream he wants to act in a way that will not shatter the illusion.

Regarding style, the most general thing that can be said of Calderón is that he was a master rhetorician, reflecting his early studies. His plays are full of speeches that are models of rhetorical construction, piling seemingly disparate image upon image and then uniting and resolving them in a few concluding lines. His most famous *auto*, *El gran teatro del mundo* (*The Great World Theatre*, 1649) is probably the finest example of this genre.

Calderón was complemented in his own time by two fine playwrights, Francisco de Rojas Zorrilla (1607-48) and Agustin Moreto (1618-69). However, no writer of real merit came along to succeed him. Spain had already deteriorated politically and economically, and after Calderón the Golden Age of drama came to an end.

THE CORRALES

In 1565 the first truly Spanish public theatres—the *corrales* or "yards"—began to develop. These temporary theatres greatly resembled the theatres in the English inn-yards, and like the English inn-yards they varied slightly from *corrale* to *corrale*. Essentially, however, the similarities that they had in common were much greater than their differences. They all had basically the same shape, being established in rectangular or square courtyards. The temporary stage was set up at one end (or on one side) of the courtyard, and thus they all had, on at least three sides, windows from which patrons could witness the play. In addition, there was always standing space in the unroofed courtyard and, in some cases, benches were set up close to the stage so that the audience in the yard, or at least some portion of it, could also sit.

The popularity of these temporary theatres indicated the need for permanent theatres, and when these were built they tended to follow the earlier, successful pattern. That is, the theatre building surrounded a square or rectangular courtyard, with the exception of the Corral de Monteria, which according to the 1625 contract was oval in shape. Generally speaking the central yard remained unroofed, as it had been for the temporary theatres, but

The entrance to the *cazuela*, the only theatre viewing room where women could be seated. Men were not allowed. (From an old print)

as early as the seventeenth century some theatres were constructed with roofed yards. Windows were placed just beneath the eaves to let in the necessary light. As in the English theatres, the yard was usually occupied by standing patrons, but there was, for men, a roofed platform (*gradas*) with benches along the side walls, and close to the stage benches (*luneta*) were set up in curved rows.

At the rear of the yard (*patio*), opposite the stage, a tavern (*alojería*) usually was located on the ground floor, and above it was a gallery reserved for ladies (*cazuela* or *corredor de las mugeres*). Above the women's gallery was yet another gallery reserved, in most cases, for the local dignitaries. The side walls of the yard were divided into galleries or boxes, with windows looking onto the yard and stage. These windows were usually covered with wrought iron grilles.

One of the most famous, and typical, of the *corrales* was the Corral del Príncipe in Madrid. Built in 1582 on the Calle del Príncipe, and modeled on the earlier Corral de la Cruz, the expense book for this theatre provides an accurate record of what was done and what the finished theatre was like. In his *Tratado historico*, Casiano Pellicer traces the progress of the building: a platform or stage was built, with a greenroom; raised and roofed seats for the men were placed about the perimeter of the yard, with ninety-five portable benches; a sequestered gallery was provided for the women; the building also had stalls, windows with iron grilles, and passageways. The yard was paved and an awning was stretched over it to provide protection from the sun, but not from rain. Four stairways were built. One led to the women's gallery, and was provided with a brick and plaster balustrade, wooden steps, and partitions, so that women who went up the stairway could not communicate with the men. Adjoining the theatre was the house of Doña Juana Gonzalez Carpio, who was paid one hundred ducats annually for allowing a passage to be built through her house as a woman's entrance to the theatre. The other three stairways ascended to the galleries where the men sat, and to the greenroom. There was also a stall or box in the *corral* in which the women could find seats before a window which looked upon the stage.

THEATRE MANAGEMENT

After the early seventeenth century the court began presenting for its restricted audience some of the finest Spanish drama. However, the public theatres began and long remained under the control of the brotherhoods or confraternities (*cofradias*) which had presented the religious drama of the Middle Ages. In many ways the theatrical organization of Madrid, which became the Spanish capital in 1560, is typical of theatrical production. In 1565 the Cofradia de la Sagrada Pasion was founded as a charitable organization to feed and clothe the poor. They soon branched out, founding as well a hospital to treat "poor women suffering from fever." In order to help provide funds for this worthy project the President of Castile, Cardinal Espinosa, and the city councilors granted to the Cofradia the license to provide a place for the production of all *comedias* (plays) presented in Madrid, and then appropriating for their holy purposes the funds collected from this enterprise. Two years later, in 1567, another confraternity, the Cofradia de Nuestra Señora de la Soledad was founded for the purpose of creating a less specialized hospital. By this time the Cofradia de la Pasion had set up three *corrales*, one of which was now given to the Cofradia de la Soledad. Then, in 1574, another brotherhood was founded to create a hospital, and applied for permission to provide a place for the presentation of *comedias*. In 1583 the General Hospital of Madrid was also given a share of the theatrical revenues. In 1615 the City of Madrid was ordered by the state to pay the hospitals a yearly sum, from which could be deducted an amount equal to the money earned from the theatrical ventures. This removed incentive from the brotherhoods, who were assured their money in any case, and so they began leasing their *corrales* to theatrical businessmen. As a result, in 1638, the city took over ownership of the *corrales*, with two commissioners appointed to administer their operation. The city continued the pattern of leasing out the theatres (and dipping into box office revenue for charitable purposes), and a truly professional theatre was the result.

Early performances took place only on Sundays and feast days, but in 1579 a *commedia dell'arte* troupe, not being Spanish and thus less than purely Christian, was given permission to play on a weekday. This was so successful monetarily that equivalent privilege was soon granted to Spanish troupes. By 1600 performances took place every day of the week except Saturday, with Sunday being the best day because no one was working except the actors.

The season was divided into two parts, part one ran from September to Lent. On Ash Wednesday the theatres were closed and remained so through Easter. Then a new season began which ran into July. As was true in London and Paris, theatres could be closed, along with all other places of public assembly, in case of plague, war, or insurrection. Productions were given during daylight hours, usually early in the afternoon, and featured introductory music, singing, and dancing. The acts were separated by the *entreméses* and the productions ended with dances.

A reconstruction drawing by Juan Comba y Garcia of a performance at the Corral del Principe in Madrid.

THE SPANISH STAGE AND ITS CONVENTIONS

Just as the elaborate, Italianate stage settings so heavily influenced seventeenth century England and France, so did they have a major effect on the theatre of Renaissance Spain. The court productions were, as might be expected, the most strongly influenced, with elaborate, expensive sets prepared for all productions. The public theatres, however, did not lag far behind. The religious drama had long had a tradition of lavish sets and costumes, and this was continued throughout the Renaissance. The theatrical contracts of the period all specify that several days be set aside for the creation of stage effects for the religious dramas, and while such provision is not as common for the secular plays, the comments of viewers in letters, journals and essays all indicate that by the middle of the seventeenth century these nonreligious dramas were quite intricately staged.

In its Medieval form the Spanish theatre, like the English, was one of portable dramas mounted on wagons (*carros*). This emphasis was continued into the Renaissance by such traveling troupes as Rueda's and by the Italian *commedia dell'arte* troupes which plied the countryside. As the Renaissance developed and permanent theatres became the rule these wagons were converted to use in the preshow pageantry; beautifully painted and decorated, they carried the costumed performers about the city in a procession that eventually ended at the site of the presentation.

The stage was an elevated platform backed by a permanent architectural façade often featuring more than one level, with the open yard in front of it, and surrounded by the galleries. The stage (at the Corral del Príncipe, for example) was apparently not large, measuring approximately twenty-eight feet in width by twenty-three feet in depth. It was backed by the traditional façade which featured a curtained "discovery" space.

Generally speaking, the staging was simple during the early years of the seventeenth century, and resembled Elizabethan English staging. That is, exits and reentries indicated changes in physical location, displays in the "discovery" area could be used to identify specific locations, and the use of mansions on the stage, a holdover from the Medieval period, could add variety, quick geographical changes, and much color and pageantry.

Mechanically the stage was reasonably simple, with traps in the floor of the stage and some flying machinery in the roofed space above the playing area. However, by the middle of the seventeenth century this simplicity began to disappear under the bombardment of complex staging learned from the Italians. Practical doors and windows became the rule in the façades, and painted flats were set in place to give verisimilitude. Set pieces were constructed to simulate gardens, trees, bowers, rocks, and even castles.

At the court, Italianate settings were fairly common, but it was not until 1626, when Cosme Lotti arrived from Florence, that the court entertainments became lavish enough to rival those of other courts in Europe. In 1633 a new palace, Buen Retiro, was completed and became the center of court dramatic productions, which more and more were acted by professional players rather than the courtiers. Spectacular outdoor productions were given on the palace grounds, with Lotti constructing floating stages, pageant floats pulled by dolphins, and even such spectaculars as the destruction of Circe's palace.

In 1640 a court theatre, the Coliseo, was designed and built by Lotti. It resembled the public theatres in general structure, but was equipped with all the machinery for the court style of show. Shortly after it opened, however, court interest in the drama began to wane and the theatre was opened to the public.

COSTUMES

If the public stage was a bit less colorful than its court cousin, it made up for this lack in terms of rich, colorful, gorgeous costuming. Generally speaking, it was contemporary costume or the "traditional" costumes that had long been worn by actors playing certain roles. In a limited manner costume aided the audience in determining locale—that is, if the characters onstage were all wearing hunting costume or were dressed for a ride in the countryside, then the audience might well suppose this to be a country or forest scene. It also identified certain character types such as fools, professionals (lawyers, scholars), and soldiers. Beyond this, however, costume provided few clues to anything. In a country only recently freed of the conquering Moors, the people (and stage costumers) were fully able to recognize Eastern dress, and so Moors onstage were costumed with some accuracy, wearing turbans and long robes.

Beyond this almost accidental realism, there was no real attempt made to achieve either historical or national accuracy. The Spanish theatre of this period was not bound by any tradition of growing realism, as later theatre would be. Costuming was designed to add color and richness to the production, and historical considerations were ignored in favor of something more important to the time. Thus, Coriolanus came onstage dressed like a central European, while the great Greek philosopher Aristotle was likely to appear in the costume of a Spanish grandé. Romans appeared in cloaks and swords or Medieval coats of mail, and even Eastern costume was sometimes befouled with such Western touches as ruffs or lace at the wrists.

The costumes for the religious dramas—the *autos*—were apparently more lavish even than those of the public theatre; most of the contracts specified rich materials such as silk and velvet, sateen and taffeta. Largely this is because the municipalities footed the bill for such productions and no city or town wanted to be found penny-pinching at the expense of the Church. In addition to the rich materials there are records of performers asking for and receiving money for additional or unusually expensive costumes.

Among the poorer traveling troupes the costumes were least rich and ornate, and the selection was obviously quite limited. Cervantes wrote of Rueda's troupe that its costumes were all carried in one sack that contained "four white pelices trimmed with gilded leather, four beards and wigs, and four staffs, more or less." While this is probably an exaggeration, the few chests that a traveling company could take with them on their *carros* certainly means limited costumes for their shows.

ACTING

The situation of the professional actor in Renaissance Spain was difficult indeed. On one hand, the profession of acting had long been anathema to the Church, and in the thirteenth century King Alfonso X, in his code of laws, had pronounced that actors were to be branded infamous. On the other hand, the public was demanding the opportunity to see plays, and the actors could even be considered employees of the cities, and by extension of the Church, in that they were hired to act in the sacred *autos*. Some churchmen never gave up their battle against actors and constantly harrassed both city and state for bans on theatrical productions. However, the municipalities, who received all of their charitable monies from theatrical performances, and who would be forced to turn to other sources if the theatres were to close, resisted just as strongly.

One of the major problems of the acting profession was the actress. Perhaps because of the popularity of actresses in the touring Italian *commedia* troupes, women were apparently active on the Spanish stage almost from the beginning. There is evidence that the Spanish did use some boys in the women's roles, but the practice never became as widespread as in England and, in 1587, women's theatrical rights were recognized and they were officially licensed to appear onstage. There were many attempts to control the actresses, such as laws requiring that actresses be married to another member of the company or the child of an acting couple. However, one suspects that the performers found little difficulty in getting around such rules. Indeed, the actresses were apparently very popular in the dances and in "breeches" roles that allowed them to appear in men's trunks and hose, thereby showing far more leg than the Church, particularly, approved. As a result, in 1599, the Royal Council forbade either sex to appear in the dress of the other, allowed only actors to go backstage, banned friars from attending productions, and prohibited secular plays being performed in churches.

Most actors were members of companies, although some became famous enough so that they could work independently, hiring themselves out to companies for a substantial daily wage. The companies operated much like the English companies, with permanent members who shared in the proceeds of the company, plus apprentices (or, occasionally, stars) who were paid a daily wage. Most such companies had formal agreements specifying the percentages that were to be paid, the hours of rehearsal, and fines for being late or absent.

Generally speaking, the life of an actor was no soft touch. They were, according to Augustin de Rojas Villandrando, up at dawn, wrote and studied until about nine, and then rehearsed until noon. Following lunch they went to the theatre to give the afternoon performance, finally leaving at about seven in the evening, either to rest or, often, to give another performance for the city fathers, the Royal Council, or some other adjunct of the court.

More than two thousand names of Spanish actors have come down to us, but unfortunately we know little of their methods or techniques. Apparently voice was the most important of an actor's commodities, for it is most often mentioned in a critical sense. The greatest actor of the period, Damien Arias de Penafiel, was especially noted for his "clear, pure" voice. He was also characterized as vivacious and possessed of a fine memory, which may mean only that he knew his lines better than most. "The graces were revealed in every movement of his tongue, and Apollo in every gesture."

While there was no formal training program, the major performers clearly had to have a number of finely tuned skills. The plays of the period

A painting by Fabier shows the great actor Augustin de Rojas rehearsing a play.

were verse dramas and audiences were especially demanding in terms of vocal presentation. In addition, actors had to sing, dance, and perform on some musical instrument, inasmuch as all productions included such entertainment.

By the end of the seventeenth century, Spain was economically and spiritually drained following nearly one hundred and fifty years of adventuring, not only in the New World but also in France and the Low Countries. As a result of this, plus continual governmental meddling and financial depredations by Church and crown, theatre lost its impetus and the new writers after Calderón became imitators of past glories rather than questing, experimenting artists. This ended the Spanish Golden Age, one of the great periods in theatrical history.

7

The English Theatre From The End Of The Middle Ages Through The Renaissance

7

The English Theatre From The End Of The Middle Ages Through The Renaissance

The English Renaissance is all too often defined, in the minds of theatre people at least, as being those few years from the time of Christopher Marlowe's first great drama, *Tamburlaine* (c. 1587), to the death of William Shakespeare in 1616. This definition does, in fact, include within its boundaries some of the greatest drama the world has ever known. However, it leaves out of consideration the late interludes, the Tudor school drama, and most of the Jacobean drama that began in the early seventeenth century, only a few years before Shakespeare's death, and that held the stage until Parliament closed the English theatres in 1642. It is with the whole panorama of English theatre during this more extensive period—a period that at its all too brief peak produced a theatre so outstanding that it is still considered one of the world's glories—that the student must be concerned.

THE ENGLISH RENAISSANCE

The Renaissance came late to England, at least in comparison to its mid-fourteenth century appearance in Italy. It had to work its way up through France and the Low Countries before it could make its appearance, and it underwent some significant mutations along the way. It is thus a much harder period to date with any exactness than the Italian or French Renaissance. By the mid-fifteenth century the Middle Ages were dying out in England, but the glories of the Renaissance would not get underway until Elizabeth I ascended the throne in 1558. Therefore, it is with those two transitional monarchs, Henry VII and Henry VIII, that it is necessary to begin.

Henry VII (1457-1509) became head of the house of Lancaster at the death of Henry VI. He invaded England from Brittany in 1485, and at the Battle of Bosworth Field he defeated the forces of Richard III. Marrying Elizabeth, daughter of Edward IV, he united the houses of York and Lancaster and founded the Tudor dynasty. In 1494 he consolidated British rule in Ireland, and five years later negotiated a peace treaty (however short-lived) with Scotland that was sealed when his daughter married Scotland's James IV. The specifics of his reign are relatively unimportant to the development of the Renaissance, beyond the all-important fact that his defeat of Richard and ascension of the English throne brought an end to the Wars of the Roses and allowed the Renaissance to develop.

While Henry VII spent his time puttering about Oxford and trying to get the ladies of the court to cover up their bosoms, a revolution was taking place within the Church. The exmonk Erasmus had a number of friends and supporters in England who made up a group commonly referred to as the Oxford Reformers because they were all—directly or indirectly—associated with the University of Oxford. Among these was John Colet, son of the Mayor of London, who went on to become Dean of St. Paul's Cathedral in London. Colet did away with a number of abuses in the Church, though unlike his friend Erasmus he was not opposed to scholasticism and monasticism. Thomas More, another member of the group, would publish his *Utopia* in 1516, seven years after Henry VII was succeeded by his son Henry VIII. More pictured a society in which all property was held in common, with order and peace maintained by the highest ideal of Christian love. All citizens of his ideal republic would be obliged to work six hours per day and spend a reasonable amount of the resulting free time in study and recreation. The distinction between master and slave, that curse of antiquity, would be eradicated, and all citizens of the republic would be free men. The government would be a senate, publicly elected, with a president who would be assisted by commissioners. There would be a system of free public education, and crime would be curbed by the reform of evil-minded citizens. Perhaps most important of all, religious toleration would be granted to all sects and individuals.

Henry VII's son, Henry VIII (1491-1547), succeeded his father in 1509. He married his brother's widow, Katharine of Aragon, who bore him a daughter, Mary. His chief minister, Thomas Wolsey, however cunning and

A portion of Visscher's engraving of London, c. 1616, showing the Globe Theatre and the Bear Garden.

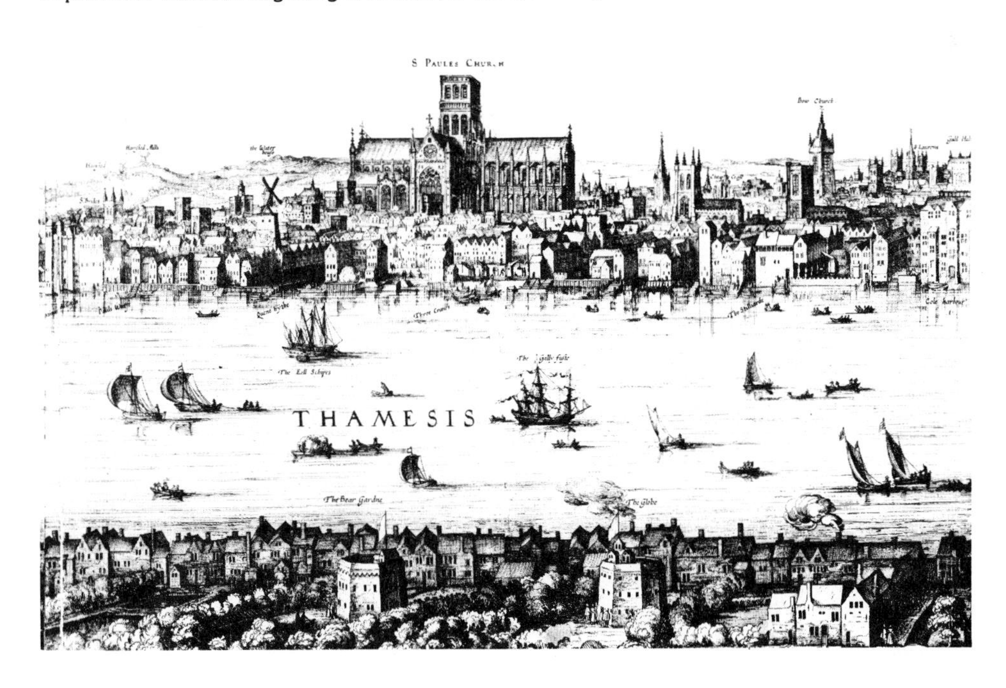

amoral, was an able administrator and England prospered. Henry's court became a center of Renaissance learning, and it nourished a number of humanistic writers. John Skelton's career spans the reign of both Henrys, and the sonneteers, Sir Thomas Wyatt (1503-42) and Henry Howard, Earl of Surrey (1517-47), came at the close of Henry VIII's reign. Along with poetry, the drama also received some impetus, especially from John Heywood's (1497-1580) interludes and the plays of Nicholas Udall (1505-56). The court became famous for its masques and costume balls under the leadership of a Master of Revels. This was an office permanently instituted by Henry in 1544, though it had been in existence off and on for many years.

Early in his reign Henry had personally received recognition from the Pope, who gave him the title "Defender of the Faith" for a treatise against Luther. However, Henry now wished to marry Anne Boleyn and Pope Clement VII resisted demands for a divorce from Katharine. Wolsey was unable to negotiate the divorce, which caused his downfall, and Thomas Cromwell became minister. Henry married Anne in spite of papal objections and was excommunicated. However, he merely transferred the papal powers to himself as divinely appointed head of the English Church, and the break with Rome was complete. His next four marriages are too well-known to require discussion, but his marriage in 1540 to Anne of Cleves, whom he disliked and soon divorced, led to the execution of Cromwell, who had urged the marriage.

Henry remained a popular king, in spite of his advancement of personal desires under the cover of public policy or moral right. And he gave England a *comparatively* benign reign, marred by two wars with Scotland, a continuing conflict with Ireland, and numerous adventures in France.

Following Henry VIII's death in 1547 there was a brief reign by the child King Edward VI, who lasted until 1553. He was followed by Mary Tudor, from 1553 to 1558, and then Elizabeth I (1533-1603) ascended the throne and the greatest period of the English Renaissance was underway.

Elizabeth was the daughter of Henry and Anne Boleyn, and she had been declared illegitimate following her mother's execution. However, in 1544 Parliament reestablished her in the succession. On her ascension, England's fortunes seemed at a low ebb. The country was torn by religious strife and was deeply in debt, primarily as a result of continual warfare in France. Her reign brought England back to solvency, resolved the religious issues, and saw a flowering of the arts unequalled since the Golden Age of Greece. It produced such men as Shakespeare, Spenser, Bacon, and Raleigh. Under Elizabeth England became the greatest naval power in the world. Commerce and industry prospered and colonization began.

It is against this broad background of civil war, religious strife, economic growth, and political adventuring that the drama of Renaissance England must be considered.

THE INTERLUDE

The interlude, as it developed during the Renaissance, was based on the earlier form, the moral interlude, that was so popular during the Medieval period. However, unlike the Medieval form, the Tudor interlude was not merely concerned with defining proper and improper conduct in terms of secular doctrine. Instead, the interlude became a form that included the comic as well as the serious, that outgrew its abbreviated length, and that provides a link between the moral religious drama of the late Middle Ages and the totally secular Elizabethan drama. Eventually, the form became so difficult to define that almost any dramatic work of the period was referred to as an interlude.

The interlude was, in most cases, a vehicle for professional actors. The interludes written by John Heywood in the mid-sixteenth century were performed by the Players of the King's Interludes. They were reasonably short works, usually containing more dialogue than action, which were designed to entertain the court of Henry VIII. There are six surviving interludes usually ascribed to Heywood. Of these the first three—*The Play of the Weather*; *A Play of Love*; and *A Dialogue Concerning Witty and Witless*—all printed in 1533, are little more than moral disputations on traditional themes. The following three—*A Merry Play Between John the Husband, Tyb the Wife, and Sir John the Priest* (c. 1520-33); *The Play Called the Four PP* (c. 1520-22); and *A Merry Play Between the Pardoner and the Friar* (c. 1513-21)—all have some dramatic value. They contain substantially more stage action, a much greater reality of characterization, and a hearty humor close to that found in the English folk materials or the works of Chaucer. Heywood's interludes do in fact reveal a dependence on the Medieval moral interlude, the *debat* (debate), and the *fabliau* (fable), but they also mark a distinct dramatic advance toward the later Elizabethan drama. At the same time, however, that Heywood's advanced interludes were being done, didactic moral interludes written in Latin and somewhat closer to their Medieval ancestry were being performed in the English public schools.

Early troupes of actors used the interlude as a means of capturing large audiences. They drew upon folk materials, the English historical past, biblical stories, and Classical mythology. Henry Medwall (fl. 1486), second to Heywood as the most distinguished writer of interludes, wrote the romantic *Fulgens and Lucres* (c. 1490-1501) in the Classical manner. He also wrote a moral interlude called *Nature* (c. 1490-1501).

TUDOR SCHOOL DRAMA

In the early sixteenth century the presentation of plays became common at the universities. With the rediscovery of the Classics came the presentation of plays by Euripides, Seneca, Terence, and Plautus. These soon led to original works based on the Classical writers. Initially these were written in Latin, and even a few in Greek, but by the 1540s they were regularly appearing in English. It was from this essentially Classical background that the plays of the Renaissance were to emerge. They used the Classic sources for forms and ideas and occasionally for material, while providing their characters with a rich style and fluency from their own Medieval background.

It is perhaps a commentary on the English sense of fun that the broad humor and the comic physical action of Plautus were preferred to the moral restraint of Terence by the scholars at the universities. It is not a coincidence that Plautus' *Menaechmi* served as the model for *Comedy of Errors*. During this period, when Medieval forms gave way to Classical, when the guilds gave way to professional companies, the total change in English life was reflected on stage.

Ralph Roister Doister by Nicholas Udall (1505-56) is one of the earliest extant examples of vernacular school drama, but its exact date is debated. Some scholars place it during Udall's service as Headmaster at Eton (1534-41), while others place it shortly after 1555, while Udall was Headmaster at Westminster.

The basis of the play is quite obviously Plautian; the braggart soldier of Plautus done anew in English. However, the play by Udall is not a translation but what is often called "Englished," that is, Plautus' play has been freely adapted to the English idiom and setting, with the influences of the Medieval English stage at times quite pronounced.

The play, in the best Roman fashion, opens with a prologue. The prologue asks the audience for its attention, disavows any insult that might be implied and acquaints the audience with the setting of the play and its background. There is also a line of deference to Plautus and Terence, which affirms the authors' fidelity to the Classical rules. The play tells the farcical tale of the duping of Ralph the braggart by Matthew Merygreek the parasite. It is told in rhyming doggerel and includes, in the attack on Dame Custance's household, one of the great mock-epic battles of dramatic literature.

The second major play of this period is *Gammer Gurton's Needle*, ascribed to William Stevenson and acted at Cambridge in 1553-54. Even more English than *Ralph Roister Doister*, it has strong Medieval links, but is a less tightly woven piece. It is a farce which deals with a missing needle. While patching the pants of Hodge, her manservant, Gammer Gurton loses her needle. Diccon the prankster hears of the loss and tells Gammer Gurton that her neighbor, Dame Chat, has found the needle but will not return it. Then he tells Dame Chat that Gammer Gurton has accused Chat of stealing and cooking Gammer's rooster. A fight ensues and the curate is called in to mediate. Diccon confuses the curate and gets him beaten by Chat and her servants, who mistake him for Hodge. Gammer suspects various people of stealing her needle, which is eventually (and painfully) discovered by Hodge to be still in the seat of his pants.

The style and life of these plays are Medieval. *Roister Doister* is sprinkled with Medieval idioms, such as "by Saint George," while *Gammer Gurton's Needle* is full of Medieval farce set loosely in a Classical framework. *Gammer Gurton* is purely Tudor in setting and flavor; its only major concession to Classic sources is its scene divisions, its five acts, and its adherence to the unities.

It might be well to point out here a problem with the school plays of this period, or rather with our knowledge of them. Many simply were not retained; manuscripts were carelessly lost or were undervalued and thrown away. This is perhaps why the period is generally ignored among texts on theatre, yet the examples that we have indicate that some particularly delightful plays were written.

THE UNIVERSITY WITS

As early as 1580 the drama took a major step forward because of a talented and often rather dissolute group of young men who are often lumped together under the title of "University Wits." When these men, who shared a common pride in their university backgrounds, began to write for the public stage, they were able to draw on their academic training to unite the several types of drama that existed in England—Classical, interludes, school plays, and folk drama—into something new and unique. The group included Lodge and Peele, both Oxford trained, Nashe and Marlowe, both Cambridge graduates, Lyly and Greene, who held degrees from both institutions, and Kyd, who was a member of the group but who never, apparently, graduated from either university.

Robert Greene (1558-92) was one of the most talented of the "Wits" in terms of reading the public taste and then giving the Elizabethan audience what it wanted. He pandered to the love for artificial romance by imitating Lyly's *Euphues* in his *Mamillia* (1583), and he imitated Sir Philip Sidney's *Arcadia* in his *Menaphon* (1589). His *Conny-Catching Pamphlets* (1591-92) filled the demand for sensational realism by "revealing" the crooked tricks of the London underworld. The growing demand for commercial drama led him to write such plays as the farcical *Friar Bacon and Friar Bungay* (c. 1589), and the pseudohistorical *James IV* (c. 1590). Greene is thought to have had a hand in the *Henry VI*, which Shakespeare later rewrote; in Kyd's *The Spanish Tragedy*; and in numerous other plays of the time. Always a writer, Greene even capitalized on his own misspent life with a final group of pamphlets. One of these, *Greene's Groats' Worth of Wit Bought With a Million of Repentance* (1592), contains our earliest reference to Shakespeare as "an upstart Crow . . . with his Tyger's heart wrapt in a Player's hide." Greene died while still a young man. The legend has it that he passed away due to a "surfeit of pickled Herrings and Rhenish wine."

THOMAS KYD: Thomas Kyd was born in London in 1558, the son of a scrivener. He attended the Merchant Taylors' School but did not, as did so many of his playwriting contemporaries, go on to the university. After leaving school he took up the family profession, becoming a scrivener for a short time before undertaking his first play. He appears to have been a fringe member of a group of literary types who revolved around the Countess of Pembroke, and under her influence transcribed into English one of the tragedies of Garnier in his *Cornelia* (c. 1593).

Kyd was a close friend of Christopher Marlowe; the two poets shared the same room and, apparently, the same unorthodox religious views. They also shared, between 1590 and 1593, the same employer (either Lord Pembroke, Strange, or Sussex) for whose players Marlowe was writing. In 1593 Kyd was arrested on suspicion of being party to the posting of certain "mutinous libels" on the walls of the Dutch church. In a search of his rooms, papers were found that also led to an order for the arrest of Marlowe. Previously, in 1588, Marlowe had posted bail for an unknown offense, and at the time of Kyd's arrest he

The title page of a 1632 edition of Kyd's *Spanish Tragedy*, showing Horatio, hanged in the arbor, being discovered by his father, Hieronimo, with Bel Imperia and Lorenzo.

was the subject of a "note" by an informer charging him with atheism and blasphemy. His death in a tavern brawl took place before this new arrest order could be carried out. Kyd, imprisoned and apparently tortured, wrote letters to Sir John Pickering, the Lord Keeper, explaining his relationship with Marlowe and denying any complicity in Marlowe's beliefs. He was released later in the year, 1593, and died before the end of 1594, impoverished and in disgrace.

Of Kyd's work, only two extant plays, *The Spanish Tragedy* (c. 1584-89) and *Cornelia* are certainly his. Other works, however, are often attributed to him, such as *Soliman and Perseda* (c. 1590), the so-called *Ur-Hamlet* (c. 1587), *Arden of Feversham* (1586), *The Taming of the Shrew* (c. 1588), the first part of *Ieronimo* (printed in 1605), and parts of *Titus Andronicus* and *Henry VI*.

Kyd's reputation as a playwright rests on only one of these many plays—*The Spanish Tragedy*. Dramatically it exhibits a somewhat older form than the works of his friend Marlowe, making much use of Senecan techniques, though popularized and invigorated by rhetorically heightened dialogue and a strong dramatic structure. Essentially romantic in an almost Medieval sense, the play is based on an imaginary situation between Portugal and Spain, which is given the semblance of true history. The other play that is certainly his is little more than a translation of an existing French tragedy.

Of the works so often attributed to him, *Soliman and Perseda* dramatizes the play within *The Spanish Tragedy* and reads like a poor imitation of the original. The lost *Ur-Hamlet* seems likely to be Kyd's because of several mentions of that title earlier than Shakespeare's play, and because Nashe, in his 1589 *Epistle to Menaphon*, links Kyd's name to a work titled *Hamlet*. How much of a hand Kyd may have had in *Titus Andronicus* and the *Henry VI* trilogy is debatable. Also, there is little substantial evidence to indicate that he really did write an early version of *The Taming of the Shrew* upon which Shakespeare eventually based his own play. However, the attribution of the earliest domestic tragedy, *Arden of Feversham*, seems likely. *Arden* begins the practice of basing plays on recent, sensational crimes, and its general level of construction has even led some critics, over the years, to attribute it to Shakespeare.

Kyd, like his friend Marlowe, died relatively young, leaving behind a great but unfulfilled promise. His works did, however, set the course for many of the plays throughout the period by popularizing the revenge tragedy. It is his most enduring contribution to English drama.

Thomas Lodge (c. 1558-1625) was, like most of the "Wits," a miscellaneous writer. He cranked out pamphlets, plays, and poetry with more energy than art. As a dramatist he was reasonably undistinguished; his *Looking Glass for London and England* (which he apparently wrote with Robert Greene between 1587 and 1591) and his *Wounds of Civil War* (1587-92), are both rhetorical and soggy. His greatest success was as a lyric poet, but his most famous work is the prose tale *Rosalynde, Euphues' Golden Legacy* (1590), an imitation of Lyly's style, which owes its renown not to Lodge's artistic talents but to the fact that Shakespeare used it as the source for *As You Like It*.

John Lyly (c. 1554-1606) was the oldest and, except for Kyd, the most influential of the "Wits." A favorite of the court, he was the protege of two of the Queen's favorites: Robert Dudley, Earl of Leicester; and Burleigh, Lord High Treasurer. Although Lyly was a miscellaneous writer like his contemporaries, his main works were romances and comedies, in which his involved and allusive style showed to best advantage. He wrote exclusively for the court audience, which savored his artificial grace and the many sly allusions to court intrigue with which he seasoned his works. His first two plays, *Campaspe* and *Sapho and Phao*, were produced in 1594 by the Children of Paul's and by the Children of the Chapel, both at court and at the Blackfriars. *Endimion, the Man in the Moon* (acted in 1588), is his best play. Two later comedies, *Midas* and *Mother Bombie* (this last in the style of Terence), were produced about 1590 by the Children of Paul's, of whom Lyly was vice-master. His last comedy, *The Woman in the Moon*, may never have been produced. In spite of his court friends and popularity, Lyly never attained his ambition to be named Master of the Revels, and he died an embittered man.

CHRISTOPHER MARLOWE: Christopher Marlowe was born in Canterbury in 1564, the son of middle-class parents: his father was a shoemaker and his mother was the daughter of a clergyman. Little is known about his early childhood. At age fifteen he entered the King's School, Canterbury, on a scholarship. He spent two years at King's School, and then in 1581 he entered Corpus Christi College on another scholarship, spending the next six and a half years in the semimonastic atmosphere of late sixteenth century Cambridge. In 1584, he took his B.A. degree and immediately embarked upon the course of studies for the M.A. He continued to receive a scholarship, but only on the condition that he take Holy Orders. His affiliation with Cambridge and the Church became steadily more distant during these last three years of study. In

A 1620 woodcut illustrating a scene from Christopher Marlowe's *The Tragical History of Doctor Faustus.*

1587 he was awarded the coveted M.A. degree, but his intention to take Holy Orders had by this time been abandoned.

By the summer of 1587, Marlowe had arrived in London and was finishing work on *Tamburlaine*. Both parts of the play were completed the following March. During his last term at Cambridge he had, apparently, started the writing of *Tamburlaine*. It was also during this period that he translated Ovid's *Elegies* and completed the first draft of *Dido, Queen of Carthage*. It is evident that the last years of his residence in Cambridge were not entirely occupied with formal studies.

Not one critic can agree about all the dates of Marlowe's writings and, worse still, about the authenticity of major works or sections of some others. For *Tamburlaine* there is only a conjectural date of composition, and the quarto of 1590 in which it was first published did not even bear the name of its author. Thus, there is no technical proof that Marlowe even wrote the play. However, no recent critic has cast doubt on his authorship, for the evidence of his poetic style is on every page.

A hypothetical date of 1588 has been given for the completion of *The Tragical History of Doctor Faustus*. By the time it was produced, Marlowe had resided in London for about two years and had associated himself with two groups of men—Sir Walter Raleigh and his circle, and the Walsinghams of Kent. He was also known to be connected in some way with the actors and managers of the Lord Admiral's Men and with Lord Strange's Company. The commonest theory, and certainly the most likely, is that Marlowe was, for a time, a member of both these companies.

In 1589 Marlowe was commanded to appear before the Recorder, at which time he was ordered to appear at the next sessions at Newgate. Most biographers agree that his trouble was in some way related to the theatre. The records show that the offense was committed within the City of London and, although not heinous or treasonable, was serious enough to warrant bail of forty pounds.

From 1588 to 1591 Marlowe wrote *The Jew of Malta, The Massacre at Paris, Edward II*, and *The True Tragedy of Richard, Duke of York*.

Another detail of Marlowe's life, one so fascinating that it sometimes gets in the way of serious critical examination of his works, is his association with Thomas Kyd. On May 12, 1593, Kyd was in trouble with the authorities and his rooms were searched for incriminating material. The "political papers" which the authorities expected to find did not appear. They did, however, find material that by the standards of the time could be labeled as "atheistic." Kyd protested that these papers had been written by Marlowe and had lain among his own papers since 1591, when Kyd and Marlowe had worked together. A warrant was issued to bring Marlowe before the court, and for the next ten days he was ordered not to leave London. On Whitsun Eve, May 26, another alarming accusation was filed against Marlowe, this time for "atheistical" and "blasphemous" sayings. Before any action could be taken by the courts, Marlowe was dead.

According to the evidence laid before the jury that viewed Marlowe's body, he had spent the day at an inn kept by Eleanor Bull, and with him were three men: Ingram Frizer, Robert Poley, and Nicholas Skeres. According to their testimony they were the only men present at the time of Marlowe's death. They testified that Marlowe attacked Frizer, who then killed the poet in self-defense. This satisfied the jury, but unfortunately it left the impression that Marlowe may have, in fact, been deliberately murdered. This sensationalism has, all too often, taken precedence over his artistic attributes, with the result that critics have spent a disproportionate amount of time on his life and death in an attempt to justify his political and religious beliefs by way of his writings.

When Christopher Marlowe came to London in 1587, English drama was more than six hundred years old, but still in its artistic infancy. As a result, Marlowe absorbed the whole tradition of the morality and hybrid morality plays. He added to these the Classical forms, and gave the English stage a dramatic form combining true poetic quality with reality of characterization. He demonstrated the unifying and spectacular value of a single dominating superhero and, together with Thomas Kyd, he paved the way for the transition from the homiletic tragedies of the 1560s and 1570s to the great Shakespearean tragedies of the first decade of the seventeenth century.

Thomas Nashe (1567-1601) was in many ways the least restrained of the "Wits," at least in terms of his writing. He first became famous for besting the Puritan Martinists at name-calling during the Martin Marprelate Controversy, and then gave better than he got in a pamphlet war with Gabriel Harvey. In terms of drama, he collaborated with Marlowe on *Dido, Queen of Carthage* (c. 1587-93), and then by himself wrote *A Pleasant Comedy, Called Summer's Last Will and Testament* (1592-93).

George Peele (1557-96) was a court writer and, as was so common to the period, a poet turned playwright. His plays generally had little real dramatic structure, but he was one of the earliest playwrights to develop blank verse

A woodcut from the 1597 quarto edition of Marlowe's *Tamburlaine the Great* shows the overreaching conqueror dressed in the Renaissance armor of a Spanish nobleman.

beyond its stiff, original form, and he began the technique of filling plays with songs and lyrical passages. In 1581 he wrote *The Arraignment of Paris*, a court comedy which he spiced up with pastoral and Classical devices. *The Love of King David and Fair Bethsabe* (1581-94) and *The Old Wives' Tale* (1588-94) are usually considered to be his best plays. *King David* is interesting in that it has no act divisions, consisting instead of a series of scenes illustrating the biblical stories of King David. *Old Wives* is the first dramatic burlesque in English drama, poking lively fun at romantic court plays of the period. This play provided the source of Milton's *Comus*. Peele went on to write *The Battle of Alcazar* (1588-89) in which he imitated Greene and Marlowe. In 1590 he wrote a court pageant, *Polyhymnia*, and followed it with the romanticized historical play *Edward the First* (1590-93). Peele was not a great dramatist, but he was a great innovator and thus his plays had real influence on the works of later and better playwrights.

ELIZABETHAN PUBLIC DRAMA

Following in the pathway blazed by the University Wits came a group of public and essentially commercial dramatists who, in slightly more than twenty years, beginning about 1588 with Marlowe's *Faustus*, made the terms *Elizabethan period* and *great drama* nearly synonymous. The Elizabethan period, in its strictest sense, refers to the period of Elizabeth's reign, from 1558 to 1603. However, literarily speaking it also includes those playwrights who were producing during the first years of the reign of James I, who ascended the throne after Elizabeth's death.

WILLIAM SHAKESPEARE: William Shakespeare, greatest of the English poets and dramatists, was born in Stratford-on-Avon in 1564. He was baptized in Holy Trinity Church on April 26, presumably a few days after his birth, which is therefore usually celebrated, appropriately, on April 23, the feast day of England's patron saint, St. George. Shakespeare died, rather neatly for those concerned with remembering dates, on April 23, 1616, and was buried in Holy Trinity Chancel. Between these two dates comparatively little is known of his life, though many theories, romantic and otherwise, have been advanced.

Because a free education was provided to children of the town burgesses (his father was an alderman and, for a period, mayor) at the King's New School, William probably attended from about age six to thirteen, which meant that he had a better than average education, though he probably did not complete the full ten years required for a degree. This seems likely because, when Shakespeare was twelve, his father was struck by some sudden but unknown misfortune. He ceased attending meetings of the town corporation, he failed to pay his taxes, he sold off a large part of his property, and he endured several suits for debt. From a position of importance in the town he sank into a penury and obscurity that lasted until his death.

MR. WILLIAM
SHAKESPEARES
COMEDIES,
HISTORIES, &
TRAGEDIES.
Published according to the True Originall Copies.

LONDON
Printed by Isaac Iaggard, and Ed. Blount. 1623.

The title page from the first folio.

In 1582 Shakespeare married Anne Hathaway, a woman eight years older than himself, who was part of a well-to-do farming family in nearby Shottery. They had a daughter, Susanna, who was born the following year, and twins, Hamnet and Judith, who were born in 1585. After this Shakespeare passes out of sight for seven years, to reappear as an actor and playwright in London.

Exactly why Shakespeare chose to leave his young family and seek his fortune on the London stage is unknown. The severe change in family circumstances, mentioned earlier, may be part of the reason. However, the most likely explanation is that he became stagestruck after seeing the plays put on by the touring companies that regularly visited Stratford, and that he eventually joined one of these companies. Certainly the opportunity was there; in 1587 at least five different companies played in Stratford, including the Earl of Leicester's Men. This troupe was likely recruiting new members, as several of the players had left to accompany the Earl and his army to the Netherlands and had then embarked on a subsequent tour of Germany.

Shakespeare's first position in theatre was certainly as an apprentice, acting small roles, writing, and probably even sweeping the stage, but his development as a playwright was exceptionally swift. By 1589 his first play was produced—either *The Comedy of Errors* or the first part of *Henry VI*. By 1592 his success was such that Robert Greene complained publicly about an ambitious actor who was writing his own plays and who fancied himself "the only Shake-scene" in the country. That same year the playwright Thomas Nashe mentioned the first part of *Henry VI*, stating that it had won the applause of ten thousand spectators. Indeed, by 1592 it is likely that he had completed the first two parts of *Henry VI*, *The Comedy of Errors*, and *Titus Andronicus*, his one attempt at writing full-blown Senecan tragedy. In terms of his later work these are surely minor plays, but they show skill in three areas of dramatic writing: comedy, the history play, and tragedy.

In mid-1592, however, the blossoming young playwright faced a real test. Following some riots in Southwark the Council closed the theatres (and other places of assembly) until autumn. By autumn, however, London was in the throes of the plague, and except for a few scattered weeks the theatres remained closed until the late spring of 1594. This was a great blow to the companies, which tried to eke out an existence by constant touring. However, at least one company—Pembroke's—went bankrupt, and all the others fell on hard times indeed. Exactly what Shakespeare was doing during the plague years we do not know, at least in terms of theatre, but he probably wrote the poems *Venus and Adonis* and *The Rape of Lucrece* during this period. By the summer of 1594, when the theatres were again open and drawing large crowds, he was one of the foremost members of the Lord Chamberlain's Men, and given the fact that both Marlowe and Kyd were dead, the foremost playwright in London. He spent the balance of his creative life with the company, and its success, in large measure due to his presence, is testified to by the fact that when Shakespeare retired in 1613 there had been no more than nineteen shareholders since it was formed in 1594.

It is, obviously, difficult to date most of Shakespeare's plays with any exactness. However, such rough dating as we can manage does shed light on

This woodcut from the title page of Kempe's *Nine Days' Wonder*, 1601, shows Kempe dancing to Norwich.

certain aspects of the playwright's creativity. For example, the comedies were written essentially in the following order: *Love's Labor's Lost* (1590-92), *The Comedy of Errors* (1592-94), *The Two Gentlemen of Verona* (1592-94), *A Midsummer Night's Dream* (1594-96), *The Merchant of Venice* (1594-96), *The Taming of the Shrew* (1594-97), *The Merry Wives of Windsor* (1597-1600), *Much Ado About Nothing* (1598-1600), *As You Like It* (1599-1600), *Twelfth Night* (1599-1601), *All's Well That Ends Well* (1600-04), *Measure for Measure* (1603-04), *Pericles* (1607-08), *Cymbeline* (1609-10), *The Winter's Tale* (1610-11), and *The Tempest* (1611-12).

It can easily be seen that Shakespeare wrote comedies throughout his career, from first to last, and that they are all of high quality. Certainly there are changes in style and periods in which he worked with varying comic types—at least one of which began when the company clown, Will Kempe, departed to dance across the Alps and his place and stock in the company were taken over by Robert Armin. Kempe had been a boisterous, peasant buffoon style of clown, and so the clown role and thus the basic nature of the early comedies tended toward the farcical and boisterous. Armin, on the other hand, was a "white-face" clown, a court jester type, and beginning with *As You Like It* the clown roles Shakespeare wrote were designed for such a performer. This change in the clown role affected the whole tone of the plays. Following this "golden period" of comedy he turned briefly to dark or "black" comedy, in *All's Well That Ends Well* and *Measure for Measure*, but he ended his career with one of his greatest lyrical comedies, *The Tempest*.

The history plays also span his writing career, but his output is uneven and such great histories as *Richard II* and *Henry IV* came almost exactly in the middle of his career. The dates of the history plays are as follows: *Henry VI*, parts 1, 2, and 3 (1590-96); *Richard III* (1593-94); *King John* (1594-96); *Richard II* (1594-96); *Henry IV*, parts 1 and 2 (1597-98); *Henry V* (1598-99); and *Henry VIII* (1612-13). All but two of these (*King John* and *Henry VIII*) are based on the war with France and the English civil wars from the last years of Richard II (reigned 1377-99) to the accession of Henry VII (1485). It was a century of rebellion and intrigue that apparently captured Shakespeare's interest above all other periods.

The tragedies are all the work of the poet's maturity. Their dates are *Titus Andronicus* (1593-94), *Romeo and Juliet* (1594-97), *Julius Caesar* (1598-99), *Hamlet* (1600-01), *Troilus and Cressida* (1601-03), *Othello* (1604-05), *King Lear* (1605-06), *Macbeth* (1605-06), *Antony and Cleopatra* (1607-08), *Timon of Athens* (1607-08), and *Coriolanus* (1608-10). The tragedies seem to have less range in matter and mood than the comedies. Every one of the tragedies follows the traditional patterns—that is, either the downfall of a single great figure, or the tragedy of a pair of lovers.

In 1597 Shakespeare, moderately wealthy from his interest in the company, bought New Place in Stratford. He likely spent an increasing amount of time there. In 1613, after the Globe caught fire and burned down during the opening performance of *Henry VIII*, he apparently sold his interest in the company and retired.

To even attempt a discussion of Shakespeare's dramatic and poetic techniques, in these few pages, would be foolhardy indeed. Over the past four hundred years enough has been written on the subject to fill a respectable library. A few things, however, may be pointed out. First, Shakespeare was not original, in the purest sense, in his plots—all but two of his plays can be traced to a specific source, and one may suspect that if the materials were available even these two works would prove to be lifted from an earlier work. Shakespeare ranged widely in his search for materials that he could dramatize—the Classical legend, history, biographies, Italian tales, English and Scottish chronicles, and even plays by earlier dramatists. However, in every case these materials were transformed by the poet into fresh, exciting, entertaining plays that are as truly his own as if he had created them whole cloth. His plots are often complex and intricate, but the action is always clear. His characters are true—that is, they hold the mirror up to life and they are always consistent. He was always a romantic, yet he mixed up the elements of comedy and tragedy as they are in life, thus providing theatre with a kind of stylized reality. He clearly

A scene from *Titus Andronicus*, c. 1595. This drawing, usually attributed to Henry Peacham, is thought to be the only existing contemporary illustration of a Shakespearean play.

knew the Classical rules for drama, but was too talented an artist to be bound by them. His great fellow poet and dramatist, Ben Jonson, could truly say of him, "He was not of an age, but for all time!"

BEN JONSON: More than any other writer of the Elizabethan and Jacobean periods, Ben Jonson was a mass of inconsistencies. He was a fine, sensitive Classics scholar, but also, in such plays as *Bartholomew Fair* (1614), he was the most vivid of contemporary realists. An egotistical satirist who mercilessly mauled many of his colleagues, he nevertheless was awarded the admiration and even the affection of most of his fellow writers. A composer of often dull formal tragedies, he also wrote some of the best and most influential comedies in the English language. He did not attend college, yet he educated himself so well that his comment on Shakespeare's "small Latin and less Greek" is certainly justified. He was a soldier in the Dutch wars and killed an actor in a duel, and yet he wrote masques for the court and in 1616 became court poet. When James I died in 1625 Jonson fell out of favor at the court, but the Cavalier poets almost worshipped him, forming the "tribe of Ben" at his table in the Mermaid Tavern. Jonson's career lasted over forty years, and he is considered by many to be the finest English playwright after Shakespeare. His dramatic output included comedy of every sort, tragicomedy, satire, tragedy, court masques, and some pieces that defy classification.

Title page of Ben Jonson's collected works, 1616.

Jonson was born in 1572, the son of a clergyman. His father died when Ben was still young and his mother remarried—this time forsaking the clergy for a bricklayer. Jonson received a solid Classical education during his early years and enrolled in Westminster School to further his learning; however, much to his disgust, his stepfather took him out of school and put him to work as a mason. The young scholar soon tired of this work and made his escape by joining the army, which was looking for recruits to fight the Spanish in the Low Countries. When he returned to England, Jonson became an actor under Philip Henslowe—theatre manager and owner of the Rose, Fortune, and Hope playhouses. He was notoriously bad as an actor, but he was so grotesque, with his great hulking body (according to legend his weight varied regularly, from gross to merely fat) and flaming red hair, that he was considered the perfect physical type to portray murderers and devils.

Jonson soon tired of acting—one may suspect that in spite of his ego he was too intelligent not to recognize his lack of talent—and turned to the writing of plays. His stepfather had put an end to Ben's formal education, but thanks to his own determination he was better educated than most of his contemporaries. Perhaps for this reason he was unusually meticulous in the care he took to follow Classical precepts.

When Elizabeth I died and King James I mounted the throne, Jonson quickly won the new king's notice and friendship. Soon he was highly popular at the court, charming the courtiers with his wit, his epigrams, his poetry, and his masques, which were produced in uneasy alliance with that outspoken designer Inigo Jones.

In 1616, the year of Shakespeare's death, Jonson was appointed court poet and given a pension for this position, thus becoming the first "poet laureate" of England. Also in that year he became the first playwright to actively collect and edit his own works for publication. It is too easy to assign the reason for this publishing venture to Jonson's inflated ego; it also must be said that Jonson took his writing—his art—with great seriousness.

As exciting and brilliant as his career had been, and as personally popular as he had been, both with the court and the public, he died miserably and alone. When King James died, Charles came to the throne, and he did not think highly of Jonson. The poet's court post was revoked, his pension removed, and his masques were no longer produced. Finally, paralyzed and ill, Jonson tried to write plays from his bed, but they were not the brilliant successes of his earlier days. In 1637, unable to write and with the Puritan influence already adversely affecting the theatre he loved, Jonson died.

Of his total theatrical contributions, Jonson's masques are of least importance. They contain some fine lyrics but, without the spectacular staging and pageantry for which they were an excuse, they are barren and skeletal. Of his many masques, the best are probably *The Masque of Queens* (1609) and *Oberon* (1611). Along with the masques, Jonson also composed some unclassifiable semidramatic pieces such as the unfinished *Hue and Cry After Cupid* (1608) and *The Sad Shepherd* (printed in 1641).

Jonson was primarily a writer of comedies, and his greatest talent seemed to be as a satirist, but he did attempt tragedy with some contemporary success. Apparently influenced by the great success of Shakespeare's *Julius*

Caesar (1599), he wrote *Sejanus* (1603), a tragedy without any real dramatic action and couched in an unrelieved Senecan style. It is, however, more playable than *Catiline*, which he wrote in 1611.

Jonson's best works are clearly his comedies, and though some of them, such as *The Poetaster* (1601) and *Cynthia's Revels* (1600-01), fail to hold up today because they are primarily satirical attacks on Jonson's long dead rivals, Dekker and Marston, many of them are still good entertainment and some of them are excellent indeed. *Eastward Ho!* (1605), for example, which he wrote in collaboration with Marston and Chapman, is a satire on the king's Scottish courtiers and it still has the capability to amuse audiences.

In terms of his own age, and succeeding ages as well, Jonson's greatest contribution to the comic drama is his creation of the "comedy of humors," in which he satirizes characters who are ruled by one of the four body humors—blood, phlegm, black bile, and yellow bile—which, according to Medieval belief, controlled human personality and behavior. His first comedy in this form was *Every Man in His Humor* (1598). It was so successful that Jonson followed it with *Every Man out of His Humor* (1599), in the introduction to which he defines the term *humor*. Basically all the humor comedies are Latinate in the sense that they follow the forms of Plautus and Terence—the action is restricted in time and place, the plot is based on intrigue, the people of the plays are contemporary "type" characters, and the scene is usually local.

Inigo Jones' dress design for Jonson's *The Masque of Blackness*, 1605.

Within this Classical framework, however, Jonson constructed brilliant satires on London life. The action is often slim, but the characterizations are vivid, the individual scenes are lusty, the comedy is hilarious, and the satire is keen.

Of all the comedies Jonson wrote, the best are probably the well-known *Volpone, or the Fox* (1605-06); *Epicoene, or the Silent Woman* (1609), a Renaissance version of *Charley's Aunt*; *The Alchemist* (1610), an epic of Elizabethan con artists; and *Bartholomew Fair* (1614), a rather shapeless presentation of London low life, based in part on a traditional cautionary tale about a king (in the play a magistrate) who goes among his subjects in disguise to discover the truth. Jonson's later comedies, which are more complex and more heavy-handed, are best characterized by *The Devil Is An Ass* (1616); *The Staple of News* (1625-26); *The New Inn* (1629); *The Magnetic Lady* (1632); and *A Tale of a Tub* (1633).

After the great triumverate of Shakespeare, Marlowe, and Jonson, came a number of fine playwrights who, on their own merits, would have made the Elizabethan period famous for its drama. The earliest of these is George Chapman (c. 1559-1634). Chapman was a poet, Classics scholar, and playwright. As both a poet and student of Classical literature he began a translation of Homer's *Iliad* in 1598 and completed it in 1610. In 1615 he completed the companion piece, his translation of Homer's *Odyssey*. The first of these translations is in rhyming lines of fourteen syllables, the second is in ten-syllable rhyming lines. The poetic capability and power that Chapman showed in his translations of these great epics had been revealed earlier when, in 1598 he completed Marlowe's *Hero and Leander*, which had been left unfinished at Marlowe's death. Unfortunately, in his own plays Chapman was less sure than in his translations. The plays contain some fine poetry, but their dramatic construction is weak and his attempt to achieve the epic qualities he so admired in Homer tends to destroy what little drama is there. His comedies—*Monsieur d'Olive* (1604), *All Fools* (1605), and *May Day* (1611)—are weak, as is his tragicomedy *The Gentleman Usher* (1606). His melodramatic tragedies comprise his best work: *Bussy d'Ambois* (1607), *The Revenge of Bussy d'Ambois* (1613), and the two parts of *The Conspiracy and Tragedy of Charles, Duke of Byron* (1608). All of these deal with the rise and fall of an upstart at the French court. They achieved substantial popularity in their own time, but today Chapman is better known from a single sonnet by John Keats, "On First Looking Into Chapman's Homer," than from all his plays.

John Marston (c. 1575-1634), more than any other of the Elizabethan playwrights, earned a reputation for satirical bitterness in all of his dramas. He was born at Coventry of an Italian mother and went on to graduate from Oxford. In 1616 he became rector of Christ Church, Hampshire, and stopped writing plays to devote himself for the rest of his life to parish work. Until this date, however, he wrote poetry and at least a dozen important plays which were exciting, realistic, and often coarse in both word and deed. The two-part *History of Antonio and Mellida* is a bloody revenge tragedy that contains so much bombast and inflated ranting and roaring that it led Ben Jonson to satirize both Marston and the play in *The Poetaster*. Marston in return collaborated with Thomas Dekker, another victim of Jonson's attentions, and wrote *Satiromastix*, *or the Untrussing of the Humorous Poet* (1601). However, he seems to have settled his literary feud for in 1605 he collaborated with Jonson and Chapman to produce *Eastward Ho!*, a savage satire on the king's Scots followers that earned the three playwrights a jail term for libel. Marston's coarse comedy *Dutch Courtesan* (1603-04), was followed by his most successful work, *The Malcontent* (1604), a tragedy in which the misanthropic hero Malvole vents his spleen regarding court intrigue and society.

After Shakespeare, Jonson, and Marlowe, the most important dramatist of the Elizabethan period was probably Thomas Dekker (c. 1572-1632). Little is known of Dekker's life, beyond the fact that he managed to eke out an uncertain living in a city that was notoriously ungenerous to its writers. He was constantly harrassed by creditors and lived in constant fear of debtors prison. He apparently failed to attract the support of a patron, which is unfortunate because he managed to carve out a highly respectable career as poet, pamphleteer, and dramatist.

Dekker, like Samuel Johnson after him, was purely a city man, in love with London and its citizens and, excepting a few attempts to imitate the romantic vogue, his writings are all of the city and its middle class. He was a careful reporter of his subject, and as a result realism and depth of human understanding became the hallmarks of his work. Even if he had never written a play he would have achieved considerable status as a writer, for his *The*

The frontispiece to *The Wits; or, Sport upon Sport*, by Francis Kirkman, is thought to illustrate the stage of the Red Bull.

Wonderful Year (1603) is an exceptional account of the London plague upon which Defoe later drew heavily on for his own *Journal of the Plague Year* (1722). Such pamphlets as *The Seven Deadly Sins of London* (1606), an allegory of God's punishment of the city, *The Bellman of London* and its sequel *Lanthorne and Candle-light* (both in 1608), which are outstanding contributions to the literature of roguery, and *The Gull's Hornbook* (1609), a primer for London fops, are all far above the average pamphlets of the time.

In writing his plays, Dekker apparently collaborated with other playwrights nearly as often as he worked alone. With John Marston he attacked Ben Jonson in *Satiromastix* (1601); with Thomas Middleton he wrote *The Roaring Girl* (printed in 1611), in which a female crook becomes a feminine Robin Hood; with John Ford and William Rowley he wrote *The Witch of Edmonton*; and with Henry Chettle and Haughton he wrote *Patient Grissel* (1600), a comedy on the theme of the patient wife. On his own, Dekker wrote *Old Fortunatus* (1599), a play based on the folk tale of the miraculous purse. His two best plays are *The Honest Whore* (1604-05, in two parts), and *The Shoemaker's Holiday* (1599). *Holiday* seems easily the best of the two plays and is regularly revived, because while the action is not always highly dramatic the comic antics of the shoemaker Simon Eyre and his journeyman Firk still delight and enthrall an audience.

One of the most important of the Elizabethan dramatists is Thomas Heywood (c. 1570-1641), an actor who tellingly defended his profession in the pamphlet *An Apology for Actors* (1612), and a playwright who, at the close of his career, boasted of having had "either an entire hand, or at least a main finger" in two hundred twenty plays. He wrote huge and rather shapeless chronicle plays such as *Edward IV* (1592-99, in two parts), melodramas such as *The Fair Maid of the West* (1607-31, in two parts), and many works dealing with classical mythology. He also wrote pageants and masques. Probably his best work is in the genre of domestic tragedy or melodrama. *A Woman Killed with Kindness* (1603) is the best of these, featuring an English middle-class gentleman, John Frankford, whose wife, Anne, is seduced by Frankford's best friend. Instead of taking revenge, Frankford merely banishes Anne to another manor house where she dies of sorrow made doubly difficult to bear because she is so conscious of her husband's kindness. A subplot that details the problems of Anne's young brother, a wastrel who at last learns true love and nobility, counterpoints the main action. In terms of his total work, Heywood probably deserves the epithet he received from Charles Lamb—"a sort of prose Shakespeare."

THOMAS MIDDLETON: As is true, unfortunately, for so many other Elizabethan theatricians, we can follow the general outlines of Thomas Middleton's career, but we still know very little about the man himself. The first record of the playwright's existence is April 18, 1580, when he was baptized at the Church of St. Lawrence in the Old Jewry, London. When Thomas reached the age of five his father, William, a London bricklayer, died, leaving the family with some acreage and a little money held in trust. Less than ten months later Thomas' mother, Anne, married an out-of-work grocer named Thomas Harvey. Anne's new husband seems to have married her primarily for personal gain, because within a short time the Harveys were fighting tooth and nail, with the property left by William Middleton and the income it provided at the center of the conflict. Whatever the reason for the marriage it seems to have been a mistake. Both parties resorted to trickery, with Anne threatening to have Harvey arrested, claiming that he had tried to poison her, which may very well have been the case. It is not clear to what extent Thomas was involved in the family feud, or in what way he was affected by the irregularities in his mother's household, but affect him it must have.

At the age of sixteen Middleton completed his first published work, a translation (or paraphrase) of a passage in the Bible. As it turned out, the piece was flat and unreadable; in attempting to be rhetorical, Middleton had carried his writing to an excess.

In April 1598, at the age of eighteen, Middleton went on to Queens College, Oxford. Although he never graduated, this experience at the university turns up in a number of ways in his later works. The passage between Tim Yellowhammer and his tutor, at the beginning of act IV of *A Chaste Maid in Cheapside* (1611), is a humorous indication of his familiarity with academic disputation, and the short history of the scholar in *The Ant and The Nightingale* shows his acquaintance with university life.

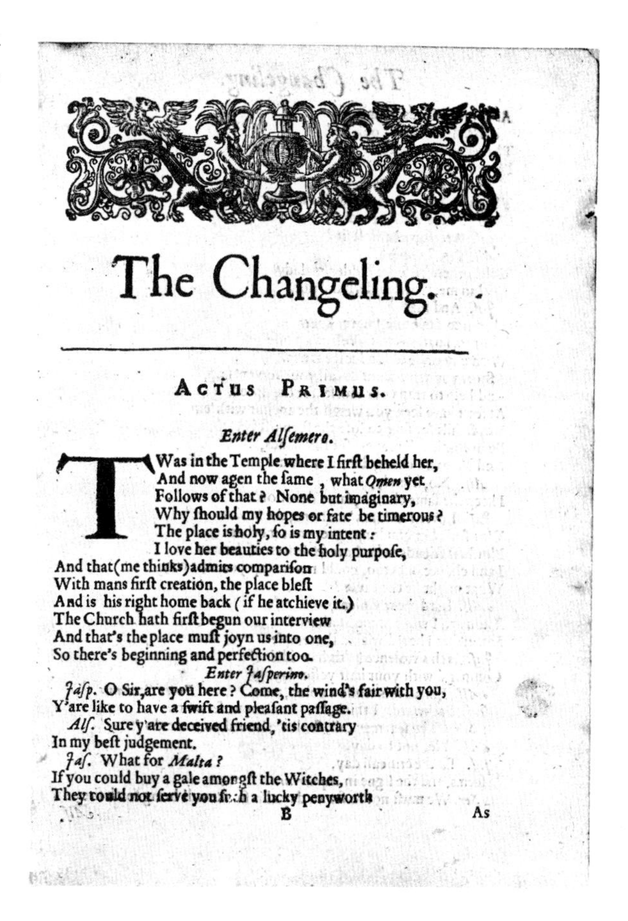

The Changeling.

ACTUS PRIMUS.

Enter Alsemero.

TWas in the Temple where I first beheld her,
And now agen the same , what *Omen* yet
Follows of that ? None but imaginary,
Why should my hopes or fate be timerous ?
The place is holy, so is my intent :
I love her beauties to the holy purpose,
And that(me thinks)admits comparison
With mans first creation, the place blest
And is his right home back (if he atchieve it.)
The Church hath first begun our interview
And that's the place must joyn us into one,
So there's beginning and perfection too.

Enter Jasperino.

Jasp. O Sir,are you here ? Come, the wind's fair with you,
Y'are like to have a swift and pleasant passage.

Als. Sure y'are deceived friend, 'tis contrary
In my best judgement.

Jas. What for *Malta* ?
If you could buy a gale amongst the Witches,
They could not serve you such a lucky penyworth

B As

The first textual page of *The Changeling* (1635), which was a popular play, but was not printed until 1653, in a cheap quarto edition.

According to Henslowe's diary, in 1602, at the age of twenty-one, Middleton began to write for the theatre. His work for Henslowe's two companies, the Admiral's Men and the Earl of Worcester's Men, should probably be considered Middleton's apprenticeship in the theatre, since the engagement was brief, and in 1604 he began writing for the children's companies. This second phase of Middleton's career, with the children's companies, marks his emergence as a major comic dramatist.

In his first plays Middleton revealed an allegiance to the declining Elizabethan romance, joined with the attraction of the new Jacobean critical spirit, but he soon became a complete Jacobean. The Jacobean age was characterized by a questioning attitude, skepticism, cynicism, satire, amusement, and an excessive preoccupation with staged horrors. Middleton especially reflects the satiric aspect, looking at the London around him and applying his vivid, barely restrained imagination to the task of reproducing, in verse, what he saw. His skill as satirist can be seen in one of his earliest works, *The Phoenix*, which was presented by Paul's Boys on February 20, 1604. In this play Middleton emphasizes contemporary dishonesty, depravity, and greed. As a corrective, he advocates the simplicity and properness of the society of the past, and introduces a theme which comes up again and again in his plays; that is, sin is blind and the sinner will inevitably grope in the darkness until he finally stumbles onto the path that will surely lead him to disaster.

After Middleton had found the direction for his own particular talents, he went on to write four major comedies—*Your Five Gallants, Michaelmas Term, A Trick to Catch the Old One,* and *A Mad World, My Masters*—all published (or at least entered in the Stationers' Register) in 1607 or 1608. These plays describe contemporary London, portraying the fascinating variety of scoundrels who inhabited it; however, they differ a good deal in tone and emphasis. In these plays Middleton shows his interest in capturing the surface manners and morals of his time, as well as the inner workings of the characters.

Sometime between 1606 and 1608 Middleton resumed writing for adult companies, and by the time he had reached his thirties he had established himself as one of the principal playwrights of the finest Renaissance company, the King's Men. From 1613 on, he was employed in a number of civic undertakings, chiefly the preparation of the Lord Mayor's shows, which he sometimes produced as well as wrote. At this time he was also writing pageants, entertainments, and masques, and it was here that he displayed an ability to turn out the type of rhetoric that appealed to the sponsors of such productions. In one of his pageants, *The Triumph of Truth*, he created such an inspiring spectacle that many thought it outdid anything that had gone before it.

Middleton, who up to this point had spent the largest part of his career writing comedies, suddenly turned to tragedy. It is not known whether the three tragedies he wrote were done with a collaborator. However, *The Changeling* (1622) was almost certainly written with the help of William Rowley. Rowley probably worked with many different dramatists of the time because he was an actor and thus knew the stage from that particular perspective. He was also, however, a hack writer whose work would not have made it alone. Whatever Rowley's personal talents may have been, his collaboration with Middleton on *The Changeling* was a successful match.

On September 6, 1620, Middleton was granted the post of Chronologer for the City of London, a position he held until his death in 1627, when Ben Jonson succeeded him. As Inventor of Entertainments for the city he composed speeches of welcome and interludes for civic banquets; as Chronologer he kept a manuscript journal of public events.

In July 1627 Middleton died at the age of forty-seven. He had written successfully for more than twenty years, producing plays that were profitable to the theatre, but that were not critical successes, even during their own time. His choice and treatment of his materials, taken from contemporary London life and from a variety of literary sources, his use of language, the breadth and depth of his interest in character, the continuity of his themes, and the concentrated thematic relevance of the various components of his dramatic structures, reveal a great individuality and independent strength of purpose. However, it was not until many years after his death that he was finally considered by many to be among the greatest of the Jacobean dramatists.

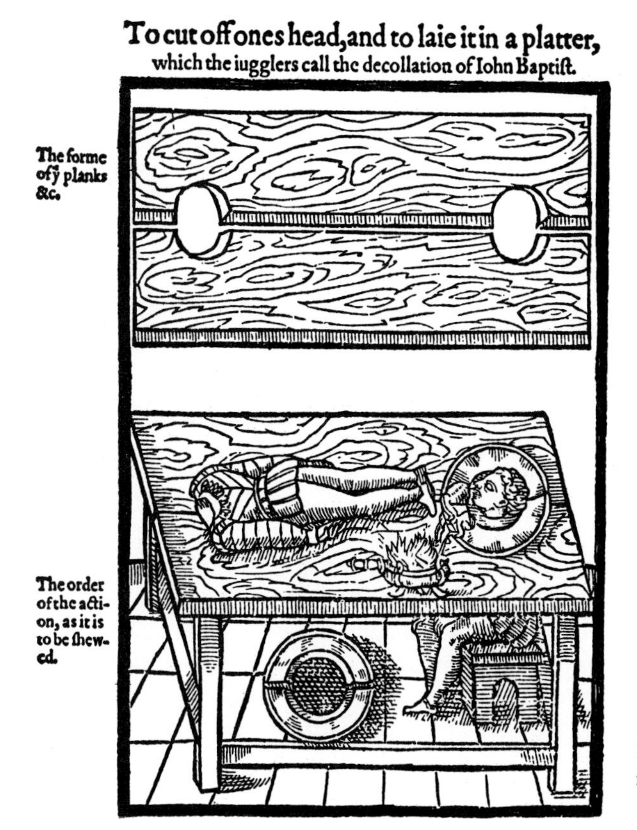

Illustration of a "beheading machine" for use in Jacobean plays.

JACOBEAN AND CAROLINE DRAMA

Elizabeth I died in 1603, but the great flowering did not end with the death of the monarch. Indeed, so pervasive was the Renaissance attitude which had developed under Elizabeth that some critics ignore her immediate successors and consider that the Elizabethan period lasted until 1642 and the closing of the theatres by edict of the Puritan Parliament at the beginning of the Civil War. This attitude, however justified in a superficial way, ignores the fact that shortly after Elizabeth's death a change did begin to occur in the English drama, probably provoked by the change in court attitudes that came about with the ascension of James I, who ruled from 1603 to 1625.

Jacobean is the term generally applied to the characteristics of the reign of James I, and it is derived from *Jacobus*, the Latin name for James. Sometimes it is confused with *Jacobite*, the term applied to supporters of James II, who was deposed by the Revolution of 1688, and sometimes with *Jacobin*, the name of a radical democratic club during the French Revolution nearly a century later.

James was followed to the throne by Charles I, who ruled from 1625 to 1649, and this period is usually referred to as the *Caroline* period. The term derives from *Carolus*, the Latin name for Charles, and is often extended to cover the literature created during the reign of Charles II, who was restored to the throne in 1660.

The Jacobean and Caroline periods are similar in many minor respects to the Elizabethan, but in major ways the drama is quite different. The great Elizabethan dramatists were concerned with exploring the grave moral, philosophical, and scientific issues of the times. They raised questions about man's nature and his place in the universe. The Jacobean and Caroline dramatists, on the other hand, tended to subjugate intellectual interests and complex characterization to the thrills and excitement usually generated by Senecan-style horrific incidents. In part this lack of substance is made up for by increased technical skills. The Jacobean writers plotted more tightly, used exposition more skillfully, and compressed the action into tight, swiftly moving episodes.

Of these writers, one of the earliest and certainly the bloodiest was Cyril Tourneur (1575-1626). Tourneur had been for many years a soldier in the Netherlands and this experience, fighting against the Spanish tyranny in one of the cruelest of all wars, may have given him the taste for brutality and bloodshed that characterizes his two plays, *The Revenger's Tragedy* (1606-07) and *The Atheist's Tragedy* (1607-11). In the whole of Jacobean drama, which reveled in incest, rape, and murder, no plays quite equal these two works. Tourneur let his horrific imagination run riot, and produced such scenes as a duke who is poisoned by being tricked into kissing the moldering skull of the girl he seduced and thus destroyed, or a group of avengers stomping their victim to death. The characters are compatible with the plots; which is to say that they are grossly exaggerated and most are overcome with evil passions. Tourneur's death, in a kind of strange poetic justice, resembled a potential scene from one of his own plays; he died miserably from wounds received in the Cadiz expedition under Sir Edward Cecil.

Two of the best of the Jacobean writers were Francis Beaumont (1584-1616) and John Fletcher (1579-1625), whose collaboration is one of the most successful in theatrical history. In fact, so closely are their names linked together that it is a common error to apply both their names to all the fifty-odd plays they turned out. The two playwrights, however, do not appear to have been at all close before 1606, and Beaumont, who was five years younger than Fletcher, died nine years before his partner. Thus, their collaboration could not possibly have covered the period of time they were both writing, and it is certain that both wrote plays alone or in partnership with some other dramatist.

Exactly how their labor on the plays was divided is difficult to tell. From all accounts Beaumont seems to have been the more serious of the two and probably responsible for most of the tragic scenes. Fletcher, on the other hand, was coarser and more comic in his inclinations, thus far better suited for comic scenes. Fletcher was also the better poet, both in terms of blank verse and incidental lyrics. Of the plays that they certainly did together, the most famous is the satirical *The Knight of the Burning Pestle* (1607-10), which mounts a savage attack on bourgeois theatrical tastes. *The Maid's Tragedy* (1608-11) is a moving and even heartbreaking play that is sometimes melodramatic but always tempered by the powerful, restrained tragic scenes. *Philaster, or Love Lies A-Bleeding* (1608-10) is a melange of heartrendering situations designed to produce a pathetic rather than tragic appeal. Although the plays of Beaumont and Fletcher are marred occasionally by Jacobean excesses, they are well constructed works with excellent single scenes and fine characterization.

Philip Massinger (1583-1640) was, from a purely technical point of view, one of the finest Jacobean playwrights. Born in Salisbury, he attracted the Earl of Pembroke as his patron and thus became free to develop his dramatic tal-

The title page of William Alabaster's *Roxana* (1630) shows, in the lower-center panel, a view of a stage with actors and spectators.

ents without the financial woes that plagued so many beginning writers of his period. Fifteen plays are usually attributed to him, many of which were written in collaboration with Fletcher, Dekker, Field, and other playwrights. His two early tragedies which he wrote by himself are *The Duke of Milan* (1620-22) and *The Roman Actor* (1626). Neither is as good as *The Fatal Dowry* (1618-19), which he coauthored with Field. *The Great Duke of Florence* (1627) is a typical Jacobean comedy which foreshadows the manners of the Restoration period. Massinger's most famous work is probably *A New Way to Pay Old Debts* (1621-25), which is an imitation of the intrigue plot developed by Middleton. The play features the nasty, scheming Sir Giles Overreach, based on the character of Sir Giles Momperson, a slumlord extortioner of the period. This play, like all of Massinger's works, is unusual for the period in that it displays a moral sense that is strongly promoted but never sentimentalized.

John Webster (c. 1580-c. 1625) was a tailor's son who went on to become perhaps the greatest playwright of the Jacobean period, displaying the power of the Elizabethans without the excesses of the Jacobeans. He wrote an undistinguished comedy, *The Devil's Law Case* (1616-22), and in collaboration with Thomas Heywood, a tragedy on classical materials titled *Appius and Virginia* (1608-30). His two greatest plays are *The White Devil* (1609-13) and *The Duchess of Malfi* (1612-14). Webster's plays tend to lack tightness in plot construction, they contain too many wordy episodes, and the characters are often overdone and even, upon occasion, inconsistent. However, he wrote some great individual scenes and managed to infuse his plays with a sense of terror that exceeds even Tourneur, but without resorting to such bloody excess. The trial of Vittoria Corombona in *White Devil* and the death of the Duchess in *Malfi* are examples of his best work.

In one of literature's most unfortunate episodes, four of John Ford's (1586-c. 1639) plays were "unluckily burned or put under pye bottoms" by Betsy Baker, the infamous cook of the antiquary Warburton. The plays which managed to survive such treatment are *The Witch of Edmonton* (1621), a domestic tragedy which he wrote in partnership with Dekker and William Rowley; *The Lover's Melancholy* (1628), a gentle romantic comedy under the influence of Burton's *Anatomy of Melancholy* (1621); *Perkin Warbeck* (1629-34), a fine historical drama about an impostor who masquerades as the son of Edward IV; *Love's Sacrifice* (1625-33), a tragedy which deals with the incentuous love of Fernando and his sister Bianca; *'Tis Pity She's a Whore* (1625-33), another incestuous tragedy, this time between Giovanni and his sister Annabella; and *The Broken Heart* (1625-33), which traces the consequences that result when a brother forces his sister to marry against her will. Ford anticipated the discoveries of many contemporary students of abnormal psychology, but as an artist he was primarily concerned with results when people substituted passion for moral law. For this reason his plays are often regarded as prime examples of Jacobean decadence.

James Shirley (1596-1666) was a graduate of both Oxford and Cambridge, a teacher, a soldier, and the last of the great Jacobean (or perhaps Caroline) dramatists. More than forty plays have been attributed to Shirley, but of these only a handful are still important. His tragedies are in the usual Jacobean mold. The best of them are *The Maid's Revenge* (1626), *Love's Cruelty*

A blowup of the stage scene on the *Roxana* title page. The stage does not seem to be one of the public theatres but, from its dimensions, seems likely to be in the great hall of a private manor house or castle.

(1631), and *The Traitor* (1641), which still stands as his finest work, in spite of the fact that it is too complicated in its plot, wordy, and highly exaggerated in its characterization. It was in the field of comedy, however, that Shirley excelled. *Hyde Park* (1632) is an excellent satire on high life in London. *The Gamester* (1633) and *The Lady of Pleasure* (1635), while not up to *Hyde Park* in most ways, are interesting to the degree that they foreshadow the Restoration comedies of Etherege and Wycherley which were still to come. Shirley died of exposure during the Great Fire of London, six years after the Restoration and long after he had come to the end of his playwriting career.

THE ACTING TROUPES

The profession of acting was not only frowned upon in early sixteenth century England, but actively discouraged by charging itinerant actors with vagabondage, which made them liable to physical punishment such as branding or jail sentences or both. This could only be avoided when the actors came under the protection of a patron. At the time that Elizabeth mounted the throne any gentleman could maintain a company of actors, and many did so. However, because of local civil and religious attitudes, the days on which even such legitimate troupes could perform were severely limited. Thus, most actors performed other duties when they were not acting—which was most of the time.

Sir Henry Paston, for example, kept a groom not because of the man's way with horses but because of his skill at playing the roles of St. George and Robin Hood.

On January 3, 1572, the activities of actors were gathered closer to the throne by making it illegal for any nobleman under the rank of baron to keep an acting troupe. At the same time, independent companies were permitted to play, though only after obtaining a license from two local justices of the peace. These licenses were difficult to obtain in many areas, required the payment of a license fee, and were good only in the area where they were obtained—which meant that every time a troupe changed location a new license had to be secured. In 1574 the actors were placed under even closer control of the court by making the Master of Revels, an official of the royal household, the licenser of all plays and acting troupes. This arrangement was not as hostile to the art as it might at first seem, and managed to preserve theatre, often in the face of strong local disapproval. Community governments, even those that had supported the cycle plays, were often strongly opposed to professional actors, and means for voiding licenses issued by the Master of Revels ranged from the danger of the plague to the interruption of religious services.

In 1604 the crown ended the right of noblemen to maintain private acting companies, providing that all companies be licensed to members of the royal family. In 1608 the final step was taken when the crown took over the specification of playing areas outside the city of London which then, as now, controlled its own property. Up until this time the permanent theatres of London had existed only outside the city limits, but now they moved into the city to escape the strict control of the crown.

Of the many troupes that existed in Renaissance London, the most important early company was the Earl of Leicester's Men, licensed in 1574 under the leadership of James Burbage. After the plague year of 1592-93 the Lord Chamberlain's Men, a shared venture between the Burbage family and the troupe's leading players, and the Lord Admiral's Men, under the artistic direction of Edward Alleyn and the financial management of Philip Henslowe, both emerged to share the limelight. After James I ascended the throne the Lord Chamberlain's Men became the King's Men, a title they kept until 1642.

THE EARL OF LEICESTER'S MEN: Exactly when the Earl of Leicester's Men began as a true acting company is uncertain. In 1559, responding to Puritan pressure, Elizabeth issued a proclamation limiting theatre to licensed troupes. Perhaps in an attempt to please Elizabeth, who resented the Puritan pressure, or perhaps in a sincere desire to protect theatre, Robert Dudley, the Earl of Leicester, became the patron of a band of actors. Exactly who they were, or when this patronage begins, is unknown. The first reference to the troupe is in 1559, the same year as Elizabeth's proclamation. Because of Dudley's power, both as Earl of Leicester and as Elizabeth's favorite, the company was relieved of the problems that beset minor troupes and, armed with their license and letter of recommendation, they set out on their travels around the provinces, returning periodically to London to perform before the court.

Following the proclamation of 1572, the Leicester players, for their own protection, petitioned to be made personal servants of their lord, and it is this petition that for the first time identifies the members of the troupe. They were, in the order their names were signed to the petition, James Burbage, John Perkinne, John Laneham, William Johnson, Roberte Wilson, and Thomas Clarke. Because Burbage heads the list it has been assumed that he was head of the company. Two of the troupe, Laneham and Johnson, would become members of the Queen's Men when that troupe was established in 1583.

The company at last gained a permanent house when Burbage erected The Theatre in 1576. The Theatre gave Leicester's Men a valuable headquarters in London, but while performances must have been immediately successful we know nothing about the plays the troupe performed, except for eight titles. However, the acrimony that developed between the City of London and The Theatre led, in 1583, to Elizabeth forming her own troupe, the Queen's Men. Two of the actors who formed this new troupe were members of Leicester's Men, and perhaps as a result of this loss the troupe disappeared for nearly two years.

In 1585 Leicester's Men made a tour of the provinces and on December 27, 1586, they made their final court appearance. In September 1588 Leicester died, leaving no heirs, and the company dissolved; some of the actors joined

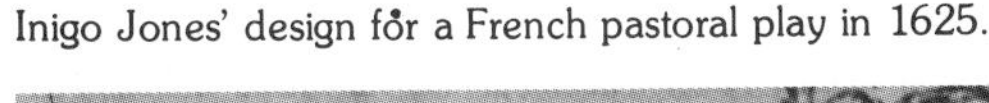
Inigo Jones' design for a French pastoral play in 1625.

Lord Strange's Men and the balance must have sought a new patron, whose name we do not know.

THE LORD CHAMBERLAIN'S MEN: The founder of the Lord Chamberlain's Men was Henry Carey, the first Lord Hunsdon, who died in 1596 without his players ever having achieved particular distinction. His son, George Carey, the second Lord Hunsdon, continued his father's tradition and kept the players in his service. The company thus had to change their name, and for a time they were known as the Lord of Hunsdon's Servants (and are so referred to on the title page of the first quarto of *Romeo and Juliet*). They were able to resume their former title, however, when the second Lord Hunsdon was, like his father, appointed to the post of Lord Chamberlain in 1597. By this time the formerly undistinguished company had become very distinguished indeed.

The aspect of the Lord Chamberlain's Men that is particularly exciting is the depth of talent the members possessed. Richard and Cuthbert Burbage, the sons of James Burbage, were both actors, and Richard was building a reputation as a tragic actor that was nearly as great as that of Alleyn. Will Kempe had already established himself as a great clown, perhaps the greatest in England. Another member of the troupe, William Shakespeare, had only two serious rivals for the title of England's greatest dramatist.

The earliest popular success of the Lord Chamberlain's Men was *Richard III*. Having Shakespeare in the company, however, guaranteed them a reasonably consistent supply of excellent new material. *Romeo and Juliet* followed *Richard III* and was an enormous success. During the Christmas season of 1594 they played at court and also at Gray's Inn, where they did *The Comedy of Errors* for the budding young lawyers as part of the season's revels. In 1595 they did *A Midsummer Night's Dream* and *Richard II*, which was Shakespeare's attempt to outdo *Edward II* by Marlowe, one of his closest rivals for playwriting honors.

In 1597 the players had a stormy time. The lease on the property on which The Theatre was built was running out, and the owner, Gyles Allen, decided not to renew it, hoping to foreclose the lease, tear down The Theatre, and sell the used lumber. James Burbage, who was at last witnessing his dream of a major popular theatre coming true, leased the dining hall of the old Blackfriars monastery and converted it into a theatre where the Lord Chamberlain's Men could perform. However, the neighborhood objected to having a theatre in their district and petitioned the Council to halt the planned opening. Burbage was ordered not to proceed further with the plan, and several weeks after receiving this notice he died, leaving The Theatre to Cuthbert and the aborted Blackfriars Theatre to Richard. Also in 1597 the players produced Chapman's *A Humorous Day's Mirth* at the Rose Theatre.

At about this time some of the Chamberlain's Men (and some of the rival Lord Admiral's Men) deserted to join a new company sponsored by the Earl of Pembroke. This new company chose as its first venture a new play called *The Isle of Dogs* by the bitter satirist Thomas Nashe in collaboration with a young actor, Ben Jonson. The play was deemed "seditious and slanderous" and the Council took a firm stand, closing all the city's theatres and sentencing three of the actors, including Jonson, to short prison terms.

The rivalry between the Lord Chamberlain's Men and the Lord Admiral's Men grew exceedingly keen. The lease on The Theatre was not negotiable and so the chief shareholders in the Lord Chamberlain's troupe all agreed to build a new playhouse. They leased a plot of land south of the Thames, tore down The Theatre, and making use of the lumber from the old building they built the Globe Theatre.

By 1600 the public theatre in London was in serious trouble, what with Puritan complaints and repressive measures by the Council. The theatres were often closed and so, seeking to make some money on the side, the great clown of the Chamberlain's Men, Will Kempe, made a bet with some gamesters that he could dance all the way from London to Norwich—some one hundred miles. He won the bet, and the event proved so popular that success went to his head. He sold his share in the Globe, left the Lord Chamberlain's Men, and departed for Europe to dance over the Alps to Rome. This loss of their clown in an already depressed season left the players on the brink of seeming disaster.

In 1603, following Elizabeth's death, the Lord Chamberlain's Men were appointed to be the King's Men and Grooms of the Chamber Extraordinary. This good fortune marked them as the city's leading company, a distinction they were to hold until the end of the era.

THE LORD ADMIRAL'S MEN: Like the Lord Chamberlain's Men, the Lord Admiral's Men was, in the beginning, a reasonably undistinguished troupe. The plague of 1593, however, forced the acting troupes out of London, and when they returned in the late spring of 1594 the rising young actor Edward Alleyn reorganized the company so efficiently that it went on to rival the Lord Chamberlain's Men. Established almost permanently at the Rose Theatre, they produced plays by Chapman, Marlowe, Peele, Greene, and Dekker. While Jonson and two of his fellow players, Gabriel Spencer and Robert Shaw, were in prison following the production of *The Isle of Dogs*, they agreed that they would join the Admiral's Men at the Rose, and upon their release they followed through with this plan, strengthening the troupe considerably. This association lasted only a few months, however, before Jonson and Spencer fell out and Jonson killed Spencer in a duel.

After the Lord Chamberlain's Men established themselves in the Globe, thereby becoming near neighbors of the Admiral's Men, the rivalry between the two fine troupes became intense. This competition, however, was cooled a bit as both troupes turned to face a common enemy—Paul's Boys. The choir boys of St. Paul's had, some ten years earlier, given musical and dramatic entertainments before the court, but now, financed by the Earl of Derby, they were set up as a semipublic theatre, playing in a private house in the precinct of St. Paul's. They immediately became one of the most popular troupes in London.

In 1599 the Admiral's Men realized that the old Rose could no longer compete with the new Globe Theatre, so Alleyn and Henslowe signed a contract with Peter Street, the man who had built the Globe, to build a new theatre in the parish of St. Giles Cripplegate to the north of the city. There were many problems and delays, but in August of 1600 the new theatre, called the Fortune, was finished.

The Queen's official choir, the "Children of the Chapel," acted their plays in the Middle Temple and Trinity Hall.

Shortly after the Admiral's Men moved into the Fortune they were faced with a new threat, the reestablishment of the Blackfriars as a boy's troupe under the direction of Nathaniel Giles, Choirmaster of the Queen's Chapel Royal. They were aided by their own one-time resident playwright, Ben Jonson, who had once again left the Admiral's Men. With Paul's Boys and the Children of the Blackfriars both drawing heavily on the gentry; that is, the highest paying part of the audiences that had flocked to see the professional players, the professional troupes faced real troubles indeed.

Following the appointment of the Lord Chamberlain's Men as the King's Men, the fortunes of the Admiral's Men went into decline, and when in 1608 the Blackfriars reverted to Burbage and the King's Men the route was complete and the era of the great troupes had effectively come to an end.

THE ELIZABETHAN PLAYHOUSE

On April 13, 1576, James Burbage, an excarpenter and exactor, obtained a twenty-one-year lease from one Gyles Allen on a piece of property in Holywell near Bishopsgate. Putting his total background to work he drew up plans for Renaissance England's first permanent theatre. The building was completed in late summer and opened during the fall of that year. It was immediately successful and thus provided a strong influence on all subsequent theatre construction during the period. In the following year, Henry Lanman leased a parcel of land near Burbage's building, in a spot called Curten Close, and constructed a theatre called, appropriately, the Curtain. Lanman apparently lacked Burbage's managerial ability, however, and within ten years he turned over control of the Curtain to the carpenter-actor, thus making Burbage the major theatrical entrepreneur in the city.

In 1579, at the same time that The Theatre and the Curtain were drawing large houses, a theatre about which we know very little, Newington Butts, was constructed. Also during this period a young man named Philip Henslowe married his exmaster's widow and thus gained control over some extensive property. He attempted a number of commercial ventures such as innkeeper and farmer, and in 1585 he purchased from the Church a plot of land on the Bankside and built a theatre on it. This theatre, the Rose, opened in 1587. As a practical businessman, Henslowe was conditioned to the careful keeping of records, and it is from his diary that much of our knowledge concerning the early Elizabethan theatre is derived.

In the twenty-six years following the Rose, five more theatres were built in London. These were the Swan (c. 1595-1632); the Globe (1599-1613, 1614-1644); the Fortune (1600-1621, 1621-1661); the Red Bull (1605-1663); and the Hope (1613-1617). Although these theatres varied in minor ways, essentially they were all based on the same plan—the plan that began with The Theatre, that lasted throughout the Elizabethan period, and that has influenced theatre design right up into our own time.

Generally speaking, the English theatres are considered to have developed out of two primary ancestors. The first and most important ancestor is the inn-yard, because in many ways the essentially Medieval English inn was quite similar in shape and basic appearance to the Renaissance English playhouse. These inns followed a standard pattern in terms of structure, with rooms grouped about three or four sides of an inn-yard that could be entered by passing through a large gateway. Early performances did indeed take place in these inn-yards, and the playing situation was probably much like it was in the later theatres. Most of the theorists of inn-yard performance propose a stage (probably one or more wagons) with a booth or mansion at the rear (to serve as a stagehouse) set up at one end of the yard. Raised bleachers around the perimeter of the yard provided seating, as did the windows of the inn that

A Renaissance English inn, seen from the back of the innyard. The public entered the enclosed yard through the gate where the horseman is making an entrance. The balconies and windows looking onto the yard became the galleries of the Elizabethan theatre, and the yard itself also was incorporated into the theatre structure.

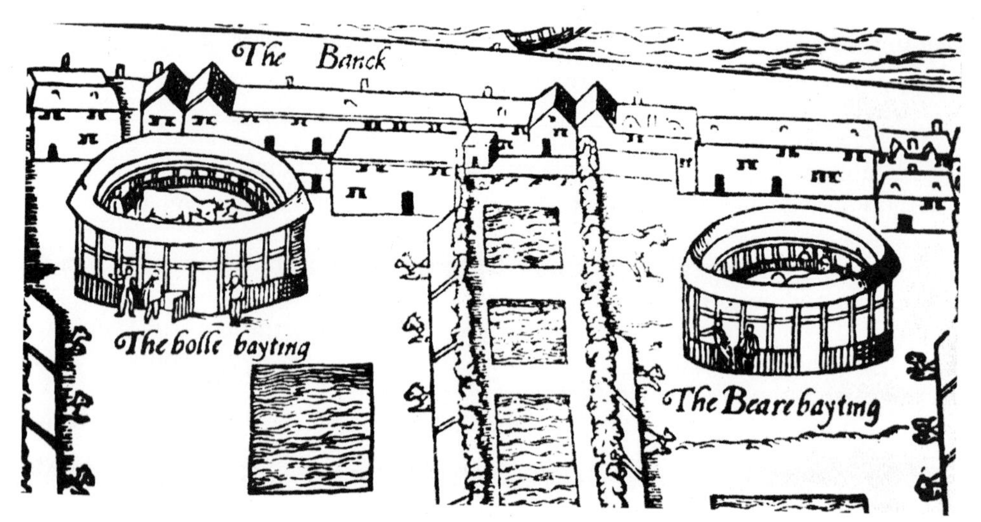

The Bull Baiting and Bear Baiting Arenas, in a detail from Aga's map of London, published between 1560 and 1590.

opened onto the inn-yard. The flat area in front of the stage, that is the center of the yard, could accomodate patrons who wished to stand or who could not afford seats within the inn or on the bleachers. Admissions were collected at the inn-yard gate, and the proprietor of the inn collected from those who wished to view the action from a window (corresponding to the later gallery boxes). This setup describes in a surprisingly accurate way the basic structure of the Elizabethan public theatre.

The second most likely ancestor, after the inn-yards, has generally been considered to be the arenas where bull and bear baiting took place. Such influence now seems rather unlikely, however, for maps of London drawn during the period show the arenas to be circular structures, fenced in, and without seats or galleries. The customers apparently stood outside the structure, behind reinforced low walls, to view the combats.

For the stage area itself the most likely ancestor seems to be the pageant wagon, probably with a flat-bed wagon drawn up before it to serve as a playing area. Such wagons likely provided the stage area in many of London's inn-yard performances.

Essentially the Elizabethan theatre was a timber and stucco building, either square, round, or hexagonal, with a thatched roof over the galleries and an unroofed central courtyard. In most cases it was three stories high; that is, high enough to contain three levels of galleries for seating patrons. At the far end of the yard, opposite the main entrance, was the stage, which projected out into the yard itself. Over the back part of the stage was the "shadow" or "heavens," a roof that protected the rear stage area from rain or even direct sunlight, and that provided a loft from which to raise and lower scenery and create such sound effects as cannon shots, thunder, and alarm bells. The size of the stage undoubtedly varied from theatre to theatre, and there is no way of ascertaining even an average dimension. However, the building contract for the Fortune Theatre has been preserved, and thus we can base our guesses on the solid facts available for at least one of the theatres. The Fortune was 80 feet square on the outside, and the inner courtyard was 55 feet square. The stage itself was 27½ feet deep and 45 feet wide. This means that there was, for the groundlings in the courtyard surrounding the stage, a standing area of nearly 27½ feet in front of the stage, and about 6 feet of standing space on either side.

At the rear of the stage was a façade containing two substantial doors that served as entrances and that allowed set pieces to be brought out to the thrust area from the tiring house. The two doors also helped, as did the doors in Greek and Roman theatres, to localize the action; thus, in *Romeo and Juliet* the Capulets and their servants would use one door and the Montagues and their people the other. Also, the rear of the stage provided a "discovery" area between the doors, sometimes called the "inner below" or study. Some scholars have depicted this discovery area as being a recess, and others as a small room projecting outward, much as if a small mansion were set between the two doors. Whatever the case, the area was one that could be curtained and large enough to contain such set pieces as a bed, chairs, or a throne. Exactly how much of the action took place within the discovery area—whether action merely began there to identify a scene and then moved out onto the thrust, or whether full scenes were played there—is another matter of scholarly disagreement.

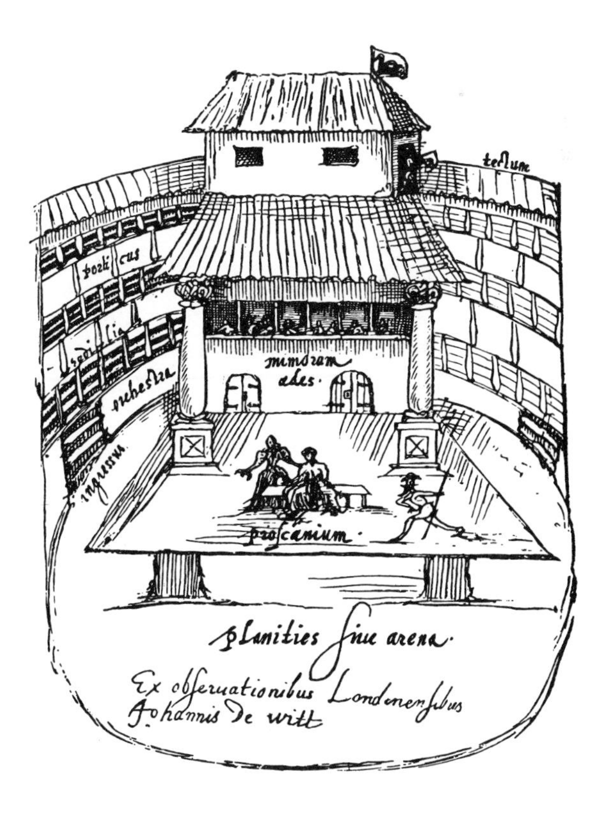

A contemporary drawing of the interior of the Swan Theatre by the Dutch traveler and scholar de Witt. His sketch shows only two doors in the lower façade, but stage directions for plays (especially at the Globe) clearly indicate a curtained alcove between the two doors. De Witt's sketch also shows clearly a balcony, used by actors, above the stage.

A third playing area existed on the second level of the façade, which could double for windows or balconies or castle walls and battlements. Exactly what the structure resembled or how it worked it uncertain. The only sketch of the interior of an Elizabethan public theatre, made of the Swan in 1596 by the Dutch traveler and scholar Johannes de Witt, shows an open gallery the width of the stage area, but other theatres may well have had variations on this arrangement, and some historians believe that the second level probably possessed a curtained discovery area similar to the one on the stage level.

Some historians have proposed a fourth playing area on a third level, sometimes referred to as the "musicians' gallery," but the evidence for this is sketchy and unconvincing. If it did indeed exist it was used only occasionally for scenes requiring higher elevations than, say, the battlements of a castle.

Somewhat less is known about the roofed-in playhouses that were called private theatres than about the unroofed public theatres. Even the title *private theatre* is misleading, for anyone could buy admission to a performance in a private theatre. However, the private theatres were substantially more expensive than the public theatres and thus the audience was generally a bit more sophisticated. There was no yard to accommodate groundlings; in the private theatres everyone had a seat, and certain of the young gallants even paid extra to secure a stool on the stage itself. This onstage seating finally became such a nuisance to the rest of the patrons that Charles II ordered the practice stopped; however, even the royal command failed to end it entirely and it took nearly another century and the backing of David Garrick to get the stage reserved for the actors.

The idea of a private theatre probably goes back into the 1570s when the London authorities exempted from regulation those dramatic performances where there was no public "or common" collection of money. This was intended to encourage productions at the Inns of Court or in the houses of noblemen, where the occasional appearance of child-actors had achieved a degree of popularity, and to discourage the troupes of professional players. In 1576, when Richard Farrant, Master of the Children of Windsor, decided to have his boys' troupe give performances at the Blackfriars, he decided to avoid charges of vagabondage by announcing it as a *private* performance in a *private* theatre, even though he did indeed collect money from the public for admission. Farrant's attempts to avoid the legal entanglements inherent in public theatre led to a series of lawsuits. In 1580 Farrant died, and in 1584 the first Blackfriars came to an end.

The second Blackfriars theatre, built by James Burbage in 1596, is certainly the most important of the private theatres. James Burbage died in 1597, willing the Blackfriars to his son, Richard, who subsequently leased it for twenty-one years to Henry Evans, who opened the theatre with a boys' company. The company was continually in trouble for doing politically objectionable plays, but from 1600 to 1608 it was one of the most successful theatres in London.

In spite of its history as the primary private theatre of the era, the dimensions of the second Blackfriars are widely disputed. It probably occupied a rectangular room that measured about one hundred feet by forty-six feet. One end of the room (perhaps up to thirty-five feet) was masked off for use as a

An etching of the Curtain Theatre, c. 1600. (From *The View of the City of London from the North Towards the South*)

tiring (and prop) room. In front of this tiring room was a stage of no more than forty-six feet by twenty-five feet, elevated about three or four feet, and separated from the front row of seats by a low railing. The audience was seated on tiers of wooden seats around the perimeter of the room and on wooden benches in the center of the room. There were also several galleries and private boxes to accommodate important members of the nobility.

SCENERY

There was apparently an almost undue use of scenic display in plays (or masques) produced at court or at the Inns of Court. Records show extensive expenditures to build a "citie" and a "battlement." Hundreds of yards of canvas was purchased to "cover divers townes and howes and other devisses and clowds." Such records imply mansion sets in the manner of Medieval stage settings, although the concept was probably toward a single, large, unified set rather than the individually conceived mansions. By the time of James I the Italianate stage practices had made their appearance in England, especially in the court performances. By 1605 they were in use for the court masques designed by Inigo Jones, and soon after they spread to private theatres. Certainly by 1636 the private theatres were using fairly lavish sets, even by court standards; the court records show that the Queen, apparently taken by reports of a private production at Oxford, borrowed both scenery and costumes for her own production of the play. Also, there are a number of allusions to sets at the Blackfriars which imply the painted "Italianate" style.

In the public theatres there was little scenic display, at least when compared to court and private theatre performances. The inner stages may well

Inigo Jones' scenic design for *The Masque of Oberon,* 1611.

have had some furniture, such as benches or a throne chair and wall hangings, but out on the thrust stage itself there was probably very little that could be defined as a set. Henslowe's list of properties includes only "i rock, i cage, i Hell mouth, i tomb of Guido, i tomb of Dido, i bedstead, i wooden hatchet, i leather hatchet, Iris head and rainbow, i little altar, i copper target, and vxii foils, iii timbrels, i dragon in Faustus, i Pope's meter, iii Imperial crowns, i plain crown." There may have been signs or "locality boards" used to identify specific geographic areas; certainly the props Henslowe lists would not have served the bill. However, in most Elizabethan plays the locale is identified quite clearly in the lines and action of the play.

COSTUMES

There has been a tendency, even in recent years, to assume that Elizabethan stage costuming consisted of little more than the contemporary dress of the time. That it was very rich contemporary dress is not debated, but the

This 1611 figure in Roman dress indicates far more knowledge of and concern with accurate historical costume than is generally credited to the Elizabethans.

implication is that little attention was paid to *creating stage costume*. Such is certainly not the case. Many of the actors did wear contemporary dress, probably of the type worn at the court, and in many cases very likely the cast-off clothing of the troupe's sponsor; however, in addition to such general costume there were apparently significant efforts to achieve national and historical verisimilitude.

In terms of historical costume, there were attempts to create Roman dress with some accuracy. Costume inventories mention "senatores cloaks," and a 1595 sketch shows an actor in such a cloak. Costumes indicating nationality were seemingly common. Henslowe lists a Moor's coat and two Danish suits; contemporary sketches show actors in Turkish trousers; and a line in a Kyd play about a "Turkish bonnet" clearly refers to a turban. Classical figures, both human and inhuman, were often given special costumes. Henslowe's list includes a robe for Dido, a coat for Juno, and a "sewtle for Nepton." Ghosts and witches were given distinctive costumes. Shylock was dressed in a Jewish gabardine robe, and such characters as churchmen, lawyers, and doctors wore their own distinguishing dress.

The cost of costumes was high—velvet, for example, cost a pound a yard. However, the contributions of the troupe's patron helped, as did a custom reported by a European visitor to London, that "when distinguished gentlemen or knights die, almost their best clothes are given to their servants, but as it is not fitting that they should wear them they sell them cheaply to the actors."

ACTING

The situation in which the Elizabethan actor was placed probably had much to do with the development of acting style. On one hand the actor was a constant target of the law, always on the verge of arrest for vagabondage, condemned and maligned as vagrant, thief, and worse; yet on the other hand, the actor was often a respected consort of the highest level of society, able to mingle with the nobility and even sought out by members of the court circles.

In addition to the irregularity of the social and legal situation, the actor also faced a repertory system that was physically more difficult and yet artistically more rewarding than anything since devised. There were no lengthy runs, not even after the troupes developed permanent homes at theatres in and around London. Playbills changed almost nightly, but plays remained in the repertory and were repeated, again for very few nights, at various intervals. For example, during the season of 1593-94 Henslowe lists thirty performances, but these performances include thirteen plays. This wide variety of materials, dredged up from memory at short notice and for short runs, allowed the players to perfect their techniques on a variety of types and styles of drama without the numbing effect of extended (or even short) runs.

There is a great deal of disagreement about acting style during the Elizabethan (and Jacobean) period. Some historians insist that the acting style was rhetorical and highly formalized. Others claim that it was basically realistic. Still others, probably rightly, claim that Elizabethan acting was a broad art that included elements of the formal along with aspects of realism. Certainly it was spirited and often fiery—such would be necessary to carry some of the long, involved speeches before an audience known for its own volatility.

The strongest arguments for acting style tend to favor realism, or at least what was considered realism by an age dedicated to explaining nature in philosophical terms. First, the theatres themselves were so intimate, with no member of the audience far from the action, that a certain naturalness would seem to be indicated. Second, such comments as we possess seem to indicate something basically natural in style. Thomas Heywood certainly wanted natural physical movement when he told his fellow performers "not to use any imprudent or forced motion in any part of the body, no rough or other violent gesture; nor, on the contrary to stand like a stiff starched man." And Hamlet's advice to the players promotes for the voice what Heywood was suggesting for the body: "Speak the speech, I pray you, as I pronounce it to you, trippingly on the tongue . . . o'erstep not the modesty of nature; for anything so overdone is from the purpose of playing, whose end, both at the first and now, was and is, to hold, as 'twere, the mirror up to nature."

The Elizabethan actor underwent a rather rigorous training, though never such a formalized one as had developed in Greece. Some actors were graduates of the boys' companies, where they had been carefully coached in singing and vocal delivery, but most came up by way of the apprentice route. That is, an aspiring young actor apprenticed himself to a member of one of the acting companies. When he had perfected his craft and art he could move up to journeyman and become one of the shareholders in the company.

The actor Richard Burbage.

From the moment of taking apprenticeship the young actor tended toward specialization. Most of the advanced actors specialized in either comic or tragic roles, and a beginning performer who became apprentice to an actor specializing in comic roles thus set certain parameters on his future acting career.

Women did not appear on the professional stage in Renaissance England. In part this may be due to the strong Puritan influence during this period; in part it may be due to the fact that England, more than most countries, gave great heed to its own Medieval traditions. In any case, the female roles were played by boys—apparently highly skilled performers.

RICHARD TARLETON: Richard Tarleton, the most famous of the Elizabethan clowns and certainly one of the great comic players of all time, was probably born at Condover in Shropshire, though no specific record of his birth has survived. The family later relocated at Ilford in Essex. According to a nearly contemporary report (by Thomas Fuller in his *Worthies of England*) his education was strictly limited in that he displayed only "a bare insight into the Latin Tongue." Fuller goes on to relate that Tarleton, during his youth, was employed at Condover keeping his father's pigs. While so employed he was, one day, accosted by a servant of Robert Dudley, Earl of Leicester, whom he so pleased with his "happy unhappy answers" that he was taken to court, where he became the most famous jester to Queen Elizabeth. Another contemporary account says that he was a waterbearer in early life, and a number of contemporary references indicate that at some time during his early life he was an innkeeper, with one tavern in Gracechurch Street and another in Paternoster Row. In William Percy's play, *Cuck-queans and Cuckolds Errants*, Tarleton is represented as "quondam controller and induperator" of an inn at Colchester.

Exactly when Tarleton gave up the profession of swineherd (or water-bearer or innkeeper) for the stage is not known, but by 1570 his name was given as author of a broadside ballad entitled "A very lamentable and wofull discours of the fierce fluds which lately flowed in Bedfordshire, in Lincolnshire, and in many other places, with the great losses of sheep and other cattel, the 5 of October, 1570." Tarleton was almost certainly not the author of this forgettable work, but his name was appended to it to take advantage of the fame he was just beginning to achieve as a comic actor.

Tarleton's name is not included in the first known acting patent granted to the Earl of Leicester's servants in 1574, but it was not long after that he was recognized as a valuable and experienced player, with his best known role being Derrick, the clown in the pre-Shakespearian *Henry V*. In 1583 with the founding of the Queen's Men, he was one of the original twelve appointed to the group. He remained one of the Queen's actor-servants until his death.

During the final five years of his life his popularity as a clown reached all of England at all levels. One contemporary account says of him that "for a wondrous plentifull pleasant extemporall wit, hee was the wonder of his time." Thomas Nashe wrote that "the people began exceedingly to laugh when Tarlton first peept out his head." It was also said that he was a prime favorite of Queen Elizabeth, able to make her smile even in her blackest moods.

Apparently the facility Tarleton displayed for improvising doggerel verse on subjects suggested by his audience was so highly admired that such

Richard Tarleton, one of the age's great clowns.

improvisations were for some time called "Tarletonizing." He was also admired for his "jigs"; that is, comic songs and dances performed to the music of tabor and pipe. The dances, unfortunately, have been lost, but the music of several of his jigs and the words to one, "The Jigge of the Horse Loade of Fools," have been preserved. His skill in movement is also attested to in another way: in 1587 he was awarded the highest degree, Master of Fence (fencing) by the School of the Science of Defence in London.

During the last years of his life Tarleton lived in "Haliwel Stret" (now High Street), in Shoreditch. The stories of his dissipated life, recantation, and reprentance are almost certainly exaggerated, but they formed the subject for many broadside ballads. In spite of his great popularity and Queenly appreciation, he died in poverty at the home of Emma Ball, a "woman of bad reputation," on September 5, 1588.

EDWARD ALLEYN: Edward Alleyn was born on September 1, 1566, in the parish of St. Botolf without Bishopsgate. His father, variously referred to as "yeoman, citizen, and innholder," was apparently quite well-off financially, for his will establishes that he had "lands and tenements" as well as "goods, leases and ready money." Edward was only four years old when his father died, and his mother subsequently married a man named Browne, who has been identified as an *actor* and haberdasher. This gives substance to a belief during Alleyn's own time that he was "bred a stage player," indicating that Browne raised his young stepson to the profession of the stage.

Exactly how young Alleyn made his start upon the stage is unknown. Perhaps he began as an apprentice to a major performer, or perhaps, given the training that he undoubtedly received from his actor stepfather, he began (as did so many boys or young men) by playing the female characters. By 1592, however, at the age of twenty-six, Alleyn had established an excellent reputation as an actor. In that same year Thomas Nashe's *Pierce Pennyless, His Supplication to the Devil* was printed, and in it Alleyn was twice mentioned as a performer of great distinction, with Nashe likening him to those great Classical actors, Roscius and Aesope. Ben Jonson, in his "Epigram" addressed "to Edward Allen" also likened the actor to both Roscius and Aesope.

Like any professional actor in an age where shows had short runs and playbills changed regularly, Alleyn must have played many roles. However, like any great actor of any age, he had certain roles in which he was outstanding and for which he was justly famous. In Alleyn's case one of these was Orlando in Robert Greene's *Orlando Furioso*, based on Tasso's epic poem. Another of Alleyn's famous roles was Barabas in Marlowe's *The Jew of Malta*. This is testified to by Thomas Heywood who mentions, in the dedication for a production of the play at Whitehall and in the Cockpit Theatre, that the part of the Jew "was presented by so inimitable an actor as Mr. Alleyn." Also, in the prologue for the Cockpit Theatre production, he inserted lines that credit Alleyn with winning the attribute of "peerless" with his "personation of Tamberlaine, the Jew of Malta, and many other characters." Other testimonials to the heights Alleyn achieved as an actor are the number of references to wagers placed on him by friends and acquaintances, that he could outact such

Edward Alleyn, shown in costume for one of his great roles—Marlowe's "Tamerlane."

various performers as Peele and Kempe. Such wagers were common during the period, and exactly how they were settled is not known. Still, the fact that a fellow actor would bet on Alleyn to outperform Kempe indicates that Alleyn was apparently as adept at comedy as at tragedy.

In addition to these well-known roles, it is evident that Alleyn also played the part of King Lear (he spells it "Leir"), probably not in Shakespeare's play but in the "Chronicle Hystorie" licensed to Edward White; Romeo, perhaps in a version earlier than Shakespeare's; Pericles, possibly in the version that Shakespeare made use of in 1608; and the "Moore in Venis," which was apparently another version of *Othello*. He also played unspecified roles in Marlowe's *Massacre at Paris* and in Marlowe and Nashe's *Dido*.

On September 1, 1592, Edward Alleyn married Joan Woodward, the daughter of the wife of Philip Henslowe (who had married a widow). From the date of the marriage, Alleyn and Henslowe entered into a partnership in their theatrical concerns, with the two families for a short time even sharing the same dwelling in Southwark.

But while it is relatively easy to prove that Alleyn was one of the great actors of his time, it is quite difficult to put a finger on exactly what it was that made him great. Perhaps the best indication of what he did onstage comes from Heywood's prologue which says, essentially, that Alleyn could so vary his physical appearance that he might be ranked with Proteus (in Greek legend, the Old Man of the Sea, who could turn himself into any shape), and that he could so vary his voice that he might be ranked with Roscius. Apparently, he employed this physical and vocal ability in an acting style that the age believed to be realistic, at least Fuller's summation of his talent seems to lead to that assumption: he was "the Roscius of our age, so acting to the life, that he made any part (especially a majestic one) to become him."

THE COURT MASQUES

The final and least important (at least from a literary or performance point of view) form of theatrical entertainment that began under the Tudors and that was developed by the Stuart kings was the masque. This dramatic form had its roots in the spectacular court productions of the Italian Renaissance and the lavish disguisings and pageants of late Medieval England. It became a court pastime under Henry VIII and was continued by his daughter Elizabeth. Under the Tudors the masques were primarily pantomime with occasional poetry, and it remained for the Stuarts, especially James I, to turn them into elaborate scenic and vocal displays. With lyrics by such great poets as Ben Jonson and John Milton, and scenic wonders by Inigo Jones, the court masques became lavish in every way. More than a hundred of these productions were put on under the Stuarts, until Cromwell and the Puritan Parliament put an end to such extravagance.

The scripts for the masques were short, little longer in terms of text than a contemporary one-act play, and consisted primarily of lyric poems written around some central theme. The characters were usually drawn from Classical mythology (Neptune, Diana, Boreas, etc.), or were allegorical (Love, Splendor, Revel, Beauty, etc.) and were portrayed by members of the court. Because of the nature of the masque, both men and women performed. Queen Anne loved to perform in masques and was responsible for getting Ben Jonson appointed as court poet to write approximately thirty masques. To provide outstanding scenic effects she brought the young English architect, Inigo Jones, back to England from her brother's court in Copenhagen.

The masques contributed little of significant value to English dramatic literature. They were of great importance, however, in the area of scenic design and stagecraft, where they popularized the lavish Italian style. Also, they managed to infuriate the ever-growing Puritan element to the point where, in 1642, using the Civil War as an excuse, Parliament closed the theatres for a period of five years. By the time five years had passed the Puritans were in control of the government and the closure act was made permanent, thereby bringing to an end one of the most exciting and productive periods in theatrical history.

INIGO JONES: Inigo Jones was born in 1573. There is no record of Jones' education, which makes it reasonably certain that he never entered either of the universities. This conclusion is supported by the fact that his writing and spelling were poor enough to make his manuscripts a problem to later scholars. In spite of this educational lack, he associated regularly with the poets and men of letters of his time, indicating a certain amount of learning, no matter how it was achieved. His position in court also implies the polish and nicety of manners which were requisite during the period. Although very little is known about the first thirty years of his life, it is thought that he may have traveled to France, Germany, and Italy, in the train of Lord Roos, between 1598 and 1601. Whatever the case, it is certain that he had some exposure to Italian scenic design during this period, inasmuch as in 1605 he collaborated with Ben Jonson on the production of the *Masque of Blackness* for Queen Anne of Denmark, making use of several Italian scenic techniques in his design, including his first use of perspective scenery.

In 1609 Jones was sent to carry letters to France on "His Majesty's service," which gave him an opportunity to observe French scenic design. By 1611 he had become Surveyor to Henry, Prince of Wales, and after the sudden death of Henry, Jones traveled to Italy in the train of Thomas, Earl of Arundel. In 1614 he returned to England, and in 1615 he was appointed to the position of Surveyor of Works. Jones began work on the new Banqueting House in Whitehall in 1619, eventually producing the first really Italianate building designed in England.

In spite of the glamour associated with being the king's Surveyor of Works, most of the duties connected with this job were mundane. In fact, the restoration of St. Paul's Cathedral was the most important piece of architectural work which grew out of the position and which can definitely be attributed to Jones.

In 1640 Jones designed *Salmacida Spolia*, which because of the Puritan and court conflicts was the last of the great masques. By 1642 civil war had broken out between the King and Parliament, and in 1645 Jones was taken prisoner at the siege of Basing House. He was then seventy-two years old. According to reports at the time, Inigo Jones was not only very well-known, but highly unpopular as well. The main cause of this unpopularity seems to be that he carried out faithfully the duties connected with his job, thereby making a number of powerful enemies. In July 1646 he was pardoned. His job had ceased to exist so Jones retired, and except for a few architectural designs (most of these for details rather than entire buildings), we known nothing of him until his death in 1652.

Jones' contributions to the English stage fall into two groups, each of which demonstrates something about Jones' theory of theatre. The first of these contributions was quite specific, that is the introduction of Italian stagecraft into England. The second contribution, more general in nature and more artistic, was the creative use he made of this stagecraft to mold the English theatre according to his vision.

Jones, during his career as a designer for masques, introduced *periaktoi*, the proscenium stage, Serlian two-sided houses, back shutters which concealed two-dimensional cut-out scenes, and a system of flat wings in grooves. He used a curtain to mask the upper and lower portions of the stage, and developed control over the lighting to create atmospheric nuances. In fact, in the thirty-five years during which Inigo Jones was involved in designing masques, he introduced to England an entire century of Italian scenic development.

When Jones began designing for masques, they were little more than masked dances. There was almost nothing to distinguish the performers from the audience because the costumes worn by the masquers were not much different from those worn by the court in general, and there was no particular place in which the performers were to be found. The point of the entire masque was the arrival of nobles, disguised and costumed, to dance a specially prepared number. This was followed by ordinary ballroom dancing between the masquers and the audience, and sometimes by a speech, song, or both.

The 1605 collaboration with Jonson on the *Masque of Blackness* was not the first occasion on which Jones applied his knowledge of Italian scenic devices. He had already used *periaktoi* and a raked stage for performances at Oxford. However, it was his first opportunity to show theatre as he thought it should be, with all the design elements completely integrated. Queen Anne of Denmark wanted to dress as a "black-a-moor," and it was around this promise that Jones created the first masque which was a unified whole and that isolated the performers from the viewers. The decor was all set up at one end of the hall, so that use could be made of perspective scenery, and this provided a separation between the royal performers and the court audience.

The concept of a unified production was probably the most important result of his adaptation of Italian scenic practice, but Jones constantly refined this concept. He added music and light to help distract attention from the scene changes, keeping the emphasis on the effect itself and not on how it was achieved. He used motion (the costumes and certain scenic effects) and light to create an effect that was dynamic rather than static.

Inigo Jones was a Renaissance man. He saw in stage design a chance to show the deeper reality below the world of surface appearance. He believed in a world that was made up of ideal proportions, and in the structural harmony of an ordered universe. Two of the marginal comments in his books make this clear: "The same numbers that pleese the eare pleese the eie," was Jones' comment on the mathematical relations found in music and which were, at that time, believed to order the universe. But Jones did not lose sight of man "as the measure" of all things. According to him, "the boddi of man well proporsioned is the patern for proportion in buildings" (and in all things).

Inigo Jones' work does represent a theory of the nature of theatre. His scenery and costume designs for masques show a concern with the production as a unified whole, emphasizing a dynamic, colorful, total presentation. It was important to his career that people marvel over his scenery, yet he was the one who used music to keep the audience's attention on the spectacle and not on his own clever ways of creating effects. It is obvious from his use of perspective that Jones' marginal comments were not just an expression of a popular philosophy of the time, but rather were an expression of his belief in the importance of harmonic principles. In total, he helped to create a theatrical form with internal integrity out of what had been essentially a masked ball.

8

French Theatre, 1552-1789

8

French Theatre, 1552-1789

At a time when the theatre in England had become one of that nation's chief glories, with Shakespeare, Jonson, Marlowe, and a number of fine but somewhat lesser dramatists creating plays for all time; when Spain had already built numerous theatres, and such great playwrights as Lope de Vega and Cervantes were hard at work; in this period of outstanding theatrical achievement France had no significant dramatists writing and Paris contained only one theatre. However, in a period lasting nearly one hundred fifty years, France would catch up with England and surpass Spain, producing numerous beautiful theatres and such outstanding playwrights as Corneille, Molière, Racine, and Beaumarchais.

THE HISTORICAL AND SOCIAL BACKGROUND

The background of this period begins with that misnamed series of battles, the Hundred Years' War, that began in 1337 and ended in 1453. In France two results of this war were of major importance. First, to meet the external threat the king was given control of the army, a control he continued to exercise after the war's end. Second, due to the resulting drain on the royal treasury, the king was authorized to collect a national tax (*taille*). The combination of these two powers made the king an absolute ruler who could (and did between 1485 and 1560) even suspend the Estates-General, the national legislature. This authority was hotly contested by some of the more powerful nobles, but the French kings stood firm and the eventual rise to power of Richelieu certified the absolute monarchy.

It was a period of religious as well as political upheaval, with the growing forces of the Reformation challenging the defenders of the established Church. The seeds of the Reformation had been sown in France, even before Luther's time, by Jacques Lefèvre (1450-1536), a neoplatonic humanist, by Guillaume Budé (1468-1540), and by Guillaume Briçonnet, a student of Lefèvre. The French kings, however, savagely resisted the introduction of Protestantism. Francis I persecuted the Waldensians and drove Calvin out of France. Henry II continued the policy of religious persecution. Charles IX, a weak king totally guided by his mother, the infamous Catherine de Medici, and by the Guises, a group of prominent Catholic nobles headed by the Duke of Guise, made matters

Frontispiece from a 1493 French edition of Terence's comedies.

even worse. The Huguenots (Calvinists) were gaining converts at a rapid rate and so the Duke of Guise started a civil conflagration by massacring a group of these Protestants at Vassy.

This original massacre began a series of eight major confrontations between the years of 1562 and 1598. Of these, the most memorable was the massacre of the Protestants on St. Bartholomew's Day (August 24) in 1572. None of the conflicts seemed to have a decisive effect, but eventually Henry of Navarre (Henry IV), one of the most influential Protestants, turned Catholic. Soon thereafter he became king and so the Reformation wars ended. Very shortly after ascending the throne he issued the Edict of Nantes (1598) in which he gave the Huguenots *almost* complete religious freedom and civil rights—that is, they could worship as they chose, but not publicly in the city of Paris, they were to have the full protection of the law, they could hold public office, they were to be admitted to all hospitals, schools and colleges, and they were to pay annual tithes to the Catholic Church.

Henry IV united the nation and ended the bitter religious strife. Richelieu destroyed the few political privileges of the Huguenots, further curtailed the power of the nobles, and abolished the Estates-General. Jules (Giulio) Mazarin (1602-61), Italian cardinal and Chief Minister of Louis XIII (and later Louis XIV), provoked and then suppressed the last rebellion of the nobles (the Fronde). Then Louis XIV came to the throne.

In both appearance and temperament, Louis XIV seemed almost designed to be King of France. He believed in the theory of Divine Right, and he practiced absolutist policies. He secured men of unusual abilities to aid him, and he managed to pacify many of the nobles who were still smarting from the loss of their privileges, bringing them to court where they lived as pensioners of his bounty and captives of his slightest whim. It was in keeping with these ideals that he erected the magnificent palace at Versailles.

Louis XIV, for all of his restrictive political thinking, was an outstanding patron of the arts, as were several of his advisors. He encouraged Molière, Racine, and St. Simon. He built up the French Academy, began the Royal Library, which eventually became one of the great libraries of the world, established an astronomical observatory, and in many other ways promoted learning and the arts.

However, he also began a series of aggressive wars designed to promote the glory of France and to extend its boundaries. The War of the Spanish Netherlands (1667-68) was over territory he claimed through the inheritance of his Spanish wife. He was finally stopped by an alliance which included England, the Netherlands, and Sweden, but at the Peace of Aix-la-Chapelle, which ended the hostilities, he was awarded a frontier strip of the Netherlands.

Angered at this thwarting of his plans, Louis isolated the Netherlands by signing special treaties with England and Sweden, and then attacked once more (1672-78). The Dutch, unable to halt the French army, broke down their dykes and flooded the country, bringing hostilities to a temporary halt. Brandenburg, the Emperor, and Spain eventually came to their aid and halted Louis once again, but in the Peace of Nimwegen, Louis gained Franche-Comté.

A France at peace seemed more than Louis could bear, and so the War of the Palatinate (1688-97) began with Louis revoking the Edict of Nantes and seizing some German districts in the Palatinate region. A coalition of England, Spain, Austria, Holland, and several German states finally managed to bring the conflict to a halt. As there was no decisive military victory, Louis was assessed no penalties for his invasion, though the territories he had occupied were restored.

The War of the Spanish Succession (1701-13) came about as a result of Louis seeking to do politically what he had been unable to do militarily. Philip of Anjou, Louis' grandson, was named as heir to the Spanish throne, and most other European rulers opposed what seemed to them a union of the continent's two most powerful and aggressive nations. A coalition was formed to promote the accession of Charles, second son of the Emperor Leopold of Austria. In the war which resulted the French were decisively defeated at the hands of the English general Marlborough and Prince Eugene of Savoy. The Peace of Utrecht followed, in which Philip was to be King of Spain on the condition that Spain and France never be united. Austria was given the Spanish Netherlands, Milan, Naples, and Sardinia; England was granted extensive Spanish territory in the New World, as well as the right to trade in slaves with the Spanish West Indies.

Louis' wars seriously hurt the French treasury, reduced her army, badly injured her commerce, decreased her colonial possessions, and left her with a five-year-old child as a ruler. It was a rather sad end to what had seemed a brilliant beginning.

Rivalry with England lasted throughout the eighteenth century. The two nations clashed in India, where the British and French East India companies were both trying to establish dominance over this huge but politically divided country. In North America the British and French clashed along the Canadian border, in the Great Lakes area, and at the mouth of the Mississippi. In addition to the wars of Louis XIV, mentioned earlier, the two countries also fought the War of the Austrian Succession and the Seven Years' War (where the conflict existed on two continents). In these last conflicts the English won, taking control of India and North America. This signaled an end to French dominance in European affairs.

Louis XIV, Louis XV, and Louis XVI all ruled as absolute monarchs, at least up to the year 1789. From 1614 to 1789, a period of nearly two hundred years, the Estates-General was never called to meet. Instead, the King and his ministers controlled all aspects of government. Even the law courts of France, the Parlements, existed under the veto power of the king. The king was not the head of the French Church, as was true in England, but due to the intercession of a number of powerful cardinals the French government was given an unusual amount of independence by the Pope.

But the question of finances was never solved after the debilitating wars of Louis XIV. The nobles made little contribution to the treasury, in part because of the king's usurpation of their traditional powers. The Church paid no taxes, though it did make a minimum gift of money to the king, at irregular periods. As was, and is, too often the case, the burden of supporting the country fell upon that great mass of people who were least able to pay. Such able ministers as Turgot, Necker, and Calonne, who sought to make tax reforms, were dismissed. On July 14, 1789, a Parisian mob stormed the Bastille and the end of the monarchy, and the great French neoclassical drama, were both underway.

THE RENAISSANCE TO RICHELIEU

From its Medieval period France inherited two types of drama. On one hand there were the great Medieval mysteries that were essentially dramatized sermons on biblical subjects. On the other hand there was farce, exemplified by *The Farce of Master Pierre Pathelin*. It became the practice, late in the fourteenth century, to lighten the sermons of the mysteries by using the techniques of farce, and this spelled the end of French Medieval theatre for it alienated many of the traditional supporters of the drama. Faced with the growing resentments of the humanists, many of whom not only disagreed with traditional knowledge but also with each other, and with the pressures brought to bear by traditional churchmen to put an end to farcical interpretation of Scripture, the Parlement of Paris decided in 1548 to ban the performance of all *mystères* that had a religious subject.

This ban did not totally end Medieval theatre, for it had no effect at all in the provinces outside of Paris, but it did pave the way for a humanistic, Classically oriented Renaissance drama. The opening gun of this drama sounded in 1552 when Etienne Jodelle's *Cléopâtre captive* (*Cleopatra captured*) became the first native tragedy to be produced. It contains 1,615 lines, has few characters, and makes excessive use of a chorus; however, it introduces the

An early humanist production of a play by Terence, probably being done in Latin by university students or faculty. (Gustave Cohen, *Le Théâtre en France au moyen âge*, Paris, 1928-31)

Senecan form (complete with dream scene, confidantes, and sententiousness) and it provides impetus for a Classical drama that is at least reasonably original and not merely translated from the Classical sources.

From 1518 onward, the only group authorized to present plays in Paris was the Confrérie de la Passion, a religious group organized at the beginning of the fifteenth century for the express purpose of presenting religious drama. In 1548, having been relocated several times, the Confrérie began construction of a theatre on land once owned by the Duke of Burgundy. As a bow to the former owner the new theatre was called the Hôtel de Bourgogne. The ban on production took place before the new theatre was completed, but the monopoly granted to the Confrérie was reconfirmed.

By 1578 this monopoly still existed, but the Confrérie no longer acted as a producing unit, preferring instead to rent its facilities and exact fees for performances. The continuing warfare that plagued France through much of this period, and the Catholic-Calvinist battles, surely slowed the development of theatre. However, in 1589, Henry of Navarre ascended the throne as Henry IV, and by the turn of the century religious peace had been restored.

While native French theatre was languishing, the Italian *commedia* toupes were playing in Paris and nearly every other city in France large enough to provide a paying audience. It is from their example, however, along with the Classical push of Jodelle and the influence of Aristotle following publication, in 1561, of *Poetices libri septem* (*Seven Books of the Poetics*) by Jules-César Scaliger (1484-1558), that a great French drama began to develop.

Henry IV ruled for twenty-one years, and during his reign there was an increase in dramatic activity, with at least two native companies performing in Paris during 1596, an increase in the number of Italian *commedia* troupes that visited the capital, and in 1598 the visit of an English company. It was, however, the advent of France's first professional playwright, Alexandre Hardy (c. 1572-1632), in 1597, that marked the beginning of a real national theatre. During the thirty-five years before his death, Hardy apparently wrote nearly five hundred plays, thirty-four of which have survived.

As a professional who depended on his plays for a living, Hardy's only artistic credo was public taste, and while this may seem a very slender reed on which to lean one's aesthetic sensibilities, it allowed Hardy to adapt the best of all early techniques to his own uses. He made use of such neoclassical devices as the five-act form and poetic dialogue, he used Senecan ghosts and messengers, and he put all scenes, no matter how violent or bloody, out on the stage. He also ignored the unities of time and place, so beloved of neoclassical theorists.

Much of Hardy's early work was done for Valleran le Conte (also Lecomte), a successful actor-manager who, in 1599, leased the Hôtel de Bourgogne and enlisted Hardy to provide plays for his company. The combination was not immediately successful and the troupe left Paris. They eventually returned in 1610, the year when Henry IV was assassinated and Louis XIII ascended the throne.

The Parisan theatrical demand throughout this period was essentially for farce. Robert Guérin and his troupe provided a steady diet of this, as did the Italian *commedia* companies, who played successfully before court and public

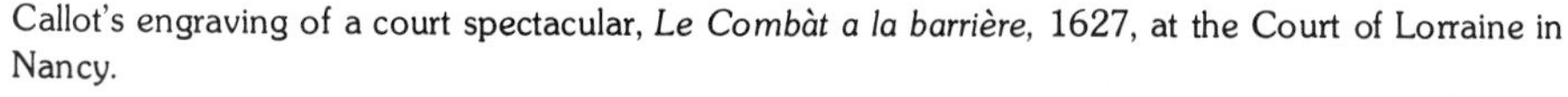
Callot's engraving of a court spectacular, *Le Combàt a la barrière,* 1627, at the Court of Lorraine in Nancy.

audiences alike. The court of Louis XIII promoted this, as Louis' mother remained exceedingly fond of her native Italy and its performers. Most of the famous Italian troupes played in Paris before the court, including the most famous of all, the Gelosi troupe featuring the famed Isabella Andreini.

Against this tide of farce, *commedia*, and pastoral (largely provided by Hardy), regular tragedy and comedy stood little chance, and it was not until the advent of Cardinal Richelieu (1585-1642), the prelate and statesman who became Chief Minister to Louis XIII, that traditional drama gained a valuable ally.

NEOCLASSICISM

The neoclassical ideal began early in France. Exposure to Aristotle and the principles of the *Poetics* produced a number of diverse interpretations that are primarily recorded in the prefaces to those minor Classical dramas produced in the 1560s. The reason for this diversity of interpretation is, in part, that the French critics and playwrights did not, in most cases, go directly to the works of Aristotle. Instead they went to the sixteenth century Italian interpreters and definers of Aristotle, such as Minturno, Castelvetro, and Scaliger. André de Rivaudeau (c. 1540-80) expounded on the necessity of complying with the unity of time. Jacques Grévin explained in his preface to *César* (1561) that he chose soldiers as his chorus as it destroyed verisimilitude to have the formal

In Dufresny's parody of Gluck's opera *Armide*, Juno, played by Pierrot, descends from the heavens not on an eagle but on a turkey, to surprise her unfaithful husband, Jupiter, played by Harlequin. (*Le Théâtre italien de Gherardi*, IV, Amsterdam, 1701)

choruses singing onstage. The most extensive neoclassical discussion of dramaturgy was written by Jean de la Taille (c. 1540-1608) in his *De l'art de la tragedie* (c. 1572), which is primarily a work devoted to supporting the unities of time and place.

This early neoclassicism tended to subside under the onslaught of farce and Italian *commedia* in the theatres, and religious contention in the streets. However, it developed new strength beginning about 1595 and lasted as the major artistic force until the Revolution. French neoclassicism from 1595 on may be divided into four quite distinct periods. The first runs to sometime around 1630 and the Fronde (a series of outbreaks during the minority of Louis XIV), with the early Pierre Corneille as its foremost representative. The second period began immediately after the Fronde and lasted to about 1660, just before Jean Racine (1639-99) began his career. This period was distinguished by a revival of comedy, by Pierre Corneille's *The Cid*, by his subsequent departure from theatre and then by his resumption of dramatic work, by Moliére's return to Paris, by the popularity of Thomas Corneille (1625-1709), Pierre's brother, and by the works of Philippe Quinault (1635-88). It is also the period in which Richelieu, convinced that France could achieve greatness in the arts only by following Italian styles, promoted neoclassicism by offering financial support to writers working in a neoclassical style. He also formed the French Academy as a hedge against the debasement of the French language and as a Classically oriented arbiter of literary good taste, and he built the first Italianate theatre in France. The third period began soon after 1660 and lasted through the reign of Louis XIV. Its four major figures were the Corneille brothers (again) and, most important, Racine and Molière (1622-73). The fourth period begins with the ascension of the child king Louis XV in 1715 and lasts until the beginning of the Revolution.

DRAMATIC LITERATURE

In the development of the great neoclassical drama that was to rule French theatre for nearly two centuries, the year 1628 is of special importance because it represents the high point of the rather irregular neoclassicism that had existed since 1595—a Classicism in which the rules were broken as often as they were followed, in which genres were mixed, and in which "faithfulness to life" was the rule by which everything was justified. In that year the last volume of Hardy's *Théâtre* was published, along with a revised edition of Jean de Schélandre's *Tyr et Sidon*, with preface by François Ogier. In this preface, Ogier made an impassioned plea for "free" theatre; that is, a theatre designed to be faithful to reality and to give pleasure. To achieve these ends, Ogier said, the dramatist must be free to mix genres—to mix tragic with comic—and to ignore the rules set up by ancient authority. Ogier's plea was answered in 1630 by Jean Chapelain in his "Letter on the Twenty-four-Hour Rule" and in his *Discourse on Representative Poetry*. Chapelain claimed that faithfulness to life—verisimilitude—could only be achieved within the rules set forth by the ancients, especially Aristotle.

The French Medieval theatre descends directly to the Renaissance in the Hôtel de Bourgogne, where Laurent Mahelot, designer for the Comédiens du Roi, produced Renaissance sets that followed a Medieval pattern. This set, done sometime soon after 1608, is for Alexandre Hardy's *La Folie de Clidamant*, and shows a ship on a seacoast, the throneroom of a palace, and a smaller side room with a practicable curtain.

In 1631 the second period of neoclassicism got underway with the production of *Sylvanire* by Jean Mairet (1604-86). This was a "regular" pastoral in the sense that it observed the Classical rules as they had been interpreted in France. More important than the play itself, however, was Mairet's preface—a manifesto promoting the rules as a way of putting an end to the disorderly, irregular theatre of the previous period. In 1634 Mairet produced *Sophonisbe*, the first fully "regular" tragedy of this second period of neoclassicism, and it was successful enough to provoke a host of imitators. George de Scudéry's *La mort de César* (*The Death of Caesar*, 1636) seemed to follow the rules in every point but one—the murder apparently takes place on stage in full view of the audience. However, in the second edition published in 1637 even that is corrected by a marginal note indicating that the compartment representing the Senate be closed so that "the stage not be steeped in blood, against the rules."

The Classical tragedies appeared swiftly after the initial breakthrough, provoked by public appetite and by the support of Richelieu, who in 1629 had become Louis' Chief Minister. The year 1634, in addition to *Sophonisbe*, saw the production of Jean Rotrou's (1609-50) *Hercule mourant* (*Hercules Dying*). The 1635 season presented Pierre Corneille's *Médée* and Scudéry's *Caesar*. In 1636 audiences were treated to *Mariane* by François Tristan L'Hermite and Pierre du Ryer's *Lucrèce*. Then in 1637 came Pierre Corneille's *The Cid*, produced in the Marais Theatre. From a historical point of view this work is probably the single most important play of the whole French neoclassical period, and from an artistic point of view it must rank as one of the greatest of French neoclassical dramas.

PIERRE CORNEILLE: Playwright, poet lawyer, and administrator, Corneille (1606-84) was born in Rouen into a family of lawyers and administrators. In school he proved an outstanding student, but he did not leave home for the university. Instead, he was educated at home by the Jesuits and then, from 1624 to 1628, he studied the practice of law in the Parlement in Rouen. Completing his legal studies, he began a busy career in various aspects of law and administration, at which he worked regularly for twenty-five years, in spite of his great theatrical success.

Harlequin, disguised as "Mahomet," is flown across the stage making lightning with fireworks. (Le Sage and D'Orneval, *Le Théâtre de la faire*, Amsterdam, 1722-32)

Corneille began to write verse sometime around 1624, but it was not until 1629 that we have any evidence of his dramatic interests. In that year he gave his first play, the comedy *Mélite*, to a traveling company under Charles Lenoir (?-1637), with Montdory as its star, which was appearing in Rouen in plays by Alexandre Hardy. The company took the play to Paris and in 1630 gave the first Parisian production of a Corneille play in a converted tennis court near Porte-Saint-Denis. The show was an eventual success, but it took a while to catch on, probably because it contained none of the traditional stock characters that the audience expected in farce, and it paid no attention at all to the unities that were being so strongly promoted by Jean Mairet.

Provoked by critical comments regarding *Mélite*, Corneille next wrote a tragicomedy, *Clitandre* (1631), in an attempt to avoid the supposed problems of his comic style. The play was a minor success with audiences, but according to tradition "the critics were then ready to implore him to return to his earlier style." Whether as a result of critical vituperation, or merely that at this stage of his career he felt more comfortable with the comic style, Corneille did return to comedy, producing four plays in rapid succession: *La veuve* (*The Widow*, 1631-32); *La galerie du palais* (*The Palace Corridor*, 1632); *La suivante* (*The Maidservant*, 1633); and *La place royal* (*Place Royale*, 1633). Possibly needing a respite from comic writing, or perhaps in an attempt to take advantage of the interest in historical tragedy that followed the production of Mairet's *Sophonisbe* (1634), he produced his first tragedy, *Médée* (1635). This was immediately followed by another comedy, *L'illusion comique* (*The Comic Illusion*, 1636).

In 1633, with five comedies and one tragicomedy behind him, Corneille was presented to Cardinal Richelieu, who granted him patronage. In 1635, following *Médée*, the Cardinal convinced him to join ranks with five other dramatists who would write the Cardinal's plays on commission. This was clearly an error, as Corneille was temperamentally unsuited for writing plays to order. Finally, having incurred Richelieu's anger by making changes in parts of a plot given to him, Corneille left in a huff for Rouen. At home, with the constraints of the Cardinal lifted, Corneille turned to Spanish drama and, using Guillén de Castro's *Las mocedades del Cid* (*The Youthful Exploits of the Cid*, 1621) as a starting point, he wrote *The Cid* (1637), the play that began the greatest period of French theatre.

Like his earlier plays, this new work was first produced in the converted tennis court—now the flourishing Théâtre du Marais—with Montdory in the title role. It was an almost astonishing success, both in France and internationally, with English and Spanish translations playing in London and Madrid during the same year. However, the great success of the production made Corneille a number of enemies, chief among them being Mariet and Scudéry, and perhaps even Richelieu himself, though the part that the Cardinal played in the *Cid* controversy is still being debated.

A pamphlet war raged around the play, with its detractors (and there were many) ranged against Corneille, Jean de Rotrou (1609-50), a fellow dramatist, the essayist Guez de Balzac, and the general audience. Scudéry, in *Commentaries on The Cid*, 1637, attacked the play as lacking in verisimilitude and the proprieties. Richelieu, as ever playing a devious role, secured Cor-

Pierre Corneille (From a contemporary edition of his works)

neille's grudging approval to submit the play to the French Academy for judgment. Nearly six months later Jean Chapelian, writing for the Academy, drew up an indictment that, "in spite of the play's unquestionable merits," finds it to be irregular in terms of the unities and based on a bad subject. This latter objection may well owe much to Richelieu, who was busy propping up an absolute monarchy. A play in which two subjects go against the king's express wishes and then justify this disobedience on the basis of personal honor must have been highly galling to the Cardinal.

In any case, the decision by the Academy that *The Cid* was deficient in several ways left Corneille with a bad case of wounded pride, and he deserted the stage for more than two years. It must be said in Richelieu's behalf that during this period of theatrical silence he did not take away his patronage and, in fact, had two performances of *The Cid* played in his private theatre.

Corneille's return to the stage in 1640 was a public triumph, and enthusiastic audiences applauded his *Horace* (1640), *Cinna* (1641), *Polyeucte* (1642), *La mort de Pompée* (*The Death of Pompey*, a tragedy, 1643), and *Le menteur* (*The Liar*, 1643), his finest comedy. As with his earlier plays, these were also produced at the Marais, but this time with Floridor (1608-72) in the lead roles due to Montdory's retirement.

By this time there was no doubt in anyone's mind that Corneille was France's leading dramatist, and in 1647, in one of history's strangest reversals,

Frontispiece from a 1664 edition of Pierre Corneille's works.

he was elected to the French Academy, the very body which had flayed *The Cid*. His *Rodogune* (1645), *Théodore* (1645), and *Héraclius* (1646), were popular successes and were probably played at the Hôtel de Bourgogne. These were followed by *Don Sanche d'Aragon* (*Don Sancho of Aragon*, 1649), a play of small merit, and *Andromède* (1650), a spectacle-opera commissioned by Cardinal Mazarin to exhibit the stage machinery designed by Torelli. It was acted by the players of the Hôtel de Bourgogne in the Petit Bourbon. Then, in 1651, he produced *Nicomède*, a play so popular that Molière chose it for his 1658 reappearance in Paris.

Corneille was beginning to show signs of exhaustion—after all, for the largest part of this demanding period as playwright he was also keeping up a full schedule as lawyer and administrator. In 1652 he produced *Pertharite*, an unqualified disaster, and then left the theatre for several years.

After nearly seventeen years Corneille returned to the theatre with the production of *Oedipe*, but his powers had failed and while he never had another disaster, he had no resounding triumphs. In 1660 he produced La *toison d'or* (The Golden Fleece), a spectacle play written for the marriage of Louis XIV and played by the Marais actors in the great hall of the castle of the Marquis de Sourdéac. *Sertorius* (1661) was also done by the Marais players, in their own theatre, and *Sophonisbe* (1663) and *Othon* (1664) were done at the Hôtel de Bourgogne. None of them were significant successes.

Corneille's last plays were only moderately successful, and only *Attila* (1667) and *Tite et Bérénice* (1670) really deserve mention. *Attila* was not a success in its time, not because of any defect in the play, but because of spectacular competition from Racine's *Andromaque* in the same year. A similar case may be made for *Tite et Bérénice*, which had the misfortune to play opposite Racine's drama on the same subject. Indeed, gossip at the time said that Henrietta, the sister of Charles II and sister-in-law of Louis XIV, had suggested the subject to both authors in order to enjoy their competition. There is no evidence to back up this story that the subject of Corneille's play was "suggested" by a powerful court personage, but it must be admitted that Corneille never did well at plays that were either commissioned or "suggested" to him by the court. It was only when he had complete control of all aspects of his art that he created great drama. In fact, it may well be that he would have been even greater working for a theatre with fewer constraints—that the formalized French tragedy which he did so much to further was not as suited to his genius as the theatre of Shakespeare would have been. However, all quibbles aside, he was one of the truly great French dramatists, and his work has never been off stage for nearly three hundred years.

While tragedy was now well established, comedy was still feeling its way. Gradually a sense of direction emerged that drew on the forms promoted by Horace in his *Art of Poetry*, and on the subjects and styles of the two more recent forms, the *commedia erudita* of Italy and the Spanish *comedia*. Jean Rotrou's *La Soeur* (*The Sister*, 1645) exemplified the turn to Italian comedy in its controlled confusion over the kidnapping of certain characters by Turkish pirates. Spanish *comedia* contributed plots less concerned with mystery and action than with the heroic deeds (and, indeed, heroic torments) of young lovers. This Spanish style, popularized by the great actor Jodelet, can be seen in Paul Scarron's (1610-60) works, especially those written for Jodelet and his later *Don Japeth d'Arménie* (*Don Japheth of Armenia*, 1651), in which a serious and sensitive love story is almost destroyed by the character of Don Japheth, the court fool of Emperor Charles V, who believes that he is the direct descendant of Noah. Don Japheth speaks in constant hyperbole; his utterances and indeed his character are a savage parody of the characters in heroic drama.

The growing French taste for the love stories of the Spanish *comedia*, the increasing popularity of the *précieux* novels, and the continuing taste for tragedy, led in the late 1650s to the development of a new form of tragedy, or perhaps tragicomedy inasmuch as many of these new plays ended happily. Based loosely on historical (usually Classical) characters, these plays may be likened to the historical love novels so popular in the late 1940s and 1950s. This new tragedy really began in 1656 when Thomas Corneille's *Timocrate* opened at the Marais Theatre and went on to run for approximately eighty performances. This may seem reasonably modest today, when a run of several years is not unknown, but in the seventeenth century a run of only twenty-five nights identified a play as a smash hit. Thomas Corneille went on to produce more such plays—*Bérénice* (1657) and *Darius* (1659)—making him one of the most popularly acclaimed playwrights of the century. Immediately after him in

The Money-Devil, his costume studded with coins, and his mistress, Lady Folly, wearing a fool's cap, greet Harlequin. (Le Sage and D'Orneval, 1722-32)

the public affections was Philippe Quinault, whose *Amalasonte* (1657), *La feint Alcibiade* (*The False Alcibiades*, 1658), and *La mort de Cyrus* (*The Death of Cyrus*, 1658), were among the most popular plays of the time.

It is appropriate that this second period of French neoclassicism should end with a work by Pierre Corneille, who in one sense began it all with *The Cid*, and with the arrival in Paris of a troupe directed by Jean-Baptiste Poquelin (Molière).

MOLIÈRE: Molière (Jean-Baptiste Poquelin, 1622-73), actor, troupe manager, and one of the world's great playwrights, was born the eldest son of a Parisian upholsterer who was attached to the service of the King. Information regarding his early years is scanty, though tradition has it that as a child he was an outstanding mimic and a frequenter of theatrical performances. If this last is true, then he probably saw Belleville at the Hôtel de Bourgogne, and Montdory at the Marais, and learned at least part of his art from the early comedies of Corneille. He certainly saw the farces of the fair troupes and his plays give evidence of close attention to the Italian *commedia* troupes.

In 1631 Molière enrolled at the Jesuit College of Clermont (which was later to become Louis-le-Grand), which he left nearly eight years later without a degree. However, he was fluent in Latin and had developed a taste for read-

In this portrait by Mignard, Molière is shown dressed for the role of Julius Caesar in Corneille's *The Death of Pompey.* He seems to be wearing some form of Roman costume, but the full, curled wig, even crowned with laurel, is contemporary.

ing poetry, drama, and the Classical materials. He made an abortive attempt to study law, and in 1642, at the insistence of his family, he went to Narbonne in the suite of Louis XIII. This was probably an attempt on the part of his family to break up the close association he had formed with the Béjarts, a family of generally unsuccessful actors, If so, the move failed completely, for in 1643 he renounced his succession in favor of his next younger brother and joined the Béjart family and some actor acquaintances in setting up the Illustre-Théâtre.

The new theatre group began life in an abandoned tennis court under the direction of Madeleine Béjart, the eldest member of the family and a woman who possessed enormous drive, talent, and physical attraction. By this time young Poquelin had taken a stage name to protect the reputation of his family, as acting was still anathema to the Church and actors were regularly denied the Mass, final rites, and even burial in consecrated ground. Why he chose the specific name of Molière is unknown, but it served the purpose of masking his identity.

Molière was, when the troupe was organized, little more than an enthusiastic amateur actor who wanted perversely to perform in grand tragedy even though he was physically, mentally and emotionally unsuited to the tragic genre. He was also, according to popular belief at the time, the lover of Madeleine, a liason that was to cause serious repercussions in his later career.

The Illustre-Théâtre failed to catch on and Molière, unable to draw on the family fortune, was imprisoned for debt. The jail term was of short duration and, together with several other young actors from the disbanded troupe, Molière left Paris for the provinces, where they remained for thirteen years perfecting their art and craft. These were the most important years of Molière's existence in that they shaped what he would later become. He achieved some distinction as an actor in comedy, and he began writing, furnishing his company with short farces in the *commedia* style.

The wanderings of the company can be traced in part, but few specifics are known. They apparently had only a brief period of hard times, swiftly developing their skills and reputation, and at various times enjoyed the patronage of the Duc d'Epernon and the Prince de Conti. It became inevitable that they would return to Paris.

On October 24, 1658, the troupe appeared in Paris, in the Guard Room of the old Louvre, before Louis XIV who was at this time twenty years of age. The audience, as might be expected, was made up of courtiers, notables, and some of the actors from the Hôtel de Bourgogne troupe. As their vehicle Molière had selected Corneille's *Nicomède*, which the audience had already seen played with Montdory's theatrics. The quieter, more natural style of Molière failed to impress, and the future of the troupe seemed in doubt. However, when the main play was done, Molière stepped forward to introduce a short farce of his

An etching of a production of *Tartuffe,* with Molière himself playing Orgon. The simple set with chandeliers is typical of the staging Molière provided for most of his plays.

own, *Le docteur amoureux* (*The Amorous Doctor*), and their success was assured.

At first Molière did everything possible to snatch defeat from the jaws of victory. In spite of the failure of *Nicomède* the company kept on doing tragedies—and kept failing. Finally, driven to desperation, Molière put on two of his own plays—*L'etourdi, ou les contretemps* (*The Blunderer*) and *Le dépit amoureux* (*The Amorous Quarrel*)—and both were successful. He followed this with *Les précieuses ridicules* (*The Affected Ladies*) and the troupe was on its way.

The balance of Molière's life was divided between theatrical success and domestic and personal misfortune. In 1662 he entered into an unsuccessful marriage with Armande Béjart, the daughter of his exmistress, and was later accused of incest, on the assumption that his wife was his natural daughter by her mother Madeleine. He was attacked by jealous fellow playwrights and by the Church for promoting atheism (they said) in *Don Juan, ou le festin de Pierre* (*Don Juan, or The Feast with the Statue*). Racine, who Molière much admired and whose first play Molière produced, threw Molière's company over for the troupe at the Hôtel de Bourgogne. Finally, in 1772, the King withdrew his favor, granting it instead to Lully and his operas.

On February 17, 1673, disappointed, ill, and exhausted, Molière performed in *Le malade imaginaire* (*The Imaginary Invalid*) and following the final curtain went into convulsions. He died that same night. The Church was determined to deny him a Christian burial, but after the intervention of the King it was agreed to bury him in holy ground, though at night so as to "avoid scandal."

A very important factor that separates Molière from Corneille and Racine, the century's other two masters of drama, is that he was the most professional, and he was more a man of the theatre than he was a man of letters. This is probably the key to the entire problem of how Molière reacted to his age and the rules the age sought to enforce; he felt stronger rules binding him to the theatre than to any literary codes. Thus, what was most important to Molière was what would please the audience. If this happened to fit into the confines of Classicism, well and good, but if it did not, Molière would not change merely to conform to a set of rules. He held to the unities, for example, only to the degree that they suited his needs, but when they did not particularly suit his needs he would disregard them, using whatever was necessary to achieve his goal.

The comedy of Molière is based on human illusion. Nearly all of his characters are reduced to their single illusion or, to say it another way, their basic motivating force. Molière reduced his characters to this illusion for several reasons, two of which are of special importance. By reducing a character to a single primary attribute, the playwright is able to observe one of the major rules of tragedy and comedy; that is, he can present a moral lesson. Though Molière frequently denied that he was writing for this purpose, in all of his plays there is a moral lesson that is pointed up by the absurdities (even though they are often very real) which motivate the character on stage. In fact, it is difficult to know whether or not Molière was writing purely to entertain his audiences. It is likely that Molière knew the psychology of comedy—that through

A 1674 performance at Versailles of Molière's *The Imaginary Invalid.* The king can be seen front and center, and the orchestra is spread across the front of the stage in a low enclosure.

an entertainment of high quality a lesson can be instilled in the mind of the audience. At any rate, he followed this dictum, and thus at least a part of the entertainment of Molière's plays is derived from the moral values, or lack of values, contained in the plays. Conversely, the lesson that the audience receives is derived from the humor of the writing. In this manner, Molière was able to follow his own artistic conscience and at the same time remain faithful to the dictates of the age.

Closely related to this is Molière's understanding of the humor that is inherent in excessive behavior. This is an understanding that Ben Jonson had already partially explored in his comedies of humor, but it took Molière to bring the concept to its ultimate goal. Molière's use of excess, both in his characters and situations, is integrally tied to his use of illusion. By reducing his characters to their outstanding motivating force, and by reducing possibilities of comparison between his characters, he creates a climate of excess. And this, of course, creates an unnatural surface appearance. There are, in the plays, the necessary characters who operate on the basis of traditional reason and thus provide contrast for the irrational and absurd types, but these characters are usually the dullest and most uninteresting ones in the plays.

Molière's greatest contribution to French drama is that he raised the traditional and often subliterary form of farce to a satiric vehicle for social comment. He is the only writer of his age to elevate French comedy to the level of French tragedy.

JEAN RACINE: Jean Racine (1639-99), playwright and poet, was born in La Ferté-Milon, a small town about fifty miles northeast of Paris. By the age of four he was an orphan and, lacking a family estate, totally without funds. An aunt who was a nun in Port-Royal saw to it that he was taken in by her religious order as a charity case, and thus he was educated in the convent schools of Port-Royal, a center of Jansenistic thought. These schools were fine ones, but unusual for their time in that they emphasized the study of logic, the study of French as a living language over the dead Classical languages, and the study of

Greek over the Latin so important to the Church. They also emphasized the doctrine of Cornelis Jansen that man does not possess free will, that human nature is basically corrupt, and that Christ did not die on the cross for all men, but only for a select few who would thus be allowed entry into heaven. In 1658 Racine left Port-Royal to complete his advanced work at the Collège d'Harcourt in Paris, where his teachers urged him to study law. Racine, however, gravitated naturally toward literary studies. He became involved with a number of literary groups and began to write poetry.

During this period he was also writing drama, and two tragedies (unfortunately lost) which he completed and submitted to the Marais and the Hôtel de Bourgogne were both turned down. Unhappy in what seemed an aborted literary career, Racine left Paris for Uzès in the eastern area of Languedoc, where he lived with an uncle between 1661 and 1663. The uncle was a canon and Racine had hopes of being selected for the priesthood. Again, however, his hopes were dashed, and when he was not selected for a benefice he began anew on his literary career, starting work on a third tragedy.

Back in Paris he had some minor success with his poetry, but his third tragedy went unclaimed. Molière refused it, though he was kind and encouraging to the young author, and in 1664 he did accept and produce Racine's fourth tragedy, *La Thébaïde (The Theban Brothers)*, which he wrote according to an

Jean Racine (French Cultural Services)

outline by Molière. The play was a failure and it was perhaps the disappointment of this failure that led Racine to break with Molière and with his old friends at Port-Royal. This parting was the most unsavory event in Racine's career. While Molière was staging Racine's new tragedy, *Alexandre*, Racine was giving the play to the Hôtel de Bourgogne. This underhanded treatment of an old friend and supporter caused cries of outrage in Paris, and so hurt and angered Molière that he never spoke to Racine again. At the same time that he was betraying his benefactor Molière, Racine was also breaking his bonds with Port-Royal by denouncing Jansenism because of its antitheatrical attitudes. The break was not a complete one, however, in the sense that Racine was never able to escape his Jansenist upbringing and it appears in some way in all of his plays.

In 1667 Racine began work on what would be a series of seven great tragedies. These plays made him a respected if not loved member of the Parisian literary societies, and by 1673 he had been elected to the French Academy. The society in which Racine moved—the literary world and the court—along with his own overweening ambition, created a number of problems for him. Plots and counterplots were much a part of his life. However, in 1677 he forsook his mistresses and got married, was appointed Royal Historiographer on the condition that he leave the theatre, and was well along the pathway to a religious reconversion to Jansenism. He did return to the theatre for a brief period, from 1689 to 1691, with two biblical tragedies which had been written at the request of Mme. de Maintenon, wife of Louis XIV. In 1698 the King withdrew his favor due to Racine's passionate embracing of Jansenism, and the following year Racine died. The plotter, the betrayer, the man of overweening ambition and pride, died an austere Christian whose primary interest had shifted from the theatre to the education of his seven children.

It was with the production of *Andromaque*, produced at the Hôtel de Bourgogne in 1667, that Racine won recognition as a great dramatist and serious rival to the ageing Corneille. It was followed by his only comedy, *Les plaideurs* (*The Litigants*, 1668), intended for an Italian comedy troupe but eventually played at the Hôtel de Bourgogne. It was based on the *Wasps* of Aristophanes and seemed destined for failure until it was applauded by the court, which turned it into a sudden success. Racine's next tragedy was *Britannicus* (1669), which was not completely successful, although its poetry was widely admired. The character of Nero, making a fool of himself by insisting on playing leads at his court entertainments, was said to have caused Louis XIV to stop featuring himself at court ballets. Racine's *Bérénice* (1670), which opened opposite Corneille's play on the same subject, fared rather well in the competition, but it succeeded primarily in making even more enemies for a playwright already well supplied with this commodity. He followed *Bérénice* with *Bajazet* in 1672 and *Mithridate* in 1673, both on Oriental subjects but treated in a contemporary French style. They were both popular successes in their time, but perhaps because of the contrasts between subject and treatment they have not held up for later audiences.

For his next two plays Racine turned to the Greek Classical period, which had come into vogue by way of the plays of Thomas Corneille and Quinault. He completed *Iphigénie* in 1674, and it was perhaps his greatest popular success. In 1677 he produced his greatest play, *Phèdre*, based primarily on Euripides' *Hippolytus*, but with some debt to Seneca's *Phaedra*. Unfortunately, Racine's many enemies, having learned that Racine was working on such a play, convinced a popular hack writer named Pradon to compose a tragedy on the same subject. The two plays opened opposite each other and, to Racine's horror and his enemies' delight, Pradon's play was the most successful. It was perhaps this, as much as his appointment to the position of historiographer, that caused Racine to leave the stage.

In 1689 he made a brief comeback with *Esther*, a delicate and tender play unlike anything Racine had ever attempted, and probably expressive of the change of heart occasioned by his marriage, subsequent family, and religious reconversion. *Esther* was followed in 1691 by *Athalie*, an even better play and again far more delicate and sensitive than the earlier, more biting works.

In spite of the emphasis that critics and biographers have placed on his generally detestable character, Racine ranks as one of the greatest of French dramatists. In the narrow, carefully defined world of French neoclassicism he had no equal. The rules that seemed to hinder and restrict Corneille, and that Molière tended to ignore, were perfectly suited to Racine's logical, scholarly, and rather cold temperament. In this field of endeavor he stands unequalled.

The third period of French neoclassicism, sometimes called the period of high Classicism, began about 1660 and lasted for approximately fifty-five years, but the productive portion of the period was short indeed. Of its three major writers, Molière, who had only burst upon the scene in 1659, died in

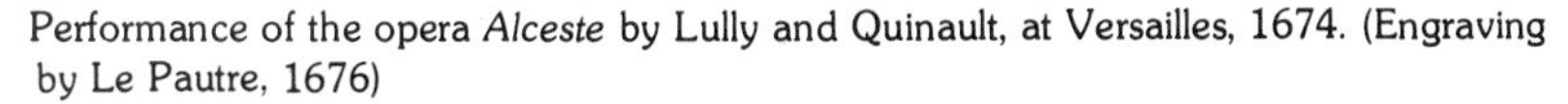

Performance of the opera *Alceste* by Lully and Quinault, at Versailles, 1674. (Engraving by Le Pautre, 1676)

1673; Pierre Corneille stopped producing in 1574; and Racine's career, excepting a brief attempt to return to the stage, ended in 1677. Of the next level of playwrights, Thomas Corneille produced less and less and finally fell into disfavor by 1680, and Quinault gave up writing plays about 1670 to concentrate on less demanding opera librettos. From about the late 1670s onward, the French theatre was alive primarily with replays of works by the giants who began the period.

The fourth and final period of French neoclassicism begins with the Regency (1715-21) and ends with the Revolution. The earliest, and perhaps most successful writer of Classical tragedy during this period was Voltaire (François Marie Arouet, 1694-1778), who began his dramatic efforts in 1718 with a production of *Oedipe*. By the time of his death, sixty years later, he had produced about twenty such tragedies, all regular in form, with strong characters and flashes of great dramatic strength. And yet, though his audiences felt him to be the legitimate successor to Corneille and Racine, Voltaire's works have not held up theatrically, perhaps because he was never able to resist the temptation to overburden his plots with his philosophical beliefs.

The comic writers of the period were, generally, even less successful than the writers of tragedy, with the exceptions of Alain-René Lesage (1668-1747), whose major work *Tucaret* (1709) came at the end of the third period rather than the beginning of the fourth, and Pierre de Marivaux (1688-1763). Marivaux wrote plays which, in tone and style, stand at the outside edge of the neoclassical tradition. He excoriated tragedy as too fixed in form and generally uninteresting, and he had no particular admiration for Molière. Indeed, his plays, which concentrate on the psychological problems of young love, are totally original and classical only in their formality.

By about 1760 two major writers arose to challenge the whole Classical tradition, especially as it applied to tragedy. Denis Diderot (1713-84) was an exponent of bourgeois drama, an offshoot of *comédie larmoyante* (tearful comedy), which contained a mixture of sentimental nonsense, staunch virtue, and narrow prudery which appealed strongly to the growing middle-class audience of the late eighteenth century. His plays have no lasting literary or theatrical value, but historically they are important because they wielded an influence out of proportion to their quality, exerting a great influence on Lessing, the German dramatist and critic, and thereby helping to change the whole of European drama. It was, however, in his *Observations on Garrick* and his *Essay on Dramatic Poetry* that he achieved the greatest success, pleading for ensemble acting, for standardized acting techniques, and for a closer relationship between actor and dramatist.

Pierre Caron de Beaumarchais (1732-99) closed out the French neoclassical period with two works important enough to elevate him to the company of Corneille, Molière, and Racine. He began his career, like Diderot, as an exponent of bourgeois drama, but it was the comedy of *The Barber of Seville* (produced in 1775), his first great play, that brought him public acclaim. Nine years later *The Marriage of Figaro* went on stage, and in its topic (the failures of society generally and of the nobility in particular), and the tricks Beaumarchais used to get it produced, it sounded clearly the theme of the coming Revolution. Beaumarchais' few later works tend to be uninteresting literarily

A singing quartet of farceurs inspects the cabinets just as the lover hides in one of them. (Le Sage and D'Orneval, 1722-32)

and unimportant historically, and by 1794 Beaumarchais was an *émigré* in Hamburg, with his wife, daughter, and sister imprisoned in Paris, hiding from the Revolution for which he had been the first great mouthpiece.

DENIS DIDEROT: Denis Diderot (1713-84) was perhaps the most complete French man of letters—philosopher, essayist, playwright, and critic. He was born in Langres, a medium-sized town in the province of Champagne, the son of a prosperous artisan. Diderot received his early education from the Jesuits in his home town, and in 1728 went to Paris where he studied in Louis-le-Grand College. Perhaps in defiance of his solidly middle-class upbringing, Diderot became involved in the life of the artists' colony in Paris' Latin Quarter, where he read widely, studied, wrote pamphlets, and drank. As part of this rebellion he married a laundress. The marriage was an unhappy one, but a daughter was born in 1753 and gave Diderot an object on which he could lavish the love he denied to his family and his wife.

In spite of Diderot's rebellious life, his nature continued to be virtuous and sentimental. This was apparent in one of his earliest works, a 1745 translation of Shaftesbury's "Essay on Merit and Virtue," from which Diderot borrowed the motto "The good, the true, and the beautiful." Following this early venture he began a lengthy battle with Christianity, for which he wished to substitute deism. He also began work on his monumental *Encyclopédie*, which took nearly twenty years to complete.

In 1757 Diderot began his affair with theatre by publishing his first play, *Le fils naturel* (*The Illegitimate Son*). It was not a very good play and remained unproduced until 1771, when it was put onstage for one performance. However, his second play, *Le père de famille* (*The Father of the Family*, 1758) achieved a modest success at the Comédie-Française in 1761. In a sense, Diderot wrote both plays as vehicles for explaining his approach to theatre to a reading rather than a playgoing public, and as a result each play was accompanied by an original essay explaining the *drame bourgeois*, of which the plays were examples, however ill-conceived.

Diderot brought to drama his own personal convictions, which were on the whole those of his century. That is to say, they were rationalistic, philosophical, mildly anti-Christian, antitraditional, and sociological in approach. In a sense his plays were tools to effect a social, economic change, and while they fully earned the neglect that was visited upon them, the theories they illustrate did not die so easily.

At the time that Diderot began writing plays the Parisian stage was given over to several types of comedy: Alain-René Lesage was continuing in the tradition that Molière had established nearly a century earlier; Pierre de Marivaux was writing witty, slightly sentimental plays featuring polished, highly sophisticated dialogue; and Nivelle de la Chaussée was writing in the genre of *comédie larmoyante*, which was not traditional tragicomedy but bathetic sentimentality. It was in this last genre that Diderot was most interested. From it he created the *drame bourgeois*.

While Diderot's plays were unimportant as works of art, his accompanying essays were very important indeed. *Entretiens sur "Le fils naturel"* (*Conversations on "The Illegitimate Son"*) and *Discours sur la poésie dramatique* (*Discourse on Dramatic Poetry*) show clearly that his ideas were far superior to his dramas, and that the essay and not the play was Diderot's true genre.

Diderot always considered the theatre as little more than a dramatic means to the end of social reform, and it is surely this attitude that ruined his own plays. The end he sought, however, was to bring out man's natural goodness and his inherent sympathy to human misery. In writing of the need for theatre to promote these natural traits he won over some of the most outstanding dramatists of the age—Beaumarchais, Lessing, Goethe, Schiller, Dumas *fils*, and Augier. Their works, more than his own plays, are testimony to Diderot's place in the history of theatre.

PIERRE BEAUMARCHAIS: Pierre-Augustine Caron (later Beaumarchais) was born in Paris in 1732, the son of a prosperous clockmaker. As a youth he was sent to technical school in Alfort to learn the family trade. Apparently a zealous student, he returned to Paris at the age of thirteen, not only skilled in clockmaking, but also proficient in Latin and adept at music, playing the flute, violin, and harp. Pierre-Augustine's spirit and love of adventure displeased his father, apparently because it distracted the young man from his trade, but he managed at the age of twenty to devise a system of regulating watches which won him a patent from the French Academy of Sciences.

Pierre-Augustine became attached to the French royal court at Versailles, primarily as a clock and watch expert and musician, and by 1755 he believed himself to stand high in the court's favor. In 1757 he married one of his customers at court and took her name, Beaumarchais. Two years later his wife died, and Beaumarchais was financially ruined by a series of lawsuits. During this period, Beaumarchais discovered that he had never had any real standing with the court. Instead he found himself alienated from the court not only because of his unfortunate legal situation, but also because of his "low birth." The enmity that this discovery engendered culminated in a duel between Beaumarchais and a courtier who was considered to be the best swordsman at court. Through sheer luck and natural agility, Beaumarchais won the duel and was pardoned through the intercession of King Louis XV's daughters, to whom he had taught music.

A scene from a production of Beaumarchais' *The Marriage of Figaro.* (A 1785 engraving after Saint-Quentin)

Back in the court's favor, Beaumarchais developed his political connections, entered into several successful business enterprises, and then was called to Madrid in 1764 by his sister to handle her legal difficulties involving a breach of promise suit. On his return to Paris the following year, having acquired some writing skill through writing burlesque sketches, Beaumarchais printed his first major work, *Eugénie*, produced in 1767. The preface to *Eugénie*, "Essay on the Serious Drama," exemplified Diderot's *drame*, the domestic drama. After the failure of his second major play, *Les deux amis* (*The Two Friends*) another *drame*, Beaumarchais was ready to turn to comedy, but instead became involved in more legal problems involving his now deceased second wife's estate.

Beaumarchais was again in financial trouble, but this time the King took pity on him and arranged for him to leave the country, to get away from his creditors. As the King's personal agent, Beaumarchais traveled extensively in England, Holland, Germany and Austria. It was during this period, in 1772, that he completed the text of his first great comedy, *Le barbier de Séville* (*The Barber of Seville*). Back in Paris, and still in the King's favor, Beaumarchais attempted to get his comedy produced. It was censored until 1775, when it finally was staged to public acclaim.

With his strong feelings about personal independence, Beaumarchais again engaged in commercial ventures, this time by sending supplies to the Americans for their struggle against England. The venture was a financial loss, but it demonstrated the dramatist's desire for human liberty. Eager to see the same liberty in France, he wrote *Le mariage de Figaro* (*The Marriage of Figaro*), which after many delays was finally produced in 1784. The play was an enormous success and with its revolutionary spirit is considered by many to be the first salvo fired in the French Revolution. With the Revolution finally at hand, Beaumarchais found that he was growing too old to actively participate, and following a bitter pamphlet war with Mirabeau, he retired.

Beaumarchais came along at the end of the greatest period in French theatre, and as a result he was able to draw on a number of dramatic styles and genres; thus, he was able to combine comedy of manners, drama of character and intrigue, and political satire. His plays seem on the surface to be based on the theatre of Molière and the *commedia dell'arte*, but in many ways they are a far more serious type of drama. Like the plays of one of his predecessors, Corneille, Beaumarchais' last three plays may be considered a form of epic drama in that the same characters are used, allowing the audience to follow them through the varying situations and periods displayed in *The Barber of Seville, The Marriage of Figaro,* and *La mère coupable, ou L'autre Tartuffe* (usually titled in English, *Frailty and Hypocrisy*, 1792). Beaumarchais' drama was a melting pot of those dramatic styles, techniques, and characters which had been historically successful, but the result of this combination was, essentially, a completely new dramatic form. Not only did this new drama gain both critical and popular acclaim because of its own unique nature, but it helped to undermine the stagnating neoclassical stronghold in France. His drama helped divert attention away from neoclassicism, thus clearing the way for future playwrights to develop, if not a more significant drama, at least a more varied one.

THE ACTING COMPANIES

As was also true in England and Spain, the acting companies of France were essentially companies of shareholders. All actors held shares in the company, with the size of the share held by each individual determined by seniority and talent. Thus, the young bit players each were given one-fourth of a share. Journeymen actors, those playing reasonably major supporting roles, received one-half a share. Master actors, who played leading roles, held a full share. In addition to his share, each actor was supplied with a small grant of money, the amount determined in the same way that share size was computed, to heat and light his dressing room or area.

The nonacting members of the company who performed the essentially technical tasks were not given shares but were paid fixed salaries. These were paid out of gross income, before the shares were determined. For a successful company, these employees might include a porter, a ticket seller, doorkeepers, a copyist, and even a playwright. In some cases the playwright, like the stage manager, might also be an actor and thus entitled to a share. If not an actor, he might still receive a share in productions of his own plays.

In most cases the playwright was expected to help in the casting and direction of his own shows, though the position of "director" as we know it today did not then exist. In this direction he was assisted (and in many cases probably superseded) by senior members of the acting troupe. Even Molière, the most famous of the actor-playwright-manager-director tribe, apparently found directing his actors a difficult business, remarking that "actors are strange creatures to drive."

An illustration featuring Agnan Sarat, one of the period's great farcial actors, sharing the stage of the Hôtel de Bourgogne with Harlequin and a milkmaid. (Bibliothèque Nationale)

In those cases where a company began work on a new production, the following sequence was usually observed. After the play had been accepted by the company manager the playwright was called in to read his work to the assembled troupe. This gave the writer the opportunity to indicate his concept of the play and the characterizations, and it gave the troupe the chance to experience the play.

The parts were assigned on the basis of special actor competence, or perhaps appearance, and though one may suspect that this was not always an amicable process, the very organization of the troupes, with the actors sharing in the profits and thus deeply concerned with the ultimate success of every show, makes it likely that there was a certain amount of unanimity. Once the parts were assigned the actors began learning their lines, and rehearsals started as soon as the lines were committed to memory.

The rehearsals were usually conducted by the playwright, with help from the senior members of the company. Because the lines had already been learned, the rehearsals concentrated primarily on blocking and stage business. This does not mean that there was no attention paid to characterization, but in a period of more stylized acting the performers had a style for each type of role, and the kind of nuance usually thought of in terms of more realistic theatre was rarely attempted.

While rehearsals were going on the "orator" or company manager was also hard at work preparing posters, working out any special house problems, and composing his nightly addresses to the audience, in which he would seek to entice them to return and see the next offering of the company.

ACTING

Persons interested in becoming players learned their craft and art in one of two ways, either by joining one of the major companies as an apprentice, and learning by watching and studying, or by joining one of the smaller provincial troupes where there was a chance to get onstage right away and learn by doing. There was always the hope, for the small provincial troupes, that a sudden shift in fortune could make their reputations and carry them to Paris, and performers could hope to establish their individual reputations and then be selected to join one of the major companies.

MONTDORY: Guillaume des Gilleberts (or Desgilberts), born in 1594 and better known by his stage name of Montdory, has sometimes been called (along with Bellerose) the first great French actor because of the energy and grandeur he displayed onstage.

Montdory's career began sometime before 1612 in the company of Valleran Lecomte, who had begun his own career twenty years earlier in Bordeaux. After the death of Lecomte, Montdory went on to join the Prince of Orange players under Charles Lenoir, an actor-manager who had been performing in Paris intermittently since 1610. Montdory remained with Lenoir's company until the early 1620s and became one of its chief actors. He left to form his own company, but the role of actor-manager was not suited to him and he eventually returned to work with Lenoir in the late 1620s.

During Montdory's second alliance with Lenoir the company toured many of the French provinces, in 1629 playing Rouen, where an unknown playwright submitted to them the script of a play titled *Mélite.* As a result, on their return to Paris in 1630, the group brought with them Corneille's first play. Beginning by performing in temporary theatres, the company was finally permitted by the Confrérie de la Passion to settle in a converted tennis court near Porte-Saint-Denis, where they became the first serious rival to the Hôtel de Bourgogne. The Corneille play began quietly but soon became a success and the company decided to remain in Paris.

In 1634 another tennis court in the rue Vieille-du-Temple was converted for the Lenoir troupe, opening as the Théâtre du Marais. Montdory was by this time the sole leader, as Lenoir along with other important members of the company had been commandeered by Louis XIII for the Hôtel de Bourgogne, probably in an attempt to annoy Richelieu, who had expressed a preference for Montdory and the Lenoir players over Bellerose and the King's players at the Hôtel de Bourgogne. In the following three years Montdory presented the newest of plays in his theatre, attracting all the major playwrights of the period, except for Rotrou, to write for him. As a result he won the favor of Cardinal Richelieu, who awarded him a pension in 1634.

Montdory, given a second chance as actor-manager, proved to be a fine businessman as well as being a great actor in the old, declamatory tradition. Of all the single honors he earned, probably his greatest distinction turned out to be that he produced *The Cid,* in which he starred as Rodrigue. Eventually, however, his moment of greatest embarrassment (and sorrow, seeing that it ended his career) came in one of his finest roles—Herod in Tristan's *Mariamne,* a role famous for its bombastic style. He was acting before Richelieu and probably ranting and raving at his bombastic best when he was striken by paralysis of the tongue, which caused his premature retirement.

Sometimes called the first great French actor, and certainly the first great French actor who never played farce, Montdory was at his best in the roles of tragic heroes. Although a declamatory actor, he was capable of extreme emotion and is said to have brought conviction to all his parts. Under Montdory's leadership, the Marais became the leading theatre of Paris, a position it was to hold until 1647.

JODELET: Jodelet (Julien Bedeau) was a member of Lenoir's company at the tennis court in 1610, shortly before the opening of the Théâtre du Marais. He was transferred to the company at the Hôtel de Bourgogne, as a result of an order by Louis XIII, but he returned to the Marais in the early 1640s, where he played Cliton in Corneille's *Le Menteur* in 1643.

Jodelet's most noted contribution was his standard role as the comic valet. This role became so popular that the dramatists of the time began to write plays especially for him. Pierre Scarron wrote *Jodelet, ou le maître-valet* (*Jodelet, or the Master Valet*) in 1645, a play that involved a great deal of farcical humor. In this comedy Jodelet played a valet to Don Juan. Don Juan calls upon his valet to impersonate him, which causes general chaos until all is finally resolved at the end of the play. Other works in this vein were *Jodelet duelliste* (*Jodelet the Fencer*) and *Jodelet astrologue* (*Jodelet the Astrologer*). As a result of his performances as the comic valet in so many plays, the name *Jodelet* entered the language as a term used to signify a person who provokes laughter by his absurditites.

During this period the critics scorned the farce and parody in the theatre. Nevertheless, farce brought frank laughter back to comedy, and at the same time provided merciless satire on certain extravagances of more heroic theatre.

In 1659 Jodelet pooled his talents with those of Molière, who induced the famous comic actor to join his troupe, probably as a way of avoiding a feared rival and also as a means of assuring himself of a highly skilled clown. Jodelet played the valet in Molière's *Les precieuses ridicules*, and Molière probably wrote the role of Sganarelle for Jodelet. He was never able to play it, unfortunately, as he died the following year.

Three rows of flats painted to resemble towers, with practicable windows through which are leaning a chorus of fools. (Le Sage and D'Orneval, 1722-32)

During Jodelet's career the financial and social position of the actor began to improve, especially since prominent people were beginning to frequent the theatre. In 1641, Louis XIII sought to remove the stigma attached to acting by issuing a decree stating his desire that "the actors' profession . . . not be considered worthy of blame nor prejudicial to their reputation in society."

In France, unlike England, there was no prohibition against women performing, and indeed several of the most popular performers of the period were women. Also, unlike the English, the French had little interest in troupes of child actors. One such troupe, the Little Actors of the Dauphin, had limited success, but the troupe's main claim to fame was that one of its members, Michel Bayron, who acted under the name Baron, went on to become one of the greatest actors of the age.

The style of acting used in comedy was a reasonably natural one, at least in terms of the conventions of the age. It was established primarily by Molière, who despised the bravura, the ranting, and the posturing that was so often identified with the Classical style of performance. It was highly successful in comedy. However, when Molière tried it in terms of tragedy it failed miserably. This was, perhaps, less due to the natural style than to Molière's own failure to operate in the tragic genre. Its failure may even have been due to the tenor of the time, for when Baron, who had graduated from the boys' troupe to Molière's company, used the technique some years after Molière's death, he was highly successful.

The eighteenth century French theatre produced a number of great performers, most by way of Comédie-Française, including Michel Baron who made an extended comeback to theatre between 1720 and 1729. Probably the most famous of these performers were Charles Chevillet Champmeslé (1642-1701); Mlle. Dumesnil (Marie-Françaises Marchand, 1713-1803); Mlle. Dangeville (Marie-Anne Botot, 1714-96); Mlle. Clairon (Claire-Josèphe-Hippolyte Léris de la Tude, 1723-1803); Henri-Louis LeKain (1729-78); Adrienne Lecouvreur (1692-1730) and Préville (Pierre-Louis Dubus, 1721-99).

Champmeslé, an outstanding actor and a dramatist of minor note, began his career with a provincial company at Rouen. From there he went on to Paris, to the Marais, and then to the Hôtel de Bourgogne. Physically a very handsome man, he soon became highly popular, particularly in tragic roles. As a playwright, his success was only nominal, but his understanding of the dramatic genre and his good taste were much admired, and as a result his advice was regularly sought by some of the best playwrights of the age. Champmeslé's plays are mostly forgotten, but *Le Florentin* (*The Florentine*, 1685), his most popular work, was produced in Paris early in this century. Both Champmeslé and his wife, the celebrated actress Marie Desmares (1642-98), were founding members of the Comédie-Française.

Mlle. Dumesnil began her acting career, as did so many others, as a member of a provincial troupe, and was so successful that in 1737 she was accepted as an understudy at the Comédie-Française. She became a full performer in 1738 and was soon famous for such passionate roles as Medea and Clytemnestra. Voltaire attributed to her much of the success of his *Mérope* (1743).

She held the stage for many years, finally retiring in 1776 after nearly forty years as the country's outstanding tragic actress.

Mlle. Dangeville, the daughter of a family that had served the Comédie-Française for three generations, was admitted in 1730. By 1733 she had become the troupe's principal comedienne and maintained this position until she retired thirty years later. She was at her best in the comedies of Marivaux, but she was able to work so well in all styles that Garrick considered her to be the finest actress on the French stage.

Mlle. Clairon, the daughter of a seamstress, showed such early talent as a performer that at age twelve she became a member of the troupe of the Comédie-Italienne. She played minor roles for a year and then moved on to La Noue at Rouen. Her fine singing voice later took her to the Opéra, but her greatest talent was, clearly, acting. At the Comédie-Française she at first understudied Mlle. Dangeville, and finally made her debut in *Phédre*, one of Mlle. Dumesnil's favorite roles. She scored a great triumph in this debut and went on to excel in a number of tragic roles, especially those by Voltaire. Together with LeKain she attempted to introduce a limited sense of historical accuracy into costuming. Also, midway in her career, she abandoned much of the declamatory style that was still so popular for tragic acting and introduced what was then considered a much more natural style of performance. Arrested in 1765, along with some other famous members of the Comédie-Française for refusing to act with a player who, they felt, had disgraced the company, she never returned to the public stage. Instead she joined Voltaire at Ferney and performed in his private theatre. A series of misfortunes, including the outbreak of the Revolution, left her nearly destitute, but she was able to live the last few years of her life on the proceeds of her book, *Memories and Thoughts on the Art of Acting* (1799).

Henri-Louis LeKain (really Cain) was a protegé of Voltaire, in whose *Brutus* he made his debut at the Comédie-Française in 1750. A man of small physical stature, with a harsh voice that seemed to defy the demands of the time for richness and resonance, he possessed a quality of genius that allowed him to surmount these obstacles and become one of the great actors of the age. According to one of his leading ladies, Mlle. Clairon, he worked feverishly at his roles, often wearing himself out physically in both rehearsals and public productions. Voltaire, who had seen all the great actors beginning with Baron, called him the only truly tragic actor, and he was regularly compared to Garrick. He was responsible for a number of theatrical reforms, including the attempt to introduce historically accurate costumes in Voltaire's *L'orphelin de la Chine* (*The Orphan of China*). His death was as tragic as any role he played. After giving a bravura performance as Vendôme in Voltaire's *Adélaide du Guesclin*, he left the theatre for the chill night air, where he caught cold. He died of this just as his benefactor and friend Voltaire was returning to Paris following thirty years of exile.

Adrienne Lecouvreur began life as the daughter of a hatter who resided and had his business in the vicinity of the Comédie-Française. Thus, brought into contact with the great actresses of the period, she determined to follow in their footsteps and began appearing in amateur productions. At first she enjoyed little success, but then her fortunes changed and she was taken in charge by Marc-Antoine Legrand (1673-1728), an actor whose stage talents were considered to be excellent and whose morals were considered to be among the lowest in the profession. Adrienne acted for a season at Strasbourg under the tutelage of Legrand and then made her debut in 1717 at the Comédie-Française. She was an immediate success with the public, though her relationships with her fellow actresses were marred by their jealousies. It is difficult to comment on Lecouvreur's artistic capabilities because even her most ardent supporters tended to accept her more as a personality than as an actress. She clearly had great physical beauty, and she was generally considered to be better in tragic roles than in comic. Her open series of love affairs, especially with Marshall Saxe, overshadowed her talent, at least in the public eye. She was the reigning queen of the Comédie for thirteen years, and when she died her reputation had become such that she was refused Christian burial by the Church and was interred quietly, at night, in a corner of the rue de Bourgogne.

Préville, the finest comic actor of the eighteenth century, first acted with a provincial company and then joined the Comédie-Française in 1753. His approach to low comic roles is especially important. Before Préville's time such characters were played entirely for physical comic effects, usually as fat, drunken oafs. Préville, a handsome, slender man, gave them a sophistication not only in the physical aspects, but also in the way he delivered his lines, that was brand new. His greatest roles were in the plays of Marivaux, which especially suited his temperament, and he won raves for his performance of six characters in a revival of a play by Boursault. With his wife, who was also a

The fair (or fairground) stages in Paris were usually set up on Saint-Germain, Saint-Laurent, and, like this one, on Place Vendôme. (From an early seventeenth-century print)

member of the troupe, he retired in 1786, just as the French neoclassical period was drawing to an end.

THE PLAYHOUSES

The French theatres varied greatly during this long and diverse period, from the temporary scaffold stages of the traveling troupes and their more elaborate court cousins, to the converted tennis courts that were a bit makeshift and not expected to last through the ages, to the beautiful and often rather ornate permanent theatres that were mostly built after the middle of the eighteenth century.

The temporary stages erected by the traveling shows at fairs, in town squares, and on city streets, varied significantly. At one end of the spectrum were the simple stages, planks set up on the equivalent of sawhorses or barrels, perhaps with a painted backdrop of muslin. These were most used by the shows which featured dancers, jugglers, and acrobats rather than dramatic works, although many of the poorer, ragtag *commedia* companies (both Italian and French) used little more than this simple stage. The richer, more famous companies performed on similar stages, but theirs were large, the drops were better painted and varied from play to play and even, in some cases, from scene to scene.

At the court, temporary stages were regularly set up at great expense for single performances of elaborate court spectaculars. These were usually erected in large, rectangular halls, though outdoor performances of such spectaculars also took place. The stages and machines for production varied greatly, from show to show—as money was no object the designer had a relatively free hand. In fact, the only thing these production facilities had in common is that they were all elaborate, ornate, and completely supplied with the necessary equipment to produce scenic marvels.

The tennis court theatres, while more permanent in location, were hardly a full step up from the best of the trestle stages of the traveling troupes. By the last quarter of the sixteenth century the ancestor of the game we call tennis—*jeu de paume* or "game of the palm"—had become highly popular in France. In Paris alone several hundred halls had been constructed so that the sport, basically an indoor game played with a short-handled racquet, could be carried on in all weather conditions. Thus, when theatre companies began searching for permanent homes the tennis courts were ideal, being rectangular in shape, with galleries already built for spectators. The theatre companies merely built a stage at one end of the rectangle, using the existing galleries and benches on the floor to seat spectators. Because Paris had been so slow in constructing permanent theatres, these courts played an important role in helping the rapidly expanding French theatre.

Of the permanent theatre buildings the first and most important was the Hôtel de Bourgogne, built by the Confrérie de la Passion. Located in the rue Mauconseil, it was completed and ready for use in 1548, the same year in which the acting of religious plays was forbidden. Thus, the theatre got little immediate use as the Confrérie was forced to struggle along without the lar-

A 1632 engraving of a tennis court, illustrating the narrow rectangular shape, the high windows, and the side galleries that made such courts perfect for conversion to theatres.

gest part of their repertory, doing an occasional farce or nonreligious drama. By 1578, when Agnan Sarat was using the theatre, the Confrérie had given up producing and was renting out their theatrical facility.

The theatre was in use from 1548 to 1783—the final years only intermittently by Italian troupes—but very little is known about its dimensions and its general plan. It was, interestingly enough, of probably the same general dimensions as the tennis court theatres. It was between forty and sixty feet in width and approximately one hundred five feet long. Around the interior walls there were either two or three galleries, the lowest probably being divided up into box seats or loges. The main floor, the pit, had an elevated bench running around its walls, with temporary benches that could be set up in a variety of ways. The stage ran the width of the interior, which means that it was no more than forty feet wide and probably closer to thirty. Estimates on stage depth vary from seventeen to thirty-five feet, and when one remembers that the Confrérie did erect Medieval-style mansions on their stage, one is tempted to opt for the greater depth.

The first major competition for the Bourgogne was the Théâtre du Marais, which opened on December 31, 1634, in a converted tennis court on the rue Vieille-du-Temple, The resident company was that of the great actor, Montdory. Little is known of this first Marais, but when it burned down in 1644 a

"Curtain Time," a painting by Charles Coypel, c. 1700, shows the smaller type of theatre that developed in the palaces and great houses of Paris. This shows the Palais-Royal, opened in 1641 in the home of Cardinal Richelieu.

permanent theatre was erected on the site. Its dimensions, probably close to that of the original building, were 115 feet in length by 38 feet in width. It had three galleries and a capacity of about fifteen hundred persons. The Marais remained in use until 1673, when the resident company was integrated with that of Moliére. The combined company played at Lully's Opera Company theatre in the rue Guénégaud and the Marais was abandoned.

Not much is certain about the theatre on the rue Guénégaud. The Palais Royal was the most elaborately equipped theatre in Paris, but from 1661 it was in the possession of Molière, and Lully was forced to take a lesser house—the theatre on the rue Guénégaud. When Molière died, Lully pulled rank and forced the Molière company out; thus, since Lully did operas, the Palais Royal became an opera house by definition. The theatre on the Guénégaud became home to the combined Marais-Molière troupe, which subsequently affiliated with the Comédie-Française in 1680.

The Comédie was evicted from the rue Guénégaud theatre in 1687 to make room for the Sorbonne's new college, and it was not until 1689 that it found a reasonably permanent home in the remodeled Etoile tennis court on the rue Neuve-des-Fossés in the quarter of St. Germain-des-Prés. The company, at the plan of architect François d'Orbay, paid 200,000 livres for the remodeling, and though it left them deeply in debt it proved a good investment and they remained in the theatre until 1770.

The remodeling that d'Orbay effected is almost a textbook on the theatrical developments that began in 1634 and continued through the rest of the period. Paying no attention to the exterior walls, d'Orbay constructed a horseshoe-shaped interior that contained a pit for standing room, with elevated bleachers along the wall. This was topped by three galleries, the lower two of which were divided into boxes. Totally, the theatre could accommodate about two thousand persons. The stage was large for its day—fifty-four feet wide by forty-one feet deep—and was equipped for both flat wings and shutters.

While the public theatre was moving toward a larger stage and simplicity of design—that is, most settings represented a single space created by flat wings—the royal or court theatres began and ended on an opulent note. The King's private theatre, in the Petit Bourbon Palace, contained a proscenium-arch stage at one end of a rectangular, highly decorated ballroom. The walls contained two galleries for spectators, but the floor was left open so that appropriate seating could be set up for the King and his entourage. This was the theatre that Molière's troupe shared with a group of Italian comedians until, in October 1660 at the order of the Superintendent of Royal Buildings, it was razed. Over Molière's objections the scenes and machines that had been designed by Torelli were given to Torelli's successor, Vigarani, who claimed to

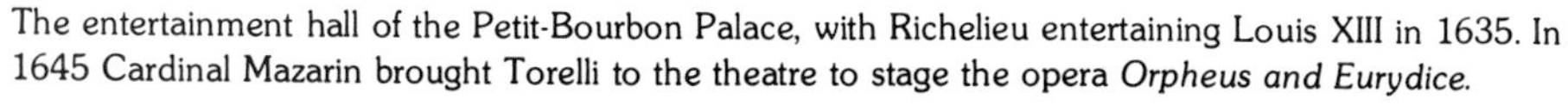

The entertainment hall of the Petit-Bourbon Palace, with Richelieu entertaining Louis XIII in 1635. In 1645 Cardinal Mazarin brought Torelli to the theatre to stage the opera *Orpheus and Eurydice.*

need them for his Hall of Machines in the Tuileries. Having gained possession of the scenes and machines, Vigarani had them burned, probably to erase all reminders of his illustrious predecessor.

The King, Louis XIV, then gave Molière the theatre in the Palais Royal. This sumptuous theatre, originally built by Richelieu as part of his private residence, contained a small, richly decorated theatre capable of accommodating about six hundred persons. Rectangular in shape, one end contained a proscenium-arch stage, decorated above the proscenium by the Cardinal's coat of arms, and the opposite end was a lobby formed of three arched arcades. Along the walls were two galleries. In 1670 it was enlarged to seat more people and to accommodate some complex stage machinery.

The Hall of Machines, which had given Vigarani the excuse for appropriating Torelli's equipment, was a theatre expressly designed to produce the court spectaculars so popular at the time. The proscenium stage was only 32 feet wide, but was 132 feet deep, to provide extensive space for stage constructions and depth for perspective sets. In terms of equipment, it contained the most extensive machinery of any theatre of its day. This was the last major Parisian theatre to be constructed until 1769 when the Opéra moved into a new theatre especially built for that troupe.

SCENIC PRACTICE

Settings during the French neoclassical period varied as greatly as did the theatres themselves. At one extreme, the sets of the traveling companies and *commedia* troupes consisted of little more than painted drop curtains and a few set pieces, though some old engravings show backdrops of what seem to be simulated Classical columns with painted-curtain doorways much like the engravings of the Terentian set.

In the Hôtel de Bourgogne the early seventeenth century designer, Laurent Mahelot, designed sets in the tradition of the Medieval mansions used to present the religious dramas. Sketches of these sets are contained in Mahelot's *Notes for the Decoration of the Plays Presented by the King's Comedians, Reported to His Majesty.* The frame and muslin mansions as described by the *Notes* represented various localities—especially necessary for the plays of Hardy, who had little interest in geographical unity—with the open central area a kind of generalized acting area corresponding to the Medieval *platea.* Given the size of the stage in the Hôtel de Bourgogne—probably about twenty-five feet wide by thirty feet deep, though some scholars claim dimensions slightly larger—these mansions must have been set up in a manner that would make them little more than curtained doorways, again similar to the stage of Terence.

Italian-style staging had made early but sporadic appearances at a number of court productions. However, it was not until Cardinal Richelieu built his sumptuous private residence (called the Palais Cardinal until after his death, when it reverted to the crown), which included the theatre that Molière would later be given, that the wide use of Italianate scenery got underway. The Palais Cardinal theatre began production in January 1641 with the staging of *Mirame,* for which Georges Buffequin designed scenery and special effects.

A design by Carlo Vigarani for a production of *Alcestis,* c. 1675. (Stockholm National museum)

In 1642, a little more than a year after his theatre opened, Richelieu died and the Palais Cardinal, becoming the property of the crown, was renamed the Palais Royal. Richelieu's successor as Chief Minister was Cardinal Mazarin, an Italian with a taste for spectacle and a love of opera, which he hoped to popularize in France. As a result of his machinations in favor of opera, and the subsequent fears of a visiting *commedia dell'arte* troupe which had seen opera replace theatre in Italy, the Queen requested the Duke of Parma to send a designer to aid the *commedia* troupe. The Duke responded by sending the most famous scenic designer in Italy, Giacomo Torelli.

Torelli refused to be tied totally to *commedia* productions and, in fact, his best work in France was probably with opera productions. However, he remodeled the Petit Bourbon into an Italian-style theatre in 1645 and the following year he did the same for the theatre in the Palais Royal, where he installed the chariot and pole system to shift scenes.

In 1659 Mazarin sent to Italy for another designer, Gaspare Vigarani (1586-1663), who became the rallying point for Torelli's many enemies. When Mazarin died in 1661 Vigarani's supporters managed to have Torelli deported and Vigarani appointed his successor. Vigarani's son, Carlos, followed his father as court theatrical designer, doing a number of highly spectacular productions such as *Les plaisirs d'île enchantée* (*The Pleasures of the Enchanted Island*), which lasted three days.

Beginning in the 1640s, ballet began to regain its popularity at the court, in part because Louis XIV, inordinately proud of the appearance of his legs, took part in many such productions. The sets and costumes for such ballets were rich indeed, especially those designed for the King's participation, and ballet began to replace opera in the court affections. There was, in 1654, an abortive attempt to marry opera and ballet, when Mazarin commissioned an opera which would feature ballet between the acts. Torelli designed sumptuous sets and Louis XIV danced six of the roles. However, the idea failed to catch on and ballet replaced opera for nearly twenty years.

The late seventeenth and early eighteenth centuries saw little significant change in the public theatres, in part because the major theatre structures remained unchanged and the Italianate spectacle of the court was too costly for a self-supporting troupe.

By the beginning of the eighteenth century there were only two legitimate public troupes in Paris—the Opéra and the Comédie-Française. The Opéra, however, beset by financial problems, authorized one of the illegitimate "fair" theatres to produce comic operas, and this eventually became the Opéra Comique. In 1716 a new troupe was added when the Duc d'Orleans, Regent for the boy king Louis XV, installed a troupe of *commedia del'arte* players in the Hôtel de Bourgogne. In 1723 the *commedia* troupe became legitimate

Antoine Watteau's painting of "Les Comédiens Français," c. 1720.

under the title Comédiens Ordinaires du Roi but they were known popularly as the Comédie-Italienne.

In 1763 the Palais Royal theatre burned down, forcing the Opéra to move into the Théâtre des Tuileries, which was the remodeled Hall of Machines. The Opéra moved to a new theatre, created especially for it, in 1769, and in the following year the Comédie-Française moved out of their old tennis court theatre and into the Tuileries. The Comédie remained there for twelve years, until its own new theatre, on the site of the present day Odéon, was opened. The Comédie-Italienne played in the Hôtel de Bourgogne from its founding until 1783, when it moved into a new theatre in an attempt to compete with the more popular Comédie-Française. All this modernization of Parisian theatres came just before the Revolution put an end to the period.

COSTUMES

Costuming throughout the period remained almost remarkably consistent—that is, for all but certain historical, fantasy, or allegorical characters, or (after the 1750s) characters with a special national affiliation, contemporary French costume was the rule. In most cases these costumes were purchased by the individual performers and became part of their professional wardrobe, which meant that the more famous and financially successful a performer was, the more sumptuously he would be dressed. However, in the vicinity of the Hôtel de Bourgogne there was a substantial business carried on in secondhand clothing, and in the middle of the seventeenth century a Parisian merchant set up what was, apparently, the first theatrical costume rental business.

The Italian players of the *commedia dell'arte* continued to wear traditional costumes through the seventeenth century, but by the eighteenth even these were modernized and some contemporary French garb appeared on the *commedia* stage.

The hairstyles that were popular on the street, and especially at court, also found their way to the stage. This meant that the men wore long, full wigs for most of the period, and the women made use of the elaborate hairstyles and headpieces that were fashionable. Makeup was commonly used off the stage, and so there is every reason to believe that it was used onstage as well to heighten features and bring a blush to the cheek.

In the middle of the eighteenth century a challenge was mounted to the traditional costuming practices. The famous actress Mme. Favart (Mlle. Chantilly, 1727-72) donned peasant costume to play the heroine of *The Loves of Bastien and Bastienne,* and in 1761, she imported a Turkish costume for her role in *The Three Sultans.*

Voltaire, who also called for reality in acting, commissioned the artist Joseph Vernet to design costumes for *The Orphan of China* that would look authentic but that would not cause the audience to laugh. The innovation was a success and Voltaire's lead was followed by his two protégé's, Clairon and LeKain, who began to insist on dressing in appropriate styles for all their subsequent roles. LeKain finally carried this too far even for Voltaire, appearing in *Sémiramis* with his arms bare, his hair tangled and unkempt, and his hands dripping with blood. The public was outraged and subsequent attempts at "realistic" costuming were carefully kept within the bounds of what the public would accept.

These were hardly heroic attempts at historical realism, and they made little impression on the costuming of the time, but they signaled the beginning of the end for the costuming traditions of the French neoclassical period.

9

The Restoration Period

9

The Restoration Period

The Restoration period in England was a brief one in terms of the years it includes—1660 until just after the beginning of the eighteenth century, at least from a theatrical point of view. It was also an unusual one in that many of the best Restoration plays came at the end of the age rather than at some peak during the middle years. It was a period of intense political and religious struggle that reshaped the English monarchy. And nothing typifies the period better than its theatre.

THE COMMONWEALTH AND RESTORATION

In a sense the history of the period begins with the final years of the reign of Charles I, who ruled Great Britain from 1625 to 1649. Charles outraged a large percentage of his subjects by favoring those religious practices that seemed to them to smack of Catholicism. To aid in bringing the Scots to heel, Charles recruited William Laud, Archbishop of Canterbury, and Thomas Wentworth, first Earl of Strafford, whose repressive measures and "High Church" policies angered all of Scotland. When they attempted to force the Uniform Prayer Book on Scotland, the country broke into open rebellion. Charles was forced to call on Parliament for aid, but because of his religious practices and his tax policies, Charles found himself with few parliamentary allies.

Instead of granting Charles money, Parliament proceeded to gain redress for a number of grievances. It imprisoned both Laud and Wentworth (later executing them), abolished the Courts of Star Chamber and High Commission, decreed that Parliament would meet each three years, whether the King called for it or not, declared Charles' "ship money" tax to be illegal, and printed its "Grand Remonstrance" to inform the country of Parliament's side of the controversy with the monarch.

Charles tried to arrest the five major parliamentary leaders who opposed him, and when that move failed both sides prepared for war. Favoring the King were the nobility, Catholics, "High Church" Anglicans, and a few members of Parliament. Opposed to him were the Puritans, shipping interests, and most of the middle-class citizenry. Charles' forces had the initial advantage, but Oliver Cromwell, who became the leader of the opposition, turned the situation around and led his forces to victory, capturing the King and ending the conflict. Charles tried negotiating with the army, Scotland, and Parliament for his return to power. However, the army leaders became convinced that Charles was deceiving them, seeking to regain power and restore Catholicism. They purged Parliament of the King's supporters, set up a special court before which Charles was tried on a charge of treason, and executed him.

For more than a decade England had no king, and Cromwell ruled by virtue of his control of the army. He suppressed rebellion in both Scotland and Ireland and controlled a hostile majority at home. Favoring the shipping interests which had supported him, he sponsored a navigation act which struck at Dutch shipping. This led to an inconclusive "sea war" with the Dutch. There was also a resumption of hostilities with Spain, during which the English captured Jamaica, a possession they refused to relinquish at the end of hostilities.

Following Cromwell's death in 1658 his son, Richard, succeeded him. The people, however, long unhappy with the repressive Puritan policies of the father, refused to accept the son. Instead they went to the son of the executed Charles I, and in 1660 he was called to the throne, where he ruled as Charles II. A far more able monarch than his father, Charles favored religious toleration, even though Parliament insisted on limiting freedom of worship to Anglicans. Charles managed to avoid dependence on Parliament, thanks largely to a substantial subsidy from Louis XIV and his Portuguese wife's large dowry. During the final years of his reign he even managed to overpower Parliament, forcing this body to accept his Catholic brother James as his successor.

James II (ruled 1685-88) was not, unfortunately, nearly as able as his brother, and his blatant attempts to restore Catholicism soon raised many enemies. Thus, the birth of his son, which certified a Catholic succession, was more than the Protestant majority could bear, and the "Bloodless Revolution" took place only three years after James had ascended the throne. James was overthrown and fled to France. William of Orange and his wife, Mary, daughter of James II, were invited to rule. Historically speaking, this marks the end of the Restoration period. Theatrically speaking, however, the Restoration lasted for nearly seventeen more years.

William was a reserved and rather sour man, highly suspicious of all things English, who was far happier in the field fighting the French than at court. As a result he was not reluctant to accept an act which confirmed certain fundamental privileges of Englishmen, and a toleration act which provided freedom of worship for all except Catholics, Jews, and Unitarians. By the end of the seventeenth century the problem of religious freedom and the issues raised by the conflict between a Catholic monarch and a heavily Protestant populace had been resolved. By 1705 the social changes that began when William and Mary ascended the throne had filtered down to the theatre and the theatre audience—and the Restoration period was over.

THEATRE DURING THE COMMONWEALTH

As the Commonwealth entered its formative years, Puritan antipathy toward the theatre was twofold. From a religious point of view the Puritans both hated and feared theatre as the devil's instrument. From a political point of view, they hated and feared it as an instrument of the court, this belief rooted in the fact that all the acting companies were licensed to members of the royal family. Thus, using the religious warfare as an excuse, the Puritan-dominated Parliament closed the English theatres in 1642. As a concession to non-Puritan factions, the closing was originally to be for only five years, but by the time the five years had passed the Puritans were in firm control of the government, and the closing was made permanent.

During the first few years after the theatres were closed, public performance came to a virtual halt. The companies disbanded, the King's Men sold their wardrobe, and the Globe Theatre was torn down. Occasionally, however, public performances were put on at such theatres as the Fortune, the Cockpit, and the Salisbury Court. Parliament made occasional moves to suppress these productions, but violations of the law were common and legal action against them was in most cases ineffectual. When the first five-year closure law ran out, enough casual companies were around to begin performances immediately. This provoked the heavily Puritan Parliament to pass a new law, permanently banning theatre and ordering that all actors be apprehended as rogues. They also saw to it that offending theatres (Fortune, Cockpit, and Salisbury Court) were gutted so that performers who escaped arrest would have no place to play. As has been true from the beginning, the actors refused to stop playing. However, performances became much more surreptitious, many taking place at the Red Bull. This theatre, built in 1600, had escaped the interior destruction visited on so many others. Perhaps because it was roofed over it continued to operate on an occasional basis throughout the period of the Commonwealth. Performances also took place at inns, tennis courts, and private homes. Because of the strained circumstances of performance, the traditional-length plays were usually replaced by "drolls"—short, farcical adaptations of the longer works.

By the early 1650s, anti-Puritan sentiment was increasing rapidly enough to convince some would-be theatrical entrepreneurs that soon dramatic activities would once more be safe and, perhaps, even legalized. In 1650 William Beeston (c. 1606-82), who had acted with his father, Christopher, and succeeded him as the head of the boy's troupe called Beeston's Boys, bought the dismantled Salisbury Court Theatre and rebuilt the interior. He also recruited and began to train a company of boy actors. John Rhodes, a bookseller, purchased the Cockpit and, like Beeston, rebuilt it and recruited a company. The most important step in the restoration of drama to the public stage, however, took place in May 1656 when William Davenant (1606-68) publicly produced *The First Day's Entertainment at Rutland House*. He justified the production on the claim that it was not a play but an opera. Also, because his early works were staged in Rutland House, Davenant's private residence, he could claim that technically they were not public performances.

Inasmuch as public performances had for so long been limited to "drolls" and other short, farcical works, the audience was hungry for full-length, serious drama, and Davenant gave it to them in the new heroic theatre form that operated under the guise of opera. *The Siege of Rhodes* (1656) was the first important specimen of the genre, but others were soon to follow.

By 1658 Davenant was presenting his "operas" in the restored Cockpit Theatre and, though some diehard Puritan members of Parliament growled their disapproval, the death of Cromwell and the public resentment of his son conspired to let the public productions go onstage. Gathering sentiment for restoration of the monarchy allowed the heroic drama to continue undisturbed, and only the fact of the Restoration was necessary to place once more a reasonably full range of drama on the public stage.

THEATRE IS REVIVED

In 1660, when the restoration of the monarchy under Charles II was assured, Davenant gave up producing in a rented theatre and in March signed a lease for Lisle's Tennis Court. He then left for France to seek a theatrical monopoly from Charles. In the meantime Sir Henry Herbert, who had been Master of Revels under Charles I, resumed his position and awarded licenses to three companies: John Rhodes' Company at the Cockpit; Michael Mohun's at the Red Bull; and Beeston's at the Salisbury Court. Charles, still in France and unaware of Herbert's independent actions, gave a theatrical monopoly in London to Davenant and Thomas Killigrew (1612-83), a pre-Commonwealth playwright who had gone to France with the court to share their exile. Herbert refused to back down on the licenses he had granted, and it was not until 1660

An illustration from Dryden's *Love Triumphant.* (London, 1735)

that the troupe of Davenant and Killigrew was able to suppress their competition. As soon as their rivals had been leveled, the two men split their troupe into two companies—the King's Company under Killigrew, which kept most of the established actors, and the Duke's Company (with the patronage of the king's brother, the Duke of York), under Davenant, which took the younger players to the theatre that had been Lisle's Tennis Court and that was now called Lincoln's Inn Fields or the Duke's House. It soon became apparent that Davenant had gotten the better of the deal; among his young players were Thomas Betterton, Mrs. Sanderson, and the comedians Jevon and Nokes, all of whom were to dominate the stage of their day.

The patent granted Davenant and Killigrew underwent one last challenge, this from George Jolly (fl. 1640-73), an English actor who may have begun his career at the Fortune. He was in Germany during the Commonwealth period, perhaps in an attempt to escape the Puritan suppression of theatrical activity. He was particularly active in the Frankfurt area when Prince Charles, who would later become Charles II, probably saw him perform. Trading on this early exposure before the newly restored monarch, Jolly was able to gain from the King a patent to perform in London. However, when he went on tour in 1662 he rented his patent to Davenant and Killigrew, who then told Charles that they had purchased it. When Jolly returned to London he continued to produce in spite of this treachery, and finally there seems to have been a behind-the-scenes deal consummated. Charles stopped Jolly from performing, and Davenant and Killigrew then hired him to run their training school for actors.

Because no theatre company, including their own, could operate in London without the specific permission of the monarch, the company (and, ultimately, companies) operated by Davenant and Killigrew took a special interest in pleasing the court. As a commercial venture they hoped, of course, to please their audience, which was primarily aristocratic, or nouveau riche pretending to aristocracy, but the major concern was the King himself. Charles very much enjoyed theatre. While he was still in exile he kept, for some time, a company of English actors, and he took pains to see performances by touring English troupes. After his restoration he not only had a court theatre (at Whitehall) which he attended, he also regularly went to see performances in the public theatres.

The King's patronage of public theatre and his occasional presence in the audience was, in a sense, an unspoken command to the members of his court. Thus, the Restoration audience was essentially an elite one. The most important members of the aristocracy sat in boxes on the sides and at the rear of the auditorium. The ladies regularly sat in the boxes, and the "fashionable" young gentlemen sat in the "pit," on benches placed on the raked auditorium floor. Here the orange-wenches hawked their wares (which included apples and sweetmeats) and the young men could engage their friends in conversation, scan the boxes, and make sure that they were "seen" to be in attendance. The actual practice of young gallants climbing up to sit on the stage itself (as had been the practice in Elizabethan theatre) did not begin until the end of the period, mostly because Charles II really did come to see the play, and as a result he frowned on this odious custom. The galleries above the boxes held the well-off but less fashionable members of the audience, often members of the growing merchant class who were attempting to imitate the courtiers. In the highest gallery, which was the cheapest area of the house, were the few working-class spectators, many of whom were servants to the fashionable people below.

RESTORATION DRAMA

When the English courtiers returned from their long exile at the French court, they brought back a taste for drama that was not quite French (though strongly influenced by French drama) and not quite traditional English, though again the influence was there. They also brought back with them a French-inspired respect for the Classical rules that had been missing from the earlier drama of the Elizabethan and Jacobean periods. At least one result of this was the belief that the great writers of the earlier periods were in error and that their plays needed correcting before being presented. Thus, *Hamlet* was given music and dance, the ending of *Romeo and Juliet* was turned into a happy one, and major excisions were made in such plays as *Lear* and *Macbeth*. Upon occasion this attitude led the writers of Restoration tragedy to go beyond correction to complete rewriting. The most notable example of this is John Dryden's (1631-1700) *All for Love, or The World Well Lost* (1677), which is a rewrite of Shakespeare's *Antony and Cleopatra*. Like its original, Dryden's play is in blank verse, but unlike its original, *All for Love* is carefully written to observe the unities of time, place, and action. The English tragedies, even *All for Love*, failed to achieve the artistic level of the plays by Corneille and Racine. They

A scene from John Dryden's tragedy *All for Love*. (An engraving from *The Dramatick Works of John Dryden, Esq.*, London, 1735)

did, however, follow similar plot patterns, with a strong emphasis on the conflict between the demands of love and honor.

Of the three major dramatic forms of the Restoration period, the least important is the form often referred to as the heroic drama. The plot of the heroic drama was in many ways similar to that of Restoration tragedy, but the heroic drama featured athletic heroes performing incredible feats of derring-do. The form grew out of the spectacular operas of Davenant, but the major works were Dryden and Sir Robert Howard's (1626-98) *The Indian Queen* (1664), Dryden's *The Conquest of Granada* (1670), and Nathaniel Lee's (c. 1653-92) *Sophonisba* (1676). The absurdities of the form were brilliantly parodied by George Villiers' (the second Duke of Buckingham, 1628-87) *The Rehearsal* (1671).

The major achievement of Restoration dramatists was their development of a distinctive form of comic drama—a comedy of manners with a hard, brilliant surface, that ridicules the social follies of the age. In some ways it seems similar to the Jonsonian comedy of humors, with type names such as Mr. Witwould, Frederick Frolick, Lady Wishfort, and Mrs. Fainall giving clues to the specific humor involved. However, the emphasis is always on the period rather than on the humor itself. As an example, Sir George Etherege's (c. 1635-91) character, Sir Fopling Flutter (*The Man of Mode*, 1676), is more a caricature of the English beau vainly trying to imitate Parisian manners than an example of the humor of vanity. The characters in this form of comedy are often given superficial comic manners, but in general the humor comes from intellectual wit rather than from broad or farcical satire. The coin of Restoration comedy of manners is dialogue rather than stage business, and though the plays concentrate on the manners of their own contemporary world, they are removed to a basically unreal world that was remote from the entire population.

A few of the plays from Elizabethan and Jacobean times were staged during the Restoration, some in corrected versions and some in their original form, in spite of their supposed faults. The most popular of these earlier plays were those by Beaumont and Fletcher, followed by the plays of Shakespeare, Jonson, Marlowe, Chapman, Webster, Middleton, Massinger, Ford, and Shirley. In addition, a few translations of French drama were staged to please the French-trained court; especially popular were the plays of Corneille.

JOHN DRYDEN: John Dryden, who was to become the outstanding literary figure of the Restoration period, was born on August 9, 1631, in the parsonage house of Aldwincle All Souls, Northamptonshire, the first child of two redoubtable Puritans, Erasmus and Mary Pickering Dryden. He was educated at Westminister School and at Trinity College, Cambridge. In 1658 he went to London where he "set up for a poet."

Dryden supported the Commonwealth in his early verses, but after the Restoration became a hard fact he accepted it and soon became an ardent royalist, writing his brilliant satires in support of the Tory cause. This occasioned a great many charges of opportunism, and Dryden was regularly accused of being a turncoat for forsaking his Puritan heritage. It was probably, however, a legitimate conversion, caused in part by his marriage in 1663 to the fiery royalist Lady Elizabeth, sister of Sir Robert Howard, Dryden's future collaborator on *The Indian Queen* (1664).

Earning a reasonably decent living by hackwork, Dryden turned to the theatre, emulating Jonson (and to some degree Fletcher) in his first play, a prose comedy titled *The Wild Gallant* (1663). Dryden eventually wrote a number of comedies, most of them in the somewhat coarser tradition of his own time, but it was not until he completed *The Indian Queen* that he found the genre in which he was to excel. The heroic drama perfectly suited Dryden's talent and temperament. Grand emotion, physical bravery, and sentimental posturing were the underpinnings of heroic drama, and Dryden's plays included the best of all three. He wrote a series of such dramas, the best of which is probably *Aurung-Zebe* (1675), even though it is not typical of the genre.

Involved in a clutch of quarrels and rivalries, literary and personal, Dryden took time out to examine the theory and practice of the drama in various prose essays, the most important of which is *An Essay of Dramatick Poesy.*

In 1677 he produced *All for Love,* a completely rewritten version of Shakespeare's *Antony and Cleopatra*; by nearly general consensus it is Dryden's finest play and almost a blueprint of the Restoration ideal of tragedy. Charles II had barely arrived in London when the demand for dramas sent theatre managers scurrying to stage such materials as they could find. There existed very few works written in the new, fashionable mode, and this led companies to unearth the greatest works of the age preceding the Commonwealth. The aristocratic audiences, convinced that they themselves represented the ultimate in sophistication, found the older plays to be inelegant, a bit coarse, and sadly lacking in the necessary Classical unities.

Dryden himself fell prey to this delusion. He had certainly seen Davenant's "altered" productions of *Hamlet* and *Macbeth* and his completely rewritten *Measure for Measure.* When he began work on *All for Love,* Dryden tells us, he consulted with those Classical writers who had treated the love of Anthony and Cleopatra, but after all his consulting his main source was Shakespeare, not only *Antony and Cleopatra,* but also *Hamlet, Othello,* and *As You Like It,* from which he took lines and passages.

Following *All for Love,* Dryden turned out a few generally undistinguished dramas, but a growing interest in the escalating strife between the increasingly licentious Catholic court and the increasingly moralistic Protestant populace led to an energy-draining involvement in political and religious causes. In 1685 Dryden converted to Catholicism and in 1688 the Revolution, his new religion, and his involvement in causes sponsored by Charles and James, led to the loss of his position as Poet Laureate, a position he had held since 1668.

Dryden tried vainly to reestablish himself in theatre, and when that failed he reverted back to the work with which he had begun his career—translation and verse narrative. So successful was he that he became England's "grand old man" of letters and, thus, a respected arbiter to whom literary disputes were regularly referred. He died on May 1, 1700, and was buried with pomp and circumstance in Westminster Abbey.

WILLIAM WYCHERLEY: William Wycherley (c. 1640-1716) wrote only four plays—*Love in a Wood, or St. James Park* (1671), *The Gentleman Dancing Master*(1672), *The Country Wife* (1674-75), and *The Plain Dealer* (1676)—but the last two were good enough to place him permanently in the first rank of Restoration dramatists.

Wycherley was born in Shropshire, the son of an old and distinguished family. When he reached the age of fifteen and had completed his early schooling, his family followed custom and sent him abroad on the traditional grand tour. He went to France, where the English court was in exile, and there he was introduced to the literary and social elite. He returned to England shortly before the Restoration and enrolled in Queen's College, Oxford, but he lasted only a short time before moving on to London where he began the study of law at the Inner Temple. London, especially in the early days of the Restoration, was a heady place for a young man of good family, literary tastes, and independent means. Wycherley soon became involved in the literary circles of the court and the study of law was abandoned. He became a friend of George Villiers, John Wilmont (the Earl of Rochester), and the others who are usually referred to as the "court wits." Eventually he even married into the group, wedding the widowed Countess of Drogheda in 1679. She proved to be a highly jealous woman (not, it must be admitted, without reason) and she gave

A scene from a contemporary production of William Wycherly's *The Country Wife* at the University of Illinois, Urbana-Champaign. Directed by Clara Behringer.

Wycherley a bad two years before dying in 1681. By this time Wycherley had squandered the family funds and he was in serious financial trouble, from which he was rescued by James II, who paid his debts and gave him a pension. Wycherley's life spanned the Commonwealth, the Restoration, and the beginning years of the eighteenth century. By the time of his death in 1716 the literary styles and subjects of the Restoration had passed on and he had become the friend of the young and promising poet Alexander Pope.

Wycherley's plays, even the last two, are often considered by literary critics to have less artistic merit than the plays of several dramatists who are usually ranked beneath him, and yet his plays were highly popular in their own time. In part this is because of the vivid life that these plays have when staged, and in part because Wycherley was such a powerful force in Restoration life and in the development of Restoration drama. The lover of the Duchess of Cleveland, tutor to the King's son, and husband of the Countess of Drogheda, he was part and parcel of his time, and his effect on Restoration comedy of manners was unequaled until Jeremy Collier appeared on the scene. He flayed the age, writing with a brutal pen of the jaded roués and their fickle mistresses. His style is hardly graceful, and his wit is not polished and fine, but his effect on his own age is incalculable.

Wycherley's four plays were all composed in a short span of little more than five years, and as far as can be determined he never attempted another drama, as if the very force with which he wrote had burned him out as a dramatist. His first play, *Love in a Wood*, is generally undistinguished and, without Wycherley's ever-present vulgarity, might easily have been assigned to Etherege. Even less successful was his second effort, *The Gentleman Dancing Master*, which is only interesting in the way it contrasts two types of foppery—French and Spanish.

After a break of two years Wycherley returned to the stage with *The Country Wife*, and his reputation was assured. In it he combines farcical action and witty dialogue in a manner previously unknown. The farcical "china" scene is one of the best in dramatic literature, and the sexual innuendo that began in *The Gentleman Dancing Master* is here pervasive and effective. Wycherley's final play, *The Plain Dealer*, is often considered to be his best. In it the character Manly, a misanthrope (who owes much to Molière), is contrasted to Fidelia, a model of purity, and to Olivia, Manly's former mistress and a model of her time. In addition the play presents a notable fop in Lord Plausible, a would-be wit in Novel, and a woman who has discovered that the law can provide entertainment in the Widow Blackacre, who has fallen in love with litigation.

Because of his style, Wycherley was often called "manly" or "brawney," or "bitter," but the most important aspect of his writing was that he captured, better than anyone else, all the vulgarity and nastiness of a society seemingly bent on its own destruction.

WILLIAM CONGREVE: William Congreve (1670-1729), more than any other writer of his time, epitomizes the genre of Restoration comedy. With only four comedies and one tragedy to his credit, Congreve achieved fame during his lifetime and even greater recognition in the generations that followed. No other playwright better represents the comedy of manners period; no historian more accurately captures the social environment of the time. Although Congreve cared little for his career as playwright, and much for the role of the English gentleman, it was his ability to transfer the wit and grace of the Restoration to the stage, to mirror the foibles of the pleasure-seeking aristocracy in his sparkling comedies, that enabled him in later life to achieve the gentlemanly existence he so much admired.

Although Congreve lived to be fifty-nine years old, his productive period as a writer was short. His first literary work, a novel entitled *Incognita* (1692), and his last dramatic work, a comedy of manners entitled *The Way of the World* (1700), spanned only the short period of eight years.

Congreve's first comedy, *The Old Bachelor*, appeared in March 1693 and was an instant success. He followed this in December 1693 with *The Double Dealer*, which was not quite so successful but which later became a popular comedy. *Love for Love* was written in 1694, but was held up for the opening of a new theatre. For contemporary audiences it was his most popular play. His only tragedy, *The Mourning Bride* (1697), although popular when it was first presented, has since failed to interest either audiences or critics. *The Way of the World*, later acknowledged as his greatest play, was not well received by the turn-of-the-century public, perhaps because the argument of the play was too complex, but more likely because the vogue for Restoration comedy of manners was already dying. Except for a few verses and a masque, *The Judgment of Paris* (1701), William Congreve never wrote again.

Details of Congreve's life are meager. As a youth he was of medium stature and was physically quite active. However, he was far too fond of eating and drinking, and by the time he was forty he had become so corpulent he could hardly tie the laces of his shoes. At all times Congreve was a very private man, guarding details of his life as carefully as he hoarded his monetary wealth. He never married, but his romances included two of the most beautiful women of the day, the actress Anne Bracegirdle and the Duchess of Marlborough, wife of Lord Chesterfield. However, time and age took their toll. In 1710, suffering from painful gout and blindness, Congreve was injured in a street accident and died soon afterwards.

Although Congreve always wished to be remembered not as a writer but as a gentleman, his obsession for respectability grew as he aged, until at last it even became disagreeable to him to hear his own comedies praised. Voltaire, who hungered for literary reknown, was puzzled and disgusted, during his visit in England, by this extraordinary whim. Congreve rejected any claim to being a poet, declaring that his plays were merely trifles produced during an idle hour, and begged Voltaire to consider him merely a gentleman. "If you had been merely a gentleman," Voltaire responded, "I should not have come to see you."

The genius of Congreve's writing—his witty dialogue—found its fullest expression in the comedy of manners. In his earliest play, *The Old Bachelor*, two gentlemen of wit marry two heiresses, one of whom is capricious and affected; a cast-off mistress is passed off as a widow; a wife is seduced by one of the wits; and a surly bachelor, hater of women and gallantry, is saved by his friends from marrying the cast-off mistress. The play was a great success with

A scene from a contemporary production of *The Way of the World* at the Stratford Festival, Stratford, Ontario, Canada. Featuring Maggie Smith as Mrs. Millamant and Jeremy Brett as Mr. Mirabell. Directed by Robin Phillips.

its sparkling dialogue. Only the mechanics of the play needed help, and this Dryden volunteered to do, preparing the play for presentation.

That Congreve's second play, *The Double Dealer*, was not as successful may have been due to Congreve's attempt to "design the moral first, and to that moral I invented the Fable . . . ." The comedy was primarily criticized by women for its attack upon married women, to which Congreve replied that no objection to his play pained him quite so much as theirs; however, innocent women would take no notice of the satire, for it did not apply to them, and guilty women might pass for innocent if they did not seem to be displeased.

His third and most popular comedy, *Love for Love*, was written to please the audience. However, in its initial production it ran into a problem when an actor named Sandford, generally seen playing a villain, was cast as an innocent man. The audience, after sitting through most of the play and waiting in vain for him to display his usual villainy, became angry when he remained honest. The plot of *Love for Love* is perhaps Congreve's best dramatic construction. The twofold moral sentiment, voiced in the final speeches of Scandal and Angelica, makes the point that parents should not deal tyrannically with their children, and that a constant lover is more rare than a kind woman.

The Mourning Bride, Congreve's only tragedy, suffers from an intricate and involved plot, and although well received when it opened, it eventually was shelved. However, some famous lines lived on: "Music has charms to soothe the savage beast," "Heaven has no rage, like love to hatred turn'd, Nor hell a fury, like a woman scorned."

With the presentation of *The Way of the World*, Congreve reached the highest point in his career, for his play is the finest example of the comedy of manners genre. The play is successful in almost every way, featuring brilliant dialogue, sharp contrasts of social types, and Restoration society at its awful best.

A contemporary production of Vanbrugh's *The Relapse* at the Guthrie Theatre, Minneapolis-St. Paul. Directed by Michael Langham.

The best of the Restoration dramatists were probably Dryden, Wycherley, and Congreve. However, after these three there were still a number of fine Restoration playwrights, most of whom are almost unknown to today's audiences.

One of the most interesting of these essentially minor dramatists was Aphra Behn (1640-89), the first English woman to earn a living by writing. Taking the pen name "Divine Astraea," a title to which she had very small claim, she wrote novels, poems, and plays designed to suit the taste of the Restoration audience. Mrs. Behn knew the theatre well, and she was quite clever at taking plots from earlier plays and refurbishing them with new, farcical situations. In her plays, especially, she provided tales featuring an almost frantic sexual activity, to the point where even some of her contemporaries considered them to be immoral, ironically referring to her as "Chaste Aphra." Pope, a bit later, disposed of her sexual dramas with two sneering lines: "The stage how loosely does Astraea tread / Who fairly puts all characters to bed."

Thomas Otway (1652-85) was, like his fellow playwright Nathaniel Lee, a failed actor who succeeded as a playwright. Also like Lee, he wenched heroically, drank too much, and died miserably in his thirties. Today his plays are rarely read and almost never staged. However, two plays of great popularity in his own time have earned him a place as one of the leading writers of Restoration tragedy. *The Orphan* (1680) tells of the love of twin brothers for a young woman who is a ward of their father. *Venice Preserved, or A Plot Discovered* (1682) is in the tradition of love-versus-honor dramas, this time with a setting of seventeenth century Venice. Neither of these tragedies, in spite of their debts to Shakespeare, are great drama, but they are highly dramatic and were theatrical favorites for generations.

Otway's fellow dramatist, mad, drunken Nathaniel Lee (c. 1653-92), spent his last five years in Bedlam, a sorry end for a playwright who had made his reputation writing mad, ranting speeches for actors in such tragedies as *Nero* (1674) and *Sophonisba* (1676). Today Lee's plays are often pointed out as horrible examples of the worst aspects of Restoration tragedy, and yet in his own time Lee's wild bombast, usually couched in rhymed heroic couplets, was taken very seriously indeed. Dryden collaborated with him on two plays, *Oedipus* (1678) and *The Duke of Guise* (1682), and Lee's blank-verse tragedy, *The Rival Queens* (1677), was long considered to be one of the great works of the period.

Thomas Shadwell (c. 1642-92), at best a second-rate dramatist, has made his mark on posterity not so much through his art as through his highly accurate eye, which recorded many aspects of late seventeenth century society far more faithfully than some of his artistic betters. To students of the literature of the period he is mostly memorable as an exfriend of Dryden who had the misfortune to quarrel with the great satirist and thus end up as the dunce-hero of Dryden's *MacFlecknoe*. Thus, "the True-Blew-Protestant Poet, T. S." has become little more than an academic footnote.

The person who brought the heroic drama to an unheroic end was George Villiers, the second Duke of Buckingham (1628-87). An important and often vicious political figure during the reign of Charles II, a heavy drinker, ribald rhymester, turncoat, duelist, and "womanizer," Villiers was later char-

An anonymous engraving, c. 1723, illustrates George Etheredge's *The Man of Mode.*

acterized by Sir Walter Scott as the "most lively, mercurial, ambitious, and licentious genius who ever lived." He is remembered mostly as the primary author of *The Rehearsal* (1671), a brilliant parody of the heroic drama and especially of Dryden's *Conquest of Granada*. Dryden, never one to turn the other cheek, later pilloried Buckingham as Simri in his *Absalom and Achitophel*.

One of the earliest and best writers of Restoration comedy was Sir George Etherege (c. 1635-91). His earliest work, *The Comical Revenge, or Love in a Tub* (1664), is an outrageous prose mixture of drunken farce and disguise, supported weakly by an awkward subplot, written in verse, on the love-versus-honor theme. By 1668, however, in *She Would if She Could*, his technique had matured; farce had given over to wit, verse had been replaced by prose, and the overdone heroics more suited to an earlier period had surrendered to a real Restoration London, where there was no contest between love and honor inasmuch as honor was usually a joke, certainly not something that a Restoration rake would agonize over, and love was reduced to a series of affairs. *The Man of Mode, or Sir Fopling Flutter* (1676), Etherege's finest play, contains almost no plot at all, mocking the follies of Restoration London and relying solely on a cutting wit and sparkling dialogue for its success. Nevertheless, it stands second only to Congreve's *Way of the World* as one of the finest Restoration comedies.

George Farquhar (1678-1707) was an Irishman who failed, first as a college student and then as an actor, in his native land. Moving to London, Far-

An early eighteenth century illustration of Farquhar's *The Beaux Stratagem.* (From *The Works of the Late Ingenious Mr. George Farquhar,* London, 1711)

quhar began his writing career with an undistinguished play promisingly titled *Love and a Bottle* (1698). However, with each of his succeeding seven plays he demonstrated major improvements in his technique and he ended his career with two outstanding works: *The Recruiting Officer* (1706) and *The Beaux' Strategem* (1707). These plays are not only highly entertaining dramas, but they also brought about a change in Restoration comedy by taking it out of the salons and streets of metropolitan London and placing it in the taverns and country roads of rural England. *The Recruiting Officer* also features two unusual character types for the comedy of the day—Captain Plume and Sergeant Kite, two swaggering, roistering recruiting officers who were almost certainly the result of Farquhar's own army service. *The Beaux' Stratagem,* which is set in suburban Litchfield, features characters more traditional to Restoration comedy, even if the setting is unusual. Aimwell and Archer are both wellborn but impoverished young men out fortune hunting. Aimwell not only does well in marriage (capturing Dorinda, the daughter of Lady Bountiful) but also learns that his elder brother, Lord Aimwell, has died, leaving him the family title and fortune. Archer also manages to do well. He has an affair with the wife of Lady Bountiful's son, Sullen, and when Aimwell comes into his fortune he gives Archer 10,000 pounds. Eventually Archer even manages to marry his mistress when Sullen promises to divorce her because he has decided that they are not one flesh but merely "two carcasses unnaturally joined together."

Sir John Vanbrugh (1664-1726), the son of an expatriot Flemish merchant, was a distinguished architect and the author of several fine comedies. *The Relapse, or Virtue in Danger* (1696), his earliest play, is usually considered

An engraving of a scene from Farquhar's *The Recruiting Officer.* (London, 1711)

to be his best. It was a cynical sequel to Colley Cibber's *Love's Last Shift,* produced earlier in the same year, and it featured Loveless, Cibber's reformed husband, suffering a temporary relapse into libertinism. The following year Vanbrugh staged *The Provok'd Wife,* which featured the cowardly, drunken Sir John Brute, staggering through the London streets in a parson's gown. *The Confederacy* (1705) is distinguished only by the fact that it is the only Restoration comedy with a middle-class setting. *The Journey to London* (1728), which Vanbrugh never finished, was completed by Cibber, who renamed it *The Provok'd Husband* in an attempt to cash in on the popularity of Vanbrugh's earlier play. Because Vanbrugh made much stronger use of farce and caricature than his contemporaries, using physical action as well as dialogue to entertain, Jeremy Collier, the antitheatre preacher, found Vanbrugh's plays to be veritable treasure troves of "immorality and profaneness."

Colley Cibber (1671-1757) is best known today for his election as King of Dullness in the 1743 version of Pope's *Dunciad*. While his verses as Poet Laureate certainly earned him that unenviable title, his career in theatre should guarantee him a much better memory. An actor, playwright, theatre historian, and comanager of the Drury Lane Theatre, Cibber did all these things well, but none outstandingly enough to earn him more than passing mention in the history books. His first play, *Love's Last Shift* (1696), added a new dimension to the Restoration fop by allowing him enough basic good sense to

A scene from the Restoration "acting version" of Shakespeare's *Richard III,* in which Colley Cibber had his greatest success. (From Rowe's edition of Shakespeare, London, 1709)

see the error of his ways and repent. Following Jeremy Collier's fiery fusillade against immorality in the theatre, Cibber obliged by writing *The Careless Husband* (1704), in which the fifth act conversion to morality is so sickening that one must wonder if Cibber had his tongue planted firmly in his cheeck during its writing. At the end of his long career he published *Apology for the Life of Colley Cibber, Comedian* (1740), which is not only frank in its assessment of his contemporaries, but does not spare the author himself. A gently amusing portrait, it is the finest work extant on this great period of theatre.

An earlier playwright, and artistically the least important of those so far discussed, was John Banks (c. 1650-1706). However, even though he comes early he is, like Colley Cibber, a transitional playwright. His history plays are less in the Restoration style than in the Elizabethan, and they never achieve artistic distinction. However, while Banks was behind the times as regards his style of writing, he was far ahead in terms of his approach. The title of just one of his plays—*Virtue Betrayed, or Anna Bullen*—indicates the type of emotional response that his plays tried to provoke. This attempt to evoke the pathetic, inherent in all of his plays, is an early indication that the ingredients of bourgeois tragedy, that had been present in English tragedy from the beginning and that would become the major dramatic genre during the early eighteenth century, had not died out during the sophisticated Restoration period.

THE RESTORATION STAGE

There was somewhat greater variety in English theatre buildings during the Restoration then there had been during the earlier periods of English drama. There was still, however, a general pattern that most theatres followed. The auditorium consisted of the pit, which was raked and set with backless benches; boxes, primarily for the aristocracy and a few of the rich tradesmen; and galleries for the poorer tradesmen and servants of the aristocracy in attendance. The theatres were rather small by previous standards, varying from about five hundred fifty seats to seven hundred fifty. The stage was in many ways a compromise between the thrust of Elizabethan theatres and the proscenium of continental theatres—that is, there was a proscenium arch, but there was also a substantial playing area out in front of the proscenium. The Drury Lane Theatre, for example, had a stage approximately thirty-four feet deep, but only about half of this was behind the proscenium. Thus, the Drury Lane stage could well be described as a shallow proscenium stage with a large apron. Most such stages were slightly raked, to complement the raked floor of the pit, and the combination of the two led to excellent sightlines.

From 1660 to the end of the Restoration period, shortly after the turn of the century, there were only three major theatres, plus a handful of others that had brief importance for reasons other than their physical structure. Drury Lane Theatre, built during the period and the most famous of English theatres, must head the list, followed by Lincoln's Inn Fields and Dorset Garden. Also of interest are the Cockpit, the Red Bull, and Salisbury Court.

The first theatre on the site of the Drury Lane (a former "riding yard") was built by Thomas Killigrew, under a charter granted by Charles II, in 1662. It was called the Theatre Royal in Bridges Street and it opened in May 1663 with a production of *The Humorous Lieutenant*. It was a small theatre, its total size scarcely equal to the stage area of today's Drury Lane. The pit was raked and furnished with benches covered with green cloth; the stage had a proscenium arch, six proscenium doors, and a large apron. The general quality of the structure was attested to by a visiting Frenchman who found the gilded upholstery and the general decor to be charming and the stage area well equipped. He pronounced it to be the best theatre he had ever seen. Refreshments were provided by the widow Mary Meggs, better known as Orange Moll. However, oranges could not be sold to the poor and apparently inconsiderate audience in the upper galleries, as the management did not wish to provide them with ammunition to fire at the actors.

The 1665 season opened brilliantly with the introduction of the actress Nell Gwynn, but it ended disastrously when the theatre was closed for slightly over a year (June 1665 to November 1666) because of the plague. Killigrew sensibly used this period to make some necessary modifications. The theatre reopened and prospered, in part because of substantial royal patronage; in 1669, at Drury Lane, Charles II heard Nell Gwynn declaim the epilogue to *Tyrannic Love* and promptly plucked her from the theatre to be his mistress.

In June 1672 the theatre was partially destroyed by a fire which also wiped out the entire wardrobe and scenic stock. The remains of the building were torn down and a new theatre, designed by Sir Christopher Wren, was

Nell Gwynn as Epilogue to *Sir Patient Fancy.* Basically her costume is Restoration, with the addition of an Elizabethan ruff.

erected on the site. It was substantially larger than the first theatre (the foundations can still be viewed under the stage of the present Drury Lane) and opened on March 26, 1674, as the Theatre Royal in Drury Lane, with both the King and Queen in attendance. It prospered for two years, with Dryden as resident playwright, but Killigrew and his actors were getting old and the competition from the younger company at Dorset Garden proved to be too much. In 1676 the theatre closed. After Killigrew's death his two sons briefly reopened the theatre, but they were unable to operate it profitably and when it closed again the Drury Lane company merged with the company at the Dorset Garden.

By this time Charles II, a great patron of theatre, was dead. As a result the court audience had ceased to attend theatrical performances on a regular basis, and the Restoration theatre had never developed a mass audience that could take up the slack. London could support only one major theatre so Betterton, head of the troupe at Dorset Garden, moved to Drury Lane in 1682, and Davenant's son, Charles, was awarded the patent to operate it. Charles did not possess the business sense of his father, and sold the patent for eighty pounds to Christopher Rich, a lawyer and father of John Rich, who built the first Covent Garden Theatre. Rich tried to run the theatre on a high profit margin, and was so tightfisted and unfeeling toward his actors that Betterton left and obtained a license from William III to perform at Lincoln's Inn Fields. The fortunes of Drury Lane sank very low indeed, and in 1709 Rich lost his patent and the theatre closed once more. It was an appropriate date inasmuch as, theatrically speaking, the Restoration period that had spawned the Drury Lane had quietly come to an end.

Lincoln's Inn Fields Theatre (alternately known as Lisle's Tennis Court and the Duke's House) was built as a tennis court in 1656 on Portugal Street and converted into a theatre in 1661 by William Davenant. Its exterior measurements were approximately seventy-five feet long by thirty feet wide. Perhaps its primary distinction is that it was the first English theatre to have a permanent proscenium arch and to make use of scenery which could be set and then struck. As was the case later with Drury Lane, Lincoln's Inn Fields had a large apron stage in front of the proscenium.

The theatre opened in June 1661 with part 1 of *The Siege of Rhodes*, Davenant's heroic "opera"; part 2 was given the next day. This production was followed by *The Wits*, an early and undistinguished Restoration drama, and then by *Hamlet*, in which, according to Pepys, Betterton played the prince "beyond imagination." This was followed by *The Adventures of Five Hours*, a box office success, and a very interesting production of *Romeo and Juliet*, in which Shakespeare's original was staged on alternate days with James Howard's adaptation, in which the young lovers are allowed to live.

Davenant managed to combine a talent for business affairs with excellent artistic judgment and an ability to handle those most difficult of creatures, actors. As a result, his theatre was so successful that he soon outgrew it, and shortly before his death in 1668 he had begun work on the theatre that was eventually to become the Dorset Garden. Following Davenant's death his widow, along with Betterton and Harris, continued to produce at Lincoln's Inn Fields until 1671, when the new theatre was completed. The old theatre then was emptied to become that which it had been in its infancy, a tennis court.

Lincoln's Inn Fields had a brief renewal as a theatre between 1672 and 1674, when Killigrew's troupe played there following the fire at the Theatre Royal. Again, in 1695, Betterton, following his confrontation with Christopher Rich, revived the theatre for a ten-year period. Again the theatre closed, though Rich, whose patent at Drury Lane had been "silenced" because of his oppressive treatment of his actors, had begun alterations before his death. It was reopened again in 1714, after the Restoration period was over. It remained open until 1732, and gained some fame for housing the first production of *The Beggar's Opera* (1727-28). It passed its final years as a military barracks, an auction house, and a warehouse for storing china, finally being torn down in 1848.

As mentioned earlier, Dorset Garden Theatre, also known as the second Duke's House, was begun by Davenant and completed after his death. Perhaps designed by Wren (some contemporary scholars have called this into doubt), it stood by the Thames, south of Salisbury Court Theatre, and featured a landing (Dorset Stairs) to accommodate those who came to the theatre by boat. Above its front doors were the arms of the theatre's patron, the Duke of York, and the resident troupe was known as the Duke's Men.

It was a larger theatre than either Lincoln's Inn Fields or Drury Lane, and was the most opulent in London's history, with statues of Melpomene and Thalia and a richly decorated proscenium arch.

An exterior view of the Dorset Garden (Duke's) Theatre. (From Settle's *The Empress of Morocco*)

On November 9, 1671, the theatre opened with an already popular play, Dryden's *Sir Martin Mar-All*, and followed that with a number of productions that audiences loved. Opera, for which the theatre would one day become famous, began with musical versions of *Macbeth* and *The Tempest* by Davenant and Shadwell. Also during this period Thomas Otway and Nathaniel Lee made beginning (but not exciting) appearances as actors in Dorset Garden productions.

After Drury Lane was gutted by fire in 1672, and until it was rebuilt in 1674, Dorset Garden was the primary theatre in London. However, after the death of Charles II the theatre audience fell off badly, and the companies of Dorset Garden and Drury Lane combined, making their headquarters at the newer Drury Lane. The Dorset was still used to produce occasional operas, and enjoyed a brief vogue when it was, in 1689, renamed the Queen's Theatre in the hope of invoking royal patronage. However, Queen Mary (William and Mary) was not the material out of which theatre patrons are made, and the hopes of the Dorset fell even lower. For a brief period it was used to stage acrobatic and "wild beast" shows, and after 1706 it was not heard of again.

The oldest of the Restoration's secondary theatres was the Red Bull, built in 1600 by Aaron Holland. While the theatres were closed (and many physically damaged) during the Commonwealth, the Red Bull managed some-

The interior of the Dorset Garden (Duke's) Theatre, looking toward the stage which is set with a scene from *The Empress of Morocco.* The stage was a proscenium arch with a pictorial setting behind it. Action also took place on the forestage, which was flanked by doors. The music room is shown above the stage, between statues of Thalia and Melpomene. The stage was slightly raked to provide excellent sightlines. (From Settle's *The Empress of Morocco*)

how to survive, perhaps because the nontheatrical Puritans got it confused with the earlier Red Bull Inn. In any case, during the Commonwealth period, with all other public theatres out of business, the Red Bull carried on with short farces and puppet shows. At the start of the Restoration a company under the direction of Michael Mohun performed there, and Killigrew made use of the theatre before moving to Vere Street, taking with him the best actors of the Red Bull Company. By 1663 it was deserted, and by 1665 it had disappeared.

The next oldest Restoration theatre was the Cockpit, later called the Phoenix, located in Drury Lane. Built to house cock fights in 1609, it was converted into a roofed "private" theatre in 1616 by William Beeston. In the following year it burned, supposedly set afire on Shrove Tuesday by a group of rowdy, drunken London apprentices celebrating the holiday. It was quickly rebuilt and renamed the Phoenix, but the public persisted in calling it by its old name. During the Commonwealth period it was, like the other theatres, closed, but there were some illegal performances given in the building, as evidenced by a raid made in 1649 by soldiers of the Parliament, following which audience members were fined. Two of Davenant's heroic "operas" were played at the Cockpit during the Commonwealth.

Early in the Restoration the Cockpit remained busy, with a troupe under Rhodes and a joint troupe under Davenant and Killigrew playing there. From 1661 to 1665 it was occupied by a company under the direction of George Jolly, who was bilked of his patent by Davenant and Killigrew. After the Theatre Royal (Drury Lane) was completed in 1663 the fortunes of the Cockpit declined seriously, and after 1665 it was heard from no more.

The last and least important of these secondary theatres was the Salisbury Court Theatre, built in 1629 by Richard Gunnell and William Blagrove on a portion of the site of Dorset House, where Salisbury Square (Fleet Street) now stands. A private "roofed" theatre, it was occupied successfully by the King's Revels, Prince Charles' Men, and the Queen's Men. In the early part of the Commonwealth period some illegal performances were produced in it, but after its interior was destroyed by soldiers of the Parliament in 1649 it stood unused until William Beeston restored it in 1660. Rhodes' company played the Salisbury Court, as did Davenant and George Jolly. Beeston himself occupied it from 1663 to 1664. It was destroyed in the Great Fire in 1666.

SCENIC DESIGN

When the English court returned from France in 1660 it brought with it a taste not only for French drama but for continental staging. As the theatres were rebuilt, because of the destruction wrought by the soldiers of Parliament in 1649, the wings, borders, shutters, and roll drops used in France and Italy were installed. Thus, after about 1661 the conventions of English scenic practice differed little from those on the continent. That is to say, sets were changed by means of grooves on the stage floor, in full view of the audience, and the entr'acte entertainments were performed in front of whatever set happened to be onstage.

Companies developed scenic holdings, or had them built at the same time a new theatre was built, for a limited number of possible sets. In large part this was due to the neoclassical concept that setting should always be general, never particular. It was also, probably, due to the very practical consideration that it was much less expensive to maintain a few generalized sets than to build specialized sets for each individual show. And for a period when an eight or nine-day run denoted a success, one can understand this practical point of view. Thus, most companies maintained a Classical set, a tomb, a city wall (with gate), a palace (interior and exterior), a street, an interior chamber, a prison, a formal garden, and a rural scene. A few specialized scenes were built for such plays as demanded them, especially the spectacular heroic dramas and operas, but generally the settings used throughout the Restoration period were simple and standardized.

Lighting during this period was apparently so simple and so taken for granted that there is little contemporary mention of it. Plays were usually given in the afternoon so that windows or skylights could provide most of the light. Chandeliers with numerous candles were usually hung behind the proscenium and out over the apron, with candle-lit footlights adding to the illumination.

Anne Bracegirdle as the Indian Queen. Her costume is basically Restoration, with a feathered headdress and fan to mark it as Indian.

COSTUMES

Restoration theatre, like the Elizabethan theatre which preceded it and also like its French contemporary, paid little attention to either historical or national styles in terms of costume. There were standardized costumes—Turkish and Roman, for example—but even with such costume the actor was was likely to wear a Restoration-style wig. When one of the characters in a historical play was famous enough so that a well-known portrait of him existed, there was some attempt to create a costume in the image of the portrait, but even this effort was usually little more than an adaptation of Restoration dress.

For the actresses there was even less concern for accurate costuming than there was for the actors. They always wore contemporary dress, no matter what the period of the play, adding a feather headpiece to indicate particularly heroic or important characters. In tragedies the actesses usually wore black velvet gowns, and for comedies the richest gowns (and jewels) they owned.

Makeup was used excessively. The men wore false noses, beards, and mustaches, along with their wigs. The actresses used powder, rouge, pencil, and lip rouge to such an extent that, as Colley Cibber pointed out, they were unable to use facial expressions for fear their makeup would crack.

ACTING

The outstanding difference between the acting companies of the Restoration and their Elizabethan and Jacobean predecessors was the fact that Restoration troupes were allowed to include women. The reason for this new (to England) dispensation is clearly the influence of the continental theatre which Charles II so much admired. Indeed, the right of the patent holders to recruit actresses was included in the patent itself, and so the use of women onstage could be justified by royal sanction. This did not, of course, satisfy some of the Puritan group who were upset by the immorality of women onstage, and so a number of specious arguments advancing the immorality of having men play women's roles were also bandied about. Whatever the reason, the addition of women to the acting companies greatly enriched the stage and one must wonder whether without them such brilliant female roles as Congreve's Millamant or Etherege's Harriet would have even been written.

At the beginning of the Restoration, because there had been no opportunity to develop new acting talent during the Commonwealth, the older players who had been active before the closing of the theatres tended to dominate the stage. It was not long, however, before a group of young and exciting actors had replaced them in the public affection. Thomas Betterton (1635-1710), the greatest actor of the Restoration stage, dominated the male ac-

A contemporary engraving of Betterton as Hamlet. The set appears box-like, but is almost certainly angle wing. The costumes and decor are Restoration.

tors, and Nell Gwynn (1650-87) and Anne Bracegirdle (1673-1748) were the leading actresses.

Actors received their training in one of two ways, either by being apprenticed to one of the licensed companies, or by studying at the Nursery, the acting school established by Davenant at Halton Garden and supervised by George Jolly. Exactly what the training program at the Nursery consisted of is not certain. It is probable that the students practiced the traditional techniques of vocal delivery, stage movements and gesture, singing, and dancing. These student performers did give public performances and most of them moved on from the school, either to one of the established London companies or to itinerant work in England and on the continent.

As had been true in companies before the Restoration, the apprentice actors performed in a broad variety of minor roles until a special talent was recognized for one particular type of role. Once a specialization was developed, and if the talent was present, the young actor moved from minor roles to secondary roles to leads. Some of the best actors were good enough to work in all types of drama—Betterton was highly regarded in both tragic and comic roles—but they were the exception rather than the rule.

The acting style of the Restoration was essentially an oratorical one. Betterton had inherited the primarily vocal tradition, and such contemporary commentators as John Downes, Thomas Davies, and Colley Cibber indicate that he never really departed from it. Cibber's description of Betterton playing a scene from *Hamlet* gives us a look at what was the most admired style of the age, and thus likely the most imitated and most common.

> *He opened with a pause of mute amazement! then rising slowly to a solemn, trembling voice, he made the ghost equally terrible to the spectator as himself! and in the descriptive part of the natural emotions which the ghastly vision gave him, the boldness of his expostulation was still govern'd by decency, manly, but not braving; his voice never rising into that seeming outrage, or wild defiance of what he naturally rever'd.*

What this passage describes is an actor who has great oratorical skills and who has not yet descended into the rant and bravado that would eventually overtake tragic acting.

RESTORATION'S END

Historically, the English Restoration ends with the ascension of William and Mary to the throne. However, for Restoration theatre the beginning of the end was marked by another quite unrelated event—the publication in 1697-98 of Jeremy Collier's *Short View of the Immorality and Profaneness of the English Stage*. The pamphlet struck out at contemporary English theatre, accusing it of corrupting English morals. What Collier did, in fact, was take the Restoration dramatists at their word (i.e., the purpose of drama is to teach and please, and it has a moral obligation not to inculcate evil) and prove that they had not done a proper job of it. What Collier failed to realize, however, was that the Restoration drama was not so much a corruptor as a reflection of a corrupt society. On the other hand, the theatre's defenders failed to realize that the society which this drama reflected was already dead, and that a whole new social milieu had formed. In any case, Collier's work brought about a reconsideration of theatre and a number of resultant reforms which, given the change in the social climate, were long overdue.

10

The Eighteenth Century

10

The Eighteenth Century

The eighteenth century is sometimes referred to as the Age of Enlightenment; it was also the age of retrenchment. In English theatre the drama swung from the libertine excesses of the Restoration to a stifling, sentimental morality. In France the neoclassical period would continue almost until the end of the century, stopped at last by the French Revolution, but the writers, except perhaps for Voltaire and Beaumarchais, were a far cry from such giants as Corneille, Molière, and Racine. In Italy the drama was almost submerged by the love of opera, but scenic design made great strides. In Germany, Johann Christoph Gottsched and Carolina Neuber were trying to renew a theatre that alternated between imported court performances and a debased combination of native farce and *commedia*. In Russia theatre was gaining a tenuous foothold, and in the United States an infant theatre that had merely imitated British and continental theatre began to emerge as a healthy art form by the middle of the century, and was aided in this growth by independence in 1776.

THE EIGHTEENTH CENTURY BACKGROUND

Probably the most significant aspect of the eighteenth century was the antimonarchial sentiment that ended in two successful revolutions—the American and the French—and that severely limited the powers of the monarch in England. It was also an age of colonialism and nationalism, with Prussia establishing itself as the major power among the Germanic states. In Russia, beginning under Peter the Great and continuing under Catherine II, artistic contacts were made with western Europe for the first time.

The accession of William and Mary to the English throne had guaranteed England a limited religious toleration. Also, as part of the articles of accession, the powers of the king were severely limited. Anne (1665-1714), the last Stuart ruler, was also the last ruler to use the veto. Her reign is notable for the unification of England and Scotland under one Parliament (1707), and as a period of transition from monarchial to parliamentary government. It was during the following reigns of George (1714-27) and George II (1727-60) that the cabinet system developed. George III, who ruled from 1760 to 1820, tried to reinstitute personal rule, and to that end found a supportive minister in Lord North. Together they pursued a policy of coercion toward the North American colonies that ended in the American Revolution. The King's ultimate insanity led in 1811 to the regency of his son, George IV.

England was eager to expand colonially, and so entered the War of the Spanish Succession (1701-13), justifying this intercession publicly by an expressed desire to maintain the balance of power and to uphold Protestantism. England emerged from the struggle with large accessions of territory. Robert Walpole, in effect the first English prime minister, then favored peace but was compelled to lead his country into the War of Jenkin's Ear (1739), a conflict caused by commercial rivalry with Spain. This war soon merged into the War of the Austrian Succession (1740-48), which England was eager to enter because of colonial rivalries with France.

In northern Europe the Great Elector, Frederick William, built up an army, gained territory, and consolidated Prussia, which originally was only a partially settled buffer state along the Baltic that had been set up to contain the Slavs. The Elector Frederick III gained the title of King (Frederick I) and increased his country's military strength. In the early years of his reign Frederick II (the Great, 1712-86) seized Silesia from Austria, thus beginning the War of the Austrian Succession. A number of European countries entered the war against him, but at the end of the war he still held the territories. Maria Theresa, the Austrian ruler, was not satisfied with this result and so began the Seven Years' War (1756-63). Frederick was surrounded by enemy states (Austria, France, Russia, Sweden, and Saxony), but again he managed to hold his own—and Silesia. In 1772 he joined with two of his erstwhile enemies, Russia and Austria, in the first partition of Poland. Two more partitions in 1793 and 1795 completed the dismemberment of that unfortunate nation.

As a child, Frederick II had been despised by his militaristic father as an effeminate esthete whose primary interests were music, philosophy, and poetry. However, after becoming King in 1740, Frederick proved himself not only a military genius but a wise, benevolent despot. He reclaimed waste lands, encouraged colonization in barren areas of his country, built canals, fostered industry, reformed the legal system, instituted religious toleration, and most importantly for drama, encouraged the arts.

During the eighteenth century Anglo-French rivalry took a serious turn. In India, where the British and French East India companies had been in operation since about 1600, the battles pitted Indian against Indian. In North America the British and French also clashed in the French and Indian War. Britain was triumphant in both India and North America, largely because of British leadership under Clive, Wolfe, Pitt, and others. In the Peace of Paris, England gained Canada, Nova Scotia, Cape Breton, Florida, and Senegal. However, the ink was hardly dry on the treaty when the American colonies began to rebel. In this the British victory worked against them, for the colonists no longer felt the need for British troops to protect them from the French. Also, France, piqued at the loss of territory and prestige, gave the colonists the necessary economic and military aid to assure a successful rebellion against archenemy England. Only thirteen years later, however, the French paid their dues and the spirit of revolution they had fostered in the North American colonies resulted in the French Revolution, which put an end to the absolute monarchy.

It was then against this background of nationalism, colonization, rebellion, and war that the drama of the century was played out.

The Eighteenth Century In England

When the Restoration drama came to an end, some fifteen years after the Restoration was over both politically and economically, it was replaced by a drama that was responsive to the social changes of the age. Restoration drama had reflected the interests of only a small, closed portion of society, but the theatre of the eighteenth century was much broader. More than anything else, however, it represented the broad and rapidly expanding middle class. Such playwrights as Thomas D'Urfey (1653-1723) began, even before the turn of the century, to reflect the changing mood of the time, adjusting such plays as *Love for Money* (1691) and *The Bath* (1701) to the everyday values of the growing middle-class audience. By the end of the 1704 season the end was clearly in sight when Colley Cibber produced *The Careless Husband*, with its overwhelming sentimentalism.

EIGHTEENTH CENTURY ENGLISH DRAMA

From a literary point of view there are, in fact, two eighteenth centuries. One is the eighteenth century of the literary arts—an age of sharp satire with such writers as Johnson, Swift, Pope, and Fielding; of brilliant conversation, with Johnson, Boswell, the Bluestockings, and all the people who gathered in the coffeehouses, clubs, and salons; of graceful and exciting casual writing in the letters of Horace Walpole and Thomas Gray; of talented, intriguing politicians such as Prime Minister Robert Walpole; and of fascinating records such as Johnson's life and the diaries of Fanny Burney. The other is the eighteenth century of the dramatic arts, and unfortunately, except for John Gay's *The Beggar's Opera*, there is little that is sharp, or satiric, or even graceful. This is probably because the drama was seeking out a mass audience in a way that other literary forms distained, and thus the drama of the age tends to strike a middle note, eschewing the savage satire of the previous age, and also avoiding the moral rigor of Puritanism. What emerges is a world of moderation, where God has imbued humans with benevolence, love, and charity toward their fellows, and the primary sin is to in any way debase these innate aspects of the spirit. As a result the theatre became the exact opposite of what Collier had pronounced it. It became a means not of urging licentiousness but of promoting a rational, moral order that was perfectly suited to the time.

Tragedy

Of the two major genres, tragedy underwent the most minimal change as the Restoration gave way to the Age of Enlightenment. This was because the pathetic (often bathetic) element that had never been part of Restoration comedy had been present in some Restoration tragedy from the beginning. The history plays of John Banks, for example, emphasized the pathetic, and even the heroic drama of Dryden and the tragedies of Lee and Otway emphasized the sentimental over the horror and grandeur of Classical tragedy. This was because the dramatists of both the Restoration and the eighteenth century subscribed to the idea, articulated by Samuel Johnson, that the purpose of tragedy was "to instruct by moving the passions." And it is this insistence on instruction that has made eighteenth century tragedy a failed art form, at least in terms of recent audiences and critics.

The early years of the century, sometimes referred to as the Queen Anne period, produced only one writer of tragedy whose work is significant. Nicholas Rowe (1674-1718) was a playwright and scholar whose plays were sentimental (see *The Fair Penitent,* 1703), didactic (see *Jane Shore,* 1714, written in careful imitation of Shakespeare), and bombastic (see any of his plays). However, while later ages may smile at this unlikely combination of ingredients, Rowe completed two highly successful domestic tragedies. In fact, the tremendous contemporary impression that his plays had can be seen in the character of "gay Lothario," whose name became part of the language and who served as model for the most accomplished literary villain of the century, Lovelace of Samuel Richardson's novel *Clarissa Harlowe.* Rowe also gave the world the first modern edition of Shakespeare's plays in 1709, a fine translation of Lucan's *Pharsalia* in 1718, and between two undistinguished versifiers (Nahum Tate and Laurence Eusden) served a three-year term as Poet Laureate.

Rowe's only challenge to preeminence during the Queen Anne period came late when Joseph Addison (1672-1719) published his only tragedy—*Cato* (1713). The play was highly successful when it appeared, and was acclaimed and produced for many years following, becoming a model for Augustan tragedy. Most audiences today would find *Cato* to be static in action and platitudinous in thought, but Addison's attempt to take a Classical theme and make it conform to the eighteenth century ideal of decorum was rewarded by nearly fifty years of sometimes slavish imitation. Addison followed *Cato* with a comedy, *The Drummer,* in 1716. However, the work was not well received and three years later Addison died without writing another play.

After Rowe and Addison, the early years of the century are filled with names, most generally forgotten, of playwrights who tried and failed to produce major drama in a society that valued sentiment and neoclassical propriety. John Dennis (1657-1734) is remembered more as a critic and an object of Pope's invective than as a playwright; James Thomson (1700-48) has an honored place in literature for his four-part poem, *The Seasons,* but his plays are quite forgotten; Edward Young (1683-1765) is equally honored for his *Complaint, or Night Thoughts on Life, Death, and Immortality,* but his two tragedies, *Busiris* (1719) and *The Revenge* (1721), reasonably popular in their time, are now known only to the literary historian.

It was not until 1731, however, and the production of George Lillo's *The London Merchant, or The History of George Barnwell,* that the eighteenth century fully realized its potential. Altogether, Lillo wrote eight plays, but only two of them, *The London Merchant* and *Fatal Curiosity* (1736) are significant. *The London Merchant* dramatized an old broadside ballad telling how a harlot (Millwood) dragged a young apprentice (George) along a rapidly descending pathway from robbery to murder to the gallows. It is melodramatic sermon literature at its best, but even after it had passed its peak as a theatrical attraction it was regularly produced at various small theatres on boxing nights to warn off potential Barnwells from a life of sin and dissipation. *Fatal Curiosity,* unlike *Merchant,* was a rather conventional blank-verse tragedy with an unfortunate resemblance to *Macbeth*.

Bourgeois tragedy hardly began with Lillo's *Merchant,* and the author gave credit in his prologue to the works of Otway, Southerne, and Rowe, for putting aside pomp in favor of a "humbler dress." In fact, it is much older than Lillo knew. *Arden of Feversham* (1586, uncertainly attributed to Thomas Kyd) began the domestic tragedy by departing from noble characters to tell of an essentially middle-class man "most wickedly murdered by the meanese of his disloyall and wanton wife." In 1603 Thomas Heywood's *A Woman Killed with Kindness* continued the genre, telling of a woman who, because of an affair, is on the verge of murdering her husband. She repents, however, and confesses and her husband treats her with such kindness that she dies of her guilt feelings. This led directly to the attitudes of the Restoration tragic writers and thus to Lillo's works.

About the middle of the century tragedy began to decline from an eminence not all that high at best. Edward Moore's (1712-57) *The Gamester* (1753) was an attempt, largely unsuccessful, to follow in the path defined by Lillo. Moore's two comedies, *The Foundling* (1748) and *Gil Blas* (1751) are both better remembered than his tragedy, in which a devoted wife tries vainly to rescue her husband from the clutches of a vicious gambler. The play was a morality on the evils of gambling and had a short but widespread vogue both in England and on the continent.

Following Moore came John Home (1722-1808), a Scottish preacher-turned-playwright whose tragedy, *Douglas* (1756) was highly popular, probably because there was literally no competition. The play is a romantic, sentimental reworking of a theme from traditional Scottish balladry, and by today's standards is flawed by a lack of stage business and interminable recitations.

Near the end of the century, tragedy gave its last gasp in the gothic, horrific tragedies of Horace Walpole (1717-97) and Matthew Gregory "Monk" Lewis (1775-1818). Walpole's *The Mysterious Mother* (1768) was the first of these plays, and led directly to the most famous of such works, *Castle Spectre* (1797) by Lewis.

By the opening of the nineteenth century tragedy had degenerated into melodrama and virtually disappeared from the stage.

COMEDY

Though eighteenth century tragedy remained narrow and actually deteriorated over the course of the century, comedy broadened its base and improved as the century drew to a close. As was mentioned earlier, the comedy of the century actually begins with that essentially transitional dramatist, Colley Cibber, whose works from the beginning (*Love's Last Shift*, 1696) displayed the sentimental attitudes that were to become the hallmark of the age. Cibber's third play, *The Careless Husband* (1704) clearly departed from Restoration convention and attitude, striking far closer to the ideals displayed in *A Woman Killed with Kindness*. In Cibber's play a betrayed wife, Lady Easy, discovers her husband's infidelity, but is quick and generous in her forgiveness. This does not drive the husband to waste away and die because of his guilt, as it does the wife in *Kindness*, but in the fifth act he is completely converted to righteous living.

RICHARD STEELE: Sir Richard Steele (1672-1729), essayist and playwright, was born in Dublin, Ireland. Little is known of his parents, who died when he was a small boy, leaving him in the care of an uncle, Henry Gascoigne. In 1684 he was enrolled in the Charterhouse to take his early education, and in 1689 he entered Christ's Church College, Oxford. In 1692 he gave up his studies, which he found dull, and joined the army, eventually becoming an Ensign in the Coldstream Guards. Whatever else army life was for Steele, it certainly was not boring or dull. He played the role of dashing young man about town, fighting a duel, fathering an illegitimate child, and engaging in drinking bouts that became legendary, even among his fellow rakehells. One of the earliest memories of Thackeray's Henry Esmond is of Corporal Dick Steele of the King's Life Guards, fresh out of Oxford without a degree, hiccuping a solemn sermon through his drunkenness, reaching for his sword when his comrades laugh at his religion and falling flat on his face, then looking up at young Henry and saying, "Ah, little Papist, I wish Joseph Addison was here!" Eventually he gave up his wastrel life, repenting his evil deeds and misadventures. As proof of his moral conversion he wrote and published a reforming tract, *The Christian Hero*, in 1701.

Steele began his career as a playwright in 1701 with the Drury Lane production of *The Funeral, or Grief a-la-Mode*. The play was inoffensive morally—a work that would please Jeremy Collier—and yet lively and amusing, pleasing London audiences without exciting them. His second work, *The Lying Lover* (1703), which he based on Corneille's *Le menteur*, was too moral for his audiences and was roundly damned for its sentimental piety; it had a run of only six nights. His third play, *The Tender Husband* (1705), at first seemed doomed to a similar fate but managed to survive without ever becoming a real success.

Steele was deeply disappointed that his plays had failed to earn him the place in the world that he expected, and so he set out in a new, though still literary direction. In 1707 he had been appointed editor of *The London Gazette*, and two years later, apparently convinced that he had found his calling, the first issue of *The Tatler* appeared. In 1711 *The Tatler* was succeeded by *The Spectator*, which in its first series ran to 1712. Joseph Addison, at this time a close friend and a contributor to *The Tatler*, was a close associate of Steele's throughout the period of the second periodical.

Politically a Whig, Steele was more and more drawn into politics. In 1713 he was elected to the House of Commons, only to be expelled the following year for having written a political satire, *The Crisis,* which his opponents claimed was seditious. However, later in that same year George I ascended the throne and the Whig cause—and Steele—was triumphant. He was appointed a governor of Drury Lane, which post he retained for the rest of his life, and in 1715 he was knighted by a grateful monarch. Steele still loved the theatre, but his literary interests remained centered on the essay and periodical writing. *The Tatler* and *The Spectator* both contained some good theatrical criticism, mostly written by Steele though some of it was contributed by Addison, and the 1720 series of essays by Steele entitled "The Theatre" still ranks as the best of the period.

In 1722 Steele produced his last and best play, *The Conscious Lovers.* It had been seventeen years since his last play, and the author had since become a person of social and political consequence, which guaranteed a substantial public and critical interest in the work. The finest available performers were cast, with Mrs. Oldfield as Indiana, Barton Booth as young Bevil, Colley Cibber as Tom, and Mrs. Younger as Phyllis. It played for eighteen nights and was revived for eight more performances before the end of the season.

In 1724 Steele retired, unhappy with his economic state, distraught over the deaths of his wife and most of his children, and angry over disputes with Addison. He moved to Wales, where he died in 1729.

The defense of Restoration comedy had been that it held folly and vice up to scorn, satirizing wrongful or foolish actions and thus making them things to be avoided. Steele, however, created characters to be emulated by the audience. There was little intent to make the audience laugh. Steele had quite clearly expressed himself on this point in the epilogue to *The Lying Lover:*

Our too advent'rous author soared tonight
Above the little praise, mirth to excite,
And chose with pity to chastise delight.
For laughter's a distorted passion, born
Of sudden self-esteem and sudden scorn;
Which, when tis o'er, the men in pleasure wise,
Both him that moved it and themselves despise;
While generous pity of a painted woe
Makes us ourselves both more approve and know.

In 1713 John Gay (1685-1732) produced *The Wife of Bath,* a rather undistinguished comedy for a man whose satirical pastorals (*The Shepherd's Week,* 1714) would, in the coming year, savage the works of Ambrose Philips. In 1716 a satire entitled *Trivia, or The Art of Walking the Streets of London,* offered a verse guide, but little solace, to strolling through a maze of slops, odors, and a foul substance faintly related to mud. It was not until 1728, however, that he produced his masterpiece, *The Beggar's Opera.* It ran an uninterrupted sixty-three nights in its first London appearance and from the beginning overshadowed all Gay's other works. Today it is remembered primarily as the first and greatest of ballad operas, or for a handful of airy songs, or for the funny and often exciting romance of Polly Peachum and Macheath the highwayman,

A painting, by the great satirist William Hogarth, of a scene from John Gay's *The Beggar's Opera,* with Polly and Lucy pleading for Macheath's life.

or as the original of Brecht's *Threepenny Opera*. However, in its time it struck home as a savage satire on both the Walpole government and the Italian opera craze that was sweeping London. Its sequel, *Polly* (printed 1729), is not nearly as good as its predecessor and was banned by the Lord Chamberlain.

Also during this period the great novelist Henry Fielding (1707-54) began his writing career—as a dramatist. Between 1728, when he arrived in London, and 1737, when the government refused to renew his license to continue as the manager of Haymarket Theatre, he wrote more than two dozen dramatic pieces—mostly comedies, farces, and burlesques. Very few people today recognize even his best plays, such as *Pasquin* (1736), or *The Historical Register for the Year 1736* (1737). In fact, the only dramatic work of Fielding to survive is *The Tragedy of Tragedies, or The Life and Death of Tom Thumb the Great* (1730), a wide-ranging burlesque of dramatic conventions that takes satiric aim at no fewer than forty-two plays, from Dryden to James Thomson.

The middle of the century was rather quiet in terms of new comedy. Only Benjamin Hoadly's (1706-57) *The Suspicious Husband* (1743), and James Townley's (1714-78) *High Life Below Stairs* (1759) achieved even popular success. Indeed, it was not until the late 1760s that dead comedy came back to life.

Oliver Goldsmith (c. 1730-74), a village clergyman's son, was born in Ireland and educated at Trinity College, Dublin. His writings span the breadth of the literary arts—satirical essays in the then popular Oriental style, a long poem in heroic couplets, short poems including some mock-elegies and beautiful lyrical works, a fine novel (*The Vicar of Wakefield,* 1766), and two excellent plays, *The Good Natur'd Man* (1768) and *She Stoops to Conquer* (1773). Of the two plays, *Good Natur'd Man* is the least successful, but is memorable for the splenetic character of Croaker. *She Stoops to Conquer,* one of the finest plays of the century and never long off the stage, is famous for the waggish Tony Lumpkin. Both plays represented a return to the busy, laughing farce of George Farquhar, and they served English drama well by ending the overserious sentimental comedy.

The last great comic writer of the century was Richard Brinsley Sheridan. When Sheridan came to theatre, comedy was just beginning to recover, with the help of Goldsmith, from the sentimental twaddle that had afflicted it for nearly seventy-five years. With only three plays, Sheridan restored comedy of manners to the stage, resurrecting much of the best aspects of the Restoration drama, but without some of its drawbacks.

RICHARD BRINSLEY SHERIDAN: Like many of the comic playwrights of his age, Richard Brinsley Sheridan (1751-1816) was born in Ireland. His father, Thomas Sheridan, had once been a minor actor and had since become a successful teacher of elocution. His mother, Frances Sheridan (née Chamberlaine), was a novelist and playwright, author of the successful comedy *The Discovery* (1763). In 1771 Thomas Sheridan settled his family at Bath where young Richard was smitten by the beautiful concert singer Elizabeth Linley. In 1772, helping her in a plan to leave England for the continent to escape the unwelcome attentions of an admirer, Richard took her to France; it was here that her father caught up with them. Elizabeth was returned to Bath and Richard followed. He fought two duels with the admirer whose attentions had precipitated these events, and in 1773 he and Elizabeth were married.

Two years later, deeply in debt and unable to support his new wife in the fashion to which she was accustomed, Sheridan wrote his first play, *The Rivals* (1775). The play was not an immediate success, but Sheridan revised the script and tinkered with the production and it soon won over the previously uninterested audiences. In the same year Sheridan followed his now successful play with a two-act farce, *St. Patrick's Day, or The Scheming Lieutenant,* and a comic opera in the ballad tradition, *The Duenna.* All three were produced at Covent Garden. *The Duenna* proved to be enormously popular, running seventy-five nights.

In 1776, when Garrick retired from the stage and left Drury Lane, Sheridan and several associates purchased the vacant theatre with the idea that they would produce their own shows and then reap all the profits rather than pay the largest share to theatre management. In January 1777 they opened with a new production of *The Rivals,* and a month later presented Sheridan's adaptation of Vanbrugh's *The Relapse* (retitled *A Trip to Scarborough*). However, their major theatrical success of the year was the production of Sheridan's new play, *The School for Scandal.* In 1779 Sheridan's *The Critic,* a derivative work in the style of Villiers' *The Rehearsal,* achieved a modest popularity,

An engraving showing a scene from Sheridan's 1777 production of his own play, *The School for Scandal,* at Drury Lane.

and then later in the same year, they produced Sheridan's *Pizarro.* It was not his best play by far, and it contained material every bit as outrageous as the material of other playwrights which he had mercilessly satirized in *The Critic.* However, audiences loved it for its patriotic melodrama and it was often staged over the next few years.

Like Steele, Sheridan was an avid political creature, and in 1780 he was elected to the House of Commons, where he remained for more than thirty years, distinguishing himself as a member of the Whig opposition. In his famous speeches against Warren Hastings on the government of India he won the admiration of such tough-minded legislators as Edmund Burke, and in 1806 he was appointed Treasurer of the Navy. In the 1790s it became necessary to rebuild and expand Drury Lane if it was to remain competitive, and this sorely strapped the ever-improvident Sheridan. When the building was destroyed by fire in 1809 he was ruined financially. In 1812 he was defeated in the parliamentary elections, and he finished out the last four years of his life a bitter, unhappy man.

When Sheridan arrived on the theatrical scene the genre of comedy, with some help from Goldsmith's *Good Natur'd Man* and *She Stoops to Conquer*, was just beginning to recover from the affliction of sentimentalism, from which it had suffered for nearly three-quarters of a century. In three great plays (*The Rivals, The School for Scandal*, and *The Critic*) Sheridan managed to restore the comic spirit of Restoration theatre. *The Rivals*, except for a few sentimental scenes between Julia and Faulkland, is a busy, high-spirited situation comedy that owes much to the works of Farquhar. *The School for Scandal*, considered by many to be his greatest work, is a satire on London manners that sparkles with wit and epigrams and that seems indebted mostly to Congreve's plays. *The Critic*, a burlesque of almost all aspects of the theatrical scene, is a worthy descendent of its ancestor, *The Rehearsal*.

The plays have long been actors' favorites because they are filled with outstanding characterizations. *The Rivals* has Mrs. Malaprop, who has given her name to the misapplication of words; Lydia Languish, the faithful patron of the circulating library; and "Fighting Bob" Acres, who chooses not to fight. *The School for Scandal* features Joseph Surface, the moral hypocrite; his brother Charles, the good but worldly apostle of actions over words; Lady Teazle, who maintains her social status with a sharp tongue; and Lady Sneerwell, who exists for scandal. *The Critic* has Puff, the play-promoting virtuoso turned playwright; Sir Fretful Plagiary, a scathing send-up of the contemporary playwright, Richard Cumberland; and that immortal (and immoral) pair of critics, Dangle and Sneer.

Sheridan's gift to the theatre was laughter, and the resurrection of that most durable of theatrical genres, the comedy of manners.

THE ENGLISH STAGE

In 1695, William III granted a license to the Betterton troupe, ignoring the exclusive patents issued by his predecessors. This established a dangerous precedent that the earlier patents were at best highly questionable. As a result, people were encouraged to try operating without patents, and so the Haymarket Theatre, built by John Potter and opened in 1720, was unlicensed. By the 1730s four unlicensed theatres were operating in London. The upshot of this was the Licensing Act of 1737, even though the primary motivation for the Act was Walpole's distress at the political satires being given at the unlicensed theatres. The Licensing Act prohibited the acting (for gain, hire, or reward) of any play not licensed by the Lord Chamberlain. It also restricted the authorized theatres to the city of Westminster. This meant that Drury Lane and Covent Garden were the only legitimate theatres in England, as no exemptions were provided for other cities. In 1752 a new bill was passed requiring all types of entertainments within a twenty-mile radius of London to secure licenses from the local magistrates. By the 1760s some of the larger cities outside London had established troupes, and a regular provincial theatrical circuit had developed. These cities objected to being denied legitimate theatres, and so Parliament was forced to authorize theatres in Bath and Norwich (1768), York and Hull (1769), Liverpool (1771), and Chester (1777). In London the Haymarket was licensed in 1766 to Samuel Foote, who received his license as compensation for being crippled by a prank begun at the behest of the Prince of Wales. Foote was allowed to present plays between May 15 and September 15, when the two patent theatres would be closed. In 1788 a bill authorizing magistrates outside the twenty-mile radius to license theatres made legitimate theatre common throughout the country.

A 1775 print of Drury Lane during Garrick's term as manager. The proportions of the print probably make the theatre seem a bit more spacious than it in fact was.

During the eighteenth century only Drury Lane, Lincoln's Inn Fields, the King's Theatre, the Haymarket, and Covent Garden had real importance. Drury Lane was refurbished several times during the century—after 1709 when Christopher Rich lost his patent and it was taken over by Colley Cibber, Robert Wilks, and Thomas Doggett; after the riot in 1737 caused by the abolition of the custom which gave free gallery admission to footmen whose masters were attending a performance; and most importantly in 1775 when the Adams brothers made extensive changes in both house and stage, so that it could seat 1800 persons.

Lincoln's Inn Fields also was affected when Rich's patent at Drury Lane was silenced, for he took over Lincoln's Inn Fields and began renovations. He died before the work was completed, but the theatre opened in 1714 under the management of his son, John. In 1731, when the structure began to decay, Rich started a subscription to build a new theatre in Bow Street which eventually became Covent Garden. In 1733 Lincoln's Inn Fields reopened with an Italian opera company in residence, and when they left it became a barracks, an auction house, a china warehouse, and was destroyed in 1848.

The King's Theatre (originally called the Queen's Theatre for Queen Anne, and then the Haymarket) was built in 1705 by John Vanbrugh, who hoped to draw audiences from Rich's mismanaged Drury Lane. He made Congreve his manager, installed Betterton's troupe in residence, and opened with an opera. The theatre lost money and Vanbrugh let it to a manager named Swiney, who left in 1711, deeply in debt. The theatre was too large for drama and became a successful opera house until it was destroyed by fire in 1789.

Covent Garden Theatre was built by John Rich in 1732 (originally called the Theatre Royal) on a piece of land that had once been part of a convent garden. The theatre, which seated around 1400 patrons, opened in December with a revival of Congreve's *The Way of the World*. It remained essentially the same until 1784, when it underwent substantial renovation to enlarge the auditorium seating area. In 1792 it was so altered that some refer to it as being rebuilt. This allowed it to seat nearly 3000 persons, making it competitive with Drury Lane, which could at this time seat 3600 persons. In September 1808 it burned

The interior of Covent Garden Theatre in 1794, just fourteen years before it was destroyed by fire.

down, but a new theatre would be built on the site. In the fire Handel's organ and the manuscript scores of some of his operas that had been produced there also perished.

The scenic practices followed on the eighteenth century English stage did not differ significantly from those followed in Italy and France. The standard units of set construction were wings, borders, and shutters, as had been true throughout the Restoration, though in this period roll drops were sometimes used in place of shutters. Sets were shifted by way of grooves on the stage floor and overhead. After the middle of the century a curtain or act-drop was used to mask scene changes, but for the first fifty years all changes were made in full view of the audience.

Toward the end of the Restoration period, when the royal presence was rarely at the theatre and thus the royal vision and sensibilities could not be blocked or injured by such antics, the earlier practice of spectators climbing up to sit on the stage was revived, primarily by the "young bucks" of London society. This unfortunate practice lasted until 1762 when Garrick, his reputation well enough established to risk offending these social luminaries, banished them from the stage.

Probably the most important aspect of scenic practice during the century grew out of a rapidly increasing demand for spectacle. Perhaps as a result of the widespread interest in Italian opera (which provided such spectacular staging), grand processions, coronation scenes, and pageantry were regularly added to plays—especially history plays where such scenes seemed appropriate extensions of the subject matter. Such spectacle not only demanded lush costuming, but also extravagant scenic designs that could be painted on flat wings and roll drops. Thus the eighteenth century became the seminal period for scene painters, and the names of such home-grown scenic artists as John DeVoto, George Lambert, Frances Hayman, and Thomas Lediard, stand beside such continental artists as Jean-Nicholas Servandoni, Giovanni Battista

Cipriani, and Nicholas Dall. Certainly the most important scenic designer of the century was Philippe Jacques DeLoutherbourg, a French artist engaged by Garrick to design and supervise the building of spectacles.

PHILIPPE JACQUES DELOUTHERBOURG: DeLoutherbourg (1740-1812), a fine scenic designer, had the good fortune and in a sense the bad fortune to be David Garrick's scenic designer. Thus, he had the support of a brilliant actor-manager in the production of his designs, but he was for many years remembered merely as Garrick's designer rather than for his own important contribution to the theatrical arts.

DeLoutherbourg was a painter from Alsace who worked for several years in France and Italy studying "stage illusion" and theatrical machines. In 1771 he went to London, where he met Garrick. The actor-manager, impressed by DeLoutherbourg's background, made him scenic director of Drury Lane, a position he filled so brilliantly that he retained it under Sheridan after Garrick's retirement.

He introduced a number of new devices to the Drury Lane stage, the most admired of which was a machine to project fleeting colors on a landscape by mounting colored silk screens on pivots in the wings, and backing them with concentrated lights. His cloud effects were particularly admired by audiences. He also introduced a series of head-lights (or border battens) behind the proscenium, which helped force the actors to stay within the scene and improved scenic focus through the intense illumination.

His designs were described as "vivid" and "arresting" and sometimes as "garish" and "bizarre" because of his preoccupation with primary colors. However, he was highly successful in creating such spectacular effects as fire, volcanoes, the sun and moon, and clouds. He created sound devices to simulate thunder, firearms, lapping waves, and falling rain and hail. He is also generally credited for doing for scenic effects what his employer was doing with acting; that is, moving away from the artificial conventions of the time toward something more natural and realistic.

He is referred to by Puff in *The Critic*, for which production he designed and built the striking Tilbury Fort, and in a 1779 revival of *The Winter's Tale* he executed some transparent effects that were applauded by audiences and critics alike. Also in that year DeLoutherbourg paid a visit to the Lake district and was so impressed with the spectacular view that he returned to London and painted it on an act-drop scenic curtain that was used until it and the theatre were destroyed by fire. Some scholars consider this to be the earliest use of an act-drop in western Europe.

Shortly after completing the scenery for the first stage production of *Robinson Crusoe*, which had eight set changes in the first act alone, DeLoutherbourg retired from the stage because of a dispute over his salary. He devoted the rest of his artistic life primarily to a remarkable scenic exhibition, the *Eidophusikon*. The influence of this scenic marvel could be seen as late as 1820 when Robert William Elliston (1774-1831) tried to reproduce some of its storm scenes for his production of *King Lear*.

Elected to the Royal Academy in 1781, DeLoutherbourg has been credited, in addition to his scenic marvels, with the introduction of realistic design, with ending the era of the "flat" scene by the innovative use of perspective, and with being the first designer in England to make use of raked set pieces (some accord this honor to Inigo Jones). His accomplishments are far too many and too significant for him to be remembered merely as Garrick's designer.

ACTING

During the century the acting styles varied greatly, from the inherited oratorical styles of Thomas Betterton, Barton Booth (1681-1733), and James Quin (1693-1766), to the more realistic styles of Charles Macklin (c. 1700-97) and David Garrick (1717-79). In the early part of the century the formal, oratorical style was prevalent, mostly because Betterton and Booth were both products of the older Restoration school. However, by mid-century the formal style and the developing realistic style were meeting head-on, with Quin and Garrick both competing for audiences. The triumph of Garrick served to establish the realistic style, and though the oratorical delivery did not totally die out—actors using the older style could, apparently, be found on the same stage and even in the same troupe as actors using the realistic approach—the realistic acting style became dominant and has remained so until the present time.

DAVID GARRICK: David Garrick (1717-79) was considered by most theatregoers in his day to be the greatest of all the English actors. There were some who disputed this; Thomas Gray was one, and Horace Walpole another. Samuel Johnson often spoke admiringly of Garrick, but there was a grudging quality in his comments, as if he resented his old pupil who, after coming to London had attained greater fame and wealth in a less intellectual pursuit than Johnson's own. Edmund Burke, Garrick's intimate friend, said of him that "he raised the character of his profession to the rank of a liberal art." An actress who had worked with him, Kitty Clive, said somewhat less eloquently, "Damn him, he could act a gridiron."

Garrick was born in Hereford on February 19, 1717, and spent most of his childhood in Lichfield. His parents were members of the middle-class, of Huguenot descent, and his family was a large one. He attended Edial Hall where, a student of Samuel Johnson, he amused his fellow pupils by peeping through the keyhole of their bedroom at Johnson and his bovine wife and mimicking what he saw. He served a brief apprenticeship to his uncle David in the wine business, which he abhorred, but his interest in the theatre was kindled by a troupe of strolling players, and subsequently he made his first appearance on the stage in an amateur performance of Farquhar's *The Recruiting Officer*.

Garrick came to London in 1737, along with Samuel Johnson, and enrolled as a student at the Lincoln's Inn acting school. This did not further his career as an actor, so he turned to managing the London office of his uncle

An engraving after Zoffany shows David Garrick in a comic scene from Vanbrugh's *The Provoked Wife.*

David's wine business. Fortunately, Covent Garden was close by, so Garrick did not concentrate all of his energy on the wine shop. In 1741 he got his first chance to act at Goodman's Fields, standing in for another actor. From there he traveled to Ipswich where, under the name of Lyddal, he appeared in a number of minor roles. At this time he did not wholly commit himself to acting, though he did continue to take whatever roles were offered. It was not until after his mother's death that he decided to devote himself to the theatrical art.

Playing the role of Richard III at Goodman's Fields, on October 19, 1741, Garrick "arrived" in the theatre. The press, especially the *Daily Post*, declared that his reception was "the most extraordinary and great that was ever known on such occasion." From this triumph Garrick went on to play roles in *The Orphan, The Rehearsal, The Lying Valet* (which he had authored), and *The Fair Penitent.* Because of the reception accorded his performances at Goodman's Fields, he found himself engaged by Drury Lane for the upcoming season. He opened on October 5, 1742, and played in *The Recruiting Officer, the Beaux' Strategem, The Alchemist, Richard III, King Lear,* and *Hamlet.*

Garrick was a generous man, often lending large sums of money to friends in need. In an age where all theatre people were suspect, in many cases for good reason, his morals were above question. He did not gamble and was considered a moderate drinker; in fact, he often warned young actors against the dangers of the bottle.

Probably the greatest of Garrick's many contributions to the theatre was the natural style of acting. As Baron Grimm said of him, he tried to become as much as possible the person he represented. Grimm also wrote that "when he turns to someone with a bow, it is not merely that the head, the shoulders, the feet and arms, are engaged in this exercise, but that each member helps with great propriety to produce the demeanor most pleasing and appropriate to the occasion."

Garrick coached many young actors, impressing on them his theory that every gesture, facial expression, and vocal intonation should be settled in "the closet" before setting foot upon the stage. He also taught that an actor was not an actor if he could not "give a speech, or make love to a table, chair, or a marble slab, as well as the finest woman in the world." To study characterizations, he sometimes visited the Old Bailey to observe the emotions displayed there, and he advised young actors to do the same. He told them to develop their intelligence and culture beyond immediate theatrical requirements, not only for their social value, of which Garrick was highly conscious, but also to develop depth on stage.

In the modern sense of the word, the director did not exist at this time, and actors were usually left to their own discretion as far as blocking, gestures, and characterizations. Garrick, as theatre manager, came closer to becoming the first modern director than any of his contemporaries. His rehearsals were long and frequent, and he disciplined actors who failed to appear. His disciplinary technique ranged from fining them to not casting them in future shows. He set up a rehearsal schedule ranging from three to eight weeks for preparation of any given play. It is interesting to note that he kept one play in rehearsal for over a year. From the very onset of rehearsals he conveyed his concept of the characters and their interpretations by acting out before the assembled cast all the roles (male and female), with appropriate facial expressions. This gave all his productions, for better or worse, his own personal stamp.

In 1747 Garrick, along with James Lacy, obtained the management of the struggling Drury Lane Theatre. Their desire was to coax back its patrons by staging worthwhile plays and such entertainments as the pantomimes of Henry Woodward. Garrick made considerable physical changes in the Drury Lane building. The first was an enlargement of the gallery, and the boxes on the Russell Street side were given a new entrance in 1750. He had the building repainted and supervised an increase in seating capacity. Finally, in 1777, a brand-new auditorium was constructed and extensively decorated.

Following Garrick's takeover in 1747, the theatre's fortunes changed for the better. Before his modifications the theatre held 1,000 people and its annual receipts were 18,276 pounds. When he retired, the house had been remodeled to hold 2,362 people and took in 33,615 pounds. Another reason for one of Garrick's structural changes, and one for which all theatregoers should be grateful, was to abolish spectators from the stage itself. The stage action was pushed gradually back from the apron to behind the proscenium arch, nearer to the scenery. This made it difficult for the young men in the audience to get to the stage, and they also knew that even if they succeeded in this venture they would only draw upon themselves Garrick's disapproval.

Thomas Otway's *Venice Preserved*, at Drury Lane, 1762, with Garrick as Jaffier and Mrs. Cibber as Belvidera. (Mezzotint by J. McArdell, 1764)

Garrick was the author of many plays, but they were not highly successful and they are seldom revived. His first play, *Lethe, or Aesop in the Shades*, hardly had the semblance of a plot, but the characters were Classic ones designed to capture audiences in terms of character alone; such as old Aesop the philosopher and Charon the boatman. Most of Garrick's plays contained outstanding roles for members of his company, and were written especially for them. He had definite ideas regarding what good comedy and tragedy should be, especially as it applied to the performer. He maintained that comedy required the more practiced actor. In a tragedy, he said, the plot and the language could carry even an indifferent actor to surprising heights.

As an actor David Garrick played over ninety roles; as an author he wrote eighty prologues and epilogues, thirty-five plays (including interludes and adaptations), and innumerable verses and songs; and as a theatre manager he watched over the fortunes of Drury Lane for twenty-nine seasons. His contributions were so many and so varied that he is certainly one of the most important contributors to the history of English theatre.

In addition to Garrick there were a number of highly successful performers during the century, especially during the early years before Garrick arrived to dominate the stage. Betterton, Booth and Cibber were, of course, actors of the old school, but by the 1730s these were all dead or retired and James Quin had become acting's leading light.

A contemporary print showing James Quin as Coriolanus in 1749, wearing a peruke, plumes, and a short, flaring skirt. He is carrying the equivalent of a swagger stick.

Quin, an English actor, somewhat reversed traditional procedures by making his first stage appearance in 1712 at Smock Alley Theatre in Dublin; only two years later he was doing bit roles at Drury Lane. It was here that he made a sudden reputation in the role of Bajazet in *Tamerlane* (by Nicholas Rowe), when the actor scheduled to play the role was taken ill and Quin went on in his place. In 1718 he left Drury Lane for Lincoln's Inn Fields, where he stayed for fourteen years, appearing in a wide variety of roles—Hotspur, Othello, Lear, Falstaff, and even the Ghost in *Hamlet*. In 1732 he left Lincoln's Inn Fields for Covent Garden, remaining for only a brief period before returning to Drury Lane, where he specialized in leading tragic roles. An orator by nature and training, Quin was the last great representative of the school of Betterton, and he carried this love of traditionalism into all aspects of stage presentation, even insisting that the costumes not be altered from what they had been during the earlier period. In 1751, defeated by audience preference for Garrick's more realistic style of presentation, Quin retired to spend the final years of his life at Bath.

Charles Macklin, an Irish actor of great talent and rotten temperament, slightly preceded Garrick in inaugurating the natural style. Born sometime around 1700, he joined a company of strolling players in 1716 and by 1720 was acting with the Bath company. In 1725 he went to Lincoln's Inn Fields, but his realistic (by the day's standards) delivery was unsuited to the ideals of the day and he soon went back to the provinces. In 1730 he returned to Lincoln's Inn Fields in Fielding's *Coffee-House Politician* (a rewritten version of *Rape upon Rape*), and soon after that he went to Drury Lane, where he spent ten years playing secondary roles. He finally managed to persuade the management to revive *The Merchant of Venice* and, in 1741, he became famous overnight for his performance as Shylock. Macklin managed to rescue Shylock from the crude jests of the low comedians to whom the role was traditionally assigned, raising him to the status of a dignified and tragic figure, of whom Pope could write "This is the Jew, / That Shakespeare drew." Macklin might well have

Macklin in costume for his greatest role—Shylock.

gone on to even greater glory, but his temper betrayed him. He killed another actor in a quarrel over a wig, and fought regularly with theatre managers, moving from one troupe to another as a consequence. He lasted well, in spite of his problems, making his final appearance (appropriately as Shylock) in 1789, though he was unable to complete the play. He died in 1797, disappointed only in playing his whole career in the shadow of Garrick.

Other than Macklin, Garrick's only other serious rival during the last half of the century was an Irish actor named Spranger Barry (1719-77), who began in 1744 at Smock Alley in Dublin playing the role of Othello. Two years later he went to Drury Lane to play Othello to Macklin's Iago. He became one of the finest "young lovers" on the stage and highly popular, remaining at Drury Lane even after Garrick took over, where he played such roles as Othello, Pierre, Bajazet, Henry V, and Orestes. Garrick and Barry both played Hamlet at different times, and their performances as the Danish prince may well be described in terms of their later performances as Romeo, about which Macklin said that Barry swaggered so much and talked so loud in the garden scene that the servants should have come out and tossed him in a blanket; Garrick, on the other hand, sneaked in like a thief in the night.

Unfortunately, Garrick's dominance of the stage tended to subordinate some fine actresses. Among the best who worked with him was Peg Woffington (c. 1714-60), an English actress born in Dublin, who came early to the stage. By the age of ten she was playing roles in a children's company, from which she went on to Smock Alley to play a wide range of roles, from old women to Ophelia to (somewhat later) her famous "breeches role" of Sir Harry Wildair in Farquhar's *The Constant Couple.* She played the role made famous by Wilks with such verve and flair that for a long time no male actor would attempt it. A

A print by R. Pyle showing Spranger Barry and Mrs. Nossiter playing the balcony scene from *Romeo and Juliet* but dressed in eighteenth-century costumes.

great physical beauty, Peg was cursed with a harsh voice which, given the ideals of the day, made her unfit for tragic roles. However, her way with such highborn ladies as Millamant and Betty Modish made her the most popular actress of her day. She was in great demand by male actors, and was known as being witty, charming, and a delight to work with. This did not, however, extend to her fellow actresses, with whom she was constantly at odds, even driving one from the stage and wounding her with a dagger during a fit of rage. She was for some years the mistress of Garrick and played opposite him in many plays. Her last "breeches" role was Lothario, and her last stage appearance was as Rosalind in *As You Like It,* where she was taken ill during the epilogue. She retired and spent three sickly years doing good works and repenting her former life, finally dying young and mourned by all the actors (if not the actresses) of the London stage.

As the century drew to a close in the 1790s, even the influence of Garrick had begun to wane, and the acting baton was passing to the Kemble family, who would greatly influence the stage during the first half of the nineteenth century.

The Eighteenth Century In Italy

In the seventeenth century nearly all significant developments in theatre technology and scenic design had come from Italy. In the eighteenth century this pattern continued and Italy remained the center of such activities. Unfortunately, the art of playwriting did not keep pace, and the drama of the period is generally insignificant. Both of these aspects of Italian theatre are due in large part to the evergrowing popularity of opera, which inhibited the writing of regular drama while, at the same time, because of its demand for spectacular staging, promoting all aspects of scenic design and stagecraft. Also, the continuing influence of the now degenerate *commedia dell'arte* made the exploration of new dramatic forms very difficult. Designers in other countries were also, during this time, hard at work in the areas of scenic design and theatre technology, and by the end of the century Italy's lead in the areas of technical theatre had all but disappeared.

EIGHTEENTH CENTURY ITALIAN DRAMA

The eighteenth century drama in Italy is, in essence, the effort of one playwright, Carlo Goldoni, to bring the Italian drama out of its dependence on the by then debased *commedia* form. Inasmuch as the *commedia* worked from scenarios rather than scripts it did not give rise to a dramatic literature. Thus, as the form lost its vitality over the centuries it degenerated into rather routine spectacles' filled with incongruities as the traditional materials and sense of purpose disappeared. Scenarios even became a bit nonsensical as set speeches that were passed on from master actor to apprentice failed to jibe with the set speeches passed on by other master actors to other apprentices. Thus, the performances began to rely more and more on meaningless vulgarities. The costumes and masks also lost their significance as the groups from which they had sprung disappeared or changed to fit new social conditions.

This, then, is what provoked Goldoni. He felt that Italian drama could only become meaningful when it was freed from outmoded traditions and allowed to take its cues from contemporary life.

CARLO GOLDONI: Carlo Goldoni (1707-93), until recently known outside of Italy only as the reformer of the *commedia dell'arte*, has now come to be known by some critics as the first naturalistic playwright in the history of the drama.

Goldoni was born in Venice. His grandfather had squandered the family fortune, and his father had to earn his living as a physician, spending much of his son's childhood away from Venice attending to his practice in Perugia. Goldoni displayed an early interest in playwriting, completing a comedy when he was eleven, and his mother was so delighted that she sent a copy to her husband in Perugia. Giulio Goldoni, in turn, was so pleased by what his precocious son had written that he brought him to Perugia and enrolled him in a Jesuit school.

Two years later his father moved to Cioggia, near Venice, and had Carlo put into school at Rimini. There, at the age of fourteen, Goldoni met a troupe of strolling players and stowed away on their boat for three days. From his own account of this initiation into the theatrical life, its greatest attraction was the plentitude of attractive young actresses. From an early age on, Goldoni was unable to resist a pretty face.

The comedies of Goldoni were played not only in the finest theatres, but also on improvised stages, as shown here in Marcola's painting of a festival in Verona.

From Cioggia his father sent him to the ecclesiastical college at Pavia, from which he was expelled within a year for writing a dramatic satire on the college. For the next fifteen years he was continually on the move, constantly retrenching as a result of his rash escapades. At the age of twenty-five he managed to gain his law degree at Venice, only to find that "his face was too jovial to attract clients," who apparently felt that a lawyer should look as stern as the law he represented. He fled to Milan to avoid his creditors, but war forced him to Verona, where in desperation he joined a troupe of strolling players and began to provide them with scenarios for their *commedia dell'arte* performances.

It is said that Goldoni saw a pretty girl sitting on the balcony of her home, sought out her father, and the next day arranged to marry her. Given Goldoni's impulsiveness in regard to women, the story may well be true. After marriage, Goldoni and his wife returned to Venice and for the next seven years he endeavored to earn his living as a lawyer. Clients were not numerous and so he was forced to write scenarios for the Venetian *commedia dell'arte* troupe under the management of a man named Imer.

In 1743, at the age of thirty-six, Goldoni left Venice with his wife and traveled to Pisa, where he again tried his hand at the law. It was here that Goldoni was approached by Cesare d'Arbes, the Pantalone of the Medebac troupe in Venice, and offered "pockets full of gold" to return to Venice to become a full-time dramatist to the Medebac company. This generous offer came about because a play, *La donna di garbo* (*The Clever Woman*, 1738), which

In this illustration of a Goldoni play, Pantaloon becomes a realistic version of a Venetian merchant. (From Antonio Zappa's edition of Goldoni's works, Venice, 1789)

Goldoni had written for Imer, had become a great success. Cesare d'Arbes, after much pleading and after agreeing to hire the Teatro Sant'Angelo and place at Goldoni's disposal the city's finest troupe of *commedia* actors, finally received Goldoni's word that he would return to Venice.

It is interesting to note that in 1750 near calamity struck the Medebac company. Goldoni was not meeting his agreed-upon quota of eight new comedies per season, and as a consequence the subscribers were not renewing their subscriptions to the Teatro Sant'Angelo. Also, Pantalone (d'Arbes) had left the troupe to take service with the King of Poland. Goldoni defiantly agreed to write sixteen new comedies for the 1750-51 season. He accomplished this monumental task, and though some of the plays are considered weak, at least three are numbered among his best.

From the age of fifteen when he discovered the national dramas of England and France in the library at Pavia, Goldoni's ambition had been to reform the decadent *commedia dell'arte* and replace it by an Italian theatre that would rival that of England and France. When he took the position at the Teatro Sant'Angelo he had begun this task by writing into his scenarios the dialogue to be spoken by the nonmasked characters. Next he tried to persuade the masked characters to allow him to write their dialogue as well, his purpose being to keep them from using their tired, obscene jokes. He had given the Imer company their first play in which all the dialogue was written for them. The success of this venture is what had brought d'Arbes to offer Goldoni the position of professional playwright. The next step involved getting Pantalone (d'Arbes) to do his part without a mask. With this accomplished, Goldoni was able to get all the actors of the company to learn their lines.

In 1748, realizing that Pantalone displayed two opposing characters, Goldoni wrote *I due gemelli veneziani* (*The Venetian Twins*), which is a comedy of mistaken identities. The performances of this play were the most successful that Venice had ever experienced, and because of the great success of this production a number of theatre people realized that the improvised *commedia dell'arte* style at last was dead. The stock characters of the *commedia* were gradually replaced by the real people of Venice, and Goldoni's "naturalistic" comedies were born.

With this great success came the jealousy of the critics and the academic dramatists. The attacks became malevolent, finally driving Goldoni from his beloved Venice. It is interesting to note that the most vicious attack came from Carlo Gozzi, who became outraged when Voltaire came unsolicited to the support of Goldoni. It was through his support that Goldoni became an international figure, leading to the offer made by King Louis XV of France to write plays for his company of Italian actors, (the comédie-Italienne) in Paris. At age fifty-five Goldoni left Venice, never to see it again.

In Paris the Italian actors were uncooperative, demanding scenarios rather than written dialogue, and as a result of this Goldoni only wrote one play, *Il ventaglio* (*The Fan*, 1763); however, it is a fine play that is generally considered to be one of his best works.

After three years in Paris, Goldoni went completely blind, though he finally regained partial sight in his right eye. He tutored the French princesses at Versailles until he was given a pension by the King and returned to Paris. In 1789 the Bastille fell and Goldoni, now in his mid-eighties, became seriously ill and died on February 6, 1793.

Goldoni successfully effected a reform in theatre, but only because the bourgeois audience had become dissatisfied with the outworn dramatic form of the times. Venice, having a more solidly developed bourgeois society than any other city in Europe, was the logical place for this reform to take place. Goldoni, sensitive to the desire of the people, felt the need for plays that reflected the customs, ideals, and problems of his society; one which would join the artistic integrity of performance to the didactic aims of denouncing excess and condemning vice.

Goldoni achieved reform gradually by first writing dialogue for scenes featuring everyday, contemporary characters, as opposed to the traditional stock figures of the *commedia*. He at first kept his characters in masks, inasmuch as they were still popular with the public in their traditional appearance. Then he gradually wrote them away, along with the unrealistic, stylized costumes. Finally the Pantalones and Arlecchinos were dressing in realistic costume, without masks, and using names and surnames. The *commedia* in Italy had come to an end.

These reforms were not achieved without opposition. Goldoni found his strongest adversaries in his native Venice, the first being Abbé Pietro Chiari (1711-85), author of several extravagant and exotic comedies that slavishly followed what the Abbé believed to be the *commedia* tradition. Abbé Chiari was followed by even stronger competition in the person of Count Carlo Gozzi (1720-1806), a nobleman who favored the old social order of a dominant nobility and who resented any change that might promote more egalitarian understandings. What made Gozzi such a formidable opponent to Goldoni's reforms, however, was that almost in spite of himself Gozzi was an excellent playwright.

Pantaloon is surrounded by admiring and independent young ladies. (From Antonia Zappa's edition of Goldoni's works, Venice, 1789)

Interestingly enough, change was inherent in the very things that Gozzi himself undertook. Essentially he tried to adapt the masks and characters of the *commedia*, or what he believed was the *commedia*, to a written and essentially literary drama. In this sense he set himself up against Goldoni, who wanted to substitute written drama of character and intrigue for the older *commedia* materials. Gozzi's first play, performed in 1761, was *L'amore delle tre melarance* (*The Love for Three Oranges*), and was a combination of fully written scenes and scenes written as scenarios so that the actors could improvise. The play was done by the Sacchi troupe, which featured Sacchi himself, the foremost actor of his day, and the brilliant Theodora Ricci as leading lady.

Gozzi's finest contribution to dramatic literature was his concept of the *fiabe* or fairy-tale play. His plays in this style achieved only a slight acceptance in Italy, where they were considered too fantastic, but they were highly successful in Germany and France as forerunners of the Romantic movement. With only slight revision to get rid of crudities and meaningless parodies of works by his hated enemy, Goldoni, Gozzi's fairytale plays still hold up. These are *Turandot*, *L'augellin belverde* (*The Beautiful Green Bird*), and *Il re cervo* (*The King Stag*) which is probably the best of the lot and is still often done in spite of some outstanding technical difficulties.

In the area of tragedy, little was written that strikes us as significant today. The French concept of tragedy tended to dominate Italian sensibilities, and it was not until *Merope* (1713) by Scipioni de Maffei (1676-1755), that this dominance was challenged. Written in verse, in five acts, and in accordance with what Maffei believed to be the Classical rules, the play achieved great audience success, both in Italy and throughout Europe.

The only other significant writer of tragedy in the eighteenth century was Vittorio Alfieri (1749-1803), who between 1775 and 1789 wrote nineteen tragedies based on biblical, Roman, and Renaissance sources. Alfieri, like most other Italian writers, looked to France for inspiration. As a result he composed in a rigorous Classical form which he found (as did Racine) congenial for powerful, tragic expression. To this form he added a depth of psychological insight that makes his plays the equal of anything written for the French stage. It is unfortunate that because he stood so alone in the Italy of the eighteenth century his works have generally been ignored outside his native country.

The most significant aspect of drama in eighteenth century Italy was the attempt to create a musical drama. Unfortunately, the aspiration never totally succeeded as even the best writers in this form—Apostolo Zeno (1668-1750) and Pietro Trapassi (Metastasio, 1698-1782)—tended to replace tragic passions with pathetic sentimentality. This writing found its musical complement in the composers of the age, such as Galuppi, Vivaldi, and Leopold Mozart, and the term *musical theatre* was replaced by *opera*. The music quickly overpowered the text, reducing it to mere libretto and, in spite of a brief, abortive movement to restore meaning to the libretto, by the end of the century the dramatic aspect of opera had lost all significance.

SCENIC DESIGN

As the eighteenth century opened in Italy the practices of the earlier century were still generally followed. That is, using wings, shutters, borders, and on some occasions roll drops, lavish and spectacular sets were created and shifted with great rapidity. Most of the scenic wonders the designers created were in the style popularized by Torelli and Vigarani, with a perspective alley faced by ornate buildings leading to some distant prospect such as an arch, a temple, or a palace. Only a few years after the turn of the century, however, this began to change, primarily as a result of the contributions of the Bibiena family.

THE BIBIENA FAMILY: One sometimes sees references to Ferdinando or Giuseppe Bibiena, but usually any mention of their scenic contributions is attributed somewhat generally to the "Bibiena family." This family formed a dynasty which guided and largely controlled the progress of European stage techniques for nearly one hundred fifty years.

The founder of the Bibiena dynasty was the mayor of the Italian town of Bibiena at the beginning of the seventeenth century. His surname, however, was Galli, and not Bibiena. Galli sent his son Giovanni Maria, who was born in 1619, to Bologna where he could receive training as a painter. To ease the confusion between himself and another Giovanni Galli who also resided in Bologna, Giovanni Maria Galli added "da Bibiena" to his name. Giovanni Maria's career was not especially distinguished. However, his two sons, Ferdinando and Francesco, started the theatrical innovations which were to pervade every European court of note for over a century.

Ferdinando Galli da Bibiena (1657-1743) originally studied to be a painter like his father; later he studied architecture and theatrical engineering, and for over twenty years he designed sets and wall decorations for the Duke of

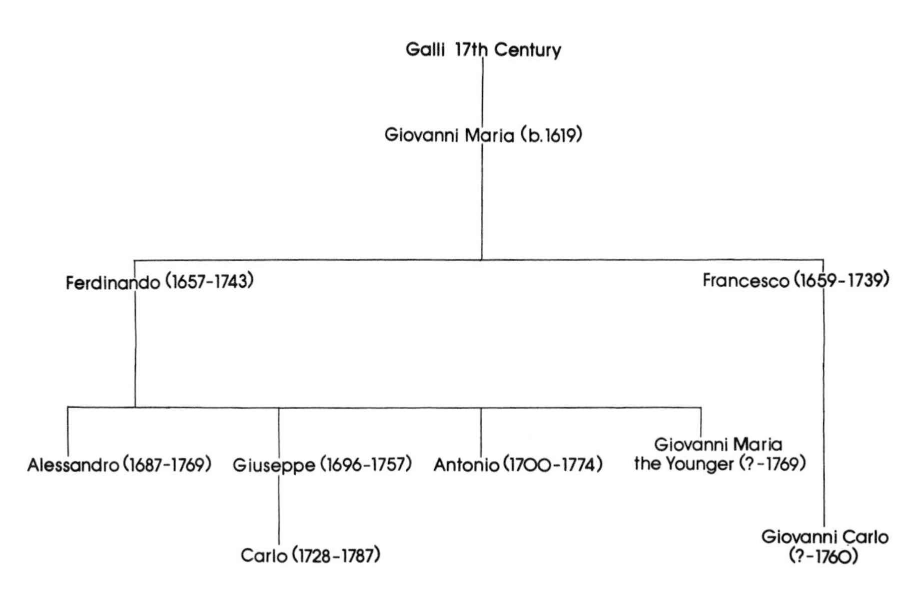

The Bibiena family tree.

Parma. During this period he also worked in Bologna, and it was there in 1703 that Ferdinando introduced angle perspective. In 1708 he staged the marriage of the future Emperor Charles VI, which had far-reaching effects in the realm of stage design. Charles VI was so pleased with Ferdinando's work that when he became Emperor in 1711 he appointed Ferdinando as court architect at Vienna, taking not only Ferdinando but also his two sons, Allessandro and Giuseppe, under his protection. Francesco had already been at the court in Vienna under Joseph I, so for almost forty years Vienna was the city in which the Bibienas exchanged ideas and formed the "Bibiena style," which they and their many admirers carried throughout Europe.

Francesco (1659-1739) contributed to the continuity of the set, from the background to the foreground. He abandoned the rule of symmetry, creating scenery which did not take its proportions from the auditorium, which is to say that he stopped considering the stage area as an extension of the auditorium. However, because he often worked closely with his brother Ferdinando, their individual contributions are difficult to distinguish.

The oldest of Ferdinando's sons was Alessandro (1687-1769), who became court architect and engineer to the Elector of Mannheim in 1719. His architectural works include the opera house in Mannheim, the Jesuit church, and the right wing of the palace. In his stage designs he created the suggestion of depth, not by using symmetry and straight lines, but by way of a zig-zag effect. His scenes draw the spectator's eye from the foreground to the center right, and then to the back left-hand corner.

The most notable member of the Bibiena family was Ferdinando's second son, Giuseppe (1696-1757). In 1716 Giuseppe collaborated with his father on the aquatic spectacle, *Angelica vincitrice d'Alcina*, and later on the opera *Coslantino*. When Charles VI was crowned King of Bohemia, Giuseppe designed the sets for the opera that was performed in honor of the occasion.

A setting by Ferdinando Bibiena, which uses oblique wings to form an architectural effect. Above we see a backdrop with painted sky and clouds. Immediately below the sketch the designer projects a perspective diagram of the set. Below that is an actual plan in which top and bottom, left and right are reversed.

Giuseppe went to Dresden in 1747, and then to Bayreuth to design the interior of the Margravine Wilhelmina's Opera House. Following this he returned to Dresden to supervise the building of an opera house, and in 1757 he went to Berlin, where he remained until his death.

Antonio (1700-74), the third brother, spent the years from 1727 to 1740 in Vienna as deputy theatrical engineer. Leaving the city with his own reputation firmly established, he began a kind of technical tour of Europe, spreading the

Bibiena style. In Bologna he designed the Teatro Communale, which was bell shaped and designed to hold twelve to fifteen hundred spectators. He also designed another theatre—the larger Redoutensaal, which was completed in 1752.

It is not known when the youngest brother, Giovanni Maria the Younger was born, but he died in 1769. During his lifetime Giovanni Maria was overshadowed by the rest of the family. He worked at the family trade, but it is now almost impossible to distinguish his work from that of the other family members. Giovanni Carlo, Francesco's son, also has an unknown birthdate. However, we do know that before his death in 1760 he and some fellow Italian artists designed such magnificant spectacles for the Spanish court that the Spaniards never found it necessary to develop their own techniques of stage design.

The fourth and last generation of the Bibienas, at least in terms of significant theatrical design, is represented by Giuseppe's son Carlo (1728-87). He worked with his father on the Bayreuth opera house, he designed for the stage in London and Berlin, and he designed sets for the opera house in Lisbon.

The Bibiena family spanned a transitional period in which scenic design changed from the baroque to the rococo. What audiences wanted on the stage was the magic escape provided by spectacle, and the Bibienas gave it to them. They gave viewers the opportunity to escape into a world of fantasy. For our time these designs seem too vast and ornate, but for their own time they were perfect; overwhelming in their grandeur.

When trying to assess the contributions of the Bibiena family it is important to remember that what they were doing is generally unrelated to what stage designers are trying to do today. They were not in the least interested in creating intimate sets or sets that captured an everyday reality. Neither were they producing backgrounds for plays. They were producing spectacle, and their carefully ordered, architectural sets were quite obviously scenic metaphors for idealized action based on Classical principles. Angle perspective enabled them to create an impression of enormous grandeur, and so they no longer used the theatre as a measure of the spectacle but as a spot where spectators might watch a presentation of much greater proportions than had been previously imagined. Illusion and vitality were the essence of the Bibiena style, which was so coherent that one is sometimes misled into considering it the product of a single vision. And yet, when closely considered, traits of individual character clearly emerge from their respective drawings. Ferdinando, who first developed angle perspective with more than one vanishing point, was a logical and methodical draftsman. The drawings of Francesco show that his work falls into the last stages of the high baroque style. Alessandro's stage sets are typically rococo, while Giuseppe, probably the most renowned of the Bibienas in his time, drew together the total family contribution. Antonio's style may have been more emotional, but it is difficult to distinguish between drawings done by him and Giovanni Carlo. Carlo drew heavily on his predecessors, yet in scale his drawings are much smaller, just as they are more regular and predictable. In spite of these differences in style, the similarities are so striking that it makes sense to talk about the Bibienas as a family when discussing their influence on the theatre.

A design by Francesco Bibiena for a production in 1703. The design uses divergent perspective, with walls leading backward and away from a common point.

The theatres designed by the Bibienas were not public theatres but were designed for members of the court. In fact, they were not even theatres from a purist point of view in that they were not designed for the presentation of plays but rather for the production of operas, ballets, and other spectacles, such as the aquatic spectacle held in 1716 in the park of the Favorita palace. This spectacle, designed by Giuseppe and his father Ferdinando, included plays within plays, processions, music, spoken dialogue, and an outdoor setting with a lake and garden.

The Bibienas started their reforms on a seventeenth century court stage which was dominated by a central perspective alley. Thus, only a few spectators who were seated near the exact center of the auditorium got to see the true perspective. The others had a more or less distorted view, according to the location of their seats. Side vanishing points and backdrops set at oblique angles, which were introduced by the Bibienas, provided a more evenhanded viewing situation—nearly everyone in the audience could now get the effect of perspective. However, it is obvious that providing equal opportunity viewing was not of the slightest concern to the Bibienas. Several of their theatres were designed with the audience sitting in a bell-shaped area, where the natural focus of every seat was directed at the point where the Prince was seated; even the Bibiena designs took a back seat to pleasing the Prince who paid the

In this design by Francesco Bibiena for a late seventeenth-century production, the painted flats and backings are not parallel to the front of the stage. Two diagonal walls meet at the back of the stage, and through the arches we see painted flats and backings.

bills for their spectacular staging. Francesco built the Teatro Filarmonico in Verona in this bell shape, and later Antonio used the same shape for the Teatro Communale in Bologna.

The achievements of the Bibiena family mark the rise of specialization in theatre design. The Bibienas made great strides in the realm of perspective, but their limited view of theatrical endeavor often hurt other aspects of the theatre at the expense of the design. In spite of this single-minded dedication to the production of spectacle, the impact of the Bibienas' reforms was great. They introduced multiple angle perspective, altered the scale of scenery, and then they spread these concepts throughout Europe, designing theatre buildings along the way. When all this is added to the two works published by Ferdinando, it is not at all surprising that they were as influential as they were.

Ferdinando's *L'architettura civile* was especially important in setting forth the Bibiena theories of scenic design. The introduction to the work calls it "the most influential document of theatre history in the eighteenth century," and while this is perhaps exaggeration, it was certainly of tremendous importance. Yet the theories behind the work of the Bibiena family are not to be found in a book. It goes back to the audience which they were trying to please. All of their efforts were concentrated on making grander, more fantastic spectacles, and to design theatres in which these spectacles could most easily be produced.

Although the contributions of the Bibienas are the most significant of the century, certain other scenic designers, including Filippo Juvarra (1676-1736), also made enormous strides in putting perspective to new, more efficient uses. Juvarra was an architect who, while working in Rome in 1708, gained the attention of Cardinal Pietro Ottoboni, a man influential in both Church and state affairs, and who had an abiding love for plays and operas. He commissioned Juvarra to design and build for him, in his Palazzo della Cancelleria, a small theatre. A number of Juvarra's scenic designs for opera productions in this theatre are still extant. Juvarra also designed sets for several other Roman theatres, but his primary work was for Ottoboni, and after leaving Rome in 1714 he gave up theatrical design for architecture. What makes Juvarra's sets unusual, and very important, is that he took a cue from the painters and designed curvilinear sets which use architectural curves to lead the eye back to the center foreground instead of off the stage, as so many of Ferdinando Bibiena's settings tended to do.

By the middle of the century a major change in scenic style was well on its way. Developing Romanticism and the concurrent fascination with ancient history, exemplified by the rediscovery of Pompeii in 1748, led to an interest in mood over spectacle. Whereas earlier designers had built clean, sharp, essentially new structures, designers now began to build ruins. Classical buildings on stage were cracked, chipped, and sometimes tumbling into ruins. Also, as a result of this growing interest in the past, the Medieval period came in for its share of attention, and as a result Gothic architecture replaced Classical in many eighteenth century designs.

To achieve the romantically misty quality of the ancient past, and to turn Gothic architecture to its best or at least most common use in some of its more eerie aspects, scenic designers began to work toward mood rather than clarity. The use of light and shadow to create effects had long been used by painters, and now scenic designers began to make use of the same techniques. At the forefront of this movement was Gian Battista Piranesi (1720-78), whose stage settings and engravings of Roman ruins promoted widespread interest in the uses of light and shadow. No longer were designers content to build a well-lit perspective avenue flanked by rather rococo-looking buildings purporting to be Classical structures. Glades seen by moonlight, interiors of Gothic castles, and grottoes were far more suited to the growing Romantic mood.

ACTING

The acting of eighteenth century Italy underwent some significant changes, but the lack of a great national drama tended to reduce the significance of these changes. As the century began there were opera performers barely trained in acting, and *commedia* troupes who followed styles long outmoded. The opera performers remained singers as the music continued to dominate the script, and the musical theatre envisaged by some writers

In Naples, late in the eighteenth century, the remains of the *commedia dell'arte* could be found in the work of the street theatres. (Engraving by G. Werti)

never matured. The *commedia* troupes, however, were forced to make some changes. Thanks to the contributions of Goldoni the traditional masked characters had almost disappeared from the stage by the century's end, and the actors had begun to learn lines and to act with an ease and naturalness unknown in earlier Italian theatre.

The Eighteenth Century In Northern Europe

Eighteenth century drama in northern Europe is primarily German drama (or, more accurately, drama of the German-language area), which by the end of the century had progressed from the weak school drama of the rediscovered Middle Ages, the work of occasional touring troupes, and a few court theatres, to one of the best and most influential dramas in all Europe.

EARLY GERMAN THEATRE

The German school drama had begun during the waning of the Middle Ages, when the plays of Hrotswitha, a tenth century nun, were published in 1501. These six plays, which used the techniques of Terence to promote Christian virtue, became popular, and by the middle of the sixteenth century similar plays were being written and produced, along with some Terentian originals, in schools and universities throughout Germany. This practice remained popular until the end of the eighteenth century. However, because these Latin productions seemed so removed from life outside the universities, which was one of continuing warfare and political struggle, they never developed into a true secular drama.

The German secular drama really begins with Hans Sachs (1494-1576), a cobbler by profession, a master-singer, and from about 1518 on a dramatist. He wrote long tragedies, comedies, and short carnival farces, and his range of subject matter was very large, from biblical materials through Classical, legendary, and historical, even including contemporary anecdotes. Like the plays of Hrotswitha, his works were designed to promote morality, and as a result only the carnival farces, which combined natural language, a rough but effective verse, and believable plots, have any contemporary interest.

Sachs had no real successors, and so the traveling troupes filled the void. English troupes played Germany regularly, mostly performing at the

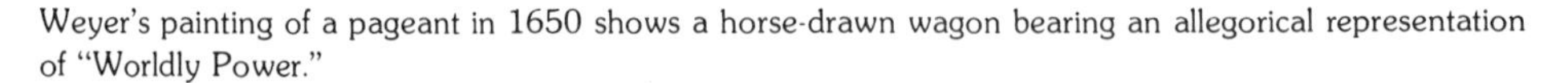
Weyer's painting of a pageant in 1650 shows a horse-drawn wagon bearing an allegorical representation of "Worldly Power."

various courts, but playing at least a part of the time for the public. *Commedia dell'arte* troupes (both Italian and French) were also touring Germany, and these groups also played primarily for the courts and only partially for the mass public audience. However, by the middle of the seventeenth century the courts, in an effort to ape the more sophisticated courts of France and Italy, were importing opera, ballet, and spectacles, and as a result the English and *commedia* troupes were more and more forced to play for mass public audiences.

As a result of this a national public theatre began to develop. It was a crude effort and largely derivative, and by the beginning of the eighteenth century it had formed around the clown character of Hanswurst. Traditionally a beer-swigging peasant, usually of Bavarian origins, Hanswurst was a descendant of the *commedia* character Arlecchino (Harlequin) and of the Medieval Vice character. The most famous actor to play Hanswurst, and the performer who succeeded in establishing him as a national symbol, was Joseph Anton Stranitzky (1676-1726).

EIGHTEENTH CENTURY GERMAN DRAMA

As the eighteenth century opened the German drama was still in its infancy. Such early seventeenth century playwrights as Martin Opitz (1597-1639), who had created a lifeless drama based on Classical aesthetics, and Andreas Gryphius (1616-64), whose lyrical dramas were morbid with their sense of sin, had no successors. The Germanic area was exhausted following the excesses of the Thirty Years' War, and ready for a national drama and not

Gottsched and his wife in a portrait by an unknown artist, c. 1750.

an imported Classicism. The most important of the dramatists immediately preceding the eighteenth century was Christian Weise (1642-1708), who began such a drama. He wrote plays that were sensible, cheerful, down-to-earth, and highly comic, making excellent use of the Narr or fool character. However, his excellent example was not followed in the intellectual and cultural vacuum that existed during the early years of the Age of Enlightenment. Indeed, following the last of Weise's plays in 1702 there was no German drama for nearly thirty years, and when it finally reappeared it was more akin to the French neoclassical models than to Weise's homegrown materials.

This French neoclassicism was largely due to the influence of Johann Christoph Gottsched (1700-66). Leipzig became, early in the century, a center for the production of French drama, especially the plays of the French neoclassicists, and after Gottsched arrived in 1723 he soon became a virtual literary dictator, enforcing German drama in the French style. He was awarded a professorship at the university, and his *Attempt at a Critical Poetics for Germans* (1730) became the textbook for dramatic writing. His Classical sources were Aristotle, Horace, Scaliger, Opitz, and Boileau, and his dramatic models came from Corneille, Racine, Destouches, and Ludwig Holberg, the "Danish Molière" who used the style of the great French dramatist to support traditional moral themes.

Without any German originals which he considered worthy, Gottsched began work on new translations of the Classical dramas—but translations that would follow his own set of rules derived from his Classical sources. By 1723 eight such plays were ready for production, including his own translation of Racine's *Iphigénie*. Between 1740 and 1745 he published these works, along with a few German originals. He also published his own *Der sterbende Cato* (Dying Cato, 1730), which contained three acts taken from Deschamps, one taken from Addison, and one composed by Gottsched himself.

Probably more than his plays and his philosophical works, Gottsched's discovery of the fine acting troupe led by Johann amd Carolina Neuber was responsible for his theatrical success. The Neubers were already committed to dramatic reform; their troupe was highly trained and tightly disciplined, and their aim was to make theatre a socially respectable profession.

Neither Gottsched nor Neuber was totally successful, though Carolina was probably more so than Gottsched. By the middle of the century most of the techniques she had espoused (minus the policing of performers' private lives) had been adopted by major troupes. Gottsched's reforms, on the other hand, were not accepted. He had sensed that the time was right for a new theatre, but he did not have the material or the vision to supply it.

CAROLINA NEUBER: Frederika Carolina Neuber (1697-1760, *née* Weissenborn), one of the earliest and best known of the German performer-managers, was born on March 9, in Reichenbach, Saxony, where she was given a comparatively good education. Her father, a doctor of laws, later settled as an advocate in Zwickau. Carolina, tired of his repressive guardianship, soon after ran away from home. In 1718, as part of this rebellion against her tyrannical father, Carolina married a young clerk named Johann Neuber.

Carolina Neuber is pictured in costume for Elizabeth in Thomas Corneille's *Essex*. (Theatermuseum, Munich)

The newlyweds joined a theatrical company under the management of Christian Spiegelberg, serving an acting apprenticeship in the city of Weissenfels until 1722 when they joined the Haach-Hofmann company. The Neubers formed their own company in 1727 and the Elector of Saxony granted them a patent to perform at the Leipzig Easter Fair.

As early as 1725, Carolina had attracted the attention of Gottsched, who planned to make use of her many talents in his attempt to reform the German theatre. She was quite willing to carry out his ideas about how to raise and purify the standards of both acting and repertory, and in 1727 she began the production of some French neoclassical tragedies and comedies that had been translated and adapted by Gottsched and his adherents. The collaboration of Neuber and Gottsched, which lasted until 1739, is usually regarded as the turning point in the history of German theatre.

After three years of touring in other cities, the Neuber company found, upon returning to Leipzig in 1737, that their patent had been given to Johann Ferdinand Müller, a proponent of the old improvised farces and harlequinades, featuring the clown character of Hanswurst, which Neuber was trying to reform. Carolina reacted by banishing Hanswurst from the stage; by refusing to allow the character of Hanswurst in any play she produced. This was probably less an aesthetic decision than a way of putting Müller on the spot artistically.

In 1740 the Neuber company was invited to St. Petersburg by the Russian Empress Anna, which prompted the introduction of modern drama to Russia. When Neuber returned to Leipzig in 1741 she found that Gottsched had allied himself with another company.

In 1747 Carolina quit the stage, but returned the following year with a new company and presented Gotthold Lessing's first play, *Der junge Gelehrte* (*The Young Scholar*). Indifferent success, however, dogged the company and following her failure to establish herself in Vienna, and her husband's death, Carolina Neuber retired. She died in 1760.

Carolina Neuber and her German contemporaries inherited what some historians have referred to as an unhealthy theatre. Certainly it is difficult to find any substantial theatrical expression prior to the eighteenth century. However, Neuber was a woman of remarkable character. Throughout her early theatrical apprenticeship she, too, was a vagabond, and thus she learned her craft in the old tradition of the German traveling troupe. With a family heritage of unusually high education she came from a background genuinely better for improving theatre than most of the strolling players of the time. Through this unique, capable woman a new hope for German national theatre was born.

During her wanderings, Neuber had observed French troupes playing in German and was especially attracted to their way of declaiming the alexandrine, a twelve-syllable poetic line. In the mid-1720s when the Neubers joined the company of Madame Hofmann, the best of its day, she put to good use the French style which she had observed. Here she became a popular actress, appearing in such distinguished plays as Corneille's *The Cid* and Pradon's *Regulus*. Although she achieved distinction as a tragic actress, her strength seemed to lie in the comic and "breeches" roles. At this point, having achieved national and even international recognition, Neuber began teaching the actresses of Germany the true manner of the alexandrine declamation.

Neuber's company became one of the finest in Europe, both for its overall quality of production and its dramatic execution. She would not allow improvisation by the actors, she demanded careful rehearsal, and she introduced order and punctuality into her company. In addition, each actor was required to work on all aspects of production; they had to work on costumes, paint posters, distribute handbills, and aid in the construction of scenery. She fought the old cliché that actors all have inborn tendencies to loose living, and she was uncompromising in her insistence that all of her players keep a high moral character.

Of all the reforms attempted by Neuber (and Gottsched), none stirred more controversy than the banishment of Hanswurst. This action had a far more serious effect than the mere exclusion of comic irrelevancies in poetic tragedy. It was Neuber's way of attacking the old improvised comedy and its stock characters. In 1737 the Neuber company performed a prelude, created by Carolina Neuber herself, in which Hanswurst was tried for his crimes against good taste, condemned, and removed from the stage. Although she fought resolutely against his return, it was a losing battle as Germany was not quite ready to surrender the traditional comic element from its national drama.

Neuber's uncompromising attempt to reshape theatre tradition led the public to desert her theatre. Insulted, she publicly denounced the Hamburg audience for its bad taste, closing the 1740 season with a satiric epilogue which

Hanswurst as a Bavarian peasant, in an engraving dating from c. 1790.

made her return to that city forever impossible. Despite her failure to remove Hanswurst from the stage, the popularity of this character soon declined.

By the late 1730s the Neuber-Gottsched alliance was weakening, their union no longer reinforced by a common, theatre-reforming zeal. The final breach occurred when Gottsched forced the unwilling Neuber company to abandon a successful translation of *Alzire* and perform an inferior translation by his wife, which further decreased Carolina's local popularity. The result was open warfare. Gottsched wrote bitter criticisms of everything performed by the Neuber company, and Carolina became acid-tongued, using the stage to openly ridicule Gottsched's concepts and personality.

Her victories over Gottsched were only temporary, and Carolina fled Germany, accepting an invitation from Empress Anna of Russia to perform in St. Petersburg. She returned to Leipzig the following year, only to find that Gottsched had since allied himself to the company of Johann Friederich Schönemann, a former disciple of Carolina's who had acted with her company in 1730. From this point on, Carolina Neuber's fortunes went downhill, and she made no more significant contributions to theatre.

The best of the dramatists during the period of Gottsched and Neuber was Johann Elias Schlegel (1719-49). He was strongly committed to Gottsched's rules and models, and he believed in reason and principle over emotion, as a good Classicist should. However, his talent led him beyond the narrow confines of Gottsched's own personal Classicism, and he managed in his best plays to create emotion through believable dialogue and powerful dramatic action. Along the way he also created strong characters and moving plots. Two of his original historical plays, *Hermann* (1743) and *Canut* (1746), are considered to be his best serious plays; all of his comedies are good, especially *Die stumme Schönheit* (The Speechless Beauty, 1748), a rococo verse comedy. As a critic he anticipated the later German fascination with Shakespeare, pointing out that Shakespeare was sometimes more true to Aristotle than were the French neoclassical writers.

Johann Christian Krüger (1722-50) was one of the earliest major dramatists in Germany proper, working in Hamburg with the Schönemann troupe. Taking Pierre de Marivaux for his model, he created a series of light comedies that were both popular and critical successes. His best work is usually considered to be *Die Candidaten* (*The Candidates*, 1747), in which a strong touch of social satire gives the play a significance missing in his other works.

The greatest German dramatist of the Age of Enlightenment was surely Gotthold Ephraim Lessing.

GOTTHOLD EPHRAIM LESSING: Gotthold Ephraim Lessing (1729-81), was born in the small Saxon town of Kamenz (Kamentz). His father had studied theology and church history at the University of Wittenberg, where he was a zealous Lutheran and wholehearted supporter of the Reformation. He had aspirations of becoming a professor at the University, but in 1717 he took a post as a catechist and preacher to the Lutheran Church in Kamenz. Lessing's mother was formed in a more common mold; she performed her household duties, revered her husband, and helped to discipline the children. Lessing's childhood was one of strict discipline, surrounded by an atmosphere of piety and learning, with a heavy thrust toward Lutheranism. In his early youth he was constantly reading and his parents, counting on this academic orientation, had high hopes that he would become a great theologian.

At the age of twelve he entered St. Afra, an academically respected boarding school. The program of study at this school was considered to be extremely difficult, but Lessing so excelled that in five years he left St. Afra because the academic load was no longer challenging. In 1746, with the encouragement of his parents, he became a student of theology at the University of Leipzig. It was at the University that Lessing's love for drama developed.

Lessing became the resident critic of the Hamburg National Theatre at the request of a man named Lowen, who was the theatre manager. As a result of Lowen's poor management the theatre was closed within a year; however, though the theatre failed, Lessing did not. His writings provided new insight into acting, Christian tragedies, Shakespeare, the French neoclassicists, and Aristotle. Lessing's main thrust was to define the nature and function of tragedy and to examine contemporary drama through a better understanding of the Aristotelian concepts.

One of his first essays was concerned with the problems faced by Christian tragedy. Lessing felt that the main fault with Christian tragic heroes was the fact that they were all martyrs. He proposed the idea that Christian legend,

A scene from Lessing's *Minna von Barnhelm*, produced in Hamburg, 1768. (Engraving by G. M. Kraus, *Taschenbuch für die Schaubühne auf das Jahr 1776*, Gotha)

and even Christian character, is essentially untheatrical. He believed that basically Christian tragedy is opposed to Classical tragedy in the sense that Classical tragedy purifies passion with passion, but Christian tragedy purifies passion through the renouncement of passion. Also, in Christian tragedy the hero or martyr is concerned with the hereafter, which is not consistent with Classical tragedy in which the protagonist is concerned with matters in the here and now.

Lessing concerned himself with acting in the three basic areas of emotion, gesture, and interpretation. He believed that emotions may be present on stage and not seen; that is, the actor feels the emotion but fails to project it. On the other hand, emotions are sometimes seen when not present because the actor's technique allows him or her to simulate emotion and project it to the audience. Since emotions can only be detected by external signs, although they are basically internal, he favored what we call today, in one of our most unfortunate overgeneralizations, a technical approach.

In discussing the actor's movements, Lessing confines them to three categories: significant, picturesque, and pantomime. Pantomime, he believed, was legitimately a separate category because each movement has a purpose and meaning, so that thought or message can be transmitted without words. In acting the movement must always be significant and coincide with the words;

in pantomime the movement is the words. To be successful, acting must always work in conjunction with the poetry, becoming a form of "silent poetry." By using the correct approach in acting, that is, by coordinating the movement and the voice, the actor can control the audience.

In one of his articles, Lessing wrote that farce must be very quick and sharp. The basis for this belief was his feeling that for farce to be successful the audience must not be allowed to think. If they have time to think, they will concern themselves with the humor of the play, with whether it is witty or stupid. This is detrimental to the aesthetic basis of farce.

Lessing also concerned himself with the dramatic uses of ghosts, specifically the ghosts created by Voltaire and Shakespeare. Voltaire's ghost, according to Lessing, was a poetical machine, whose only purpose was to assist in unraveling the plot. It held no interest, of its own account, for the audience. The Ghost in *Hamlet* he found to be quite the contrary. It concerned the audience with its own fate; exciting pity and fear as a distinct character.

Lessing's comments on comedy center around his belief that comedy should mirror human life; it should make us aware of our faults. Although it cannot cure our faults it can remind us of them and thus prevent us from further faults. It serves as a valuable medicine in this sense, for it acts as a preventative.

The French neoclassicists were, according to Lessing, deficient to the degree that they tried to follow their own misunderstanding of Aristotelian principles. The Greeks were mainly concerned with action, Lessing wrote, while the French were concerned with time and place. Moreover, the French were more influenced by the Spanish than the Greeks. What the French actually did was to modify the Greek rules involving time and place, inasmuch as

An etching depicting Iffland in the title role of Lessing's *Nathan the Wise*. (From Henschel Brothers, *Ifflands mimische Darstellungen*, Berlin, 1811)

they did not have the courage to reject them. The French, especially Corneille, also misinterpreted Aristotle's concept of pity and fear. For the French, fear became terror. Lessing contended that this change in meaning was too great. The fear that is aroused in a viewer of Classical tragedy is a fear which arises due to the similarity of circumstances between the audience members and the sufferer. This fear then creates compassion which is referred back to ourselves.

The Hamburg Dramaturgy, along with his plays, was Lessing's major contribution to the theatre. He was the first German to truly upgrade the quality of German theatrical language, with *Miss Sara Sampson* (1755) becoming the first bourgeois tragedy to be written in natural dialogue. His *Minna von Barnhelm* (1767) was Germany's best comedy for many decades. *Emilia Galotti* (1772), though a popular play in its day, is perhaps his least significant work. *Nathan der Weise* (*Nathan the Wise*, produced posthumously in 1783) is, next to *Faust*, perhaps the noblest expression of Western idealism. It was a failure in its first production and was not well received until Goethe revived it at Weimar in 1801.

By this time—the late eighteenth century—the same philosophical and political uncertainty that caused the American and French revolutions was seriously troubling the Germanic area, and it resulted in two dramatic movements: "sentimentalism," which did not differ markedly from the English sentimental movement; and "storm and stress" (*Sturm und Drang*), an eruption of pre-Romanticism. Lessing was primarily responsible for provoking the sentimental movement with his emphasis on English materials, though by way of some Swiss literary philosophers (Bodmer and Breitinger) the movement became stronger and more visceral than Lessing would have wanted.

Storm and stress was a brief but violent literary, dramatic, and philosophical upheaval that lasted from about 1760 to 1785. Essentially Romantic—wildly Romantic in some of its aspects, storm and stress took its cues from a variety of sources—the neomysticism of the Pietists; the "graveyard" melancholy of Edward Young; the exaggerated and false Medievalism of James Macpherson's gaelic bard, Ossian; the ravings of the East Prussian prophet Johann Georg Hamann, whose wildly visionary works began appearing in 1759; the anticultural "natural" philosophy of Jean Jacques Rousseau; and from such literary geniuses as Homer, Marlowe, and Shakespeare.

The Germanic fascination with the dramas of Shakespeare was a prominent aspect of storm and stress and, in fact, of all German drama in the latter half of the eighteenth century. The greatest Shakespeare lover of all was the critic-playwright Jakob Michael Reinhold Lenz (1751-92). He wrote that Shakespeare was the total natural genius who had created a universe equal to the one created by God, and then went on to say that any genius who could shed the inhibitions of Classical criticism and let his imagination roam as freely as Shakespeare, could also achieve this pinnacle of greatness. His ecstasy and visions ended in insanity, but during the four years of his creative period he completed very good prose translations of five Plautian comedies and two original comedies—*Der Hofmeister oder Die Voritele der privaterziehung* (The

An engraving of the first German production of *Hamlet,* featuring Franz Brockman in the title role, in the Royal Theatre, Berlin, 1788. (From Otto Weddigen, *Geschichte der Theater Deutschlands,* Berlin, 1904)

Family Tutor, or The Advantages of Private Education, 1773), and *Die Soldaten* (*The Soldiers*, 1775).

Friedrich Maximilian Klinger (1752-1831), one of the leading dramatists of the storm and stress school, was a bundle of inconsistencies: a man of spartan discipline; a passionate moralist; and a man of action. He wrote plays that come closest to Gothic melodrama, but outlived the storm and stress period long enough to repent his dramatic excesses. Ultimately he decided on a military career and finally ended up as a general in the Russian army.

The greatest dramatist (and poet and philosopher) of the storm and stress period was Johann Wolfgang von Goethe. His works achieved worldwide praise, and he worked in nearly every literary form. Eventually he became the acknowledged master in storm and stress, in the German Romantic movement, and eventually in German "Weimar" Classicism. His *Faust* is still considered by many critics to be the greatest of all Romantic dramas.

JOHANN WOLFGANG VON GOETHE: Johann Wolfgang von Goethe (1749-1832) was born at Frankfurt-on-Main. He spent his first sixteen years studying the Bible, Hebrew, English, Italian, French, the Classics, music, and science, with the French seemingly having more influence on him than any other language or culture. Frankfurt-on-Main was a busy mid-eighteenth cen-

Goethe began his theatrical career as an amateur actor. This engraving shows him as Orestes to Corona Schroeter's Iphegenie in c. 1775. (Goethe Nationalmuseum, Weimar)

tury town, and young Goethe witnessed fairs, ceremonies, the coronation of the Emperor in 1764, and the events of the French occupation.

Goethe emerged from the protective cocoon which had been placed around him by his family in 1765, entering the University of Leipzig, where he stayed until August 1768. He returned home, remaining for nineteen months in poor health, and then returned to the university life, this time at Strasbourg. It was also in Strasbourg that Goethe met the writer and critic Johann Gottfried von Herder who, it is believed, inspired in Goethe the belief and determination which would eventually result in the birth of modern German literature.

In 1771, inspired by the plays of Shakespeare, Goethe began work on his first drama, *Götz von Berlichingen* (completed in 1773), celebrating the sixteenth century robber-knight of that name. In 1774, in four weeks, he produced the short romantic novel, *Die leiden des jungen Werthers* (*The Sorrows of Young Werther*). These works had great success, making him the leader of the young Romantic writers, and the literary movement known as *Sturm und Drang* began. It was also during these years in Frankfurt that he wrote the original of *Faust*, sometimes called *Urfaust*.

In 1775 Duke Karl August invited Goethe to the Duchy of Weimar, where he was to make his home for the rest of his long and influential life. For the next ten years Goethe spent most of his time working on affairs of state, leaving himself little time for literary work. His state duties involved him in agriculture, mining, finance, and military affairs. He also became interested in scientific studies, especially in zoology, botany, mineralogy, and geology. In 1774 he even contributed to the development of evolutionary doctine, discovering rudiments of the intermaxillary bone in man.

Goethe came to regret his state duties, and in 1786 he escaped to Italy for twenty-two months disguised as a merchant named Moller. While in Rome he completed *Iphigenie auf Tauris* (*Iphigenia in Taurus*, final version, 1788), *Torquato Tasso* (1789), and *Egmont* (1787), all works that he had begun previously. After his return to Weimar, Goethe found it impossible to continue his former duties, and so he began his literary work in earnest. In 1794, he began his friendship with Friedrich von Schiller. This friendship encouraged both men to prodigious literary efforts which were to change the face of German letters forever. After Schiller died in 1805, Goethe became something of a recluse, and in 1807 he married Christiane Vulpius, a young factory worker whom he had earlier taken as a mistress. Goethe did, however, continue to direct the Weimar Theatre until 1817.

In 1832, the year of his death, Goethe completed his work on *Faust*. His work on this philosophical drama had spanned sixty years. He was buried beside Schiller and Karl August in the ducal vault at Weimar.

Goethe's contributions to all areas of literature are important, but his contributions to theatre are perhaps greatest of all. When he first arrived in Weimar, Goethe took over the duties of managing the court theatre. He also began acting and directing, but his efforts were half-hearted and prompted more by boredom than anything else. However, after he returned from Italy and began his friendship with Schiller, he returned to the theatre.

A contemporary print showing a crowd scene from Goethe's 1798 production of Schiller's *Wallenstein's Camp* at the rebuilt Weimar Court Theatre.

As a director Goethe was a dictator, ruling his actors and his audiences with an iron hand. His real accomplishments were the creation of ensemble acting and the standardization of stage speech. Considering the fact that his actors came from all over Germany and were not accustomed to actor training programs and rehearsal schedules, it was probably necessary that the company have an autocrat at the helm in order to accomplish what they did.

Goethe introduced the rehearsal system in Germany, and his standards of speech and ensemble acting techniques were later to influence the Duke of Saxe-Meiningen's troupe, who in turn influenced Stanislavsky and the rest of Europe; thus, theatre outside of Germany also owes a great deal of its practice to Goethe.

Goethe was not an especially sensitive director. He thought the box set was an abomination and was not at all concerned with realistic acting. He considered it ridiculous for actors to talk to each other when they had an audience to which they could speak. His actors never performed with their backs to the audience, and he even discouraged profiles. He had a list of rules printed up that gave instructions to the actors, both on the stage and off, but on the whole they are rather shortsighted and indicate that Goethe was much more proficient at writing plays than at staging them.

Goethe created complex scenic designs and stage pictures that were harmonious and rich. His meticulous attention to detail was something never before seen in German theatre. He was one of the first theatricians to bring harmony to movement, picturization, setting, and sound.

Although Goethe's directorial influence was felt strongly in the German theatre and, indirectly, by the rest of the Western world, it was his plays, novels, poetry, critical essays, and philosophical treatises which were to influence the mind of Western man, helping to change his vision of himself and, thus, his art.

Perhaps the second greatest dramatist of the age was Johann Christoph Friedrich von Schiller, a genius who suffered most from living and writing in the shadow of his friend Goethe.

FRIEDRICH VON SCHILLER: Friedrich Schiller (1759-1805), the son of an army medical officer, was born in Marbachs Württemberg. The family atmosphere was a strict one, owing to the military doctor's career. Money was not in plentiful supply as a military career, though somewhat stable, was not rewarding in terms of pay. Due to this economic reality Captain Schiller decided to send his son, Friedrich, to a military school in Stuttgart.

Life in the school consisted of rising at six, marching to breakfast where an overseer gave orders to pray, eat, pray, and then march back again. Curfew was at nine. Such was the disciplined, confined, militaristic atmosphere in which Schiller evolved. The outside world was shut off from the young poet and he resented it. Not knowing about the normal world outside of school, he romanticized it, conditioning his mind to passion and sentimentality. Such a conditioning is evident in his first major work *Die Räuber,* (*The Robbers*, produced in 1782).

A scene from *The Robbers* at the Royal Theatre in Berlin, 1782. Scenic design by Karl Friedrich Schinkel. (An engraving by Chodowiecki in *Theatre Kalendar auf das Jahr 1788*, Gotha)

While at the academy he studied medicine for the purpose of becoming an army physician as had his father. During his off-duty hours he wrote *The Robbers*, reading it to his peers as he composed it. After graduating Schiller found himself without money and with an overwhelming ambition to write. He accepted a post as an army doctor and embarked upon a literary career with the passionate determination to eventually earn a living by his pen.

No theatre manager was interested in staging *The Robbers*, so Schiller had the work published, hoping that someone would read the manuscript and take interest. A bookseller named Schwan did take an interest in it, showing the play to Baron Dalberg, manager of the Mannheim Theatre. Changes were made in the script to ready it for stage production. While these changes were being made, Schiller went back to Stuttgart, trying his hand as poet in writing an anthology. The young poet produced nothing more than meaningless analogies, with no basis in the realities of life. However, *The Robbers* was more or less well received, and as a result Schiller was appointed editor of a magazine.

With the success of *The Robbers*, Schiller returned to Mannheim for a visit. At this time Schiller was absent without leave from his army post, and as a result of the unauthorized visit he was arrested and confined for two weeks. At the time he wrote *Die Verschwörung des Fiesko zu Genua* (*Fiesco, or The Conspiracy of Genoa*, 1783) and *Kabale und Liebe* (*Love and Intrigue*, 1784), Schiller was again absent without leave, broke, and living under an assumed name. *Fiesco* was curtly rejected for production so Schiller had it published as a literary drama called *A Republican Tragedy*. It proved to be a disappointment and it was general opinion that historical tragedy was obviously over his head.

On January 14, 1783, Schiller completed *Louise Miller*. Dalberg read and wanted to produce it. However, he demanded certain revisions in the piece. The major revisions apparently were in the female characters. Even in this best of his early works, Schiller still had problems developing his females, making them overly sentimental and unusually stupid. A "pestilent fever," certainly an early sign of tuberculosis that would eventually kill him, halted Schiller's work on the revisions.

On the strength of his works Schiller was at last elected to the "German Society," which gave him a social status above that of his army father and family. *Fiesco* was performed on January 12, 1784, but the public in Mannheim showed little interest. However, Berlin and Frankfurt audiences responded well, making the play a success. On April 15 of the same year *Kabale und Liebe* opened in Mannheim, where it did well, as it subsequently did in all of Germany.

Schiller was, however, unhappy in the intellectural climate of Mannheim, apparently bitter over the trouble he had in getting his works on the stage. Brooding over what he conceived to be his literary failures, he turned to medicine once again to earn his living.

August Wilhelm Iffland's production of Schiller's *The Maid of Orleans* in 1801. This shows the coronation procession to the cathedral, which required one hundred forty-five active participants and fifty extras all on stage at once.

The Duke of Weimar read the beginning of *Don Carlos*, Schiller's first historical tragedy, and appointed him to the Weimar Council. He became an ardent friend of Gottfried Körner, who stimulated Schiller intellectually, and the outcome of this new friendship was "Song of Joy," with music by Körner. The friendship also stimulated in Schiller a deep interest in history, and he began reading intently about the world's past wars.

Don Carlos was caustically received by the critics, and rightly so, for Schiller had not yet really developed a feeling for theatrical writing, for creating a work that can be brought to life by actors. The play is more a literary exercise than a theatrical text, too complicated to allow any artistic or dramatic flow to develop.

In 1788 Schiller was introduced to Goethe. They more or less interviewed each other, each feeling for the other a somewhat grudging respect but no real liking. The two writers saw literature from diametrically opposed points of view and as a result each wondered what the other could possibly mean by his work. Eleven years later the differences dissolved and the two men formed a solid friendship.

In the meantime Schiller became something of a Classical historian, producing *Geschichte des Abfalls der vereinigten Niederlande* (*The Defection of the Netherlands*). The work was so well received that he was appointed professor of history at Jena. With his philosophical approach to history, Schiller became one of the most popular professors at Jena, yet to his dismay he still remained poorly paid.

While still at Jena he married Lotte von Lengefeld, and with the advent of a young wife, his outlook changed and his growing moodiness reversed its trend. With spirits high and a new lease on life, Schiller tried his hand at writing a novel. Fortunately, this one attempt convinced him that the novel was not his genre. He turned again to history and his book on the Thirty Years' War made him the champion of Classical German literature in the eyes of certain of his followers. As a historian and lecturer, Schiller consciously attempted to make his endeavors highly interesting to his readers and listeners. Thus, he was more often referred to as an "aesthetic philosopher" than as a historian.

In 1791 Schiller experienced an attack of pneumonia, undergoing a siege of doctors treating him with leeches, purgatives, and vomitives. In his weakened condition, he began doing translations, producing Vergil's *Aeneid* in a highly readable form, though not doing justice to the original author's intent. A second attack occurred, weakening him still further. Friends from Holland sent money, setting up a trust fund that enabled him for three years to do whatever he wished. During this period of recuperation he did not write, totally immersing himself in the philosophy of Kant and metaphysics. Also during this time he at long last became friends with Goethe; the two writers still disagreed regarding the correct approach to literature, but they proved to be powerful intellectual stimulants for each other.

With the insight gained from his earlier attempts, and with the materials from his historical studies at last thoroughly digested, Schiller went on to produce his mature works: the dramatic trilogy *Wallenstein* (1799); *Maria Stuart* (*Mary Stuart*, 1800); *Die Jungfrau von Orleans* (*The Maid of Orleans*, 1801); *Die Braut von Messina* (*The Bride of Messina*, 1803); and *Wilhelm Tell*

A scene from a play by Iffland, produced at Mannheim in 1786. (An engraving by Heinrich Anton Melchior in *Theater Kalendar auf das Jahr 1788*, Gotha)

(*William Tell*, 1804). *William Tell* was his last play, and is probably still his best-known work.

The tumultuous eighteenth century in the German language areas ended with both storm and stress and sentimentalism gasping out their short lives and German Classicism in firm control. The period had produced three great playwrights, two of whom were still writing and who would go on to make significant contributions in the coming century. August Wilhelm Iffland was already writing, beginning in 1784 with his *Verbrechen aus Ehrsucht* (*Crime from Ambition*), and his plays were huge popular successes, dealing with ordinary men and women idealizing a simple life that was little more than a modified Rousseauian naturalism. Another writer who began his career at the end of the century was August Friedrich von Kotzebue (1761-1819), whose more than two hundred plays would make him one of the greatest influences on drama during the coming century.

SCENIC DESIGN AND COSTUMES

Scenic design in eighteenth century northern Europe was highly restricted in the early years by the lack of permanent, well-equipped theatres. During the first quarter of the century most acting troupes, working in concert halls, inns, fencing rooms, and tennis courts, kept their settings simple out of necessity. Touring companies rarely had more than three basic sets—a pastoral scene, a palace hall, and a cottage. By the middle of the century the settings had become more numerous and a bit more spectacular, but this grew out of the competitive nature of such theatre and the resulting need to in some way outshine rival troupes. However, in the 1770s, with the establishment of a national theatre, major innovations for the production of spectacles were swiftly made.

The first state theatre was established in 1775 at Gotha, out of the old Hamburg National Theatre troupe. The Gotha Court Theatre was a nonprofit enterprise under the direction of Konrad Ekhof (1720-78). Each actor was a state employee with a guaranteed salary and pension rights. The theatre was only moderately successful, in spite of Ekhof's reputation as Germany's finest actor, and it closed, following his death, in 1779.

The Deutsches Nationaltheater in Vienna was the next state theatre to be organized, under the personal supervision of Emperor Joseph II. Usually called the Burgtheater, after the theatre building in which it performed, this group was organized after the model of the Comédie-Française.

A third national theatre was established at Mannheim in 1779 when Karl Theodor moved his court to Munich. As a departing gift to his subjects he established the Hof-und-Nationaltheater under the supervision of Baron von Dalberg. After the 1780s national theatres were established at all the major population centers in the Germanic area.

The effect these national theatre groups had on developing scenic effects was great indeed. The chariot and pole method of scene changing was installed in most permanent theatres, even though it had passed its peak as a technical device. Artists were commissioned to design historically accurate sets for such plays as *Minna von Barnhelm* and *Götz von Berlichingen*. By the end of the century the vogue for bourgeois drama and the excessive dramatic action of the storm and stress school had created a need for practical sets—with some doors and windows that would open, and even such items as practical bridges.

The few attempts at historically accurate costuming in the early part of the century were greeted with audience disdain. The French influence prevailed, and until the 1770s most tragedies were played in French court costumes. Heroes in Classical drama wore a stylized Roman costume and Eastern characters wore the standard turbans and baggy pants. By the 1770s, however, the historical concerns that affected scenic design also influenced costuming, to the point where many authors insisted on writing into their plays, in detail, the types of costume and even the colors that their characters should wear. By the end of the century costuming had still not reached the spectacular accuracy of scenic design, but at least most troupes had become convinced of the necessity for creating individual costumes for different characters instead of pulling all stage clothing out of a trunk.

Opposite. A view, section, and plan of the Stuttgart Opera House designed by the French architect De la Guépierre in 1759. There are no actors on the stage, but the proscenium arch, the forestage, and the orchestra can be seen. (An engraving by Bernard, from Diderot's *Encyclopedie*, Paris, 1751-65)

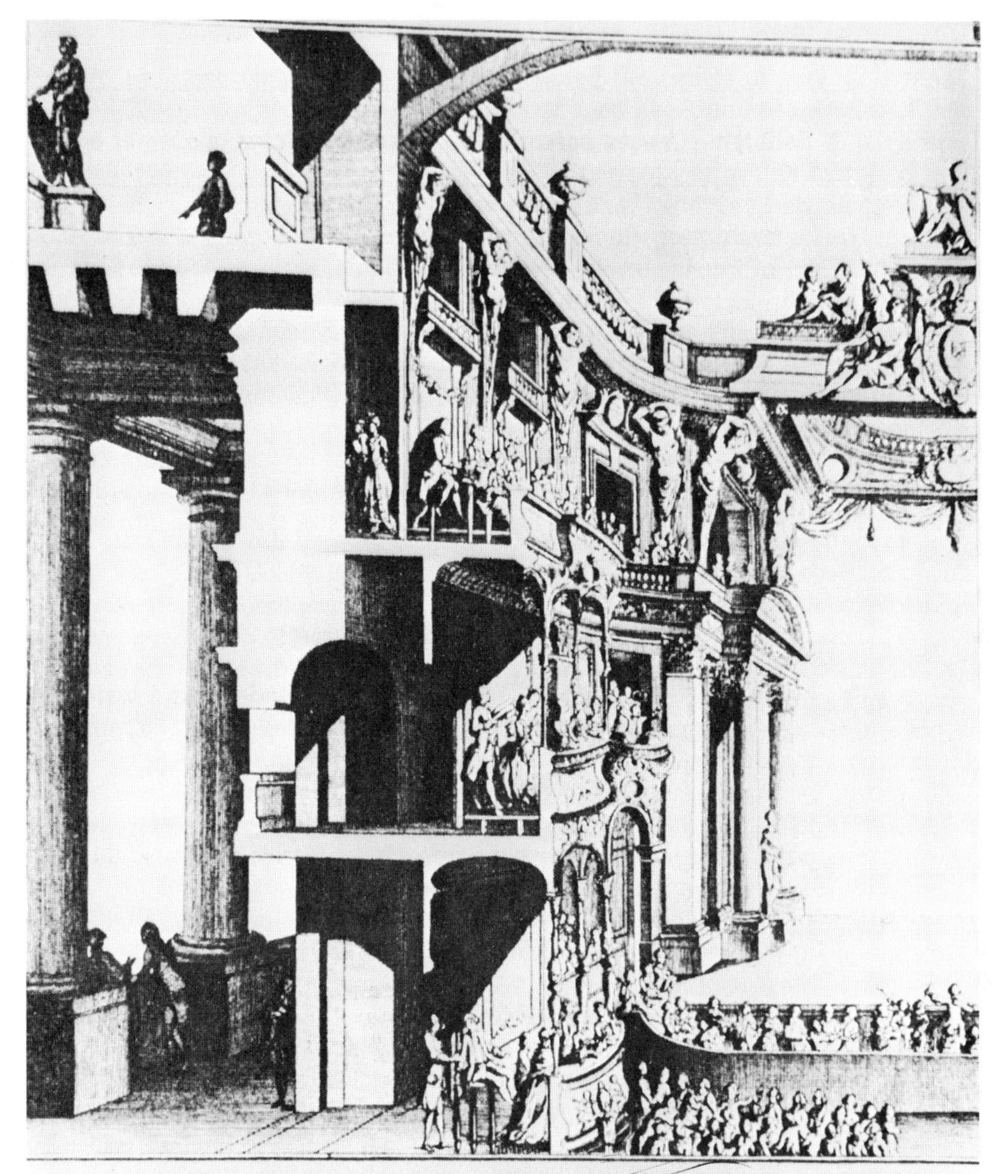

Coupe du nouvel Opéra de Stuttgardt esquissé pour en voir l'effet sans aucunes regles de Perspective

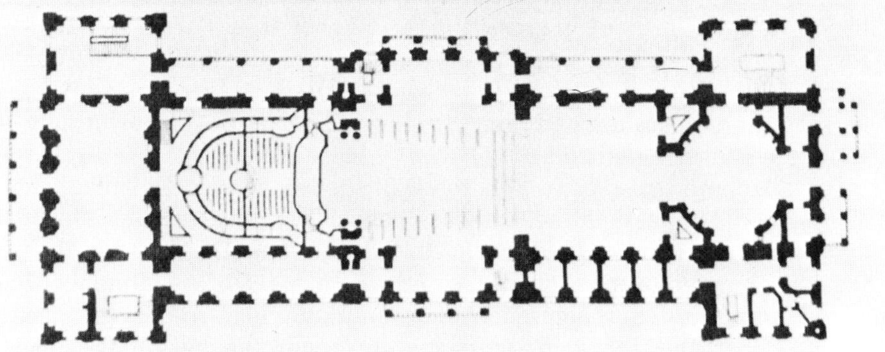

Plan du Projet de la restauration de l'Opéra de Stuttgardt

The Eighteenth Century In Russia

The beginnings of Russian theatre were really not very different from the beginnings of theatre throughout Europe. That is, at pagan (and to some degree, Christian) seasonal rites there were produced a number of folk dramas. The wandering minstrels of western Europe had their counterpart in the Russian *skomorokh,* who sang, displayed trained animals, put on puppet shows, and in some cases acted with troupes of *skomorokhi* put together by rich princes and early tsars.

However, because of Russia's vast geographical distances, its remoteness from European capitals, its political isolation and, indeed, long-lasting political oppression, the history of Russian theatre until the nineteenth century is very spotty.

THE WESTERN INFLUENCE

The history of contemporary Russian theatre—indeed, the history of modern Russia—begins with Peter the Great, who ruled from 1682 to 1725. Peter saw theatre as a kind of propaganda weapon (as it still tends to be viewed in modern Russia) that would help him achieve his ultimate goal of separating Russia from the old Byzantine ways and move her toward Europe. Thus, late in the seventeenth century he imported a German theatrical troupe under the leadership of Johann Kunst.

The idea was good but the execution needed help, and so in 1702, to achieve a larger audience, he moved the Imperial Theatre from the palace grounds to Moscow's Red Square. In 1709, continuing his theatrical bombardment, he established the St. Petersburg Imperial Theatre in his new capital city. Peter's use of the theatre can be seen in the way it aided him to mold public opinion when he decided to get rid of his unlovely empress in favor of an attractive German princess. His theatre produced a version of *Esther* in which the biblical king is shown to have lofty and virtuous motives when he exiles his homely wife and marries in her place a beautiful foreigner.

The Empress Anna (ruled from 1730 to 1740) continued Peter's infatuation with German theatre, importing the Neuber troupe from Leipzig in 1740. However, she was also freer to allow other theatrical influences. *Commedia dell'arte* troupes began to play in western Russia, a few making it as far as Moscow, and the Italian and French ballet companies began performing before enchanted Russian audiences.

Elizabeth (ruled from 1741 to 1762) succeeded Ivan IV (ruled from 1740 to 1741) and her taste in theatre was French. The plays of Corneille, Molière, and Racine soon dominated the stages of the national theatres and the private theatres that had been authorized by Elizabeth in 1750. The influence was pervasive, so that the first significant Russian playwright, Alexander Sumarokov (1718-77), carefully followed French dictates regarding the unities.

Catherine the Great ascended the throne in 1762 and like Peter she quickly began to use the theatre for her own personal ends—to shore up what she was afraid might be a weak hold on the throne. This self-glorification worked well and Catherine became so enamored of theatre that she took to writing plays herself, or at least signing as author some plays written by court poets. She also founded the Bolshoi Theatre in 1779 as another imperial theatre.

Russian theatre remained purely derivative until 1781, when a young playwright named Denis Fonvizin (1745-92) produced the first Russian comedy *Nedorosl* (*The Minor*). The son of a nobleman, Fonvizin had been educated at Moscow University and had subsequently gone to St. Petersburg as court translator, attached to the office of the Supervisor of Theatres. *The Minor* had been completed in the years between 1762 and 1765, when he put it aside in favor of another play, *Brigadir* (*The Brigadier-General*), which he read with great success before the court in 1766. Pleased with his reception he rewrote *The Minor*, a play contrasting the crude, uneducated provincial nobility with the cultured nobles of the court. In his rewrite he sharpened his satiric attack on these corrupt provincial landowners and their politics. However, as this group had a great deal of quiet influence with the court, Fonvizin was disgraced and following the death of his patron in 1783 he was forced to retire from public life.

The Minor remains a small classic of the period, and though it is a bit French in its form, the dialogue and humor are clearly Russian. Thus, the century ended on a promising note for the future of Russian drama—and it was a promise that would be richly fulfilled.

The Eighteenth Century In America

The eighteenth century American theatre was quite limited, and yet it is interesting because it followed the pattern of the American political and social evolution and, in its closing years, it laid a large part of the foundation for the theatre that exists in the United States today.

COLONIAL THEATRE

American theatre, as distinct from any dramatic ritual that might have been produced by the native Indians, began in 1665 when three young men in Virginia Colony were taken into court and accused of the heinous crime of putting on a play. The play was titled *Ye Bare and Ye Cubb* and had been written by William Darby, who was also one of the accused performers. Many inhabitants of the colony were shocked and offended, but the magistrate, an educated and apparently somewhat sophisticated man, found that the young men were "not guilty of fault."

That there was some dramatic activity in the American colonies following *Ye Bare and Ye Cubb* is clear from a few sketchy references, but it was sporadic and slight and the references are mostly unreliable. A man named Richard Hunter, sometime between 1699 and 1702, petitioned for a license to present plays in New York City; the petition was granted but there is no record of subsequent performances and Richard Hunter is not heard from again. In 1703 a traveling player named Anthony Aston wrote that he acted in Charleston and New York, but there is no record of such performances. In 1714 came the first original play to be published in America—*Androboros, a Biographical Farce in Three Acts,* usually attributed to Robert Hunter, the Governor of New York. Whether or not Hunter wrote it is not certain, but it seems likely as the play is a bitter satire that flays all of Hunter's political enemies. In 1716 the first theatre in America was built in Williamsburg, Virginia, for the acting team of Charles and Mary Stagg, but what they played there and with whom is not known. In 1745 the building was converted into a town hall.

In New York, in 1732, Farquhar's comedy *The Recruiting Officer* was performed and in 1735, in Charleston, South Carolina, Otway's tragedy, *The Orphan,* was played in the town courthouse. Charleston also has the honor of being the site of the first opera performed in America. The work, also played in 1735, was called *Flora, or Hob in the Well,* an unpromising title at best. The following year the students at William and Mary College produced Addison's *Cato* and a series of three comedies.

That theatrical production in the American colonies was limited is only too obvious, and the attitude that caused this limitation becomes evident in Boston in 1750 when *The Orphan* was presented in a city coffeehouse. The authorities, up in arms over the abomination of such theatrical performance, quickly passed a law forbidding all forms of theatrical entertainment and establishing fines to be levied against actors and owners of buildings where theatrical performances took place.

The American colonial theatre continued to be just that—a colonial theatre that aped English productions and produced English plays. After all, most of the settlers continued to think of themselves basically as Englishmen residing outside of England. It took the American Revolution to bring an end to that state of mind, and along with this the Revolution—and not Puritan objections—also ended theatre, at least temporarily. In October 1774 the Continental Congress passed a declaration, apparently to promote the war effort, that discouraged "every species of extravagance and dissipation," including "shews, plays, and other expensive diversions and entertainments."

THE EARLY PROFESSIONAL COMPANIES

The first professional company to play in America was a group headed by Walter Murray and Thomas Kean. They made their debut in Philadelphia in 1749 and then moved to New York in 1750, where they played for two seasons before leaving to tour the area of Virginia and Maryland. The company soon faded away, perhaps because of competition from the newer and more lively Hallam company.

William Hallam, a bankrupt London theatre manager, along with his brother and sister-in-law, Mr. and Mrs. Lewis Hallam, their three children, and ten other failed London actors, organized a company based on the sharing plan common to English provincial troupes, to play in the colonies. When they arrived, the troupe, calling themselves the London Company, went to Williamsburg, the capital of the Virginia Colony and a city more well disposed than most to actors. The governor quickly granted their request for permission to perform, and the company moved into the Williamsburg Playhouse, which had been built the previous year to house the touring Murray and Kean company. They remained in Williamsburg from September 1752 until March 1754, when they moved on to Philadelphia. In 1755 they departed for Jamaica, apparently intending to spend one season in the West Indies, but they did not return until 1758, by which time the character of the company had been totally altered.

Lewis Hallam had died shortly after arriving in Jamaica, leaving the troupe without a manager or cosponsor. However, another English troupe, headed by David Douglass, had been in Jamaica since 1751, and Douglass was eager to try his luck in the American colonies. In 1758 he married the widowed Mrs. Hallam, united the two companies, and departed for New York. The company, renamed the American Company because of growing anti-British sentiment, dominated American theatre until the Congressional Declaration in 1774.

POST-REVOLUTIONARY THEATRE

The economic, political, and social upheavals of the Revolution damaged theatre badly, but by the 1780s a theatrical revival was underway. In part this

An engraving of the Chestnut Street Theatre, which Dunlap, among others, characterized as being the finest in the new world. (From *The New York Magazine; or, Literary Repository*, April, 1794)

was sparked by the rapidly growing population. At the beginning of the Revolution there were only about two and a half million people in the colonies; by the end of the century the population had more than doubled. More people meant greater audiences, and the number of professional companies increased markedly.

Most of the new companies were offshoots of the American Company. Popular or dissatisfied members of the troupe departed to found their own competing companies. Thomas Wall left in 1782 to found a company. He was followed in 1785 by Mr. and Mrs. Allen, who established their own company, and by Mr. Godwin who, with a partner named Kidd, also formed a troupe. In 1791 Thomas Wignell, the most famous and popular performer in the company, left to form a partnership with Alexander Reinagle and establish a Philadelphia troupe.

Gradually the early discriminatory theatre laws were repealed. In 1789 Philadelphia canceled its antitheatre laws, and in 1793 Boston, the Puritan stronghold, followed suit. By the end of the century the laws forbidding theatre performances had been repealed in almost every major city. There were still restrictions on the days and hours when theatrical performances could be staged, and on the type of material that could be presented, but essentially the antitheatrical period had come to an end.

By the end of the century the American drama, as opposed to imported British drama, had made a small but important start. In 1767 *The Prince of Parthia,* written by Thomas Godfrey (1736-63), was produced by Douglass' American Company. It was the first major production of a play by a native-born playwright. The play was not a good one, or even especially American in nature. It was modeled on British drama of the Elizabethan period and, indeed, in its mediocre blank verse it contains variations on lines from at least five plays of Shakespeare.

The developing sense of national identity occasioned by the separation from Britain began, very slowly at first, to bring about a truly national drama. In 1767 Thomas Forrest composed *The Disappointed, or the Force of Credulity,* the first American comic opera. It satirized a number of American types and is memorable today only because it was first and because it contained the first American stage Irishman, a figure that would become a staple of comedy for years to come. Robert Munford (c. 1730-84) wrote a play, *The Patriots* (1775), which tried to promote common sense and moderation with both Whigs and Tories, and Mercy Otis Warren (1728-1814) wrote two satires (*The Adulateur,* 1773, and *The Group,* 1775) on her fellow citizens who were sympathetic to the British cause.

It was not until 1787, however, that *The Contrast,* the first truly American drama appeared. Written by Royall Tyler (1757-1826) in three weeks, the play was modeled on the comedic style of Sheridan, specifically on *The School for Scandal,* but its characters and its theme—the foolishness of imitating European styles and manners—are all American.

Born in Boston, Tyler graduated from Harvard, served in the army, and was then admitted to the bar. In New York he met Thomas Wignell, who at that time was still the leading comic actor in the American Company. It was due to Wignell's influence that *The Contrast* was produced at the John Street

A scene from Royall Tyler's *The Contrast*, as recorded by William Dunlap, from the first printed edition of the play.

Theatre. In return for this intercession in behalf of his work, Tyler gave Wignell the copyright of the play, which was published in 1790 with George Washington at the head of the list of subscribers. The play was a great success, though when it played in Boston it had to be disguised under the billing of a "Moral Lecture." Tyler wrote several plays after completing *The Contrast*, but never managed to attain the excellence of his first drama.

Tyler was followed as playwright by William Dunlap, a total man of the theatre who, before ending his career, was able to work successfully as playwright, manager, producer, and theatre historian. More than any other single person he earned the title of "Father of American Theatre."

WILLIAM DUNLAP: William Dunlap (1766-1839) was born the son of a merchant, Samuel Dunlap, in Perth Amboy, New Jersey. He grew up during the Revolutionary War, witnessing the riots, the battles and the eventual victory of the Colonies. At the war's end the Dunlap family, who had fled for their safety, returned to Perth Amboy. There, at the age of thirteen, William went to work as a clerk in the family looking-glass and china shop. The store was quite lucrative, providing Samuel with a comfortable living and William with an easy boyhood. At about this time he began painting portraits; also, having witnessed a production of *The Beaux' Stratagem* given by English soldiers, he began to try his hand at writing dramatic pieces. His father placed him under the tutorship of Leslie and Thomas Steele, but after an accident in which he suffered the loss of his right eye, William went back to clerking for his father. His first dramatic piece was entitled *Arabian Nights*.

In 1783 he met General Washington and painted his portrait. This work encouraged his father to send William to England to study under the famous Benjamin West at the Royal Academy. Upon arrival in England, however, William immediately went to see performances of *The School for Scandal* and *The Critic*, which prompted him to join an eating and drinking club, supporting himself with his father's endowments. William rarely saw Benjamin West, and he later remarked that he had neither the courage nor the fortitude to introduce himself to the Academy.

His father received news of William's two-year vacation and summoned him home. Upon his arrival he continued in his artistic ways, setting up his own studio but receiving few portrait commissions. William's main interest continued to be the theatre, prompting him to write his first comedy, *The Modest Soldier*, which was accepted by several theatre managers but never produced. In spite of a lack of success in his artistic endeavors, William decided to abandon life as clerk and merchant and earn his living as a playwright and painter. He married Elizabeth Woolsey in 1789, the same year that he saw his first plays produced: *The Father, or American Shandyism*, and *Darby's Return*. *The Father* was especially well received.

A scene of the interior of the John Street Theatre in 1767.

From this success Dunlap turned to poetry, becoming one of America's first poets and publishing his works in *American Poems* (1793). One year later he became an anonymous drama critic with the *New York Magazine.* Only two years later, in 1796, he purchased a quarter interest in the John Street Theatre, now run by Hallam and John Hodgkinson, and became comanager of the house and its troupe, the American Company. After two years the company moved to the new Park Theatre where Dunlap soon became the sole manager. During this time he turned to translating plays. His first was *The Stranger* by August Kotzebue, presented in 1798. He also wrote and produced *André* (acted in 1798), a tragedy which Dunlap based on an incident during the War of Independence, thus making it the first native tragedy based on American material. The play tells of the capture and subsequent execution of Major André, a British agent. André is such a good and honest man that the American captain Bland seeks to save him, as do Bland's mother, brothers, and sister. Even André's sweetheart arrives from England to plead for his life. The play was highly patriotic, and the presentation of General Washington made the man seem almost a god. However, it was not successful with audiences because there was no comic relief, the individual speeches tended to run on and on, and the spectacle of Captain Bland dashing his red, white, and blue cockade to the earth was roundly booed.

During Dunlap's life the American theatre elevated itself above the stature of colonial theatre. Boston, by the post-Revolutionary years, had attained enough culture and population to cancel some of the old antitheatre laws and allow theatrical performances. Lewis Hallam and John Hodgkinson had established their company in Boston and sought the services of Dunlap. The theatre was growing in America and they hoped that Dunlap could aid in promoting the respectability of the performing arts. He was given the power to choose plays, establish rules and policies, and decide casting. His initial thrust was to enlighten and uplift the American audience, which he attempted to accomplish by writing plays, managing, acting as theatrical critic, and performing a host of other duties.

The year 1805 saw the decline of Dunlap as theatre owner-manager. His company was declared bankrupt and he retired with his family to his mother's farm in Perth Amboy. However, in 1806 he returned to the Park Theatre to help Thomas A. Cooper, who was more an actor than manager, run the house. This arrangement lasted until 1811, when Dunlap retired from theatre management. He began serving as assistant paymaster-general of the New York Militia in 1814, but after two years he resigned this post to continue his painting. In 1838 he declined reelection to the National Academy because of poor health, and one year later, on September 28, 1839, he died.

Along with writing plays and managing theatrical companies, Dunlap was also America's first theatre historian. *History of the American Theatre* (1832) is simple and straightforward, placing all the facts in strict chronological order and in an easily readable form. He remained largely objective, splicing together the stories he had heard about American theatre's earliest days. His work is invaluable as a resource—almost the only resource—on early American theatre.

A painting by William Dunlap of a scene from *The School for Scandal*, probably as performed at the Southwark Theatre in Philadelphia, 1791.

Dunlap's contributions to periodicals cannot, in most cases, be identified inasmuch as they were published anonymously. Some, however, have been traced by historians through the medium of his diaries. He once started his own magazine, *The Monthly Recorder*, but he found it so dull that he stopped printing after only six months.

As an artist, Dunlap contributed to scenic design in a small but remarkable way. Theatre in America usually took place before minimal, painted scenery consisting of no more than one backdrop. This was due as much to the travel requirements of the companies as to a lack of artisans and proper funds. Dunlap, from what can be ascertained, helped to introduce perspective scene painting, borrowing from what he had learned in England.

The work of William Dunlap was never artistically significant, except perhaps in the case of *André*. But it was far superior to the work being done around him. Because of this distinction alone he stands as an important theatre artist. No American in his time can be said to match him in comedy, tragedy, translations, and adaptations. Dunlap is a major figure, not only for his plays, but also for his history of the early American theatre.

11

The Nineteenth Century

11

The Nineteenth Century

The nineteenth century was an important period of transition for the theatre, opening with the flowering of the Romantic movement and ending with a strong movement toward realistic theatre. At the beginning of the century most drama was provided by a relatively few professional companies, most of which toured for a large part of the year. At the end of the century theatre had become a major business, companies had proliferated, and most theatre centers had several permanent troupes that were in residence the whole year. It was not an important period for the production of great dramatic literature, except at the beginning and closing of the century, but it was a time of change and preparation for the dramatic explosion that would follow.

THE NINETEENTH CENTURY BACKGROUND

From an historical point of view the nineteenth century was packed with significant events and movements. Among these were the ascension of Napoleon as Emperor of France in 1804, his defeat in 1815, and the brief restoration of the French monarchy. A second French revolution followed and a short-lived republic was set up under Louis Napoleon, who became Emperor in 1852. In 1848 both Italy and Germany began to move toward unification, and in 1870-71 both countries were at last united. This was also the century which saw the triumph of the Industrial Revolution.

When Napoleon rose to power in 1800 France was reeling from the excesses of the Revolution. He centralized the administration, making himself supreme ruler. He was conservative in his tax collection, frugal in his government expenditures, and essentially honest in his dealings with the people, ending official corruption. He reformed the legal system with his Napoleonic Code, and he set up a complete system of schools, ranging from elementary schools to the University of Paris. In addition he built highways, drained marshes, and beautified Paris. In 1804 he was crowned Emperor.

A complete history of Napoleon's rule is not in point here, even though what he did had highly significant effects both inside and outside France. In 1813, following the Russian debacle, Napoleon was defeated by a new coalition at Leipzig. He abdicated the throne to become ruler of the Island of Elba. However, he soon escaped the island and again took power in France. In 1815 he was defeated at Waterloo and banished to the Island of St. Helena, where he died in 1821.

Following Waterloo, France restored the Bourbon monarchy and Louis XVIII ascended the throne. Economically the country was in good shape, thanks to Napoleon's nationalization of Church property. The new king began as a liberal, keeping many of Napoleon's reforms, but the assassination of his nephew by a liberal fanatic convinced him that conservatism was the only course, and when he died in 1824 the government was firmly in the hands of the Ultra-Royalist party.

The next king, Charles X, was so repressive in his measures that a revolution seemed imminent and he abdicated in 1830. He was followed by Louis Philippe of Orleans, who also practiced a number of repressive measures. In 1848 a second French revolution took place. Called the February Revolution, it overthrew Louis Philippe and set up a second republic under President Louis Napoleon. In 1852 he was made Emperor.

In Italy the revolutionary spirit of 1848 brought insurrections in a number of major cities, but Austrian troops crushed these small flare-ups. However, Sardinia remained unbowed and in 1859 annexed Lombardy. In 1860 four more states overthrew their princes and voluntarily joined Sardinia. Garibaldi expelled the King of the Two Sicilies from Naples and led southern Italy into the growing union, In 1861 the Kingdom of Italy was created. In 1866 Venetia joined the Kingdom and in 1870, when the Franco-Prussian War broke out the French troops stationed in Rome were withdrawn. The city then became the capital of the new Italian government, and unification was complete.

In Germany 1848 saw the overthrow of the Metternich government at Vienna, and the Prince fled. Revolutionists seized control of Berlin, and the crown of a united Germany was offered to the King of Prussia, who rejected it out of fear that Austria would immediately declare war on the new kingdom. However, the necessity of Prussian leadership in any unification movement was made clear. Finally, William I of Prussia, with his Prime Minister, Bismarck, used war to unite the German states. First he went to war with Denmark, with Austria as his ally, and then with Denmark defeated he immediately started another war with ex-ally Austria. The crisis of war and the Prussian victories drew the German states into the North German Confederation. The name was changed to the German Empire, and the King of Prussia was made Emperor, with Bismarck as Chancellor. The new empire was proclaimed from the Hall of Mirrors at Versailles in 1871.

England in the nineteenth century was, as a result of the wars and insurrections of the previous one hundred years, more politically and economically stable than any other European country. England had become the leading maritime and colonial power in the world, and had also established the strongest capitalistic system. The Industrial Revolution that would strike most countries in the nineteenth century, after political and social unification, had begun during the previous century in England, and her natural resources, especially iron ore and coal, allowed her to outdistance all industrial rivals.

In the United States, following the adoption of the Constitution in 1788, the first part of the century was one of enormous and rapid expansion. Already possessing an abundance of natural resources and unsettled land, the country expanded even more rapidly than the populace, purchasing the Louisiana Territory from France in 1803 and Florida from Spain in 1819. The annexation of Texas led to war with Mexico, but when the war was over the United States not only had control of that state, but also an immense piece of land from Texas to the Pacific Ocean. These two purchases and the annexation led an expansionist drive that finally ended when there was no territory left to conquer.

The slavery that proved economically profitable in the cotton economy of the South was not profitable in the industrial North. People saw its evils and began to demand an end to this inhumane institution. Tension grew between the two sections, finally bringing on the Civil War (1861-65), a bloody conflict eventually won by the antislavery forces, who also stood for preservation of the union. Three amendments to the Constitution officially ended slavery forever.

Following the Civil War the population grew with great rapidity, swelled by succeeding waves of immigrants who were attracted by the potential of employment in the industrializing cities, and the promise of cheap and fertile land. A war with Spain in 1898 over Cuban independence demonstrated the military capability of the United States, added the Philippine Islands and some other smaller territories to the list of colonial possessions, and assured the country of major power status as it entered the twentieth century.

It is against this background of growing nationalism, colonialism, and industrialism that the theatre of the nineteenth century played its role.

The Romantic Movement

The early nineteenth century is probably most distinguished as the period of one of the most pervasive literary movements of all time—Romanticism. Like all *isms*, Romanticism is difficult to pin down regarding all its possible meanings. Its dates, however, are reasonably simple; in most cases it begins just prior to the beginning of the nineteenth century, and is essentially over by the middle of the century. In France it came a bit late and is usually dated from the publication of *De l'Allemagne* (*Of Germany*) by Mme. de Staël (1766-1817), following her visit to Weimar in 1810. In England it begins as early as the 1760s, but as a major movement it is usually dated arbitrarily as beginning in 1798, the year in which Wordsworth published his *Lyrical Ballads*. In Germany Romanticism is identified with the *Sturm und Drang* movement, and becomes a major force right at the turn of the century when, according to tradition, Goethe, Schiller, and some of their writer friends gathered on New Year's Eve, 1799, to toast "the dawn of a new literature."

In most areas of Europe Romanticism burned itself out early. In England it is usually considered over in 1832, the year of Sir Walter Scott's death and only five years before Queen Victoria ascended the throne to put her stamp on English literature for the rest of the century. In France it was over by 1838, when a neoclassical revival seemed imminent. Germany essentially ended its affair with Romanticism in the late 1830s, though in that country the end point is not as neat as it is in France and England. Indeed, there was still a substantial Romantic drama on the German stage until that year of decision, 1848.

The "Battle of Hernani" that took place on the opening night of Hugo's romantic play at the Comédie Française, February 25, 1830. (Painting by Albert Besnard, Paris, Victor Hugo Museum)

To define Romanticism is much more difficult than dating it. Victor Hugo said, far too simply, that it was "nothing more than liberalism in literature," and others have called it the "predominance of the emotional life" and even "literary antiauthoritariansim." These are all true, but they are only aspects of a movement, rather than the movement itself. In its broadest sense, Romanticism represents a tendency to represent life as it is not—that is, it distorts the real world in order to escape from it. Thus, Romanticism stands opposed to realism. Romanticism is also the product of the artist seeking to express himself outside of and even in defiance of the established artistic rules. In this sense, Romanticism is the opposite of Classicism.

THE CASTLE SPECTRE;

A DRAMATIC ROMANCE IN FIVE ACTS.—BY M. G. LEWIS.

An illustration of "Monk" Lewis' *Castle Spectre*, the greatest of the Gothic dramas.

In any case, Romanticism in all countries and at all times (for Romantic traits exist to some degree in nearly all literature) has displayed at least five major tenets. The first is faith in the imagination. This meant that the artists were willing to make reason subordinate to feeling and intuition, and to substitute new artistic forms for the older, stylized methods. Faith in the individual was the second tenet, and this was clearly a result of the growing new idealism that had already resulted in the American and French revolutions. It also reflected the steadily growing humanitarianism evident in such revolutionary commonplaces as "life, liberty, and the pursuit of happiness," and "liberty, equality, fraternity." Third was an intense interest in the past, especially the Medieval or Gothic period. The continuing discoveries of the archaeologists and the increasing influence of such literary antiquarians as Walter Scott helped elevate this curiosity about times past into an aspect of literary style. Fourth was a growing interest in nature as a positive force in man's existence. The theories of Rousseau were popularized and nature was conceived of as "good," in opposition to society, which was "bad." This was, of course, part and parcel of the Romantic rebellion against the immediate past and its institutions. It also reflected, perhaps, a fear of the growing industrial age and the sudden need of man to compete with machines. And last was the belief in the "Free Man." The concept of the rebel or outlaw standing outside the evil influence of society and thus "good" was something that the great romantics—Byron, Goethe, and Hugo—all believed in implicitly. This dedication to individualism was Rousseauian, and it was also anticlassical in that it tended to view man in isolation and as a creature of emotion instead of man as part of a social order and a creature of reason.

Finally, the Romantic movement did not produce great drama, but it managed to free theatre from the bonds of Classicism, and that was a necessary service if theatre was to move on toward the new genres yet to come.

The Nineteenth Century In France And Southern Europe

France When the French Revolution came to an end, many new theatres sprang up, most designed to attract their audiences from the masses. As a result, a number of new, light theatrical forms became popular, such as comic opera, vaudeville, and melodrama. This last was especially popular in the boulevard theatres, and by way of its best practitioners (especially Guilbert de Pixérécourt, who was theatrically active from 1797 to 1835) provided a substantial basis for the later Romantic drama.

The French theatre of the nineteenth century falls rather neatly into three distinct periods: first is the age of Romantic melodrama, from just before the turn of the century until the 1840s; second is the midcentury development of realistic melodrama; and third is the period of naturalistic and symbolistic drama that came late in the century.

NINETEENTH CENTURY FRENCH DRAMA

Following the Revolution and the subsequent development of a semiliterate and sometimes even illiterate mass audience for theatrical productions, it was the boulevard theatres, frowned upon by the theatrical establishment, that developed the first of the popular new dramatic forms—melodrama. Melodrama was not totally new; aspects of it had been incorporated into a number of dramatic genres as far back as Classical Greece, but it was in the boulevard theatres that for the first time all of the traditional crowd-pleasing elements were incorporated into one dramatic package.

The term "melodrama" did not come into use until the form had already been set—about 1800—and it is descriptive only of a part of the form it identifies: "mélo" from the Greek *melo(s)*, meaning song, plus "drama." In its earliest form, melodrama meant a slight but exciting tale in which virtue is pitted against evil, and virtue only triumphs after overcoming a series of hazards designed to thrill audiences. To complement these slender and often episodic plots, the writers of melodrama added music and song, spectacle, and such plot incidents as disguisings, coincidence, and concealed identity. Eventually, as production costs mounted and the vogue for melodrama spread to Germany,

A French melodrama as illustrated by Daumier.

England, and the United States, the music and spectacle were played down and the term was applied to popular plays which featured such devices as hairbreadth escapes, unjust suffering, poetic justice, and happy endings.

Essentially the melodrama tends to be lurid rather than quiet; it is sentimental, emotional, and exaggerated rather than intellectual and restrained. Basically it can be said that melodrama is related to tragedy in the same degree that farce is related to high comedy.

The foremost practitioner of melodrama, and the man to whom the title "Father of Melodrama" is often given, was René-Charles Guilbert de Pixérécourt (1773-1844). Alone or in collaboration he wrote nearly one hundred twenty plays, at least fifty of which are truly melodramas. Pixérécourt had survived the Revolution and done some casual writing, but in the 1790s, penniless and with a wife and child to support, he began writing in earnest. He had written sixteen plays, some of which had been accepted by various theatres but not yet produced, when in 1797 the Ambigu-Comique staged his *Les petits auvergnats* (*The Children from Auvergne*). It was quite successful, and in the following year he produced *Victor, ou L'enfant de la forêt* (*Victor, Child of the Forest*). It was the first of the long series of melodramas for which he is remembered.

Melodrama held the French stage in thrall through the first quarter of the nineteenth century, and then it was replaced by a Romantic drama that used many of the melodramatic devices to assure its own popularity.

While the boulevard theatres were offering their mass audiences a menu of essentially light entertainment, the Comédie-Française continued to supply its establishment audience with the standard fare of neoclassical tragedies and prerevolutionary comedies. Neither was wholly satisfactory—the first often lacked substance and the second often lacked charm—and a change in the theatrical diet was badly needed. This change began in 1827 when Victor Hugo (1802-85) published *Le préface de Cromwell*, the first theatrically oriented manifesto of Romantic doctrine. Mme. de Staël's *Of Germany,* which described in glowing terms the Romantic movement at Weimar, was suppressed until 1814, but following that date it was openly distributed and led to a widespread debate between Romanticists and Classicists. Stendhal (Henri Beyle, 1783-1842) joined the controversy on the side of Romanticism, arguing that the plays of Shakespeare were more suitable models for emulation than the plays of Racine.

Hugo agreed with Stendhal. He had attended, in 1822, some performances of Shakespeare by a traveling English troupe, and was so impressed that he began to seek contemporary equivalents for the older drama. He envisioned, especially, historical plays that would be produced with all the richness of costume and scenic design that had been denied the earlier playwrights. These plays would be full of color and passion, and most importantly they would not be restricted by the neoclassical concept of the unities. Instead they would be free to move through time and space, and to mix tragic and comic genres in support of a noble theme. These plays, he felt, should emphasize the Romantic hero in the tradition already solidly established by Byron in England. That is, they would feature an individualist, set apart from society for unjust reasons, engaged in a worthy quest, and inspired by the highest form of love for either a pure heroine or his own or his family's honor.

The Classic versus Romantic controversy came to a head in 1830 when Hugo's *Hernani* opened at the Comédie-Française to howls of audience support or disgust, and with fights between the spectators a regular occurrence. For forty-five nights the noisy fracas continued, often completely drowning out the actors onstage. Both sides were adamant, perhaps because they sensed, quite rightly, that this play represented a turning point in theatre. At length the

A scene from the original 1830 production of Hugo's *Hernani.* This sketch shows less excessive Romanticism in both costumes and sets than might have been expected—in fact, the overall feeling is one of simplicity and reality.

Romantics triumphed. It was, however, a short-lived success, and by 1843 when Hugo's *Les burgraves* (*The Governors*) failed critically and at the box office, the movement was essentially over.

Victor Hugo, who contained in himself something of the philosopher, was the acknowledged leader of the Romantic movement, but Alexandre Dumas *père* (1803-70) was the better dramatist. A highly successful novelist (for which he is best remembered today) and one of the truly great storytellers of all time, Dumas *père* was also a brilliant and inventive Romantic dramatist. His *Henri III et sa cour* (*Henry III and His Court*) was performed in 1829, the year before *Hernani* was almost howled off the stage, and audiences were quite willing to accept it, perhaps because of his outstanding reputation as a novelist. He began by writing vaudevilles, but the historical romance was his forte in drama, just as it was in the novel. His *Antony* (1831) was produced at the Théâtre de la Porte-Saint-Martin and was extremely successful. He followed this with his most popular work, *La tour de Nesle* (*The Tower of Nesle*, 1832), which had more sheer terror, rapid action, and (eventually) corpses, than almost any work before or since.

Probably the most unusual talent of any Romantic playwright was displayed by Alfred de Musset (1810-57), whose plays (all but one, his first one-act, *La nuit vénitienne*, translated as *A Venetian Night*) were written to be read rather than staged. Musset was, first and foremost, a poet and his short affair with the dramatic genre came fairly late in his all too brief career.

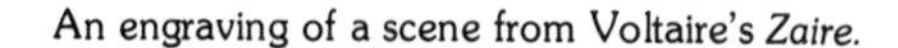
An engraving of a scene from Voltaire's *Zaire*.

ALFRED DE MUSSET: Alfred de Musset, generally considered the youngest of the great French Romantic poets, was born in 1810 and, creatively speaking, matured early. As early as 1828 he had been pronounced a prodigy by Alfred Victor de Vigny and by that master of French Romanticism, Victor Hugo. This judgment seemed to receive support from Musset's first volume of verse, *Les contes d'Espagne et d'Italie* (*Tales of Spain and Italy*, 1830), which received much favorable notice; perhaps too much, for in it he imitated the popular exotic melodrama and, as a result, during his lifetime he was unable to escape being characterized as the daring young Romantic who was unafraid to describe the moon as "a dot on an i."

In 1831 Musset left popular Romanticism behind him, publicly eschewing exoticism and political-social idealism for a poetic, though highly Romantic, realism. Indeed, in his best dramatic work he attacks the Church, traditional education, civil law, and Romanticism with equal vigor. Unlike his fellow Romantics, who devoted themselves to literature with a capital *L*, Musset devoted himself to life with a capital *L*—and perhaps this is just as well, for his creative life, at least, proved very short indeed.

The years from 1833 to 1837 are easily the most important in Musset's artistic career, for they encompass the beginning and the end of his liaison with George Sand. This affair, which ran alternately hot and cold for both parties, was the most important and formative emotional experience of Musset's young life. Like Rousseau in impassioned pursuit of his elusive noble savage, Musset spent a large part of this four years in urgent pursuit of his ideal woman, convinced that finding her was indeed possible and would resolve all of life's problems. For Musset, and for so many other young writers of the period, romantic love—that is, love between man and woman—was the ultimate reality and desired end of human experience. Musset, after his first encounter with the magnetic personality of George Sand, felt that he had found his ideal. The "ideal woman," however, proved all too human, and after a series of stormy confrontations, usually provoked by George's procession of lovers, there was a permanent break between them. Following this break Musset shared a brief passion with Aimée d'Alton in 1837; suffered through a period of unrequited love for Princess Belgioioso in 1841; and entered into an extended affair with his final and greatest love—the bottle.

Musset wrote most of his major works early in his life (several volumes of poetry, an analytical novel titled *Confession d'un enfant du siècle*, translated as *Confessions of a Child of the Century*, a number of short tales, and seven or eight plays). This was, at least in part, because by the time he reached the age of thirty he had found the dream of an ideal love to be, if not false at least unattainable, and the search for purely physical pleasure both boring and futile.

Though Musset thought of himself primarily as a poet, which seems justified in view of the fact that most of the recognition he achieved during his lifetime was for his poems, the works which have best survived the test of time have been his plays. His first dramatic work to be produced, a short and floridly dramatic melodrama titled *A Venetian Night*, had been whistled off the stage, and Musset made a public vow never again to write for such a rude audience. He kept his vow, writing his subsequent plays for readers rather than for a public audience. This decision ultimately proved to be a wise one, for he was thus able to ignore the strictures of his own stage and avoid the problems inherent in the well-made play.

The dramatic form was, essentially, a perfect one for Musset, in that the requirements of intelligible dialogue forced him to avoid the overly Romantic sentimentalism that characterized so much of his poetry. Also, the drama forced him to deal directly with its characters, and thus his plays are concerned *first* with people who, in their actions, manage to make evident the moral truths that tend to get lost in the excesses of his poetry. Indeed, because his characters are true and take precedence over philosophy, these moral truths are never overstated and come through not as moral philosophy but as truths of the human heart.

In displaying the human heart, however, Musset's plays are often far from pleasant exercises. He believed that the selfishness, deceits, and myriad daily cruelties that humans practice on their fellows, even those they love, can turn the very act of living into a horrible nightmare. Thus, we can imagine him saying with his Perdican: "Oh, this life itself is such a painful dream. Why should we mingle our own dreams with it?"

Musset's plays are often painful and are never really hopeful, but they illuminate life's universal problems and they point the way out of the Romantic period.

By 1838 the Romantic movement was already losing momentum, which became obvious when the best known actress of the day, Elisa Félix Rachel, ap-

A scene from Balzac's *Mercadet* performed in 1871 at the Théâtre Gymnase, Paris. (Bibliothèque de l'Arsenal)

peared as Camille in a revival of Corneille's *Horace*. This proved so successful that she went on to do a number of such neoclassical works. In 1843, while Hugo's *Les Burgraves* was failing, a production of *Lucrèce*, a second-rate neoclassical tragedy by François Ponsard (1814-67) was warmly received.

Perhaps the most ironic aspect of the early death of Romanticism was that the two greatest Romantic plays were still unwritten. Alexandre Dumas *fils* (1824-95), the illegitimate son of Dumas *père*, dramatized his Romantic novel, *La dame aux camélias* (usually translated in English as *Camille*) and produced it in 1852. It was an astounding success, coming nearly ten years after the Romantic period was over, and it remained one of the most popular dramas of the latter half of the nineteenth century. Also, in 1897, some fifty years after the close of the Romantic period, Edmond Rostand's (1868-1918) *Cyrano de Bergerac* was produced. The play is still regularly done and stands as a monument to all the things that the early Romantics were trying to achieve.

While the Romantic drama could never be described as realistic, it did contribute in several ways to the rise of realism during the middle of the century. It modified the alexandrine in which earlier serious plays had been written, and which had been codified for all tragedy; it introduced a whole new vocabulary previously frowned upon as lacking tragic dignity, which made it easier to write realistic dialogue; and it completely destroyed the slavish attitudes about the necessity to follow Classical precepts and unities. As a result, even while Romanticism held the stage the new, more realistic style of play was gradually gaining recognition, so that by the time the Romantic drama faded away a new dramatic genre was set to take stage center.

The Classical revival that seemed ready to succeed the Romantic movement never fully developed, perhaps because it was never more than a curiosity, a necessary antidote for the excesses of Romanticism, or perhaps because the genre was still beset with the problems that had led to its downfall soon after the Revolution. Instead a new genre made its appearance, led by Eugène Scribe and his somewhat less illustrious successor Victorien Sardou. The genre that Scribe devised and popularized was called the "well-made play."

Essentially the well-made play contained nothing new. Rather, it was a compendium of the best dramatic devices from the history of Western theatre. In recent years the term has been used in a pejorative sense, but what it meant for Scribe and his followers was a formula, based on the best examples, for creating good drama. It simplified structure by using only three acts; exposition was used with great care to set up the action; all events grew out of a cause-effect relationship; scenes were carefully built to achieve a peak of suspense, and these peaks were carefully built to a climax; the most popular dramatic devices, such as screen scenes, reversals, misunderstandings, and wrong identification were used to create suspense.

EUGÈNE SCRIBE: Alexander Dumas père once said of Eugène Scribe (1791-1861), "He was a marvelous juggler." This statement rather succinctly sums up the essence of Scribe; he is known for his manner of juggling plot and situation rather than for his philosophical or moral concepts.

Eugène Scribe was one of the most prolific and versatile writers of all time. His writings comprise over sixty volumes and won him a seat in the highly selective French Academy. Scribe's most important contribution, however, was not so much the quality of his plays but rather his formula for the well-made play. This formula has influenced the playwrights in and near his own time such as Dumas *fils* and Sardou, as well as such modern writers as Ibsen, Shaw, Wilde, and Miller. Many playwrights and critics since Scribe have criticized the nature of his well-made play, yet while criticizing Scribe they have often used his formula themselves. One such playwright was Emile Zola, the founder of naturalism. Although his philosophy was diametrically opposed to the philosophy of the well-made play, Zola was not above using Scribe's techniques in his own work; *Thérèse Raquin*, his best drama, was well-knit and contained exposition, climax, and denouement in the most approved Scribian style.

Scribe was born in 1791 and began to write for the stage before he was twenty. He was not an instant success, and it took fourteen failures before he wrote his first hit. One of his many talents was obviously perseverance. His early plays were attempts to imitate such playwrights as Picard and Duval, but soon Scribe started to write in his own style about contemporary events. His first "human interest" play to attract attention was *Une nuit de la Garde Nationale* (*A Night With the National Guard*, 1815) which was really a vaudeville in one act. Because it poked fun at the currently fashionable citizen-soldier the play caused some turmoil. However, the play made people laugh and Scribe began to file the devices for future reference, thus beginning to establish a set pattern for writing plays.

Between 1820 and 1830 Scribe achieved his greatest output. During this time he completed more than one hundred fifty pieces, most of which were vaudevilles. He enlarged the one-act vaudeville form into three acts, developing the little vignettes of everyday life into comedies. He tried to develop these three-act comedies into drama, but in this he was unsuccessful.

Scribe relied on situation rather than on character development, getting his characters in and out of intrigues mostly because of ingenious situation manipulation rather than their own internal qualities. For this reason, Scribe's characters, like those of the *commedia dell'arte*, developed into stock types. Like the *commedia*, Scribe emphasized plot and situation rather than character and dialogue. However, unlike the *commedia* there was no improvisation.

Scribe was an eclectic, borrowing from anything he could find. He took from his contemporaries as well as from playwrights of the past, and he even borrowed from himself, doing his own plays over and over again—rewriting them until they worked. To achieve this volume, Scribe had numerous collaborators, some of whom became famous in their own right. His critics, of course, accused him of running a "play-factory."

Although Scribe's plays were very popular and made him a great deal of money, time has not dealt kindly with them. He tended to rely on witty, pointed puns, and on jokes pertaining to the immediate period in which he lived, and thus what seemed so alive to his own contemporary audiences seems dead to later periods. He wrote to be immediately popular, which he was, and did not venture into any kind of noteworthy experimentation, using what he knew from experience to be successful.

Scribe was conscious of the fact that a good plot alone can draw the public, yet what he apparently did not know was that in time, unless a play contains characters who are human, it will die. For example, Molière's plots are for the most part contrived, but such characters as Tartuffe will always be remembered. Today, nobody remembers any of Scribe's characters; his immortality is not in his plays, but rather in his structural concepts.

The well-made play tends to be a bit like Mark Twain's weather; that is, everybody talks about it, but very few people ever bother to find out exactly what it is. In his introduction to *Camille and Other Plays*, Stephen Stanton defines the form quite neatly:

> *First, the well-made play contains a plot which is based on a secret that is known to the audience, but that is withheld from certain characters. The secret is revealed and this is the climactic point. At this moment the antagonist is exposed and the protaganist is restored to dignity and gets his just deserts.*
>
> *Second, the first act is almost entirely composed of exposition, while the remainder of the plot uses contrived entrances, exits, letters and props to increase the suspense.* The Glass of Water, *for example, is a play in which a large percentage of the action revolves around a particular prop.*
>
> *Third, the hero has a series of failures and successes which are caused by his battle with the villain. Therefore, the action tends to hang in the balance between these two poles and switches from one side to the other throughout the action and up to the climactic point.*
>
> *Fourth, there are discovery scenes in which the antagonist learns of secrets which can usually hurt the protagonist in some way. The protagonist does not know until later on that the antagonist knows as much as he does.*
>
> *Fifth, there is a misunderstanding that is known to the audience, but that is unknown to the participants. This increases suspense and anxiety on the part of the audience.*
>
> *Sixth, there is a believable and logical denouement.*
>
> *Seventh, there is a repetition of the general action pattern in the individual acts themselves.*

Scribe did not invent any really new aspect of drama. Rather, he gathered techniques and ideas, arranged them, and then used all of them all the time. For this he was roundly damned by some of his contemporary playwrights, and copied by others. Certainly his facile structure led to much superficial drama, but some fine playwrights, such as Ibsen and Shaw to name just two of many, have made use of Scribe's technique.

The degree to which critical venom or flattering imitation would bother Scribe is open to question, as his only measuring stick for success was the box office. Pleasing the public, which he did as well or better than any other playwright, was his ultimate concern.

Scribe, the master of the form, was followed by Victorien Sardou (1831-1908). His first successful play was a comedy, *Les pattes de mouche* (1860, usually translated as *A Scrap of Paper*), but he also wrote a number of histori-

A 1901 revival of Sardou's *Patrie,* with a highly realistic, almost overwhelming street setting.

cal dramas, the best of which is probably *Madame Sans-Gêne* (*Madam Devil-May-Care,* 1893). Sardou is usually underrated, yet many of his plays were written expressly for Sarah Bernhardt and contained great acting roles. Sardou wrote in nearly every known dramatic genre, and he was perhaps the most uniformly successful playwright of his century. However, the critics have complained that most of his characters lack life, and recent audiences have tended to agree, with the result that his plays are now rarely seen onstage.

The well-made play certainly dominated the midcentury French stage, but the greatest drama of the period came from two playwrights who borrowed the basic structure, but not the internal devices, to create their "thesis" or "problem" plays. The two men were Alexandre Dumas *fils* and Emile Augier (1820-89).

Emile Augier was, along with François Ponsard, one of the first major dramatists to rebel against the excesses of the Romantic movement. His first play, *La cigüe* (*Hemlock,* 1844) was produced at the Odéon, and with its success Augier gave up the study of law and began to make his living as a dramatist. His first few plays followed the traditional verse format, but he soon switched to prose, writing domestic social dramas—problem plays—that dealt with the questions of the time. His best-known work in France is probably *Le gendre de Monsieur Poirier* (*Mr. Poirier's Son-in-Law,* 1854), but in English *Le mariage d'Olympe* (*Olympe's Marriage,* 1855) is perhaps best known. In this play Augier takes the basic situation created by Dumas *fils* in *Camille,* allows the prostitute to marry into a respectable family, and then displays the lamentable result.

Although Zola, the naturalist, despised Augier's dramas, Jules Lemaître (1854-1914), a far better critic, enjoyed them. Augier was always more of a realist than either Dumas *fils,* Scribe, or Sardou, and in such work as *Les lionnes pauvres* (*A False Step,* 1858), which displayed the breakup of a family because of the wife's adultery, and *Les effrontés* (*Faces of Brass,* 1861) and *Le fils de Giboyer* (*Giboyer's Son,* 1862), both political comedies, he tackled serious domestic and civil problems.

Dumas *fils* was almost the literary opposite of his famous father, who seems to have had no real influence on his son's career. His first theatrical work was the dramatization of *La dame aux camélias* (*Camille*), but this Romantic tale of the repentant consumptive courtesan who coughs out her life was unique in terms of his total dramatic output. Following the enormous success of this first play, Dumas *fils* turned to the thesis or problem play, using the stage as a pulpit for expounding on social problems. While he was himself an agnostic, Dumas *fils* nevertheless sought to promote Christian morality through his dramas. As a child he had been brought up in the free-thinking society of artists that surrounded his father, and his reaction to it was bitter indeed. In fact, he gave this group a permanent title in his play, *Le demi-monde* (1855). His obsession with his own illegitimacy provoked *Le fils naturel* (*The Illegitimate Son,* 1858), and his relationship with his father resulted in *Un père prodigue* (*A Prodigal Father,* 1859). He aired the social problems of the day in *La question d'argent* (*A Question of Money,* 1857), *L'étrangère* (*The Foreigner,* 1876), and *Francillon* (1887), his last work. The prescription he offered for almost all social ills was the united, supportive family unit, perhaps because he had never had such a family situation and was romantically mourning its loss. In any case, like so many others of their kind, his problem plays tended to die when the problem that provoked them no longer existed. Today he is remembered only for his great Romantic drama, because the character of Marguerite Gautier transcends period and type and style.

While the first realistic plays in the middle of the century were dominated by the well-made play form, the latter half of the century saw the first stirring of a new movement that would mark the beginning of modern drama. The new movement was naturalism, an aspect of realism that had been evolving in the novels of Emile Zola. The world had been shocked, excited, and intrigued when Charles Darwin (1809-82) published his *Origin of Species* in 1859. His ideas on the relationship between the evolution of species and the environment was taken up, simplified, popularized, and turned into a school of thought sometimes known as "social Darwinism." The social Darwinists held that men, like the animals Darwin had studied, were purely and simply products of their environment—and this idea, in the hands of Zola and some of his fellow artists, turned into naturalism.

The relationship between dramatic realism and naturalism is a close one, but there are some areas where they differ. Realism, as a form, has no philosophical axe to grind. The only requirement for realistic theatre is that whatever is treated onstage must match the offstage reality. Thus, realism can deal with kings and millionaires or, at the other extreme, workers or tramps, and the only requirement is that they be dealt with fairly in terms of their own particular reality. Naturalism, on the other hand, begins with the philosophical proposition that man is purely the product of the total (physical, social, and economic) environment. Thus, for anyone except another naturalist, reality must be bent in order to display dramatic evidence of the philosophical proposition. Such beliefs were part of the growing faith in the new and rapidly expanding scientific establishment. People in all areas of endeavor, looking at the experiments of the physiological researchers, decided that science and not art offered the best hope of understanding man.

EMILE ZOLA: The opening gun of the naturalistic revolution was sounded when Zola dramatized his novel *Thérèse Raquin* (1867). The play was staged in 1873, and while it failed as a play it did make possible the later naturalistic works of such playwrights as Henry Becque. In subject, *Thérèse Raquin* came very close to the traditional domestic tragedy established by *Arden of Feversham* more than two hundred years earlier, dealing with an unfaithful wife and her lover who, together, kill her husband. Then, somewhat like the wife in *A Woman Killed with Kindness* (by Thomas Heywood), they are overcome by their guilt and commit suicide.

But if the play failed aesthetically, Zola's "Preface" did not fail in its purpose. Essentially it was a manifesto calling for a naturalistic revolution in theatre. Zola demanded the scientific study of heredity and environment on stage. That is, the stage could become a laboratory for the scientific dissection of the human condition, especially the condition of the lower middle class, where naturalistic theory seemed most clearly borne out. The views he expressed were not so much Zola's own original thoughts as an expression of the views of Auguste Comte (1798-1857), the positivist, and Hippolyte Taine (1828-93), the historian who saw the past in terms of environmental determinism.

Emile Zola (1840-1902), the acknowledged leader of the nineteenth century naturalistic movement, was born during his family's temporary residence in Paris. They then returned to Aix-en-Provence, where his father was a civil engineer. As a youth, Emile idolized such Romantic authors as Victor Hugo and Alfred de Musset. In secondary school he became a friend of Paul Cézanne (1839-1906), who sparked an early interest in painting. At seventeen, ten years after his father's death, Emile returned to Paris with his mother in hopes of overcoming financial difficulties through the aid of friends. He left school at nineteen to seek employment and finally, at twenty-two, he found a job with the publishing firm known as Hachette. Here he met Hippolyte Taine and other authors, and these associations were an important aid to the publication of his first works.

Zola's continued relationship with Cézanne enhanced his interest in painting. Between 1865 and 1868 Zola's main influences were, in general, ideas derived from the impressionist painters and the rapidly expanding realm of science. As a result of this he renounced his early Romantic leanings in favor of a literature based on the study of reality. His first critical work on writing appeared in 1865, disparaging traditional values in literature and espousing ostensibly new ideas. His argument for exposing truth, no matter how ugly, brought him his first public attention, and in 1866 he embarked on a career in writing, encouraged by contracts for newspaper articles and the success of his early stories.

Zola first wrote of "experimental" theatre in 1873 for *Le Bien Public*. "Experimental" literature as he used it was analogous to scientific experimentation. By this time the word *naturalism* was a fairly common term meaning a literary form based on observation and experimentation. But if Zola did not invent the accepted literary meaning of the term, he did manage to shift its emphasis toward the growth of scientific observation and experimentation in all disciplines.

Zola believed that experimental medicine as formulated and practiced by Claude Bernard could be used in the literary examination of character and society, and the object was to study the social manifestation and then trace its underlying root by discovering the way in which they are related. Zola, however, strongly disagreed with Bernard's statement, provoked by what he considered to be an artistic invasion of the scientific realm, that artistic creation is personal and spontaneous and has nothing to do with the scientific observation of phenomena. The literary naturalist, Zola said, must display the same scientific objectivity as a biologist, limiting himself to recreating life as he observes it, without favoring any of his characters and without making judgments of right or wrong.

Zola's doctrine was a product of the nineteenth century's worship of science as the tool for discovering truth, and its ultimate result was a view of the human personality as the end result of its genes, its racial instincts, and the effects of the physical and social environment. Humans were reduced in this view to objects subject to natural law, that would respond to laboratory tests in the same specific and thus predictable way as chemicals. Morality, from this point of view, has no special significance and is merely an arbitrary by-product of the blind workings of nature.

Zola's primary influence on the theatre of his time came by way of his critical articles which appeared in the Paris press from 1876 to 1881. He cried out against traditional theatrical conventions that reduced the horizons of the stage, arguing that the theatre should be as free as the novel. The Romantics, he felt, had overthrown the Classical stereotypes and forms and now the naturalists must attack the self-limiting concepts of morality that opposed reality in the theatre. The contempt in which he held sympathetic characters and conclusions in which virtue is rewarded helped to do away with the sentimental drama and bring on the work of such writers as Becque and Strindberg and Ibsen.

Zola's first important play, *Madeleine* (1865), was not produced until 1889. *Les mystères de Marseille* (*Mysteries of Marseille*, 1867), based on his *La confession de Claude*, was written and produced in collaboration with Marius Roux and was Zola's first play to be produced. It was a trite and even silly play, written only to make money, and its well-deserved failure taught Zola a far greater respect for theatre. His next two plays were *Thérèse Raquin*, based

A contemporary sketch of André Antoine's Théâtre Libre production of Ibsen's *The Wild Duck*. (From Rudolphe Darzens, *Le Théâtre-Libre Illustré*, Paris, 1890)

on the novel of the same name, and *Les héritiers Rabourdin* (*The Rabourdin Heirs*, 1874). These were far more serious tries than his earlier efforts but failed to win critical acclaim, probably because in spite of his principles his plays are little more than domestic tragedies. Becoming irked at the failure of his plays, in contrast to the great success of his novels, he wrote a farce, *Le bouton de rose* (*The Rosebud*), which was an expression of his contempt for the dramatic genre which failed to appreciate his talent.

Between 1865 and 1889 Zola wrote five plays that were produced and published (*Madeleine, Thérèse Raquin, Les héritiers Rabourdin, Le bouton de Rose* and *Renée*). In addition, eighteen of his prose works, of which seventeen were produced and eleven published, were translated into dramatic form. In spite of this output, Zola never won the popular appeal he so badly wanted.

Although Zola wanted greatly to write for the theatre he was generally unsuccessful, probably because he was never truly a theatre person and he never understood the limitations of naturalism on the stage. He died leaving plans for an immense cycle of plays, but he never was able to encompass the diversity of life that must be created as the essence of the dramatic experience.

Zola was followed by a number of gifted writers who worked in the naturalistic form, but none approached the genius of Henry Becque (1837-99). A misanthropic and quarrelsome man, Becque began his literary career with a libretto (1867) for the composer Joncières. His first play was a four-act comedy, *L'enfant prodigue* (*The Prodigal Son*, 1868), and this was followed by *Michel Pauper* (1870), a fine play that was ignored until its revival in 1886. In 1882, Becque wrote *Les corbeaux* (*The Vultures*) the first of the two great naturalistic plays on which his reputation is based. The second play, *La Parisienne* (*The Woman of Paris*) was written in 1885. Both plays presented rapacious and amoral characters in the *tranche de vie* (slice of life) manner prescribed by Zola, even though Becque disagreed with much of Zola's philosophy. Becque battled long to get the plays produced, and it was not until André Antoine (1858-1943) provided a new stage for them that Becque received his full due as a dramatist.

Naturalism, as a viable dramatic form, continued well into the twentieth century, but in the closing years of the nineteenth century it was challenged by a new and seemingly even more revolutionary form of theatre, the symbolist drama. Paul Fort's (1872-1962) Théâtre d'Art was producing a new type of drama based on the discoveries and theories of the symbolist poet Stéphane Mallarmé (1842-98). Using nonobjective staging techniques, he sought to portray the inner truth by way of the outer reality. One of his actors, Aurélien-Marie Lugné-Poë (1869-1940), succeeded Fort as manager, changing the name of the theatre to the Théâtre l'Oeuvre. Here, from 1892 until 1929, he worked as manager, director, and chief actor. Under his direction the symbolist drama attained distinction, especially in the plays of Maurice Maeterlinck (1862-1949), the Belgian poet and dramatist.

The nineteenth century in France ended with all the major dramatic genres established and with the playwrights still experimenting. It was a hopeful way to finish a complex and fruitful period.

ACTING, AND THE RISE OF THE DIRECTOR

Just as in its literature the theatre moved from the prerevolutionary Classical theatre through Romanticism and into realism, so acting moved from the declamatory Classical style, through the stylized attitudes of Romanticism, to realism. The shifts from one style to another were not, however, as neat as they sound, and also it is necessary to remember that one generation's "realistic acting" may be considered quite stylized by the next.

The melodrama and the ensuing Romantic drama both dealt with highly emotional materials—injustice, violence, and death—in a tabloid fashion. In one way this struck audiences as being realistic; after all, for the first time they were able to view onstage scenes that had been banished from Classically oriented theatre, and the result seemed to be almost stark reality. Audiences moaned in pity and terror at some death scenes, according to contemporary reports.

And yet actors had little chance to play naturally, for they were placed in unnatural positions, forced to move into place downstage when they had lines, deliver these lines to the audience and not, really, to the character for whom they were intended, and then retire upstage. This practice only came to an end after the middle of the century when the growing power of the director and the increasing emphasis on realism allowed the actors to be placed onstage in a realistic manner and deliver their lines to each other and not the audience.

The great French actor, Talma, playing the role of Hamlet. The costume is not Elizabethan or contemporary French, but what the French designers judged appropriate for a Medieval Danish prince.

The great tragic actors of the period were Talma, who is often said to have been the greatest of all French actors, and his usual partner, Mlle. Duchenois. Among the comic performers, Fleury and Mlle. Mars dominated the stage. These actors are all four from the early part of the century, but except for Sarah Bernhardt and Constant-Benoît Coquelin, no performer in the latter part of the century ever seemed to quite match them in either critical or public acclaim.

François-Joseph Talma (1763-1826) was born in Paris but spent a large part of his early years in England before returning home. As a young man he went back to London to study dentistry under his father, a successful and fashionable society dentist, but spent most of his time performing in amateur theatricals, where he did well enough to be offered professional work at one of the patent theatres. However, his father was unimpressed by the theatrical life and shipped his son back to Paris. Unwilling to give up his dream of an acting career, Talma enrolled at the relatively new Ecole Royale de Déclamation (founded in 1786), where his tutors were his good friends Molé (1734-1802), a player of young lovers, Fleury, who had already established his reputation for comic acting, and Dugazon (1746-1809), who was a well-known performer of farcical roles.

He made his debut in 1787, playing a small role in the Comédie-Française production of Voltaire's *Mahomet*. An extremely handsome man with a fine voice and real flair for speaking verse, he continued to get minor parts until 1789 when he took the role of Charles IX in Chénier's play. The role had been turned down by all the leading actors because of its political ramifications (Charles was a weak and vascillating king, dominated by his mother, and the parallels between Charles and Louis XVI were too obvious to miss) and when Talma went onstage and delivered Charles' lines with great passion, many of the older actors refused to appear on the stage with him. The audience, however, and particularly the great revolutionary hero Mirabeau, loved him.

Talma seemed not to lose his powers in his late years, and in fact seemed ever to grow more successful. He performed in London in 1817, attended Kemble's farewell performance, and in 1826, the year of his death, he was outstanding in an otherwise undistinguished play.

Talma's influence on the French stage was as extraordinary as the rest of his career. He began a reform of stage costuming and was the first actor to play Roman roles dressed in a toga instead of contemporary costume. He toned down the traditional declamatory stage speech, and insisted that actors speaking verse allow the sense rather than the meter to dictate their delivery. He also left behind some interesting reflections on the art of acting.

Talma's usual partner in tragic drama was Mlle. Duchenois (Catherine Rafuin 1777-1835), who made her debut in 1802 in the role of Phaedre. She did not have the effect on the French stage that Talma did, but she was a highly skilled actress with a large and devoted following. Most contemporary accounts describe Mlle. Duchenois as being physically (one assumes facially) "ugly," and yet her skill onstage, her "tenderness," and her "melodious" sorrow allowed her to transform herself into a variety of tragic heroines. Following Talma's death she went into semiretirement, and in 1830 she left the stage for good.

The famous French actress, Rachel, in costume for her role as Rosalind in *Bajazet.*

Abraham-Joseph Bénard Fleury (1750-1822) did not dominate the stage in the manner of Talma, but he was the century's outstanding actor of high comedy. His father managed a theatre at Nancy, and it was here that Fleury began his stage career. In the beginning he was undervalued—considered only suitable for minor roles—but with his actress sister and her husband he went to Geneva and was given the opportunity to act at Ferney. Here he was seen by Voltaire, who encouraged him and in 1774 he made his first attempt to join the Comédie-Française. He was told that he had promise, but that he should return to the provinces for further work. In 1778 he made his second attempt, was accepted, and stayed with the Comédie-Française until he retired in 1818. It was said of him that he had a nobility of carriage and character, and was a master of polished comedy. His most famous role was that of Alceste in *Le misanthrope*.

Fleury's counterpart in high comedy was Mlle. Mars (Anne-Françoise-Hippolyte, 1779-1847), the youngest daughter of the actor-dramatist Monvel (Boutet). Being born a member of an acting family she began her stage career as a child, appearing at Versailles and Paris, and in 1795 she made her debut at the Comédie-Française. Her best work was done in the comedies of Molière, but she also played serious roles in such romantic dramas as *Henry III and His Court* and *Hernani*. She was said to be a beautiful woman with a lovely voice, and her career gives substance to this in that she continued to play the roles of beautiful young women until she was in her sixties.

The great Coquelin in his most famous role as Cyrano at the Théâtre-Porte-Saint-Martin, 1897.

The middle years of the century produced such performers as Bocage (Pierre-François Touze, 1797-1863), regarded by many as the greatest stage lover of the day; Jean-Gaspard Deburau (1796-1846), who specialized in the role of the lovesick Pierrot; Frédérick Lemaître (1800-76), the most famous romantic actor of his day; and Rachel (Elisa Félix, 1820-58), one of the first "star" performers whose salary demands were so exorbitant that as a result the Comédie-Française gave up forever the star system billing. However, the actor whose name is best known today is Constant-Benoît Coquelin (1841-1909), by tradition the greatest Cyrano of all. Coquelin spent most of his acting life at the Comédie-Française, but eventually his reputation became so great that he left for a triumphal tour of Europe and the United States. In 1892, shortly after he returned, he left the Comédie. In 1898, six years later, he appeared at the Porte-Saint-Martin in his greatest role as Rostand's Cyrano de Bergerac. He was a large, robust man with a resonant voice capable of infinite modulation. Coquelin was one of the greatest technical actors of his age—perhaps of all time—and he became embroiled with Tommaso Salvini, the epitome of emotional performance, over the relative superiority of their two systems. He was rehearsing another Rostand play, *Chantecler*, when he died.

The most famous actress in the latter part of the nineteenth century—perhaps the most famous French actress of all time—was Sarah Bernhardt (1845-1923). Madame Sarah was well-known not only in Europe, but also in North and South America, Australia, and even in Egypt, where she often toured. Perhaps because of her immense popularity so many legends grew up about her that it is difficult to separate fact from fiction. Her main physical attribute as an actress was probably her voice, which has been described variously as a "golden bell" and a "silver stream." Unfortunately such descriptions, while poetic, fail to tell us much. Apparently her voice was resonant, more powerful than might be expected from a woman of her slight stature, and had an astonishing range.

She began her acting training in 1858, at the age of thirteen, and in 1862 she made her first appearance at the Comédie-Française. Her subsequent appearances at this already venerable establishment tended to be tempestuous, as her temperament was too unrestrained to accommodate that theatre's strict rules. She tried unsuccessfully to create a career singing in burlesque, and finally gained national attention at the Odéon in 1869. In 1872 she returned to the Comédie-Française to play Cordelia in *King Lear* and the Queen in *Ruy Blas*. It was a double triumph and boosted her to the peak of her profession. In 1880, after a spectacular row with the management of the Comédie, she left that theatre for good to "tour the nations of the world." The tour was such a great success that others followed, and the remainder of her theatrical career was divided between touring and managing several Parisian theatres. Bernhardt's greatest roles were Camille, Phaedra, Tosca, Adrienne Lecouvreur, Doña Sol, and the title role in Edmond Rostand's *L'Aiglon* (*The Eaglet*).

The changes in acting styles that took place during the nineteenth century were due not only to the changes in dramatic literature, but also to the rise of the director as a major theatrical force. When the century opened the idea of a director was unknown, at least in the way we now define the term. Theatre managers (or theatre directors) sometimes worked with the plays in a

The great actress Sarah Bernhardt in costume for her role as the Queen in *Ruy Blas.*

perfunctory manner, and senior actors occasionally gave the other players some guidance, and authors sometimes stepped in to give vocal guidance in the delivery of their lines. However, the director as a powerful theatrical entity did not exist. Interestingly enough it was melodrama that made obvious the need for someone to carefully supervise all aspects of a production. Because melodrama contained so many interlocking elements—spectacle, music, drama, and sometimes dance—and because it so often depended on such plot devices as accidentally overheard conversation, or accidental sightings, or seemingly misplaced prop items, or even just plain coincidence, there was a real need for someone to draw it all together.

This need for coordination and precision led Pixérécourt to take control of the staging for all of his dramas, and near the end of his career he gave as much credit to his directing as to his writing for the success of his plays. His lead was followed by a number of other playwrights as drama moved into the Romantic and realistic periods.

While the authors made sure that their plays worked; that is, that lines were learned and props properly set and entrances and exits made on cue, they seem to have made no attempt to achieve a realistic stage picture. That development is usually assigned to Adolphe Monsigny (1805-80), the second director of the Théâtre du Gymnase-Dramatique. Under Monsigny, the Gymnase (which had been playing mostly vaudevilles) began to accept serious dramas, and Monsigny was determined that their presentation would match the subject matter. In the early 1850s, producing and directing plays by such outstanding dramatists as Dumas *fils*, Sand, Augier, and Feuillet, he began the practice of placing a table and chairs in the downstage area to break up the semicircular formation in which French actors had traditionally tended to group themselves, while addressing their lines to the audiences instead of to each other. His next step was to get the actors to sit in the chairs and speak their lines to the proper character on stage. When he achieved this, a major step toward realistic theatrical presentation had been taken. Monsigny also must be given credit for beginning the practice of dressing the set. To complete the illusion of reality that he was seeking with his actors, he arranged realistic prop materials, such as cigar boxes, letters, journals, and handkerchiefs about the stage. This accentuated the illusion of reality and also provided realistic motivation for his actors to move about the set.

In spite of Monsigny's example and the success of the Gymnase, which under his management began to rival the Comédie-Française, the first significant French director, André Antoine, did not make his appearance until late in the century. Antoine founded the Théâtre Libre in 1887, primarily to produce the new naturalistic playwrights that were beginning to appear throughout Europe. Thus, he went first to the master naturalist, Zola, for his inspiration. Zola had demanded that theatre put a "man of flesh and bones on the stage, taken from reality, scientifically analyzed, without one lie." Antoine undertook to do exactly this, and in an early adaptation of Zola's *Jacques Damour* he even provided a totally realistic facsimile stage by using furniture and props brought from his own home.

Working in a genre that held the environment to be all-important—the total shaping force on man—the appearance of reality supported by a meticulous attention to detail was absolutely necessary. In describing his directorial techniques, Antoine said that his first problem was to create the environment and the setting, without worrying about what would take place on the stage. Then, with the actors placed within this environment, he would strive to make them all conscious of it and react to it. He was, in this sense, the first French promoter of the ensemble techniques of acting, and though he may have learned it from the Meininger troupe, what he did went far beyond the Duke's accomplishments. If Antoine had a fault as director it was his unswerving belief that naturalism was the only possible genre for theatre, and thus he attempted to impose it on any and all works. The Théâtre Libre failed financially in 1894, but Antoine moved on to Odéon and then to the Théâtre des Mensus-Plaisirs, taking his concept of the total director, the *metteur en scène*, into the twentieth century.

SCENIC DESIGN AND STAGECRAFT

Just as the melodrama provoked the rise of the French director, so did it cause at least a minor revolution in stagecraft, especially in the boulevard theatres. The melodramas depended on spectacle, which held and excited their audiences, and the playwrights provided it in abundance. Pixérécourt's production of *La ruine de Pompèi* (*The Destruction of Pompeii*, 1827) featured Vesuvius in eruption, and his earlier *Coelina, ou L'enfant du mystère* (*Coelina, Child of Mystery*, 1799), required a wild countryside with rocks to be climbed, a Devil's Bridge, and a raging storm with constantly flashing lightning.

Understandably this tradition of spectacular staging carried over to the Romantic drama, which also demanded pomp, spectacle, and (because so much of it was based in Medieval times) pageantry. This spectacular staging also carried over to the problem drama, so that Paul Meurice's 1850 drama, *Paris*, required a panoramic view of Paris that would create the feeling of the city being an ant-heap of humanity.

A few such sets were achieved by use of the panorama, a device developed by a Scottish painter and first displayed in an Edinburgh theatre. The Scotsman was followed by Robert Fulton (1765-1815), an American, who displayed a panorama in Paris in 1799. These two devices had been continuous paintings, carefully lit, that could be viewed from the center of the hall. Louis-Jacques Daguerre (1787-1851), who had begun his career as a scene painter at the Ambigu-Comique, designed his "optical show" on a somewhat similar basis. However, it went inside a stage setting, with the front rather dark, while the brilliantly illuminated background changed continuously, thanks to shifting lights from above, to show a series of different perspectives and various atmospheric conditions. Because the scenes were painted on both sides of a transparent cloth, Daguerre called it a diorama (or see-through).

Moving panoramas—that is, continuous scenes painted on long rolls of cloth and then attached to spindles on either side of the stage area, were also introduced early in the century. When the spindles were turned the background seemed to flow across the stage.

Treadmills were also introduced. With a treadmill in front of a moving panorama, chariot races, horse races, or chase scenes could be realistically done, with the background moving while the horse or runner galloped furiously in place.

In 1822 the new Opéra opened, complete with equipment to produce all of the popular spectacles. It also had gas lighting and even a system of water pipes to produce fountains, rain, and waterfalls. So popular were these scenic devices that even the staid Comédie-Française commissioned new, historically accurate settings for some of its plays. By 1840 the Parisian critics were spending almost as much space on descriptions and criticism of the scenic wonders as they were spending on the plays and the acting.

By the last quarter of the nineteenth century the demand for realistically produced historical spectacle had reached its peak. Settings and costumes had become almost prohibitively expensive—Sardou's *Hatred* cost over sixty thousand francs—and so the growing demand for naturalistic plays featuring reasonably inexpensive sets displaying middle-class reality was an economic if not an artistic boon.

COSTUMES

The innovation in historical costuming begun in the middle of the eighteenth century by Voltaire and Mlle. Clairon had been accepted, but without any particular enthusiasm. Other attempts at even more accurate historical detail had even been whistled off the stage. Thus, when Talma made his first appearance onstage in a true Roman toga the event was sensational. Because actors provided their own wardrobe, his fellow actors were as shocked as the audience, and thoroughly outraged because they felt upstaged by the young bit player in the sensational costume. However, most of the audience applauded and historically accurate costuming was on its way.

The Romantic vogue for rich historical drama encouraged the trend, and at the Paris Opéra the designer Paul Lorimer continued to press for accuracy in costuming. However, it was not until the last quarter of the century that accuracy of costuming caught up to the accuracy of scenic design. The culmination of all this (as with scenic design) was probably Sardou's *Hatred*, which used Medieval armor costing 120,000 francs, twice the cost of the settings, and costumes that cost 192,000 francs, more than three times the cost of the settings. Costuming had come of age with a vengeance.

Italy

The drama in nineteenth century Italy remained, as it had in the previous century, a minor art form at best. Partly this was due to the upheavals of the *Risorgimento*, that long, drawn-out struggle for independence that was not fully completed until the 1870s. However, even more than these internal struggles, the Italian love affair with opera reduced interest and support not only for theatre, but for all the performing arts. The operas of Verdi, Mascagni, and Puccini were Italy's only major contribution to the theatrical art of the century, and when the dramatic part of their operas—the librettos—are examined, one must admit that it is a very tiny contribution indeed.

There were some playwrights at work, but in the early years of the century their propensity to continue imitating the Classics was their undoing. Ugo Foscolo (1778-1828) wrote a number of literary tragedies based on both Classical sources and Medieval Italian historical legend. Silvio Pellico (1789-1854), on the other hand, wrote serious dramas so bursting with patriotism and the need for Italian unification that they could be of no interest to anyone outside of Italy.

By the middle and late part of the century a school of writers began creating a serious historical drama based in most cases upon Medieval materials. The best of the early members of this group was probably Leopoldo Marenco (1831-99). Their works tended toward a literary, unplayable style, with dialogue couched in verse and including for verisimilitude many archaic words and usages. However, the school did produce the only internationally famous dramatist to arise in Italy during the century—Gabriele D'Annunzio (1863-1938), who came late and spanned the end of the nineteenth and the beginning of the twentieth century. His Medieval tragedies, such as *Francesca da Rimini* (1901), are rather bookish, but his masterpiece, *La figlia di Iorio* (*The Daughter of Iorio*, 1904), which is sometimes called a pastoral tragedy, is Classically perfect, sincere, and truly dramatic. Unfortunately a large part of his international reputation is due to the great actress, Eleonora Duse, who championed his works and appeared regularly in them.

In creating comedy, the Italian playwrights ignored their own important predecessors, such as Goldoni and Gozzi. Their works were rewritten and even imitated, but no writer picked up Goldoni's realistic style or Gozzi's flights of pure fantasy. The only two writers who tried to write significant comedy were Giovanni Giraud (1776-1834), whose *l'Ajo nell'imbarazzo* (*The Embarrassed Tutor*, 1807) and *Il galantuomo per transazione* (*Gentlemen by Arrangement*, 1833) still hold up, and Francesco Augusto Bon (1788-1858), whose *Trilogia di Ludro* (*Trilogy of Ludro*, 1832-37), in the styles of Goldoni and Beaumarchais, presents a vivid, sardonic picture of contemporary Italian life.

The epitome of emotional acting, the great Italian actor Salvini in costume for his most famous role as Othello.

The naturalistic drama that swept most of Europe late in the century only caught on in the northern area of Italy. Girolamo Rovetta (1851-1910) was one of the best of the naturalists, but his plays seem totally isolated in the middle-class Italian conventions of the time, without ever using them as metaphors for more universal problems.

As far as scenic design and stagecraft, in which Italy had excelled for nearly two hundred years, the nineteenth century remained barren. France had taken over the leadership in this area, and the Italians were content to follow. Lorenzo Sacchetti (1759-1829) and Antonio de Pian (1784-1851) were both fine designers, but they contributed nothing original, continuing like their fellows to follow ideas and practices inherited from a previous century or imported from France.

It was only in the area of acting that Italy made significant contributions, primarily by way of two performers, Tommaso Salvini and Eleonora Duse.

Salvini (1829-1916), born into an acting family, was on the stage by his early teens and achieving great success, especially in the plays of Goldoni. In 1847 he became a member of the relatively new troupe of Adelaide Ristori, and with this troupe he began a highly successful career in tragic drama. He toured Europe regularly, visited England many times, and made five triumphant visits to the United States. Salvini made his reputation as a fiery, passionate, highly emotional actor who brought tempestuous life to the tragic roles he undertook. The best of these roles was Othello, but he was also extremely popular as Macbeth and Lear. Among non-Shakespearian roles his best was Conrad in Giacometti's *La morte civile* (*The Outlaw*, 1861). He retired in 1890 and published a book of memoirs, but his most famous passages, though brief, are probably the lines he exchanged at long distance with the great French actor, Coquelin. Salvini was the epitome of the emotional style of acting, while

Coquelin was an outstanding technical actor. Their debate, over the relative merits of their own particular styles, shows the strengths and weaknesses of each.

ELEONORA DUSE: Eleonòra Duse (1859-1924) was born in Italy on a train while her father was on an acting tour. She made her debut at age four. At fourteen, the proper age, she played Juliet at the appropriate place, Verona. It was probably from her grandfather, Luigi Duse, that Eleonora inherited her acting talent. Luigi was a comedian who used the Venetian dialect and the plays of Goldoni as the basis for his improvisations. It was Luigi who established the company of which Eleonora's father was a member, and it was Luigi who made it successful. After his death the company began to lose bookings, and by the time Eleonora was born it was constantly touring and always on the verge of economic disaster. Her childhood was not a happy one, with her mother too sick to pay her much attention and her father too busy caring for the mother. When they stopped touring long enough for Eleonora to enroll in school the other students made fun of her because she was from the theatre. This life may have been the reason that instead of comedy, Eleonora played mainly tragic roles. Finally, her mother died of consumption and her father retired to paint, leaving Eleonora alone in the traveling company. After a brief affair, which resulted in a child who died soon after birth, Eleonora had an even harder time. In 1881 she married an actor, Tebaldo Checchi. He was not ambitious for himself, but he managed and forwarded Eleonora's career until their separation.

However, in spite of these early hardships the most disastrous event in Duse's life was her affair with Gabriel D'Annunzio. It not only hurt her emotionally but nearly ended her career when she insisted on playing only in her lover's usually mediocre dramas. D'Annunzio was an Italian poet, fascist, hero, and according to E. M. Forster, a cad. He used his affairs as the basis for his novels, and while Eleonora was advising and encouraging him to write plays he also wrote a novel detailing their affair. He described his "aging lover" (she was forty) in intimate detail, even enumerating the positions which they used to make love. Duse ignored the book and the pity of her admirers, continuing to make successes out of the plays of the Italian poet.

By the time she retired from her acting career, Eleonora was recognized all over the world as perhaps the greatest of tragic actresses. Because of her poverty and her innate restlessness the retirement did not last long and Eleonora returned to the stage after the First World War. She had, however, weakened considerably, so the energy necessary to her style of acting left her sick and exhausted after every performance. During a tour of the United States she was kept waiting in the rain outside the stagedoor of a theatre in Pittsburg and as a result developed pneumonia, from which she died.

One of the things which characterized Duse's acting career was her very personal interpretation of the roles she played. Because of this, she usually played roles where the character was indicated but not fully developed. Verdi, after seeing Duse in *Camille*, said that if he had seen her interpretation before he wrote his opera he would have changed the opera.

Duse wore no makeup, using her mobile face to create a wide range of expression. Her costumes were simple, but she created effects with them which were as innovative as her characterizations. The colors of these costumes were always in harmony with the character which she was playing. The sets on which she played also had to fit the character of the play.

In spite of this careful attention to the details of costume and set, Duse was very casual about rehearsing. Since her technique was to live her part rather than acting it, she felt that it was more important to her to have time alone to feel the part than to rehearse. This method worked very well for Duse, but was rather difficult on the rest of the cast.

As an actress Duse was ahead of her time in many respects. She felt that anyone who did not advance artistically would go backward, so she was always attempting new interpretations of old roles. Her style was highly natural for her time, yet she recognized that the theatre would become even more so. In her later years, having failed in her attempt at acting for film, Duse said, "My mistake and that of many others lay in employing theatrical techniques despite every effort to avoid them. Here is something quite, quite fresh, a penetrating form of visual poetry, an untried exponent of the human soul." Finally, one must agree with Helena Modjeska in saying, "What ever school she belongs to, she is a great actress."

Spain

Unlike the theatre in Italy during the nineteenth century, the theatre in Spain was a veritable hotbed of activity, growing from only a few companies when the century opened to more than fifty when it closed. The French styles of acting, scenic design, and stagecraft were studied and imported, and theatre architecture also underwent some major changes. However, all this activity was merely updating; that is, the Spanish theatres were merely catching up with theatrical developments that had in the previous century passed them by. Spain made no significant discoveries and developed no important new understandings. This was especially true in the area of dramatic literature.

As the century opened, Spanish drama was still feeding on its own Golden Age, with the major dramatists primarily imitating Lope de Vega and Calderón. However, in about 1835 the Romantic movement, already nearly over in the northern European countries, arrived belatedly in Spain. Even the advent of Romantic drama was unable to break the hold of the past, and the Spanish Romantics merely imitated the styles of the French, while going back to the Golden Age for many of their themes and plots.

Probably the best of the Spanish Romantic playwrights was Angel Saavedra, Duke of Rivas (1791-1865). He wrote the first Romantic play to make a major impression on the theatre-going populace, *Don Alvaro, o La fuerza del sino* (*Don Alvaro, or The Force of Destiny*, 1835). In this play Don Alvaro, the noble half-breed son of an Inca princess, having killed the father of Leonor, the girl he loves, joins the Spanish army, hoping to die in battle. Instead, he ends up killing his beloved's older brother. Entering a monastery to seek relief from his anguish, he is discovered by Leonor's youngest brother. Leonor, coincidentally, is in seclusion at a nearby hermitage. The final scene leaves them all romantically (and very bloodily) dead.

The only other significant Romantic play, *Don Juan Tenorio* (1844), was written by José Zorrilla (1817-93). This Don Juan, a romantic villain rather than hero, is totally evil and depraved. In this play, unlike Molina's original, he is not saved from hell because of his pure love for Doña Inés, but because that good woman intercedes with God, pleading with him to spare the soul of her dissolute lover.

A reaction to Romanticism, which was never fully acceptable to the Spanish middle class, set in just before the turn of the century. Generally speaking, this reaction spawned a drama unlike any other dramatic genre except perhaps for the English sentimental drama. Celebrating middle-class morality and values, the movement is memorable only in terms of Manuel Bretón de los Herreros (1796-1873), who wrote more than one hundred seventy-five plays; Manuel Tamayo y Baus (1829-98), who created one marvelous play in which Yorick, a player in Shakespeare's company, murders his wife's lover during the performance of a new Shakespearian play; and José de Echegaray (1832-1916), who was awarded a Nobel Prize, but whose plays are all but forgotten.

The failure of Spanish theatre to forge ahead during the nineteenth century is a loss, inasmuch as it was a period of great energy and inventiveness. However, there was too much catching up to do. Also, in spite of a willingness to learn technical theatre from France, and the brief flare of Romanticism, Spain remained physically and emotionally isolated from the rest of the world, and as a consequence produced only insular drama.

The Nineteenth Century In England

The nineteenth century drama in England is all too often characterized as dull, uninteresting, and trivial, except for its last few years with the advent of Wilde and Shaw. A close look at the period, however, proves that such a belief is not justified. There were many fine dramatists throughout the century, and if none of them attained greatness at least there was a uniform level of quality to their work. In all, it was a transitional period and very necessary to the achievements of English drama in the twentieth century.

NINETEENTH CENTURY ENGLISH DRAMA

According to tradition, the Romantic period in England begins in 1798 with the publication of Wordsworth's *Lyrical Ballads*, or in 1800 when Wordsworth prefaced the second edition of the *Ballads* with his "Observations." At this time Romanticism, by way of several "pre-Romantic" writers, had been underway for nearly forty years. However, it was not until Wordsworth wrote out at least one aspect of its underlying philosophy that it burst in a flood over the country, with a group of great Romantic poets such as Wordsworth, Keats, Shelley, and Byron, and such fine novelists as Sir Walter Scott at the crest. But in England, as elsewhere, the Romantic period did not last long. In part it burned itself out through its own excesses; the deaths of Byron, Keats, Shelley, and Scott left it nearly leaderless; and the ascension of Victoria to the throne in 1837 brought a change to the social and political atmosphere.

During this brief—less than forty years—period the great Romantic writers created an outstanding body of literature. Unfortunately, almost none of it is dramatic. Most of the Romantic writers tried their hand at the dramatic form, but none of them totally succeeded. George Gordon, Lord Byron (1788-1824) seemed the most likely to produce great drama. He was deeply interested in all aspects of theatre, not merely the literary, even serving as a member of the board of governors at Drury Lane. And he tried various dramatic forms: Romantic closet dramas (*Manfred*, 1817; *Cain*, 1821; *Heaven and Earth*, 1823; *Werner*, 1823; and *The Deformer Transformed*, unfinished, 1824); Classical tragedies (*Marino Faliero*, 1820; *The Two Foscari*, 1821; and *Sardanapalus*, 1821); dramatic soliloquies (*The Lament of Tasso*, 1817; and *The Prophecy of Dante*, 1821). None of these works were successful theatrically. Of Percy Bysshe Shelley's (1792-1822) two plays, *Prometheus Unbound* (1819) is poetic closet drama; and his best dramatic work, *The Cenci* (1819), while not a bad play and certainly an influential one, has never been successfully staged. Samuel Taylor Coleridge (1772-1834), wrote several verse plays, one of which, *Remorse* (1797), was staged at Drury Lane in 1813 as *Osorio*. It was moderately successful.

In 1811 the Kembles staged *Henry VIII* in the dress of its own period. The production featured Mrs. Siddons and helped give to Covent Garden the prestige that Drury Lane had formerly enjoyed.

The main problem facing the Romantic playwrights seems to have been an overreliance on the techniques of Shakespeare. The early plays of the century are mostly literary attempts to imitate the Bard, by such writers as Joanna Baillie (1762-1851) and Henry Hart Milman (1791-1868). As a result they are naive, abstract, and moralizing, without significant dramatic action or believable characters. In fact, the only two decent playwrights of the period were James Sheridan Knowles (1784-1862) and Edward Bulwer-Lytton (1803-73), both of whom came late, after the excesses of Romanticism's early years had passed.

Knowles must be given credit for trying to reform a drama that badly needed correction. To that end he wrote serious plays, including the verse tragedies *Caius Gracchus* (1815) and *Virginius* (1820), and comedies such as *The Hunchback* (1832) and *The Love-Chase* (1837). *Virginius* is a starkly simple Classical tragedy with the same theme as Chaucer's "Physician's Tale," and it is generally considered to be Knowles' best work. Eventually giving up any hope of reforming an unrepentant drama, Knowles left the stage and entered the Baptist ministry, where he spent his remaining time writing polemical works against Roman Catholics.

Bulwer-Lytton was not as devoted to the drama as Knowles, but when he took time out from bickering with his wife and his public, and from producing footnote-ridden historical novels, he managed to write two quite good plays. *The Lady of Lyons* (1838) was a surprisingly long-lived Romantic comedy, considering that the poetry is trite and the dialogue often absurd. The plot, however, provides a saving grace. A young woman, Pauline, is deceived into thinking that a poor young man is a prince. After marrying him she discovers that he really is poor, but by this time she has fallen in love with him and decides to stay with him in spite of his poverty. The abject sentimentalism proved popular indeed. *Richelieu* (1839) is derived in spirit, if not substance, from the French Romantic-poetic tradition of Hugo and Dumas *père*, and it proved quite popular, thundering from the stage for nearly fifty years.

During the middle years of the century several of the more minor dramatic genres—melodrama, farce, and burlesque—held the stage. The most popular of these was, of course, melodrama, but burlesque did have a widespread appeal, and its two foremost practitioners were James Robinson Planché (1796-1880) and Henry Byron (1834-84).

Planché, of Huguenot descent, was a prolific writer of burlesques, extravaganzas, and pantomimes. His first burlesque was produced at Drury Lane in 1818, and during the next decade he wrote several such works per year, most of which were produced at the Adelphi. He became associated with Mme. Vestris and Charles Mathews at the Lyceum and wrote for them what most consider to be his best work, *The Island of Jewels* (1849).

Henry Byron, at best a minor dramatist, became known for a series of burlesques, beginning in 1857 and ending in 1881. Produced at the smaller theatres around London—the Olympic, Strand, and Adelphi—his plays were minor popular successes that made use of themes taken from mythology, nursery tales, opera, folk legend, and even well-known topical events. His characters tend toward stock types and his treatments lack profundity, but audiences were kept amused by his wordplay, puns, and farcical humor.

Sketch of a scene for Herbert Beerbohm Tree's production of *King John* in 1899. (From an original program of the production)

The most popular dramatic genre during the middle years of the nineteenth century was melodrama, and its most important playwright was Douglas Jerrold (1803-57). Jerrold avoided the dramatic pilfering from French and German melodrama, and as a result he managed to recast the form and spirit of the genre into something more truly English. His most important work in this sense is *Black-Ey'd Susan* (1829), because in it for the first time are all the ingredients that would shape English (and American) melodrama for the coming century. Basically these ingredients are a simple story that steers clear of controversial topics to concentrate on a generally accepted moral principle; some type of musical accompaniment; one-dimensional characters who represent good or evil; much complex physical action; and a last-second triumph of good over evil, usually the result of some type of intervention (often divine). Some other of Jerrold's better plays are *The Prisoner of War* (1842), *Time Works Wonders* (1845), and *The Catspaw* (1850).

The popularity of burlesque and melodrama provoked a revolutionary reaction that sought to restore serious drama, and the leader of this revolution was Thomas William Robertson (1829-71). Faced with the inanities of farce and melodrama, Robertson tried to replace it with drama that was original in subject and plot, serious in theme, and expert in craftsmanship. There were a few other attempts in this direction, such as Tom Taylor's (1817-80) *The Ticket-of-Leave Man* (1863) that gave the language "Hawkshaw the detective," but only Robertson was determined enough to continue in this vein. With such plays as *Society* (1865), *Caste* (1867), *Progress* (1869), *School* (1869), *Birth* (1870), and *War* (1871), Robertson created a realistic (sometimes naturalistic) form whose inheritors would be Henry Arthur Jones, Oscar Wilde, Arthur Wing Pinero, and even George Bernard Shaw.

Although his plays fail to hold any interest for most contemporary audiences, Henry Arthur Jones (1851-1929) deserves an honored place in English drama for his work in bringing to theatre the everyday problems of everyday people. A prolific writer who was deeply influenced by Robertson's works, Jones turned out at least three distinct types of plays. *The Silver King* (1882), *Heart of Hearts* (1887), and *The Middleman* (1889) are basically melodramas, though without the music and excessive physical action of an earlier age. *Saints and Sinners* (1884), *Judah* (1890), *The Masqueraders* (1894), *The Triumph of the Philistines* (1895), *Michael and His Lost Angel* (1896), and *Mrs. Dane's Defence* (1900) are all in the "thesis" or "problem play" genre, which is to say that they use an essentially melodramatic form to treat outstanding social problems. Jones' last plays, probably influenced by the success of Wilde in the 1890s, tend to be in the comedy of manners tradition—especially *The Liars* (1897) and *Dolly Reforming Herself* (1908).

The program of the original production of *Lady Windermere's Fan*.

ST. JAMES'S THEATRE,

Sole Lessee and Manager - - Mr GEORGE ALEXANDER

To-Day, at 3 o'clock punctually,

A New and Original Play, in Four Acts, by OSCAR WILDE, entitled

Lady Windermere's Fan

Lord Windermere	Mr. GEORGE ALEXANDER
Lord Darlington	Mr. NUTCOMBE GOULD
Lord Augustus Lorton	Mr. H. H. VINCENT
Mr. Charles Dumby	Mr. A. VANE TEMPEST
Mr. Cecil Graham	Mr. BEN WEBSTER
Mr. Hopper	Mr. ALFRED HOLLES
Parker	Mr. V. SANSBURY
Lady Windermere	Miss LILY HANBURY
The Duchess of Berwick	Miss FANNY COLEMAN
Lady Plimdale	Miss GRANVILLE
Mrs. Cowper-Cowper	Miss A. DE WINTON
Lady Jedburgh	Miss B. PAGE
Lady Agatha Carlisle	Miss LAURA GRAVES
Lady Strutfield	Miss M. GIRDLESTONE
Rosalie	Miss W. DOLAN
Mrs. Erlynne	Miss MARION TERRY

ACTS I & IV. Morning-Room at Lord Windermere's, Carlton House Terrace (H. P. Hall)
ACT II. Drawing-Room at Lord Windermere's (Walter Hann)
ACT III. Lord Darlington's Rooms. (W. Harford)

The Incidental Music by WALTER SLAUGHTER. The Furniture and Draperies by Messrs. FRANK GILES & Co., Kensington. The Dresses by Mesdames SAVAGE and PURDUE. The Wigs by Mr C H FOX. The Etchings and Engravings in the corridors and vestibule kindly lent by Mr. I. P. MENDOZA, King Street, St James's

PROGRAMME OF MUSIC.

OVERTURE... "Haydee"	Auber	WALTZ & MAZURKA "Copelia Ballet" ... Delibes
OVERTURE "Morning, Noon and Night in Vienna"	Suppe	CANZONETTA ... Godard
Two Songs without words	Mendelssohn	LOIN DU BAL ... Gillet
OVERTURE ... "Nozze de Figaro"	Mozart	SERENADE À NINETTE ... Bauers
ENTR'ACTE & BALLET MUSIC "Rosamunde"	Schubert	

Doors open at 8. Commence at 8.15. Carriages at 11

The Attendants are strictly forbidden to accept gratuities, and are liable to instant dismissal should they do so. Visitors to the Theatre are earnestly begged to assist the Management in carrying out a regulation framed for their comfort and convenience.

Photographs of the Artistes may be obtained from ALFRED ELLIS, 20, Upper Baker Street, N.W.

Afternoon Performances of "LADY WINDERMERE'S FAN" Every Saturday, & Wednesday, April 6th, at 3 o'clock.

NO FEES. [illegible] NO FEES.

PRICES—Private Boxes, [illegible]

Box Office open daily [illegible]

Stage Manager ... ... Mr. ROBERT V. SHONE. Musical Director ... Mr. WALTER SLAUGHTER.
Business Manager ... ... Mr. ALWYN LEWIS.

Printed for the [illegible]

In addition to writing some sixty plays, Jones worked unceasingly in the cause of a "modern national drama" that would express "all that is vital and preservative and honourable in English life." He recorded the struggle this entailed in *The Renaissance of the English Drama* (1895) and *Foundations of a National Drama* (1913).

Oscar Wilde (1854-1900) wrote just five significant plays during the 1890s, but they were enough to permanently establish his reputation as one of the outstanding English dramatists. Wilde was born in Dublin but attended Oxford, where in the late 1870s he became inspired by the teachings of John Ruskin and Walter Pater. Preaching the gospel of "art for art's sake," he toured England and then "crossed over" to America where, in flowing tie and knee-breeches, his hair drooping and sniffing a lily, he offered his philosophical *bon mots* to thrilled Boston debutantes and to sullen, suspicious miners in Leadville, Colorado. Because he was almost a living caricature of the esthete, it is too easy to take Wilde at surface value. He was, however, seriously concerned with what he considered the repressive ugliness and hypocrisy of Victorian England, and most of his work was designed to strike out at this unpleasant environment.

Except for *Salomé* (published in Paris, 1893), a sensuous pagan tragedy which Wilde originally wrote in French, his plays are all comedies—*Lady Windermere's Fan* (1892), *A Woman of No Importance* (1893), *An Ideal Husband* (1895), and *The Importance of Being Earnest* (1895). Written in the comedy of manners tradition, his comedies feature brilliant if artificial dialogue and sparkling epigrams. *The Importance of Being Earnest*, his best work, has been made into a successful musical comedy and is never long off the stage.

The last of this group of writers, and one who in a small way worked on into the twentieth century, is Arthur Wing Pinero (1855-1934). A solid craftsman who drew upon the realistic "cup and saucer" dramas of Robertson and Jones, the "social problem" plays of Ibsen, and the well-made play structure of Scribe, Pinero put onstage some of the most daring topics of his day. If he proved incapable of dealing with these problems at any depth, he must still be credited with making the English stage a place to consider major issues rather than minor tempests.

Pinero first became popular for a series of successful farces that he wrote for the Court Theatre: *The Magistrate* (1885), *The Schoolmistress* (1886), and *Dandy Dick* (1887). He also tried his hand at the sentimental domestic drama, gaining public if not critical acclaim for *Sweet Lavender* (1888), *Lady Bountiful* (1891), *Trelawny of the "Wells"* (1898), and *Letty* (1903). However, his significance as a major dramatist rests entirely on the Ibsenian problem plays that feature a character or characters in conflict with the strictures of society. In *The Profligate* (1889) he presented a man trying to live down his past. He followed this with *The Second Mrs. Tanqueray* (1893), and then in *The Notorious Mrs. Ebbsmith* (1895) he writes about a woman who makes a daring attempt to rebel against social conventions, but who finds that absolute social disapproval is too powerful a force to combat. *Iris* (1901) and *Mid-Channel* (1909) both concern themselves with women who, given the social restrictions

A production of a musical farce in Drury Lane, c. 1812.

of the time, are unable to maintain their marriages. *Thunderbolt* (1909), is the worst and last of the group.

Pinero's best work is clearly *The Second Mrs. Tanqueray*, which shows the opposite side of *The Profligate*. Paula Ray, a woman with a "questionable" past, marries a widower who has a young daughter. They move to her new husband's country home, where they are ostracized by the neighbors. Paula begins to regret her decision to marry, but is able to carry on because of her devotion to her new stepdaughter. However, she is visited by an old friend who brings along her aristocratic but profligate husband. Paula recognizes him as an old paramour and he, in turn, does the right thing and leaves rather than expose her past. However, the stepdaughter guesses the reason and is shocked by this revelation about Paula's past. Knowing that the house is now hopelessly divided, and feeling deeply the outrage of the stepdaughter, Paula commits suicide. The point of the play, however, is not contained in the suicide but in the stepdaughter's recognition of her own guilt in the affair.

It is tempting to round off the nineteenth century by invoking the work of George Bernard Shaw (1856-1950). After all, he began writing plays as early as 1885 (*Widowers' Houses*). However, his first productions were not until the 1890s and the bulk of his work, and his influence, was in the twentieth century.

Thus, the nineteenth century drew to a close. Burlesque and farce had run their course, a degenerate melodrama was no longer significant, and the problem drama pioneered by Ibsen had combined with English realism to create a drama of social conscience.

THE ENGLISH THEATRE

As the nineteenth century opened the population of London was on its way to reaching well over a million persons. This meant a large potential audience and a demand for theatrical entertainment that the patent theatres

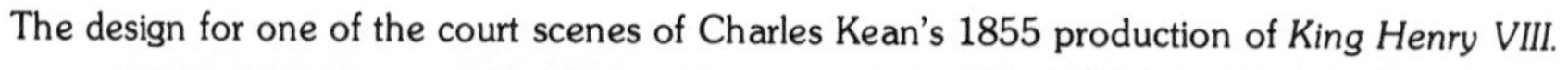

The design for one of the court scenes of Charles Kean's 1855 production of *King Henry VIII.*

(Drury Lane, Covent Garden, and Haymarket) could not fulfill. Thus, a group of minor theatres began to appear. At first they were all outside the City of Westminster, according to the law passed in 1752, but in 1804 the Earl of Dartmouth became Lord Chamberlain, and his reinterpretation of the law—that minor theatres could be allowed in Westminster as long as they did not interfere with the patent theatres—meant that at last London proper could have a full theatrical diet. In 1807 he began issuing permits for such theatres, requiring only that they not play regular drama.

The effect of this decision was twofold: it not only made more theatre available, but it also provoked the creation of a number of minor dramatic forms which could legally be played outside the patent houses. Thus, the emergence of farce, burlesque, and melodrama was almost a direct result of the Earl's decision. While farce was a native form, and melodrama was immediately recognizable in its translation (usually) from French or German, burlesque (or burletta) was almost beyond definition. It had come into England some fifty years earlier as comic opera, but had developed into so many varieties that the Lord Chamberlain was forced to act. He defined it as a work of no more than three acts that included at least five songs. This opened the floodgates, and almost immediately the minor houses were doing regular drama which had been restructured to three acts (when necessary) and provided with the minimum five musical numbers.

Charles Kemble as Hamlet in a Covent Garden touring production, Paris, France, 1827. (Lithograph by Gauguin, after Boulanger and Deveria)

And just as the minor theatres began producing regular drama the patent theatres began doing farce, burlesque, and melodrama. The competition was keen indeed. Playbills were extended to include regular dramas, farces, and burlesques, and an evening's entertainment ran as long as six or seven hours. The upshot of all this was that in 1843 the Theatre Regulation Act did away with patents, allowing all theatres to produce all types of dramatic material.

In the early years of the century the direction of staging became evident in the work of John Philip Kemble (1757-1823), the best and most famous of the acting family, who took over the management of Drury Lane in 1788 under Sheridan. Unable to get along with the famous playwright, whose political forays and constant economic mismanagement brought on a series of crises, Kemble left in 1802 for Covent Garden. Before he retired in 1817 he made this theatre the outstanding one in London.

A large part of Kemble's success was due to his careful but lavish approach to staging. The emphasis on spectacular production that in France had grown out of melodrama, in England grew out of the production of historical plays. Kemble began to produce versions of Shakespeare that rivaled the earlier productions of the Bibiena family in spectacle and that exceeded them in historical accuracy. His designer was William Capon (1757-1827), an architect and painter of plodding, pedestrian temperament, and an antiquarian who did away with the old flats and wings and designed a number of accurate new sets copied directly from the architectural remains of the period. While with Kemble, Capon also earned the more dubious distinction of introducing aquatic spectacle and live animals to the English stage.

Kemble's (and Capon's) move toward historically accurate sets and costumes was aided significantly when in 1823 James Robinson Planché, the well-known writer of burlesques and a passionate antiquarian, persuaded Charles Kemble (1775-1854), John Philip's younger brother and successor as manager of Drury Lane, to costume Shakespeare's *King John* with total historical accuracy. The actors, supposedly, were uneasy, afraid that they would be laughed off the stage, but the production was successful and pointed the way toward future theatrical practice.

After the retirement of John Philip Kemble the most important theatre manager and theatrical reformer was probably William Charles Macready (1793-1873). One of the finest tragic actors of his own or any time, Macready also became a manager, according to his diary, in an attempt to reform existing theatre traditions. He managed Covent Garden from 1837 to 1839, and Drury Lane from 1841 to 1843. Because of his reforming zeal he became the first English theatre manager to take on most of the duties of the director. He stopped the practice of letting actors select their own stage positions, and having blocked their movements he insisted on full rehearsals, even for supernumeraries, to set the blocking and the lines. Many of the senior actors were upset by what they considered this cavalier treatment, but Macready persisted and while his techniques were not immediately adopted by other managers, they pointed the way to a number of important staging reforms.

Macready must also receive credit for restoring the supremacy of the text to the English stage. He produced many of Shakespeare's plays, and to the

The theatre in Windsor Castle was the location of this 1849 command performance for Queen Victoria, with Charles Kean as Hamlet. (From *The Court Theatre and Royal Dramatic Record,* London, 1849)

best of his ability sought to work from texts as close as possible to the original. Modern scholarship has cast doubt on some of Macready's texts, but it is amazing to discover the accuracy of his restorations.

The other major manager of the period was Mme. Vestris, who was born Lucia Elizabetta Bartolozzi (1797-1856) and assumed the famous Vestris name when she married the dancer Armand Vestris. After being deserted by her husband she had a highly successful career on both the Paris and London stages, primarily because of her singing ability. The possessor of a grand opera voice, she preferred light entertainments and was reportedly at her best in burlesques.

In 1830 Mme. Vestris took over the management of the Olympic Theatre and opened with a burlesque by Planché, who thereafter provided her with a number of burlesques and farces. In 1838 she married Charles Mathews, an actor in her troupe, and from then on their careers are too entwined to totally separate them. However, most comments of the period credit all management successes to the "madame." An unusually strict manager, she controlled all aspects of production and thus was able to present a totally unified show. With the help of James Robinson Planché, in his role of antiquarian and designer, she became conscious of the need for historically accurate costumes and sets and, on those rare occasions when her contemporary or allegorical comedy demanded such accuracy, she took pains to provide them, thus anticipating the reforms of Charles Kean and the Bancrofts. As well, she is usually given credit for introducing the box set to England in November 1832; however, this is doubtful as several earlier designs seem to indicate that box sets had already been used. What she certainly did do, however, was to perfect the art of set dressing, producing such lifelike effects that the audiences probably felt as though they were seeing a box set for the first time. She also insisted on practicable scenery, with doors and windows capable of opening and closing.

The baton of historical accuracy was picked up by Charles John Kean (1811-68), son of the great English tragedian Edmund Kean and himself a fine actor. With the aid of his wife, the actress Ellen Tree (1806-80), Charles became manager of the Princess' Theatre, the last theatre opened in London before the passage of the Theatre Regulation Act, and here he established a style

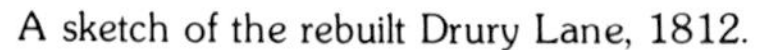
A sketch of the rebuilt Drury Lane, 1812.

of management that lasted throughout the rest of the century. Following the examples of Kemble, Macready, and Vestris, his productions were lavishly but accurately costumed and staged. His 1853 *Macbeth*, for instance, with scenic design by Dayes, featured the banquet hall of a Medieval castle, complete even to the cross-beams in the ceiling. Kean's careful staging and carefully blocked crowd scenes had a major effect not only on English theatre, but also on the Meininger Company, whose director, Georg II, Duke of Saxe-Meiningen, became familiar with Kean's work.

The final step toward theatrical realism was taken by the Bancrofts (Marie Wilton, 1839-1921, and Squire Bancroft, 1841-1926) and their playwright-director Thomas William Robertson. The Bancrofts had remodeled the old Queen's Theatre, renamed it the Prince of Wales' Theatre, and collected one of the most talented acting troupes in England. The Bancrofts had done much to upgrade the acting profession, paying top salaries to good performers and then insisting on careful rehearsals and meticulous staging. However, when they teamed up with Robertson they made an even greater theatrical breakthrough. Robertson not only wrote for the Bancrofts, he also directed their plays during the early years of their partnership, establishing a whole new style in which the accuracy and spectacle that heretofore had been lavished on historical plays was transferred to modern plays. They worked on three-dimensional sets, many designed by Edward Godwin (1833-86), that were solid, three-wall structures with ceilings, and in the tradition of Vestris the doors and windows and set pieces were practicable. In 1880 the Bancrofts moved to the Haymarket where they continued their successful venture, in spite of an opening night riot over the abolishing of the pit, and in 1885 they retired.

A final step, and one equal to anything that preceded it, came late in the century following Edison's invention of the incandescent light, making it possible to light a stage electrically. Gas had been used selectively for stage lighting since early in the century, and after the 1840s it had become almost the exclusive method of providing illumination. The limelight (hydrogen and oxygen directed against a column of lime) had been invented in 1816, and the carbon arc in 1808. By the 1840s both were in common use and, with the controlled intensity provided by gas, these instruments lit the stage as never before. The major steps in lighting were made by Henry Irving (1838-1905), who worked primarily with gas but made use of incandescent lighting for specials. Irving experimented with colored glass lenses to provide a variety of hue and light distribution, and though some critics found this distracting it led directly to the stage lighting of the twentieth century.

ACTING

In the early years of the century, English acting was dominated by the Kemble family. The first of the acting Kembles was Roger (1721-1802), a hairdresser turned strolling player and theatre manager. Roger had married Sarah Ward, daughter of a provincial theatre manager, and together they toured England, playing mostly in the provinces and, along the way, having twelve children.

The oldest of the children was Sarah (1755-1831) who, like all the Kemble children, was onstage early. At the age of eighteen she married William Siddons, a reasonably undistinguished member of her father's company, and as Sarah Siddons went on to become one of the greatest tragic actresses of the English stage. After her marriage she and her new husband continued playing the provinces, but finally a role at Cheltenham won Sarah enough recognition for Garrick to bring her to Drury Lane in 1775. This first appearance was a failure, perhaps because she was overawed by Garrick and the London audiences, and afraid to use the emotional tragic style for which she would eventually become famous.

Following this first failure the couple returned to the provinces, playing at York and Bath, and in 1782 they decided once more to try London. This time the attempt was successful and Mrs. Siddons was acclaimed by audiences and critics alike as the greatest tragic actress of the age. This was a position she would hold, without serious challenge, until her final retirement in 1819.

Probably the worst that can be said of Mrs. Siddons is that many critics believed that she could have been even greater than she was—that she never quite fulfilled her potential. She began her London career as a mature actress, apparently near the peak of her powers, and while she did not seem to decline she never developed beyond that point. Critics were unanimous in their praise of her ability—of her beauty, nobility, and most of all her tenderness. Perhaps the truest compliment of all came from the critic William Hazlitt, who found her to be "tragedy personified."

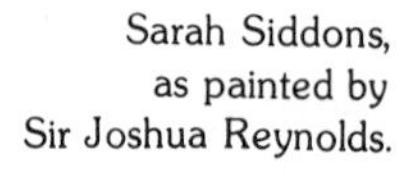

Sarah Siddons,
as painted by
Sir Joshua Reynolds.

Behind the scenes, however, was another story, and Mrs. Siddons was cordially disliked by many of her fellow performers. She was accused of being unapproachable, tightfisted, and bad-tempered. Almost pathologically shy of publicity, she even insulted some of her admirers. However, she was also apparently intelligent and sensible and the close friend of such greats as Dr. Johnson and Walpole; Gainsborough loved to paint her, immortalizing her beauty in the "Tragic Muse."

A statuesque beauty with a rich, resonant voice, Mrs. Siddons excelled in tragic and heroic parts, especially as Lady Macbeth; on the few occasions when she appeared in comedy (for example, as Rosalind in *As You Like It*) she was apparently mediocre.

She retired from the stage in 1812, but in 1818 she returned in a benefit given for her brother Charles and his wife. It was not a successful return, however, and Macready referred to it as the "last flicker of a dying flame."

The other great actor in the Kemble family was John Philip (1757-1823). Like the other Kemble children, he spent his childhood onstage but his theatrical career was seriously threatened when his father, a devout Catholic, sent John Philip off to Douai to study for the priesthood. The studies did not take and John Philip returned to the stage; however, the ascetic aspects of his priestly training left him a more reserved and dignified man than his earlier career would have indicated.

Like his older sister, Kemble spent several years in provincial repertory and in 1783, a year after Sarah's London triumph, he made his debut as Hamlet at Drury Lane. His interpretation was a new one for London audiences and critics. He eschewed the more traditional approach as a fiery warrior prince, appearing rather as a gentle, intellectual, philosophical Hamlet driven by duty into deeds foreign to him. At first his interpretation bothered audiences, and his reception was ambivalent, but he soon won over both audiences and critics.

While his sister established her great roles early in her career, John Philip Kemble began much weaker but grew steadily more powerful in his performances. One by one he undertook the great tragic roles of his day—Wolsey, Brutus, Cato, Coriolanus—playing them so definitively that they became inseparable from the Kemble name.

As a player Kemble worked primarily in the grand tradition, giving his audiences few surprises. When he did depart from traditional interpretations, as he did with Hamlet, he tended toward a reserved, poetic, philosophical reading. He was generally considered to be a very handsome man, but a harsh voice, what has been described as labored breathing, and a stiffness of gesture and movement kept him from the physical perfection so beloved in his day. Also, like sister Sarah, his natural reserve, reinforced by his religious training, seemed to make him unlikely material for comic acting and he rarely attempted such roles.

His acting, together with his significant contributions as a theatre manager, made John Philip Kemble one of the most important theatre people of the age.

John and Sarah's younger brother, Stephan (1758-1822), also began his career early, being practically born on the stage while his mother was playing Anne Boleyn. He was, like all his siblings, a child actor in his father's company,

An 1827 production of *Romeo and Juliet* done in Renaissance costume. The production featured Charles Kemble.

but he left early to seek a career as a chemist and apothecary. However, after Sarah and John had become London successes he returned to the stage, where he had a successful though unspectacular career. His greatest role was Falstaff, perhaps due to the weight he put on late in life, which allowed him to play the role without padding.

Charles (1775-1854), the youngest of the Kemble clan, also grew up on the stage, left it for the civil service, and then returned as the family name became famous by way of Sarah and John Philip. His early years on the stage had convinced him that he had no talent. Certainly he was awkward and without the rich, resonant voice considered necessary for the great tragic roles. However, he was an intelligent actor who recognized his limitations, concentrating on such nontragic parts as Mercutio, Orlando, Mirabell, Charles Surface, and Benedick. Romeo was his greatest role, perhaps because he had a

A contemporary engraving (c. 1815) shows Edmund Kean as Richard III at Drury Lane.

real flair for the poetic and the emotional. He spent twenty-five years on the London stage, one of its most successful players, and also did an outstanding job as a theatre manager.

A number of other Kembles also made their marks in the history of English acting: Roger Kemble's daughter Elizabeth (1761-1836), as Mrs. Whitlock, became famous as the American Kemble; Charles' daughter, Frances Anne (1809-93), was outstanding as Juliet, Portia, Beatrice, and Bianca; and Henry (1848-1907), Frances' nephew, was an excellent comedian and character actor who was long a member of the excellent troupe assembled by the Bancrofts.

In addition to Sarah, three more of Roger's daughters had successful stage careers, but none were as outstanding as Sarah, John, Stephan, or Charles.

While the Kembles seemed to be holding the London stage in thrall, a story was developing about John Philip's major competition, the tragedian Edmund Kean (c. 1787-1833), which is even wilder than the worst Romantic novels of the age. The most probable account of his birth is that given by Macaulay, who has him descended from George Savile, Marquis of Halifax, by way of Savile's natural son Henry Carey. Henry fathered George Savile Carey, whose wild daughter Anne ran away to be a strolling player at the age of fifteen. Failing at acting she was working as a hawker in London when she came to the attention of Aaron Kean, a man of questionable background. He told some friends that the girl was pregnant and asked them to take her to George Savile Carey at Gray's Inn. Her child was born, but other than the mother's statement, which cannot be relied upon too heavily, there is no real evidence that Aaron Kean was the father.

At some point Anne deserted her child, leaving him in a basket in a doorway, where he was fortunately found by a couple who reared him through his early years. Later, Anne came back to reclaim him, obviously hoping to use the young boy as a partial support. One of the jobs she found for him during this period was posing as Cupid in a Covent Garden ballet sequence. Stories of these early years onstage have so often been sensationalized that they have tended to get in the way of a real appreciation of Kean's artistry. And yet, perhaps unfortunately and perhaps not, many of the stories are probably true and account at least in part for the volcanic, intense actor he was to become, greater in the roles compounded of villainy than any other actor.

While John Philip Kemble epitomized the handsome, dignified, tragic hero, Kean embodied the opposite type. Not blessed with a particularly handsome body, and with a voice so harsh that it was described as "creaking," Kean lacked both grace and tenderness. He was a failure as Lear and Romeo, and his Shylock, clutching a knife and ravening for blood, was admired for all the wrong reasons. Neither could he do comedy, and cognizant of that fact he refused most comic roles and all sophisticated ones. However, given a role with even a touch of evil he was magnificent. His Richard III and Iago were accounted the best ever, and his Sir Giles Overreach and Barabas were models for villainy.

The constant scandals and, more importantly, his ever-growing practice of nonappearance finally managed to alienate even Kean's staunchest supporters. In 1833, playing Othello to his son Charles' Iago, he fell ill. He died less than two months later.

While Kemble was developing one extreme of the tragic style, while Kean was busily exemplifying the other extreme of tragic performance, and while Sarah Siddons was being acclaimed as the greatest English actress, a third tragedian, William Charles Macready, appeared to make the early years of this century probably the greatest in the history of English acting. The son of a provincial actor-manager, he made his debut in Birmingham in 1810 playing Romeo. He played Hamlet the following year at Newcastle, and in 1816 he was Orestes in the Covent Garden production of *The Distrest Mother*. Within eight

William Charles Macready in costume for the role of Iago.

years he had progressed to the point where he was generally considered to be Kean's outstanding rival.

For some reason, perhaps the spirit-trying early years in which he was forced to do one bad role after another in provincial repertory, Macready always professed to despise the profession of acting, and this did not endear him to his fellow players. However, his Lear, Hamlet, and Macbeth were widely admired, and among his parts in later plays the title role of Richelieu in Bulwer-Lytton's play earned him admiration throughout Europe and America. He appeared twice in the United States, first in 1826 and again in 1849, when his appearance in New York, supposedly as a rival to the American Edwin Forrest, led to the Astor Place Riot. In 1851 he gave his last performance, appearing as Macbeth at Drury Lane.

The middle years of the century, as if to make up for the great number of fine actors in the early years, were relatively undistinguished. Kemble and Kean were dead, Macready was retired, and it was not until 1856 and the professional debut of Henry Irving (1838-1905) that acting—and in fact all the theatrical arts—received a new impetus.

Born John Henry Brodribb at Keinton Mandeville in Somerset, Irving was sent to London at the age of ten to study at the City Commercial School. A stutter caused him to seek elocution lessons, and it was as a result of these lessons and the student plays they involved that he turned to theatre as a career. His debut was at the Lyceum Theatre, under the the stage name of Henry Irving, following which he went to Edinburgh to play in repertory. He returned to London in 1859 to act for Augustus Harris (1825-73) at the Princess' Theatre. His return was hardly triumphant—his best role was that of Osric—and again he departed for the provinces. Six years later he was back in London. This time he was far more successful, though he was most highly thought of for his portrayal of villains. It was not until 1871, when he played the terrified Polish Jew in *The Bells*, an adaptation of Erckmann-Chatrian's *Le juif polonais*, that Irving attained real fame as a performer.

Irving followed his first success with another as the pathetic Charles I, and then, perhaps too eager to pit himself against the memories of Kean and Macready, he attempted Richelieu. As would be true throughout the balance of his career, the reviews were mixed; some loved him, some hated him, but no one was indifferent. He followed this with a controversial Hamlet, a prince so gentle that he is driven to everything he does by an excess of tenderness. Audiences were baffled and critics outraged. This critical division dogged Irving for the rest of his career. Even when he had scaled the theatrical peak there were those who came to see him perform in the hope that he would fall off.

In manner Irving was quietly intense. He avoided the oratorical, traditional style of his predecessors and based his technique in movement. Each aspect of his performance was plotted with care and single-minded concentration, so that he took advantage of what seemed to be his natural faults. His native Cornish pronunciation, the stutter that the elocution studies barely managed to mask, his weak voice, and his less than stately physique were all worked into his characterizations so carefully that they seemed just right and he was given credit for achieving them.

A production of Henry Iving at the Lyceum in the late 1890s. The play is *Becket* and the scene shows the strong scenic influence of the Meininger troupe.

In addition to acting, Irving was one of the most successful theatre managers of the time, beginning at the Lyceum in 1878 where, with the fine actress Ellen Terry, he put an end forever to the remaining Victorian objections to theatrical performance. In 1895 he became the first actor to be knighted for his services to the theatre.

The Nineteenth Century In Germany And Northern Europe

Germany As the nineteenth century opened in Germany the Romantic drama forged ahead of dying Classicism, seeking to explore the directions already made evident in the later works of Goethe and Schiller. However, while German Romanticism would have a major influence on the rest of Europe, it produced very few significant German playwrights.

In Germany, as elsewhere, Romanticism was short-lived, and following Napoleon's conquest it rapidly disappeared, weighed down by the pessimism that grew out of military defeat and ignored by a brassy nationalism that was promoting German unification.

Late in the century the theatrical work of Georg II, Duke of Saxe-Meiningen, the music drama of Richard Wagner, and the developing schools of naturalism and expressionism once more filled German drama with a vital, driving force.

NINETEENTH CENTURY GERMAN DRAMA

The earliest of the nineteenth century Romantics was Ludwig Tieck (1773-1853), whose first plays were written just before the turn of the century but who went on to become a major force in nineteenth century theatre. A Romantic poet, his early plays were supernatural tragedies in the Gothic style. *Der Abschied* (*The Farewell*, 1792) and *Karl von Berneck* (1795) were both tragedies based on the vagaries of fate. In the latter part of the decade he began his fairy-tale satires done in an almost Aristophanic style. *Der gestiefelte Kater* (*Puss in Boots*, 1797), romantically put aside all the Classical rules, making use of a play-within-a-play and even interaction between the players and audience. In 1799 he wrote *Leben und Tod der heiligen Genoveva* (*The Life and Death of Saint Genevieve*), which was a mixture of nearly everything he had done to this point. Moody and yet lyrical, it contained folk elements, legend, and fantasy. This same basic combination was used in *Kaiser Octavianus* (*Emperor Octavian*, 1804), which took a mythological, schoolbook account of Octavian's life and added varieties of verse and fairy-tale enchantments.

An illustration of Tieck's production of *A Midsummer Night's Dream*, Berlin, 1843. (From *Leipziger Illustrirte Zeitung*, 1844)

In 1824 Tieck was made director of the Dresden Court Theatre, where he simplified the Romantic but cumbersome sets and staging techniques, and insisted that the actors rehearse thoroughly and practice their diction. He also became a respected critic, and his writings reveal much the same thing as his plays—that he was a man of excellent taste and sharp insight, but without any real moral force or direction.

The effect of Tieck's plays was great, however, especially those dealing with fate, and he had a number of imitators, the most important of whom were Zacharias Werner (1768-1823) in Germany and Franz Grillparzer (1791-1872) in Austria.

Probably the most important thing that the early Romantics did in terms of the developing German drama was to provide good translations of Shakespeare, Jonson, Lope de Vega, and Calderón. Tieck provided some excellent translations of Jonson, his daughter Dorothea completed Schlegel's translations of Shakespeare, and Zacharias Werner provided access to the theories of Calderón and Lope de Vega.

Both of the followers of Tieck, Werner and Grillparzer, and also Heinrich von Kleist, were part of the Romantic period, and yet, in an odd way, stood apart from it. Werner eventually concocted his own dramatic formula, and it was not basically Romantic. A thoroughly grounded theatre scholar, Werner based his formula on the plays of Calderón and on the German baroque tradition. In this formula, men and women were shown overcoming tragedy and achieving salvation through faith and a willingness to renounce worldly goods and ambitions. In spite of the way it may sound, the formula was not designed to promote Christianity or any faction thereof. Instead, it was an attempt to create a basic poetic myth to serve the nineteenth century in much the same way that the Greek myths had served the Classical period.

Heinrich von Kleist, on the other hand, had no formula at all, which may account for Goethe's rejection of his work as displaying a "confusion of emotions." In fact, Kleist was a driven man desperate to outdo Goethe and Schiller.

HEINRICH VON KLEIST: Heinrich von Kleist (1777-1811) was born in Frankfurt, Germany, to Prussian army captain Joachim Friedrich von Kleist and his second wife, Juliane Ulrike Pannwitz. Little is known about Kleist's childhood and early development. His father died when he was eleven, and his education was given over to a clergyman named Samuel Catel.

In 1792 Kleist entered the army at Potsdam, and one year later his mother died. Between 1793 and 1795 he took part in the Rhine campaign and two years later he was promoted to the rank of lieutenant. In the same year he published his first essay and, convinced that a scholarly or philosophical career was in the offing, he resigned his commission in order to study at the University of Frankfurt. He attended the university for three semesters, concentating on mathematics and physics in an effort to create a logical mental approach to life and its problems.

In 1800 Kleist became engaged to Wilhelmine von Zenge, and the emotional problems that were to plague him until his death also appeared. He took a mysterious trip to Würzberg, apparently to resolve what some historians be-

A sketch by the Duke of Saxe-Meiningen for his production of Heinrich von Kleist's *The Battle of Arminius.*

lieve was a sexual problem, and Kleist later spoke of the one-day trip as the most important day of his life.

Moving to Berlin, Kleist began studying the philosophy of Kant and avoiding any kind of permanent employment. Moral and emotional crises began to develop, feeding the pattern of emotional instability that was steadily becoming more evident. The study of Kantian philosophy failed to fulfill Kleist's need, whatever it was, and he sought escape in travel, going to Paris, Frankfurt am Main, and finally Switzerland. In Switzerland he lived a hermit's existence on an island, studying the works of Rousseau as a counterbalance to Kant. It was while he was in Switzerland that his fiancée broke off the engagement.

In the first years following the turn of the century Kleist completed two dramatic works. After the first he became almost violently sick, the first of many such spells of illness. The second play, a tragedy, he read to the writer-philosopher Christoph Wieland (1733-1813), apparently receiving fulsome praise for the work, but on a trip to Paris he had another of his spells and destroyed the manuscript. At about this time he was overtaken by a desire for death and sought to join the French army for Napoleon's projected invasion of England. Instead he was hospitalized because of a physical breakdown.

Returning to Germany he found civil service employment and continued his education, this time in economics, but in 1806 he quit his government post to concentrate totally on writing. He completed *Der zerbrochene Krug* in 1808, which is still considered one of the finest comedies in the German language and which (as *The Broken Jug*) has been quite successful on the English stage. In it a Falstaffian village magistrate tries a case in which he himself is the culprit. Also in 1808 he completed *Penthesilea*, a tragedy based on the story of the Amazon queen. *Die Hermannsschlacht* (*The Battle of Hermann*) was completed

An 1883 production of Goethe's *Faust* that makes use of a set design developed by Tieck in 1843 for *A Midsummer Night's Dream*.

in 1809, and in 1810 *Das Käthchen von Heilbronn (Kathy from Heilbronn)*, a play on the theme of devotion. Also in 1810 he finished his masterpiece, *Prinz Friedrich von Homburg (The Prince of Homberg)*, which deals with the conflict between unrestrained Romanticism and the need for order. *Der zerbrochene Krug* was presented in Weimar, but it failed and a long illness overtook Kleist. He returned to Frankfurt at last, totally bankrupt.

From Frankfurt he went to Berlin, where he found work as editor of that city's first daily newspaper, but some censorship problems and his failure to get *Das Käthchen von Heilbronn* produced once again left him too ill to work. He sent a request to the King for a civil service position or a grant of money to continue his writing, but received no answer. A number of similar failures ensued and in November 1821 he made a suicide pact on the shore of the Wannsee with a Fraulein Vogel. She was dying from cancer and he was suffering emotionally. They wrote six letters that comprise a kind of death litany, and then Kleist shot Vogel and himself.

Perhaps partly because his genius went unrecognized in his own lifetime, Kleist's work tends toward the pessimistic. He was a man ruled by two seemingly opposed qualities—logic and passion—and the conflict between these two aspects of his personality may well have resulted in his tragic death. As a young man he had accepted the optimism of the eighteenth century. He had believed that human beings were destined to achieve happiness on earth. However, his reading of Kant had confused him and by the time he wrote his tragedies he felt that reason and passion had both failed him. Thus, he turned to Rousseau, who seemed to say that the natural instinct of humans is unerring and infallible to the degree that it is not corrupted by society and its institutions.

Kleist's plays, while not popular in their own time, have held up reasonably well. *The Prince of Homburg* was an outstanding success as recently as 1951 in the Avignon Festival and was used as the libretto for an opera by Hans Werner Henze, first performed in 1960.

As it did everywhere, the Romantic period burned out early in Germany, perhaps because even its strongest adherents found that it led nowhere and thus could say with Goethe, the onetime arch Romanticist, that Romanticism was disease, and Classicism was health.

Probably the most popular playwright in Germany during the first half of the nineteenth century, and indeed the most popular playwright in the Western world, was August von Kotzebue, whose over two hundred plays were translated into nearly all languages, and who numbered Sheridan in England and Dunlap in the United States among his adaptors. Kotzebue was assassinated in 1819 by a fanatic German student who resented Kotzebue's antipathy to the youth movement in the German universities, and who suspected him of pro-Russian plotting. However, his plays were long-lived and very popular. In them he combined a semblance of reality with sensational subjects and an unshrinking sentimentalism that in the hands of his successors became merely melodrama. However, his semblance of reality helped German drama along the pathway toward realism.

At the other extreme was Christian Dietrich Grabbe (1801-36), who along with Georg Büchner was one of the early spokesmen for the German

A watercolor of the set for Hauptmann's *Hanneles Himmelfahrt*, as produced in 1893 at the Königliches Schauspielhaus, Berlin. (Painting by Eugen Quaglio)

youth movement. His brief life was spent at an emotional high, savaging a world which he felt was totally unworthy, and as a result his plays are filled with grand emotional scenes. They are chaotic and often seem little more than sketches loosely strung together. However, his *Scherz, Satire, Ironie und tiefere Bedeutung* (*Jest, Satire, Irony and Deeper Meaning*, 1822) is a strikingly modern work in which the historical forces at work in society are presented as being totally absurd.

Standing with Grabbe just outside the mainline of German realism was Georg Büchner (1813-37), a potentially fine dramatist who died before his promise could be fulfilled. A student of science and medicine, Büchner became outraged with what he considered to be the repressive policies of the German state and became a revolutionary. Fleeing the country he soon died of typhus in Zurich. His one complete play, *Dantons Tod* (*Danton's Death*, first produced in 1902), is unusual for a revolutionary activist in that it portrays the great revolutionary, Danton, as a disillusioned man sickened by the bloodshed of the revolution he helped to begin and seeking death at the hands of Robespierre. Büchner's other play, *Woyzeck*, was a mass of dramatic fragments at the author's death. However, it has been assembled with varying degrees of accuracy and is occasionally produced. In it the hero, Woyzeck, is crushed by his environment, by poverty and sickness and his wife's infidelity, and all of this while the social institutions either stand by or actively participate in his destruction.

Grabbe's *Don Juan and Faust* at the Hoftheatre, Meiningen, 1897.

But Grabbe and Büchner did indeed stand outside the development of German realism, which was carried on without distinction through the middle years of the century by such writers as Heinrich Laube (1806-84), Charlotte Birch-Pfeiffer (1800-68), and Ernst von Wildenbruch (1845-1909).

Friedrich Hebbel (1813-63), the son of a poverty-stricken north German mason, was obsessed by the tragedy of life and searched unendingly for its causes. Interestingly, he did not find those causes growing out of the social or economic environment, but rather out of human fraility and the resultant guilt growing out of incidents caused by the fraility. In seeking to dramatize this philosophy he created a number of powerful middle-class tragedies which totally avoided the sentimentalism that was destroying German realism. Many of his plays are studies of women wronged, as in his first play, *Judith* (1840), and *Maria Magdalena* (1844), in which the repressed heroine Clara destroys her suitors and herself because of the fear and respect inspired by her stern, self-righteous father.

Gyges und sein Ring (*Gyges and His Ring,* 1856) is often considered to be his best tragedy inasmuch as it is his most human and emotional. However, its legendary theme takes it out of the severe realism of his other early works and leads toward Hebbel's late plays in which he tried to impress his essentially realistic vision on Germanic folk materials. His last completed work was a trilogy, *Die Nibelungen* (1862).

The final scene from Part II of Hebbel's *The Nibelungs,* "The Death of Siegfried," produced in 1861 at Weimar. (From the *Leipziger Illustrirte Zeitung,* 1861)

Hebbel's late developing interest in Germanic myth was not totally accidental or even internal, but the result of a nationalistic movement, prevalent in Germany from the 1840s through the 1870s, ending in the unification of the German state. In part it was merely a reflection of the patriotism engendered by this politically and socially troubled time, and in part it was a reaction against sentimental realism. German writers were looking for roots, and they found them in the heroic myths of their ancestors.

Probably the most famous example of this trend is a man not usually associated with theatre—Richard Wagner, a composer of operas. A difficult, violent person who made enemies and friends with equal ease, his theories on music and drama, which he put to work in his operas or music-dramas, have led many critics to consider him the greatest operatic and dramatic genius of his time.

WILHELM RICHARD WAGNER: Wilhelm Richard Wagner (1813-83), one of the world's most important composers of opera and a major theorist of the necessary relationship between music and drama, was born in Leipzig. His "legal" father, Karl Friedrich Wilhelm, held the post of Police Actuary in Liepzig, but his greatest interest in life was the theatre. As a result of his interest, Karl Friedrich was the intimate friend of many actors, among whom was a man named Ludwig Geyer who, according to the rumors of the time, might conceivably have been Richard Wagner's real father. Whether or not the rumor was true, Karl Friedrich Wilhelm died when Richard was three months old, and less than two years later his mother married Ludwig Geyer.

Although the theatre was naturally a constant force in the Geyer household, neither Geyer nor Wagner's mother wanted Richard to enter the theatrical profession. Instead, Geyer wanted his stepson to become a painter. When Wagner's stepfather died, Richard was only eight years old, but his family was far from destitute. His oldest brother, Albert, was already supporting himself as an actor and singer in Breslau; his sister, Rosalie, was a member of the Royal Court Theatre in Dresden; and another sister, Luise, also went on the stage, joining Albert at Breslau.

In 1826 the family moved to Prague, and Richard was left, rather haphazardly it would seem, with a family friend in Dresden. In school Richard did quite poorly, refusing to work on subjects that did not appeal to him. After a year in Dresden, Wagner rejoined his family in Leipzig when they moved back to that city. Here Richard fell under the beneficial influence of his uncle Adolph. Adolph Wagner was the most distinguished member of the family. He was a respected scholar and a kindly man who was happy to open his library to Richard, to talk with him, and even to read Greek drama to him.

When Wagner was twelve years old his mother reluctantly engaged a piano teacher for him, but the duration of the lessons was short. He developed the idea that he would set his drama to music only a short time after his piano lessons were terminated, and he realized that he needed some knowledge of composition. He taught himself as much as he could, and that which he could not extract from his books he learned from a musician named Müller.

Max Brückner's 1882 stage design for a Wagner production at Bayreuth. Gurnemanz and Parsifal on the way to the castle of the Holy Grail.

His family was away during the summer of 1829, and during this time Wagner composed almost constantly. When the family returned, they discovered that he had not attended school for six months. It was decided that he would be allowed to study music only if he went back to school. This he did, but continued to avoid his lessons, and the music teacher who was engaged to tutor him was the same Müller under whom he had studied just a short time before.

In 1831 Wagner succeeded, after a great deal of effort, in gaining entrance to the University of Leipzig. He had no particular interest in studying, but the student life seemed to him to be free, romantic and, most importantly, dissipated. Enthusiastically he plunged into the traditional student excesses. He joined a club, he hastily practiced swordsmanship, and he was quickly challenged to three duels. Fortunately none of his opponents showed up to duel with him. One was killed in another duel, the second was badly hurt, and the third sustained severe but inglorious injuries while drunk in a brothel.

In the spring of 1833, Wagner accepted a temporary position training the chorus in the theatre at Würzburg, where his brother Albert was manager. He was not reengaged but remained in Würzburg until January of the following year, not only to continue work on his opera, *Die Feen* (*The Fairies*), but also because he was enjoying himself.

While Wagner was on a pleasure trip through Bohemia an offer came to join the theatrical company of Magdeburg as musical director. He went to look the situation over, and found that the company was artistically inept and economically questionable. But before he could totally reject the offer he met Minna Planer, and that chance meeting changed his life. Wagner was so smitten that he notified the director of his acceptance and agreed to conduct *Don Giovanni* the following Sunday.

After his marriage to Minna Planer, Wagner's financial situation became rapidly worse. This, and the fact that they quarreled constantly, caused Minna to leave Wagner after less than a year of marriage. At first Wagner tried to follow her, but his funds were insufficient. He somehow found the money to go to Dresden, where he stayed with his sister and her husband; and there, in Dresden, he found his wife. He finally persuaded her to again live with him, but in a few weeks she fled again, and this time Wagner did not try to follow.

After several months in Dresden, Wagner went to Riga, where he had been engaged as a conductor. In Riga, the theatre was small and the working conditions were bad, but it was here that he completed his first significant work, *Rienzi.* At last, disillusioned with the prospects in the small theatres of Germany, he decided to make an assault on Paris. By this time his wife had returned to him, apparently unsolicited.

In 1839, when Wagner arrived in Paris, he showed *Rienzi* to Giacomo Meyerbeer, who had established himself as the master of French grand opera. However, success was still far away, and in 1840 his financial state became so bad that he was sent to debtors prison for several weeks.

In the summer of 1840 Wagner began to write occasional articles for the *Gazette Musicale.* He wrote ten essays for the *Gazette* and about a dozen more for German journals. Most of the essays reflect his homesickness and his growing idealization of Germany. Wagner always enjoyed expressing his opinions,

Appia's set design for "Gotterdammerung," in Wagner's *Ring* at the Stadttheatre, Basel.

but the only attraction of journalism at this time was the money it paid. Ironically, it brought him a reputation that his musical efforts had so far failed to achieve.

While in Paris, Wagner completed *Derfliegende Holländer* (*The Flying Dutchman*). In March 1842 the Berlin Opera accepted *The Flying Dutchman* and Wagner felt justified in returning to Germany, whatever the cost. Paris had done for Wagner what nothing else could—it had made him a German. His dissatisfaction with French and Italian opera, and also with the operatic tastes of the French public, created in Wagner the belief that only in Germany would his work be appreciated. During his stay in Paris he had delved deeply into German history and legend. Lonely and homesick he began to feel a deep, mystical sympathy with his fatherland.

Rienzi marked the end of Wagner's apprenticeship as a conventional opera composer, and *The Flying Dutchman* set him squarely on the road to "music drama." The term *music drama* is normally applied to all his works after *Lohengrin*, but while it is a convient distinction, the broader term *opera* still rightfully applies. Wagner himself did not entirely approve of the term *music drama*, but he was never able to find a satisfactory substitute.

In 1843 Wagner became Kapellmeister at the Dresden Opera. The productions in Dresden of *Rienzi* and *The Flying Dutchman* kept Wagner away from his composition for several months, but by spring 1843 he had managed to complete the poem of *Tannhäuser*. The composition of the music proceeded steadily, and by the middle of April 1845 the score was complete. During rehearsals of *Tannhäuser*, Wagner began work on his next musical drama, *Lohengrin* which was completed in 1848.

In that year revolution broke out in Paris and some groups in the German states, eager for liberal reform, were quick to follow. Unsuccessful uprisings took place in Berlin and Vienna. In Dresden, one of the leading advocates of reform—by revolution if necessary—was Wagner's friend and assistant, August Rockel. The two men talked frequently, and it is almost certain that Wagner was delighted to see connections (however spurious) between his dreams of theatrical reform and the revolutionary dreams of political reform.

Wagner began speaking and writing in support of the revolution, and when his political position caused the cancellation of a production of *Lohengrin*, it only succeeded in making him increase his open criticism. When revolution broke out in Dresden in 1849, and the King's forces gained control of the city, Wagner escaped to Weimar, where he was aided by his friend, Franz Liszt. When a warrant for Wagner's arrest was issued, however, he and his wife were forced into exile in Switzerland. He did not return to Germany for twelve years.

While in Switzerland, Wagner wrote several prose essays. Among them are *Art and Revolution*, *The Art Work of the Future*, *Opera and Drama*, and *Art and Climate*. The least defensible and most potentially dangerous of his prose writing is entitled *Judaism in Music*. A movement toward anti-Semitism was gaining acceptance among German intellectuals and nationalists, and Wagner merely picked up the notion, as he had a habit of doing, and adapted it to his own problem. The principle on which his anti-Semitism rested was his belief in the importance of "das Volk" in the development of art. While he said much that was uncomplimentary, he did not insist on the inferiority of the Jewish race. He did, however, consider the Jewish people a foreign element. The internal enemies of German art he found in the watered-down "Beethoven and Handel styles" of Mendelssohn and the commercialized French-Italian style of Meyerbeer.

In considering Wagner's essays, one must avoid the trap of believing that Wagner's whole purpose can be discovered in his prose writings; that the great music dramas grew out of Wagner's adherence to the principles he enunciated. Such is clearly not the case. However, a close examination of his essays reveals a surprisingly comprehensive and astute view of the theatrical arts.

Art and Revolution, Wagner's justification for participating in the Dresden uprising, includes four major points: theatre is the center of national culture; the highest art is public art, which results in the creation of a free and healthy folk such as existed in ancient Greece; commercialization of society destroys the proper condition for art; not until social revolution trains men to seek beauty and strength will the conditions for art be right.

In *Opera and Drama*, Wagner attacks squarely, from the standpoint of opera, a problem that has concerned a number of critics: "The error in the art-genre of opera consists herein: that a Means of Expression (Music) has been made the object, while the object of expression (Drama) has been made a means." The essence of his argument is that music, the most powerful organ of expression, cannot be specific about the feelings it expresses. Poetry, on the other hand, speaks directly to the understanding. The two arts must be unified to serve the higher drama of feeling. The potential of each will be raised in combination, and the result will be, not opera in the old sense, but complete drama. The proper subject for this music drama is myth, because it embodies truth in terms of feeling.

The other performing arts must be included in this complete drama inasmuch as sight and gesture are important. All these elements will then be united by the orchestra which, expressing the unspeakable, will join with gesture in suggesting emotions past and future. Finally, however, everything must serve the drama. Even the melodies that recall or predict may not be used for purely musical reasons. There will be no chorus and there must be no set numbers merely for the sake of abstract musical form. The form of the drama will be molded only by the poetic idea.

In 1856 Wagner began the composition of *Siegfried.* However, before completing his masterpiece, *Der Ring des Nibelungen* (*The Ring of the Nibelungs*), he took time off for the composition of *Tristan und Isolde.* In 1861 he went to Vienna, where he heard *Lohengrin* for the first time, thirteen years after it was written. His wife died in 1866, but they had hardly corresponded since their last meeting in 1862. Wagner remarried in 1870 to Cosima Liszt, who was the illegitimate daughter of Liszt and the Countess Marie d'Agoult. Wagner and Cosima had two daughters and a son.

In 1872 Wagner took his family to Bayreuth, where he took charge of the construction of the Bayreuth Festival Playhouse, in which the first performance of the *Ring* took place in 1876. This playhouse was designed to provide a clear view of the stage and outstanding acoustics.

His last work, *Parsifal,* was completed in 1882. In 1883 Richard Wagner died in Venice.

The scientific revolution that had been so prominent in the previous century and that had been looked upon by such artists as Zola as man's last, best hope, in the late nineteenth century suffered a backlash. The result was a scientific skepticism that can be seen in the plays of Büchner and Hebbel in Germany and Musset in France. Ibsen was regularly produced in Germany after 1872, and in 1889 Otto Brahm (1856-1912) opened his new theatre, the Freie Bühne ("Free Stage"), based on Antoine's Théâtre Libre. The result of this welter of thought and activity can be seen in the work of Gerhardt Hauptmann (1862-1946) and Frank Wedekind (1864-1918).

Hauptmann, a Silesian by birth, studied to be a sculptor in Germany and Italy before becoming attracted to the Freie Bühne. His first play, *Vor Sonnenaufgang* (*Before Sunset,* 1889) was produced at the Freie Bühne as a grim naturalistic drama in which a dogmatic liberal, voicing all the progressive slogans of the day, is revealed as a moral coward who allows tragedy to befall the girl whose life he has destroyed. *Before Sunset* was followed by several more plays in the same unrelieved style, such as *Einsame Menschen* (*Lonely Lives,* 1891) and *Die Weber* (*The Weavers,* 1892), a drama of social comment based on the revolt of the Silesian weavers in 1844.

In 1893 Hauptmann turned to satiric comedy with *Der Biberpelz* (*The Beaver Coat*), which pierced the bubble of Prussian officiousness and bigotry.

A design by Karl Walser for Hauptmann's *The Sunken Bell,* produced at the Royal Court Theatre, Wiesbaden, 1899. (From *Bühne und Welt,* Berlin, 1899)

However, always somewhat of a Romantic at heart, Hauptmann immediately produced the fantasies of *Hanneles Himmelfahrt* (*The Assumption of Hannele,* 1893) and *Die versunkene Glocke* (*The Sunken Bell,* 1896).

Hauptmann continued writing for many years, with constant shifts from realism to naturalism to fantasy to history. In 1912 he was awarded the Nobel Prize for literature, and his last work, a cycle of four plays on the doom of Antrides, was completed just before the outbreak of the Second World War.

The works of Frank Wedekind also show the influence of the realistic school, but like the works of Hauptmann their infusion of fantasy and symbolism point directly toward the expressionism that was to become a major dramatic movement in Germany after the turn of the century.

Wedekind began his career as a journalist, became secretary to a circus, developed a cabaret act in which he sang songs he had composed, and ultimately joined Carl Heine's company at the Krystal Palast in Leipzig as an actor. It was then that he began to write. In his early plays he attempted to destroy the curtain of secrecy that a "repressed generation" had imposed on sexual matters. He was especially upset at the way this secrecy was enforced on adolescents. His first four plays, *Die Junge Welt* (*The Young World,* 1890), *Frühlings Erwachen* (*Spring's Awakening,* 1891), *Der Erdgeist* (*Earth Spirit,* 1895), and *Die Büchse der Pandora* (*Pandora's Box,* 1903), all deal with some aspect of sexuality; the earliest two with sexual repression and the last two with the more lustful aspects of sexual behavior.

Along with his dramas of sexuality he also produced some fascinating portrayals of gentlemen crooks (*Der Marquis von Keith—The Marquis of Keith,*

1900) and grotesque and lively cranks (*Hidalla*, 1904). Wedekind's most popular play in English is probably one of his earliest, *Spring's Awakening*, which is subtitled "A Children's Tragedy" and which shows two fourteen-year-olds who are destroyed by the moral dishonesty of their overbearing parents.

The period that began with Romanticism ended with naturalism and symbolistic fantasy. The two most prominent writers of the last years of the nineteenth century would continue to write during the first quarter of the twentieth, and thus the German drama maintained a continuous development until the horrors of the First World War shocked it into a new form.

SCENIC DESIGN AND STAGECRAFT

The century's primary theatrical movement in scenic design and stagecraft was, in Germany, much as it was elsewhere—that is, there was an increased emphasis on achieving historical accuracy in sets and costumes and a growing dedication to realism, whether in the realistic-naturalistic plays or the spectacles of Romanticism. August Wilhelm Iffland (1759-1814), who came to

Antonio de Pian's design for Schiller's *Wallenstein*, produced in 1814 at the Viennese Burgtheatre. (An engraving by Norbert Bittner, 1816)

Berlin after a long and highly successful career managing the National Theatre at Mannheim, was meticulous in demanding realistic presentations. His 1801 production of Schiller's *The Maid of Orleans,* designed by Karl Friedrich Schinkel (1781-1841), was the delight of audiences for its historical accuracy in costumes and sets and for its spectacle, which was as yet unknown in Germany except for operatic productions. Iffland died early in the century, but his place was taken by Count Karl von Bruhl (1782-1837), who was even less imaginative than the calm, almost reactionary Iffland. However, the Count was more insistent on "corrections," and so the Berlin theatre led the way in the reform of theatrical design.

By the middle of the century the concept of historical accuracy in sets and costumes was well established, and Franz Dinglestedt (1814-81) was one of its leading exponents. He was appointed to control of the Munich Theatre in 1851 and achieved renown with his productions of Shakespeare. In 1854, for the Munich Industrial Exhibition, he made theatre history with productions so elaborate that he imported actors from all over Germany. For the exhibition Dinglestedt rearranged the texts, added music and dance, made use of lush settings, and had more actors onstage in crowd scenes than had been seen since the Medieval pageants. However, the experiment which began so brilliantly ended in disaster, brought on by a sudden attack of cholera in the city, which reduced his potential audience, and by the outcries of local performers who felt they had been slighted. As a result of this furor, Dinglestedt prudently withdrew to Weimar. He was later appointed as director of the Vienna Burgtheater, where he continued his outstanding productions.

Throughout most of the century the usual means of creating sets was with flat wings and a backdrop painted to represent trees or buildings. As the century progressed the flat wings were linked together with hinges to provide new angles instead of merely placing the flats parallel to the proscenium arch. This probably evolved into the box set when, late in the century, doors and windows were added to these hinged flats. The box set had appeared occasionally quite early in the century, but as the realistic movement gained momentum and it became increasingly necessary to provide a variety of usually middle-class interiors, it became the dominant set of the period.

ACTING

In nineteenth century Germany, acting was dominated by the Dutch immigrant Devrient family. The first of the family to make his reputation as an actor, and probably the best of the lot, was Ludwig (1784-1832), an outstanding and emotional performer who might have achieved greatness even beyond the German language areas except for his fiery temperament that refused to be disciplined. Ludwig was almost the stereotype of the Byronic Romantic hero, with wildly tossed dark hair, a pale face, and a reserved, remote manner that contrasted with his excessive emotionalism. In his early career he specialized in romantic roles, but he was never happy trading on his appearance. A fine comedian, he was most applauded for his Falstaff, but he perversely preferred to act in tragedy, where his favorite roles were Franz Moor (in Schiller's *The*

Ludwig Devrient is shown as Franz Moor in Schiller's *The Robber.* (A contemporary lithograph by an unknown artist, c. 1815)

Robbers), Shylock, King Lear, and Richard III. He appeared in all the major theatres of Germany, right after the turn of the century, but in 1815 he took Iffland's place in Berlin and remained there until his death.

Ludwig had three nephews, all of whom made successful careers on the stage. The oldest was Karl (1797-1872), who was considered excellent in such tragic roles as Wallenstein, Faust, Lear, and Shylock—the very roles in which his uncle had wanted so desperately to excel. For most of his early career Karl was with the Court Theatre in Dresden, but he went on to play with the troupes at Karlsruhe and Hanover.

The next oldest nephew, Eduard (1801-77), began his career as a singer who, with Mendelsshon, put on a revival of Bach's *St. Matthew Passion,* himself taking the role of Christ. He became the director of the Hoftheater at Karlsruhe in 1852, where he established a reputation for meticulous if conservative performances and ensemble acting. He produced many of the German classics which had fallen into audience disfavor, along with his own translations of Shakespeare. These translations, published in 1869-71, are not as accurate as some more literary works, but they are probably the most playable translations of Shakespeare produced in the century. Eduard was also a theatre historian, publishing in 1848 a detailed and quite accurate version of the development of the German stage.

The third nephew was Emil (1803-72), a handsome and talented actor who specialized in youthful heroic and young lover roles, even into his middle age. He spent nearly forty years at the Dresden Court Theatre, but to keep him satisfied they allowed him leaves of absence during which he could go on tour. He played all the major theatres of Germany and even acted Hamlet in London, where he received a surprisingly good reception.

Emil's son, Otto (1838-94), began his career under his father at Karlsruhe and then went on to the Weimar Court Theatre. There he was quite successful as an actor, but achieved his primary renown as a director, especially for a production of both parts of Goethe's *Faust.* He designed the production like a Medieval mystery play, using a three-level stage and mansions. From Weimar he went to Jena, where he wrote and staged a pageant play for a festival honoring Martin Luther. In 1884 he went to Oldenburg, where he remained until his death.

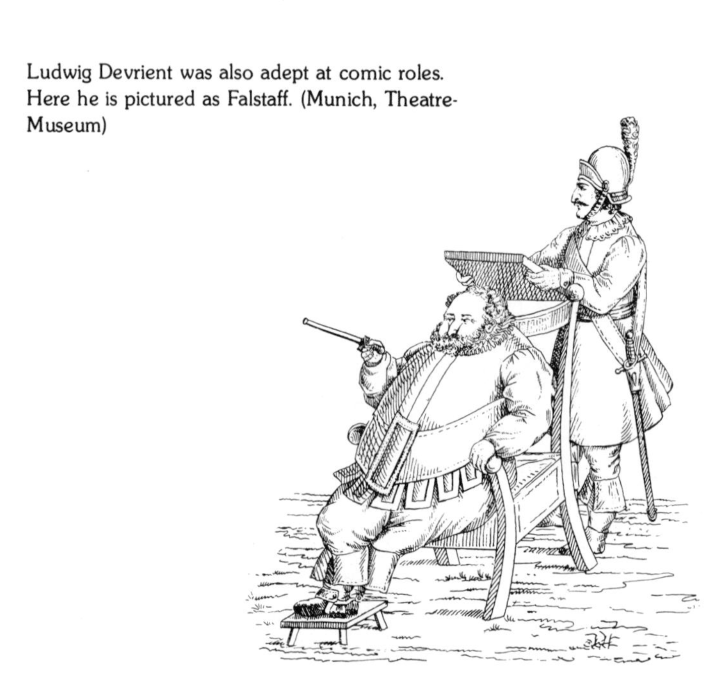

Ludwig Devrient was also adept at comic roles. Here he is pictured as Falstaff. (Munich, Theatre-Museum)

Du ungezogener Schlingel!
Act II. Scene IV

Max (1857-1929), the son of Karl by his second wife, first appeared onstage in Dresden in 1878. He played all the major theatres in Germany, and in 1882 joined the company of the Vienna Burgtheatre. A large, handsome man with a commanding stage presence, he was especially admired in the great tragic roles. He could, however, also play comedy, and one of his greatest successes was in the role of Petruchio in *The Taming of the Shrew.*

NINETEENTH CENTURY REBELS

While the history of nineteenth century German theatre tends to flow fairly smoothly, in spite of the generally turbulent political and social conditions, there were several rebels who were not satisfied with traditional theatrical practice. Some, such as Grabbe and Büchner, operated only in theatre's literary arena, but others were important in all areas of theatrical endeavor. Two of the most important innovators, Adolphe Appia and Georg II, Duke of Saxe-Meiningen, had major international effects. However, alongside these two giants there was one other theatrical rebel, Karl Immermann (1796-1840), who tended to stand outside the boundaries of nineteenth century theatre, but whose contributions were major enough to deserve special consideration.

Immermann was deeply influenced by Goethe's work at Wiemar and by the productions of Ludwig Tieck. For five years, from 1833 to 1837, he was the manager of a small theatre at Düsseldorf, and it was here that he began to develop (or at least integrate) his theories of theatre. Because his theatre was basically a small, provincial one, without the great actors and directors of the major companies, Immermann learned some important lessons. The company

The old stage of the Obergammergau Passion Play influenced such nineteenth century designers as Karl Immermann.

was under the direction of an actor of Italian descent named DeRossi, who attempted to overcome the lack of major talent by working for an integrated performance in which all aspects of the production came together in perfect balance. This meant that there was no excessive emphasis on spectacular staging techniques or starring roles.

At last Immermann put his theories to the test at the Stadttheater, with a repertory that included plays by Shakespeare, Calderón, Lessing, Schiller, and Goethe. He had, by this time, become a friend and admirer of Tieck, and even tried a production of *Bluebeard*, but it failed.

The public did not respond to Immermann's productions and so he resigned as manager and began to apply his theories in private productions. For a performance of *As You Like It* he created an architectural façade with all the basic features of the Elizabethan stage, though arranged to fit his own conceptions. The play was a financial disaster, but the idea of integrated performance and historically accurate staging would later receive support from both Wagner and the Duke of Saxe-Meiningen.

GEORG II, DUKE OF SAXE-MEININGEN, AND THE MEININGER COMPANY: The "Theatre Duke," Georg II (1826-1914) was born in the Duchy of Meiningen in Germany. He was the son of Bernhard II and enjoyed an education that accorded with his artistocratic birth, studying under the guidance of

A sketch by the Duke of Saxe-Meiningen for the final scene of *Romeo and Juliet,* 1897.

the theologian Johannes Klug and also with Wilhelm Lindenschmit, an admired painter of historical murals. Georg was later tutored by a captain of the army, and when he entered the University of Bonn he emphasized law and political economy, but his major interest seemed to be art. During a semester at the University of Leipzig he became acquainted with the composer Felix Mendelssohn. He also traveled to Berlin where he continued his drawing and painting under the guidance of Peter von Cornelius and Wilhelm Kaulbach.

In 1848 Georg was ordered by his father to return to Meiningen because of the growing political unrest and soon after he married Princess Charlotte. It was shortly after this return to Meiningen that he became interested in the Court Theatre. The theatre had been originally established in 1781 in the castle of his granduncle, Duke Karl. It was later moved by Bernhard II to a new theatre in the town of Meiningen.

In 1855, having given birth to three children, Charlotte died and Georg sought the consolation of his art and music, traveling to Italy with the painter Andreas Müller. He was married again in 1858 to the Princess Feodora.

Duke Bernhard, fearing his sovereignty was endangered by Prussia's hostile attitude toward the smaller German states, requested a military pact with Austria in 1866. This proved to be a major error as Prussia sent two battalions to occupy Meiningen, forcing Bernhard to abdicate in favor of Georg, who was known to be sympathetic toward the Prussian desire to unify Germany. As Duke, Georg served in the Franco-Prussian War of 1870 and was present at Versailles in the Hall of Mirrors in 1871 when the King of Prussia, Wilhelm I, was proclaimed Emperor of Germany.

His second wife and the mother of two more sons died in 1872. In his sorrow Georg devoted more time to the Court Theatre, even falling in love with the leading actress of the company, Ellen Franz (1839-1923). He soon entered into a morganatic marriage with Ellen, an act highly disapproved of by the Meiningen court because of her low birth. After the marriage Ellen acted only on occasion and assumed the responsibility for proposing the repertory, supervising stage speech, and adapting the texts.

The third member of the Meiningen Court Theatre's ruling group was Ludwig Chronegk (1837-91), who came to Meiningen in 1866 as a comic actor. Chronegk proved to be only a second-rate actor, but he was adept at communicating with the other players, and as a result he was appointed stage manager and company disciplinarian. It was through his advice and leadership that the Meininger company undertook the famous European tours that made them one of the moving forces of contemporary theatre.

Between the years 1874 and 1890 the Meininger company made eighty-one appearances in more than thirty-six major European cities, performing more than forty historical and contemporary plays. Georg, occupied with state duties, remained in Meiningen during the tours and saw only three road performances; he never neglected his governmental obligations in spite of his love for the theatre. With Chronegk in bad health the touring company was disbanded in 1890 in Odessa. The productions staged at the theatre in Meiningen continued, and the Duke continued to take an active interest in them until his death at the age of eighty-eight.

Friedrich von Bodenstedt (1819-92), the Duke's theatrical advisor, had been to London where he had observed Kean's adherence to historical accuracy in the settings and costumes of Shakespeare's plays. Bodenstedt discussed this with Georg, who incorporated these principles in his own designs for the Meiningen Court Theatre. Georg also contributed a concept of choreography because of his belief that stage movement should match the setting and costume in style and concept, so that the sum of the whole would be a single picture. To accomplish this, the Duke drew elaborate plans plotting the movement of each actor, and these schematics were then executed by Chronegk.

Although the idea of a unified production concept and careful blocking seem to be standard today, when the Meininger first toured to Berlin in 1874 the theatre was still ruled by the leading actors, who had no interest in the production other than to achieve their own individual effects. Stock sets were still used over and over, and costumes were merely pulled from the storeroom, except for those worn by the leading performers who provided their own costumes and generally dressed as they pleased. Stage movement generally amounted to little more than the speaking actor delivering lines downstage center and then yielding this position to the next speaker. There was little relationship established between the actors, and the scenic elements were often totally irrelevant and sometimes even opposed to the setting and mood of the play.

The Duke insisted that every actor had to participate in the action of the play and that each action must be related to the other actors. The setting was

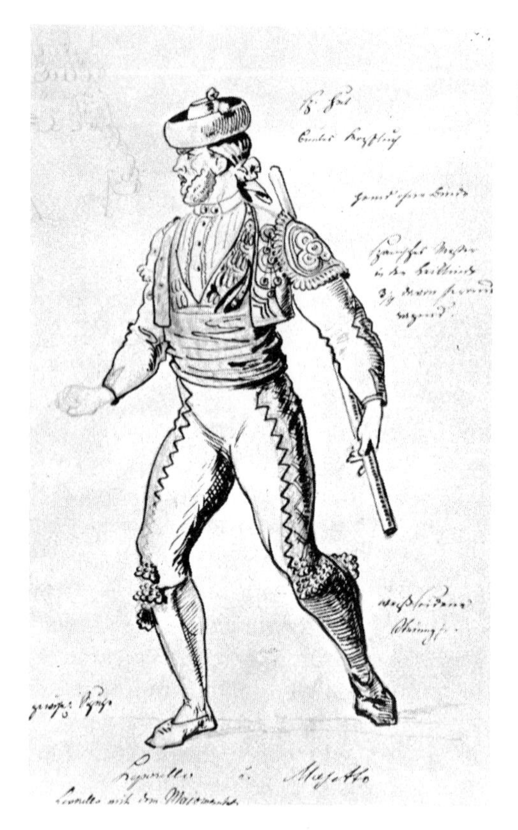

A costume design by the Duke of Saxe-Meiningen for a character in *Don Giovanni.*

designed to present an accurate reflection of the play's mood, geographical location, and period, and actors were expected to relate to the setting. The costumes were carefully designed to fit the setting and even the physical movement required of each actor. The Duke demanded adequate rehearsals, many times in full costume and with appropriate props. Every element was coordinated to relate to the whole visual picture.

As a director, the Duke was especially concerned with stage composition. He did away with the tradition that always placed the high point of a scene at stage center, insisting that the middle of the scene must not necessarily correspond with the center of the stage. In his blocking he worked from the concept that when blocking begins at the geometric middle, two halves are created, left and right. This overly formal arrangement results in a near perfect symmetry, which usually appears wooden, stiff and boring. The Duke also paid close attention to the relationship between the actors and the scenery, especially if the scenery was designed with forced perspective. His actors were never placed next to a painted object which would appear out of proportion to the performer's size; the scenic pieces (that is, furniture and props) near which an actor might be placed were always in the same proportion to the size of a person as the real ones would have been.

One of the most important innovations of the Duke's was his effective staging of crowd scenes. His success in this was due to his having complete control of the entire production, which gave him the capability of shaping these difficult scenes into unified and harmonious entities, which in turn were integrated into the whole production. The Duke, knowing the damage that an untrained supernumerary could do to his crowd scenes, used only regular company members in such scenes, and all actors were required to perform as extras. The extras were divided into subgroups, each led by a skilled actor who covered the group by standing in the foreground. This group leader was responsible to the director for his subordinates, seeing to it that all blocking was handled accurately and on cue. Each actor in a crowd scene was individualized with special characteristics and specific vocalization. They were also placed on different levels to avoid a uniform level. Crowd scenes were always extended into the wings, thereby suggesting an even larger crowd continuing offstage.

The Meininger's authenticity in their costumes, weapons, furniture, and props aroused both admiration and emulation. The Duke paid careful attention to historical accuracy, attempting to create the atmosphere and spirit of the period. The Duke himself, with his background in painting, designed all costumes, props, and scenery. All the actors and actresses wore exactly what the Duke designed for them, with no change in even the smallest detail. If a play demanded an unusual costume to which the actor was unaccustomed, the Duke arranged costume rehearsals several nights before dress rehearsal. He

Sketch by the Duke of Saxe-Meiningen for his production of *Julius Caesar.*

wanted to be sure that the actor would feel comfortable in the unfamiliar historical costume.

In the beginning, the Meininger company worked quietly, and very few people outside the Duchy were even aware that something significant was happening to theatre. In 1870, however, the most important of the critics, Karl Frenzel, was invited by Chronegk to visit the Meininger and view *The Taming of the Shrew* and *Julius Caesar*. Frenzel subsequently wrote an article on the troupe for the *Nationalzeitung*. His attitude was a bit reflective of the big city critic looking down at the little Court Theatre, but German theatrical circles became aware for the first time of the activities in Meiningen.

Chronegk talked the Duke into making a Berlin tour, despite Georg's fear that a failure would cost too much money and make him look ridiculous in the bargain. The tour was, in spite of his fears, a great success. More than anything else, the Berliners were delighted by the crowd scenes in *Julius Caesar*. The battles were so carefully staged that they gave the appearance of real fighting and Caesar's ghost was a sensation because of the Duke's use of electric lighting effects, something still quite new. The subsequent scenes of conspiratory whispering proved to be a dramatic contrast and an effective way of expressing powerful emotions. Due to popular demand the Meininger's four-week appearance was extended to six weeks, a run of unusual length by the standards of the day.

The Meininger company was not so much something new as the culmination of trends which had begun as far back as the Renaissance. To accurate costumes, props, and sets, the Duke added the concept of a completely unified production. The Duke brought the idea of a single, overriding and unifying force to theatrical production, making him the first director in the modern sense.

ADOLPHE APPIA: Adolphe Appia (1862-1928), product of a conservative, Calvinistic home, became a revolutionary whose influence profoundly changed the art of stagecraft. Nothing in his background, except perhaps the availability of drama in the rich library of his home, would have indicated the nature of his subsequent career as a radical innovator in the theatre.

Appia was born in Geneva, Switzerland, on September 1, 1862. His father, Louis Paul Appia, was a distinguished surgeon and one of the founders of the Red Cross. His family counted among themselves an unusual number of clergymen: his grandfather had been a Protestant pastor, and four uncles and a number of cousins were pastors of Calvinistic and Lutheran churches.

Appia's first opportunity to view live theatre came rather late when, at the age of nineteen, he was allowed to attend a performance of Gounod's *Faust*. The experience was an aesthetic disaster, but in the long run, it inspired Appia to correct the problems he so unexpectedly found. In his imagination, he had created an expectation of how the opera would come to life on the stage, and the reality of the performance was in opposition to his vision. He had pictured a three-dimensional presentation, but following contemporary theatrical practice, the set consisted of painted wings and backdrops, and there seemed to be no real relationship between the plot line and the set. It was an aesthetically

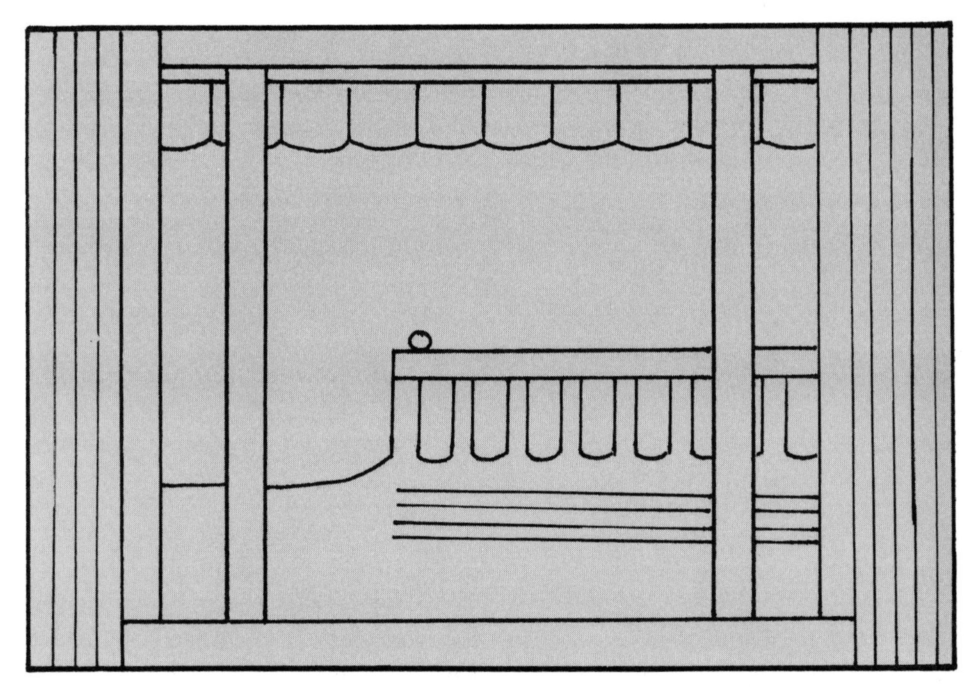

As Appia grew older his sets became more simplified and severe, as can be seen in this sketch of his design for Ibsen's *Little Eyolf.*

unfortunate experience, but one that helped form his own desire to express new, more artistic concepts.

In spite of his restricted background, Appia's family encouraged his study of music. After completing his secondary education he continued his musical studies, spending the year 1881 in Paris and then two more years at the Komnservatorium in Leipzig. He continued his musical education in Dresden, where he began one of his several friendships with men equally interested in the musical and dramatic arts.

One of these men was Houston Stewart Chamberlain (1855-1927), an ardent admirer of Wagner, an English producer and playwright, and a Germanophile. The two men shared a mutual enthusiasm for Wagnerian opera, but Appia never subscribed to the racist, Nordic supremacy views of Chamberlain.

Appia felt strongly that the traditional presentation of Wagner's works disfigured the composer's achievement. Years later, in *L'oeuvre d'art vivant* (*The Work of Living Art,* 1921) he wrote: "so different were his [Wagner's] intentions from their visual realization that all his work was weak. . . . One can assert without exaggeration, that no one has yet seen a Wagnerian drama on the stage."

In 1890 Appia returned to Geneva and began creating designs for productions of *The Ring* and *Tristan,* striving to give each of these music dramas a setting that would be appropriate and more effective. While working on this project he published his first essay, *La mise en scène du drame Wag-*

nerien (1895). Four years later he elaborated these early studies in a second volume, *La musique et la mise en scène*.

The exciting and revolutionary quality of Appia's work can only be seen and understood against the background of scenic design as it was practiced in his own time. He began his work at a time when realistic settings had replaced the Romantic but had retained too much of Romanticism's ornate and often garish aspects. Stage settings still made use of painted drops, which meant that even doors and windows were not yet fully practical. This was not only artistically objectionable in itself, but for audiences it created the unfortunate paradox of watching real people move about in front of an obviously unreal background.

To avoid the problems inherent in trying to create a realistic scene by painting it on a flat background, Appia suggested a three-dimensional setting which would be simple and unobtrusive, using lights to create the mood and intensify the communication between the actor and the audience.

According to Appia the emphasis in staging should not be on the set but on the actors, with all aspects of the staging designed to aid them in fulfilling their roles. Light should be used to create a new dimension, adding to the plasticity of the total performance by contrasting lights and shadows. Always at the heart of Appia's work was his consideration of the mise en scène and his determination that his design would work to fulfill its totality and not seek to exist for itself alone.

Essentially Appia was taking action against the excessive detail of scenic realism with its pseudo-historical details. In its place he was promoting a far more fundamental concept of theatre characteristic of the Greek theatre and the Elizabethan stage.

After 1900, living on the income of a small legacy, Appia concentrated on theatrical designing and staging. In 1903, with the recommendation of Chamberlain, he was asked by the Comtesse de Bearn to design and stage a production, in her Paris home, of scenes from Byron's *Manfred*, with music by Schumann and from Bizet's *Carmen*.

In 1906, in his home city of Geneva, Appia found another friend who supported and enlarged his concepts of theatrical art, Emile Jacques Dalcroze, (1865-1960), the creator of the theory of "eurythmics." Dalcroze theorized that each individual had his own particular rhythmic pattern. Working in a school that he had established in Geneva, he set up a system of training to help students develop a sensitivity to their internal pattern, and then to inculcate the necessary discipline for the actors and dancers to capture the rhythmic detail of a composition in body movement. Appia understood this to mean that the musical and acting elements must be synchronized to achieve a unified production. This concept supported his quest for a method that would insure the full realization in the theatre of Wagnerian music drama.

Appia insisted that the inner rhythm that motivates the performance must be understood—or at least felt—so that the mise en scène could be made to express that rhythm. To achieve this, Appia began designing sets for Dalcroze's recitals and productions. In these designs for the Dalcroze students Appia expressed his belief in the ideal of rhythmic space by using platforms of various levels, steps, ramps, flat walls, and pillars. His designs were always simple, uncluttered, and austere. Perhaps the most famous of the designs Appia created for Dalcroze is the one titled "Shadow of the Cypress." A shadow in the shape of a cypress was formed across the stage and broken against the left wall. The shadow could be controlled through fluctuations in the light, and these changes could be made to correspond to a particular musical rhythm.

In 1910 Appia was asked to become director of a new institute to be especially built for him at Hellerau. He was given the title of lecturer when the institute was established, but his primary work was done at his home in Geneva, where he continued to experiment with stage design. Together with the Russian artist, Alexandre von Salzmann, he planned the first Hellerau festival production, designing severely stylized settings for a dance drama with music by Dalcroze and a performance of the Hades scene from Gluck's *Orpheus and Euridice.*

Appia devised the plan for the large Hellerau auditorium, in which the acting area and the audience were separated only by a sunken orchestra pit. Even as his settings demanded the participation of the audience, so his theatre design provided for that possibility. His aspiration was for a production involving the entire audience in the experience of the drama. "Dramatic art," he wrote, "is directed to our eyes, our ears, our understanding—in short, to our whole being."

In 1922 Arturo Toscanini, the artistic director of La Scala, invited Appia to collaborate in preparing a new mise en scène for *Tristan und Isolde.* The result of this collaboration was a series of settings that were extremely simple

Appia's design titled "Moonlight," based on his work with Dalcroze.

and classic in their lines; their simplicity stood in stark contrast to the lush scenery of Italian opera and the traditional Wagnerian settings used at Bayreuth. In fact, the Wagnerian performances had become so stylized that any effort to change them was doomed to widespread resentment. The performance at La Scala was a musical success, but Appia's mise en scène was loudly and bitterly denounced.

The criticism did not discourage Appia from further attempts to restage Wagner. His last attempts were made at Basle in 1924-25, for the *Rhinegold* and *Valkyrie* from *The Ring* cycle.

Appia, the passionate idealist, often seemed to be a prophet without honor in his own time. He tried to stop the theatre's impossible attempt to imitate physical reality, or, in all too many cases, bedecking reality with such a clutter of rich decoration that the fragment of delicate life being created was destroyed. His approach to theatre was founded on his belief that the theatre, and indeed all art, is a joy that is compounded to the degree that we share it with others.

THE DRAMA IN NOTHERN EUROPE

Northern Europe At the beginning of the nineteenth century, theatrical activity in northern Europe was primarily centered in the major cities of Germany proper, with some important work going on in Austria.

The first major Austrian dramatist to gain prominence in the early part of the century was Franz Grillparzer (1791-1872), who remained all his life a mystery to friend and foe alike. He was a threatre scholar, like Zacharias Werner, who knew thoroughly the German traditions, the works of Lope de Vega and Calderón, the early Romantic drama, and especially the theories of Goethe and Schiller. He never developed a formula on the lines of Werner, but he did develop an abiding concern for what he saw as the tragic conflict between human aspirations and the world around us that dooms them to defeat. He worked in most of the Romantic forms: *Blanka von Kastilian* (*Blanca from Castile*, 1809) followed the form and style of Schiller's *Don Carlos; Die Ahnfrau* (*The Ancestress*, 1817) was full of folk materials and ballads and concentrated on fate in much the same way as the plays of Tieck; and *Sappho* (1818) was a Classical exercise in the manner of Goethe. His late historical plays, however, are really his own in form, and without the worst of the Romantic claptrap they explore that aspect of human existence in which he was most interested.

The playwrights who followed Grillparzer in Austria tended to fall into two groups. The first and largest group based their dramas on the formula popularized by Kotzebue, producing forgettable sentimental melodramas and comedies. The second and smaller group concentrated on more individualized works. The best of this group was probably Johann Nestroy (1801-62), whose broad comic lampoons and biting satires depend so much on native dialects, untranslatable puns, and local customs that his plays have never achieved popularity outside the German-speaking areas.

The drama in northern Europe, outside of Germany, finally narrows down to four major dramatists: Henrik Ibsen, August Strindberg, Arthur Schnitzler, and Hugo von Hofmannsthal.

A drawing by Franz Grillparzer in illustration of the final scene of his *The Argonauts.*

HENRIK IBSEN: Henrik Ibsen (1828-1906) was born in Skien, Norway. His birth came at approximately the same time as the death of an older brother, and after him were born one sister and three brothers. Henrik's father was a lumber merchant with adequate finances to support a family and the relatives of both parents were among the patricians of Skien. Ibsen's childhood was extremely happy, but in 1836 the British market changed and Knud Ibsen went bankrupt, losing all of his property except for a small farm to which the family moved. After the financial disaster the Ibsens abandoned their social position and Henrik's father earned a very modest income as a jobber, finding buyers for the cargoes that arrived in Skien harbor. The family's poverty meant that Henrik was unable to attend the town's more important schools, the "Latin School" or the "Burgher's School," and was forced to go to the "Middle School," a small institution conducted by two theological candidates. No Latin was taught in this school, and without Latin he would be unable to attend the university or enter any profession.

When Ibsen was fifteen his family returned to Skien, but this time to a much humbler part of the town called Snipetorp. It was here that he was confirmed, and his first Communion made quite an impression on the boy. Ibsen's mother, who was deeply involved in pietism, did everything in her power to instill in all her children a firm belief in the Church dogmas, but in Henrik's case she failed. He grew more and more convinced that he had absolutely nothing in common with his brothers and sister, and he never wrote to them or his mother once he left home.

At sixteen Ibsen left Skien for Grimstad, a town not much bigger than Skien in the southeastern corner of Norway. The town was not poor, receiving much trade from the building of sailing vessels, but it was far from being a cultural center. In this community he found a job as an apprentice druggist, but his pay was so meager that he often went about in winter underfed and underdressed. His work took up most of his day, but in the evening he lived in the world of books which he obtained at the library in Grimstad. While in Grimstad he wrote his first poetry. A short piece called *In Autumn* was sent by a friend to the *Christiania Post,* and when it was printed by this newspaper Ibsen's hopes for his future career suddenly became much brighter.

A turn-of-the-century production of Ibsen's *Ghosts* at the Vienna Burgtheatre, with Oswald played by a former Meininger performer, the famous German actor Josef Kainz. (From *Bühne und Welt,* Berlin, 1905-06)

In 1848, still working as an apprentice apothecary, he wrote his first play, *Catilina* (*Catiline*), which he sent to the Christiania Theatre. It was rejected, but Ibsen soon recovered from this blow, concentrating his energies on a girl named Clara Ebbell. This time it was Ibsen himself who was rejected, when Miss Ebbell announced her engagement to her own uncle.

In 1850, after studying Latin on his own, Ibsen decided to take the qualifying examinations for entrance to the University of Christiania. Before going to Christiania he made a visit to his hometown of Skien, and this was the last time he was to go there. The memories this visit reawakened of humiliating poverty and the atmosphere of orthodox religion was an uncomfortable experience for Henrik, and he never went back again. When he finally arrived in Christiania he enrolled for a brief time in "the student factory," whose purpose was coaching candidates for the university entrance examination. When after taking the exam Ibsen learned he would have to take a portion of it again, he abandoned his goal of a university education and joined two new friends in the publication of a liberal, satirical weekly called *The Man* (changed later to *Andhrimmer*). The paper was forced to suspend publication after nine months because it was losing money.

A scene from the Moscow Art Theatre's production of Ibsen's *Brand*, 1906. (From *Bühne und Welt*, Berlin, 1905-06)

Shortly after Ibsen's arrival in Christiania, he wrote his second play, *Kjaempehøien* (*The Warrior's Barrow*), under the pen name of Brynjolf Bjarme. It was performed three times by the Christiania Theatre. In 1881 a national hero of Norway named Ole Bull was responsible for the appointment of Ibsen as theatre poet, stage manager, and Bull's assistant at the Norwegian Theatre in Bergen. This came about because Norway was beginning to feel conscious of its own traditions, seeking to escape the cultural dominance of Denmark, under whose rule Norway had been from 1397 to 1814. Ibsen left for Bergen in 1851, painfully aware of his lack of knowledge regarding the technical and practical aspects of the theatre. However, he learned so quickly and so well that the Board of Trustees awarded him a stipend the next spring to enable him to travel to Copenhagen and Dresden for the purpose of learning more. On this journey Ibsen came in contact, for the first time, with productions of Shakespeare. When he returned to Bergen he had in his baggage the manuscript for his next play, *Sancthansnatten* (*St. John's Night*).

In 1855 Ibsen entered into another one-sided love affair, this time with a girl named Henrikke Holst. Although the affair itself never amounted to anything, it did result in the writing of Ibsen's *Fru Inger til Østraat* (*Lady Inger of Ostraat*, 1854). The reception of his plays up to this time can be summed up by a line from a review of *St. John's Night* in a Bergen paper: "The play is a failure, but there are a few beautiful details." Ibsen's plays were such failures, in fact, that he refused to tell anyone that *Lady Inger of Ostraat* was his work until one night at a performance when there were enthusiastic calls for the author. In 1855 Ibsen wrote *Gildet paa Solhaug* (*The Feast at Solhaug*), which was performed in that year at the French court. It was Ibsen's first play to achieve recognition, but the critics were not delighted and pounced on Ibsen like a pack of wolves.

At the age of twenty-eight Ibsen found his future wife, the daughter of Dean Thoresen of the Cross Church in Bergen. When they met Susannah was writing plays anonymously, and Ibsen staged one of them at the Bergen theatre. A few weeks after their first meeting, Ibsen wrote her a poem in which he proposed marriage. In 1857 Ibsen returned to Christiania and started work on the tragedy, *Haermaendene paa Helgeland* (*The Vikings at Helgeland*). On June 26, 1858, he and Susannah Thoresen were married.

During the next five years Ibsen wrote only two plays, *Kjaerlighedens komedie* (*Love's Comedy*, 1862) and *Kongsemnerne* (*The Pretenders*, 1863). While these plays were being written, Ibsen and his wife were living in extreme poverty. *The Pretenders*, which he finished in two months, was the first of Ibsen's plays to represent his own thought and personality, instead of merely imitating the spirit of Schiller, Shakespeare, or Scribe.

In 1864. having received a traveling fellowship, Ibsen left Norway for Rome, where he and his wife remained until 1868. In 1866 he wrote his poetic

Set design for Ibsen's *The Vikings at Helgeland*. (Painting by Eugen Quaglio, Theatre-Museum, Munich)

drama, *Brand*, the episodic history of a fanatic, and in 1867, his last great verse drama, *Peer Gynt*, the episodic history of an audacious libertine.

Through the kindness of a fellow Norwegian dramatist, Ibsen found a new publisher, Hegel, in Copenhagen. Hegel published his works in editions worthy of the poet, paid him royalties that forever ended Ibsen's poverty, and became his devoted friend. However, neither *Brand* nor *Peer Gynt* were accepted for what Ibsen had intended them to be. The plays, Ibsen felt, were treated as political pamphlets. However, with *Des unges forbund* (*The League of Youth*, 1869) Ibsen inaugurated his realistic period and, some critics feel, founded the modern drama.

In 1873 he wrote *Kejser og Galilaeer* (*Emperor and Galilean*). After a visit to Norway he settled for a few years in Munich where he wrote *Samfundets Støtter* (*Pillars of Society*, 1877). After returning to Rome in 1878 he wrote *Et dukkehjem* (*A Doll's House*, 1879), *Gengangere* (*Ghosts*, 1881), *En folkefiende* (*An Enemy of the People*, 1882), and *Vildanden* (*The Wild Duck*, 1884). In 1885 he returned to Munich, where he composed *Rosmersholm* (1886), *Fruen fra havet* (*The Lady From the Sea*, 1888), and *Hedda Gabler* (1890). In 1891 he returned to Christiania, where he lived until his death in 1906. In Christiania, he wrote *Bygmester Solness* (*The Master Builder*, 1892), *Lille Eyolf* (*Little Eyolf*, 1894), *John Gabriel Borkman* (1896), and his final play, *Naar vi døde vaagner* (*When We Dead Awaken*, 1899).

H. L. Mencken has said about Ibsen that he has lived down his commentators, and is now ready to be examined and enjoyed for what he actually was, namely, a first-rate journeyman dramatist, perhaps the best that ever lived. Forty years ago he was

> *hymned and damned as anything and everything else: symbolist, seer, prophet, necromancer, maker of riddles, rabble-rouser, cheap shocker, pornographer, spinner of gossamer nothings. Fools belabored him and fools defended him; he was near to being suffocated and done for in the fog of balderdash. There was no crime against virtue, good order and the revelation of God that he was not accused of. The product of all the pawing and bawling was the Ibsen legend, that fabulous picture of a fabulous monster, drenching the world with scandalous platitudes from a watchtower in the chilblained North.*

This picture drawn of Ibsen is, of course, untrue:

> *The genuine Ibsen was anything but the anti-Christ thus conjured up by imprudent partisans and terrified opponents. On the contrary, he was a highly respectable gentleman of the middle class, well-barbered, ease-loving and careful of mind; a very skillful practitioner of a very exacting and lucrative trade; a safe and sane exponent of order, efficiency, honesty and common sense.*

AUGUST STRINDBERG: Probably more than any other playwright of his day, Johan August Strindberg's (1849-1912) plays were autobiographical. His lifelong battle with schizophrenia, his traumatic experiences with women, and his varied and frustrating associations with nearly all the people with whom he came in contact provided him with a vast amount of material for creative works. His brilliant mind, ever wavering between reality and illusion, sought expression in practically all forms of literature, including dramatic writing.

Franklin S. Klaf, in *The Origin of Psychology in Modern Drama,* states that Strindberg's desire "to know how and why he functioned, (and) also how and why everything around him functioned" kept him from going insane. Certainly Strindberg suffered from and fought against a schizophrenic illness for the largest part of his creative life.

Strindberg's early childhood in Stockholm was intensely unhappy. He reacted to his parents' marriage with humiliation because his father had married, he thought, beneath his station. The elder Strindberg had married a domestic servant girl who had been his mistress for many years and was the mother of his three children. The size of the family increased, but the family financial fortune did not. When Strindberg reached age thirteen his mother died. His father married again in less than a year, an action for which Strindberg never forgave him. Nothing else in his life affected him more than his mother's death. She was to appear, in one guise or another, over and over again in his novels and plays. Her religious spirit dominated him throughout his early life and remained present in varying degrees throughout the remainder of his career.

As a young man, Strindberg attended the University of Uppsala, but the lack of money forced him to leave before he had a chance to graduate. He became a medical apprentice, but the sight of blood was abhorrent to him. However, the growing scientific spirit of the age remained with him throughout his life, and he was regularly involved in varying scientific experiments. For

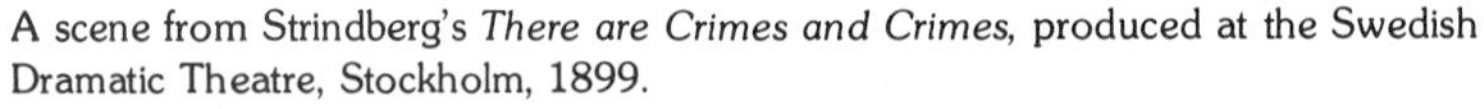
A scene from Strindberg's *There are Crimes and Crimes,* produced at the Swedish Dramatic Theatre, Stockholm, 1899.

example, during one of his schizophrenic attacks, he tried to inject morphine into plants to test his theory that plants had human characteristics.

Although Strindberg hovered on the brink of insanity during long periods of his life, his mind was always active, exploring all aspects of life, including his own illness, and creating out of his explorations a drama that would exert great influence on the drama of the twentieth century. He experimented not only with modern psychological drama, but also with the expressionistic style, which has had a constant effect on theatre since the end of the nineteenth century.

Strindberg was a prolific writer at least in part because his bouts with insanity seemed to heighten his creative abilities. He wrote fifty-eight plays, fifteen novels (including some autobiographical seminovels); over one hundred short stories, sketches, and fairy tales; three volumes of verse; a number of historical works; some pseudo-scientific treatises; a multitude of essays; and articles on chemistry, botany, politics, economics, philosophy, religion, philology, drama, music, and art.

An early influence upon Strindberg, at least during his naturalistic period, was the great French writer Emile Zola. Zola insisted that the characters in a play should be real flesh-and-blood people, placed in a realistic and clearly defined milieu, which is then shown to be responsible for their lives and actions. The characterization, he said, should depend on a psychological analysis that is firmly based on physiological findings. Zola clearly believed that characters in a drama should lead lives determined by the forces of heredity and environment.

Strindberg's best work in the naturalistic genre is probably *Fadren* (*The Father*, 1887), a theatrical adaptation of his novel titled *The Confessions of a Fool.* The plot is simple, concentrated, and explosive, and while the evil of the mother and the monomania of the father seem not to be totally the products of environment, they are soundly based in psychological analysis and in physiology.

Having worked well in the naturalistic genre, Strindberg entered a transition period, and *Fröken Julie* (*Miss Julie*, 1888) is its result. Often lumped with his naturalistic dramas, *Miss Julie* is in fact a linking of environmental determinism, psychological insight, and the mystic folk force that seems to grow out of the Midsummer's Eve celebration that is part of the play's milieu. Thus, it was only a short step from *Miss Julie* to the expressionistic plays with which Strindberg ended his career.

After working so well in the naturalistic style, Strindberg discovered expressionism before the critics and historians had devised a name for it. It was an inevitable path for him to take; his life left him no alternative. Little has been said about his psychotic relationships with women, but with each new marriage (there were three) Strindberg regressed more and more into his schizophrenic turmoils, until he finally underwent his "inferno" period. This period, which followed closely on the breakup of his third marriage, was the closest he came to total insanity. His feelings of persecution, his guilt complex from past experiences, his agoraphobia, his fear of communication with others, and his delusions regarding outer manifestations all haunted him during this five-year period. During one attack he imagined that severe shocks of electricity were going through his body. However, the reasoning faculty that always managed to keep him from going over the edge was still with him and so he took an instrument to bed with him to check the voltage reading. Discovering that no electrical current was registering, he concluded that the electrical shocks were merely products of his mental illness.

Following this inferno period his expressionistic style became dominant, resulting in such plays as *Ett drömspel* (*A Dream Play,* 1902) and *Spöksonaten* (*The Ghost Sonata,* 1907). This last play came from a grouping generally referred to as his "chamber plays." The others, a bit more realistic in style, are *Oväder* (*The Storm*) and *Brända tomten* (*After the Fire*), both written in 1907. The other plays in which Strindberg sought to explore the mystic reaches of the subconscious are *Advent, ett mysterium* (*Advent,* 1898), *Till Damaskus* (*To Damascus,* 1898, parts 1 and 2), *Paask* (*Easter,* 1900), *Dödsdansen* (*The Dance of Death,* 1901, in two parts), and part 3 of *To Damascus* (1904).

Although Strindberg is not often performed, he has influenced many playwrights through the reading of his plays; two of America's greatest playwrights—Eugene O'Neill and Tennessee Williams—are among them.

Arthur Schnitzler (1862-1931), one of the most undervalued writers in the history of theatre, was like Chekhov a practicing physician who wrote plays and short stories. However, unlike Chekhov, who so lovingly involved himself in his characterizations, Schnitzler seemed to bring to his plays an almost scientific detachment combined with a gentle warm humor. His first play, and one that is still regularly staged, was *Anatol* (1890), a series of

A scene from Schnitzler's *Anatol.* (New York Public Library, Lincoln Center)

sketches about a young Viennese gallant busily playing the games of love. It must be remembered that Schnitzler's Vienna was also the Vienna of Freud. The two men were friends and both saw sexuality at the heart of human motivation. Schnitzler, however, was determined to show that love was too important to serve as a mere game. The consequences of Anatol's game-playing are not severe, though at the end of the play there is an indication that too many games have destroyed his capability to love completely. However, Schnitzler followed up this concern in 1894 with *Liebelei* (*The Game of Love*), a somewhat darker picture of the love game in which a young working-class girl tragically destroys herself when she learns of the death of a young aristocrat who, the audience knows, has merely been playing with her.

In 1889 Schnitzler carried his game theory into the social-political area with *Der grüne Kakadu* (*The Green Cockatoo*). The play tells of some Parisian gallants who in 1789 play revolutionary games—until it actually happens. His most famous play, *Reigen* (*La Ronde*, 1900), is in the episodic style of *Anatol*. In this drama ten characters play sexual games with changing partners. Again the author's touch is light but his theme is serious—human sexuality is the center of life, the most exalted aspect of man in that through it he can, like God, create life, and to use it casually for mere egotistical enjoyment is to cheapen it and ultimately destroy it.

Schnitzler did, occasionally, depart from his concern with game playing. *Professor Bernhardi* (1912) is a problem drama exploring the evils of anti-Semitism among a group of Viennese doctors, and *Der Junge Medardus* (*Young

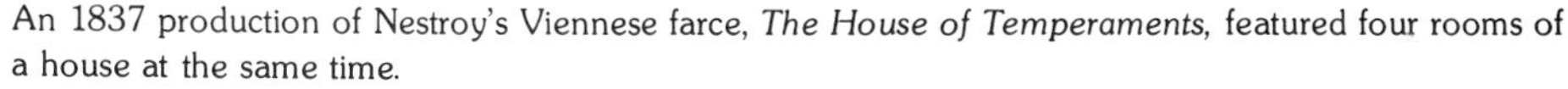
An 1837 production of Nestroy's Viennese farce, *The House of Temperaments*, featured four rooms of a house at the same time.

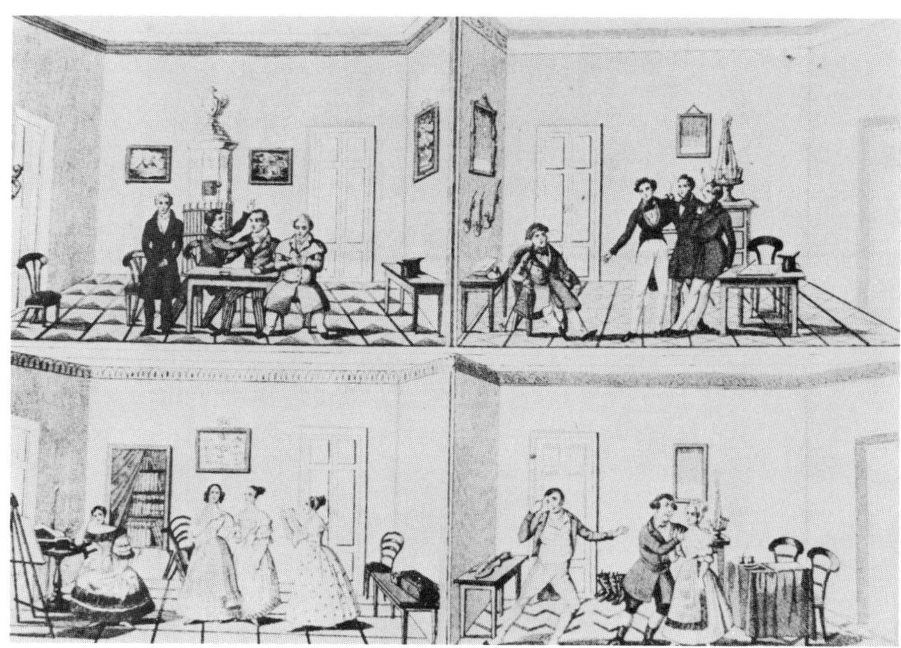

Medardus, 1910), based on a story by E. T. A. Hoffmann, is a tormented tale of self-deception. However, in his most experimental work he returns to his primary concern and makes the ultimate statement on gamesmanship. *Zum grossen Wurstel* (*The Great Punch and Judy Show*, 1910) presents a hand-puppet play, a string-puppet show, and a stage play before an onstage audience. All the shows are exposed as false, and the onstage audience that stands for the audience in the auditorium is asked to judge whether they are themselves any less false.

Hugo von Hofmannsthal (1874-1929) brought the Viennese theatre to the close of the nineteenth century and into the twentieth. A poet as well as playwright, Hofmannsthal was one of the leaders in the reaction against naturalism, using his poetry and verse drama to consider an inner rather than outer reality. Among these early verse plays were *Gestern* (*Yesterday*, 1891), *Der Tod des Tizian* (*The Death of Titian*, 1892), and *Der Tor und der Tod* (*Death of a Fool*, 1893). His early plays indicate Hofmannsthal's love of the beautiful and mysterious, but they also indicate a rather practical fear of carrying mystical intuition too far in an attempt to resolve nonmystical social problems.

Just as the twentieth century was about to open, Hofmannsthal began experimenting with new directions. The plays of this period, from 1898 to about 1905, indicate a quest for a form that could combine with verse drama to provide something dramatic and theatrical. The search ranged widely, from pagan mystery to Greek mythology to Elizabethan revenge tragedy.

It was not until 1911, however, that Hofmannsthal found his form—the Medieval allegory. In that year he wrote *Jedermann*, an adaptation of *Everyman*. The play attracted Max Reinhardt, and when the two men created the Salzburg Festival this play was produced on the steps in front of the cathedral, subsequently becoming an annual event. Hofmannsthal continued his work with the morality form, basing *Das Salzburger Grosse Welttheater* (*The Great Salzburger Theatre of the World*, 1922), a play dealing with what he conceived to be a European spiritual crisis, on Calderón's *El gran teatro del mundo*. His last play, *Der Turm* (*The Tower*, 1925), was also based on a play by Calderón, *La vida es sueño*. The play deals with the conflict between materialism and spirituality, a common concern of the Medieval morality writers and something that would be especially attractive to the artists during the early twentieth century.

The Nineteenth Century in Russia

For most western Europeans and Americans, unfortunately, Russian theatre begins and ends with Chekhov. In fact, however, the Russian theatre, which began with imported European drama in the eighteenth century, underwent a dramatic renaissance in the nineteenth. There developed an intense interest in all things theatrical, with dramatic and aesthetic theories debated in the press, in the literary societies, and even onstage. Proponents of Romanticism and Classicism and realism did verbal battle, but the primary issue soon came to be more than dramatic literary philosophy, centering on the need for a national theatre. Those critics who had cried out against the German or French or English influence on the Russian drama, demanding a truly Russian theatre, found supporters flocking to their side after the Napoleonic invasion hastened a sense of national unity and purpose. The Russian drama became far more independent and original, and it discovered a direction in the plays of Pushkin and Gogol.

NINETEENTH CENTURY RUSSIAN DRAMA

In the first quarter of the nineteenth century the German theatre was still exerting a major influence on Russian drama. The primary source of this influence was August von Kotzebue, who from 1781-1795 was a civil servant at St. Petersburg, and whose melodramatic sentimentality infected the Russian drama even more easily than it did the French, English, and American. However, productions of the "national school" were also being written; they were mostly satiric comedies by Ivan Krylov (1768-1844), a prolific composer of popular fables, and Prince Alexander Shakhovskoy (1777-1846), whose plays happily savaged the Germanic sentimental drama and the French drawing-room comedy with equal abandonment. The battle between the developing national drama and the foreign-style drama was finally decided by Alexander Griboyedov (1795-1829) with his play *Gore ot uma* (*Wit Works Woe,* completed

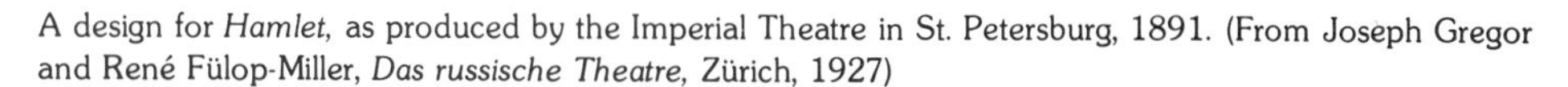

A design for *Hamlet,* as produced by the Imperial Theatre in St. Petersburg, 1891. (From Joseph Gregor and René Fülop-Miller, *Das russische Theatre,* Zürich, 1927)

in 1823, produced in 1831). Griboyedov's verse comedy hit Moscow with enormous impact, scathingly picturing the pseudosophisticated Moscow society as a group of idle layabouts, parasites, reactionaries, and fools. This unsavory group is contrasted with a radical, patriotic idealist named Chatsky, who is uninteresting in traditional dramatic terms, but whose passionate speeches make him a precursor of the Russian revolutionary movement. The official censors saw the direction of the play, and only allowed it to be produced in an expurgated form some two years after Griboyedov's death. An unexpurgated script of the play was not printed until 1862.

Because of the isolation of the Russian artistic centers, and in part, perhaps, because of the ever-growing emphasis on native drama and the consequent rejection of European styles and modes, the Romantic movement that swept western Europe at the beginning of the century did not reach Russia until the 1830s, when its European vogue had nearly passed. As a movement, European Romanticism had little influence on Russian drama, probably because from the beginning serious Russian drama has contained an almost ponderous native Romanticism that refused to be moved. Some native Romantic dramas were reasonably popular, but even such early and outstanding works as those by Alexander Pushkin (1799-1837) or Mikhail Lermontov (1814-41) were rarely produced.

Pushkin, Russia's first and greatest national poet, was born in Moscow, where his father was a government functionary. He was educated privately, with help from his uncle Vasily, who was a well-known poet, and according to popular tradition he began to write plays (in French) at the age of eight. By fifteen his favorite writers included Molière, Racine, Voltaire, Byron, and Shakespeare, with the latter two having the greatest influence on his subsequent plays. Under the influence of Shakespeare, Pushkin began his greatest drama, *Boris Godunov* (1825). He was already highly conscious of the fact that Russia had no national drama, and so while he learned from Shakespeare he went to Russian themes and folklore for his major work.

Boris Godunov was not published until six years after its completion, and it failed to achieve real popularity until the 1870s, when Moussorgsky used it as the book for his famous opera. A similar fate was meted out to Lermontov's *Maskarad* (*Masquerade*, 1835), which was not produced for more than eighty years, finally taking the stage on the eve of the 1917 revolution.

Just before his death in a duel, Pushkin completed a series of "little" tragedies—*Skupoy rytsar* (*The Avaricious Knight*), *Pir vo vremya chumy* (*The Feast During the Plague*), *Motsart i Saleri* (*Mozart and Salieri*), and *Kamenny gost'* (*The Stone Guest*)—one-act psychological portraits which he hoped would bring to life people and periods. He also completed *Rusalka* (*The Water Nymph*), a short play based on a folk tale, in 1832.

In the same year that the censors were banning Lermontov's *Masquerade*, Nikolai Gogol (1809-52) was producing *Revisor* (*The Inspector General*), and the clamorous delight with which audiences received it indicated that the native or "natural" drama had at last completely triumphed. The play shocked and delighted audiences with its comic indictment of the bureaucratic regime and its dishonest officials. It was also greeted with applause by the critics, who saw it as a continuation and a justification of the Russian-style

A scene from Pushkin's *Boris Godunov*, performed at the Alexandrinsky Theatre, St. Petersburg, 1878.

satiric drama. While this was good for Russian drama on one hand it was bad on the other because of Gogol's distinctive and inimitable style. For the next fifty years too many Russian comedies were merely bad Gogol.

At the middle of the nineteenth century the theatre was especially dependent on the work of Ivan Turgenev (1818-83), a novelist and dramatist whose best play, *Mesyats v derevne* (*A Month in the Country*, 1850) is still regularly produced. A member of a wealthy family, Turgenev entered Moscow University, where his literary tastes led him to translating Shakespeare and writing poems and articles. Finishing at Moscow, he went on to Berlin University to complete his education.

In 1843 Turgenev completed his first play, a Romantic cloak and sword drama set in Spain. He followed this, in 1846, with a Gogol-like satire titled *Bezdenezhye* (*Penniless, or Scenes from the Life of a Young Nobleman*). Two years later, his "Gogol period" apparently past, he was working in the style of Musset, publishing a one act titled *Gde tonko, tam i rvyotsya* (*Where It's Thin, It Breaks*).

In 1849 Turgenev, at last writing in his own style, published *Kholostyak* (*The Bachelor*), a delicate, sensitive comedy, and he followed this with *Nakhlebnik* (*The Boarder*), a touching study of old age. In 1850 he completed *A Month in the Country,* but it ran afoul of the censors and was not staged until 1872. It was a psychological drama, sometimes comic but not in any traditional style, and it helped prepare the way for the plays of Chekhov.

During the thirty years following the middle of the century the movement toward dramatic realism developed and eventually triumphed. In part this is due to Gogol, whose plays depended on the realistic presentation of some as-

A drawing of the final scene of Gogol's *The Inspector General*, produced in 1836 at the Alexandrinsky Theatre, St. Petersburg.

pect of life, usually that of the peasant and lower bureaucratic class. Mostly, however, it was due to the influence of the leading playwright of the period, Alexander Ostrovsky, whose more than fifty original plays formed the basis for the first truly national Russian repertory.

ALEXANDER OSTROVSKY: It has been said that Alexander Ostrovsky (1823-86) revealed the Russian soul in his great dramas. He lived his life prior to the October Revolution, which saw the start of Soviet Russia and the end of Tsarist rule, but he did, however, sow the seeds of a nationalist drama that was to speak for both Tsarist Russia and the Soviet Russia which was to come. Ostrovsky lived in a Russia still composed primarily of nobles and serfs, and all of his major dramas reflected his love for the folk ways of the Russian serf and disgust at their plight. He was also deeply concerned with the character of the provincial merchant class as well as the character of the petty government officials who were largely responsible for the corruption of the small Russian villages. Born in south-central Moscow to a minor government official in the senate and the daughter of a baker of sacramental wafers, Ostrovsky was in constant association with two groups in which he was most interested—the merchant class and the lower class of government officials. This close association with both these classes was responsible for his creation of numerous dramas whose themes and characters reflected their lives.

Ostrovsky went to Moscow to the provincial gymnasium, after which he entered the law school of Moscow University. However, he left the university within a year because of a disagreement with a professor. He then became a court clerk, which furthered his observation of the Moscow merchants and small officials from both a professional and personal point of view.

Soon Ostrovsky joined a literary group called the "Pogodin Circle" whose existence revolved around the magazine called *Moskuityanin*. Many of Russia's leading literary men were a part of this circle, and most of them had a mutual love for the poetry and ritualistic nature of Russian peasant folk materials. Because of this rather exclusive interest, the circle began to closely observe the lives of the Russian serfs, which eventually led most of them to a heightened appreciation of the Russian common people. The art of observation was one of Ostrovsky's talents, and it was this plus a sensitive awareness that was largely responsible for the realistic details of speech and manner evident in his characters.

Ostrovsky also borrowed from the newspapers, paying much attention to the actual words and speech patterns of the common people. This exceptional attention to native speech patterns was revealed in Ostrovsky's early works, and was quite typical of him; the wonderful pointedness and power of the language, and historical and folk authenticity were the fruit of his constant observation. Ostrovsky even kept an extraordinarily complete notebook of local proverbs and sayings, which he referred to from time to time in his plays.

The first Russian professional playwright who employed realism to any large extent, Ostrovsky was concerned with making theatre more available to the masses. He was, in a way, the forerunner of Stanislavsky in his belief that the inner essence of a character was the thing that the actor must understand in order to be believable. Like Stanislavsky, Ostrovsky felt that the theatre should above all mirror the "truth of life."

Ostrovsky's views on the theatre were formulated in a memorandum that he wrote in 1881 expressing his concern that theatre might collapse as a result of too many amateurs and incompetents. Because of this inadequacy the audience ended up seeing something that did not resemble life. Ostrovsky also felt that the spectator must at all times be involved in the action even to the point of forgetting that he is in the theatre. He felt that the necessary theatrical professionalism could only be reached by unceasing labor and the rigorous study of technique. An actor is a plastic artist, but he will not be an artist or even a skillful artisan without mastering the techniques of his art.

Ostrovsky wanted to avoid spectacle and stage tricks as a means of sustaining interest. He was concerned with characters and their relationship to one another. Most of all, he got away from the stylized language and stereotyped characterization of so many earlier playwrights; his characters spoke the language of the Russian people. This change toward realism helped Ostrovsky to create characters who were both real and deep, which in turn led to a greater need for truly competent and intelligent actors and actresses. It was Ostrovsky's characters that helped lead to the development of Russian acting schools to train actors to be sensitive and to explore the art of bringing the interior of a character to light.

Another of Ostrovsky's contributions to theatre was his involvement in the Russian Society of Dramatic Authors and Composers. This organization established a kind of union of playwrights which guaranteed certain sums of money to the playwright upon each performance of his play. It performed the necessary function of improving the monetary security of playwrights, a security that was obviously lacking even for Ostrovsky himself.

Before Ostrovsky, Russian theatre had been restricted to a limited repertoire. It had enough vaudeville and soul-tearing melodrama, but very little good original drama. As a result of this condition, Ostrovsky began a new period of Russian theatre when he put on stage his uncouth, petty officials, his rough tradesmen, and his overworked peasants whom he portrayed with painstaking realism without giving up command of the dramatic form. As a result of his work the genre of realism was established on the Russian stage, where it has held sway to our time.

Groza (*The Storm*, 1859) considered to be Ostrovsky's greatest tragedy, also became one of the most widely produced plays of Soviet Russia. Within *The Storm*, however, there is a combination of things that make it much more than a revolutionary drama of Tsarist oppression. There is poetry combined with realism and symbolism combined with social comment. Each person in the play is a true and living character lifted directly from life and yet they are all clearly the products of the poet's art. Because of its central theme *The Storm* was thought by many critics to be a symbolic protest of conditions among the weak and the oppressed, and the character of Katherine was connected with the up-and-coming revolutionary movement. Ostrovsky became the "writer of the people"; his dialogue was their speech and his themes reflected their problems.

An extremely prolific writer, Ostrovsky wrote plays that fall into four basic groupings. The largest group of plays were those dealing with the merchant class. Here Ostrovsky revealed a world which was relatively new to Russian literature. The second group of plays dealt with native customs. The third group was concerned with corrupt, petty government officials. The fourth portrayed ironically the foibles of fashionable society. In 1873 Ostrovsky published *Snegurochka* (*The Snow Maiden*). This is the only exception to his realistic form, for in this beautiful play he explored the world of fantasy rather than the world of realism, combining lyrical poetry and folk tales, but emphasizing the poetic essence of the folk rather than their plight. Gorky called it "the merger of romanticism with realism."

Ostrovsky did not just write in an ivory tower. He was very concerned with the physical techniques of the theatre. He spent numerous hours with actors helping them to understand the inner reality of his characters. His growing concern for developing new techniques in both acting and production led him to become the administrator of the Moscow Crown Theatres. It was under his direct leadership, both as playwright and manager, that Russian theatre began to improve.

Alexander Sukhovo-Kobylin (1817-1903), after Ostrovsky the foremost playwright of the period, produced one trilogy: *Svadba Krechinskogo* (*Kerechinsky Wedding*, 1854), a picaresque comedy; *Delo* (*The Case*, 1861), an ironic satire; and *Smert Tarelkina* (*Tarelkin's Death*, 1869), a farce-fantasy. From a literary point of view, Kobylin must rank high. His comedies are brilliantly crafted, the plots are forceful, his humor ranges from light to dark, and his characters have an emotional intensity that imparts an unusual degree of stage life.

Along with the development of contemporary realism came an interest in historical drama, and the greatest practitioner of this form was Alexei K.

Tolstoy (1817-75). A diplomat and friend of Alexander II, Tolstoy was a patrician, a poet, and a Romantic antiquarian who was more interested in idealizing the old feudal Russia than in presenting an historically accurate picture. He began his trilogy on the "era of troubles," the period including the end of the sixteenth century and the beginning of the seventeenth, with *Smert Ioanna Groznogo* (*The Death of Ivan the Terrible*, 1866). In 1868 he completed *Tsar Fyodor Ioannovich* (*Tsar Fyodor Ivanovich*), and two years later, in 1870, the final play, *Tsar Boris*. At first the plays achieved only a modest success, but *Tsar Fyodor Ivanovich* eventually became very popular after Stanislavsky chose it for the opening of the Moscow Art Theatre in 1898.

MAXIM GORKY: Gorky (Alexei Maximovich Peshkov, 1868-1936) was born the son of Maxim Savvatyevich Peshkov and his wife, Varvara Vassilyevna, both members of the lower middle class in the province of Perm. In 1869 the family moved to Astrakhan, and three years later Alexei contracted cholera. His father, caring for his young son, also caught the disease, and in 1873 he died. Alexei and his mother moved in with his grandparents, and the grandfather took over the primary responsibility for the boy's education. He taught Alexei Church Slavonic by having the boy recite from the Book of Psalms and the Book of Hours. When he was satisfied with the boy's progress, the grandfather let Alexei play with the other children of the area, but Alexei was unable to cope with the usual cruelties that children seem regularly to inflict on each other, and he was often confined to the house.

Maxim Gorky.
(Tass, from Sovfoto)

In 1876 Alexei was at last sent to a regular school, but a case of smallpox ended his studies almost before they had begun. After his recovery he found out that his mother was going to remarry, and to a man Alexei disliked. The relationships within the family went from bad to worse and before long, after seeing his stepfather strike his mother, Alexei stabbed the man, though not seriously, with a bread knife. Again he was sent to live with his grandparents, and this time, because of the family poverty, he had to go to work. Every afternoon and weekend he went out to gather bones, rags, and scraps of iron, for which he was paid thirty to fifty kopecks. At school things were not much better. The children called him "ragman" and "beggar" and the teacher would not let him sit next to anyone because they all said he smelled bad.

At the age of ten, having passed the third grade examination, Alexei's grandfather apprenticed him to a relative who worked as an illustrator. Living with the family, he was treated so miserably that he became terribly depressed, and in the spring he ran away, living on handouts until he found a job as a dishwasher on a steamboat. The cook for whom he worked told the boy to read as many books as he could to prepare himself for life, and young Alexei took his advice.

Accused of stealing, Alexei was fired and went home to his grandparents, who sent him back to the illustrator. Nothing had changed, except that now Alexei was devouring books, begging and borrowing them from whoever he could. In 1881 he again struck out on his own, this time getting himself on as an apprentice in a shop where icons were painted and sold. After work he read constantly—works by Turgenev, Scott, Dickens, Gogol, and Dostoevski. He loved the first three, but for Gogol's *Dead Souls* and Dostoevski's *Memoirs from the House of the Dead* he felt a strong aversion.

In 1884, on the advice of a friend, Alexei left for Kazan to enroll in the university. He found a part-time job in a bakery shop and immediately was swept up in the campus political movements. The seeming futility of student life so depressed Alexei that he tried suicide, shooting himself four times in the chest. However, he was no more successful at suicide than at anything else he had tried, and in several months he recovered with only minor injuries to one lung.

In October 1889 he was imprisoned by the secret police for alleged revolutionary activities. According to his later testimony the two friends with whom he had been sharing an apartment were the guilty ones, but they escaped. The police kept him four weeks for questioning, and during that time General Posnaski read Alexei's confiscated manuscripts. He suggested that they be shown to Korolenko, a well-known writer, and that Alexei keep on writing.

Late that same year Alexei decided to follow the General's advice and made an appointment to see Korolenko and show him his poem, "The Song of the Old Oak Tree." Korolenko apparently tried to be gentle in his criticism, but Alexei was so upset that his writing was not unquestioningly accepted that he swore never to write prose or verse again—a vow he kept for nearly two years. In addition to his writing difficulties he also met his first love, Olga Kaminskaya, the companion of a revolutionary who had just returned from exile. She was ten years older than Alexei, and she could not make up her mind to leave her present lover. Partly ill and convinced he was going insane, Alexei decided to leave town. His departure turned into a two-year journey across Russia.

Late in 1891, having arrived in Tiflis, Alexei met some old friends and together they formed a commune and began to turn out revolutionary propaganda. A friend, Alexander Kalyushny, suggested that Alexei write down all of his experiences during the two-year odyssey, especially a story that Alexei had learned from an old horse guard. The story was written and Kalyushny placed it in the Tiflis paper, but in the meantime Alexei had been jailed as a vagabond. Freed before the story appeared, Alexei changed his author's byline to Gorky, meaning "the bitter one."

Encouraged by his story's success Gorky, as he now called himself, immediately wrote another story, "From the Life of a Prostitute," which was rejected because the material was "inappropriate and compromising." He moved on to Nizhni Novgorod, where he was born, and there, when he was twenty-four, he was joined by Olga, who had left her revolutionary lover. He also renewed his acquaintance with his earliest critic, Korolenko, and under the older man's guidance began to cultivate a prose style that was clean and simple. The *Moscow Journal* and the *Volgan* began publishing his stories, and Gorky was at last underway as a writer.

In 1895, mostly to get away from Olga, with whom he was becoming rather disillusioned, Gorky moved to Samara, where he became editor of the *Samarskaya Gazeta*. With his position secure he sent some of his works to Anton Chekhov. The two met at Yalta and became fast friends.

A turn-of-the-century Berlin production of Gorky's *The Lower Depths*. (Munich, Theatre-Museum)

By 1899 Gorky had become famous, but his continuing revolutionary activities got him banished to Arsamas. His poor health at last worked in his favor, however, and he was permitted to live in the Crimean. He had begun to write a play, *Meshchane* (*The Petty Bourgeois*), but because he was unfamiliar with the dramatic form the work progressed slowly. Stanislavsky urged him to hurry and finish it as the Moscow Art Theatre was doing a summer workshop at Yalta, near the Crimean, and he wanted his theatre to produce Gorky's first play.

The Petty Bourgeois was performed by the Moscow Art Theatre in St. Petersburg in 1902. In it Gorky portrayed the people he had known all his life—the lower middle class. *Na dne* (*The Lower Depths*), also performed in 1902, dealt with an even lower group, but it moved people because it so artistically captured the sufferings of its characters and it expressed a deep and abiding faith in a better future for the Russian people. Gorky was awarded the Griboyedov Prize for *Lower Depths,* and the play went on to become one of Max Reinhardt's greatest successes. It has remained one of the high-water marks of stage naturalism.

On January 11, 1905, Gorky was again arrested and this time imprisoned in the Peter-Paul Fortress for political prisoners. The action provoked a worldwide response in favor of the writer, and soon Gorky was free once more, though in exile. While in prison he wrote *Deti solntsa* (*Children of the Sun*), which he called a "gay comedy." During his exile he finished *Chudaki* (*The Odd Men*) and *Vassa Zheleznova,* both of which portrayed the indecisive, backward, and even reactionary world of the petite bourgeosie.

In 1913 Gorky was granted amnesty and settled in Finland close to St. Petersburg. In 1928, on his sixtieth birthday, a national celebration was held in his honor.

Gorky never again quite attained the dramatic height he had achieved with *The Lower Depths*. Between 1931 and 1934 he worked on a trilogy which would depict the decline of the bourgeosie and the victory of socialism, but only two of the plays were completed: *Yegor Bulichev* (produced at the Moscow Art Theatre, 1934), and *Dostigayev* (produced in the same year at the Vakhtangov Theatre).

ANTON CHEKHOV: Anton Pavlovich Chekhov (1860-1904) was born in the town of Taganrog on the Sea of Azov. His grandfather was a serf who managed to purchase his freedom twenty years before the abolition of serfdom in Russia. Chekhov's father, Pavel, after his marriage to the daughter of a local cloth merchant, opened his own grocery shop in Taganrog. There were six children born to this couple. It was not a happy household. Pavel, a fanatic about religious observances, beat the children for any infraction of the rules until they grew afraid of any close human relationship.

By the time Anton was sixteen his father, whose business was bankrupt due to unwise investments, left town to escape the creditors. The family followed him to Moscow, except for Anton, who stayed in Taganrog to finish school. He lived with a family friend, whose child he tutored in exchange for board and lodging. At seventeen he suffered a serious illness and as a result

Anton Chekhov. (New York Public Library, Lincoln Center)

became interested in medicine, making up his mind that he would become a doctor. This time was especially important in forming Chekhov's personality. Being on his own taught him independence, responsibility, and a contempt for pettiness and meanness.

In 1879 he passed the examinations and obtained a scholarship for medical school. He joined his family in Moscow but was forced to assume the role of head of the family, for which his father was now too weak.

Encouraged by his older brother, Chekhov began sending short pieces to humorous magazines in order to earn money. In 1880, at the age of twenty, he sold his first story. During the first seven years of his literary activity, he wrote over four hundred stories, novels, and sketches, using such pseudonyms as Antoshe Chekhonte, Brother's Brother, A Doctor Without Patients, A Quick-Tempered Man, A Man Without a Spleen, Rover, Ulysses, and several others.

In 1884 he received his medical degree and began the practice of his new profession. His patients, however, were poor, and writing became increasingly important to him as a means of support. He liked to say that medicine was his lawful wife and literature his mistress.

In 1885 Chekhov discovered that he was a celebrity among influential people in the publishing world, and that his stories were favorites with the public and admired in literary circles. He was encouraged by the leading Russian writers to take his work seriously and not waste his talent by continuing to write for the comic journals. He tried a novel but was not successful.

The theatre had long held an interest for him as a form of amusement and forgetfulness. At school he had enjoyed vaudevilles and French farces. He began his career in theatre by writing such one-act plays as *Medved* (*The Bear*, 1888) and *Predlozheniye* (*The Marriage Proposal*, 1889). He then tried writing a lyrical play, but it was a failure and Chekhov gave up playwriting for several years, returning to his short stories. In 1887 he was awarded the Pushkin Prize by the Russian Academy of Sciences.

His health began deteriorating but his obligations to his mother and younger sisters continued to drain him of what little energy he had left. He met Lidiya Avelova and fell in love, but she was married, a mother, and virtuous. In 1890, dissatisfied with his life, Chekhov traveled to Sakhalin Island to take a census of the penal colonies. He wrote the book *Sakhalin*, which helped to bring about prison reform. His experiences at the island caused him to want to do something about the evils of Russian society.

Chekhov was finally able to buy an estate near Moscow, where he hoped to live with his family and write. But a cholera epidemic broke out and he became involved in treating the peasants in the surrounding areas. Due to his tubercular condition he was forced to go to Yalta, where he began work on *Chayka* (*The Sea Gull*). The play was given at the Alexandrinsky Theatre in St. Petersburg in 1896, but the director and the actors were unable to understand the concept of a drama in which mood and talk was more important than plot and action, and the play was a failure. Discouraged, Chekhov returned once again to short-story writing.

The Moscow Art Theatre's first production, *Tsar Fyodor*, was a success, but its staging of *The Merchant of Venice* was a fiasco, almost wrecking the organization. Vladimir Nemirovich-Danchenko approached Chekhov and persuaded him to let the theatre do a revival of *The Sea Gull*. Given a group of talented actors, trained on Stanislavsky's principles, Chekhov's play of characters, desires, and moods was an overwhelming success.

During the rehearsals for *The Sea Gull*, Chekhov met Olga Knipper, the actress who played Mme. Arkadina, and fell once more in love. But he would not speak of marriage because of his failing health. He felt tied to a family he had allowed to possess him; he was desperately ill; he knew that, at best, dying could only be delayed. Although it took Olga two years to convince him—she had to do the proposing—they were married on May 25, 1901.

Chekhov continued to write for the Moscow Art Theatre. In 1899 they did a successful production of *Dyadya Vanya* (*Uncle Vanya*), and in 1901 presented *Tri sestry* (*The Three Sisters*). However, his strength continued to fail, and the enormous effort required to finish *Vishnyovy sad* (*The Cherry Orchard*, 1904) and to attend Moscow rehearsals, brought about a complete collapse in the winter of 1904. In the hope that the fresh air of the Black Forest might delay the end, Olga took him to the sanitarium at Badenweiler, Germany. He died there July 2, 1904.

The early failure of Chekhov's plays is easy to understand, if only on a technical level. They had almost nothing in common with either melodrama, the naturalistic drama, or the grand historical drama that was so popular, and actors trained in the old school were unable to come to grips with his characters. In fact, it was not until the Moscow Art Theatre developed its ensemble techniques and its system of internal characterization that his plays could hope to succeed.

As a writer Chekhov was, from first to last, gentle and humane—allied always on the side of his characters. But his plays do not contain a Pollyanna brightness or false semblance of happiness. Rather they grow out of his own

A scene from the Moscow Art Theatre's 1899 production of Chekhov's *Uncle Vanya.* (From *Bühne und Welt,* Berlin, 1906)

combination of decency, kindness, understanding, and intelligence. Chekhov saw his fellow man as he was, with all his foibles, his selfishness, his failures and successes, his evil deeds and his good, and loved him not in spite of his shortcomings, and certainly not for them, but because he was able to accept man as he in fact existed. Particularly dear to him were those qualities which he thought of as "cultured," by which he meant a respect for the human personality, forbearance, gentleness, and courtesy. It is these qualities with which Chekhov filled his plays—and the plays tend to some degree to be laments for the passing of these qualities and efforts to clear the darkness that Chekhov felt had fallen over Russia and that was masking and destroying these qualities.

Chekhov's plays occupy a special place in the world of theatre, not only for audiences and critics, but for actors as well. The repertoire of nearly all great performers contains at least one character from a Chekhov play because they provide an almost matchless opportunity to create a full, complete, rounded character onstage. It is this quality, probably more than any other, that makes Chekhov's dramas so timeless.

By the last twenty years of the century the increasing censorship of both Church and state and the reactionary policies of the Imperial Theatres produced an unhealthy theatrical climate. By the end of the 1890s, however, a reaction had set in, and the Moscow Art Theatre was offering the public old works newly considered along with important new works. The plays of Anton Chekhov were not exactly new, but they were products of the period in which they were produced, and they were then (and now) clearly the greatest plays ever to come out of Russia. It was an encouraging note on which to end the century.

THEATRE AND POLITICS

It is difficult to think of a country where theatrical development was not greatly influenced by political conditions, and it is impossible to find a country where this influence was greater than in Russia. Throughout the nineteenth century the rapidly growing theatre existed under close government supervision, and for a large part of the century the government censors severely restricted the dramatic potential of a number of talented writers.

During the first quarter of the century Prince Alexander Shakhovskoy (1777-1846) was the Director of Repertory for the Imperial Theatres, and under his benevolent eye the theatre seemed well-off indeed. Himself a playwright and satirist who was eager to cast off the western European theatrical influence and establish a truly Russian national theatre, Shakhovskoy initiated a number of important changes. In 1805 he established a state theatre in Moscow, purchasing an acting company of seventy-four serfs to perform. Four years later he opened an actor training school as an adjunct to the theatre, hoping to make it competitive with the more Westernized companies in St. Petersburg. Shakhovskoy also visited Paris to observe the general operation and stagecraft of Western theatre, and when he returned to Russia he drew up a set of rules for theatrical companies that remained in effect from 1825 to 1912.

In spite of the century's impressive beginning, in 1825 theatrical conditions changed for the worse. Tsar Alexander I had started his reign as a reasonably liberal ruler. Under the influence of Metternich, however, he grew rapidly more conservative. The discovery of an assassination conspiracy among the officers of his guard and an abortive rebellion led to ever more stringent civil controls. In 1825, when Nicholas I took the throne, the repressive atmosphere was complete.

Nicholas I immediately moved toward strict theatrical control. In 1826 Shakhovskoy was relieved of his directorship and a strict censorship was instituted. The rules were relaxed slightly after Nicholas died in 1855, but there was no significant change in government policies until the ascension of Tsar Alexander III in 1881.

From their inception the state theatres in St. Petersburg and Moscow had held restrictive rights to all theatrical production in those cities, and the rest of Russia made do with touring troupes or community theatre put on by various literary or artistic societies. In 1882, however, the state theatre monopolies were abolished and a number of troupes immediately began performing in the two population centers. Within five years there were more than twenty-five companies performing in Moscow and St. Petersburg.

Scene from the first act of Turgenev's *A Month in the Country*, produced at the Maly Theatre, Moscow, 1872. (Painting by Mstislav Dobujinsky)

While Alexander III seemed to loosen the government hold on theatrical performance, in fact, he tightened it, clamping down tightly on freedom of expression. The assassination of his predecessor by a terrorist had left the new Tsar a frightened man, and so with the help of Plehve, his police chief, and a highly efficient secret police, he successfully stamped out all articulate revolutionary discontent.

ACTING

In the early years of the century, while the Imperial Theatre at St. Petersburg dominated the theatrical scene, the outstanding performer was Ekaterina Semenova (1786-1849), the daughter of a serf, who was sent to the theatre school in St. Petersburg at the age of ten. She made her debut in 1803 and soon achieved major status in the tragedies of Ozerov. She went on to play both comedy and tragedy, but she seemed to have an affinity for the great tragic roles, especially those of Shakespeare, Racine, and Schiller.

She was reputedly a great beauty with a lovely contralto voice. Pushkin said of her that she had no peer on the Russian stage, though her performances lacked continuity because they were interrupted by gusts of emotion.

After a brief retirement and then a two-year comeback in 1823, Semenova retired permanently. She was followed by Vasily Karatygin (1802-53), who was the outstanding performer on the St. Petersburg stage for the next twenty-five years. Karatygin's father, an actor and producer at St. Petersburg's Dramatic Theatre, was strongly opposed to his son making a career on-

Swan Lake, as performed at the Bolshoi Theatre, Moscow, 1877. (Drawing by Gontcharov)

stage. Thus, Karatygin's early career consisted only of amateur community theatricals and some college performances. However, while at the Cadet College he was so outstanding in a production of *Oedipus the King* that he was invited to join the Imperial Theatre company. At first he refused, because of his father's desire that he continue his studies, but in 1820 he reconsidered and in that same year made his debut as a professional actor.

Karatygin was, throughout his career, noted as a perfectionist. He studied his roles carefully, researched them if they were historical personages, and studied their period if they were not. He insisted on accurate historical costume, sets, and stage decor, even though he objected to a totally realistic acting style. Unlike Semenova, Karatygin was not a passionate actor; rather, he was a supreme technician, which allowed him to play successfully an unusually wide variety of roles, though he was apparently at his best in Classical tragedy.

After the first quarter of the century the reputation of the Moscow troupe overtook the St. Petersburg company. This was mostly due to the presence in Moscow of several gifted actors, the most talented of whom was Mikhail Shchepkin (1788-1863). Shchepkin was born in the province of Kursk, the son of a serf, and was given his first reading lessons by the wife of the local baker. He became interested in theatre when he accidentally saw a play put on in the private theatre of a provincial nobleman. Completing school, where he made a reputation as an avid reader and promising scholar, he found an opportunity to work at the Kursk theatre as a prompter and music copier. He also began acting in private theatricals.

In 1805 the Kursk theatre presented a benefit for an actress, and when the leading actor showed up too drunk to go onstage Shchepkin volunteered. His performance was so well received that he began receiving good roles, and he remained with the troupe until it disbanded in 1816. He immediately joined the Kharkov troupe run by Stein and Kalinovsky, and thus he was with them when the troupe accepted an invitation from Prince Repin to play in Poltava. The Prince was so impressed that two years later he initiated a movement to purchase Shchepkin's freedom from his owner. As soon as this was completed, and Shchepkin was at last liberated from serfdom, he was invited by the manager of Moscow's Maly Theatre to join the Imperial troupe. He made his debut in 1822.

From 1825-1828 he played with the St. Petersburg company, where he was especially successful in *Wit Works Woe* and *The Inspector General*. Returning to Moscow he triumphed in a series of comic roles drawn from Shakespeare, Schiller, and Gogol. Throughout the 1840s he was clearly Russia's outstanding actor, though during the last ten years of his career his art seemed to weaken.

Shchepkin was the first realistic Russian actor. He was so believable onstage that critics said he blended the technique of Karatygin with the passion of Semenova. As it did in other Western countries, the realistic school

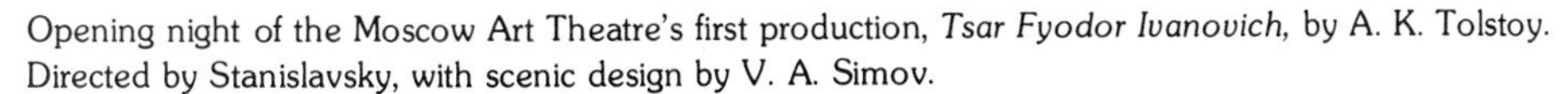
Opening night of the Moscow Art Theatre's first production, *Tsar Fyodor Ivanovich,* by A. K. Tolstoy. Directed by Stanislavsky, with scenic design by V. A. Simov.

of acting eventually triumphed over the earlier, stylized, oratorical school. Shchepkin's leadership in this area brought about a style of acting that would be necessary for the great dramas of Ostrovsky, when the Maly Theatre would gain the nickname, "The House of Ostrovsky."

The realistic movement and the growing number of fine native plays increased the acting opportunities in Russia, and the end of the playing restrictions in 1882 brought about a theatrical boom. However, except perhaps for Prov Sadovsky (1818-72), who was Shchepkin's successor at the Maly, no significant performers appeared on the stage until just before the turn of the century. In 1898 Stanislavsky and Nemirovich-Danchenko opened the Moscow Art Theatre and began emphasizing an ensemble style of acting that would have an enormous effect on the theatre of the twentieth century.

The Nineteenth Century in America

The most important influence on American theatre in the nineteenth century was the expansion of the country itself. As the century opened the United States was a new country, only twenty-four years from its birth in independence. Except for a population belt along the East Coast, a few cities in the Southeast, and a small and largely Spanish population in the Southwest and along the southern part of the West Coast, the country was a frontier. Before the century was over the great central plains and the West had been opened up and populated, the country had survived the trauma of a debilitating civil war, and just before the end of the century the frontier, that powerful shaping influence on all aspects of American thought, had officially been declared closed. It was a lusty boom period in American history, and theatre spent a large part of it galloping frantically to keep up.

NINETEENTH CENTURY AMERICAN DRAMA

The late eighteenth century example of Royall Tyler's *The Contrast* was not immediately seized upon in the nineteenth. Tyler had written his play on an American topic, and his theme was basically the moral superiority of the native American to foreigners or those who imitated foreign styles. However, as the new century began most American writers were still looking to Europe for their subjects and their themes.

One of the most interesting and important of the early writers is James Nelson Barker (1784-1858), in part because he was one of the rare writers who stuck closely to American subjects, in part because he wrote the first American play on an Indian theme, and in part because he was the first American playwright to be given a London performance. The play that so intrigued the English was *The Indian Princess, or La Belle Sauvage*, first performed in Philadelphia in 1808 and, as *Pocahontas, or The Indian Princess*, at Drury Lane in 1820.

Altogether Barker wrote ten plays, only four of which have survived. The earliest of these is *Tears and Smiles*, a comedy of manners which was played in Philadelphia in 1807. A dramatization of Sir Walter Scott's rhymed romance, *Marmion* (1808), at first billed as being by an English author, was highly popular. It was a favorite of James W. Wallack, the English actor turned American theatre manager, and its last recorded production was in 1848. Barker's final play, and certainly the best of those that have survived, is also on an American theme. *Superstition* (1824), a blank-verse historical drama, tells the story of a Puritan refugee from persecution who leads his American village in a battle against the Indians. The play stresses the evils that grow out of intolerance and the persecution of witchcraft.

Robert Montgomery Bird (1806-54), a doctor and leading light of the Philadelphia group of dramatists, wrote in the best of two worlds, going back to Europe for his subject matter, but finding themes to express the American ideal of independence from tyranny. He had written a number of unproduced plays when, in 1831, the famous tragedian Edwin Forrest produced *The Gladiator*, Bird's Romantic tragedy. Forrest played the hero, Spartacus, with muscular vigor, and the play was an immediate and long-lasting success.

An illustration of a farcical scene in Burton's Theatre, New York, dating about the middle of the nineteenth century.

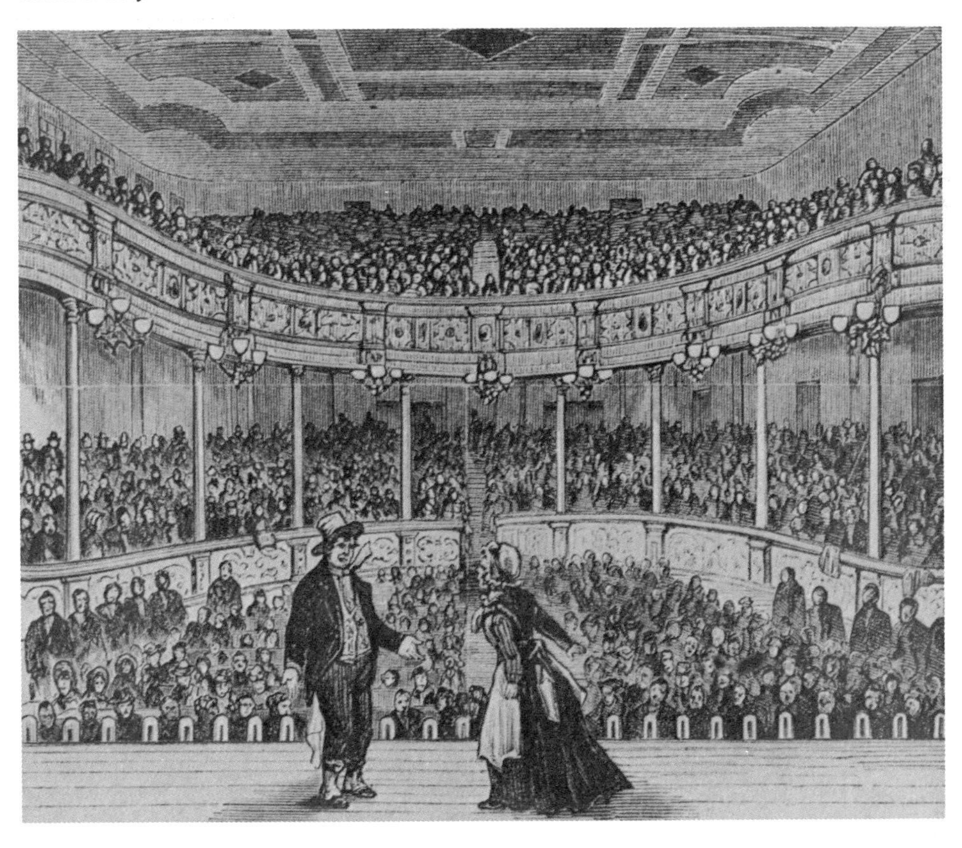

Forrest made it part of his permanent repertory, chose it for his opening performance at Drury Lane, and continued to revive it until his retirement in 1872. Other actors, of course, picked it up and it was still being produced in the 1890s. Bird wrote two more original plays for Forrest: *Oralloosa, Son of the Incas* (produced in 1832) was another heroic melodrama and was played by Forrest with only moderate success; *The Broker of Bogota* (produced in 1834) is also a melodrama, but a far more subtle and believable one. It is probably Bird's best play. Forrest loved it, even over *The Gladiator*, but audiences of the time preferred rant and bombast to the sincere tragedy of Febro the money-changer. Bird also revised for Forrest the *Metamora* of Augustus Stone. Because of the lack of copyright protection, and the fact that Forrest fearfully refused to let plays written for him be printed, Bird made no decent amount of money from his plays and so retired from the theatre in disgust to concentrate his writing talents in nondramatic genres.

Augustus Stone, whose play *Metamora* (produced in 1829) was eventually revised by Bird, was a mediocre actor who wrote his one successful play as a result of a contest, sponsored by Forrest, for a play featuring an American hero. He won the contest, but his subsequent Romantic historical plays went

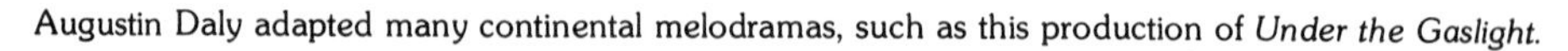

Augustin Daly adapted many continental melodramas, such as this production of *Under the Gaslight*.

unproduced. Disappointed at his failure in all aspects of the theatrical profession, he committed suicide by throwing himself into the river at Philadelphia. *Metamora* did, however, succeed in establishing the American Indian as a Romantic hero.

Melodrama, that staple of European theatre, appeared in America as an imitation of the continental format; however, it was soon adapted to American concerns and became the most popular fare on the American stage. Stock native types also developed during this period, so that Royall Tyler's shrewd down-east Yankee Jonathan and William Dunlap's stage Irishman Dennis O'Bogg were followed by such types as the rural Yankee, the frontiersman, the Bowery Boy, and the famous (or infamous) Jim Crow.

Romantic tragedy in the Elizabethan style remained popular through the first half of the century. Nathaniel Parker Willis (1806-67), a drama critic and playwright, wrote one of the best of these, *Tortesa the Usurer* (1839), for James W. Wallack, and George Henry Boker (1823-90) wrote the best of them all, *Francesca da Rimini* (produced in 1855). Boker's blank-verse historical dramas were *Calaynos* (1849) and *Leonor de Guzman* (1853), both founded on Spanish materials, and *Francesca,* based on a Medieval Italian legend. *Francesca* was not only popular in its day, but was revived in 1882 by Lawrence Barrett and again in 1901 by Otis Skinner. Boker also wrote three comedies, but they were only moderately successful and have since been forgotten.

The dramatizations of *Uncle Tom's Cabin* began appearing immediately after Harriet Beecher Stowe's novel was published in 1852. The growing antislavery sentiment in the northern states that would eventually lead to the Civil War was fed by this sentimental and melodramatic presentation of the black man, and in a variety of adaptations it was, during the 1850s, the most popular play on the American stage. In most of its versions the play is almost a textbook on the standard devices of American melodrama. It contained spectacle in a chase scene across a river filled with ice floes, "artistic" tableaus, at least two songs, a saintly hero, and a totally evil villain. The popularity of the play died with the advent of the Civil War, but it was revived in the 1870s and remained for nearly thirty years a staple of American touring companies.

One of the interesting playwrights in the middle of the nineteenth century was Anna Cora Mowatt (1819-70). Primarily an actress, Mrs. Mowatt is now remembered mainly for her one fine play, *Fashion* (1845). A delightful, satiric comedy of manners in the tradition of Royall Tyler, *Fashion* pokes wonderful fun at well-off Americans who blindly worship the false god of European culture. The play was quite successful in its day and has several times been revived, most recently as a musical, but Mrs. Mowatt's real effect on American theatre goes far beyond the success of one play, no matter how good. In a period when blue laws and antitheatrical prejudices were still rampant in rural America, she proved that an American lady could work in the profession without any lowering of the acceptable moral standard.

Probably the most interesting and talented theatrician during this period was Dion Boucicault (1822-90), an actor and playwright who managed to have highly successful careers in both England and the United States. The earliest theatrical record of his career has him appearing as an actor in the English provinces playing under the name of Lee Moreton. As a dramatist his first success was *London Assurance* (1841), a comedy produced at Covent Garden and featuring Charles Mathews and his wife, Mme. Vestris, in the leading roles. Following the success of *Assurance,* Boucicault went on to write a number of plays for the English theatre, the most successful of which was *The Corsican Brothers* (1852) and *Louis XI* (1855).

It was in the 1850s that Boucicault paid his first visit to America, where he wrote and produced *The Poor of New York* (which became *The Poor of London* and *The Poor* . . . of any major city in which it subsequently was played). Boucicault went on to write and produce such popular plays as *Jessie Brown* and *Dot* and a whole series of Irish dramas, the best of which is probably *The Colleen Bawn* (1860). He was the first writer to do a play based on the American Civil War (*Belle Lamar,* 1874), and the first to deal seriously with miscegenation and the plight of the American black (*The Octoroon; or, Life in Louisiana,* 1859). Boucicault wrote more than one hundred fifty plays, many of which still exist only in manuscript. Eventually, unable to maintain a life on two continents, he settled in America and became a teacher in a drama school.

The advent of the Civil War (1861-65) did not halt the production of drama, but it did effectively stop anything new or experimental. However, almost as soon as the hostilities ceased new plays began appearing, and interestingly the most important of these had nothing to do with the recently concluded conflict. *Rip Van Winkle,* Washington Irving's Americanized re-creation of a European folk legend, had already been produced in several dramatic versions, but it was not until Dion Boucicault completed his own adaptation of the story in 1865, and Joseph Jefferson II appeared in it, that the story was on its way to becoming an American stage classic.

Jefferson played Boucicault's version of the play in 1865 at the Adelphi in London, and it had its American debut with Jefferson the following year in New York. The play was a huge success, in part because of the performance of Jefferson in the title role, and also because in its folk origins the play manages to touch on an archetypal pattern of human existence. Jefferson played the role almost exclusively until 1880, and over the years he made so many changes and corrections in the script that most printed editions either ignore Boucicault as author, or list Boucicault as author with the added credit "as played by Joseph Jefferson."

The plays about the Civil War itself took a while to be written, at least the good ones; long enough for the special horrors of civil war to be put into some kind of perspective. The best of this group are *Shenandoah* (1888) by Bronson Howard (1842-1908), and perhaps *The Reverend Griffith Davenport* by James A. Herne (originally Ahern, 1839-1901). Howard, who began his career as a Detroit journalist, achieved his first success in 1870 with the production of *Saratoga,* a farcical comedy that, as *Brighton* (1874), achieved an equivalent success in England. He followed this first farce with several more comedies which played to moderately enthusiastic audiences. *A Banker's Daughter* (1873), retitled *Lilian's Last Love,* was quite successful in New York and then repeated that triumph in England under a third title, *The Old Love and the New.* From an artistic point of view, Howard's best play is probably *Young Mrs. Winthrop* (1882), which also had a moderate vogue in England without retitling or alteration. However, *Shenandoah,* at first a failure, was an outstanding success both in New York and on tour, and it established a long running interest in the Romantic treatment of America's worst conflict.

James Herne was a popular dramatist who collaborated with David Belasco (1854-1931) on several plays including, most importantly, the melodramatic *Hearts of Oak* (1879). His first important play was *Margaret Fleming* (1890), a serious play about marital infidelity which, in both its subject and the attitude it displayed toward the subject, was years ahead of its time. It was, however, ignored in its time and only moderately successful in subsequent revivals in 1907 and 1915. *Shore Acres* (1892), after a slow start, became a highly popular play, and *Sag Harbor* (1899), a rewrite of the earlier *Hearts of Oak* without the Belasco melodrama, was his last play. Herne was acting in it when he died.

The last of the major nineteenth century American playwrights was Augustus Thomas (1857-1934). By this time a concentration on American materials and themes had become the prevailing mode, and Thomas furthered it by writing all of his plays on themes dealing with American life and thought. His first play, *Editha's Burglar,* was originally undertaken as a one-act play for a St. Louis amateur dramatic association, where it was so successful that Thomas revised it for production as a full-length drama in 1889. Thomas worked as an adapter of foreign plays at Palmer's Madison Square Theatre, and in 1891 produced *Alabama,* a play successful enough to encourage him to quit Palmer and strike out on his own as a playwright. Thomas never succeeded in writing profound or challenging plays, but his best, such as *In Mizzoura* (1893), *Arizona* (1899), *Colorado* (1901), *The Witching Hour* (1907), and *The Copperhead* (1918), are all very good plays, and their use of American geography and the resulting sense of place are important in the history of American theatre.

THE AMERICAN STAGE

By the end of the eighteenth century, theatre was firmly established on the American East Coast. The leading theatrical center was Philadelphia, primarily because of the activities of Thomas Wignell (1753-1803) and Alexander Reinagle, who established the Chestnut Street Theatre in that city. The theatre building was modeled on the Theatre Royal at Bath and featured seating for 2000 persons with an exterior decorated with Corinthian columns. This, plus its modern well-equipped stage, made it the finest theatre in the country. Wignell began performances there in 1794 with an outstanding troupe of actors.

Theatre in New York, at the turn of the century, was in second place to Philadelphia. The Old American Company founded by Hallam and Henry had fallen on hard times, thanks in part to dissension in its management brought about when John Hodgkinson (c. 1765-1805) replaced Henry. Also, the John Street Theatre, the company's home base, was inadequate in terms of seating and staging. Thus, it was not until both Hallam and Hodgkinson resigned from management, and the new Park Theatre was opened in 1798, that New York could make a real bid for theatrical supremacy.

The performance of a comedy at the Park Theatre, New York, 1822.

The third theatrical center at the turn of the century was Boston. In 1793 prohibitive laws against acting were repealed, and the Federal Street Theatre was completed before the year was out. It opened with a hastily recruited English company in residence, and it was not until 1802, when Snelling Powell (1774-1843) took control, that the productions attained any degree of quality.

The fourth and least important theatrical center at the turn of the century was Charleston. The city had been host to a few early touring companies, but it was not until 1795, when John Joseph Sollee was made manager of the City Theatre, that a resident troupe was established. An interesting sidelight to Charleston theatre is that following the French Revolution and the slave uprisings in Santo Domingo a number of French immigrants flocked to the city. They brought with them a taste for sophisticated theatre, and many of the plays done in the city, because of the immigrants, were in French, which gave the Charleston dramatic effort a foreign and vaguely transitory quality.

By 1800, however, due especially to a rapidly expanding population, New York was giving evidence that it would soon overtake Philadelphia as the young nation's theatrical center. In 1800 the population of New York City was only 60,000 persons. By 1820 it had more than doubled and by 1840 it was over 312,000. The Park Theatre was widely regarded as being a distinct advance, even over the Chestnut. It was a solid stone building with three tiers of boxes, a gallery, and a pit. It could seat approximately two thousand people. From its establishment until 1805 it was managed by William Dunlap, whose struggles with quarrelsome actors and a divided company management finally ended in financial failure. It was then sold to John Jacob Astor and John Beekman, who put it in the care of the actor Thomas Cooper. The new management immediately instituted some enterprising policies. Cooper reshuffled the resident company, adding such new but well-known performers as the comedian William Twaits (?-1814), and began a star system in which established performers were brought in for short seasons or for just a single play. These innovations, though they did severe damage to the stock company concept and set American theatre on a course that many have since decried, succeeded in turning New York theatre fortunes around.

In 1820 the "old" Park Theatre burned, and a "new" Park with more comfortable seating and better lighting facilities was immediately constructed. It seated 2500 persons in comfort and featured the latest "patent" oil lamps in four chandeliers, each boasting thirty-five lights. The theatre was easily the best of its time and helped New York attain a theatrical dominance that would last for more than a hundred years. It was here that Junius Brutus Booth made his New York debut in 1821, beginning an American theatrical dynasty.

But if the Park Theatre had won the rivalry with Philadelphia's Chestnut Street Theatre, it soon found new competition right on its own doorstep. The Chatham Garden Theatre opened in 1824 with an outstanding troupe of actors that included Joseph Jefferson I (1774-1832). The theatre was a beautifully appointed throwback to an earlier age in that it had a forestage, something that

John Brougham's Lyceum Theatre in 1863. The proscenium doors had disappeared and the picture-frame stage had assumed the form with which we are most familiar.

had almost disappeared as action had been pushed back behind the proscenium. It also had proscenium doors set in a tudor-style frame that gave it the appearance of something out of the Elizabethan period. Technically, however, it was no period piece and the stage was a fully equipped, workable area.

Inspired by the success of the Park and Chatham Garden, the Lafayette Theatre was opened in 1826. It was hailed by many as the finest theatre in the country, especially from a technical point of view. Spectacles and melodramas had captured the public imagination and the Lafayette was fully equipped to handle such popularity. The Lafayette suffered the fate of so many theatres, burning down only a few years after it went into operation, but by this time the Bowery Theatre was already operating.

The Bowery Theatre was large, seating 3500 people, and it was one of the most exciting buildings of its time. The stage was unusually spacious in proportion to the auditorium, and it was lit by gas. It was the first theatre in New York to feature this innovation and the third in the whole country. Like the Lafayette, the Bowery burned down shortly after opening, but a new Bowery was immediately raised to replace it. This new Bowery had an even larger stage area, and there were a few improvements made in the house. However, again fire struck and in 1836 the second Bowery burned to the ground. The third Bowery opened in 1837 and burned within a year. It was followed by a fourth Bowery in 1839. The fourth Bowery burned six years later, whereupon its unusually determined sponsors erected a fifth Bowery. This building escaped the fate of its predecessors, lasting well into the twentieth century.

By the 1830s, with its population nearing 275,000, the New York theatrical facilities began to develop almost frenziedly. In 1833 the Italian Opera House opened. Eleven years later Palmo's Opera House opened, followed in 1847 by the Astor Place Opera House. By mid-century the Academy of Music was in business. This was the extent of opera houses in New York until the Metropolitan opened in 1883.

The period from the mid-1830s through the 1860s saw a number of theatres constructed, from the intimate Franklin Theatre (1835), seating only 600 persons, to Booth's Theatre (1869), seating over 1800. Booth's was almost the ultimate theatre of the age. The flat stage could be lowered, there were elevators to raise scenery from the shop in the basement, and there was an unusual amount of fly space and machinery. The stage floor had no grooves for flats, with box sets being used almost exclusively, and because of the hydraulic equipment there was no forestage. Edwin Booth produced his plays on such a lavish scale that only five years after opening his theatre he was bankrupt, but the house continued to produce.

While New York was growing so rapidly another event was taking place of even greater importance to the country and, thus, to theatre; that is, the West was opening up and the frontier was providing opportunities on a grand scale. The influence of the frontier on American society has been considered in numerous volumes and is far too great to cover here. One of its important aspects, however, was that it provided a safety valve for the social structure, or perhaps an escape hatch. As long as the frontier and free land existed, the failures, the malcontents, the antisocial, and the adventurous all had a place they could go in the hope of resolving their problems. This was also true for theatre.

A scene from Augustin Daly's production of *A Midsummer Night's Dream.* (New York City Public Library)

No sooner had the Ohio Valley and the basin of the Mississippi been settled than the traveling troupes were there, ready to offer entertainment to the culturally starved pioneers. In most cases these troupes (or individuals) working the frontier settlements were the failed performers of the Atlantic coast or England, but as the western cities grew larger and richer, and after the discovery of gold at Sutter's Fort in 1848, even the finest of American companies began to tour the West.

By 1807 the St. Pierre Theatre had opened in New Orleans. In the following year the St. Philippe opened, and in 1809 the Orleans Theatre began to produce. In 1817 Noah Miller Ludlow (1795-1886) brought his fledgling American Theatrical Commonwealth Company to New Orleans, and he was so successful that James H. Caldwell (1793-1863) followed his lead and built the American Theatre in 1822. Caldwell soon had nearly complete control of New Orleans theatre, in part because of his desire to provide the city with the finest theatrical facilities in the United States. He was one of the first three producers in the United States to install a gas system of theatrical lighting, and his St. Charles Theatre (1835), built for the then astronomical cost of $350,000, was for many years the finest theatrical facility in the country.

In 1824 Ludlow, who had been quite active touring the lower Mississippi River cities, built a permanent theatre at Mobile. Then, in partnership with

Solomon Smith (1801-69), the stagestruck, flamboyant, troubled son of a midwestern farmer, he opened a theatre in St. Louis that gave him a virtual monopoly over that city's theatrical scene until 1851. A large (seating 1500 people), three-tiered building, it received its first competition when John Bates opened his theatre, followed by the Varieties in 1852, the People's Theatre in 1852, and the Olympic Theatre in 1866.

In Chicago, at the turn of the century, there was little of theatrical significance. Indeed, Chicago itself was not yet the major city it would soon become, and its only "theatre" consisted of a trestle stage set up in a hotel dining room. However, the city was beginning to boom and in less than fifty years the first permanent theatre building had been raised. In 1857 the McVicker's Theatre was built—one of the finest facilities in the country—and it was followed by Crosby's Opera House in 1865. By the time of the famous fire in 1871 the Chicago theatrical momentum had so increased that even Mrs. O'Leary's mythical cow could not slow its advance.

Along the Mississippi River and its tributaries there was an active exciting theatre that existed entirely on river craft. The showboat, that particularly American institution, began early in the century when minor troupes traveled the river on rafts or keelboats and landed close to villages, where they moored their craft, drew a crowd by means of trumpets, flags, and processions, and then put on their show either aboard their raft or in some village facility.

The first recorded instance of such a company is in 1817 and the company is, appropriately, that of Noah Miller Ludlow, who took his American Theatrical Commonwealth Company down the Cumberland River to the Mississippi, and then down the great waterway to New Orleans, on a flatboat with a sleeping shelter at one end. The company did play at villages along the way, but usually on land rather than on the boat.

The honor of running the first true showboat goes to William Chapman (1764-1839), a minor London and New York actor who left the competitive metropolitan stage for the rigors of pioneer theatre. With his wife and five children he operated a large flatboat with a house built on it. Above the house flew a flag bearing the word *Theatre*. The inside of the house was, given the shape of the flatboat, long and narrow. At one end was a shallow stage, and across the width of the boat, in front of the stage, were benches. The light was provided by candles.

Near the end of the century the most famous showboat was probably *The Water Queen*, built in 1895 and run by Captain E. A. Price. The boat was nearly twenty feet across, could seat nearly two hundred people, and had a company of some fifty players and crew. The shallow stage was lit by oil lamps, there was a large scenery hold, and the appointments were in plush and gold. And its greatest claim to fame was that most necessary of all items, a giant steam calliope.

The Great Plains for a long time proved inhospitable, awaiting such technological developments as barbed wire, improved windmills, and even repeating rifles before they could be settled. However, in the Far West there was an active theatrical movement spurred by the discovery of gold and the resulting economic boom.

California's first (or perhaps second) playhouse, the Eagle Theatre in Sacramento, was a rough affair with a canvas roof, which opened in 1849 to provide entertainment to the gold seekers.

There was some minor Spanish theatre in early California, but the first theatrical production in English was given at Sacramento's Eagle Theatre in 1849, only one year after the gold strike. Early performances were also staged at Monterey's First Theatre sometime around 1850. As long as it remained a boisterous mining town, Sacramento's theatre remained primarily little more than tent shows and occasional appearances by touring troupes. Mostly this was because performance conditions were primitive indeed, as a newspaper article pertaining to a tent show near the Sacramento River displays. Apparently a melodrama was being produced and, between acts, an actor came out to perform a jig. The miners in the audience, obviously unhappy with the quality or vigor of the dancing, drew their guns and began firing into the floor at the dancer's feet. According to the article this spurred the performer on to tremendous speed of foot and leaps of prodigious height. After the performance the miners were so delighted with the exhausted young man's exhibition that they showered the stage with gold.

San Francisco soon became the theatrical center of the Far West. In 1850 the first theatre opened over a saloon. By the following year there were three permanent theatres. Fires, which regularly took their toll of theatres all over the world, seemed especially bad in San Francisco. As theatre after theatre burned new ones were built to take their place, and the greatest performers of two continents played in them. The first major theatre was the Metropolitan, erected in 1853 by Edwin Forrest's exwife, Catherine Sinclair. Her resident company was considered to be the best on the West Coast, and her theatre was the Mecca for actors until John McCullough and Lawrence Barrett opened the California Theatre in 1869.

While theatre was firmly established on the East Coast and as far inland as the Mississippi River, and on the West Coast in San Francisco, Sacramento, and Monterey, there was little between these two areas. However, in Utah the Mormons, who had a history of theatrical interests, began doing shows as early as 1849 in a small building called the Bowery, and later in their social hall. In 1860 Brigham Young began the construction of a major theatre building, which was completed and dedicated in 1862.

Theatre came to St. Paul in 1851 in a converted meeting hall, to Omaha in 1857 in a converted general store, and to Denver in 1859 in a room of the Apollo Hall, It was not yet a major artistic movement, but the theatre was on its way and before the end of the century would penetrate even the distant rural areas of the United States.

THEATRICAL JACKS-OF-ALL-TRADES

The experience of the American frontier produced a myth about the American "jack-of-all-trades" who could do everything well if not brilliantly. In part the myth was grounded in fact—it was impossible to live on the frontier and not be able to do a variety of jobs well. The myth seems to have transferred to the theatre, because the nineteenth century produced two such men—James Steel Mackaye and David Belasco. These men did everything in theatre well, and some things they did brilliantly. They were both successful actors, playwrights, directors, producers, designers, and theatre technicians.

JAMES STEELE MACKAYE: Steele Mackaye (1842-94) is all too often remembered as the father of Percy Mackaye. He also should be noted, however, for fathering many new ideas in theatre which we today take for granted.

From his earliest days, Mackaye was interested in all the arts—especially painting, sculpture, and theatre. While serving in the army during the Civil War, he entertained his fellow troops in an amateur performance of *Hamlet,* and after the war he left the country for Paris to study art. In Paris he not only learned to be a competent artist, but he also began to develop the grandiose schemes and plans for which he would become famous. He became the American sales representative for a large group of French painters (including Rousseau) and started producing small realistic statuettes of famous people which were called photo-sculpture. Most importantly, he became excited about theatre and began to study acting under François Delsarte (1811-71) and François-Joseph-Pierre Régnier (1807-85).

Mackaye found that Delsarte's system of controlled gesture and physicalization matched a system which he himself had been developing years before in America. Régnier, on the other hand, was a retired actor of the

Comédie-Française, who had specialized in the French Classical comic roles and who had no new or exciting systems to offer—merely hard work and the traditional acting techniques. Given Mackaye's character, it is no wonder that Delsarte most engaged his interest.

In 1871 Mackaye was back in America and lecturing on the Delsarte system. He also went back to his own early experiments and began teaching his version of the system as well, even arranging performances of plays using his system—naturally starring himself. His first such effort was in 1872, when he starred in his own adaptation of a little known play titled *Monaldi.* At the same time he began working as a playwright, adapting Feuillet's *Julie* into his own play titled *Marriage.*

In 1872 Mackaye returned to Europe, where he did two productions of *Hamlet*—one in French and one in English—with himself in the title role. Europe raved over them, and he was compared favorably with the great actors of the past. For several years after this he successfully toured in England and Ireland. He returned to America in 1874, convinced of the future of his system, and began preparations for a new American school of acting and playwriting. He began a New England tour during which he became the first American actor to dispense with footlights and use only overhead lighting. He also continued to write plays, such as *The Vagabond* and *Rose Michel.*

Mackaye's association with Dion Boucicault began when he produced *The Arran Islands.* The unlikely partnership continued through several of Boucicault's plays, and was only broken off when Mackaye began preparations to produce what would become his most famous play, *Hazel Kirke* (1880). The play was enormously popular and was hailed by critics as being the epitome of the new realism. In fact, it was basically romantic melodrama and its only claim to realism was that it was set in a mill and dealt primarily with people of the middle class.

In 1879 Mackaye rebuilt the old Fifth Avenue Theatre—calling it the Madison Square Theatre—because he needed a playhouse in which he could exercise total control of the acting, play selection and technical presentation. Mackaye's new theatre had a double stage—that is, a stage set on an elevator so that while one stage was in view of the audience, the other would be above or below it, being reset for the next scene. The theatre had no orchestra pit, with the orchestra being located in a box above the proscenium. The lighting was all overhead, and there were no footlights. The theatre was equipped with chairs which had folding seats—the first theatre ever to have them.

In 1880 the Madison Square Theatre opened with *Hazel Kirke* and the production was not only an immense success in terms of the play's critical reception, but also because of the technical aspects of the production. Following this technical triumph, Mackaye kept producing new theatrical inventions, including an automatic prompter, a gyratory stage, a new system of electric illumination, a new combination of orchestra chairs and Turkish baths, and an "honest" mechanical doorkeeper.

By 1884 Mackaye had established the American Academy of Dramatic Art, the first such school of acting in New York. He bought the Lyceum Theatre, after being forced out of the Madison Square by business associates, and with the aid of Thomas Edison he made it the first electrically lighted theatre.

As time passed, Mackaye aimed his skills at perfecting such theatrical spectacles as Wild West Shows, and in 1891 he began planning for a great new theatre in Chicago which would open as part of the Columbian Exhibition. The theatre was to be called the Spectatorium and would present a Mackaye play about Columbus. He planned to include sailing ships and theatrical effects never before or since attempted. It was an amazingly bold and exciting plan, worthy of Mackaye's vision, but his poor health and equally poor financial planning kept it from being realized.

Mackaye died in 1894 after the immense disappointment of his Spectatorium. His grandest dream, which could have won him fame, collapsed, and less creative men, such as the Wallacks, became famous while he faded into undeserved oblivion.

The Delsarte system fell into disrepute and so did Mackaye. His plays, regardless of the predictions by contemporary critics that they would become classics, dated rapidly. His theatrical inventions, however, live on even though Mackaye himself is largely forgotten.

DAVID BELASCO: David Belasco (1854-1931) was born into an old Portuguese-Hebrew family, the name of which was originally Valasco. The family had fled Portugal because of that country's relentless persecution of Jews, and as a result David's father, Humphrey Abraham Belasco, and his mother, Reina Martin, were both natives of London. Relatives on both sides of the family were poor and held a social position which was humble at best.

Humphrey Belasco was a harlequin by occupation and apparently quite proficient in his calling. In an attempt to improve his condition, with his wife's agreement and approval, they set out by sailing vessel for San Francisco, hoping to make their fortune out of the "easy money" that accompanied the gold rush. The Belascos were almost destitute on their arrival in San Francisco, and their first lodging was in a cellar room in an old house on Howard Street. It was here that their first child, David, was born. The Belascos lived in San Francisco for several years, and Humphrey achieved a moderate prosperity as a tradesman, keeping a general store. Early in 1858 they migrated to the coast town of Victoria, where Humphrey continued in business as a dealer in tobacco, fur, and other commodities. Young David received the rudiments of an education from his mother, who was intellectual, romantic, and imaginative, and at an early age he was sent to a Victoria private school called the Colonial. The school was conducted by an Irishman named Burr who supposedly was vile-tempered and a harsh disciplinarian. From the Colonial, David went on to a school called the Collegiate, which was conducted by a clergyman named T. C. Woods. David was still only seven years old when one of the teachers, a Roman Catholic priest named Father McGuire, noticed that the child had an uncommon intelligence and precocious talent. With the persuasion of David's mother, his father finally consented and the boy was sent to Father McGuire's monastery for more intensive scholarly work. David remained at the monastery about two and a half years, benefiting greatly in his study habits, patterns of thought, willingness to work, drive to excel, and general demeanor.

David Belasco—actor, adaptor, director, manager, designer, technician—produced a variety of shows, both realistic and spectacular. This production of *Sweet Kitty Bellairs* took place close to the turn of the century.

Eventually, however, Belasco became discontented with the seclusion of the monastery and ran away to join a wandering circus. This was his first theatrical venture, and from it he learned to ride horses bareback and to perform as a miniature clown. An illness so serious that he could not be moved caused him to be left behind in a small country town, and if it had not been for Walter Kingsley, a clown from the circus, Belasco would have died. Kingsley stayed with Belasco, nursing him through the malignant fever. While Belasco was convalescing, Kingsley died of this same fever, which he had caught while caring for the boy. By this time Humphrey Belasco had located his son and took him home to his mother and a new school.

By 1862 David's strong desire for a theatrical career, nourished by his brief stint with the circus, was leading him toward acting. He appeared frequently in juvenile parts at the Victoria Theatre Royal, and when Charles Kean appeared for a short engagement at the Victoria in 1864, Belasco appeared as the little Duke of York in *King Richard III*. He also appeared as a supernumerary in *Pauline*, produced during Kean's engagement.

In 1865 Belasco returned to San Francisco when his family decided to move back to that city. David was then sent to the Lincoln Grammar School, where he was given training in elocution. Belasco attended every theatrical performance to which he could gain admission, and his frequent visits to the theatre enabled him to make personal acquaintance with a number of theatrical people. He left school for good in 1871 and immediately began his career by acting a minor part in a play called *Help*. In 1871 he met Cecilia Loverich, and in 1873 they were married.

From 1871 to 1879 Belasco lived the life of a nomadic Bohemian, roaming the streets of San Francisco at night, visiting saloons and waterfront dives in which he would recite. He lived off whatever money the people threw him for his readings. He also earned money by writing articles for the local newspaper. Belasco acquired his writing material by visiting every gambling house, opium den, hospital, and police station in the city. With the material he gathered he would write brief stories which he then sold to any newspaper that could buy them. The experience that Belasco gained through this observation of the night life of San Francisco contributed greatly to the melodramas he later wrote.

Between 1873 and 1879 Belasco worked in several San Francisco theatres as actor, manager, and play adapter, occasionally touring with shows. One such show was *Hearts of Oak* (1879) which he wrote in collaboration with James A. Herne. A business alliance was formed between Belasco and Herne in which both parties received one-half interest. A lawsuit was later filed against Belasco and Herne because *Hearts of Oak* was not an original play but an adaptation of *The Mariner's Compass*. However, inasmuch as it was unprotected by American copyright, *The Mariner's Compass* could be used by any person in the United States. The success of Herne and Belasco in Chicago and other cities outweighed this awkward situation and thus relieved the two plagiarists of any public embarrassment.

In 1880 Belasco moved to New York, where he became associated with Daniel Frohman as stage manager at the Madison Square Theatre. During his thirteen odd years of hard work at this theatre he displayed a talent in skilled stage management, the ability to adapt or doctor plays, and good judgment in casting of parts.

In 1902 Belasco leased the old Republic Theatre. The owner, Hammerstein, spent more than $150,000 in remodeling the theatre, which was renamed the Belasco Theatre. The work took five months to complete and the result was the finest and best-equipped theatre in the world. "The theatre," Belasco had often said, "is, first of all, a place for the acting of plays." Accordingly, the stage of the Belasco Theatre was designed to prevent the disadvantage of restrictive space, allowing for every possible mechanical aid to the acting of plays.

Due to pressures created by the monopolistic theatre syndicate, Belasco built his own theatre in 1906, David Belasco's Stuyvesant Theatre. Meyer R. Bimberg built the theatre according to Belasco's designs, and Belasco supervised every step of the project. The stage was designed to facilitate in every way the setting and shifting of scenery.

Belasco was the first American producer whose name alone could

A scene from Belasco's *Rose of the Rancho,* 1906. (New York Public Library)

attract an audience to come to the theatre, and this served him well as he became famous for picking unknown actors and bringing them to stardom. Although he was attacked by a number of people for being cruel to his actors, the hard work and demanding training he insisted on proved fruitful. The actors that worked under Belasco's direction testified to having great respect and admiration for him.

Belasco also preferred working with playwrights whose success depended upon his own collaboration. Some critics view his preference for playwrights who would collaborate with him as mere egotism. Whether or not this is true, the success and popularity of his work cannot be overlooked. Other aspects of Belasco's reputation were his minute attention to detail, his sensational realism and lavish settings (which often overshadowed productions, leading to charges of "Belascoism"), his exciting technical effects, and his experiments with lighting.

As a producer, Belasco was noted for his capability of making stars out of unknowns. He carefully selected his actors, coached them tirelessly, and then tailored plays to suit their abilities. Some of his stars were Mrs. Leslie Carter, Blanche Bates, Frances Starr, and David Warfield.

Belasco is especially well remembered for his staging. He insisted upon controlling every aspect of his productions. Being a naturalist, Belasco went as far as reproducing a "Childs Restaurant" on stage, with real food supplied by Childs. His extensive experiments with stage lighting led to the elimination of footlights, replacing them with the first lensed spotlights.

ACTING

The nineteenth century saw a number of outstanding actors working in the United States—some of them, like Edwin Forrest, American-born, and some of them, like Helena Modjeska, born in Europe but making their greatest theatrical impact in the United States. It was, in spite of the popularity of some foreign-born favorites, a period of growing nationalism for actors. Early in the century John Howard Payne (1791-1852), a native-born actor, reversed the usual procedure and went to England to establish his reputation. Edwin Forrest (1806-72), another native-born performer, achieved such a reputation that when Macready toured to the United States, in seeming competition with the American, the Astor Place Riot resulted. By the end of the century a strong native tradition of acting had established itself and the United States was no longer dependent on the importation of foreign stars.

Today, unfortunately, John Howard Payne is better known as the lyricist who wrote the song "Home, Sweet Home" than as the first major American-born actor. He was, however, the most successful American actor at the turn of the century. He went on the stage in New York at the age of seventeen, in spite of parental disapproval, and soon earned limited fame in such roles as Young Norval, Romeo, Tancred, and even Hamlet. By the age of twenty he had toured all the major cities and was appearing at the Chestnut Street Theatre in Philadelphia as Frederick in his own adaptation of Kotzebue's *Lovers' Vows.*

Perhaps because of his successful tours, Payne was unable to reestablish his popularity when he returned to New York. As a result he reversed the trend of young English actors coming to America to seek reputations and boarded a ship for England in 1813. There he played the provinces and appeared at Drury Lane, both with great success. A visit to Paris won him the

Edwin Forrest in costume for one of his favorite roles—Spartacus.

friendship of Talma, and as a result Payne spent considerable time translating and adapting French plays for the English stage.

Payne never returned home, but his European success helped establish American acting as something beyond the colonial or pioneer stage. In 1842 he was appointed American Consul to Tunis, where he remained until his death.

In the early and middle years of the century no name in the acting profession stands out like that of Edwin Forrest. Born in Philadelphia, he made his first stage appearance at the age of ten in an amateur production. By the age of fourteen he was playing Young Norval at the Walnut Street Theatre. Because of his later fame and popularity these early years are often overlooked, but they were hard years indeed, always haunted by the spectre of poverty. However, due to a tremendous drive to succeed and a great but never quite disciplined talent, Forrest eventually triumphed and dominated American acting for nearly thirty years.

Personally Forrest always remained something of an enigma. He was often described as brutal, selfish, vain, proud, and self-seeking, but others found him gentle, generous, and unselfish. Whatever may have been the truth, Forrest was a highly talented man with many physical attributes. He had a brooding but expressive face, a rich, powerful voice, and a powerful physique. Early in his career his voice led him astray and he was accused of ranting. However, he learned to control this tendency and became highly successful in roles that demanded forceful delivery, such as Lear, Macbeth, and Richelieu. Among the plays written especially for him the roles of Spartacus and Metamora were outstanding.

In 1836 Forrest toured to London, where he played with only limited success. In 1837 he married Catherine Norton Sinclair (1817-91). It was never a happy marriage and ended in 1850 in divorce. Catherine Sinclair went on to become a successful theatre manager in San Francisco.

In 1845 Forrest repeated his tour to London, hoping this time to score the major success that had been denied him on his first visit. This time, however, he was greeted with hostility by London audiences and critics. Forrest was sure that this was due to the machinations of Macready, and indeed this may be true. More likely, though, audiences and critics were merely reacting against this vainglorious American who dared to match talent with their own outstanding tragedian. In any case, the enmity that resulted from this tour erupted later in the Astor Place Riot in New York when Macready next visited America.

During his last years Forrest's talent seems to have deserted him and he went from failure to failure. His final stage appearance was at Boston's Globe Theatre in 1872 in one of his great roles—Richelieu.

The nineteenth century in the United States also saw the development of theatrical families. In Europe this had long been a commonplace, with families of designers or actors—such as the Bibienas or the Kembles—dominating the stage for periods as long as a century. However, the theatrical tradition in America was too short in duration and had been too dependent on England for its performers for such family traditions to develop. This was changed in 1795 with the arrival in Boston of Joseph Jefferson I (1774-1832).

Joseph's father, Thomas Jefferson (1732-1807) was an English actor of good reputation who was for some time at Drury Lane under Garrick. He had a large family, most of whom went on the stage but failed to achieve distinction. Joseph, however, decided to seek his theatrical fortune in America. After a short stay in Boston he moved to New York, appearing first at the John Street Theatre and later at the Park, where he was a popular performer, especially in the comic roles of elderly gentlemen. However, the constant bickering of the management and the unfortunate influence of Hodgkinson forced him to leave the Park. He joined the company of the Chestnut Street Theatre in 1803 and remained there until 1830, when his career began to dissolve, probably because his powers were diminishing. The final two years of his life were spent on tour through most of the major cities. Throughout his career Joseph was held up as a model of the gentleman-family man-actor, which contributed greatly to American provincial acceptance of theatre, but his greatest contribution came in terms of his son and grandson. Like his own father, Joseph Jefferson had a large family, all of whom went on the stage. Only one of these children, Joseph Jefferson II (1804-42), made a memorable contribution.

Joseph II was, according to tradition, much like his father in terms of temperament, which is to say he was honest, likeable, a gentleman, and a family man of unassailable virtue. He was not, unfortunately, much of an actor, in spite of the training he received from his father. He did, however, excel in art and did some of the most outstanding scene painting of the age. Unlike his father he had a small family, consisting of only two children, but the second of these, Joseph Jefferson III (1829-1905), became one of the outstanding actors in American theatrical history.

Joseph III made his stage debut at the age of four when he was unceremoniously dumped out of a sack by the famous (or infamous) Jim Crow, whose song and dance act he then imitated. The family, like so many semisuccessful theatrical groups, toured incessantly, costing Joseph his formal education and the traditions of childhood outside the theatre. By 1850, however, the long years of work began to pay some small returns and his popularity increased. By 1856 his income had increased to the point where he was able to travel to Europe.

Returning from the continent he joined the Laura Keene Company where he became an instant success in the roles of Dr. Pangloss (in *The Heir-at-Law*) and Asa Trenchard (in *Our American Cousin*). Moving on from the Keene Company he joined the Winter Garden troupe where, under Boucicault he played Caleb Plummer in *Dot* and the shrewd, honest Salem Scudder in *The Octoroon*. In 1861, his career assured, tragedy struck by way of his wife's death. Anguished, Jefferson left the country on a four-year tour of Australia. In 1865 while in London on his way back from Australia, Jefferson played the title role in Boucicault's version of *Rip Van Winkle*. It was highly successful and, a year later, Jefferson repeated the role in New York to even greater applause.

Adaptations of Washington Irving's story had been around in American theatre for a number of years, and Joseph III had even played the Innkeeper in a version by his half-brother, Charles Burke. However, it was not until the combination of Boucicault's script and Jefferson's characterization of Rip went onstage that the public paid attention. The role, eventually, almost overwhelmed the actor. For fifteen years Jefferson played Rip almost exclusively, changing the script along the way and making it his own. From *Rip* he went on to stage *The Rivals*, with Mrs. John Drew as Mrs. Malaprop, which he toured successfully for several years. In 1904, after seventy-one years on the stage, Jefferson made his final appearance, appropriately in the role of Caleb Plummer, which had been his first major success.

Contemporary with the Jeffersons was another important American theatre family—the Booths. Junius Brutus Booth (1796-1852) was the first of this family to make his career on the stage. His father was a lawyer of Republican sentiments—hence his name—and Junius was given a good education and prepared for legal studies. However, at age seventeen, in spite of some rigorous family objections, he went on the stage. After several years of touring the provinces he arrived at Covent Garden, where he scored a major success as Richard III. In at least one way this was unfortunate, for it established him as a leading rival of that specialist in great villainous roles, Edmund Kean, and Junius Brutus was never quite up to such rivalry. He went on to play Leonatus Posthumus, Sir Giles Overreach, Shylock, and Lear at Covent Garden, and two years later left for Drury Lane to act with his exrival. He played Iago to Kean's Othello, Edgar to his Lear, and Pierre to his Jaffier.

In 1821 Booth deserted his wife and son and, with a Bow Street flower girl, he took ship for America. His reputation got him immediate roles, and shortly after his arrival he appeared in Richmond, Virginia, as Richard III. Moving on to New York he repeated the role late in the same year. He went on to play most of the great classic roles and was very popular in some of the better modern parts. Except for two short visits to England to play at Drury Lane he remained in America until his death while touring the West. He died, appropriately, while aboard a Mississippi River showboat.

With his Bow Street flower girl Booth had ten children, several of whom died young. The eldest, Junius Brutus Booth, Jr. (1821-83) followed his father on the stage, and while he seems not to have inherited his father's acting talent, he was a fine theatre manager and producer. He did, however, spend all his career doing some acting as well as managing. For many years he was part of the company at the Bowery Theatre, and in later years he moved to the Booth Theatre. His youngest son also went onstage as Sydney Barton (1873-1937) and was for many years a successful leading man with such fine actresses as Maude Adams and Lillian Russell.

The second son of Junius Brutus Senior was Edwin Thomas Booth, one of the great American actors and the first to win the European reputation that Edwin Forrest so coveted. Edwin's younger brother, John Wilkes Booth (1839-65), brought a different kind of fame to the family by assassinating President Lincoln on April 14, 1865, during a performance at Ford's Theatre, Washington, D.C., of *Our American Cousin.* There are a number of theories about John Wilkes, both as an actor and as a man. The most popular is that he was highly talented but wild and undisciplined, jealous of his brother Edwin's success and seeking fame through what he conceived to be the ultimate criminal act.

EDWIN BOOTH: Edwin Booth (1833-93) is considered by many to be the greatest actor America has ever produced. He was also a major innovator in theatre architecture and staging, and one of the first managers in this country to cross the line between actor and the job we now call director. He was a man touched personally by the most unforgettable crime of his century (his brother, John Wilkes Booth, assassinated President Lincoln), visited by major personal tragedies, and tortured by alcholism. He outlived the prime of his creative power by nearly twenty years, and his last performances were described as pathetic. Yet when he died the eulogies, from the greatest theatre people of the day, put him in the rarefied company of Garrick, Marlowe, and the playwright he most loved, Shakespeare.

Edwin was born at Belair and spent the largest part of his childhood traveling with his father. The elder Booth constantly discouraged Edwin from making the theatre his profession, but Edwin at last managed to make his stage debut in spite of Junius Brutus' disapproval. His father's company was at the

An engraving of Edwin Booth's *The Winter's Tale,* which in its handling of a crowd suggests that Booth anticipated the work of the Duke of Saxe-Meiningen and Henry Irving.

Boston Museum and the prompter had a walk-on he did not want to do, so Edwin arranged to make himself the stand-in. Junius Brutus found out a day or so prior to opening, but he gave in and on September 10, 1849, the sixteen-year-old Edwin made his debut as Tressel in *Richard III*.

For nearly three years Edwin toured with his father's company, playing a variety of minor roles, and in 1852, when the company was ending a tour in California, Junius Brutus told his son that if he wanted to become an actor he had to strike out on his own. Edwin stayed in California while the company toured toward the east. After a performance in New Orleans the elder Booth became ill and on November 30, 1852, he died. Edwin received word of his father's death while snowed in at a remote town. Using the last of his money to "buy in," he joined an adventurous and determined crew who planned to escape the snowbound and starving town. He managed to get to San Francisco where, his brother Junius Jr. had a theatre. He remained there until 1854, when he toured the Pacific, appearing in Australia, Tahiti, Hawaii, and Samoa. While in San Francisco he played utility roles, then leads, then more utility parts, making the cycle three times. It was during his first series of leads that he did the role of Hamlet for the first time. This immature Hamlet received good critical reaction for its vitality and power, but was criticized for lack of control.

After returning to the East by way of the mountain circuit, he worked the eastern seaboard, gaining in technical skills and popularity. In 1858 he met Mary Devlin, an actress, and in 1860 they were married. It was his love for Mary that led him to attempt to stop drinking, a growing problem that had plagued him for several years, and it was her death in 1863 that brought the resolution he needed to conquer his "demon." They had one child, Edwina, in 1861. Mary's death affected Edwin so deeply that he retired, but not for long. Toward the end of 1863 he was back at work, this time in collaboration with his brother-in-law, who owned the Winter Garden Theatre. It was at Winter Garden in 1864 that Booth first triumphed in *Hamlet*.

This production, artistically controlled by Booth, was new in every respect, even featuring entirely new sets, costumes, and furniture. It opened November 26, 1864, at the Winter Garden, and ran for a record one hundred performances. Edwin Booth became the new idol of American theatre—for five months. On April 14, 1865, John Wilkes Booth shot President Lincoln, who died the following day, and the world Edwin had so carefully built collapsed. For nearly a year Booth left the stage, shamed by his brother's act, living the life of a near recluse. However, because of debts that had to be paid, and his love for the "grand and beautiful art" of the stage, he was forced to return. Booth opened *Hamlet* at the Winter Garden on January 3, 1866, to the warm cheers and ovations of an audience who refused to blame this great artist for his brother's mad act. It was a heartening reception for Booth, who had expected anger or cloying sympathy, neither of which he could stand.

Following his triumph in *Hamlet* Booth next staged *Richelieu* in the same sumptuous and "authentic" style. Out of debt, thanks to the popularity of these productions, he bought the Winter Garden Theatre, which promptly burned to the ground. Booth then set out to open a new era in theatre. His production of *Hamlet* and his historical re-creation of Richelieu's period had been the first major breakthrough in realistic setting. He now set out to make a major change in theatre architecture. In 1869 the new Booth Theatre opened with a delicate yet elegant production of *Romeo and Juliet.* The theatre was both sumptuous and tasteful. Because of the Winter Garden loss, Booth saw to it that his new theatre was as fireproof as possible. It was the first theatre with a sprinkler system, the stage crew held fire drills regularly, and a fire bell was built into the proscenium. It was the first theatre with a high stagehouse, high enough to effectively fly scenery and the first to eliminate grooves for wing and border sets. The orchestra was sunken, there was no forestage, and the stage itself was not raked. It had traps in the floor, and sophisticated hydraulic elevators to lift scenery into place.

Romeo and Juliet was very popular, as was the subsequent *Othello,* despite the "too hard, sharp, and midwestern" Juliet and Desdemona of Mary Runnion McVicker. Miss McVicker soon after retired from the stage when she married Edwin Booth. After *Othello,* Booth sponsored a series of productions by some of the great actors of the day, including Joseph Jefferson in a highly regarded production of *Rip Van Winkle.*

According to most critics, Booth's 1870 production of *Hamlet* was his masterpiece. The reviews ranged from ". . . a genuine feast of reason, of beauty . . . of histrionic intelligence and splendor" to "a magnificent honor, not only to the American stage, but to the drama of the entire civilized world." The sets for the production were rich and grand, featuring romanesque arches, vaulted ceilings, grand staircases, and broad vistas. The costuming was elaborate and elegant, the lighting (gas) was subtle and artistic, and the performances were inspired (if all the critics are to be believed).

Booth was at his height as an actor. In previous years he had displayed the power and physical energy requisite to great acting, but lacked maturity; in future performances he would grow more mature but lose the power and energy. At age thirty-six he combined all these qualities. Booth, in acting style, appears to have verged on modern realism—to have been natural in manner rather than declamatory and affected. He would often use the device of turning his back to the audience, something that was never done by the older-style actors standing at the front of the stage, near the audience. But his greatest talent was the ability to take the script into himself and synthesize it into a living character. He did this best with Hamlet, and his daughter had a sound idea of why: "It was long before I could thoroughly disassociate him from the character of Hamlet, it seemed so entirely a part of himself. Indeed in that impersonation, I think, his confined nature and pent-up sorrows found vent. He told me that the philosophy of *Hamlet* had taught him to bear life's vicissitudes." His acting was superior in most of the roles Booth attempted. His Iago, Richard III, and Richelieu were all considered outstanding. Yet Hamlet was always his best characterization. The word "naturalness" appears over and over again in reviews, and so does "believability." This is important if it is remembered that this was an age when reviews normally praised "declamation," "gesture," and "emotion."

The 1870s and the early 1880s were Booth's greatest years. He suffered more tragedy in 1874 when he went bankrupt and lost his theatre due to an unscrupulous partner, but for the most part it was a period of awards and triumphs. His tour of England drew great acclaim as did his tour of Germany. Yet at the same time tragedy struck again. Mary McVickers Booth's health declined, and she died in 1881. After losing his theatre, into which he had put so much of himself, he never attempted again to manage, produce, or own a theatre.

Booth's triumphs during his tours of England and Germany were not entirely without problems. The German critics especially began to notice flaws in his work. Some pointed out that he would alter or forget lines, and others disliked his realistic interpretation on the assumption that it drew from the audience feelings of sympathy instead of tragic pity and terror. When he returned to the United States for the 1883-84 season, Booth was very tired. Despite his exhaustion, however, he had to compete with an American tour by Henry Irving. For the American actor it was a demoralizing season. He was just fifty years old, but his hair was graying, his voice and physique were breaking down, his concentration was weak, and his health generally was poor. The following season he seemed to have recovered to a degree, but each year the signs of age became more and more pronounced. Yet, when all things came together properly, the mature Booth could still give stunning performances. His Hamlet especially continued to draw fine reviews and outstanding audience response.

In April 1889 Booth suffered a mild stroke on his way to a performance and temporarily lost his voice. His letters to his daughter contain several references to relaxing his schedule so that he could rest, and to that end he eliminated one-night stands and matinees. On April 4, 1891, he was booked into a Brooklyn theatre to do *Hamlet,* and when word got out that he planned to act no more, at least three thousand persons stormed the theatre for seats. The performance was reviewed, but the review read like an epitaph. After suffering another stroke, Edwin Booth died on June 8, 1893.

Before his death, which ended a theatrical era, Booth managed to remotely touch the new generation by recording two Edison cylinders. He also had some association with realistic theatre as it now exists, and according to William Winter, he loathed it. He felt that accuracy, or "realism," is useful only insofar as it supports the romance of art.

No one can ever again experience Booth's *Hamlet,* yet it was his portrayal of that beleaguered prince that caused his greatest fame. He performed a great Hamlet because he knew what Hamlet meant to him, and what theatre and art meant to him.

Also during this early period in the century an insignificant actor and vaudeville performer named Thomas Dartmouth Rice (1808-60) gave the American public, and also English audiences, their taste for impersonation of blacks and subsequently for minstrel shows. Eventually he became known as Jim Crow, from a line in his famous song and dance act which was supposedly based on a song and shuffling dance which Rice observed being done by an old black groom. First performed in 1828 in Ludlow and Smith's Southern Theatre as an intermission entertainment, it quickly became popular and spread across the country. In 1836 Rice performed his Jim Crow act at the Surrey Theatre,

London, and was so well received that the vogue for American-style minstrel shows can be traced to his appearance.

While the early years of the century were dominated by the first English representatives of the great acting families, and the middle years by the most distinguished members of these families, the later years of the century saw a number of distinguished native-born performers on the American stage. Of these, one of the most significant was William Gillette (1855-1937), a playwright-actor whose career spanned the nineteenth and twentieth centuries, but whose greatest successes came in the 1880s and 1890s. As an actor his best work was done in plays he wrote or adapted himself, especially *Esmeralda* (1881) and *Sherlock Holmes* (1899), which he played with great success both in the United States and in England.

Probably the outstanding actress on the American stage was Minnie Maddern Fiske (1865-1932). The daughter of a theatrical agent, she came to the profession early, appearing at the age of three under the stage name of Little Minnie Maddern, which she later retained in preference to her own (Marie Augusta Davey). By the age of five she was an accomplished performer, appearing as Little Eva in *Uncle Tom's Cabin*, as the young Duke of York in Cibber's version of *Richard III*, and as Little Alice in *Kit the Arkansas Traveller*. By age thirteen she was appearing in the roles of adults, such as Widow Melnotte in *The Lady of Lyons*. During the early years of her career Minnie was praised for her vivacity and also for the "naturalness" of her acting. It was this naturalness on which the latter half of her career was founded.

In 1890 Minnie Maddern retired from the stage to marry Harrison Grey Fiske (1861-1942), editor of *The New York Dramatic Mirror* and a promoter of the "new" drama—that is, the realistic social drama appearing in Europe. Thus, in 1893 Mrs. Fiske, as she was now billed, returned to the stage to apply her "natural acting" techniques to her husband's *Hester Crewe*. She subsequently appeared as Nora in *A Doll's House* and as Tess in a dramatization of Hardy's novel. The Fiskes finally rented the Manhattan Theatre and there, with an outstanding company, Mrs. Fiske starred in a series of fine dramas, such as *Hedda Gabler* and *Rosmersholm*.

Along with Mrs. Fiske, Maude Adams (1872-1953) also made her mark on the late nineteenth century stage. The daughter of an actress in a Salt Lake City stock company, she was onstage early, and by the age of five had received rave critical notices for her portrayal of Little Schneider in *Fritz* at the San Francisco Theatre. She went on to play all the major child roles, especially Little Eva, and then left the stage to complete her education. In 1892 she returned to play opposite John Drew in *The Lost Paradise*. Her two greatest triumphs were as Juliet in 1899 and as Lady Babbie in *The Little Minister*, a role which Sir James M. Barrie rewrote and padded especially for her. Barrie was an excellent judge of performers, and she went on to popularize *Peter Pan*, *What Every Woman Knows*, *Quality Street*, and *A Kiss for Cinderella*.

The century ended with a remarkable group of performers, such as Lionel and Ethel Barrymore, just beginning their careers (Lionel's first appearance was in 1893 and Ethel would score her initial triumph in 1901). It was an end that saw realism established as the basic American acting style, and that held great promise for the coming century.

12

Oriental Theatre

12

Oriental Theatre

The theatre of the Orient is, at the same time, both ancient and contemporary; it is also complex, colorful, exciting, meaningful, and virtually unknown to all but a handful of Westerners or Occidentals. There are a number of reasons for this lack of Western knowledge regarding Eastern theatrical forms. First is the traditional separation that for so long existed between Western and Eastern civilizations and that, comparatively speaking, only recently was bridged. Second, there has been little significant crossover or cross-fertilization to attract the students of Western theatre to devote much consideration to the theatre of the East. Only in the second century B.C. in India, when the Greeks may have had some slight influence on the developing Indian drama, and in our own century by way of such men as Artaud, Brecht, and Claudel, has there been any direct influence of one theatre upon the other. Third, our training in a theatre which deals almost exclusively with the realistic surface of life, and which has tended toward sociological rather than philosophical significance, has left us ill-equipped to deal with a theatre that is as

Much oriental theatre exists to demonstrate spiritual control over the body. Such is the semi-dramatic "fire-walking festival" at Kataragama in Ceylon.

much interested in the invisible world of the spirit as it is in visible manifestations of life.

For most Westerners, Oriental theatre is all of a class, with the theatre of Japan generally undistinguishable from the theatre of China, India, Java, or Bali. There is some justice in this vision—these theatres are similar in some respects, just as Western theatre, no matter in what part of Europe or America it originated, is alike in many ways. However, because the differences are more important than the similarities, it is necessary to look at the Oriental theatre in terms of its country of origin.

THE THEATRE OF CHINA

The earliest records of Chinese drama are fragmentary. Music and dance came early to China, but how much these were affected by activity that could truly be called dramatic is open to question. In the ancient temples the votaries danced as part of the sacrificial ceremonies, and in the homes of the nobles of the early dynasties the temple dance was secularized. Taking the roles of such wild animals as tigers and bears, the dancers, accompanied by lutes and pipes, danced to amuse the nobility and even accompanied armies into battle. These dancers are depicted in the bas-reliefs on the bombs of the Han period (206 B.C.-221 A.D.).

During the Tang dynasty (618-907) the music-dance aspect of drama continued to develop, eventually assuming the form of the "Great Songs," which contain a musical prelude in which the tempo is the choice of the performer, a vocal chorus that begins in slow tempo and gradually builds, and a subsequent dance. Also, the court jester or buffoon was joined by another character, the *ts'an-chün,* who essentially served as straight man (and second actor) for the jester's improvisations.

Beginning in 960 and ending in 1280, the Sung dynasty brought trade, craftsmanship, and economic prosperity to most of China. This prosperity brought about a significant social change in that all forms of entertainment previously found only in the emperor's palace were now performed in the marketplace. Dancers, wrestlers, jugglers, acrobats, and minstrels all performed for a new middle-class audience of tradesmen. Jesters acted out their comic scenes and story tellers began extending the short literary forms with long tales from the lives of the religious martyrs and military heroes. During the Sung dynasty the colloquial language became acceptable for literature and the novel also appeared.

The access to India and Central Asia, which had begun under the Tang dynasty, was now greatly expanded. Trade began to flow regularly along the caravan routes, and it was in this way that the drama came to China. The music-dance performances were given plots and eventually became formalized into a spoken prologue, two short acts in which the story was told, and a satirical epilogue. The concept of dramatic performance as it developed in the West had still not been reached. There were five actors, but the stories were developed along the line of the story teller's narratives, with the actors speaking in the third person rather than in dialogue.

It was not, however, until the hordes of the Mongol khans swept into China and destroyed the Sung dynasty that drama—the operas of the Mongol period—truly got underway. Under the Yüan dynasty (1280-1368) the educated men who had been intended for government service were pushed out of public life by the Mongols and forced early into an unwanted retirement. Turning their attention to the folk arts—the conquering Mongols had taken over the official literary arts—these men began writing plays with music, and this was the beginning of the great Chinese classical theatre. In these music plays of the Mongol period the action is not narrative but progresses through dialogue that is spoken or sung by several actors.

The early Chinese stage reached its peak of development when Europe was in its Medieval period, and has since remained virtually unchanged. Backgrounds were painted on curtains. Sets were little more than tables, chairs, and painted banners.

While the exact origins of the drama that arose during the Yüan dynasty are still somewhat obscure, the course that this drama followed during the succeeding seven centuries is fairly clear. There have been a number of significant changes made in the form, but some of the usages even today are the same as they were in the late thirteenth and early fourteenth century. Also, because the drama was regarded as a special form existing only in production, the texts of the Chinese drama have often gone unidentified as far as the author goes, and the existing texts have regularly been rewritten, updated, and changed to fit the circumstances of the production.

Yüan drama had a fairly large repertory of plays, but these plays were so regularly rewritten that very few really new plays appeared. The subjects which the plays covered were famous historical happenings, popular contemporary events (for which existing dramas were adapted) and the traditional literary fables, and they featured, principally, emperors and their concubines, wise judges, generals, ministers of state, poor young scholars, and the wives and daughters of the great families. They began with a prologue which introduced the major characters and set the tone for the story. The prologue was followed by four acts, in which one actor sang while the rest spoke their lines. The actors were all male but they could easily move from male to female roles. The plays that were written in the north of China followed the classic four-act form; they used simple melodies performed only on the lute, and they usually were tragic. The plays written in the south often ignored the four-act structure, using as many short scenes as necessary to tell their story and all of the actors could sing. The southern drama also introduced a variety of tunes, more complex scoring for the music, vocal duets, and even full choral numbers.

Probably because it had by far the most interesting of the two dramas, the southern area became dominant at the beginning of the Ming dynasty (1368-1644). In addition to the principal type of opera (*ch'uan-ch'i*), three other types of drama developed in the southern countryside—the operas of Hai-yien, Yü-yao, and I-yang. These operas retained their popularity until the sixteenth century, but by this time they had become well nigh incomprehensible to audiences. Wei Liang-fu then used the music from these local "folk" operas to reform the classical opera, setting the old stories and themes to this popular local music. His new style of opera was named *K'un-ch'ü*, after the place where Wei Liang-fu lived. Ultimately nearly two hundred plays were written in this new style and these, along with some standard works from the Mongol period, form the basis for most of the contemporary classical opera, with *The Hall of Long Life* by Tsung-sheng and *The Peony Pavilion* by T'ang-Sien-tsu being the two best known examples in the style of the Ming dynasty. This remained the major operatic form until the eighteenth century, and the basic form is still with us today.

Under the Manchu dynasty (1644-1912) new tunes were added to the traditional stories, and new forms of local operas also developed such as the *I-yang-ch'iang* in the province of Chiang-si, the *Han-tiao* from Hupeh, and the *Ch'in-ch'iang* from Shensi. In the early nineteenth century the older *K'un-ch'ü*, and the somewhat newer *I-yang-ch'iang* and *Ch'in-ch'iang*, were combined by a troupe of actors from central China and taken to the capital. This new, combined form became known as the Pekin *Tyin-si* and today is known in the West as the Peking Opera.

In many respects the Chinese opera resembles certain types of ancient Western dramas that concentrated not on individuals but on stock characters. In both cases the basic idea of the stock character is that this character is a synthesis of a general type of person. The contemporary opera has not changed much from the traditional opera in this sense. The male roles are all types: an elderly and respectable man, a young man, an elderly warrior, a young warrior, a comic warrior (much like Capitano of the *commedia dell'arte*), and such other comic types as thieves, servants, and tramps. The female roles consist of an elderly woman, usually noble and of fine character, a virtuous woman, a flirt, a courtesan, an unmarried young woman, a war heroine (quite popular in recent times), and several comic roles. All of these types not only have a traditional appearance, they also have traditional styles of speaking, movement, posture, and even gait. It should be pointed out that from the beginning until after World War II and the revolution, with its resulting emancipation of women, all female roles were played by male actors.

The Chinese actor begins his training at age eight to ten, and his training never ceases. It is conducted along the lines of master and apprentice, with the older experienced actors tutoring the younger, inexperienced performers. These older actors also act as codirectors, taking responsibility for rehearsing the play for eventual public performance.

The young actor, as was common for Western actors at earlier periods, concentrates on learning the roles for one of the stock types for which he seems best fitted. He then trains under a master actor who also specializes in this particular characterization. From the master the beginning actor learns the traditional movements and gestures and the vocal qualities ascribed to this character type. This would seem, on one level, to be a repetitious and perhaps boring theatre, when movements and vocal qualities are passed on so exactly, but it is not at all boring because the Chinese actor is also urged to study life and bring to his role a uniqueness of spirit. This spirit must be carefully conceived in relation to the basic role and its requirements, however, for only in such harmony does the actor achieve art.

For a Westerner viewing a traditional Chinese drama, one of its most striking aspects is the makeup worn by the actors. Originally makeup was simple—black and white were the only colors used—and it was used sparingly. The complex, colorful makeup used today began to come into vogue about five hundred years ago. At first the eyebrows were the focal point and were swept up to give the impression of dashing manliness and courage to the men's faces. Gradually the makeup area was expanded to include the eyes, nostrils, and mouth. The oldest of these makeup patterns is the "three bricks" or *san-k'uai-wa,* in which stripes are made above the eyebrows and across the eyes. This divides the face into three separate parts—the two sides of the face and the brow. In some cases fanciful designs are then painted on the three plain sections. The "broken" face (*suei*) is achieved by painting curves and spirals of color, with some aspect such as an eye or the nose distorted by paint. The "old" face (*lao-lien*) is painted either gray or pink, with only the eyebrows made up to give the face a minimum of vitality. The young face is the opposite of

An authentic American production of the Chinese classic *The Rainbow Bridge*, staged by James Zee-Min Lee. At stage left, standing and smoking imperturbably is the omnipresent and "invisible" prop man. (From *Milestones of the Theatre*, an MGM production)

this. It is snow white and touched with pink only in the middle of the brow. For actresses or men playing female roles the makeup is a pale pink base with peony color used on the cheeks and around the eyes. In addition to these basics, war heroes or generals have primarily red, martial faces; devoted civil servants and men of firm personal convictions have black faces; men who are reflective by nature have blue faces; and evil spirits and devils have green faces. Actors playing gods and symbolic characters design their makeup to resemble that for which they stand. Thus, the God of Fire would appear with his face masked by flames. Upon occasion a beard is part of the makeup. The beard itself has meaning, so that an actor wearing a beard reaching to his waist represents wealth and strength, and whiskers hanging in three parts from the ears and chin indicate a learned character.

The costumes worn by Chinese actors are as colorful as the makeup, but are somewhat less standardized in terms of meaning. Usually made from rich silks and brocades, their colors indicate the nature of the character who wears them. They also have such additional symbolic trappings as fish, clouds, flames, plants, or animal heads stitched into or applied to the material. A few of the costumes are traditional in style. Warriors wear shoulder padding and fish-scale mail; the war costume simulates the metal armor of olden times; and the *mang* robe, made of brocade, is worn by an emperor or high court official. Only emperors wear yellow. Military commanders below the rank of general wear red when out of uniform. Generals and great statesmen wear green. Senior generals may wear orange, and junior generals and ministers of lower rank wear white. Evil noblemen wear black, and dishonest ministers wear blue. Other court officials and scholars wear purple. Commoners wear light blue. Female costumes are much like the male costumes, with only slight alterations. For instance, the *mang* robe for women is just like the man's in style, but is cut shorter and worn over a narrow skirt.

In recent years the Chinese theatre has been a world divided—that is, the classical drama is still presented, is still highly popular, and in fact accounts for the largest part of Chinese dramatic activity. However, alongside the classical drama, and in some ways patterned after it, there has developed a communist theatre of propaganda which reflects the several phases that Chinese communism has passed through. Even some of the traditional dramas, because of their championing of the poor and oppressed, have been taken over by the propagandistic theatre. Thus, such a drama as *The Wealthy Fool*, in which a wealthy, conceited official is made to look foolish by a peasant lad, is still popular both as a traditional play and as egalitarian propaganda.

Ultimately, the Chinese theatre may be characterized as a theatre without walls, where the total experience is created by the actor, who needs no more than a playing space with a rear curtain for entrances and exits, an audience area, and if possible a table and a few chairs. Song and dance are frequent; the whole production is, in fact, so stylized that it might be said to have been choreographed. And yet, in spite of this standardization and simplification, the Chinese theatre digs deeper beneath the surface of human emotion and motivation than most other theatres of the world.

THE THEATRE OF JAPAN

Perhaps more than any other country, East or West, Japan has remained devoted to theatre. For over a thousand years, with no break, the Japanese drama has played regularly. During this period the drama developed into several major and quite distinct forms, the four major types of which are the Noh, Kabuki, *Kyogen*, and the Bunraku puppet theatre.

Noh

The Noh (or Nō) drama is perhaps the most important type of Japanese drama, even though it is not as well known in the Western world as the Kabuki. The name itself (*noh*) is sometimes translated as "accomplishment," meaning a perfected skill, and in a sense this definition clearly fits the form, which is a limited but highly polished type of dramatic art.

The Noh drama, which combines in perfect balance, and thus harmony, the arts of poetry, dance, music, mime, and acting, achieved its present form in the fourteenth century. Its earliest history is unknown, but some aspects of Noh drama can be found in a variety of early dramatic forms. One of the most important of these was *gigaku*, a satiric, festival type of entertainment that included music, dance, and mime. A regular part of religious festivals, in spite of

Gagaku, ancient court music and dance, is shown being performed by a troupe of the Imperial household. Gagaku is an esoteric form of art brought to Japan from China in the eighth century. (Photo courtesy of the Japanese Tourist Association)

its satire, the Korean-originated *gigaku* was highly popular and amazingly long-lived. It may have entered Japan as early as 612 A.D., and one aspect of it, the "lion dance," is still popular today.

Another contributor to Noh drama was the *bugaku*, a group of courtly dances that through mime and limited vocal narration told a story. The third major contributor to Noh was *sarugaku*, a popular street entertainment that was generally comic in its outlines. A form of *sarugaku*, the *dengaku*, broadened the comedy and included acrobatics and, apparently, much physical horseplay. Some of the founders of Noh drama had been trained in *sarugaku* and had worked in *dengaku*.

The Noh drama began as an entertainment for the feudal Japanese aristocracy, and thus it presented scenes from the life of people in that class. The fact that this dramatic form managed to survive the audience that spawned it, without ever changing its traditional emphasis, is a tribute to the perfection Noh drama has achieved in its limited field.

Basically Noh was an intellectual drama designed for an educated, upper-class audience proud enough of themselves and their own heritage to, upon

A seminal part of Japanese dramatic art reached the island from China in the seventh century, when ancient tales were acted out on raised, railed, open-air platforms, as depicted in this painting of c. 850 A.D. (From *Japanese Drama*, Tourist Library, Tokyo, 1935)

occasion, ban attendance by any other than the aristocracy. The plays were, in the beginning, produced during the festivals, and like the Classical Greek festival theatre in the West, they were produced in series. Each series contained five Noh plays dealing with serious subjects, separated by short, farcical scenes, usually of indelicate character, called *kyogen*. Ultimately a formula developed for the presentation of these plays that was rigidly followed.

In the fourteenth century two men, Kan-ami and his son Zeami Motokiyo, wrote almost half of the Noh plays still in the repertory today, and it was under their guidance that Noh achieved its final distinctive form. The degree to which this form was (and is) followed becomes apparent when it is realized that no significant Noh plays have been written since the early seventeenth century, and all the nearly two hundred forty plays that are currently in the repertory of Noh companies date from considerably earlier periods.

To follow the total production plan for Noh drama, including order of production, acting style, makeup, costume, and even the design of the stage, it is necessary to understand the types of Noh drama and how they work. First is the *shin* play. This is usually the first in order of performance because of its high seriousness and usually religious character. The *shin* play is in most cases devoted to singing the praises of a deity, and it is accompanied by a solemn dance in the deity's honor.

The next play in order of production is the *asura* play, which is devoted to praising one of the great warrior-heroes from the epic period of Japanese history. Following the *asura* play comes the "female wig" play. This play, acted by a man, is often about a woman who is mad, and as a result of this madness the play always ends tragically. Next comes a play where a choice is available to the artist—it can deal with people or with ghosts and spirits. In either case, this fourth play is always highly emotional, featuring violent or otherwise sensational action. If the subject matter of this play deals with characters from the world of the living, it is called the *genzai-mono* play. The final presentation in the Noh series, more dance than drama, is called *kiri*. The dances featured are usually warlike in nature, and the dialogue expresses a sincere, dignified approval of whatever occasion the current festival represents.

The rules regarding all aspects of Noh plays are extensive indeed, covering not only the order of presentation and the subject matter of the plays, but also the characterizations, acting style, makeup, costume, scenic design, and even the shape of the stage and the relationship between the stage (and performers) and audience. The music and dance for each play are traditional and must be performed exactly as specified. Such a compendium of rules is too great to be covered in a brief examination of the form, but some of the major aspects must be touched upon.

In terms of the characterizations, most Noh plays are in two parts, which allows the main character to be depicted in two major aspects. In part one this character (*shite*), either god or hero, appears disguised as a humble human being. In part two the god appears in his heavenly form and the hero appears in his spiritual form. The hero, in this spiritual form, must do penance for his actions while a human being.

The staging of these plays is unique, though some relationship to other forms of Japanese drama such as *kowaka* or Kabuki can faintly be seen. Basically the Noh stage must be square, measuring 19 feet, 5 inches. It must be raised precisely 2 feet 7 inches above the floor of the auditorium, into which it projects much like the Elizabethan stage. At the back of the stage is a panel on which is painted a gnarled and venerable pine tree. At the left rear of the stage is a delicate bridge which leads to a curtained doorway through which the principal characters enter and exit. Three dwarfed trees are spaced regularly on the bridge. The whole of this stage has a roof resting on four corner posts exactly 15 feet high. Behind the stage is a small, shallow enclosure, and in it, completely visible to the audience, are four musicians. Reading from left to right, they play the horizontal drum, the large hand-drum, the small hand-drum, and the flute.

The way in which the actors may use this stage is just as strictly prescribed as its structure. The corner where the bridge joins the stage square is reserved for the first actor (*shite*). The pillar area diagonally across from this belongs to the second actor (*waki*). The area between the rear of the bridge and the back of the stage belongs to the "stage manager," who relates program notes between the two parts of the play. The chorus is seated to the right of the stage. While the actors have no choices in terms of their stage areas, they may

Scene from a Noh play. Originally Noh drama was a rustic form of lyric drama played between functions at Shinto festivals. In its ultimate development, Noh drama features rhythmic recitation of texts, classical music, and symbolic movement. Masks are used by the actors to indicate the characters they are portraying. (Photo courtesy of Japanese Tourist Association)

introduce aspects of the character they are playing as long as they stay within the bounds of traditional movement, gesture, and vocalization.

The presentation as well as the subject matter is refined and elevated. Verse is used for most of the lofty scenes with the *shite,* and the minor characters usually speak in a delicate, balanced, rhetorical prose. The stories themselves are almost all from religious literature or classical secular literature. Of the religious literary contributions, the largest number come from Buddhist texts, followed by materials from Shinto writings.

The primary virtue of Noh drama is its attempt to bring the audience into a state of delicate, cultured aestheticism. Zeami Motokiyo wrote that the first goal of Noh was to attain a state of *yūgen.* This word does not translate easily into English, but if one could combine tranquility and beauty with meditation, and consider it as an ultimate gratification, it would be close to the Japanese concept. The second goal, according to Noh's founder, is to bring the audience to a state of sublime exaltation. Largely this is achieved by the "build" of a Noh presentation from the opening play, which is stately and of high seriousness, to the fourth play, which is highly emotional. This growing emotion is controlled by the continuing religious relevance that exists throughout the structure and by the religious thanksgiving of the fifth and final play in the series.

Kabuki

From the early years of the seventeenth century until sometime around the 1960s the Kabuki was the most popular theatre in Japan. Unfortunately, the popularity of Kabuki is now declining. Several reasons can be advanced for this decline: production costs have skyrocketed; Japan has continued to Westernize itself and has developed a preoccupation with Western styles, customs, and drama; and the old moral values expressed by Kabuki now seem outmoded and even obsolete. And yet, in spite of all this, Kabuki is still one of the most vital theatrical forms in existence.

According to a somewhat questionable tradition the Kabuki had its beginning sometime around 1620 when a young temple attendant named Okuni began to present dance programs in a dry streambed on the outskirts of Kyoto. Eventually she added more women to her performances and she dressed as a man. These programs attracted large audiences. Exactly when the name Kabuki was applied to this form of entertainment is unknown, but it was probably early in its development, for its root is a verb meaning to behave ec-

The Kabuki includes many romantic historical plays. In this scene from *Imoseyama Onna Teikin*, a pair of "star-crossed" lovers stand before their respective houses, the interiors of which are visible. (From *Travel in Japan*, winter edition, 1935-36)

centrically or, perhaps, outrageously. In any case, by the year 1629 there were several female Kabuki troupes performing in Kyoto. The nature of these performances can be surmised from the fact that they were primarily designed to entice men into purchasing the sexual favors of the female performers.

While the performances were popular with the monied public, they were highly unpopular with the high officials of the Tokugawa shogunate. The officials feared that the dancers would corrupt the samurai, who were the center of power in the whole structure of the period's caste society. As a result of this fear, women were forbidden to appear in Kabuki. This did not put an end to the form, however, as a number of pretty, young men, who had been studying the basic dance forms of Kabuki, took over the female roles in the performances. It took only a few years before the high officials realized that the young men were corrupting the samurai in much the same manner as the young women, and so the pretty, young male Kabuki performers were also forbidden to appear.

It was this that forced serious Kabuki performers into developing their performances into a real art form. Music and dance had been banned, and the potential distribution of sexual favors no longer existed to draw customers. Thus, dialogue, drama, and acting skills had to be developed to replace the lost attractions, and they had to be developed in a style that would compete with the still popular Noh drama, the *kyogen*, the various puppet or doll theatres, and the other forms of incidental entertainment.

The result was the development of a theatre that was less esoteric and aristocratic than Noh, that was, in fact, more realistic. The Kabuki performers developed new styles of makeup; they emphasized the beauty of costume over the symbolic; and they created styles of movement and vocal delivery to separate men playing men from men playing women (the men playing women used exaggerated female movements and spoke in falsetto voices). Thus, between 1652 when the young Kabuki males were outlawed and 1664 when the first extensive play was performed, the artistic basis of Kabuki theatre was developed.

Once the full-length play had been accepted by the audience, the external trappings of Kabuki began to develop. Curtains and scenery were added to the stage, and they were used in a much different way than the scenic materials of Noh. The modern Kabuki stage, that is a result of this early development, is not really like the early Kabuki stages, except in its size and its highly polished wooden floor, but it indicates the direction that the early Kabuki masters sought to follow. The Kabuki-za in Tokyo, the most famous of the theatres built in the nineteenth century, has a proscenium nearly ninety feet wide and twenty-one feet high. The stage depth is thirty-five feet. From the left side of the stage, but not up against the auditorium wall, there extends a ramp (*hanamichi*), five feet wide, that runs through the entire auditorium. This serves the major characters for entrances and exits and allows for ceremonial processions. Several entrances and exits on the main stage serve the minor characters. In the center of the main stage there is a revolving platform that became part of the Kabuki technical inventory in 1757. The main stage also has two or more trap doors, one at the center of the revolving platform and the other about twelve feet in front of the ramp.

A drawing of the Kabuki theatre (the Great Theatre of Yedo in the late eighteenth century) showing the stage, the bridge ("Flower Way"), the draped front curtain (stage right), and audience seating. (From *L'Art du Théâtre*, Paris, 1901)

The early Kabuki interest in the curtain has developed, and contemporary Kabuki makes use of several stage curtains. The main curtain is the large one that separates the stage from the auditorium and pulls open from the sides to reveal the stage. This front curtain is rather clearly a late innovation based on Western theatre, for the early Kabuki stages were of the thrust style and the curtains were used in the rear.

The audience-performer arrangement has also changed slightly from earlier periods, which attempted to create an intimate relationship while preserving the isolation of the groups who came to see the show. Private boxes ringed the auditorium much as they did in Western opera houses until the present century. The auditorium floor was then divided into small enclosures, seating from six to eight persons, with narrow walkways in between. Seating was on the traditional Japanese mats. Contemporary Kabuki theatres have dispensed with the boxes and mats and seating is on comfortable chairs arranged in the European fashion. The auditorium is still small, however, and the old concept of Kabuki as an intimate theatre has been preserved.

The sudden emergence of Kabuki as Japan's most popular theatrical form took place during the years between 1673 and 1735. This was, by a somewhat liberal interpretation, the *Genroku* period. It was a time of extensive economic and social change in Japan. During these years a new class of tradesmen emerged. As had been true in China and the West, this new monied group changed the social life in the cities, and in the arts that their money supported.

They accepted the severe, aristocratic aestheticism of Noh, but alongside it they demanded something flashier and more emotional. Kabuki was the perfect vehicle to provide this new drama. Also during this period appeared Sakata Tōjūrō and Ichikawa Danjūrō, the two most famous actors of the early Kabuki. These men, each with a different approach to the drama, blazed the two major paths that Kabuki would follow to the present day. Sakata Tōjūrō worked primarily in Kyoto, which contained the emperor's court, and Osaka, which was the Japanese commercial center. As a result his works were elegant (reflecting the court demands) and realistic (reflecting the attitudes of the hard-headed businessmen of Osaka). Ichikawa Danjūrō, on the other hand, worked mostly in Tokyo, which housed the great military rulers of Japan, and as a result his work was full of bravado—heroic and flamboyant.

Basically the Kabuki is a dance and musical theatre in which the musicians, traditionally costumed, have several positions, depending on the work being produced, but they are almost always visible. In most plays they are on the left of the stage area, but when doing one of the highly ceremonial plays or dance dramas they occupy the rear of the stage. A chanter (*joruri*) who narrates parts of the action, together with an accompanist who plays the samisen, sits on a small revolving platform at the right. This is a technique derived from the ancient puppet or doll theatre. Offstage are sound specialists who provide a variety of effects.

The famous Kabuki actor Mitsugoro Bando plays the role of the aged warrior, Ikyu, in the play *Sukeroku*, one of the most popular plays in the Kabuki repertoire. (Photo courtesy of the Japanese Tourist Association)

There are three types of Kabuki plays—the *sewamono,* which is a fairly realistic treatment of middle and upper-class life; the *jidaimono,* which is a period play done in a stylized manner; and the *shosagato,* which is a dance-drama. Performances in all these forms, however, have tended toward the eclectic in the sense that aspects of each form appear in the others. Thus, in almost any given play there will be portions of realism, of stylization, and of dance. All the plays are long, so that such a variety of style can be supported. In its earlier years a Kabuki performance began early in the morning and lasted until midnight or even later. Such performances are no longer common, but the very long plays may be presented over a period of several days.

The acting of the Kabuki is as varied as its ancestry. Once the form was established, Kabuki performers were trained from early childhood to play certain types of roles, and gradually families of actors developed much like the family troupes of *commedia dell'arte* players in the West. The social status of Japanese actors, also much like that of their Western counterparts, has been hazy. In the earlier periods they were often oppressed or treated harshly by the authorities, and in almost all periods they existed as a group set apart—essentially outcasts. However, at the same time the great actors were idolized by the public. The most famous actors were those specializing in female roles because, except for the early female troupes, women have not acted in the Kabuki until the last few years after the Second World War.

Ultimately, Kabuki is a stage spectacle with actors who are skilled mimes, dancers, and acrobats. It uses a huge, spectacular stage, colorful, rich costumes, and much music and sound effects. It is a pictorial theatre; in fact, its scenes are referred to by the Japanese as "stage pictures." While words are spoken, the manner of speaking is at least as important as the words themselves. This perhaps accounts for the conservatism of the Kabuki repertory. Most of the favorite plays come from the seventeenth and eighteenth centuries, with a few from the nineteenth and none from the twentieth.

Kyogen

The *kyogen* are the ancient, traditional farces of Japanese drama, and they are among the best of such forms to be found in the East or West. Their origins have long since been lost in time and there is no definitive material relating to their earliest period. Their often coarse style and broad buffoonery indicate to most scholars a peasant ancestry, probably growing out of the entertainments of rustic festivals. In any case, they became the leading comic form in a country devoted to drama, and their period onstage far exceeds that of their closest counterpart in the West, the *commedia dell'arte.*

Today there are no troupes dedicated exclusively to the playing of *kyogen,* but existing dramatic troupes specializing in other forms sometimes present one or more of them as a matter of dramatic and national interest. This is important inasmuch as the humor of the *kyogen* is a sparkling compound of satire and ridicule which presents a delightfully lopsided view of life and art.

The exact period when the *kyogen* were born may be in doubt, but by the fourteenth century a strong tradition of performance had been established.

Unfortunately, like some of their Western counterparts, the scripts of the *kyogen* were not then written down but were passed along in an oral tradition from master actor to apprentice. It was not, in fact, until the middle of the seventeenth century that any of the *kyogen* materials were written down and preserved.

Basically the *kyogen* were short, farcical pieces that provided much opportunity for physical action, and yet in contrast to most Western farce there was, apparently, always a strong emphasis on the spoken word. This is apparent in the name of the genre—*kyogen*—which is usually translated as "play," meaning theatrical performance. However, tradition has it that originally the word *kyogen* meant something equivalent to "wild words" or "mad words." In the manuscripts that are available there is, as might be expected, a great deal of mime, but there is also a substantial amount of crisp, literate dialogue designed to skewer many areas of human pretension and folly. In the *kyogen* all men have their faults, and the more wealth and power a man possesses the more faults he is likely to accumulate. And yet the *kyogen* never really present a sad view of man's plight. Men may be knocked down and battered by the exigencies of fate and the foolishness of their fellow mortals, but they bounce back and soldier onward. In this sense the *kyogen,* like all great comedy, become a celebration of life, recognizing every man's faults and problems, laughing at them, and then moving on without lingering to lament the unchangeable.

Perhaps the most interesting aspect of the *kyogen's* long history is the influence that they exerted on the serious, aristocratic, and often tragic Noh drama. The *kyogen,* which were already an established form, were performed as entr'actes between the five pieces of the Noh, and in fact many of the *kyogen* that have come down to us parody the Noh dramas. Later, the Kabuki also drew on the *kyogen* in much the same fashion as did the Noh, and today the few *kyogen* that are performed are seen as part of Kabuki performances.

Bunraku

Bunraku received its name from Uemara Bunrakuken, a puppeteer and entrepreneur who, in 1871, opened a puppet theatre in Osaka. The traditional puppet theatre had fallen off in popularity, even in Osaka, which was the center of puppet drama, and the opening of a new theatre must have seemed the height of foolishness. But Bunrakuken's theatre, which he named Bunraken-za, was highly successful and in a short time the whole classical puppet theatre, generally known as *ningyo shibai* or doll theatre, came to be called Bunraku.

Japanese puppet (or doll) theatre had been a minor entertainment form for more than a thousand years when, in the early seventeenth century, it was caught up in the exploding Japanese cultural movement and translated into a major art form. The main school for puppetry was established in Osaka by Takemoto Gidayu shortly before his death in 1714. It was called the *jōruri,* in honor of the narrator who spoke for the puppets, and it concentrated on training the narrator to reach the highest artistic level in terms of his performance and in terms of the materials developed for his use. What had been merely simple narrative was turned into an elocutionary art.

A scene from a Bunraku puppet play. The Bunraku puppet drama employs "three-man" puppetry, which means that each of the puppets is operated by three manipulators. The home of Bunraku is the Bunrakuza Theatre in Osaka, but performances are sometimes given in Tokyo. (Photo courtesy of the Japanese Tourist Association)

To upgrade the materials available to the narrator, Gidayu was able to turn to Chikamatsu Monzaemon, a famous Noh playwright who had been unable to make the transition to Kabuki drama. Monzaemon found that writing for puppets, rather than restricting his imagination, freed it, and he wrote his greatest plays for these nonhuman performers. In fact, his puppet plays were so widely admired that they were later adapted for the Kabuki theatre, which had rejected Monzaemon's earlier efforts on its behalf.

Japanese puppetry reached a degree of technical and artistic excellence almost unrivaled in the Eastern or Western world. In the time of Gidayu only small puppets were used, and these were manipulated very simply and had limited movement. By the end of the century, however, the puppets had become nearly half of life size and the manipulation had become so complex that three persons were necessary to work each puppet. These manipulators were fully visible onstage. This tradition has lasted until today, though now the leader of the manipulating team is the only one to wear the traditional garb, and his helpers are masked and dressed all in black.

The stories told by the puppet plays can be divided into two major groups: the heroic plays that take as their source the epics and stories from the feudal age; and the domestic melodramas, farces, and mythological fantasies.

By the opening years of the nineteenth century the Bunraku had lost much of its initial popularity. It was unable to compete with the Kabuki, which took from the puppet theatre its best plays and adapted them for live performers. Kabuki even borrowed the character of the narrator and made him a regular part of the Kabuki tradition. Ultimately the competition from other forms and the invasion of Western films and plays ended the Bunraku. The only remaining Bunraku theatre is in Osaka, where it exists on government grants. It is a sad ending for a theatre with such an extensive history and that made so notable a contribution to all the other theatrical forms.

THE THEATRE OF INDIA

In India all things are handed down from the gods, and that especially includes the classical theatre, often called the Sanskrit drama because it is usually written in that language. For Indians the four sacred *vedas* were the great storehouse of wisdom and knowledge, but they were available only to the higher classes of society. So, according to the tradition, Indra, along with the other gods, approached Brahma and asked him to create something which all persons might enjoy, which would not be the exclusive preserve of a privileged few—essentially a fifth *veda*. Brahma felt that the request was fair and so he created the *Natyaveda* by taking the element of recitation from the *Rigveda*, the element of music from the *Samaveda*, representation and mime from the *Yajurveda*, and sentiment from the *Atharvaveda*. The task of producing drama, the gods decided, must be left to mortals, and so the sage Bharata was entrusted with the task. Bharata compiled the *Natyashastra* (2nd or 3rd century B.C.), a huge work, both speculative and specific, which contains all the basic concepts of traditional Indian drama, and in his account of its composition he makes it clear that this is, essentially, a fifth *veda*.

At the time that Bharata produced his great work India was totally under religious control. When the Aryans had invaded India a sharp division had developed between them—the conquerors—and the Dravidians already living there—the conquered. As a result the Aryans established a caste system, which was designed to maintain their own racial purity and which gave them a handle to control the native people. Within this caste system the priestly caste, the Brahmin, soon became supreme and assumed absolute authority in both ecclesiastical and secular matters. This put a severe restriction on all things artistic and especially the arts dealing with popular entertainment. Entertainers were relegated to the lowest possible caste, the Shudras or the Dravidians. Thus, it was necessary for Bharata to establish divine authority for his work on drama. He had to convince his audience that all the gods, Aryan and non-Aryan, were in favor of drama and that his pronouncements on drama had religious authority behind them.

The *Natyashastra* is voluminous, detailed, complex, and highly exacting in setting forth the specifics of theatre. In fact, it is so complete in its pronouncements that it has no parallel anywhere else in the world, and it has given scholars a rare vision of an early though hardly primitive drama. First it contains a description of the divine origin of drama. It then goes on to cover the types of playhouses, the types of plays that may be produced, styles of representation, the poetic requirements, the emotional states that drama may deal with, and the sentiments that drama should evoke. It also contains directions for the invocation to the gods, to be given before the play begins, and a host of materials on the art of performance.

Because the *Natyashastra* is so complete and so much emphasis is put on it, it is easy to forget that it is not the only early work on Indian drama. There is also the *Dasha-rupaka* (11th or 12th century), a critical work which deals with the ten forms of dramatic composition; and the *Saraswati-Kanthabharana* (11th century), which deals primarily with poetic composition. In addition there are various early treatises, such as the *Kavya-Prakasha*, the *Sahitya-Darpana*, and the *Sangita-Ratnakara*, which deal with various aspects of drama.

It may be well, at this point, to expand on a comment made earlier in this chapter—that the presence of the Greeks in India during the period that the *Natyashastra* was composed, may mean that the Greeks influenced the early Indian drama. Many arguments, both pro and con, have been put forth regarding the possible influence of Greek theatre on the Indian—far too many to summarize here. Perhaps the strongest argument for Greek influence is that the Indians were impressed with the importance that the conquering Greeks put on theatre and so determined to have an equivalent theatre of their own. Beyond this kind of influence it is difficult to find a true link between the early theatres of Greece and India. The Greek world view and the Indian were quite dissimilar, and the drama that developed from the two cultures reflects this, with the Greek drama imitating the action and the Indian drama exploring the state or condition in which the action is undertaken.

The Indian drama was conceived as having three forms: drama (*natya*), gesture with language; pantomime (*nritya*), gesture without language; and dance (*nritta*), which tells a story without words, using music and movement, but without the gestures of drama and pantomime. The drama was then subdivided into realistic drama (*lokadharmi*) and theatrical drama (*natyadharmi*). These divisions are a bit suspect, however, because while the realistic drama means in fact that the actors portray normal people living out normal situations, there are a number of unrealistic conventions that pervade the form. The theatrical drama, on the other hand, does not mean theatrical in the sense that we generally understand it, but rather poetic, lyrical, and imaginative.

In terms of this division, plays were arranged in two groups—regular plays (*rupakas*) and minor plays (*uparupakas*). Regular plays were then subdivided into ten different types, and there were eighteen types of minor plays. This presents a panorama of dramatic types too large to be examined individually, but within this welter of types two were of major importance: the *nataka* and the *prakarana*.

The *nataka* identified a play in which the story was always taken from mythology or based on a great historical episode. The hero was always a person of high standing, such as a king, a demigod (similar to the Greek hero characters), or a god. The plot featured a specific passion, such as love, duty or heroism. These plays had between five to ten acts, but the time of action was rather short, elongated only by intervals of narration.

The *prakarana* was less elevated than the *nataka*, but was still exalted in comparison to ordinary life. In this type of play everything was pure fiction—nothing could be drawn from another source. Its theme was always love,

Scene of a pantomimic dance performed in a harem in seventeenth century India. (From *Der Tanz in der Kunst*, Ausstellungs-Katalog der Staatlichen Museen, Berlin, 1934-35)

and its characters were from the higher social levels such as priests, government ministers, great military leaders, and wealthy merchants. The heroine could be (and often was) a courtesan, if one understands by this term something closer to the Japanese geisha than the Western harlot.

The presentation of one of these early plays was always a ceremonious occasion, beginning with an invocation to the gods. The invocation was followed by an introduction and an appeal, and usually a compliment, to the audience. This introduction was performed by the *Sutradhara*, somewhat equivalent to an Elizabethan chorus, who established the time and place of the action and provided any background material necessary for the audience to pick up the spine of the plot. Two other characters who were not part of the plot commented on the action, remarked any changes of scene and generally provided the plot with continuity. One of these was a jester or fool figure called *Vidushaka*, a fat, ugly, vulgar character given to ribaldry and bawdiness. Somewhat surprisingly, he was always a Brahmin, as this allowed him to speak to any of the play's characters and even act as comic go-between for the hero. We may guess that a large part of the audience also enjoyed seeing a Brahmin make a fool of himself.

The hero and heroine were always drawn from the nobility, for after all the purpose of the play was to examine the condition or state in which an action is performed, and who could better exemplify the highest state or condition than the pure nobleman. In addition, while drama was designed as the art to give pleasure to all people, in fact it was usually performed for the nobility in their castles. Thus, it was to an author's advantage through some rather torturous interpolations, to indicate a distant relationship between the pure hero and the ruling patron for whom the play was to be performed.

While the *Natyashastra* provided some interesting specifics about three types of playhouses—the oblong, triangular, and square—there is no evidence that these playhouses ever existed. Instead the plays were produced almost exclusively in the royal palaces of India's highest nobility or in the great halls of the lesser nobles. In spite of the divine injunction that theatre was to give pleasure to all, it was still a princely entertainment, staged on such occasions as a coronation, royal marriage, birth of a son, royal birthday, and so forth.

Ultimately this early Sanskrit drama declined, probably as a result of the series of invasions that weakened the national spirit, plus the fact that India, the opposite of Japan and that country's isolation, was changing rapidly and the drama that had satisfied the needs of an earlier culture soon became meaningless.

Along with the classical Sanskrit drama, India has long had a tradition of popular theatre, sometimes called folk theatre because it existed for the lower castes and was not cultivated by people in the higher economic and educational groups. This is not to say that the higher castes did not attend performances of popular theatre productions, and even enjoy them, but the creative impulse and the need to keep such theatre alive clearly springs from the folk of the lower classes.

A photograph from India, early in the present century, shows a stage, set up in a palace, ready to present a Hindu religious drama. (From William Ridgeway, *The Dramas and Dramatic Dances of Non-European Races*, Cambridge, 1915)

Over the years very few plays from the popular drama were set in print and recorded for posterity. Largely this is because these were less traditional plays than an ever-changing series of skits, scenes, music, dance, and spectacle. Over the years these works have maintained an amazing likeness, though in most cases they vary from production to production. Unlike the folk drama of early Europe, the Indian folk drama never seems to have existed in an oral tradition. Rather, one or two authors would create each work anew out of the vast reservoir of material—adding, changing, and adapting, but always remaining true to the spirit of the material.

After the Sanskrit drama had declined in about 1000 A.D. the popular drama surfaced as a major theatrical form. It had already been around for years as simple folk entertainment, but after the literary Sanskrit died out it was the only dramatic form, and as a result it took on added importance. Drawing its materials from folk music and dance, from the legends, epics, and even the old Sanskrit plays, it freely adapted these materials into something possessing the folk spirit. This, along with a strong, vital tradition of performance, provided a theatre that has lasted until the present day.

The strong point of the Indian popular theatre has always been rich spectacle, music, and dance, rather than meaningful drama. However, when a topic is paramount in the public concern the drama has not hesitated to deal with it in the strongest terms. Thus, the popular theatre agitated for freedom from British colonial rule. Religious plays propagandized for their particular beliefs, and territorial dramas have promoted a particular geographic area.

Alongside and paralleling the development of folk or popular drama was Indian dance-drama. It is perhaps the most complex and, to its audiences, clearly the most meaningful dance-drama in the world. Abstaining from vocalization, the Indian dancer learned to "speak" with his body, especially his hands. Over many years a whole silent language developed so that, ultimately, the audience was able to see the dancer "speak" and understand what he said with as much clarity as they could hear and understand the actor.

The sources of material for dance-drama were the same as for the folk drama—that is, the poetic epics and the old Sanskrit plays. Thus, the dancers were telling stories that were familiar to their audience, and so the symbolic movement of the dance was able to develop in correlation to known material. In some cases, dance-dramas even made use of narrators who told the story while the dancers interpreted it and, in fact, retold it through their own movement.

Because it requires an audience educated to its "language" or brought up in its mysteries, Indian dance-drama has had little appeal outside of India. However, it is India's greatest contribution to theatrical form since the demise of the classical Sanskrit drama.

THE THEATRE OF JAVA AND BALI

The major Javanese theatrical form is a puppet theatre called *wajang kulit,* with *wajang* meaning "puppet" and *kulit* meaning "leather." Basically, what all this means is "shadow play with leather puppets." The history of *wajang kulit* plays is lost in time. Whether they began in Java and were exported to China, India, and Bali, or whether they were imported, is difficult to determine. There are a number of early accounts of *wajang kulit* plays in the epics composed at the Hindu-Javanese court in the eleventh century, but this is hardly conclusive evidence in either direction. It does, however, indicate the extensive history of shadow puppets in Java.

The *wajang kulit* dramas are controlled by a lone puppeteer (*dalang*). The *dalang* speaks all the dialogue for the various characters, he provides the narration between the scenes, he sings songs to create the proper mood, he provides cues for the musicians (*gamelan*), and he manipulates the flat leather puppets in front of a light so that they cast their shadows on a white screen. This is all even more difficult than it at first sounds, for the characters in any given play will be about sixty in number. Also, he is in full view of the audience, which sits on both sides of the white screen, so that half of them see a puppet show and the other half see a shadow drama cast on the screen.

The *wajang kulit* plays fall into four divisions, but only one is of major interest. The animistic group contains only about six plays, all of which tell of the creation of plants and animals. The second group also contains about six plays that tell of Ardjuna Sasra Bau's victory over Rawana, the ogre king. The third group contains eighteen plays that tell of Prince Rama's banishment from the kingdom of Ayodya, the kidnapping of Sinta, Rama's wife, by the ogre King Rawana, and the final battle between Rama and Rawana in which Rawana is

A scene from a Balinese Barong drama in which the citizens, in a graveyard, prepare to resist the witch Rangda.

killed. The fourth group of plays, and the primary one, is the Pandawa group which contains over one hundred fifty plays.

The Pandawa plays tell of the great battle for the jeweled kingdom of Astina between the five virtuous Pandawa brothers and their opponents, the ninety-five evil Kurawa brothers. The plays have large casts made up of gods, nobles, comic servants, ogres, and peasants. Owing little to the traditional epics, most of the Pandawa plays deal with side issues merely touched upon in epic literature, and in some cases their plots are totally invented. A part of this group called the "branch plays" does display an unusual dramatic format, with a three way conflict between the Pandawas, the Kurawas, and an ogre kingdom apparently located outside of Java.

While the *wajang kulit* is the most interesting, ancient, and influential form of Javanese drama, there is also a recent, popular, and somewhat Westernized type of drama. This drama is of two types, the *ketoprak* and the *ludruk.* The *ketoprak* drama tells of events in Javanese history, while the *ludruk* plays concentrate on contemporary social problems in Javanese life. The *ketoprak* plays tend toward romantic melodrama, while the *ludruk* plays strive toward realism, in spite of the fact that women are not allowed to act on the *ludruk* stage.

In Bali, as in most Oriental areas, the drama is firmly based on religion, but in Bali this relationship has not weakened in recent years and the Balinese drama must still be regarded as religious drama. There are a number of Balinese entertainments that have strong dramatic elements, but the primary dramatic types are the *wajang kulit,* the *barong* dance-drama, the *wajang wong* dance-drama, and the operatic *ardja.*

The Balinese *wajang kulit,* like its counterpart in Java, includes the Pandawa plays; it also includes several plays based on Balinese legends. Whether the Balinese version of the shadow play was imported from Java in ancient times, or whether it originated in Bali and was exported to Java, is still debated. Because the Balinese puppets are not as refined and realistic as those in Java, some experts believe that they were imported from Java in the period before that area's contact with the arts of Islam, but even that speculation is open to question.

The Balinese *wajang kulit* performance is accompanied by four xylophone-like instruments (*gender*). This is a far simpler type of musical accompaniment than the large, complex musical ensembles used in Java. In length the Balinese plays usually last four to five hours, though occasional performances have lasted as long as ten hours. Sometimes performances are given in daylight, without the screen, as a combination of serious religious rite and puppet show. On such occasions the manipulator performs with his torso naked as a sign that he is functioning as a Brahmin priest.

The *barong* dance has always fascinated visitors to Bali because at its climax the dancers hold sharp daggers to their chests and roll about on the floor in a trancelike state. The concept of the dance is that they are trapped between the two major forces in life, evil represented by the witch Rangda, who is attempting to thrust the daggers into their bodies, and good represented by the lion (*barong*), who tries to save them from Rangda's evil magic. This dance

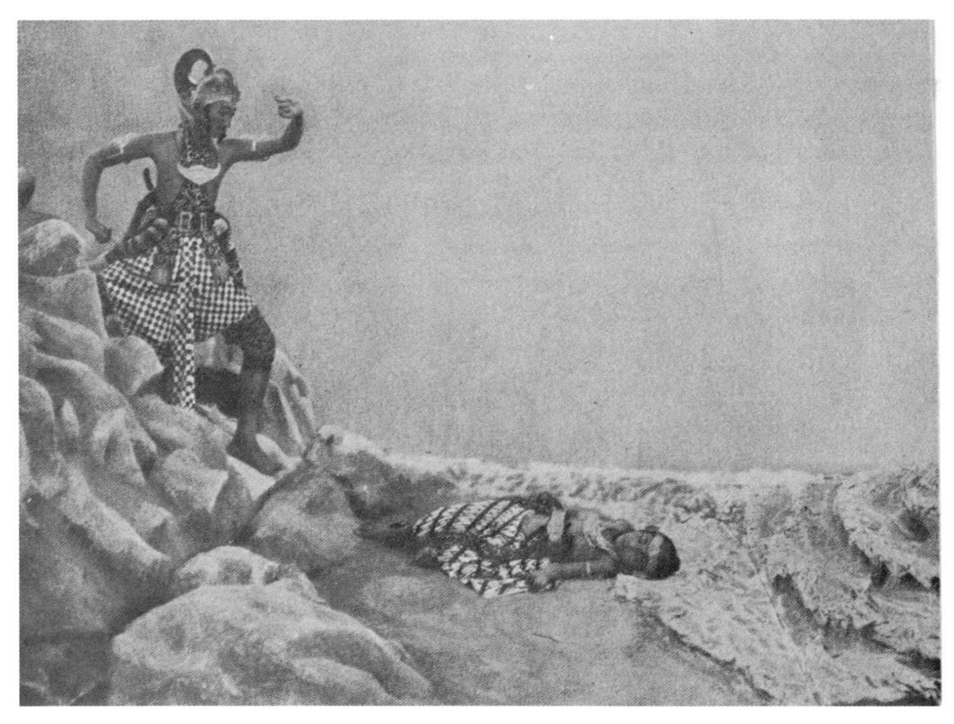

A scene from a Javanese *wajang-wong* play. Most such productions use minimal scenery, but in some productions, such as this, the scenery grows elaborate and realistic. (From *Tourism in Netherland India*, IX, 1, Batavia, 1934)

symbolizes the major belief of Balinese religion—that the world contains both good and evil spirits which constantly do battle to dominate man. Thus, the *barong* dance is a religious rite and is performed to keep the evil spirits from gaining ascendancy.

The *wajang wong* is a dance-drama that features masked dancer-actors who dance and recite lengthy poetic narratives. Most of these plays feature Rama in materials drawn from the *Ramayana*, but some of them—the plays dealing with the Pandawa brothers—are almost totally original.

The operetta-like form called *ardja* deals primarily with the stories of Prince Pandji, a legendary hero who is known, under other names, in such other Eastern countries as Thailand, Cambodia, and Burma. The *ardja* troupes are professional (unlike the *wajang wong* and *barong* troupes) and perform whenever and wherever they are hired. Thus, they are not considered to be religious performers and they are the only nonreligious performers in Bali. The plays about Prince Pandji (who is played by an attractive female) feature dance and song, in swift rotation, with much romantic interest and an unusually fast pace that is closer to Western vaudeville than any other Eastern entertainment. Along with the tales of Pandji the *ardja* troupes also perform a few plays based on the Pandawa epic, the *Ramayana*, Javanese classical legends, and some ancient Chinese romances.

13

The Twentieth Century

13

The Twentieth Century

By the time the twentieth century began, the theatrical movement that would dominate the century—realism—was already well underway. This did not preclude experimental movements in theatre, however. Expressionism became a significant force during the decade following World War I; fantasy remained a viable genre in the hands of such playwrights as Percy Mackaye; Brecht's epic theatre or theatre of alienation affected much that happened in the 1930s and 1940s; and the excesses of the absurdist playwrights changed the face of traditional drama during the 1950s and 1960s. The century saw the birth of the American musical, the development and phenomenal rise of motion pictures, and the equally spectacular beginning and explosion of television. Live theatre was several times pronounced dead, the casualty of an increasingly technological age, and final rites were performed by otherwise dependable critics; but each time theatre not only survived but came back stronger than ever so that today, as the 1970s draw to a close, it is a lively, exciting, and endlessly fascinating art form.

THE TWENTIETH CENTURY BACKGROUND

The twentieth century has been a busy, sometimes frantic period and a highly complex one. Much of what has happened is interrelated and, essentially, inseparable. Technology has exploded, partly as a result of two world wars and two extensive but isolated conflicts. Motion pictures, advanced medical practices, a swiftly growing industrialism, rapid and economical transportation, television, electronics, and of course, the resulting shortages of fossil fuels, living space, and unpolluted environment have been pervasive. As a result, the century that began so confidently secure in the belief that education and technology could assure the perfectability of humanity, has floundered so badly that its later years might well be characterized as the Age of Uncertainty.

In Europe the early, seemingly peaceful years of the century were violently disturbed by World War I (1914-1918). Imperialism—the desire to secure colonies or establish control over foreign lands and peoples—provided a major basis for the conflict. The scramble for possession of Africa and parts of Asia, the bitter competition for markets, Germany's intense desire for economic control of Turkey, and Russia's determination to secure a foothold at Constantinople and in the Straits all led to fear, anger, and ultimately war. The conflict broke out when, on June 28, 1914 the Archduke Francis Ferdinand, heir to the Austrian crown, was assassinated by a Serbian nationalist in Bosnia. Austria declared war, then Germany declared war on Russia and France. To attack France, German troops entered Belgium, which brought England into the conflict. Other European powers entered the war, choosing sides, and finally in 1917, as a result of German submarine attacks on American ships, the United States entered the conflict. Slightly more than four years after it began, on November 11, 1918, the Armistice disarmed Germany and put an end to the most widespread conflict in history.

In 1917, while World War I was still going on in western Europe, the Russian government was overthrown. There had been an earlier, abortive revolution in 1905, but this time, due to the defeat of the Russian army at the hands of the Germans, the revolution was a success. A number of political parties began struggling for control of the national government and, for a time, it appeared that the Liberals would assume command. However, because of a much stronger central leadership the radical socialists finally managed to establish the dictatorship of their own party. They were led by Lenin, a Marxian

Remigius Geyling at the Burgtheater was one of the early twentieth century pioneers who developed techniques of theatrical projections. This is his setting, projected onto a rear screen, for *The Little Clay Cart.*

socialist who assumed party leadership, and Leon Trotsky, who became Commissar for Foreign Affairs. The government was called the Council of People's Commissars, and the Commissars were led by the Party Chairman, the first of which was Lenin. When he died in 1924 he was succeeded by Joseph Stalin, who began a repressive regime designed to secure absolute power by removing potential rivals. Among these was Trotsky, who was banished from Russia.

In 1918, with the Russian Revolution over and World War I ended, new states were formed, old ones redefined, and old territories given independence. Poland was re-created out of territory taken from Germany, Austria, and Russia, with the new boundaries essentially following the old ones—except for the "Polish Corridor" which gave Poland access to the free port of Danzig, thereby cutting Prussia in half and providing a major cause of World War II.

Czechoslovakia, a new state, was formed out of the provinces of Bohemia, Moravia, Silesia, and Slovakia. The population was largely Slavic, but large German and Hungarian minorities made this a troubled state from the beginning.

Yugoslavia, also a new state, was created out of the provinces of Bosnia, Croatia, Dalmatia, Herzegovina, Montenegro, and Serbia. Again the population was largely Slavic, but there were so many differing religious, social, and political beliefs, and so many ancient tribal feuds, that troubles began almost as soon as the state was formed. Italy moved in to conquer Fiume, and kept it in spite of worldwide objections, and in 1941 Yugoslavia was easily conquered by Germany, with the help of internal dissension.

Theatrical experimentation has been a hallmark of this century, as evidenced by the imaginative use of masks in this 1939 production of J. B. Priestley's *Johnson Over Jordan.*

Finland, previously a province of Russia, gained its freedom as a result of the overthrow of the last Romanov Tsar. Also, Estonia, Latvia, and Lithuania all emerged as independent republics.

The postwar period was one of boom and bust, except in Germany where the boom was cancelled by extensive war reparations. The reasoning was that if Germany was responsible for the war, then it followed that Germany should pay the bills. Thus, the Germans were saddled by long-term debts, and their industrial potential was crippled by attachments for war debts that took trainload after trainload of industrial machinery out of the country. By 1929, however, even the conquering nations had joined Germany in a major economic breakdown. This worldwide depression began in 1929, after nearly a decade of overspeculation, and a wave of frightened reaction kept prices falling. A world economic conference met in London in 1933 to try and shore up the economy, but American refusal to cancel war debts or to return to the gold standard scuttled the conference.

After more than ten years of effort, the National Socialist Party, led by Adolph Hitler, took power in Germany, with Hitler assuming the position of Chancellor and *Führer*. The party was highly nationalistic and violently opposed to communism, Jews, and the Treaty of Versailles. Finally, in violation of the Treaty, Germany began conscription to raise an army and signed the anti-Comintern pact with Italy and Japan. This pact, along with the Rome-Berlin Axis developed by Hitler and Benito Mussolini, formed the basis for the Axis alliance of World War II.

World War II probably began as early as 1935, when Mussolini invaded and annexed Ethiopia. In 1938 Germany took over Austria and then the Sudetenland. The Munich Conference, designed to prevent any further aggression, merely rewarded the aggressors for their actions, and full-scale war was soon underway. For a time Japan refused to convert the anti-Comintern pact into a military alliance, but on December 7, 1941, Japanese carrier-based aircraft attacked Pearl Harbor. On December 8 the United States declared war on Japan, and England followed suit. Within one month the battle lines had been drawn, with twenty-six nations pledged to fight the Axis powers.

The war lasted until 1945. In that final year Germany was caught in a vise, with the Russians moving in from the east, capturing Vienna, Warsaw, and Budapest, and England and the United States attacking from the west and destroying the German hold on Scandinavia. Hitler was finally reported to have committed suicide, and victory in Europe came on May 8, 1945. Japan, refusing to accept unconditional surrender, fought on until the atomic bombs were dropped on the cities of Hiroshima and Nagasaki, at which time the Emperor surrendered all of his forces on September 2, 1945.

Following World War II there was a brief period of economic recession in the late 1940s and then, in 1950, North Korean troops invaded South Korea. The Security Council of the United Nations (which in 1945 had replaced the old League of Nations) approved military action against the aggressors, and a United Nations army was sent to Korea. In 1953 this "police action" came to an end when an armistice was signed by United Nations and Communist delegates at Panmunjom.

The 1950s saw a series of crises brought about by French colonial adventuring, by the establishment of the State of Israel, and by Egyptian attitudes about the Suez Canal Zone. Also, in the late 1950s problems began developing in Vietnam (once French Indo-China) between the North Vietnam Communist regime and the South Vietnam republic. What began as a decision by the United States to fulfill an earlier treaty and act as advisor to South Vietnam led to ever more deepening involvement, the commitment of American combat troops, and finally a geographically limited but intense war, with the United States supporting a corrupt South Vietnam against a hardly less corrupt North. It was a highly unpopular war, both in the United States and Europe, and it dragged on interminably, finally coming to an end in 1972 with the withdrawal of American troops.

The century, now into its fourth quarter, has been one of great technological change and a resulting social instability. Instant worldwide communication and its potential for swaying mass audiences has made splinter political movements, urban guerrilla warfare, and a flock of *-isms* the standard of the time. The theatre of the century has reflected this unrest, with its movements, its experiments, and its uncertainty. While the realistic theatre has dominated, it has been deeply changed by its environment, and the directions theatre may take during the final quarter of the century are still unclear.

The Twentieth Century In France, Italy, and Spain

France French theatre in the twentieth century has been almost everything that a discriminating viewer could ask it to be. It has preserved the best of French Classical theatre, primarily by way of the Comédie-Française, which in 1980 will have been producing for three hundred years with very few interruptions. The other state supported theatre, the Théâtre de France or Odéon, has presented the best of the more contemporary playwrights. Outside the state theatres the dramas of such experimental playwrights as Beckett, Ionesco, and Genet often received their first public production in Paris. Indeed, France has been home to some of the most profound dramatic experimentation of the twentieth century.

TWENTIETH CENTURY FRENCH DRAMA

The opening of the twentieth century differed little from the late years of the nineteenth. Most of the best early playwrights spanned the two periods. Thus, the early years, before World War I, tend to be dominated by themes of adultery, domestic realism, and the well-made play. A few playwrights were, however, beginning to move in new directions, and the most important of these was probably that graduate of Antoine's experimental theatre, Eugène Brieux (1858-1932). A dedicated naturalist who used the theatre with reforming zeal in the correction of social ills and injustices, he somehow managed to avoid the cold didacticism of his contemporaries and substituted for it a warm human concern for individual human beings. His best play is probably *La robe rouge* (*The Red Robe*, 1900), a study of judicial abuses, *Les avariés* (*Damaged Goods*, 1902), a study of venereal disease which created a sensation in its time, and *Maternité* (*Maternity*, 1903), an examination of birth control.

At the other end of the dramatic spectrum from the naturalism of Brieux was the symbolic, poetic drama of Maurice Maeterlinck (1862-1949), whose *Monna Vanna* (1902), *L'oiseau bleu* (*The Bluebird*, 1909), *Les fiançailles* (*The Betrothal*, 1917), and *Le bourgmestre de Stilemonde* (*The Mayor of Stilemonde*, 1919) provided a second direction for the emerging twentieth century drama.

In 1896 a crude, obscene, nihilistic farce, *Ubu roi* (*King Ubu*) by Alfred Jarry, (1873-1907), set a third direction that would be pursued in part by the existentialists after World War I. This play, considered by many historians to be the basis of most avant-garde theatre, was written when Jarry was only fifteen years old and was first performed in 1888 as a marionette play. The play's main character, Père Ubu, is vicious, cowardly, obscene, and cruel—the prototype of the later anti-hero, and many of the play's effects, first developed for the puppet stage and then included in the stage directions for live dramatic performance, provided a pattern for playwrights such as Ionesco and Brecht.

While these playwrights and their works set patterns, and while such directors as André Antoine, Jacques Copeau, Charles Dullin, and Louis Jouvet supported an essentially experimental drama, the bulk of French drama through the 1920s remained the standard well-made plays and the domestic dramas dealing primarily with adultery themes. Jules Romains' (1885-1972) *Knock, ou Le triomphe de la médicine* (*Doctor Knock, or The Triumph of Medicine*, 1923), with Louis Jouvet in the title role, was an outstanding success, both with audiences and critics. However, the success was more due to the play's departure from traditional themes than to any inherent artistic significance. In the 1930s and 1940s, however, a number of outstanding playwrights appeared on the scene. In some cases they were men who had already established reputations in the areas of literary endeavor, and so they brought to the stage a kind of artistic sanction that had become lost during a period of mediocre productions.

The earliest of these writers was Paul Claudel (1868-1955), who began his literary career as a poet and disciple of Stéphane Mallarmé. At the age of twenty-four, Claudel took a position with the French diplomatic corps and was posted to America, where he came under the influence of Walt Whitman and where he gained the background for *L'echange* (*Exchange*) one of his early plays that is set in the East Coast of the United States. From America he went on to China, where he worked on his *Grandes odes*, which display Whitman's influence, and in 1908 he was appointed as French Consul at Prague. From there he went on to similar posts at Tokyo, Washington, and Brussels.

Claudel's earliest publications were anonymous, as he feared that his zeal in promoting Catholicism might damage his diplomatic career. However, in 1912 his play *L'annonce faite à Marie* (*The Tidings Brought to Mary*), was produced in Paris by the Théâtre de l'Oeuvre. Its success was recognized by an immediate production of *L'echange*, which he had written in 1893. He went on

The scene design for the second act of Paul Claudel's *L'annonce faite à Marie*, by J. Variot. Produced at the Théâtre de l'Oeuvre, December 22, 1912.

to write *L'otage* (*The Hostage*), *Le pain dur* (*Crusts*), *Le Père humilié* (*The Humiliation of the Father*), and *Le soulier de satin* (*The Satin Slipper*), his best-known work, which was written shortly before 1924 but was not performed until 1943 at the Comédie-Française. His *Jeanne d'Arc au Bûcher* (*Joan of Arc at the Stake*), with music by Arthur Honegger, had its first performance at Basle in 1938; *Protée* (*Proteus*) and *Christophe Colomb*, both with music by Darius Milhaud, have been produced in Paris.

While Claudel's dramas have often been popular, they tend to stand outside the traditions of French drama in the twentieth century, largely because the ardent Catholicism that infused his poems also pervades the plays. Indeed, Claudel's is the only dramatic voice of the century that continues the French Christian tradition in theatre.

Just a dozen years after the first production of a Claudel play, in 1924, came Jean Cocteau (1889-1963). Cocteau later managed to make his mark in almost every area of French art—as poet, novelist, and critic—but his first major recognition came by way of his plays. The play that sparked his career was *Orphée* (*Orpheus*, 1924), produced at the Théâtre des Arts by Georges Pitoëff. An earlier translation of Sophocles' *Antigone* (1922) had achieved a modest success, and these two works were followed by Cocteau's most famous work,

A scene from *The Madwoman of Chaillot* by Jean Giraudoux, as produced at San Diego City College. Directed by Lyman Saville.

and third adaptation of Classical Greek materials, *La machine infernale* (*The Infernal Machine*), which makes use of the Oedipal myth. However, Greek Classicism did not remain Cocteau's only source. He wrote fantasies, *L'aigle à deux têtes* (*The Eagle Has Two Heads*); Ibsenian problem plays, *Les mariés de la Tour Eiffel* (*The Eiffel Tower Wedding Party*); tragicomedy, *Les chevaliers de la table ronde* (*The Knights of the Round Table*); and an *opera parle*, *Renaud et Arminde.* Cocteau's plays, and his films, made the French drama between the two world wars one of the most exciting and controversial in the world.

One of the most important playwrights, because he managed to pull French drama back from the edge of banality, was Jean Giraudoux (1882-1944). He began his career as a novelist and his first play, *Siegfried* (1928), was not produced until he was forty-five years old. However, age seemed no handicap and the minor success of *Siegfried* was followed in 1929 by the major success of *Amphitryon 38,* a slight but witty and sophisticated retelling of the Classical legend. In 1931 Giraudoux turned to a Christian theme with *Judith,* which was his first failure. However, he followed this with *Intermezzo* (*The Enchanted,* 1933), a blend of realism and fantasy which proved to be his best genre. In 1934 he produced *Tessa,* a minor work, and then in 1935 he did *La guerre de troie n'aura pas lieu,* which was a major success in France, and as *Tiger at the*

Gates has been highly successful in England and the United States. The play tells of the last moments before the outbreak of the Trojan War, when it seems that the conflict can still be avoided; then, because of a lie and a misunderstanding, the war becomes a reality. This drama possessed a special significance, coming as it did on the eve of World War II. In the same year Giraudoux also produced *Supplément au voyage de Cook* (*The Virtuous Island*), based on the Electra myth.

The play was a failure with audiences and critics alike, and this may have provoked Giraudoux's two-year silence and then his 1937 *L'impromptu de Paris* (*The Paris Impromptu*), a savage attack on drama critics, written in the style of Molière. In 1938 he produced a one-act play, *Cantique des cantiques* (*Song of Songs*), and one of his finest works, *Ondine*. This last retells the legend of the water-nymph who falls in love with a mortal man, and it blends some of Giraudoux's finest poetic fantasy with a realistic approach toward the material.

The outbreak of World War II silenced Giraudoux for several years, and it was not until 1943 that he returned to the stage with *Sodome et Gomorrhe*. The play was a failure, in spite of the fact that it contains some of Giraudoux's best poetry, perhaps because the atmosphere of the Occupation was incompatible with lightness, which was always his forté. In 1945, the year the war ended, he produced *La folle de Chaillot* (*The Madwoman of Chaillot*) one of his most popular plays not only in France but also in the entire Western world. Giraudoux's last two plays were produced posthumously in Paris—*L'Apollon de Bellac* (*The Apollo of Bellac*, 1947) and *Pour Lucrèce* (*Duel of Angels*, 1953).

Giraudoux's influence on French theatre is almost incalculable. He combined realism with fantasy and found themes in Classical legend that made for powerful contemporary comment. The constant revival of his works, even those from the late 1920s and 1930s, proves that they have great theatrical vitality and are likely to endure.

In 1932, just four years after Giraudoux appeared on the scene, came **André Gide** (1869-1951), already a highly successful novelist and author of two slight and unsuccessful plays—*Le roi Candaule* (*King Candaules*) and *Saül*. It was not until his *Oedipe*, however, that he made a marked impact on the theatre. This play, which dramatizes a major Gide concern regarding the problem that exists when the individual comes into conflict with demands for religious submission proved popular with audiences, which saw it as an examination of the tension between the French intellectual community and the Catholic Church.

Gide's greatest contribution to French theatre, however, was his translations of Shakespeare. He began a translation of *Hamlet* in 1928, but it was not completed until 1946, when the Barrault-Renaud company used it to open their season. In 1947 Gide also adapted Kafka's *The Trial*, which has since been revived several times.

In the same year that Gide had his first success came one of the most prolific of French dramatists, and perhaps the single most important French playwright in this century, Jean Anouilh (1910-). His first play to take the stage, *L'hermine*, (*The Ermine*), was produced in 1932 by Aurélien-Marie Lugné-Poë, and in 1933 he followed this success with *Mandarine*.

Most critics tend to follow Anouilh's own lead and divide the body of his work into two parts—the *pièces roses* ("rose plays"), in which the themes are handled by comedy and quick wit, and the *pièces noires* ("black plays"), where the comedy turns dark and the wit becomes savage satire. In his early works Anouilh tended to construct plays in which absolute purity is confronted with total depravity, and the resulting conflict is one of purity struggling to maintain itself. Thus, in his *Antigone* (1944) the problem facing Antigone is not so much the conflict between religious duty and civil law as it is the difficulty she has in remaining true to herself, in maintaining her purity.

In 1951, however, Anouilh's dramas underwent a significant thematic change, and the pivotal play is *Colombe.* In this play, for the first time, Anouilh shows less dedication to either absolutely pure characters, or to absolutely evil ones. Instead he creates much more rounded characters who contain both good and evil, albeit they have a surfeit of one or the other quality. Thus, Julien, the pure hero, is so puritanical, so demanding, so boorish in his crusade for purity, that he is totally unlike any of Anouilh's earlier creations.

A full listing of Anouilh's plays would be too much, considering his productivity; however, his major works are *La sauvage* (1938, which as *The Restless Heart* became the first in a long string of international successes), *Le bal des voleurs* (*Thieves' Carnival,* 1938), *Eurydice* (1942), *L'invitation au Château*

Having conquered France, King Henry II of England and his Lord Chancellor, Thomas Becket, lead a triumphal parade in the Guthrie Theatre Company's 1973 production of Jean Anouilh's *Becket*, directed by David Feldshuh.

(*Ring Round the Moon*, 1947), *Colombe* (1951), *La valse des Toréadors* (*The Waltz of the Toreadors*, 1952), *L'alouette* (*The Lark*, 1953), *Becket* (1959).

Anouilh, more than any other playwright in the twentieth century, created a popular worldwide market for French drama, and he has managed to do this without sacrificing anything in terms of the materials or his treatment of them. Such plays as *The Lark, Becket,* and *The Waltz of the Toreadors* are still very popular on the professional stage, and nearly all of his other plays are produced with some regularity. Indeed, his urbane, witty, and often satiric style, plus his major theme (what happens to the essential purity of man when faced with the brutalizing influence of the world around him) have influenced countless writers both in and out of France.

After Anouilh the French dramatists of the first half of the century drop off sharply in terms of popular appeal. Albert Camus (1913-60), a dramatist and novelist, began in 1936 as actor-producer with Le Théâtre du Travail in Algiers, a left-wing organization that saw theatre less as an art than as an instrument for social revolution. For them he dramatized one of André Malraux's novels in 1936, and in the following year he struck out on his own, organizing the Algerian Théâtre de l'Équipe, where he adapted Gide's *Retour de l'enfant prodigue*. In 1944 he wrote *Le malentendu* (*The Misunderstanding*) and in 1945 his only widely popular play *Caligula*. In 1948 he completed *L'état de siège* (*State of Siege*) and in 1949 *Les justes* (*The Just*), his last major original work. Throughout the 1950s he worked only on adapting other men's works. Camus was, at best, a second-rate dramatist. However, as an early purveyor of existentialism he had great influence on many substantially better playwrights. In this sense, his most representative work is perhaps *L'état de siège*, in which the plague is used to symbolize the repressive totalitarianism that destroys man in his search for total liberty. The protagonist is able to overcome the plague-establishment inasmuch as he is a totally free individual. This makes for interesting philosophy but rather poor drama.

Along with Camus, Jean-Paul Sartre (1905-) also promoted the existentialist philosophy, not only in his plays but also in novels and essays. Probably this essentially negativistic view of life would not have rated even a footnote in theatrical history had it not come in the late 1940s, right after World War II, when people everywhere were seeking rational reasons for the carnage and cruelty of this war, and finding such reasons highly elusive. Sartre did not give his audiences rational reasons; instead he gave them an understanding of why such reasons did not exist. His first play was *Les mouches* (*The Flies*, 1943), and it used the legend of Orestes (and a plague of flies in Argos) as its subject matter. This was followed by *Huis-clos* (translated as *No Exit* in the English version), *Morts sans sépulture* (*Men Without Shadows*), *La putain respectueuse* (*The Respectful Prostitute*), *Les mains sales* (*The Red Gloves*) and *Le Diable et le Bon Dieu* (*The Devil and the Good Lord*), which has attracted little interest outside France, perhaps because the vogue for existential drama has passed. *Nekrassov* and *Les séquestrés d'Altona* (*The Condemned of Altona*) have also been pretty much ignored except by people who are more passionately addicted to philosophy than theatre.

Up to the middle of the century French drama had undergone three reasonably distinct periods—that is, from the beginning of the century to World

War I, when the drama was largely that inherited from the nineteenth century; from World War I through World War II, with the new drama of Giraudoux and Anouilh outstanding; and the late 1940s, which featured especially the philosophical drama of Camus and Sartre. In the 1950s, however, a fourth period began, sparked by four major writers who were to form the core of that movement dubbed by Martin Esslin as absurdism.

The first of these writers to get a play onstage was Jean Genet (1910-), a playwright, novelist, and poet. As a youth and young man his life alternated between the physical exclusion of being imprisoned in correctional facilities and prisons and the social exclusion imposed on homosexuals, and as a result his work seems as much an act of rebellion against organized society as the creation of living drama. His first play *Les bonnes* (*The Maids*, 1947), began his preoccupation with the drama as a ritual of the unreal, a "reflection of a reflection." In 1949 he produced *Haute surveillance* (*Death Watch*), and several years later his most famous play, *Le balcon* (translated as *The Balcony* and produced in England in 1957, though not played in France until 1960). *Les nègres* (*The Blacks*, 1959), was his last generally successful play, with an extended New York run.

Trying to assess the impact of Genet on contemporary drama is difficult. Certainly he gave back to a basically realistic theatre some of its illusionary sense, with his insistence that theatre should be like looking at life through a house of mirrors. Beyond that, his choice of subject matter broadened the potential choices of more traditional playwrights.

After Genet came Eugène Ionesco (1912-), one of the most popular of the absurdists and perhaps the most important of that group from a purely theatrical point of view. A Roumanian who has lived most of his life in France, Ionesco early on took the position that theatre can never be realistic; that no matter how hard one tries, the cracks, the joints, the editing, and the puppet strings all show. Thus, the best thing that theatre can do is use nonrealistic means to get at the truth that is buried right under our noses. And that truth, more often than not, is buried in a mass of words. For Ionesco, and most other absurdists, language is not only a failure as far as communication goes, it actually hinders communication in its absurd complexity. Ideas and emotions tend to get lost in it, and it is necessary to simplify it before it can be even a partially useful tool. Thus, Ionesco reverted to a kind of child's primer dialogue for his earliest and best works.

La cantatrice chauve (*The Bald Soprano*, 1950) is his first play. A one act, it was presented in Paris under the billing of "anti-play," and it is a marvelous satire of the realistic theatre Ionesco so despised. He followed this with two more one acts, *La leçon* (*The Lesson*, 1951) and *Les chaises* (*The Chairs*, 1952). In each of these Ionesco returned to his attack on language, but in *The Lesson* he also found a number of secondary targets, such as traditional education and scholarship, social organizations, including the Church, and such accepted fields of study as mathematics.

Ionesco's major success has been in the one-act form, in part because the almost farcical absurdity of his characters defies the depth of examination necessary to the full-length form. However, in his first significant full-length work, *Rhinocéros* (1960), he introduced the character of Bérenger, who stands far enough outside the boundaries of his earlier absurdism to allow the necessary development. This was followed up in *Le roi se meurt* (*Exit the King*, 1963), which is a delightful combination of absurdism, fantasy, and characterization.

It is fashionable to rank Ionesco a bit below Genet inasmuch as, unlike Genet, Ionesco failed to create the primitive, ritualistic theatre specified by Antonin Artaud. However, this is merely a misunderstanding of Ionesco, who wanted something at least as valid as Artaud, a "puppet theatre" full of color, action, limited dialogue, and a direct commentary through word and deed on the ills of the world. In creating this Ionesco has, on the whole, succeeded brilliantly and his ultimate effect on Western drama may be great indeed.

Like Ionesco, Arthur Adamov (1908-70) was not a Frenchman by nationality but by choice, He was born in the Caucasus, but in 1912 he left Russia and in 1924 became a member of the surrealist group in Paris. It was a group that would make its greatest mark by way of the graphic arts, through such fine painters as Georges Braque, but Adamov was destined to give surrealism coinage in the drama. His first play was *La parodie* (*The Parody*, written, 1947; produced 1952). Two other plays, *La grande et la petite manoeuvre* (*The Big and the Small Maneuver*) and *L'invasion*, (*The Invasion*) were written after *La parodie* but were produced earlier, in 1950. These early works exemplify the surrealistic approach, using a dream world to express a superreality in which man is exposed as isolated and helpless. By 1955, however, in *Le ping-pong*, Adamov had developed a new form, based more closely on political and social reality. He followed this with *Paolo Paoli* (1957), probably his most important play, which concentrates on exposing the corruption that lies below the bright surface of French society.

The last of this group, Samuel Beckett (1906-   ), was born in Ireland but has been a resident of France since 1938 and has written primarily in French since 1945. A novelist and poet as well as a dramatist, Beckett gained renown by way of three novels, *Murphy* (1947), *Molloy* (1951), and *Malone meurt* (*Malone Dies*, 1951), before his first play, *En attendant Godot* (*Waiting for Godot*) was produced in 1953.

SAMUEL BECKETT: The curtain opens. On stage is a pile of trash and garbage. Ten seconds of silence. Heavy breathing is heard for another ten seconds. Ten seconds of silence. A baby cries. The curtain closes. The audience has just seen Samuel Beckett's play, *Breath* (1970). On the whole it follows the pattern that Beckett's audiences have come to expect. But what is its basis, rational or irrational? What are the intellectual tools of a man who creates *Acte sans paroles* (*Act Without Words*, 1958), in which a mute man is goaded and teased by sticks traveling on wheels from offstage and cubes or water bottles lowered from the flies, or who creates *Fin de partie* (*Endgame*, 1957), in which characters talk endlessly in eternal immobility or are buried up to their chins in sand?

It should, in all fairness, be pointed out that by his own admission Beckett is not a philosopher, but one must be careful about accepting at face value Beckett's statements about his own work. William York Tindall once tried to pin Beckett down on the meaning of two of his characters' names, Watt and Knott. "Watt is a question. Knott is a nothing. Anglo-Saxon *Ic ne wat* and *Ic nat,* which suggest Watt and Knott, mean *I do not know.* Beckett studied Anglo-Saxon at Trinity. Asked if he had these words in mind while writing *Watt,* he said 'No.' " In view of Tindall's experience the scholar would (and probably should) be inclined not to believe Beckett. Perhaps his statement about not being a philosopher can be at least partially explained by his 1931 essay on Proust in which Beckett seems to arrive, early in his career, at a rejection of philosophy since "concept and logic are helpless in a world of confusion." Although a philosopher cannot really be said to exist without a philosophy of some kind, one can hardly argue that Beckett's often repeated theme of "the impossibility of a logical philosophy" is as logical a philosophy as could be maintained.

Whether or not Beckett is a philosopher, he certainly uses philosophy (or the lack of it) as a tool with which to create his characters. He could perhaps be labeled more correctly as a "thinker." Beckett's pseudoscholarly paper *Whoroscope* (1930), even with its pedantic footnotes, hardly measures up to our notion of "philosopher" when we read about Descartes brooding over the relative age of several eggs as he questions, "Are you ripe at last / my slim pale double-breasted turd?" Unless one were familiar with the extensive knowledge exhibited in the whole of the work, one would be tempted to reject this sentence as crude and unskilled. Such would also be the temptation in

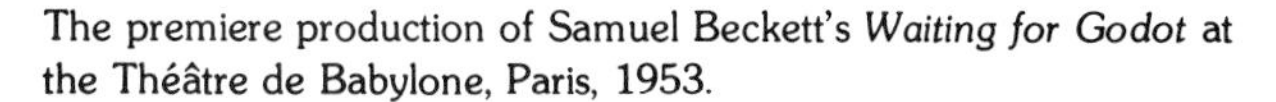
The premiere production of Samuel Beckett's *Waiting for Godot* at the Théâtre de Babylone, Paris, 1953.

terms of several of Beckett's individual plays, unless one becomes familiar with enough of them to appreciate the demonstrated literary skill of this associate of Joyce, Kafka, and Dylan Thomas. Beckett's novels (*Watt, Malloy, Murphy, Malone Dies*) are complex penetrating probes into the working of the human mind; failure to read at least one of these novels would almost certainly lead to false conclusions about Beckett's motives and his "simple," "monotonous" view of theatre.

The answer to the question, "What are Beckett's plays about?" is obvious and uncomplicated. One needs only to look at Estragon's opening line, "Nothing to be done"; or Murphy's opening sentence, ". . . nothing new"; or Clov's beginning, "Finished, it's finished, nearly finished, it must be nearly finished"; or Krapp's plaintive, "Now the day is over" followed by a coughing fit; or Winnie's first line, "Another heavenly day. For Jesus Christ sake Amen. World without end Amen." Beckett is "about" nothing and "about" death or the approach of nothing. But while one may question the validity of writing about "nothing," it is necessary to delve deeper into Beckett's writing to discover the profound exploration of human intellectual dislocation which arrives at nothing. Beckett himself, an Irishman by birth, felt this dislocation so strongly that he turned to writing in French where he was forced by his own limitations in the language to use a simpler manner of expression in order to be even intelligible. His dislocated characters, who exist in a dislocated place that is not society (because that does not exist either), all maintain a tragic dignity as they are dying. But it would probably be an error to view this process as decay or even as a loss of consciousness. Beckett's characters start with nothing, with the absence of consciousness. What this nothingness means to the viewer is what makes Beckett a playwright. The sociologist may be truly moved when he equates *Endgame* with the problems of aging in a callous society; but the inmates of San Quentin Prison knew to a man what *En attendant Godot* (*Waiting for Godot,* 1953) was all about—waiting for nothing. Beckett seems to know that his beliefs could be accepted as having *some* meaning by an audience, and so he has Murphy take genuine delight in proceeding from "taking delight in nothing" to "taking delight in Nothing!" To Beckett, *nothing* is more real than *Nothing.*

The Beckett style of playwriting is free, theatrical, difficult to view, and—at the same time—repetitive. He must have realized this when he quit writing for five years in 1951. His 1956 statement, "There's no way to go on," was a prelude to *Endgame, La dernière bande* (*Krapp's Last Tape,* 1958), and *On les beaux jours* (*Happy Days,* 1961). Beckett, for all his searching and probing, manages to retell the same experience over and over again in the same style. The themes are nothingness and death. The set is usually a sterile space flooded with nearly blinding light. The characters have either an abundance of business, which Beckett spells out in detail, often giving the exact length of pause desired, or they have a total absence of business. There are many interruptions, both of action and dialogue. All of the characters have extreme difficulty in remembering things and when they do remember, the "things" are so meaningless that they then try to remember why they were trying to remember in the first place. There is no development of action or situation because when a playwright starts with nothing there is no place to go. With the exception of several children, Beckett's characters all vary from old to very old. The memory of their past hopefulness is always framed with the hopelessness of the present. All his plays are concerned with the passage of time or the refusal of time to pass, and all his characters are concerned with time that does not pass but that stays around them, or that passes too quickly, or too slowly, or in too great a quantity. Beckett ridicules the existence of God. Pozzo (which means "cesspool" in Italian) says, "You are human beings, of the same species as myself . . . made in God's image." Frequent use is made of the monologue; characters speak to or for themselves in incredibly long passages.

For many critics the dignity of Beckett's characters is both profound and tragic. The viewer must feel their frustration (and also Beckett's) when all attempts at logical reason become futile to the extent that this very futility is accepted as logical. Poor Watt, in an attempt to find harmony in his life, invites piano tuners to work on his piano. But mice have eaten away at it to the point where the existing nine hammers correspond to the existing nine strings in only one place—so the tuners tune that string to any one note. Watt is perplexed by the fact that nothing has happened which relates to anything else, and he tries to find some meaning in the experience. He sprawls in a ditch and hears a round being sung on one note, in four parts; this causes him to think of time, which, in turn, causes him to try and determine exactly how many weeks there are in a year. He divides the number of days in a year by the number of days in a week. The answer, 52.14285714285714 . . . perplexes him, and his search for harmony and logic leads only to monotony.

To evaluate Beckett's impact on theatre, it is necessary to remember that he created a style of drama which has almost become a cliché now, but which had a tremendous impact at its beginning. Many people of the theatre are concerned with the direction in which this style led Beckett and his disciples. His dictatorial stage directions and insistence on the exact timing of pauses reduce the creative actor or director to robots, and his recent insistence upon expressionless faces and voices have led to a theatre which is in many respects dull and untheatrical. A quick perusal of *Va-et-vient* (*Come and Go*) reveals nearly twice as much stage direction for inactivity as there is dialogue.

This exploration, however, of all possible aspects of theatre expression is very much like Beckett's mind. He has written radio plays, television plays, stage plays, sketches for the stage, and mimes. He has explored. It is unfortunate that this dramatic exploration will probably not have the same lasting value as his prose writing, but *Godot, Endgame,* and *Krapp* will remain and one cannot discount the effect that these works have had and will continue to have on younger writers. These young writers may eventually be even more successful than their mentor, but Beckett may be assigned the one undeniable quality given him by Ronald Hayman: "With purity and integrity, he has maintained fidelity to his theatre vision—he has never compromised his values to present what is fashionable."

After the 1950s the interest in absurdism began to fall off rapidly, and French drama seemed to follow suit. Interesting young dramatists were beginning to write—Roland Dubillard, Georges Schehadé, Henri Pichett, François

Billetdoux—but they have not yet attained the eminence of those earlier practitioners who helped change the style of Western drama.

THE FRENCH DIRECTOR

The theatre in twentieth century France is less a history of writers, or designers, or actors than it is a history of directors, for more than any other group they influenced the paths which French theatre would explore. As the century opened, France was blessed with two such directors—André Antoine, who began his Théâtre Libre during the final years of the nineteenth century, but who lived on to become the outstanding spokesman for naturalism in the twentieth; and Aurélian-Marie Lugné-Poë, who stood directly opposed to Antoine in his determination to create a theatre out of dreams, fantasy, and poetry.

ANDRÉ ANTOINE: André Antoine (1858-1943) was a clerk in the Paris Gas Company in 1886, nearly thirty years old, and trying to come to grips with an earlier desire to become an actor. When he was a child his mother had taken him to see comedies and operettas, and this experience with the theatre made a deep and lasting impression on him. The oldest of four children, he was forced by family poverty to go to work rather than continue on in school. He

A scene from André Antoine's famous production of *King Lear*, which won him a directorship at the state theatre, the Odéon.

worked first as an errand boy for a small businessman, and later was employed by the Firmin-Didot publishers on the Left Bank. He was an avid reader and at an early age consumed Dumas père, Eugène Sue and George Sand. At Firmin-Didot a coworker took an interest in his education and, among other things, introduced him to the "realist movement." Antoine visited art museums, read widely, attended the theatre, and went to lectures given by Taine on the history of art.

In 1875 he joined the *claque* of the Comédie-Française and then, later, became a supernumerary, studying the actors and the roles and learning by heart whole scenes. In 1876 he applied for admission to the Conservatoire, but without a private recommendation he was turned down. He then gave up the idea of making the theatre his career. He was called into the military service, and in 1883 he returned to Paris and became a clerk at the gas company.

Amateur dramatic clubs were common in the Paris of 1886, and a friend introduced him to one called the Cercle Gaulois, which put on productions once a month for friends and relatives. His buried interest in the theatre surfaced, but it was not long before he decided that "these people were wasting their time," and undertook to renovate their repertoire. Later, Antoine's competitive spirit was piqued by an annual revue put on by a neighboring society—the Cercle Pigalle. It was written by a member and reviewed by the critics, and Antoine suggested that the Cercle Gaulois also find original plays to do.

On hearing of the Cercle Gaulois decision, a friend introduced Antoine to Arthur Byl, who submitted a play. According to Antoine "it was naive and violent, but still, it was something unpublished." Byl also introduced him to Jules Vidal, a famous, published, and established writer, who gave him a one-act comedy, *La Cocarde* (*The Cockade*). Vidal in turn introduced him to Paul Alexis, who gave him *Mlle. Pomme*, a one-act farce (apparently found in the papers of the dead novelist Duarty). All this delighted Antoine, and even more was to come. Alexis told Léon Henneque about Antoine, and Henneque sent him his play *Jacques Damour*, based on a work by Zola. It had already been refused for production at the Odéon, but Antoine realized that the name Zola would attract the critics' attention and that by producing it he would achieve his goal of outstripping the Cercle Pigalle.

In his own Cercle, however, trouble awaited him. A retired army officer named Krauss, who was president of the Cercle Gaulois and owner of the group's theatre, was as horrified by Zola's name as Antoine had been pleased. Fearing the publicity that the naturalist drama would bring, Krauss refused Antoine the use of the Cercle's resources, including the name. He did offer, however, to rent Antoine the theatre for the night of the performance, but would not allow rehearsals in it. This was a blow to Antoine's plans, as it meant that he would have to finance the whole production himself. There is no indication that he ever seriously considered giving up the project.

Somehow, Antoine and a few close friends managed to overcome all the difficulties of production. Programs were printed, publicity was secured, and the date of March 30, 1887 (payday at the gas company) was set for the opening. Organized on a subscription basis, the Théâtre Libre—as Antoine titled his new venture—was open only to members and therefore was exempt from censorship.

André Antoine's production of *Julius Caesar* at the Odéon.

Not many critics showed up for the first performance, but those who did (such as Henry Fouauier of *Le Figaro*) were high in their praise. Antoine's second performance, two months later, was attended by all the major critics, by many famous actors and artists, and by Porel, the director of the Odéon. This program contained a realistic one-act prose play, *In the Family*, by Oscar Méténier, and a three-act tragicomedy in verse by Emile Bergerat. All the critics wrote lengthy reviews, and this convinced Antoine that the Théâtre Libre could become a permanent organization.

During the years that Antoine ran the Théâtre Libre, a continuing controversy surrounded the French theatre, and the Théâtre Libre was always right in the middle of the dissension. Zola with his naturalistic theories of the drama, stood at one extreme of the controversy, and the critic Sarcey stood at the other. In between were all shades and variations of opinion, with Antoine staunchly defending Zola.

Despite the primary purpose of the Théâtre Libre, which was to stage new French playwrights, Antoine was beginning to fill out his seasons with foreign plays. The first was Tolstoy's *The Power of Darkness*; next came Ibsen's *Ghosts* and *The Wild Duck*. These were followed by Strindberg's *Miss Julie*; Hauptmann's *The Weavers* and *The Assumption of Hannele Mattern*; and Björnstjerne Björnson's *A Bankruptcy*. These foreign plays were all reviewed by the critics and did much to broaden the French theatre.

Interest in the Théâtre Libre never waned, but Antoine, worn out from unceasing debt and wearied by continual controversy, resigned in 1894. He turned the Théâtre Libre over to a man named Larochelle, giving him all the theatre's assets and himself retaining all debts.

It was Antoine's theory, at the time of the establishment of the Théâtre Libre, that a generation gap existed between the old and the new French dramatists. The old group, which included Augier, Dumas *fils*, and Sardou, still dominated the French stage, keeping talented younger writers from being produced. Therefore, a primary purpose in establishing the Théâtre Libre was airing the work of new, young French playwrights. A little later on, when the changes that he anticipated were not happening fast enough to suit him he protested that "young dramatists have the right to expect financial remuneration for their plays in addition to moral recompense." By the end of its third season the Théâtre Libre had already staged fifty-one new authors, forty-two of whom were under forty years of age, and by 1894, the last year of Antoine's supervision, the theatre had produced the plays of ninety-four different authors.

Antoine quickly saw that the old style of acting would not work for the new primarily naturalistic plays, so starting with amateurs he began training them according to his own ideas. He taught them not to recite their lines but to speak as though they were the character they were playing. Physically they were to act as though they lived in that setting. In other words, they were to live their parts and to identify with the scene on stage, not with the audience. He insisted that the play is more important than any single actor, and that each scene has its own movement which is in turn part of the total movement of the play. Impressed by Meiningen's crowd scenes—that is, believing them right pictorially but wrong vocally—he had his actors in the crowd scenes speak at different times to produce a more authentic sound.

Antoine felt that the director performs the same function in the theatre as descriptions do in a novel, and thus he divided directing into two parts: finding the right decor and proper actor composition for the action; and interpreting and aiding the flow of dialogue. It was his belief that environment determines the movement of the characters, and therefore that all rehearsals should be held in the environment—on the finished set. He believed that the set should always be authentic, whether a landscape or an interior. In an interior the whole house should be included in the original design, so that all the exits, halls, and connecting rooms would be architecturally accurate. Only after the entire interior had been designed did Antoine remove the famous "fourth wall."

In 1888, after viewing the Meininger Players and Irving's company, he sought even more realism, and in an attempt to reproduce environment exactly he even went so far (in *The Butchers*) as to hang real carcasses of beef on the stage. Even at that time a reaction against all this realism was starting, mainly with Aurélien Lugné-Poë, yet Antoine's belief in the importance of environment helped establish the concept that each play required its own setting. Later, at the Odéon, though he still used realistic methods, Antoine did modify this realistic extreme.

After leaving the Théâtre-Libre, Antoine went on an extended tour abroad, eventually returning to France to free-lance in various theatres as an actor. Finally, in 1897, he opened a fully professional theatre called Théâtre Antoine, where he revived some of the best works he had produced at the Théâtre Libre.

In 1906 he was made director of the Odéon, where he stayed until shortly before the war broke out in 1914. There he produced Tolstoy, Hauptmann, Ibsen, as well as Balzac, Flaubert, Daudet, Villiers, Zola, and Becque.

After retirement he became a critic, reading manuscripts brought to him by new and established writers and, if he thought they merited it, helping the plays get produced.

Lugné-Poë (1869-1940) began his theatrical career at the Conservatoire, where his work was done under Gustave-Hippolyte Worms, and where he was awarded a prize for comedy. He appeared as an actor at Antoine's Théâtre Libre, but the naturalism of Antoine ran counter to Lugné-Poë's poetic spirit. He went on to act under Paul Fort at the Théâtre d'Art, and found the atmosphere far more congenial. Eventually he took over the theatre, renaming it the Théâtre de l'Oeuvre. Between 1892 and 1929 he worked at making this one of the world's outstanding theatres. He introduced works by a number of young playwrights, beginning with Maurice Maeterlinck, and while he never gave up his belief in poetic drama, he was not as one-sided in his tastes as Antoine, producing dramas by Ibsen, Björnson, Strindberg, Hauptmann, D'Annunzio, and Echegaray. He was one of the first to recognize the talent of Claudel and helped to popularize his work by producing *L'annonce faite à Marie* (*The Tidings Brought to Mary*) in 1912. Lugné-Poë's services to the theatre were great indeed, and may someday prove to be greater even than those of Antoine. He gave theatre a sense of balance in theatrical style; he encouraged many young authors to work in their own forms, rather than imposing on them a special dramatic philosophy; and he put before his audiences not only the best of contemporary French theatre, but also the best contemporary work from other countries.

Jacques Copeau (1879-1949) learned much from Antoine and Lugné-Poë—perhaps most from Lugné-Poë—but he was as hostile to unrelenting naturalism as he was to the well-made play with which Scribe's imitators were cluttering the French stage. In 1913, after a brief association with André Gide during the founding of *La Nouvelle Revue française*, he began his own theatre, the Vieux-Colombier, with the stated objective of bringing back to French theatre the beauty and poetry that had gotten lost during the domination of the well-made play. He had a very strong troupe to open his theatre, numbering among his actors Louis Jouvet, Charles Dullin, and Valentine Tessier.

Like Antoine and Lugné-Poë, Copeau was determined to provide opportunity for young, rising playwrights, but his best productions were of those playwrights who provided in their scripts the truth, beauty, and poetry that Copeau so much admired—Shakespeare and Molière.

From 1917 to 1919 Copeau was in New York, where his troupe performed in the Garrick Theatre as part of a French promotional program. When he returned to France he spent more and more time working with his acting students, and far less time directing. Finally, in 1924, he retired from active theatre production and, with some students, left for the Burgundy countryside to concentrate entirely on the acting process. The group achieved some success and a few of its members went on to distinguished careers with the Compagnie des Quinze under Copeau's nephew and student Michel Saint-Denis. In 1936 Copeau was made a director of the Comédie-Française, and in 1941 he retired in favor of a career of quiet scholarship.

While the previous three directors were all interrelated in the sense that they studied with the same men and, in a way, with each other, Gaston Baty (1885-1952) was a French original. To learn directing he went not to his esteemed fellow countrymen but to Germany. Returning to France with the techniques of German production assimilated, Baty worked wherever a directing slot was open, usually on the experimental new dramas that had no interest for more traditional resident directors. In 1930, ready to give up the touring life, he returned to Paris and took over the Théâtre Montparnasse, which he renamed the Théâtre Baty. Here he produced a wide variety of plays, foreign and domestic, contemporary and Classical. He also staged his own adaptations of major novels, some of which proved highly popular. In 1936 Baty accepted an appointment as one of the producers of the Comédie-Française, where with his concept of rich staging and his deep knowledge of the French neoclassical period, he was able to breathe new life into the Comédie's almost moribund Classical repertory.

Charles Dullin's 1928 production of *Volpone*, by Stefan Zweig and Jules Romains, was mounted on a multiple set designed by André Barsacq.

Charles Dullin (1885-1949), an actor and director, in a sense closed out the period of Antoine in that he began his theatrical career as a pupil of Firmin Gémier, who had himself been a pupil of Antoine. Gémier had taken the methods of Antoine and added to them the techniques of improvisation. These he passed on to Dullin, who added still more, including work in dance and mime that he learned from Copeau, and then passed these on to such great figures in French drama as Jean-Louis Barrault and Jean Vilar.

After his original work with Gémier, Dullin was accepted by Copeau as part of the original troupe which opened the Vieux-Colombier. Dullin remained with Copeau until the troupe returned from the two-year stay in the United States. He absorbed Copeau's methods and ideals and then, assembling his own troupe, he left on a long training tour of the provinces. Returning to Paris, Dullin established his troupe in the Théâtre de l'Atelier and through hard work, dedication, and sheer artistry soon made it one of the most significant theatres in the city.

In terms of his early teachers, Dullin represented most nearly the view of Copeau—that is, he wanted to restore to French theatre the magic, the beauty, the poetry which had become lost during the domination of the well-made play. As a result, the breadth of plays and styles he attempted was great indeed. He exhumed all the great French neoclassical works, he produced Shakespeare and Jonson, he gave Pirandello his first French production, and he gave a number of new authors a hearing.

An excellent actor on his own, Dullin never quit performing, and ran a training school for actors as part of his theatre. In this school he passed along the methods and ideals of his mentors, along with his own additions. In 1936 he was made a producer of the Comédie-Française, and during World War II he toured the "unoccupied" zone of France presenting Molière.

LOUIS JOUVET: Louis Jouvet (1887-1951), actor, producer, and director, was described by Sir Michael Redgrave as "the true *homme du théâtre.*" The description was certainly deserved. Jouvet was a true Renaissance man of the theatre, equally adept in all of his many roles, and also an outstanding scholar who was called upon to be president of the Société d'Histoire du Théâtre.

His early years in no way indicated the success that Jouvet eventually earned in his theatrical career. On the contrary, as an adolescent he was tall, ungainly, and even awkward. He had, in addition, a severe stutter which required much hard work to overcome, and the clear, precise diction that marked him as an actor was a result of this handicap.

Jouvet's father died when he was fifteen and he moved to his mother's village of Rethel in the Ardennes. Here he received his first opportunity to submerge himself, handicaps and all, in an acting role when he was cast in a student play at Notre-Dame de Rethel, a secondary school that had its own small theatre. As a result of this experience, in spite of his family's desire that he study pharmacy, a career in the theatre was his only ambition.

While following the family injunction, studying pharmacy in Paris, he tried to enroll in the Conservatoire. Three times he tried to pass the entrance auditions, and each time he failed. Within a year after his third failure, how-

Louis Jouvet's design for his own production of Giraudoux's *Ondine*, which was staged at the Théâtre l'Athénée, 1939.

ever, he made his first contact in the theatre world and was offered free enrollment in acting classes offered by Leon Noël, one of France's foremost performers in melodrama and Romantic drama. Eventually, Noël included Jouvet in a small student company with which he toured the continent.

Leaving Noël's company Jouvet played a small role in Jacques Rouché's production of *The Brothers Karamazov* staged at the Théâtre des Arts. He spent a rewarding two years with Rouché, during which he gradually developed his own theory of the theatre, at the heart of which was a respect for the playwright's intention and a devotion to the text. He would determine what the text revealed about the characters and their conflicts, and once he had made that determination he always respected it.

In 1913 Jouvet auditioned and was accepted for membership in a company being assembled by Jacques Copeau, actor, director, and producer, to play at the Théâtre du Vieux-Colombier. With this company, Copeau was determined to reform the Parisian commercial theatre and its elaborate *mise en scène*. Strongly influenced by Appia, the Swiss designer who promoted the movement for symbolic staging, Copeau brought freshness and integrity of design and action to the theatre.

The new company was put through a rigorous ten-week training program, living in the country near Paris, under a regime designed by Copeau to help them become masters of their voices and bodies and skilled in dramatic techniques. Toby Cole has pointed out that "in one year Copeau created a community of actors and workers which laid the basis of a modern theatre."

The company was reassembled after World War I, and with Jouvet as a leading actor toured the United States. Upon their return to France, Copeau again installed the company in the Vieux-Colombier. Jouvet remained with the company until 1922, when he accepted an offer to become technical director of the Théâtre des Champs-Elysées. It was here, and twelve years later at the Athénée, that he had his most productive years. His first major success in his new position came in 1923, with his production of Jules Romains' *Doctor Knock, or the Triumph of Medicine,* which he directed and in which he played the title role.

While at the Champs-Elysées, Jouvet also began his long association with playwright Jean Giraudoux, who brought him his first work, *Siegfried*. The play was a major success, running for two hundred ninety performances. The ensuing collaboration between playwright and director was enduring and creative, with Jouvet producing all but two of Giraudoux's fifteen plays.

When the German army marched into Paris in 1941, Jouvet went into voluntary exile. His company undertook a short tour of Switzerland and then visited eight countries in Central and South America. While in Brazil, Giraudoux told Jouvet that *The Madwoman of Chaillot* would be ready for production upon his return to Paris. Giraudoux died in 1944, but before his death he wrote on the manuscript of his play, "*The Madwoman of Chaillot* was presented on October 15, 1945, by Louis Jouvet at the Théâtre de l'Athénée." Jouvet missed the date by two months, but enjoyed one of his greatest successes as an actor in the role of the ragpicker.

In addition to the works of Romains and Giraudoux, Jouvet was also devoted to the plays of Molière. His love of Molière began while he was an actor in Copeau's company. Under his direction Jouvet had played major roles in *Le médecin malgré lui* (*The Doctor in Spite of Himself*), *Le misanthrope, L'avare* (*The Miser*), and other of the dramatist's works. His greatest success with Molière was achieved later, however, in his own productions of *Tartuffe* and *Don Juan,* in which he also played leading roles.

Jouvet's approach to his craft was an essentially intellectual one. Thus, he rejected Stanislavsky's insistence upon the "sincerity" of the actor, and emphasized that the actor must see himself as "both the instrument and the instrumentalist." The actor must accept and admit his own "double nature, living in the limbo of half-being and half-seeming. What he used to call his art, he recognizes as a craft, a trade."

As a theatrical philosopher and theoretician, Jouvet was ever more widely recognized. The Conservatoire, which in his youth had three times denied him enrollment as a student, asked him in 1934 to become a professor. He also taught at the University of Paris and the Alliance Française. His outstanding scholarship gained him invitations to contribute articles on the theatre for the French encyclopedia. The most signal honor was conferred in 1936 when he was appointed a director of the Comédie-Française. Still at the peak of his creative powers, and engaged in producing Graham Greene's *The Power and the Glory,* he suffered a stroke in 1951 and died soon after.

JEAN-LOUIS BARRAULT: Jean-Louis Barrault (1910-) has been for many years the most consistently fresh, and moving force within the French theatre. By way of background, a few facts relative to Barrault's theatre ex-

The 1937 Louis Jouvet production of *Tiger at the Gate* by Jean Giraudoux.

perience should be noted. In his early years he studied at the Atelier with Charles Dullin, but in 1935, at the age of twenty-five, Barrault was persuaded by Armand Salacrou to act for him at the Goncourt. On several occasions, however, he returned to the Atelier to do productions for Dullin, whom he loved and highly respected. Barrault's next enthusiasm was for the great French Classical works which were performed at the Comédie-Française. There he worked under another famous theatrician, Charles Grandval. In 1946, following the passage of several new government decrees which many young artists of the Comédie found intolerable, Barrault resigned. By this time he had earned a solid reputation as an actor and had become close friends with many other talented artists. For several years he had been suppressing a desire to form his own group, and now, with Madeleine Renaud, he founded a company at the Marigny. Many of their friends from the Comédie followed them, even though there were no contracts, out of devotion to theatre and total belief in the two founders. The company began its new venture, and after six weeks of rehearsal the Barrault-Renaud Company opened their first play, *Hamlet*. It was successful enough so that Barrault never looked back.

As early as 1935, when Salacrou was working at the Marigny, Barrault had told him that the theatre should be used primarily as a place for students and young writers. The time was not quite ready for this idea, as André Antoine had earlier discovered, but by 1946 ideas had changed. After the war the French Cultural Ministry had accepted the proposition that young poets, who had not yet made a reputation, needed progressive stages or schools where they could attempt experiments which might frighten the cautious Comédie which was used to dealing with already well-established classics. Barrault had long believed this, and now he had the opportunity to practice his beliefs.

Barrault was convinced that only a repertory configuration could create the type of atmosphere in which his goals could be achieved. Unfortunately, however, history had already proved that private companies would not be able financially to keep alive repertory systems designed to produce works by unknown playwrights. Without the subsidy afforded to state theatres, private companies attempting repertory programs had failed. Barrault, however, was determined to fly in the face of history. He believed that the rhythms created by alternating plays maintained a freshness and vitality crucial to good theatre. Actors who move from lead to supporting roles, according to Barrault, widen their range and discipline their talent. In addition, casting becomes easier for the director who has seen a wide range of roles from an actor. Barrault did admit that a continuous change of plays would require many technicians and thus increase operating costs, but he felt that the increase in skills which the technicians would gain from such alternation would eventually result in better productions.

Barrault believed that a company derives sustenance, mental gratification, and financial salvation from producing the classics. With the aid of this sustenance, a company in repertory can then go on to explore other aspects of dramatic art. Only in repertory, he pointed out, can a theatre "serve modern authors and help them with the creation of their work."

The Barrault-Renaud Company remained at the Marigny until 1959, at which time they moved into the Odéon. It is important to consider the unprecedented success of those thirteen seasons. Fifty-four plays were produced (thirteen Classical, three pantomines, one variety show, and thirty-seven contemporary plays). Twenty of these were new plays. The plays were by ten French Classical authors and twenty-one modern writers, including such outstanding authors as Anouilh, Camus, Claudel, Cocteau, Gide, Obey, Salacrou, Giraudoux, and Fry. Only two foreign plays were produced because for six months out of each year the company toured internationally and found that foreign audiences wanted to see French plays. Of the fifty-four plays produced, only five lost money and fourteen had long runs and did very well at the box office.

Undoubtedly responsible for the success of the Barrault-Renaud Company is an experimental approach and carefully mounted, craftsmanlike productions. As France's foremost actor-director and the power and talent behind the Théâtre de France, Barrault cultivated an early interest in mime and transformed it into a near religion which is "*the* approach" to theatre, and is followed by all who surround him. Barrault's approach is not new, but it is radically different from the traditional and Classical approach to mime. Barrault is captivated by mime and its application to theatre, insisting that all dramatic gesture and stage business be treated as mime. Mime and gesture, for

Barrault, are actions in the present which stand independent of speech, springing instead from thought. Action, according to Barrault, can be reduced to a state of mind, and he has devised a series of complex and exhausting sensory exercises to develop that state of mind. True acting then is an acute awareness of the senses.

Unlike many of his more experimental contemporaries, Barrault still believes, even with his emphasis on mime, that the essence of theatre lies in the spoken word. Thus, Barrault's first rule for actors is to make themselves heard and properly understood. To achieve this, diction and phrasing are basic tools which an actor must develop. Actors' voices are as essential as their minds and bodies if they intend to perform "spoken theatre." At least half of the notations in Barrault's promptbooks concern *how* a line is to be delivered—the pitch and tempo, how it should be phrased, where the accent is, and how heavy the accent should be. The lines are treated as music, and such musical terminology as *aria, recitative,* and *timbre* are used to describe the desired quality.

Perhaps the line which best describes Barrault and his contribution to the theatre is his own definition of the theatre experience as "a spiritual rendezvous which spectators and actors make with the author."

The last of this great company of directors, who all emerged during the same approximate period and who made the French drama of the 1930s and 1940s so outstanding is Jean Vilar (1912-71), a disciple of Charles Dullin. Vilar began his artistic career in music, but a chance visit to a rehearsal of Dullin's *Richard III* converted him to a theatrical career. Managing to wangle a job as Dullin's stage manager, he played a number of small roles and, after serving in the French army during World War II, he joined La Roulotte Company to tour the provinces.

Vilar began his career as producer-director at the Vieux-Colombier, but it was his production of T. S. Eliot's *Murder in the Cathedral,* done on the steps of the Abbey of Bec-Hellouin, himself playing the role of Becket, that first gained him national attention. As a result of this outdoor production, Vilar was asked in 1947 to assemble an open-air summer dramatic festival at Avignon. His opening play was Shakespeare's *Richard II,* in which he played the title role. The play had not previously been done in France, and it was a huge success, making the Avignon Festival an annual event, with Vilar's troupe in residence.

Vilar's success at Avignon brought him appointment to the Théâtre National Populaire. The theatre, a great barn of a structure in the Palais de Chaillot, had many problems. It provided space for an audience too large (perhaps) and too removed (certainly) for traditional live theatre. Vilar determined to use techniques of spectacle and audience involvement, and to seek out the mass suburban audience who were unable to afford the entry fee at the more intimate theatres. In this he was amazingly successful, but his techniques and his "theatre for the masses" offended many of the French traditionalists. Indeed, even some nontraditionalists objected to Vilar's approach, pointing out that it was essentially snobbish, and that a mass audience could be attracted to good theatre, well done, at modest prices, and that theatrical tricks were not necessary. In any case, a large house specializing in spectacular productions is not cheap to operate and in 1962 Vilar resigned his post in protest against what he conceived to be inadequate financial support by the French government.

The directors that followed this outstanding group have not yet seemed to quite measure up to their predecessors, perhaps because this first group was so outstanding and perhaps because theatre since the 1950s has tended to move in one of two directions—either toward a less experimental, more traditional form of presentation, which is almost certainly a reaction against the excesses of absurdism; or toward a street-guerrilla theatre style that may be highly meaningful sociologically but that tends to be quite uninteresting from a theatrical point of view. Such fine directors as Roger Blin (1907-), a disciple of Artaud and the director who was closely associated with the absurdist movement, who staged Ionesco's first play and later most of Beckett's works, failed to make the transition from the freer period to the more structured. In fact, among the newer French directors only Roger Planchon (1931-), who made his reputation by way of a Classical repertory, has attracted wide attention. And even Planchon's reviews are mixed, due to an unfortunate desire to use any play, no matter what the subject or theme, as a vehicle for social comment.

STAGING

The basic structure of the French stage has changed little during the twentieth century. That is, most productions have taken place behind the proscenium arch, or at one end of a rectangular hall, which merely means proscenium without wings. The experimentation with thrust and arena staging that has marked twentieth century theatre in the United States has failed so far to make an impression on French staging. In part this is because so many companies were working in existing facilities and had neither the time, money, nor desire for such change. Also, French stagecraft itself fell on hard times during this period thanks to the inordinate influence of the directors.

Antoine inspired a whole new era of scenic design at his Théâtre Libre. Always convinced of the need for a realistic approach to setting, Antoine went to see the visiting Meininger troupe and came away dedicated to a superrealism which inhibited imaginative stage design. The real environment was to be re-created in every detail. He designed his own sets, in most cases, working from a room with four real walls. Only after the set was completed did he decide which wall would be removed. He even went to such lengths as, for a production of *The Butchers*, hanging real beef carcasses onstage. In a sense, Antoine was the French equivalent of Belasco, who also insisted on this superrealism. However, Antoine's was successful as it was undertaken in support of realistic or naturalistic plays, whereas Belasco was using his realistic sets to support, in most cases, romantic melodrama.

Lugné-Poë, working in an opposite direction from Antoine, sought a kind of poetic simplicity in his attempts to bring poetic drama and fantasy to the stage. His settings were merely backdrops in poster styles or mere lines and colors to create mood and an undefined locale. In many respects, what Lugné-Poë was attempting was far more difficult artistically than the realistic sets of

A scene from Gaston Baty's 1936 production of his own adaptation of Flaubert's novel, *Madame Bovary*. The production required twenty-three sets and was produced on wagons moved by electric motors.

Antoine, and his success is due primarily to such outstanding artists as Toulouse-Lautrec, Maurice Denis (the muralist), and Pierre Bonnard (famous for his luminous and decorative use of color), who designed his sets.

Copeau, following Lugné-Poë's lead, reduced his sets to the point of symbol and, indeed, sometimes pure abstraction, working primarily with line and color to create mood. Louis Jouvet, working to capture a broader repertory, designed his own early sets, which were not imaginative except for a lush decor that he maintained throughout his career. Later, after he achieved his initial success and as his attention was more and more drawn to acting, he employed Christian Bérard (1902-49), a designer who had already achieved fame by way of his designs for dance productions. Jouvet praised Bérard's visual qualities and was impressed by the way Bérard always designed to serve the text rather than his own ego. A large part of Jouvet's reputation for subtle lighting must also be credited to Bérard.

Barrault left most design work to a series of competent but not terribly imaginative designers, but Gaston Baty put so much emphasis on the presentation of a lush decor that some critics accused his sets of overwhelming his productions.

French scenic design in the twentieth century has always been interesting, but only in the case of Lugné-Poë has it approached the brilliance that

Robert Edmond Jones was giving it in the United States and Gordon Craig was displaying in England.

ACTING

Acting, like directing and stagecraft, was largely dominated by the same group of actor-director-producers. Jacques Copeau, one of the earliest stylists, excelled in lyrical roles and especially in comic roles that depended on language. Thus, his best work was done in Shakespeare (especially *Twelfth Night*) and Molière. He also excelled as a teacher of acting, turning out not only Michel Saint-Denis but a number of fine performers who became members of the finest companies in France.

Charles Dullin, one of France's finest actors, began his professional career in melodrama, but quickly changed his interest when he became a member of Copeau's troupe at the Vieux-Colombier. There, under the influence of Copeau, he mastered dance and poetry. A fine teacher of acting, Dullin always sought to establish a personal relationship between the actor and the audience that would aid in establishing a world of imagination into which both could enter.

Louis Jouvet became an actor several years before he joined the Copeau troupe, but it was the training that he received from Copeau that helped establish him as one of France's premiere performers. Like his mentor, Jouvet did his best work in poetic drama, especially Shakespeare (in which he gained fame as Aguecheek and Autolycus) and later in the poetic drama of Giraudoux. Also, like Copeau, he loved Molière and one of his great roles was Géronte in *Les fourberies de Scapin* (*The Rogueries of Scapin*). While the other great actors who moved on to directing and producing tended to give up acting, or at least to curtail it severely, Jouvet never left the stage, and it was his performance, more than the quality of the play, that turned Jules Romains' *Doctor Knock* into a major success.

Antonin Artaud is perhaps the most difficult of the French theatricians to place. An actor, producer, and director, his work was never entirely successful with either critics or audiences. However, his theories had such a strong effect on the development of French drama during and after the 1930s that his contributions must be considered in full.

ANTONIN ARTAUD: Antonin Artaud (1896-1948), essayist, actor (film and stage), director, playwright, and poet, was born in Marseilles, France. Artaud dabbled in all of the theatrical fields, but his essays on the theatre are his major contribution. The child of a wealthy family of shipfitters, Artaud suffered from severe meningitis when he was five. A wide variety of diseases of both the body and mind were to plague him for the rest of his life, keeping him in and out of nursing homes and mental institutions.

In 1920 Artaud went to Paris to write. His early works were rejected, and it was then that Artaud began contributing articles and poems to a magazine called *Demain*. Many of these early works have been lost, but what remains seems to have been influenced by Poe and Baudelaire. While in Paris,

Artaud became involved as an actor in Charles Dullin's Théâtre de l'Atelier, one of the important little theatre groups of the period. Dullin rejected naturalism in acting and Artaud, in total agreement with this philosophy, stressed the mechanics of acting, although he consistently refused to have anything to do with diction.

Artaud's writing before the 1930s is substantially more subjective than his later works. *Le théâtre et son double* (*The Theatre and Its Double*, a collection of his essays published in 1938), *Heliogable* (*Heliogabalus*, 1934), *Les nouvelles révélations de l'être* (*The New Revelations of Being*, 1937), and *D'un voyage au pays des Tarahumara* (*A Voyage to the Land of the Tarahumara*, 1936), all illustrate Artaud's rejection of normal discursive language (or language based on reason) and his dislike of Western society and its theatre, which exemplify the traditional Western faith in the power of logic and reason.

For Artaud, the theatre of his day was dull and boring, and he felt that a new concept of it was needed—the elite playgoer turned away from it, and the crowds or masses went to movies, music halls, or circuses for the spectacle they wanted and perhaps needed to see. Theatre, he felt, should be compounded of ritual and spectacle, which would give it a direct and meaningful impact on the audience. It should not concern itself with the day-to-day aspects of love, personal ambition, or banal squabbling; instead it should focus on famous persons, atrocious crimes, and superhuman devotions. These things fulfill needs of the masses and are thus more important than those things which merely cater to the desires of the individual. All psychological theatre, since Racine, turns away from *violent* and *immediate* action, and yet this is exactly what is needed in the theatre.

Artaud's name has sometimes been attached to the surrealist movement, in which the universe was often portrayed as being menaced by some inexplicable, malevolent force. This is, however, a misunderstanding of surrealism and Artaud, who believed that the sight of brutality and savage eroticism would encourage man to unleash his own repressed instincts and thus recover his buried psychic energy. In 1937 Artaud did meet at least three surrealists (André Breton, Robert Desnos, and Roger Vitrac) with whom he shared a common objective—they all wanted to destroy traditional modes of European thought and culture.

For Artaud, theatre could only function as a "theatre of cruelty." He believed that cruelty in the theatre did not necessarily mean the dramatization of physical violence, or man pitted against man, but it did mean the presentation of cruelty that exists outside of man; "the cruelty of the universe itself, in all its natural violent force." Thus, theatre on one hand should be the massing and arranging of spectacle that affects the total organism, and on the other hand it should be an organization of objects, gestures, signals, and signs that in some ritual way represent the inherent cruelty of the universe.

Artaud uses the Balinese theatre as his model for building a theatre for today—a nonverbal theatre in which essential words are used in a "ritualistic, incantatory sense." Nicola Chiaromonte, in her analysis of Artaud's concept of drama, underlines the basic fault of Artaud's philosophy:

> *On the one hand, his theatre must strive for spiritual intensity and purity. On the other, it must cling furiously to the corporeal, to the actual*

> *presence, to the brutal and exterior effect. If we separate these drives we reduce each of them to a series of banal propositions. It seems to me that the source of their significance and evocative power is the spasmodic tension between them and the irresolute immobility resulting from it.*

In other words, Artaud's inner conflict was between his hatred of his restrictive body and his desire to arrive at a spiritual state free from the enslavement of the flesh. He kept trying to separate the two in his personal life and in the theatre.

Artaud had several bad experiences that grew out of having to compromise his theories and out of the failure of some of these theories when they were put to the theatrical test. In 1927 Artaud founded the Théâtre Alfred Jarry (named after the author of *King Ubu*). Artaud's only original play, *Le jet de sang* (*Jet of Blood*), was produced here. The theatre failed in 1931 due to lack of finances. In 1935 Artaud directed and acted in *Les Cenci* (*The Cenci*) at the Théâtré de la Cruauté. From 1937 to 1946 Artaud spent most of his time in mental hospitals writing very subjective poetry obsessed with the functions of the body. He contracted cancer in 1947 and died of it in 1948.

Of the fine French actresses, perhaps the most interesting is Edwige Feuillère (1907-   ), a student at the conservatoires of Dijon and Paris, who went on to play light comedy under the name of Cora Lynn. At the age of twenty-four she made her debut at the Comédie-Française, where she is reported to have displayed grace, beauty, and an authority onstage unusual for an ingenue. Two years later she left the Comédie-Française for a brief fling in films, but within a year she returned to the stage. One of her greatest roles was as Marguerite Gautier in *Camille*, by Dumas *fils*, but she also received excellent notices as Lia in Giraudoux's *Sodome et Gomorrhe*, the Queen in Cocteau's *L'aigle à deux têtes*, and Ysé in Claudel's *Le partage de midi* (*Break of Noon*). In her later years she also achieved fame as the Queen in Ugo Betti's *La regina e gli insorti* (*The Queen and the Rebels*).

Jean-Louis Barrault began his remarkable career at age twenty-one, playing a servant to Charles Dullin's Volpone, in the Jules Romains' translation of Jonson's play. He spent several years with Dullin, learning technique, and at the same time he applied himself to the study of mime, which became an important aspect of all his future productions. Following the fall of France in World War II he worked for Copeau at the Comédie-Française, where he made his first appearance in *Le Cid*. Barrault's acting style is elegant, sophisticated, and almost casual, but always present underneath this surface quality is the iron control developed by the exercise of an outstanding intelligence, a body kept in perfect physical shape, and years of work on mime designed to perfect every gesture. His finest roles are usually considered to have been Hamlet and Jean Cordet in Armand Salacrou's *Les nuits de colère* (*Nights of Anger*).

Jean Vilar, more than most actor-producers, appeared on the stage quite regularly. A slim, reserved-looking man, he made his acting debut in small roles for Dullin at the Atelier. After several years of touring during World War II, he played Paris in John Millington Synge's *The Well of the Saints*, and then went on with his own company to play an outstanding variety of roles, including Becket (in Eliot's *Murder in the Cathedral*), Macbeth, Richard II, Don Juan, and Ruy Blas. Of more contemporary roles, his most memorable was the gangster in Brecht's *Arturo Ui*.

The most recent of this group, and perhaps the actor with the greatest potential, was Gérard Philipe (1922-59). After studying at the Paris Conservatoire, he made his debut in 1942, during the German occupation, in Giraudoux's *Sodome et Gomorrhe*. It was not until 1945, however, that he attained national recognition playing the title role in Camus' *Caligula*. Over the next several years he built an international reputation by way of a series of outstanding performances on both stage and screen, and in 1951 he joined Vilar's Théâtre National Populaire, where his opening performance as Roderigo in *Le Cid* was perhaps his greatest role. He remained with Vilar until his early death in 1959 robbed the French theatre of one of its finest performers.

Italy The naturalistic drama that had begun its brief life in northern Italy at the end of the nineteenth century, died in the early years of the twentieth. D'Annunzio, once a champion of the realistic attitude, became more and more enmeshed in a floridly Romantic theatre, and Turin-based Guiseppe Giacosa sank into a sentimentalism that robbed his works of any serious social commentary. After World War I the "theatre of the grotesque" of Luigi Chiarelli (1884-1947) had a brief popularity, but its attempt to put onstage the many contradictions of a class-conscious society still wedded to nineteenth century economics and civil law was doomed to failure. The "futurist theatre" of Tommaso Marinetti (1876-1944) was an exciting attempt to free the drama from sentimental Italian realism, and Pier Luigi Maria Rosso di San Secondo (1887-1956) attempted the same end with a literary and often lyrically beautiful theatre. After World War II Italian theatre fared a bit better, but just as opera drained much of theatre's vitality during an earlier period, now film came along to provide formidable competition. The "new wave" of filmic realism was born in Italy after World War II and ever since Italian filmmaking has held—and deserved—a far greater reputation than its theatrical cousin.

TWENTIETH CENTURY ITALIAN DRAMA

Only three Italian dramatists have achieved deserved critical acclaim in the twentieth century: Luigi Pirandello, whose work achieved international acclaim; Ugo Betti, whose bitter predictions of the decline of the West achieved some international notice; and Eduardo De Filippo, whose dialectical dramas for the Neapolitan theatre have achieved little note outside of Italy.

Luigi Pirandello (1867-1936) was a Sicilian by birth, but only in his early prose works could he be accounted a regional artist. His family was well-off during his first twenty-nine years, until his father's sulphur mines failed, but in spite of this Pirandello was almost singularly unhappy. In 1894 he married a woman afflicted with hysteria, and who sank rapidly into deeper mental illness that essentially incapacitated her. Pirandello never ceased to love his wife, and the tender care he lavished on her until her death in 1918 required him to sublimate much of his own creativity. It is likely that his own domestic tragedy provided the basis for his later concern with mental aberration.

The scenic design for Pirandello's *Six Characters in Search of an Author*, as envisioned by L. Baldesari.

Pirandello began his career as a poet and philologist, but soon established himself as a major writer in the areas of the short story and the novel. He came to theatre late, but he had a deep and abiding love for the drama and his influence on its course, in his plays and critical works, has been great indeed. He inspired Chiarelli's "theatre of the grotesque," and some of his own later plays continued the early themes that Chiarelli explored. The primary influences on Pirandello were Ibsen and Shakespeare, but his plays are often simple and almost Classical in structure.

Beginning in 1917 with *Cosi è (se vi pare)* (*Right You Are, If You Think You Are*) he created a slim but important volume of plays that had little influence in his native Italy, where audiences persisted in preferring the Pirandello of the early Sicilian sketches written before 1917. He followed with *Il giuoco delle parti* (*The Rules of the Game*, 1918), *Sei personaggi in cerca d'autore* (*Six Characters in Search of an Author*, 1921, revised 1925), *Enrico IV* (*Henry IV*, 1922), *Ciascuno a suo modo* (*Each in His Own Way*, 1924), *Questa sera si recita a soggetto* (*Tonight We Improvise*, 1929), *Come tu mi vuoi* (*As You Desire Me*, 1930), and *Quando si è qualcuno* (*When One is Somebody*, 1933).

A consideration of Pirandello as an Italian author is a bit misleading in that his effect on Italian drama has been very limited. Italian theatre paid attention to him only after the rest of Europe and the United States began to pay him homage, and then his influence tended to be unfortunate rather than salutary as Italian writers tried to imitate his dramatic paradoxes rather than learn from them.

Along with Pirandello, Ugo Betti (1892-1953) helped to enliven the generally empty, escapist drama between World Wars I and II. Like Pirandello, Betti was first a poet and came late to theatre, which provided him with a podium from which he could express his sense of mankind's guilt for the mistreatment of the individual and warn his fellows of the breakup of values which was contributing to the growth of fascism. Betti's answer to these problems was a return to God, whose justice is true and whose charity is infallible.

Betti was deeply influenced by the works of Pirandello, but unlike his fellow Italian dramatists Betti took Pirandello's interest in the conflict between truth and illusion, added to it his regret for man's loss of earthly paradise in which there was no illusion, only truth, and made the resulting drama totally his own and not merely banal Pirandello. Perhaps his best play is *Corruzione al Palazzo di Giustizia* (*Corruption in the Palace of Justice*, 1949). Himself a High Court judge during the final years of his life, Betti was deeply concerned with the errors inherent in human justice, when contrasted with the perfection of God's charity.

Betti, like Pirandello, left theatre only a slim legacy of plays. His best works were serious dramas, beginning with *Un albergo sul porto* (*A Hotel on the Port*, 1933), followed by *Frana allo scalo Nord* (*Landslide*, 1936), *Ispezione* (*The Inquiry*, 1947), *Le regina e gli insorti* (*The Queen and the Rebels*, 1949), and *L'aiuola bruciata* and *La fuggitiva* (*The Burnt Flower-Bed* and *The Fugitive*, both produced posthumously, 1953). Two light pieces, though not exactly comedies, are *Una bella domenica di settembre* (*A Beautiful Sunday in September*, 1937) and *Il paese delle vacanze* (*Summertime*, 1942).

The most significant contemporary dramatic work in Italy is that of Eduardo De Filippo (1900-). Unfortunately, perhaps, his work has been done exclusively for the dialectical Neapolitan theatre and, thus, is largely unknown outside of Italy. The Neapolitan theatre in the nineteenth and twentieth centuries was a continuous development from the *commedia dell'arte* tradition. Southern Italy was, during this period, an isolated area, separated not only from Europe but, in many ways, from the rest of Italy as well. The scenarios and *lazzi* that began to develop during the nineteenth century were new in material, but rough and colorful, and everything was subordinated to the art of the actor. It was in this theatre that Eduardo De Filippo received his training and made his mark.

De Filippo was one of three children (also Titina and Peppino) of an acting family and was onstage from an early age. The three children performed all over Italy with some fine troupes—in 1929 they appeared with the Molinari Company—eventually settling down in Naples, where they opened a theatre. They soon earned an outstanding reputation for their *commedia*-style productions. All three of the De Filippos wrote plays, but those of Titina and Peppino were never more than scenarios for *commedia*. Eduardo, on the other hand, began to write early in the 1920s. After World War II he turned to full-length plays in the *commedia* style, exploring some of the same issues as the plays of Pirandello and Betti, and was soon recognized as one of the foremost Italian dramatists.

Scenic design for D'Annunzio's *The Ship*, by one of the best modern Italian scenic designers, Guido Marussig.

Because of their requirement for stylized presentation, and their dependence on dialectical materials, De Filippo's plays have not had much success outside of his native Italy. However, his *Napoli milionaria* (*Millionare Naples*, 1945), *Questi fantasmi* (*These Ghosts*, 1946), *Filumena Marturano* (1946), *Le voci di dentro* (*Inner Voices*, 1948), *La grande magia* (*The Big Magic*, 1949), *La paura munero uno* (*Fear Number One*, 1950), *Bene mio e core mio* (*My Darling and My Love*, 1955), and *Il figlio di Pulcinella* (*The Son of Pulcinella*, 1959) are all fine plays and, given good dialectical translations, may yet make their mark on Western theatre. In recent years he has directed and acted in several of his plays at Britain's National Theatre.

Spain The beginning of the twentieth century meant little to Spanish drama, and the sentimental middle-class drama that was popular at the end of the previous century continued unabated. Spain's decision not to participate in World War I caused the pattern to continue by creating a further isolation from western Europe, and indeed it was not until 1931 and the creation of the Republic that drama showed some change. Even this change was minimal, for the government that seemed so liberal politically did not encourage experimentation or even freedom in the arts. Thus, most of Spanish theatre in the twentieth century is really only nineteenth century material revisited.

TWENTIETH CENTURY SPANISH DRAMA

Dramatic production in twentieth century Spain is basically the history of two disparate playwrights—Jacinto Benavente and Federico García Lorca.

Jacinto Benavente (1866-1954) was the major figure in Spanish theatre during the first half of the century, winning the Nobel Prize for literature in 1922. Solidly grounded in stage techniques, knowledgeable about the total of European drama from its earliest to his own time, and immersed in the prolific tradition of Lope de Vega and Calderón, he dominated the theatre of his time to such a degree that it may ultimately have caused more damage than good. He translated into Spanish some of the plays of Shakespeare and Molière, he wrote one hundred sixty-eight plays, and he worked in such varied forms as social drama, fantasy, and drama for children.

Benavente was aware that his audience was not interested in seeing serious problems treated seriously, and so he gave them what they wanted—an escape into a generally light and airy dream world. However, in his best works the basic intelligence and sensitivity that he brought to playwriting shines through: *La noche del sábado* (*Saturday Night*, 1903) displays Benavente's belief in the power of individual will; *Los malhechores del bien* (*The Evil Doers of Good*, 1905) and *Más fuerte que el amor* (*Stronger than Love*, 1906) are smiling, ironic exposés of the vanities and vices of contemporary Spanish society; *Los intereses creados* (*The Bonds of Interest*, 1907), perhaps his best work, is a fantasy in *commedia dell' arte* style; *Señora Ama* (1908) deals with the lot of the peasant; *El príncipe que todo lo aprendió en los libros* (*The Prince Who Learned Everything Out of Books*, 1909) is a play for children; and *La malquerida* (*The Passion Flower*, 1913) is ironic social commentary.

Federico García Lorca (1898-1936) was born in Granada, a city alive with both Classical and Arabian traditions, and as a result Lorca found his principal sources of inspiration in the richness of the Spanish scene that surrounded him. Lorca began his literary career as a poet, and his plays are inseparable from his poetry; indeed, they are natural emanations from it. Even in his first play, *El maleficio de la mariposa* (*The Butterfly's Evil Spell*, 1920), written at the same time as his early symbolistic verse, he managed to turn lyric poetry into acceptable dramatic dialogue.

In 1927 Lorca seriously began his career as a dramatist with *Mariana Pineda*. In this play he attempted to join elements from both the Classic and Romantic theatre, and to do this in a contemporary manner. From the Classic theatre he took the tradition of working with known, meaningful materials—in this case an old folk ballad. From the Romantic theatre he took the concept of the heroic theme and a heroine of great virtue who is sacrificed on the altar of love.

Between *Mariana Pineda* and his next major work, Lorca wrote some short plays and prose farces. They are all better constructed than *Mariana*, though of lower emotional intensity. There are three of the prose farces, written between 1929 and 1931, and these constitute a group by themselves. The earliest is *El amor de don Perlimplín con Belisa en su jardin* (*The Love of Don Perlimplin for Belisa, in His Garden*). It was not produced until 1933, but it was written long before. Then came *La zapatera prodigiosa* (*The Shoemaker's Prodigious Wife*), first presented in Madrid's Teatro España in 1930, and later, in an enlarged version, in the Coliseum Theatre (1935). These were followed by *El retablillo de don Cristóbal* (*In the Frame of Don Cristobal*), a farce for puppets, dated 1931.

To this point, Lorca had been experimenting, trying out new forms. However, it was not until *Bodas de sangre* (*Blood Wedding*), a peasant tragedy which had its premiere in Madrid in 1933, that he finally found the proper medium to display the passionate intensity that informed his best poetry. He followed this with *Yerma* (1934), which is similar in its main theme and its technique. In some ways *Yerma* is the better play of the two, carefully crafted into a more finished product. Also, the subject is somewhat more ambitious than any Lorca had yet attempted in his drama, even though he had been elaborating on it for many years in his poetry—love frustrated because of man's incapacity to respond to woman's passion. In spite of this, *Yerma* does not quite achieve the artistic level of *Blood Wedding*. In *Wedding* everything is basic, earthy, related to the land itself. In *Yerma* the elements all tend toward abstraction.

A scene from Federico Garcia-Lorca's *The House of Bernarda Alba*. Directed by Michael McPherson.

Yerma was, more than anything else, a necessary step for Lorca to take along the pathway toward intense tragedy. Such tragedy was achieved in his last play, *La casa de Bernarda Alba* (*The House of Bernarda Alba*, 1936), a study in female frustration that occurs in a household of daughters ruled by a tyrannical mother. The play was to be, with *Yerma*, part of a trilogy dealing with sexual obsession and unfulfilled love. This topic had long fascinated Lorca, who found in it the basic conflict between pagan and Christian standards, which he felt had long troubled the Spanish soul.

One of the poet's friends later said that every time Lorca completed a scene he exclaimed "Not a drop of poetry! Reality! Realism!" This was, apparently, Lorca's ultimate goal—to write a cold, objective tragedy that would capture truth without lyrical intrusion.

Shortly after completing the final draft of *Alba*, Lorca was arrested by the Governor of Granada, who ordered the poet's death. On November 1, 1936, shortly after his thirty-eighth birthday, Lorca was marched out into an olive grove, shot, and buried. The reasons for his arrest and execution are still not clear.

The Twentieth Century in Germany, Northern Europe, and Russia

---

Germany and Northern Europe The twentieth century in Germany began as a period of experimentation. Wedekind was still challenging most social theories of pre-World War I Germany, laying bare its sexual restrictions and sensual proclivities. Expressionism was developing the basic techniques that would make it, after World War I, the most important vehicle for expressing the anguish and doubt that the holocaust had raised. The late 1920s and the 1930s saw the emergence of neorealism, and while the movement produced few major dramatists it did manage to temper the excesses of expressionism. The rise of National Socialism ended Germany's lively drama using political controls to enforce a superpatriotic drama that extolled the Teutonic superman, military might, and political unification under the Party. By 1945 the drama in Germany was essentially dead, though German-language drama was in good hands in Switzerland.

TWENTIETH CENTURY GERMAN-LANGUAGE DRAMA

Expressionism, a movement which embraced all the arts, began in Germany shortly after the opening of the twentieth century. The movement had its inception in Paris in 1901 when Julien-Auguste Hervé exhibited his paintings under the title of "Expressionismes" to indicate his repudiation of the popular art forms. But while the movement began in Paris, it was in Germany, under the influence of the theorist Kasimir Edschmid, that it achieved real significance.

Basically, German expressionism was two things rolled up into one: it was a revolt by young artists against the more repressive aspects of their society and the popular art forms of that society; and it was an attempt to portray the "reality" that existed under the surface. The philosophical basis of expressionism, like the basis of naturalism, was found in the scientific revolution. The naturalists went to social Darwinism for their concepts, and the expressionists went to popular Freudianism. The social condition in Germany before World War I was one that seemed stifling and narrow, particularly to the young artists. It was a patriarchal society that promoted a repressive, puritanical life-style, with an emphasis on authority that began with the patriarch and ended with the state. Rebelling against this situation, the young playwrights began looking for a method of displaying the seething inner passions that their society repressed, and they found it in popular Freudianism.

Freud had promoted the idea that man's internal, subconscious desires come to the surface in the dream, and the young artists accepted this. Thus, they decided to use the dream form or dream vision as a method of concretizing their own internal desires, and the result was to give a special dramatic form to expressionism. Expressionism, the playwrights felt, should deal with reality—should in fact be considered realism—but the reality it would deal

Sketch of a stage design by Cesar Klein for Georg Kaiser's *From Morn to Midnight*, 1923.

with would be internal rather than external. Also, just as Freud found the sexual drive to be the primary motivating force for the human animal, and just as Wedekind had concentrated on the hypocrisy of human sexual relationships, so the expressionists concentrated on the sexual aspects of human existence.

Following World War I, which destroyed much of the society against which the expressionists had been rebelling, expressionism's emphasis shifted from the family and inhibited sexual relationships to the guilt left behind by the horror of war. After the middle of the 1920s expressionism came to a dead end. It had produced little drama of lasting value but had contributed ideas and techniques to the traditional theatre that would be used by playwrights on both sides of the Atlantic.

One of the earliest of the German expressionists was the poet Reinhard Johannes Sorge (1892-1916). Sorge began his adult life as a disciple of Nietzsche, changed metaphysical allegiance to Catholicism, and was unfortunately killed in the war. His finest play, *Der Bettler* (*The Beggar*, 1912), was not produced until 1917. A strong drama of social criticism, it is in the expressionistic tradition of the rebellious young artist protesting against the

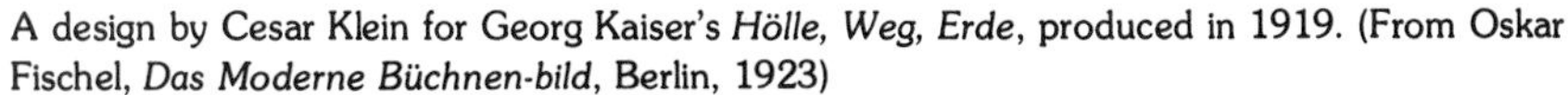

A design by Cesar Klein for Georg Kaiser's *Hölle, Weg, Erde*, produced in 1919. (From Oskar Fischel, *Das Moderne Büchnen-bild*, Berlin, 1923)

strictures of an older generation and lamenting the lack of spiritual values in contemporary society.

Oskar Kokoschka (1886-), an Austrian, is justly better known as a painter than as a playwright. His *Mörder, Hoffnung der Frauen* (*Murder, Hope of Women*, produced in Dresden in 1916 but written several years earlier) is one of the best and earliest expressionistic plays. In this dream-play the battle of the sexes is played out in nightmare terms—against a background of knights and ladies. Man and Woman face each other with instinctive hatred. They rail at each other, growing quickly hysterical. Man has Woman branded, after which she stabs him and locks him in a cage. She taunts him as he lies wounded, but he recovers enough to stumble out of the cage and kill her. Kokoschka continued this unfortunate vision in several other plays, but none with the strength of *Murder*.

August Stramm (1874-1915) was essentially a failed dramatist; he had little popularity in his own time and his plays are now all but forgotten. However, his dramas such as *Erwachen* (*Awakening*), *Kräfte* (*Forces*), and *Geschehen* (*Happening*) written during 1914 and 1915, are almost textbooks on the potential excesses of expressionism. His plays are pantomimes on the evils of social repression, with an occasional word or phrase thrown in almost as a sop to the oral tradition of drama.

Stefan Zweig (1881-1942) was an Austrian whose primary fame rests on his biographies and novels. He did have, however, a fairly distinguished theatrical career. He was not specifically a part of the expressionistic drama, but his *Tersites* (1907) was exciting in its attempt to demonstrate the spiritual superiority that grows out of physical incapacity. His *Jeremias* (*Jeremiah*, 1917) falls much more into the expressionistic school, partly because this play deals with the horror of war and expressionism offered a form that allowed Zweig to strengthen his antiwar message and keep the audience's concentration squarely on the character of the prophet.

The best of the German expressionists—certainly the most prolific and inventive—was Georg Kaiser (1878-1945), who became the acknowledged leader of the expressionist school of drama. His early plays, such as *Rektor Kleist* (*Schoolmaster Kleist*, 1905, produced in 1918) and *Die jüdische Witwe* (*The Jewish Widow*, 1911) are somewhat in the tradition of the antiromantic satires written just at the turn of the century. However, the opening of World War I gave him something new to criticize. The spectacle of a nation blindly diving into the holocaust made him seriously question the entire ethical structure of society, and as a result his middle plays, such as the historical drama *Die Bürger von Calais* (*The Citizen of Calais*, 1914), the melodramatic *Der Brand im Opernhaus* (*Fire in the Opera House*, 1919), and the sombre *Von Morgens bis Mitternachts* (*From Morn to Midnight*, 1916), all portray the failures of the machine age, which destroys all humanity in man, turning people into robots. The *Gas* trilogy (*Die Koralle*, 1917; *Gas I*, 1918; *Gas II*, 1920), carries this preoccupation one step beyond the middle plays, symbolically showing the industrial civilization falling to destruction. In his last plays, such as *Der Soldat Tanaka* (*Soldier Tanaka*, 1940), and *Das Floss der Medusa* (*The Raft of the Medusa*, 1948), Kaiser combined expressionistic techniques with neorealism, and the result, while not as experimentally interesting as the earlier works, was some of his finest drama.

Georg Kaiser's *Gas*, produced at the Schiller Theatre, Berlin, 1928, with settings by Emil Pirchan. (Munich, Theatre-Museum)

While expressionism was at its peak, and neorealism was just beginning to assert itself, the young Bavarian playwright Bertolt Brecht began to create. The effect of his plays and his dramatic theories was and has been great, but to characterize the German drama of the last fifty plus years, as some historians have done, as the Age of Brecht, is a serious error. Brecht was as much a product of his age as a creator of it.

BERTOLT BRECHT: Bertolt Brecht (1898-1956), poet, playwright, and theoretician, has been a major influence on modern drama, chiefly because of his theory of epic theatre and his concept of "alienation." Brecht's theories reveal an unquenchable, intense interest in transforming society and improving the relationships between human beings. In his determination to develop a new form of theatre that would aid in this grand design, he rejected the prevailing representational theatre and worked to create a new drama that would provide a different relationship with the audience. No more would the spectators be allowed to empathize with what happens on stage, thus giving up the ability to evaluate critically the ideas being presented.

To aid in this new relationship, Brecht created methods of freeing himself from traditional staging, intentionally devising stage events that would be unfamiliar and different, so that the audience would ask questions rather than merely accept them. The German word, *verfremdungseffekt* ("alienation effect", also translated as "estrangement," "defamiliarization," and "distancing") was the term Brecht chose to characterize his new dramatic style. His dramatic form he titled "epic" theatre.

Brecht was born in Augsburg, Bavaria, where he lived until 1924. He studied medicine and served in an army hospital as an orderly until 1918, when he wrote his first play, *Baal*. In 1919, resuming his studies at Munich University, he became drama critic of the socialist newspaper, *Die Augsburger Volkswille*. Between 1919 and 1921 he wrote more than two dozen theatre articles for that paper.

Brecht followed up *Baal* with three more plays, all of which were produced: *Trommeln in der Nacht* (*Drums in the Night*, 1922); *Im Dickicht der Städte* (*In the Swamp*, 1923); and *Mann ist Mann* (*A Man's a Man*, 1926). In 1928 Brecht collaborated with the composer Kurt Weill on *Die Dreigroschenoper*, which as *The Threepenny Opera* proved to be his greatest popular success. Brecht and Weill again joined forces, this time writing *Aufstieg und Fall der Stadte Mahagonny* (*The Rise and Fall of the City of Mahagonny*). Their goal was the creation and development of a new, innovative kind of musical theatre, as they both considered the current opera to be static and dead.

By 1933, at age thirty-five, Brecht had begun to achieve fame and limited financial success. However, Hitler was gaining a following throughout Europe

Helene Weigel in a scene from Bertolt Brecht's *Mother Courage* at the Berliner Ensemble. (Courtesy of the Berliner Ensemble, Hainer Hill)

and Brecht felt that it would be unwise to remain in Germany. Because of his socialistic beliefs, his name was high on the Nazis' liquidation lists. As a result, in 1933, Brecht left Germany with his wife, the actress Helene Weigel, and their two children. Except for a brief trip to New York they lived alternately in Switzerland, Denmark, and Finland until 1941, at which time he came to California to remain until the end of the war.

The brief trip to New York took place in 1935 when the Theatre Union was to perform one of his plays. The production of his play, *The Mother* (*Die Mutter*), at the Civic Repertory Theatre, apparently was deeply unsatisfying to Brecht. He disliked the English text, the staging, and the sets. In fact, there was little about the production that he did like, and he left the country very dissatisfied.

From 1940 on Brecht continued to strive to make his theatre highly instructive, and yet sufficiently entertaining. He wrote some of his finest plays during this period—*Mutter Courage und ihre Kinder* (*Mother Courage and Her Children*), *Das Leben des Galilei* (*Galileo*), *Der gute Mensch von Sezuan* (*The Good Woman of Setzuan*), and *Der kaukasische Kreidekreis* (*The Caucasian Chalk Circle*). Also, he ceaselessly refined and reworked his theatre theory and practice, acknowledging that his epic theatre was not necessarily *the* way, but rather *a* way; specifically, it was the way he chose to work for achievement of his goals. His *Kleines Organon für das Theater* (*A Short Organum for the Theatre*) was finished in 1948, becoming Brecht's most important theoretical work. From then until 1956 he was active, in East Berlin, in his own theatre with his company, the Berliner Ensemble, staging productions of his own plays and those of others.

His fame as a theatrical reformer spread, increasingly, to western Europe and further abroad, leading to successful appearances of his Berliner Ensemble in Paris and London. In Moscow in 1955 he was awarded the Stalin Peace Prize. The following year, Brecht died of a heart attack.

Brecht's theories of theatre are often discussed—sometimes praised and as often damned—but the degree to which they have in fact influenced the course of Western theatre is questionable. To achieve his "alienation effect" he developed a number of techniques to create that special relationship—a critical one—between the spectator and what was happening on stage. Brecht wanted to explain the world to spectators who wished not just to see the world as it is, but to change it. Thus, he made his lighting instruments visible, placed his musicians on the stage, used didactic projections, and interrupted the flow of the plot with songs, narrative passages, and even verbalized stage directions, all designed to call attention to the basic theatricality of the experience. In addition, since a good part of the traditional theatre's "illusion" grows out of the darkened environment of the auditorium, Brecht would often leave the lights on. As a result, he believed, the audience would stay fully conscious and intellectually alert.

Other Brechtian practices were revealed in his essay, "Theatre for Pleasure or Theatre for Instruction," in which he spoke of the things he had been doing in Berlin prior to his flight from Germany:

> *The stage began to tell a story. . . . Not only did the background adopt an attitude to the events on the stage—by big screens recalling other simul-*

taneous events elsewhere, by projecting documents which confirmed or contradicted what the characters said . . . but the actors refrained from going over wholly into their role, remaining detached from the character they were playing and clearly inviting criticism of him.

Speaking of the performer, Brecht wrote in a "Short Description of a New Technique of Acting Which Produces an Alienation Effect," that "there are three aids which may help to alienate the actions and remarks of the characters being portrayed: 1) Transposition into the third person; 2) Transposition into the past; and 3) Speaking the stage directions out loud. Speaking the stage directions out loud in the third person results in a clash between two tones of voice, alienating the second of them, the text proper."

Such theories are clearly difficult to put into effect, and one may legitimately wonder whether, even if they are achieved, they produce an effect worth the effort. A number of critics, with the hindsight provided by the twenty years since his death, have decided that Brecht's theories are unworkable and essentially antidramatic, and that as a playwright his dramas succeed in spite of his theories and not because of them. Whether or not this is an accurate assessment of Brecht the theorist is not yet clear. What is clear is that Brecht the dramatist has been one of the most important forces in twentieth century theatre.

Franz Werfel (1890-1945), an Austrian novelist who turned to drama, began with an overlong and slow-moving *Die Troerinnen* (1915). This recreation of Euripides' *Trojan Women* has a Wagnerian quality, combined with a deep religious fervor that made it a partial failure with audiences. In 1920, however, he followed his early work with *Der Spiegelmensch* (*The Mirror Man*), an interesting trilogy on the Faust-Mephistopheles theme. Its success encouraged him and he followed it with two interesting but basically undistinguished historical plays, *Juarez und Maximilian* (1924) and *Paulus unter den Juden* (*Paul Among the Jews*, 1926). In 1936 his *Der Weg der Verheissung* (*The Eternal Road*) was given an elaborate New York production by Reinhardt, but with little success. Werfel's most interesting contribution to German-language drama is probably *Bocksgesang* (*Goatsong*, 1921), which he adapted from his novel of the same name. In it a satyr—half goat and half man—leads an eighteenth century peasant rebellion that bloodies the countryside to no point. At the play's end this monster is killed, but he has already passed on his basic brutality and bloodlust by way of a young nobleman's wife. Werfel's most popular play, however, was his last, *Jacobowsky und der Oberst* (*Jacobowsky and the Colonel*, 1943), which deals comically and sensitively with an uneasy relationship that develops between a Jew and a Junker colonel during the terrors of World War II.

The rise of neorealism as a major aspect of post-World War I German theatre comes with the advent of Carl Zuckmayer (1896-   ), certainly one of the finest dramatists of this century. After serving as a soldier in the German army during the war, Zuckmayer found himself gripped by the postwar depression. He wandered from job to job, finally drifting into theatre by way of a stint as producer in a small, provincial theatre. His earliest plays, *Am Kreuzweg* (*Crossroads*, 1920) and *Pankraz erwacht* (*Pankraz Awakens*, 1925) were unsuc-

Alfred Roller's set for Reinhardt's production of Gozzi's *Turandot*, produced at the Salzburg Festspielhaus in 1926.

cessful with both audiences and critics, probably because in them Zuckmayer was trying to write in the currently popular expressionistic form, which was totally foreign to his nature.

In the same year that *Pankraz* failed, Zuckmayer wrote *Der fröhliche Weinberg* (*The Merry Vineyard*, 1925) in a realistic style. It was immediately successful; Berlin audiences gave it an almost unprecedented welcome, perhaps in part because they were tiring of the excesses of expressionism. Two years later he followed up this success with *Schinderhannes* (*Jack the Ripper*, 1927), a play based on the legendary-historical character of the Napoleonic Wars who, like Robin Hood, robbed the rich and gave to the poor.

In 1929 Zuckmayer wrote a circus drama, *Katharina Knie*, concerning the circus artist's determination to keep the show going even though it means sacrificing love and security, and in 1930 a children's play entitled *Kakadu Kakada*. In 1930 he completed what may be his best play, *Der Hauptmann von Köpenick* (*The Captain from Köpenick*). The story, taken from an actual happening, tells how a shoemaker, disguised as an army officer, is able to carry off the deception and attain his ends due to the Prussian trait of always obeying someone in uniform. It was a sharp, satiric attack on the reviving militarism that was bringing down the Weimar Republic.

Following the advent of Hitler and the rise of National Socialism, Zuckmayer departed Germany for Austria, where he wrote *Der Schelm von Bergen* (*The Rogue of Bergen*, 1934) and *Bellman* (1938), both historical dramas. The war was clearly getting close, however, and he left Austria for the United

States, where he achieved his greatest popular success with *Des Teufels General* (*The Devil's General*, 1946). The play deals with a patriotic German officer's gradual realization that he has been a servant of the devil—Hitler.

Zuckmayer's late plays never quite achieved the satiric bite or the unrelenting realism of the earlier works. *Barbara Blomberg* (1949) tells of the agonies of the illegitimate mother of a king; *Der Gesang im Feuerofen* (*The Song in the Fiery Oven*, 1950) deals with the French underground during World War II who condemn one of their own as a traitor; *Das kalte Licht* (*The Cold Light*, 1955) is based on the case of Klaus Fuchs; *Die Urh schlägt eins* (*The Clock Strikes One*, 1961) tells of the moral problems caused by the miraculous economic recovery in postwar Germany; and *Das Leben des Horace A. W. Tabor* (*The Life of Horace A. W. Tabor*, 1964), tells of a playboy American businessman.

Ferdinand Bruckner (really Theodor Tagger, 1891-1958) was an Austrian dramatist who sought to deal with some of the same themes as Zuckmayer, but without Zuckmayer's gift for satire. His first play, *Krankheit der Jugend* (*Disease of Youth*, 1926), concerned itself with suicide as the answer to disillusionment. His second play, *Die Verbrecher* (*The Lawbreakers*, 1928), began a series of attempts to deal with contemporary problems under the guise of history. *Timon*, based on the play of Shakespeare, was written in 1933, along with *Die Rassen* (*The Races*), which deals with the evils of racism. *Napoleon der Erste* (*Napoleon the First*, 1937) and *Heroische Komödie* (*Heroic Comedy*, 1942) continued the use of historical material to focus on more immediate problems, in this case the rise of Adolph Hitler. Bruckner's later plays—*Der Tod einer Puppe* (*The Death of a Doll*, 1956) and *Der Kampf mit dem Engel* (*The Fight with the Angel*, 1957)—had a popularity in Germany and, in translation, throughout the rest of western Europe, which their quality did not justify.

Another Austrian, Fritz Hochwälder (1911-   ), who moved to Switzerland at age seventeen, began his theatrical career in 1943 with *Das heilige Experiment* (*The Holy Experiment*) a morality play on the subject of the destruction of the Jesuits in Paraguay in the eighteenth century. He followed this with *Der Flüchtling* (*The Fugitive*, 1945), a contemporary drama. Returning to historical drama, this time the French Revolution, he wrote *Der öffentliche Ankläger* (*The Public Prosecutor*) in 1947. *Donadieu* (1953) is also sited in French history—the Hugenot Wars—and like the earlier plays it also examines the moral issue of revenge. *Die Herberge* (*The Inn*, 1956) is again a moral tale about a stolen bag of gold. During the course of investigating the theft a far more serious crime is revealed. Finally, *Der Unschuldige* (*The Innocent One*, 1958) is Hochwälder's only comedy, a satiric ramble in which a skeleton is dug up in the garden of an innocent man. He is charged with murder and, while the skeleton eventually proves to be that of a Napoleonic soldier and the man is found innocent, the experience causes him to realize his ultimate guilt.

Since World War II the German-language drama has found its most effective voice outside of Germany—in Austria and in recent years especially in Switzerland. One of the most important of these voices is Max Frisch (1911-   ), a Zürich-born student of Brecht. He began writing at the war's end with *Nun singen sie wieder* (*Now They Sing Again*, 1945), an expressionistic antiwar drama in which representations of those who were killed in the conflict mix with the living—who are unaware of their presence—to cry out their desire for peace. Frisch followed this with one of his best plays, *Die chinesische Mauer* (*The Chinese Wall,* 1946), a kind of pessimistic "theatre of the world" which allows comment on the atom bomb by importing famous characters out of the past to show that history cannot be changed and that all warnings will go unheard. In the same year, almost unnoted, he also wrote *Santa Cruz,* a light, rather romantic piece. *Als der Krieg zu Ende war* (*When the War Was Over,* 1949), is another morality play that postulates suicide as an alternative to the immorality of war and contemporary life. This was followed by *Graf Öderland* (*Count Öderland,* 1951), a nightmarish and vaguely expressionistic mishmash that tries to capture what Frisch perceives as the chaos of Western civilization.

In 1953 Frisch seemed to retreat from the didactic style of the social problem drama and produced one of his finest works, *Don Juan, oder Die Liebe Zur Geometrie* (*Don Juan, or The Love of Geometry*). Like the earlier *Santa Cruz, Don Juan* is a somewhat romantic work that, ironically, shows the great lover as the victim of women rather than their despoiler. In the play, Don Juan has no real interest in women; rather, he loves the study of geometry. However, because of the essential perversity of humanity, the women take his disinterest as a challenge and constantly seek to seduce him. Finally the poor mathematician is forced to seek refuge in marriage.

In 1958 Frisch wrote *Biedermann und die Brandstifter* which, as *The Fire Bugs* or *The Fire Raisers,* received a great deal of play in both the United States and England. In the same year he also finished *Die grosse Wut des Philipp Hotz* (*The Great Fury of Philipp Hotz*), a rather slight farce. *Andorra* (1961) was perhaps Frisch's greatest audience-pleaser. Dealing with racial prejudices, the play tells of an illegitimate Christian child who is raised as a Jew. By the time he learns the truth about himself he is unable to discard the identity of Jewishness and maintains it even in the face of death when he is murdered by anti-Semitic invaders who bear a strong resemblance to the German Nazis.

After Frisch, the most important contemporary German language playwright is Friedrich Dürrenmatt (1921-). In his book *Theaterprobleme* (*Problems of the Theatre,* 1955), Dürrenmatt states that the chaotic and disintegrating contemporary world is more suitable to comedy than to tragedy, but his plays often come close to the tragicomic. His earliest work, *Es steht geschrieben* (*It Is Written,* 1947), is a fine absurdist comedy, but received little critical notice, perhaps because it depends for its humor on certain Baptist proceedings. *Romulus der Grosse* (*Romulus the Great,* 1949), was a major success, both critically and at the box office. In the Brechtian tradition, it mocks heroic legend and uses revised history to make a social statement. In 1956 Dürrenmatt completed *Der Besuch der Alten Dame,* which as *The Visit* has had widespread popularity in both the United States and England, with many stage productions and a popular film. In 1962 he followed up with *Die Physiker* (*The Physicists*) again a major success.

Like Frisch and most other young European writers who lived through the experience of World War II, Dürrenmatt is especially concerned with questions of guilt and innocence. This is perhaps truest of the Swiss, who by re-

The Alley Theatre's production of Friedrich Dürrenmatt's marital satire, *Comedy of Marriage*. Directed by Robert Symonds.

maining neutral while the drama of the Nazi concentration camps was played out, feel the need to explain and justify their failure to take action against a monstrous evil.

THE DIRECTOR

The contributions of the German directors during the twentieth century were great, especially when it is remembered that they were made, essentially, by three men: Bertolt Brecht, Max Reinhardt, and Leopold Jessner. Brecht's career was covered earlier in this chapter, but both Reinhardt and Jessner need careful consideration.

MAX REINHARDT: Max Reinhardt (1873-1943) developed his theatrical interests as a seventeen-year-old student at the Vienna Conservatory. While studying there he was seen in a student production by producer-critic Otto Brahm, at that time director of the Deutsches Theatre. Reinhardt did a walk-on character part of an old man, and his naturalistic characterization caught Brahm's eye. The young actor was below average height, square and stocky in build, and with angular, strong-boned features that projected age well. He approached his part with originality and force, and was dramatically effective. In 1892 Brahm again saw Reinhardt, this time in Salzburg. The youth was still playing old men, and Brahm engaged him for the company of the Deutsches Theater.

Even while he was working with Brahm, carving out for himself a successful career in acting, Reinhardt began expanding his theatrical horizons, turning to a new and highly popular theatrical area—the cabaret. Reinhardt was attracted by the intimacy that cabaret theatre provided and by this new form's freedom from traditional staging practices. He joined a group interested in this new theatrical form and together they founded the Brille, a private organization which put on Reinhardt directed cabaret productions for its members. In 1901, this group opened a small, intimate theatre, the Schall und Raush ("Sound and Smoke"). In 1902 it was renamed the Kleines Theater. Until this time Reinhardt had continued his work with Brahm and the Deutsches Theater, but now he was ready to turn his energies to directing. By this time Reinhardt felt that he had learned all he could from naturalism, and he wanted to experiment with new theatrical forms. The main style of the early Kleines Theater productions was expressionism, and during this period Reinhardt introduced Strindberg to the German playgoer, along with Wedekind, Wilde, and Maeterlinck. From 1902 to 1905 Reinhardt produced over fifty plays representing several countries and styles.

In 1905 Reinhardt replaced Brahm as director of the Deutsches Theater. Under Brahm the Deutsches had been the most important theatre in Germany, but within his first two years as its director Reinhardt managed to give it international prominence. One of Reinhardt's most important innovations was the opening in 1906 of the three-hundred seat Kammerspielhaus, located next to the larger theatre. This smaller theatre gave the producer an opportunity to stage a variety of works. Because of its flexibility the multihouse system became standard for European state theatres and for many educational theatres in the United States. It was also exactly what Reinhardt needed to fulfill his own ideal of what theatre should be.

Reinhardt had given up his early emphasis on realism because he believed that the realistic details distracted audiences from the inner story. He saw theatre, with its potential for the communication of ideas, not as a unified form but as the production of individual works of art. He believed that the production style of each play must grow organically from the play itself, and as a result he worked in virtually all dramatic styles except historical reproduction. He did not feel that historical styles should be re-created. Instead he felt that they should be adapted in a manner that would make them vital to their audiences.

A Midsummer Night's Dream may have been Max Reinhardt's favorite play. He staged it many times in many styles. This rich production took place in Vienna, 1925.

To expand his potential for variety, Reinhardt introduced the revolving stage at the Deutsches Theater and employed designer Ernst Stern to work out the complex settings that the revolving stage required to achieve greatest effectiveness. The revolving stage remained one of Reinhardt's favorite technical devices and was soon taken up by producers and designers throughout Europe. Reinhardt toured America in 1912, but he did not bring his revolving stage and it was not fully utilized there until three years later, when it was popularized by Harley Granville-Barker. Reinhardt made substantial use of stage machinery, but he kept technical effects within certain guidelines. In a program note for *Das Mirakel* (*The Miracle*), by Karl Vollmöller, he wrote: "Do not spare stage properties and machinery where they are needed, but do not impose them on a play that does not need them."

Feeling limited even in the large Deutsches Theater, Reinhardt turned to the traditional European indoor circuses for staging productions of *Oedipus the King*, *Orestes*, and *Everyman*. These circuses, unlike their American tent-show cousins, were large, permanent structures. For these circus productions of Classical Greek and Medieval plays Reinhardt used the arena floor in much the same manner as a Greek orchestra, closing off one end of the arena with a Greek façade. At the center of the façade were huge brass doors, and out in front was a platform with an altar in the center. These productions were so successful that Reinhardt toured them throughout Germany and even took *Oedipus* to Covent Garden.

Reinhardt had, early in his career, perfected the techniques necessary to achieve success. At age thirty-two he came to the Deutsches Theater already prepared to be a master *regisseur.* Early in his career Reinhardt developed a concept of the *regiebuch* as a total blueprint for a play—including gestures, movement, and line readings—which had to be carefully worked out before the production began. As well, the *regiebuch* included sketches of blocking, philosophical ideas regarding actor motivations, and instructions to various members of cast and crew. Because of this planning the director was able to visualize his entire production even before rehearsals began. This provided a kind of yardstick to measure how well the play was developing. After rehearsals were finally underway, copies of the *regiebuch* were made and distributed to certain assistants, assuring uniform control of the productions.

Rehearsals were conducted in a practical, efficient, businesslike way. Some people, who observed Reinhardt throughout his career, have said that he

If this scene from Max Reinhardt's production of *The Lower Depths* is compared with the scene shown from his *A Midsummer Night's Dream*, it is possible to get an idea of the range of styles in which the director worked.

was very strict in his early years, but that he relaxed as he developed more control over his craft. Because of this control his productions were always carefully crafted and he was able to extract excellent performances from mediocre actors. It also promoted an ensemble effect that became a Reinhardt trademark.

While at the Deutsches Theater, Reinhardt initiated an acting school which taught the Dalcroze system of dancing to train the actors to move musically and to express physically thoughts too deep for words. Elocution, posture, gesture, and characterization were also taught. This system established Reinhardt as a major innovator in actor training.

Along with Appia, Craig, and other great theatricians of his time, Reinhardt helped create in Europe the movement called the new stagecraft. It was a movement away from kitchen-sink realism, emphasizing instead a theatre of spectacle, of depth, and of unabashed theatricality. The new stagecraft broke from the traditions of the picture-frame stage, using open sets, symbolic designs, and lighting to create mood and setting. This stagecraft also developed and even expanded the use of exciting new stage machinery, such as the revolving stage. Gordon Craig and Adolphe Appia were the main theorists of the new stagecraft, but from a practical point of view it was Reinhardt who was most responsible for its success. Putting the theories of Craig and Appia into practice, he was, because of his reputation, able to make these innovations accepted on a wide scale. Finally, in 1912, Reinhardt brought the new stagecraft to America.

By 1912 Reinhardt had begun to develop the concept of an ideal theatre. His vision grew out of the experience of staging plays in circuses and was surprisingly similar to an ideal set down by Gordon Craig. Essentially, Reinhardt envisioned a "Theatre of the Five Thousand"—a vast temple of theatrical art. By the end of World War I, Reinhardt was able to turn this dream into reality.

In 1919, Reinhardt acquired Berlin's Circus Schumann and converted it into the Grosses Schauspielhaus, a theatre not for the desired five thousand, but at least for somewhat over three thousand. It contained a horseshoe-shaped audience area, a Greek-style orchestra, and a fully equipped deep stage. The audience seating was steeply raked far up and away from the stage, with stadiumlike tunnels providing entrances for the audience and the actors. Unfortunately the cost of conversion and the limitations imposed by the structure itself led to many compromises. The result was an inner stage that was not fully usable, lighting that was not flexible enough, and a seating capacity that was far less than had been desired.

Reinhardt always tended toward spectacle as his major form, a tendency which ultimately led to his circus productions. The Grosses Schauspeilhaus provided him with a perfect arena for spectacle, but very few plays are spectacular from beginning to end; intimate scenes failed in its vastness. Thus, less than three years after its opening Reinhardt withdrew from the first failure of his career and returned to Austria.

Back in Salzburg, Reinhardt began anew his attempt to revolutionize theatre architecture. The Salzburg Festspielhaus, unlike the Grosses Schauspielhaus, was designed from the ground up to avoid the problems Reinhardt had experienced with the converted circus. The orchestra and stage were inte-

A drawing of the converted ballroom of Maria Theresa's palace in which Reinhardt produced for one year. This drawing, by Robert Edmond Jones, shows a scene from *The Marriage of Figaro.*

grated and audience sight lines better arranged. The house was designed with a moveable ceiling which could be lowered to cut the seating capacity from four thousand to fifteen hundred, thus creating the possibility for spectacle and intimate drama within the same house. Unfortunately, the financial situation in postwar Germany was so bad that the theatre was designed but never built.

In 1922 Reinhardt took the position of director at the Redoutensaal, an intimate theatre located in the ballroom of Maria Theresa's palace in Vienna. Here, on a small stage built at one end of the ballroom, before minimal settings, he produced plays by Gozzi, Goethe, Calderón, and Molière. These productions were quite successful, but Reinhardt left after only one season, probably due to the fact that he found the theatre too limiting. Returning to New York in 1924, Reinhardt put on his acclaimed production of *The Miracle.* For this spectacular production, Norman Bel Geddes turned the Century Theatre into a cathedral, through which the actors moved to create in pantomime the story of Sister Beatrice. Reinhardt then returned to Germany, working in the capacity of producer-director and establishing a small empire that included Berlin, Vienna, and Salzburg.

Reinhardt left Germany in 1933, and came, by way of Italy and England, to the United States, where he settled in Hollywood. At first he worked only as a consultant to the studios, but eventually he produced *A Midsummer Night's Dream* at the Hollywood Bowl and later turned it into a film. The critics tended to find this film unsuccessful, due to Reinhardt's lack of understanding of film techniques, but now, more than forty years later, the film holds up rather well, confounding the critics and proving that perhaps Reinhardt understood film better than his detractors. He remained in America until his death in New York in 1943.

LEOPOLD JESSNER: From 1919, the year in which he became director of the State Theatre in Berlin, Leopold Jessner (1878-1948) aroused audiences with his startling productions. He had previously worked in Hamburg and Königsberg, but it was in Berlin where he won his international reputation. With his designers, Emil Perchan and Cesar Klein, he did away with the trappings of traditional representational theatre, substituting instead flights of stairs, symbolic set pieces, and new and exciting concepts of costuming and lighting.

In the 1920s Leopold Jessner seemed, in his forceful theatricality, destined to succeed Reinhardt. But Jessner insisted on separating his art from what he called the "impressionism" of Reinhardt and the realism of the Meiningen-Brahm tradition. Instead, he offered a concentrated, intense, symbolic theatre rather than the detailed but often meaningless verisimilitude of the realists, or the spectacular illusions of Reinhardt. He strongly believed that theatre, which combines within itself the essence of all the arts, can express with urgency and immediacy the whole modern search for meaning and purpose. To that end he sought new theatrical forms to express contemporary realities. He insisted that new forms in theatre could be created by the insistence and determination of the *regisseur,* who had the artistic right to revise and rearrange each script in accordance with his own interpretation.

The actual practices of symbolistic theatre are outlined in Jessner's commentary on his most famous production, *Richard III.* The play was designed so that all the major action took place on an enormous stairway (*Jessnertreppen*) that occupied the whole center of the stage. Richard's bloody rise to power was symbolized by blood-red costumes and crimson light; however, as Richmond's forces began to succeed, the costumes and light both changed to white.

Jessner's concept of stage space was similar to that of his contemporary, Alexander Tairov, in that Jessner wanted to provide movement that was vertical as well as horizontal by using steps and platforms. This, he felt, would provide three dimensions—length, depth, and *height.* Jessner's placing and movement of actors about these forms also resembled Tairov's, in that both sought to establish dimension and symbolic meaning through the use of form. Jessner also tried to express emotional and psychological relationships by use of gesture rather than words. Jessner was, throughout his career, deeply concerned with generating "intensity" of expression—sometimes, especially when he was staging poetic drama, at the expense of beauty. To achieve this

Leopold Jessner's architectural setting for *Richard III* featured the steps which the director made famous. (From Julius Bab, *Das Theater der Gegenwart*, Berlin, 1928)

intensity, Jessner demanded that his settings support the verbal expression in a functional way. That is, it had to have symbolic value but it also had to be playable. The actual structure of the set on which the actor performed, Jessner believed, determined the rhythm of the actor's movement, and the rhythm of movement governed its intensity.

Jessner's main contributions to theatre were his symbolic sets, his expressive lighting, his simplified, intense performances, and his determination that theatre should exceed the restrictions of the representational tradition.

In recent years, the most important contribution to world theatre to come out of northern Europe has been made by Poland—specifically by the director and theorist Jerzy Grotowski.

JERZY GROTOWSKI: Jerzy Grotowski, (1933-) along with Ludwik Flaszen, the group's literary advisor, founded the Polish Laboratory Theatre (The Laboratory Theatre of the Institute of Actors Research) sometime prior to 1959 in Opole, Poland. He was searching for new truths about theatre, and his followers, few but devoted, willingly involved themselves in a laboratory situation in which the results of each theatrical experiment would be analyzed and codified into a philosophy. It took nearly five years for this early experimentation in acting to be completed and objectified into a program—"Actor Training, 1959-1962"—and nearly eight years for the resulting disciplines of the Laboratory to escape from behind the iron curtain into the rest of western Europe. Peter Brook, then director of England's Royal Shakespeare Company, invited Grotowski and his group to England in 1967, and the results were far-reaching indeed. The Western world was shocked (and amazed) to realize that such "radical" ideas could be the result of a small theatre group working in conservative and Communist Poland. Peter Brook overcame his shock, if not his amazement, praising Grotowski for being unique in the sense that no one since Stanislavsky had investigated the nature of acting so completely, with such depth and thoroughness.

Europe and especially the British were not quite so ready to accept Brook's accolades about the Laboratory Theatre, and the United States was even less so; therefore, it was a venture that took some courage when, in 1969, Grotowski inevitably crossed the Atlantic to America. Generally speaking, our theatre-going audience was already having difficulty in understanding the philosophies about visceral theatre that were then being explored by Megan Terry, Sam Shepard, Jean-Claude van Itallie, Maria Irene Fornes, and others. For that reason it was small wonder that the work of this group (which performed only in Polish) was loudly praised by a few Americans and as roundly condemned by a much larger number.

Peter Brook, in his video-taped introduction to a film of the Laboratory production of *Akropolis*, analyzed Grotowski's techniques for American audiences. Brook felt that the barrier of language communication (the actors speaking only in Polish) should present no problems to the viewers; that the discipline of the performers would form in the audience an understanding of life's rhythms, ever-shifting but under perfect control. The visceral response to these rhythms is communicated almost musically to the audience, in much the same way that jazz communicates, and this leads to a visceral response to and contact with the performers.

The text—that is, the verbally meaningful material delivered in a language that is foreign to most American audiences—is delivered through ritual rhythms and discipline. Grotowski's players commit their extreme acts before witnesses (audience) and, like a man who commits suicide by jumping from a building after a crowd has gathered, they *need* those witnesses but do not necessarily need to communicate with them. The Polish Laboratory Theatre has little to do with communication in any traditional sense. This concept is indeed a radical one in terms of theatrical history; theatre has always existed to communicate. For the Laboratory, however, the audience does not have to understand technically, or be moved to action, in order to perform the function of witness.

The Laboratory's approach to theatre, basically, attempts to accomplish three primary things: (1) to evolve a definition of that which is quite distinctly the craft of theatre, not of other arts; (2) to provide performers with an acting technique that is based on discipline and frees the body and mind completely; and (3) to arrive at an understanding of the actor-audience relationship.

Grotowski's collection of writings on theatre is titled *Towards a Poor Theatre* (1968), and it is an appropriate title because, according to Grotowski, that is the one thing that theatre can be and film and television cannot—*poor*. Theatre, like the art of acting, must be stripped of all that is not essential to it. There must be no illusionary and exotic lighting effects. With a stationary source of raw light, the actor can work deliberately with shadows and bright spots. There must be no makeup. The actor transforms himself in front of the audience, using only his highly trained body and his craft. With proper muscle control, an actor can create a "facial mask" that is not a trick of makeup. There must be no costuming. Since costume has no autonomous value in itself, it, like everything else in theatre, can be created by the actor, who, if he has proper control, can show himself to be wearing any desired costume, even if he is in fact dressed only in a loincloth. There can be no realistic settings or set pieces. By controlled use of gesture, the actor can turn anything or nothing into that which he wishes an audience to perceive. There must be no music other than that which the actors create. The total performance, in this way, becomes the music of the ensemble, and all sound created by the ensemble is music. These, essentially, are the fundamentals of Grotowski's "poor theatre."

The Laboratory approach to acting has been, of course, modified by experimentation through the years, but some generalizations can be made. First, it must be clearly understood that the heart of Grotowski's theatre is the personal and scenic technique of the actor. For Grotowski an actor cannot be taught a technique. The approach must be strictly negative, in which the actor's resistance as an organism to a "psychic process" is eliminated. This process, dubbed by Grotowski the *via negativa*, eradicates the actor's mental, psychological, and physical blocks, so that there is no time lapse between impulse and body reaction. In Grotowski's system impulse is reaction, and what the spectator sees is only a series of visible impulses. Through the continuous uninterrupted performance of a set of highly demanding (both physically and mentally) exercises, the actor develops "involuntary" skills; that is, he or she does not "want to do something" but becomes incapable of not doing it, which is the exact opposite of theatre's traditional "bag of tricks." All of the Laboratory's exercises and the resulting involuntary processes work toward creating a formal articulation and disciplined structuring of a role. Gesture, within these exercises, becomes an uncommon and extremely disciplined *sign*, which is the Laboratory's basic unit of expression. In this sense, technique leads to theory, and not the other way around, as is so often the case. Grotowski's productions do not lead to an audience awareness, but are products of the actor's awareness, which is transmitted through a technique that eliminates all of the traditional blocks.

To mention briefly the third accomplishment of the Laboratory—examination of the actor-audience relationship—it must be pointed out that Grotowski completely eliminates the stage-auditorium physical plant in order to rearrange the theatre. That is done in a manner that enables the creation of an actor-audience relationship that is distinctive and appropriate to each individual production. Frequently caught up in the action of the play, not by choice but through this special physical arrangement, spectators may find themselves in the acting area, where they also begin to play a part in the

Grotowski's production of *The Constant Prince* at the Laboratory Theatre.

performance. But they had best understand the "mystery" before taking part in the work. Most Grotowski audiences prefer to remain witnesses. The physical arrangement does not always permit action to take place among the spectators. In one production, Grotowski found it stimulating to seat the audience above the action and behind a high fence, through and over which they could surreptitiously peep at the work taking place.

The roots of Grotowski's theatre obviously lie deeply within such reasonably traditional theatrical approaches as mime, Stanislavsky, Noh theatre, Brecht, Artaud, and Indian traditional drama, but it should also be understood that constant experimentation and unification has bred a totally new approach that seems to delve deeper into the basic beliefs of those European and Eastern models through an attempt to logically combine them. Looking backward at sources, however, does not clearly define Grotowski's impact upon today's theatre. Many young companies, experimenting with his exercises, are finding them useful in the development of actor discipline and ensemble unity. It is also interesting to note Grotowski's obvious influence on such older artists as the "new" Jean-Louis Barrault, who, in an interview of several years ago, spoke about the necessity for the actor to free his mind and body completely and to revel in this newfound freedom.

There is, today, a tide of antitheatre (seemingly ebbing) that utilizes some of Grotowski's methods and philosophies. The ultimate success of this new antitheatre movement will, however, be decided not by the needs of its audience but by the talent and discipline exercised by the ensembles in approaching their own individual goals.

Finally, the experimental qualities of Grotowski's productions often tend to obscure the fact that, in terms of the drama it elects to play, the Laboratory leans a bit toward the conservative, with a repertoire that includes Byron's *Cain*, Kalidasa's *Shakuntala*, Calderón's *The Constant Prince*, Marlowe's *Doctor Faustus*, and Shakespeare's *Hamlet*. It is this last aspect, this marriage of contemporary techniques and approaches to the great works of drama, that makes Grotowski and his Polish Laboratory Theatre so interesting and so important.

Russia

The twentieth century really begins, in Russia, after the Revolution of 1917. Before that, Gorky, Chekhov, and Leonid Andreyev were the only major voices of the theatre and they were, essentially, a holdover from the previous century. The Imperial Theatres still held a virtual monopoly on major theatrical production. All this came to an end in 1917, and for ten years, before the Soviet government began to demand artistic obedience to political credo, the arts flourished in Russia.

Leon Bakst's design for a scene from Diaghilev's Ballets Russes production of the opera, *Boris Godounoff*, Paris, 1913. (From *Comédie Illustré*, Paris, 1913)

When Lenin died in 1924, power passed to Joseph Stalin, who immediately set about his plan to modernize Russia. This meant not only industrialization, but an attempt to make all components of the state serve the political ends Stalin had decreed. After the Revolution the Russians had placed theatre under the control of the Commissar of Education, partly to make it serve propagandistic ends, but also, partly, to assure that this art form, which had for so long been available only to the wealthy, would now serve the proletariat. However, given Stalin's objectives, theatre could no longer be responsible only to itself. In 1927 a program was initiated to train and place party members in positions of theatre management. "Artistic Councils" were set up in major theatres and given substantial power to control repertory, artistic style, and management policy.

These new policies contributed much to the suppression of Russian experimental theatres. Again the major houses came to the fore—the Alexandrinsky, the Maly (renamed the State Academic Pushkin Theatre) and the Moscow Art Theatre (renamed the House of Gorky in 1932)—and these theatres concentrated on a formalized, traditional realism. The death knell of Soviet theatre was sounded in 1939 when Vsevolod Meyerhold made his last public appearance for a speech before the First All Union Congress of Directors. Admitting that he had erred against proletarian theatre, he nevertheless added that "the pitiful and wretched thing called socialist realism has nothing in common with art." He went on to tell the directors that though Russia once had the best theatres in the world, "in hunting formalism you have eliminated art." Shortly after giving this speech he was arrested for "offenses against the state" and disappeared, never to be heard from again.

TWENTIETH CENTURY RUSSIAN DRAMA

Chekhov died early in the century, but Gorky survived him, lived on into the Soviet regime, and eventually became the most honored of the Soviet dramatists. The Moscow Art Theatre was renamed for him and he was accorded the questionable honor of inventing "socialist realism." The third member of this early group, Leonid Nikolaivich Andreyev (1871-1919), began as a realist but ended as a symbolist, unknown in western Europe and without honor in his own country.

Andreyev graduated from the Moscow and St. Petersburg universities with a degree in law, but instead of practicing he became a journalist on a Moscow newspaper. His literary aspirations began, as did Chekhov's, with the short story and in 1897 one of his stories caught the eye of Gorky, who had already achieved fame and who called this beginning writer to the attention of Russian literary circles.

In his early period Andreyev was a supporter of the revolutionary movement in Russia, and his realistic plays express proletarian support. However, his enthusiasm gradually waned and after the October Revolution he emigrated to Finland and remained there until his death. Andreyev's plays, which deal primarily with the chaos and deterioration that existed between the revolutions of 1905 and 1917, fall into two distinct groups—realistic and symbolic. The symbolic plays are substantially the best, especially *K zvezdam* (*To the Stars*, 1906), *Zhizn cheloveka* (*The Life of Man*, 1906), and *Milye prizraki* (*Cherished Ghosts*, 1916).

Andreyev was deeply influenced by Chekhov, Tolstoy, Dostoevski, and Maeterlinck, but he was never a member of any specific literary movement. Neither did he join any political or religious groups. His *Life of Man* was attacked with equal vigor by the Russian Church for blasphemy and the Communist Party for petit-bourgeois negativism. As a result he long remained a nonperson in Soviet Russia, and it is only in recent years that his genius has been recognized, not only in Russia but also in western Europe and the United States.

In the early years of the Soviet regime there was an artistic freedom that had not, to that point, been experienced in Russia. Anatole Lunacharsky (1875-1932), the first Commissar of Education and thus the supervisor of dramatic production, encouraged experimentation. Along with the traditional realism that now existed merely to sing the praises of the Revolution, there were pageant dramas, symbolic plays, and "futurist" plays, primarily by the poet and playwright Vladimir Mayakovsky (1893-1930).

Meyerhold's 1934 production of Mayakovsky's comedy, *The Bug*. (From *Soviet Travel*, Moscow, 1934)

Mayakovsky was born in Georgia, the son of a forester, and he joined the Communist Party in 1908 at the age of fourteen. He was arrested several times for revolutionary activities and was finally expelled from the School of Painting in which he had been enrolled. Encouraged by David Burliuk and Gorky to take up writing, he completed his first play in 1913. It was a forgettable effort, but Mayakovsky produced it and acted in it and was encouraged enough by its reception to complete, in 1918, the first Soviet play, *Misteriya-Buff* (*Mystery-Bouffe*), which sought to break down all barriers between the actors and the audience and show the triumph of revolutionary communism throughout the world. In 1929 he wrote *Klop* (*The Bedbug*), which tells of a future world in which only one prerevolutionary human being and one prerevolutionary bedbug manage to survive the revolution. Their attempts to fit into the new Communistic society provide satiric comment on all nonrevolutionary activity. In 1930, the final year of his life, he completed *Banya* (*The Bath House*), which, similar to *The Bedbug*, satirized the remaining elements of Russian prerevolutionary life. On April 14 of that year Mayakovsky committed suicide.

The growing Communist Party control exercised over theatrical events, the purges of the middle 1930s, and World War II conspired to put an end to significant Soviet drama. Within Russia itself certain plays from the early period are much admired today, such as *Bronepoyezd 14-69* (*Armored Train 14-69*, 1922) by Vsevolod Ivanov (1895-1963), *Vragi* (*Enemies*, 1927) by Boris Lavrenyov (1892-1959), *Lyubov Yarovaya* (1926) by Konstantin Trenyov (1884-1945), and *Aristokraty* (*Aristocrats*, 1934) by Nikolai Pogodin (1900-62). In more recent years a few fine plays have come from such Soviet writers as Alexei Arbuzov (1908-). He wrote *Tanya* (1938), *Gorod na zare* (*City at Dawn*, 1940), *Gody stranstvy* (*Years of Wandering*, 1953), and in 1960 his finest work, *Irkutskaya istoryia* (*It Happened in Irkutsk*). This play adheres faithfully to the ideals of socialist realism, but is mildly experimental in its use of chorus and narration to go beyond literal reality.

THE DIRECTOR

If twentieth century Russia has failed to produce many internationally acclaimed playwrights, it has provided the world with a crop of talented and influential directors. One of the earliest and most inventive, and probably the most articulate opponent of realism was Nikolai Evreinov (1879-1953), who explained his artistic views in two works: *The Theatre of the Soul* (1909) and *Theatre for Oneself* (1915). He attacked the whole concept of theatrical realism, pointing out that theatre is an artificial medium at best. Theatre grows, he said, out of two basic forces—the desire for self-expression and the mimetic instinct. The second of these two forces, the human need for acting and impersonation, he found to be the very foundation of theatrical activity. Given this belief, Evreinov logically concluded that theatre should clearly be "play acting"; it should not imitate life but be clearly an exaggeration of life. It should be highly stylized, as a puppet show is stylized. Carrying this one step further, he decided that the theatrical ideal could be realized only when actors could be replaced by perfect puppets. Because this ideal seemed to be unattainable, Evreinov sought the next best thing—actors who were trained like athletes to have perfect control over their bodies. This was, he felt, far more important than teaching them to "live" or "feel" or even to understand roles.

Putting his ideals into practice he produced two essentially pantomime dramas: *The School of Stars* and *The Eternal Dancer*. He also directed symbolist plays, such as Fyodor Sologub's (1863-1927) *Zolozhniki zhizni* (*The Hostages of Life*), *Nochnye plyaski* (*Nocturnal Dances*), and *Melky bes* (*The Little Demon*). In 1919, using 8000 soldiers, sailors, and workers, Evreinov produced a mass spectacle, titled *The Taking of the Winter Palace*, on the actual site of the historical event. This was, he believed, appropriate in that its importance was not in dialogue but in the revolutionary actions of the masses.

As a playwright Evreinov's influence was negligible, but as a director and theorist he directly affected the work of such talented followers as Alexander Tairov and Vsevolod Meyerhold.

KONSTANTIN STANISLAVSKY: Konstantin Sergeivich Stanislavsky (really Alexeyev, 1863-1938), whose theories are often corrupted by his followers, was a brilliant theatrician. He believed that theatre should be entertaining, should develop people's taste, and should raise the level of culture. Serving such a theatre, he felt, should be an actor's main objective. To meet these ends, Stanislavsky developed a system emphasizing the actor's inner technique. The historical significance of Stanislavsky lies in his discovery of "laws" governing an actor's creativity and the development of his theory of physical action.

Stanislavsky was born in Moscow in 1863, and at the age of ten made his debut on his family's stage in an amateur show. Always literate and highly cultured, in 1888 he helped to organize the Society of Art and Literature, and he also created a drama company of amateur actors who became associated with it. Three years later he undertook his first important independent directing work—Leo Tolstoy's *Plody prosvescheniya* (*The Fruits of Enlightenment*). In 1897, at the age of thirty-four, he encountered Vladimir Nemirovich-Danchenko, and the result of this encounter was their decision to found a theatre company. The company became the Moscow Art Theatre, and in 1898 it opened with a series of plays, one of which was Anton Chekhov's *The Seagull*, as directed by Stanislavsky himself. The play was a great success and heralded not only the true birth of the Russian theatre but also that of a great playwright. In the early 1900s Stanislavsky began formulating his theories on the actor's creativity, later to be known as the Stanislavsky System. In 1912 he opened the First Studio and tried out some of his ideas on his students. In 1918 he became head of the Bolshoi Theatre's Opera Studio. Here he continued to develop his system by using various exercises, by developing the feeling of rhythm not only in movement but in inner sensations, and also by studying the art of singers to include in his theories of acting. In 1923 the Moscow Art Theatre toured the United States and American audiences were impressed with the realism, ensemble acting, and overall technique of the players. While in the United States he picked up some American disciples. In 1928, because of illness, Stanislavsky abandoned acting to concentrate on directing and on

A scene from Stanislavsky's production of Gorky's *The Lower Depths*. (New York City Public Library)

teaching young actors. Until his death in 1938, he continued to make new discoveries in the method of creating a role and, of course, a performance.

The Stanislavsky System of acting, as set forth in *My Life in Art* (1924), *An Actor Prepares* (1926), *Stanislavsky Rehearses "Othello"* (1948), and *Building a Character* (1950), is far too complex to deal with simply, but in its essence it is primarily concerned with the understanding and use of physical actions. Stanislavsky felt that the subconscious—that uncontrolled complex of emotions that seethes below the conscious level—is not altogether unreachable. He tried to find a key to turn on this inner mechanism, a conscious means to reach and make use of the subconscious. He finally came up with a method that uses an understanding of physical actions. He stated that there is always a relationship between physical action and psychological aim. That is, every psychological aim is expressed physically (through words or movement or posture—it is with our bodies that we transmit to others our inner experiences), and conversely every physical movement has its psychological aim. Stanislavsky felt that if actors understand the inner emotions and desires (or "needs" or "wants") of the character they are playing then what they do physically on stage (movement, talking, reaction) will be truthful. To define an action, he said, an active verb should be used, expressing precisely and logically the end that the actor wants to achieve. The actors must remember that their reason for being on stage is to convey what they do and why they do it at a given moment. Knowing their actions helps actors to be truthful and aids in building a logical, consecutive performance, and also helps them to assimilate their roles.

Stanislavsky did not want his system to be considered an end in itself, but simply as a means to an end. It suggests a way of finding and using the actor's personal truth in the creation of a fictional stage character.

VSEVOLOD EMILIEVITCH MEYERHOLD: Vsevolod Meyerhold (1874-c. 1940), the eighth child of a German vodka distiller, was born thirty-five miles southeast of Moscow in the small village of Penza. Sixty-five years later, in 1939, Meyerhold made a futile speech against the state-ordained school of social realism. He was arrested for offenses against the state and disappeared. Two weeks later his wife was brutally murdered. Meyerhold was reported to be alive in Siberia, where he was said to have died in 1942. In the 1961 edition of *Teatralnaya entsiklopediya*, however, his death is said to have occurred on February 2, 1940. The cause of death is not mentioned.

Meyerhold entered Moscow University to study law, but in his second year he was admitted to the Moscow Philharmonic Society's drama school. There he studied under Vladimir Nemirovich-Danchenko, and in the final examinations of February-March, 1898, Meyerhold received one of the only two silver medals for acting given by the Society that year. In 1898, when Stanislavsky and Nemirovich-Danchenko formed the Moscow Art Theatre, Meyerhold was invited to join. In that initial year he acted in three-quarters of the group's productions, his most celebrated role being that of Konstantin Treplev in the historic premiére of Chekhov's *The Seagull*.

During the next four years Meyerhold played eighteen roles, ranging from character to juvenile, and he also acted as assistant director. However, when the theatre became a joint stock company in 1902, Meyerhold was not among the shareholders. Many thought that this was an attempt to force the actor out of the company due to his angular, grotesque style of acting, which seemed not to blend with the naturalism of the Stanislavsky-trained performers. He was increasingly assigned smaller roles and this, coupled with his own desire to work as an independent director, caused him to leave Moscow with a colleague, Alexander Kosheverov, and assemble a new group in Kherson, the Ukraine.

In their first season the company presented *The Seagull, Three Sisters, Uncle Vanya*, and plays by Ibsen and Hauptmann. In these productions Meyerhold was still following the method of Stanislavsky. However, in his second season Meyerhold turned to the symbolism of Maeterlinck and Stanislav Przybszewski (1868-1927). His production of Przybszewski's *Snieg* (*Snow*, December 19, 1903) was Meyerhold's first vague attempt at nonrepresentational staging. Reactions to the season were mixed, but Meyerhold's reputation began to grow, helped along by the company's literary manager, the poet Alexei Reinizov, who had connections with the influential Moscow symbolist periodical *Vesy*.

In the meantime, Stanislavsky had reached a dead end, trying to produce the new abstract dramas within his own realistic conventions. In 1905, he asked Meyerhold to open an experimental studio. The resulting production of Maeterlinck's *The Death of Tartagiles* was highly successful, but Meyerhold and Stanislavsky could not agree on how to use actors and Stanislavsky found the uprising of October 1905, which closed most theatres, sufficient cause to close the doors of Meyerhold's studio. Meyerhold and Stanislavsky cautiously disagreed for the next thirty-three years. Then, at Stanislavsky's invitation,

A scene from Meyerhold's 1922 production of *The Magnificent Cuckold*, done in constructivist style. (From *Soviet Travel*, Moscow, 1934)

they joined forces for a production of *Rigoletto*—which was the last joint production for both men.

The work done in the studio had never been seen by the general public, but Meyerhold's reputation had grown enough so that Vera Komissarzhevskaya (1864-1910), the well-known actress-manager, decided to entrust her theatre to the renegade. The next two seasons (1906-1907) were a constant battle between the actress and the young director. An impressionistic *Hedda Gabler* was the partnership's first production, but it was Andreyev's *Life of Man* and Alexander Blok's *Balaganchik* (*Puppet Booth*) which became the most famous productions of their collaboration.

Two years later Meyerhold and Komissarzhevskaya were still doing battle. Meyerhold felt that the theatre was mainly the province of the director, and Komissarzhevskaya, unwilling to become Meyerhold's puppet, requested him to leave. Meyerhold was not long out of work. V. A. Teliakovsky, director of the Imperial Theatres and the most influential theatre person in Russia, heard that Meyerhold was at liberty and appointed him as one of the Imperial Theatres' director-producers. This mutual agreement indicated Meyerhold's desire to retreat from his extreme position on the supremacy of the director and also the desire of the Imperial Theatres to inject vitality into their highly traditional productions. The result of this accommodation was productions that had increased flamboyance, spectacle, and theatricalism, and less cerebral symbolism. Meyerhold gradually came under the influence of the circus and music hall, with the result that he never again produced Maeterlinck or Hauptmann, and did not stage Ibsen for ten years. His chief concern seemed to be retreat from a literary style and an emphasis on theatrics, which resulted in a far greater range of dramatic literature.

Meyerhold worked as drama director at the Alexandrinsky, as opera director at the Marinsky, and under the comic pseudonym of Doctor Dappertluto he staged private productions, but in all cases he aimed to create new theatrical forms and new approaches to nonrealistic, stylized art. New approaches required new actors, and Meyerhold set about to create them. The next nine years were spent in experimentation, and the result was a *cabotin* (troubadour, minstrel, mime, histrione, juggler) of the twentieth century.

In 1917 the Bolsheviks were victorious and in 1918 Meyerhold joined the Party. He retained his position in the former Imperial Theatre and became instructor of production techniques in Petrograd, where he was appointed Deputy Commissar of the Theatrical Department of the Commissariat for Education. It was in Petrograd, in 1918, that Meyerhold produced the first Soviet play, Mayakovsky's *Mystery-Bouffe*.

In May 1919 Meyerhold entered a sanatorium in Yalta for treatment of tuberculosis. Later in the same year he was appointed chief of theatre for the Soviet Union. He immediately assumed editorship of *The Theatre Herald* and turned it into a propaganda organ to turn out polemics "on behalf of the prole-

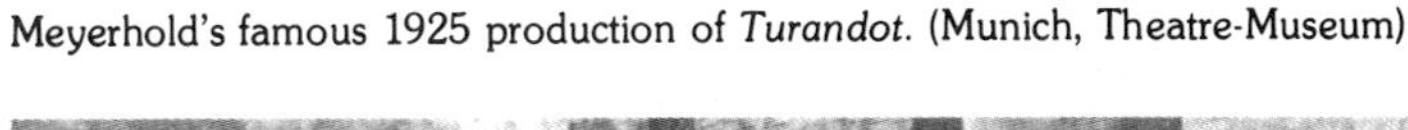

Meyerhold's famous 1925 production of *Turandot*. (Munich, Theatre-Museum)

tarian, provincial, non-professional and Red Army Theatres." The "academic theatres" which had received special support as repositories of "Russian theatrical tradition," soon came under his attack. The Bolshoi, Maly, Moscow Art Theatre and its studios, Tairov's Kamerny Theatre, and the Moscow Children's Theatre were especially singled out because of their conservative repertoires and anachronistic styles.

Lunacharvsky was deeply troubled by Meyerhold's attack on the academic theatres and in retaliation put those of Petrograd and Moscow directly under the Commissariat for Education. With his theatrical power severely reduced, Meyerhold resigned his position.

In 1921 Meyerhold was appointed Director of the State Higher Theatre Workshop in Moscow and began experimenting with "biomechanics," a series of exercises superficially resembling the time-and-motion studies of Frederick Winslow Taylor, an American, and his Russian disciple Gastev. This superficial resemblance was exploited by Meyerhold to encourage belief that his system was in tune with the machine age. His early experiments were clearly failures, but eventually the system became workable and was used for the physical training of actors in all Soviet drama schools.

Meyerhold began to leave political theatre behind in his search for aesthetic theatre. He became an experimenter—a seeker of methods and modes to fit the new century. He had actually begun these experiments in his Doctor Dappertluto period. He felt true theatre existed in his earlier concept of the *cabotin* (the strolling player), a master of technical virtuosity, a dancer, juggler, clown, singer, musician, and actor who, to Meyerhold, was the essence of theatre. Only the *cabotin*, he reasoned, could save Russian theatre from becoming the slave of literature.

Meyerhold's developing concept of theatre, which was based on the *commedia dell'arte* and the *cabotin*, led to biomechanics and scenic constructivism. Biomechanics, which was a method directly opposed to that of Stanislavsky, was based on the belief that the actor's special talent was the ability to react creatively to external stimuli. It seemed to many critics that Meyerhold was creating automatons, or puppets to dance on the director's strings, but he believed he was merely creating a performer who was physically more highly disciplined than the traditional actor—who was a dynamic representation of the "new Soviet man."

Constructivism was another aspect of Meyerhold's experiments, even though he put less emphasis on it than on his theory of biomechanics. Constructivist art had first been used by Vladmir Tatlin's "Relief Construction" of 1914. Usually, however, it is dated as beginning in 1917 when Tatlin decorated Moscow's Cafe Pittoresque. Meyerhold, in 1921, had a stage designed in terms of what he had seen at a constructivist exhibition. It was in this fashion that he produced Fernand Crommelynck's (1885-1970) *Le cocu magnifique* (*The Magnificent Cuckold*, 1922) and *Tarlekin's Death* (1922). The designs and even the concepts were essentially those of graphic artists rather than Meyerhold, but he created an atmosphere receptive to such new and startling ideas.

Another reason for Meyerhold's eager embrace of constructivism was that it was inexpensive. His theatre was poor and virtue was created out of necessity. For Meyerhold, biomechanics and constructivism were not ends in

Sketch of a constructivist set model for the Meyerhold production of Ostrovsky's *The Forest.*

themselves. He thought of them as freeing devices, designed to help both actor and audience become detached from the traditional reality of the characters and their environment. He was more interested in the "how" of things than in the "why," which made his theatre the Russian model of comedy and satire.

TAIROV: Alexander Jakovlevich Kornblit (1874-1954), who took the stage name of Tairov, was born in Romny, in the district of Poltava. The son of a local schoolteacher, he was exposed to the arts from early childhood, and his interest in the theatre stemmed from having seen a performance of *Faust* when he was still a schoolboy. While attending the gymnasium in Kiev, Tairov fed his love of the theatre by constant attendance at the city opera house. In 1904 he was accepted as a law student at the University of Kiev, but by this time his love for the theatre had become an uncontrollable passion, and in the following year he joined a company formed by Michail Borodai. With this company he played Lysander in *A Midsummer Night's Dream* and the Burgomeister in Hauptmann's *The Assumption of Hannele,* and then moved to St. Petersburg to join the resident company at the newly formed theatre of Vera Komissarzhevskaya. There he was deeply influenced by Meyerhold, who directed him in Maeterlinck's *Socur Béatrice* (*Sister Beatrice*) and Blok's *Puppet Booth.*

By this time Tairov was no longer a stagestruck student but an intense and serious young artist. He watched the growing social revolution and anticipated an equivalent artistic revolution. For a time it seemed that his anticipation would be fulfilled. Symbolist drama and futurist drama seemed to be on the doorstep, and at the Komissarzhevskaya Theatre he was able to meet and work with such leading theatrical innovators as Meyerhold and Blok. However, by the end of the season he had become disillusioned. He felt that Meyerhold's principle of putting total power in the hands of the director was to rob the actors of their rightful place as creative artists. This ran counter to Tairov's vision of the theatrical future, and so he left the Komissarzhevskaya and joined the Mobile Theatre.

With the Mobile Theatre Tairov toured Russia for two years, beginning as an actor but soon getting his chance as director. By 1912 Tairov had thoroughly grounded himself as actor and director, and he had worked extensively in both realistic and stylized theatre. However, neither had satisfied him and so he left the stage—he thought forever—to practice law. This defection lasted less than a year, and 1913 found him in Moscow directing a pantomime, *The Veil of Pierrette,* for a new venture called the Free Theatre. It was here

A scene from Tairov's 1921 production of *Romeo and Juliet*, with setting and costumes designed by Alexandra Exter. (From Tairoff, *Das entfesselte Theatre*, Potsdam, 1923)

that Tairov found the kind of theatre for which he had been searching, and he called it "synthetic" theatre.

Tairov used the term "synthetic" for two reasons: first, his theatre would incorporate in one company all the talents usually associated separately with theatre, ballet, opera, circus, and music hall; and second, it would combine all the arts of spectacle (scenic design, costuming, and lighting) into a single unified expression. It would be a theatre that took the best from Meyerhold and Stanislavsky, while avoiding their excesses. Tairov did not consider this selective use of other director's methods to be imitative. The elements he borrowed were to be transformed by the process of fusion into a new, complete, "synthetic" theatre.

Tairov based his theory of theatre on the belief that there are two truths—the truth of life and the truth of art. He pointed out that occasionally they coincide, "but for the most part what is true in life is not true in art, and artistic truth rings false in life." The truth of art, at least on the stage, cannot be captured by empty forms, no matter how decorative or pleasing to the eye they may be, but only by forms which are devised from real, creative, theatrical emotion. These forms, he said, must express the emotion of the drama clearly and vividly.

One of Tairov's main interests was the place that literature should occupy in the theatre. He believed that, ideally, literature had no place in theatre—that the theatre was an art unto itself and should not merely pass literature on to audiences by way of actors. Tairov believed that, though he used literature as raw material, the theatre really should create its own scenarios, with the actors creating the dialogue extemporaneously.

Like his mentor, Meyerhold, Tairov believed that the actor's art should be conscious as should the audience's appreciation. Also like Meyerhold, Tairov believed that "gesture" was more important than "word." However, he considered Meyerhold's use of gesture to be merely decorative, in contrast to his own, which he believed to be a masterpiece of emotion. Tairov believed that emotional gesture, or perhaps more accurately, emotional form, was the key to theatrical creativity. Unlike Meyerhold, Tairov believed that in the ideal theatre the main creator must be the actor. Logically, then, if the actor is the heart of theatre art, it is necessary to construct around him or her a setting which emphasizes the actor, supporting graphically the emotional material expressed by the actor through voice, movement, and gesture.

In 1914 in Moscow Tairov founded the Kamerny Theatre as an expression of his opposition to the realistic technique of Stanislavsky's Moscow Art Theatre. Tairov wanted to theatricalize the stage and began doing nonrealistic plays such as Oscar Wilde's *Salome*. Complementing such plays, Tairov insisted on abstract scenic design, and he made use of stylized gestures and movement so stylized that his productions were sometimes compared to the ballet.

Tairov's theatre was subjected to considerable criticism even before the Revolution. Its crusade against dramatic literature, its emphasis on form and feeling over (according to critics) intellectual content, and the importance placed on the unadorned body as the key to rhythmic design were all made the objects of intense criticism.

The American Conservatory Theatre's American premiere of *Valentin and Valentina* by Mikhail Roschin, one of Russia's leading contemporary dramatists. Directed by Edward Hastings.

After 1917 criticism of Tairov and his productions became so intense that Tairov wrote a pamphlet called *Proclamations of an Artist,* in which he declared that art is independent of politics and insisted that the political events after the Revolution had nothing to do with the Kamerny Theatre. Although Tairov's announcement had no immediate consequences, he was under pressure for the balance of his career to give up his experiments and produce plays with acceptable ideological content and a style more acceptable to the masses.

Tairov's only work on the subject of his theatrical experiments is *Notes of a Director.* It is a glowing, fervent memoire of the first six years of his attempt to create a new theatre in which he could practice a self-contained art, independent of dramatic literature, of the graphic arts, and of political ideology.

The Twentieth Century In England and Ireland

England

In a very real sense, the twentieth century in England begins in the 1890s, with such playwrights as George Bernard Shaw, Arthur

Wing Pinero, Henry Arthur Jones, and James Matthew Barrie, and such producers as J. T. Grein and his Independent Theatre. The Edwardian period ended in 1910, but even then there was no major change in the basic theatrical pattern. In fact, it was not until World War I that a major change took place in English theatre. During the war the actor-manager system that had been prominent for more than a hundred years was discarded in favor of producers, often independent, who sought long runs rather than repertory as the key to commercial success.

Between World Wars I and II old theatres took on new charges—the Old Vic became the house of English classics—and essentially new theatres, such as the Lyric, the Gate, and the Mercury, appeared to shoulder the responsibility of the newer drama. The little theatre movement, that had begun earlier in France and Germany, really got underway in England after World War I, with the assistance of the British Drama League (founded in 1919).

The Royal Shakespeare Theatre, Stratford-on-Avon, presents *A Midsummer Night's Dream*, 1977. Directed by John Barton.

Also during this period between wars a number of major performers took the stage—such as Sybil Thorndike, Edith Evans, John Gielgud, and the young Laurence Olivier, whose career began to blossom in the late 1930s. Few major playwrights appeared on the scene, but the ones who had begun their careers before World War I had unusual longevity and remained popular throughout the period.

After World War II, English theatre took the same turn that American theatre had taken many years earlier with the Theatrical Syndicate. By the late 1940s more than three quarters of all the theatres in England were controlled by "the Group," which also was a majority stockholder in H. M. Tennant, Ltd., the largest of the London producing organizations.

At first there was a dearth of good new plays. The old guard, except for Shaw, was gone and Shaw himself was long past the peak of his productivity. However, beginning in 1946 with Christopher Fry, a series of fine dramatists such as John Osborne, Brendan Behan, Shelagh Delaney, and Harold Pinter helped to enliven the British drama.

All in all, by the late 1950s English theatre had reestablished itself as one of the most vital in the Western World.

TWENTIETH CENTURY ENGLISH DRAMA

The twentieth century drama does indeed begin with George Bernard Shaw; his *Widowers' Houses*, begun in 1885 and produced in 1892, was the opening gun of the twentieth century drama. Produced at the Royalty Theatre by J. T. Grein as part of his Independent Theatre venture, it set a tone for drama that would stay with English theatre for the next fifty years.

GEORGE BERNARD SHAW: George Bernard Shaw (1856-1950) was born in the shabbily genteel precincts of 3 Upper Synge Street, the only son and youngest child of a tippling teetotaler, George Carr Shaw, and the rather cold and forbidding Lucinda Elizabeth Gurley. Shaw's father, doomed by a character of almost miraculous ineptitude, nonetheless was fortunate enough to inherit a corn mill, which maintained him for the rest of his life. His lack of business sense was only excelled by his ineffectuality in romance. His wife, the cold Lucinda, a lover of music and the owner of a mezzo-soprano voice of reasonable purity, became the student of George John Vandaleur Lee, whose "method" of singing was then in vogue. Mr. Lee, showing great aplomb, soon moved into the Shaw home where he ensconced himself as music master and resident philosopher.

The education of Shaw, in the formal sense, lasted only a short time, ending when he was fifteen. Perhaps it was just as well, for he looked on schools as places of incarceration. Shaw's education continued at home. Music was always present, but religion and philosophy took some hard knocks from his uncle Walter Gurley's dignified irreverence, his father's whimsical and usually unintentional paradoxes, and music master Lee's authoritarianism.

At fifteen Shaw became a junior clerk in the business of Mr. Uniacke Townshend. The next year his mother sold the Dublin house, left her husband,

Joan of Arc kneels before the Dauphin in this Ahmanson Theatre, Los Angeles, production of George Bernard Shaw's *Saint Joan*.

and moved to London to pursue a career as music instructor. Shaw did not see her for five years. His father was apparently happy to be well out of a miserable home situation.

Shaw rose to the position of cashier, but when placed under the authority of Mr. Townshend's untrained nephew he resigned and embarked for London and his mother's house. He was determined to become a writer and his next nine years, interrupted only by a brief and regretted position at the Edison Telephone Company, were spent in self-education at the London Museum and the National Gallery. Being able to accompany on the piano, and blessed with "a suit of evening clothes," he gained entrance to certain of London's musical and artistic circles. During this period he earned an average of one cent a day writing advertisements, verse, and music criticism, and his mother supported him, much to sister Lucy's ire.

In 1879, at the rate of five pages per day, he began a novel. It was appropriately entitled *Immaturity*, and was never published. His four subsequent novels were printed in socialist magazines, but were considered failures. Undaunted, Shaw soldiered on, becoming book reviewer for *The Pall Mall Gazette* (1885), art critic for *The World* (1886), music critic under the name Corno di Bassetto for *The Star* (1888), and Fabian socialist tract writer and orator (1889). In 1891 he championed Henrik Ibsen (and Shaw) in *The Quintessence of Ibsenism*, which he continued to enlarge until Ibsen's death.

This last work gave Shaw the opportunity to promulgate concepts which later would be central to his own work. In it he attacked "the policy of forcing individuals to act on the assumption that all ideals are real, and to recognize and accept such action as standard moral conduct, absolutely valid under all circumstances, contrary of any advocacy of it being discountenanced and punished as immoral." Shaw found this to be the essential of "idealism," and he thought it ridiculous. He put up against idealism his concept of realism, which he derived from Plato rather than Zola or Maupassant. The realist, he wrote, has no patience with the idealist who has, the realist feels, in hatred and shame, taken refuge in the illusion of ideals—a social conformity that is false.

He also dismissed the Golden Rule as poppycock, declaring with finality that the justification of conduct must be found in its effect on life not in its "conformity to any rule or ideal."

To Shaw the center of any play was the discussion, which had to be unreservedly didactic. This was the greatest test of the playwright's powers. He did not want mere fables untrammeled by morality, and he insisted that morality had nothing to do with the lurid "commonplaces" of the daily press. Nor, he felt, should plays be wrapped neatly around some splendid personality of the stage.

It was problems of conduct and character of a personal nature that Shaw wanted to present to the audience, and thus all the commonplaces of the box office had to be disregarded. The Shavian play was to be an argument of a case, with the drama arising from a conflict of unsettled ideals. Right or wrong, Shaw felt, should not be the issue. The interest should not be in the conflict, in the struggle between hero and villain, but rather in *who* is the hero and *who* is the villain.

For Shaw the spectators were to become the *dramatis personae* in a play which expounded upon their lives as real lives and not theatrical pretensions, with the play and discussion becoming "practically identical." The old stage trickery which induced interest in unreal people and improbable circumstances was to be "tossed into the dust bin."

It is essential to remember that Shaw was not merely a theorist who wrote plays. He was thoroughly grounded in the theatre in the most practical way; he had acted as an amateur. One of his more memorable moments on the boards was in the role of Krogstad in the first English performance of *A Doll's House*.

Although he had performed in the style of Ibsenesque naturalism, that mode of acting was not Shaw's ideal. It was not the drawing-room actor associated with Ibsen that he wanted for his plays. It was the classical actor he wanted for his work. Ristori, Salvini, and Barry Sullivan were his models. They had not learned to balance the tea-cup but they harkened back, in Shaw's mind, to Kemble and Siddons. He wanted players who could bring music to what he had written.

Barry Sullivan (1821-91) particularly influenced Shaw's thinking about the actor. As a young man Shaw had seen Sullivan and considered him a great actor. He was a player in the style of the eighteenth century, and it was in him that Shaw found the ancient line coming from Burbage through Betterton, Gar-

George Bernard Shaw's *You Never Can Tell* as produced by The Alley Theatre, Houston. Directed by Ted Follows.

rick, Kean, and Macready. Sullivan was an actor and proud of it. In Shakespeare, Shaw considered Sullivan equalled only by the actress, Ada Rehan (Crehan).

In his own productions, Shaw found his ideal in Sir Johnston Forbes-Robertson (1853-1937), whom he characterized as "the most natural actor of the age," and at the same time "classic" and "heroic." He wanted his actor to present a naturally heroic figure, which could be achieved by development of the actor's innate artistic sense. This could not be accomplished by the standard technical exercises, and thus the director must endeavor to stimulate "vigilant artistic sensitiveness" and awaken and cultivate the actor's "artistic conscience."

Shaw also directed, and in a letter to a friend he set down the principles of holding a rehearsal. At its core was "making the audience believe that real things were happening to real people." The director, Shaw felt, must be prepared for rehearsal in complete detail, which meant movement, business, position, and vocal delivery. No lines were to be learned until after the first week of rehearsal, then the "perfect" rehearsals (without books) should begin. From this point forward the director should move into the auditorium with his notebook.

Ultimately, Shaw's greatest contribution to drama was as a playwright. A complete list of his plays is unnecessary, and dates for original productions are difficult to establish because so many of the early plays were produced privately. However, *Widowers' Houses* (1892) is particularly important in that it began not only Shaw's career as dramatist but also a new wave in English drama that would, in time, destroy the Victorian traditions. It was not until Shaw joined forces with John Vedrenne, a business manager and public relations specialist, and Harley Granville-Barker, an up-and-coming young director, that his plays achieved real popularity. They produced eleven plays in repertory between 1904 and 1907: *Candida, John Bull's Other Island, How He Lied to Her Husband, You Never Can Tell, Man and Superman* (without act III, which was produced separately in 1907 as *Don Juan in Hell*), *Major Barbara, The Doctor's Dilemma, Arms and the Man, Captain Brassbound's Conversion, The Philanderer*, and *The Man of Destiny* (a one act). They also produced *The Devil's Disciple*, which had been seen in New York about 1897, and *Caesar and Cleopatra*, which had been performed in 1906 in Berlin. He wrote *Misalliance* in 1910, *Fanny's First Play* in 1911, and *Androcles and the Lion* in 1913. *Pygmalion* was first produced in Vienna in 1913, and *Heartbreak House* appeared in New York in 1920. *Back to Methuselah*, considered by Shaw to be his masterpiece, appeared in 1922 in New York, and *Saint Joan* was first produced in New York in 1923. In spite of Shaw's opinion, *Joan* is probably the most common critical choice as his best play. *The Apple Cart* in 1929 was followed by *Too True to be Good* in 1932, *Geneva* in 1938, and then Shaw's last memorable play, *In Good King Charles' Golden Days*, 1939. Shaw also wrote a number of short plays, a few of which are very good, including *The Dark Lady of the Sonnets* (1910) and *Great Catherine* (1913).

Beyond the wit and satire which are so often mentioned when Shaw's plays are discussed, he also provided plays of real intellectual substance. Disregarding the popular conventions of the well-made play, he set out to appeal to the intellect of his audiences. He put on the stage subjects previously confined to the courts, the pulpits, and the political platforms. That is, slum landlords, prostitutes, war, religion, health, economics, and even language. Thought, rather than emotion or action, was at the heart of all Shaw's plays, but it was made entertaining by wit and eloquence and his plays were far more fun than anything on the English stage since Sheridan.

Also contemporary with Shaw was John Galsworthy (1867-1933), a playwright and novelist whose primary claim to fame is *The Forsyte Saga*. Galsworthy came to the theatre in 1906 with *The Silver Box*, the same year that Shaw, with Vedrenne and Granville-Barker, had made social drama fashionable. The play dealt with the inequality of rich and poor before the law, and was hailed as a realistic masterpiece. *Joy* (1907) was less successful, but *Strife*

(1909), a play about early unionism, made Galsworthy one of the most talked about and admired dramatists of the day. *Justice* (1910) continued his venture into social drama, and its famous scene of a nervous prisoner cast into solitary confinement led directly to a number of prison reforms.

In 1912 Galsworthy produced two plays, *The Pigeon* and *The Eldest Son*, but neither was very successful. *The Fugitive* (1913) and *The Mob* (1914) continued the foray into social problem drama, but perhaps, seduced by his earlier success into concentrating on the problem instead of the drama, neither was wholly successful. It was not until after World War I that Galsworthy returned to the stage with *The Skin Game* (1920). This was followed by *Loyalties* and *Windows* (both 1922), *The Forest* (1924), and *Escape* (1926). None of these were successful, perhaps because the times were changing swiftly and Galsworthy, even after the war, was still writing as he had in 1906.

Sir James Matthew Barrie (1860-1937) preceded both Shaw and Galsworthy—his first work coming in 1888—but in a way he is separated from them and, indeed, even from his own time. The son of a poor Scottish handloom-weaver, he attended the Academy in Dumfries and then went on to Edinburgh University. His early plays were failures, but *The Little Minister* (1891) provided an insight into the sentimental impishness that would eventually make him one of the most popular playwrights of his day, and an 1897 production of the play made him a wealthy man.

In 1902 he produced *Quality Street* and *The Admirable Crichton*, *Little Mary* in 1903, and then in 1904, *Peter Pan* made theatre history. He never quite equalled it again, but he went on to write some very fine dramas, such as *Alice-Sit-by-the-Fire* (1905), *Josephine* (1906), *What Every Woman Knows* (1908), and *Rosalind* (1912). He completed such fine short plays as *The Twelve-Pound Look* (1910), and occasional pieces like *The Old Lady Shows Her Medals* (1917). *Mary Rose* (1920) was a strange, delicate juxtaposition of the natural and the supernatural, and in *The Boy David* (1936), his last play, he again evoked the childhood that was so much a part of his earlier plays. At his best, Barrie was indeed a great playwright—a master craftsman who combined a Puckish humor with a Victorian sentimentality.

More in the tradition of Shaw and Granville-Barker was William Somerset Maugham (1874-1965), dramatist and novelist. Truly a citizen of the world, Maugham was born in Paris, educated at King's School, Canterbury, attended Heidelberg University, and studied medicine at St. Thomas' Hospital. His earliest literary efforts were as a novelist, and even at the peak of his theatrical career he continued to write novels and short stories.

In 1904 his first play, *A Man of Honour*, was produced at the Avenue Theatre, and by 1908 he was clearly the most popular playwright in London, with four plays being performed at the same time, making himself his own best competition. For more than twenty years Maugham managed to maintain his position as a writer of well-crafted, urbane, witty, and sardonic plays, turning out such memorable works as *Lady Frederick* (1907), *The Land of Promise* (1914), *Caroline* (1916), *Our Betters* (1917, in New York), *Home and Beauty* (1919), *The Circle* (1921), *East of Suez* (1922), *The Letter* (1927), *The Constant Wife* (1927), *The Sacred Flame* (1928), *The Breadwinner* (1930), and *Sheppey* (1933). His best work is probably *The Circle*, which has been described as an

The interior of the Mermaid Theatre, Puddle Dock, Blackfriars, London, opened in 1959. It is in the shell of a Victorian warehouse destroyed in the blitz.

almost perfect serious comedy, but in all his plays, like his novels and short works, he gave the public an interesting and meaningful story.

Two fairly minor writers of the period, but writers who were highly popular in their time, were St. John Ervine and Harold Brighouse. Ervine (1883-1971) was a playwright and critic who did his early work at the Abbey Theatre in Dublin and then moved on to London. An outspoken social critic, he used his plays as a platform from which to launch attacks on various abuses. His best work is probably *John Ferguson* (1915), a moralistic tragedy which was produced at the Abbey Theatre. Other fine plays are *Jane Clegg* (1913), which tells of a worthless womanizer married to a good woman who eventually finds the courage to face life alone and tells him to leave. *Robert's Wife* (1937) is an Ibsenian problem play that chronicles the trials and tribulations of a woman doctor who seeks to establish a birth control clinic. Ervine was quite prolific, but Harold Brighouse (1882-1958), a playwright of what has generally been called the "Manchester school," wrote only one truly memorable play, *Hobson's Choice* (1916). The play was produced at the Apollo Theatre, and its tale of crusty, old Hobson whose managing daughter, Maggie, insists on marrying Hobson's timid employee, was an instant success with both critics and audiences. An earlier play by Brighouse, *The Northerners* (1914), was never a popular success, perhaps because it is based on the Luddites, but it is certainly as good as Ernst Toller's play on the same subject.

As World War I came to an end, Sir Noel Coward (1899-1973) stepped forward to maintain the English tradition of comedy of manners. An actor, producer, composer, and playwright, Coward embarked on his stage career at an early age, appearing in 1911 in a fairy play. His first attempt at writing was a melodrama, *The Last Trick,* written in 1918 but never produced. In 1920 *I'll Leave It To You,* his first produced work, went onstage with Coward himself in the cast. He was also in the cast of *The Young Idea* (1922), a somewhat overcute work about two precocious teenagers who manage to reunite their separated parents. In 1924 *The Vortex* ran for over five months in London, and Coward's reputation as a playwright was established.

Coward wrote some fine serious dramas; after *The Vortex* he wrote *Easy Virtue* (1926), *This Happy Breed* (1942), *Peace in Our Time* (1947), and *A Song At Twilight* (1966), which tells of an aged writer frantically trying to keep an old actress friend from publishing his letters to her, and also trying to hide his homosexuality from the world. The character of the writer is generally thought to be based on Somerset Maugham, but Coward once said that aspects of the character came from Max Beerbohm. However, Coward's greatest contribution to theatre is a collection of light, deft, witty comedies that usually present rather stylish people acting out an unconventional morality. The first of these comedies to take the stage was *Fallen Angels* (1925), in which two married and slightly drunken ladies await the arrival of their former lover. *Hay Fever* (1925), with its aging, eccentric actress and her strange family, has proved quite durable, as has *Private Lives* (1930). *Design for Living* (1933) presents two men and a woman who decide that their *ménage à trois* is a perfect design for living. *Tonight at 8:30* is a collection of nine one-act plays, at least three of which are outstanding. *Blithe Spirit* (1941) tells of a widower who, remarried, is haunted by the funloving ghost of his former wife. *Present Laughter* (1943) has an actor maintaining a wildly unconventional household with the help of his former wife, who is obviously more important to him than casual affairs in which he is almost singlemindedly engaged. *Relative Values* and *Suite in Three Keys* are generally below the best of Coward's work.

Coward's two autobiographical volumes *Present Indicative* (1937) and *Future Indefinite* (1954) provide a lively guide to the first fifty years of twentieth century theatre.

One of the most prolific playwrights to begin his career in the early part of the century was J. B. (John Boynton) Priestley (1894-   ), who began his dramatic career when he collaborated with Edward Knoblock in adapting his own novel, *The Good Companions,* for the stage. It opened in 1931 and ran for almost one year. In the same year, on his own, Priestley completed two new plays, *The Roundabout* and *Dangerous Corner. Laburnum Grove* (1933), an outstanding example of ingenious plotting in which a counterfeiter lives quietly in a respectable neighborhood, established Priestley as a major force in English theatre. *Eden End* (1934) is a gently nostalgic mood piece, rich in humor, in which an actress visits her "every day" family after several years' absence and then leaves again. This was followed by *Time and the Conways* and *I Have Been Here Before,* both moderately successful.

In 1938, with *Music At Night,* Priestley began a short experimental period. The play, unfortunately, attempted to present the internal monologues of some people listening to a concert. *Johnson Over Jordon* (1939) continued Priestley's experimentation with dramatic form. In this case a recently dead businessman examines his life—his career, his pursuit of pleasure, and his happiest memories. The play was a failure with most critics and all audiences.

After his experimental failures, Priestley went on to write *They Came to A City* (1943), *An Inspector Calls* (1945), *The Linden Tree* (1947), *The Scandalous Affair of Mr. Kettle and Mrs. Moon* (1955), and *The Glass Cage* (1957). Also, in collaboration with Jacquetta Hawkes, his third wife, he wrote *Dragon's Mouth* (1952) and *The White Countess* (1954).

More than anything else, Priestley is an earnest—often too earnest—social reformer. To the degree he manages to avoid this trait, as in *When We Are Married* (1938), he is also an outstanding dramatist.

Probably the most important writer of the period, though not necessarily the best playwright, was T. S. Eliot (1888-1965), an American by birth but an Englishman by temperament and adoption. In 1935, with *Murder in the Cathedral,* Eliot began an abortive revival of poetic drama and also provided English theatre with one of the finest plays of the century. *Cathedral,* which tells of the martyrdom of Thomas à Becket, is unique in its verse forms and the way it makes use of its chorus. Eliot followed this with *The Family Reunion* (1939), which was a flawed poetic retelling of the Orestian myth, and then moved to a less poetic, more natural style in *The Cocktail Party* (1949), *The Confidential Clerk* (1953), and *The Elder Statesman* (1958), which resembles an Ibsenian problem drama of the Theban myth. While these late dramas were far more realistic than *Cathedral,* they did demonstrate that Eliot's verse, depending on stresses for its rhythm, was a better contemporary choice for verse drama than the traditional blank verse.

Eliot's move toward poetic drama was picked up after World War II by Christopher Fry (really Harris, 1907-   ), a schoolmaster, actor, and poetic dramatist who in the late 1940s and early 1950s achieved a popular and critical success. Fry actually began his career in 1937 with *The Boy with a Cart,* a religious drama about St. Cuthbert, but it was in 1947 with his short play, *A Phoenix Too Frequent,* that he achieved serious attention. *Thor with Angels* (1948), was done at the Canterbury Festival and in 1949 *The Lady's Not for Burning* made Fry a prominent figure in the national drama. *Venus Observed* (1950) was written for Laurence Olivier, and that year he also translated Anouilh's *L' invitation au château* as *Ring Round the Moon.* In 1954 his *The Dark Is Light Enough* was produced with Edith Evans, and in 1955 Anouilh's *L'alouette* as *The Lark,* and Giraudoux's *La guerre de troie n'aura pas lieu* as *Tiger at the Gates.* Fry then underwent a long fallow period and it was not until 1961 that his *Curtmantle* was produced at the opening of the Stadsschouwburg Theatre in Holland.

One of the most interesting playwrights to appear in the years shortly after World War II was John Whiting (1917-63), a playwright and actor who achieved limited notice when his *A Penny for A Song* was produced at the Haymarket in 1951. The play received limited critical acclaim but was a failure at the box office. In the same year he wrote *Saint's Day,* and then in 1954 he completed *Marching Song.* In 1959 he translated two plays of Anouilh and then in 1961, after a fairly successful period of writing screenplays, he came back to

In November, 1973, the Long Wharf Theatre, New Haven, Connecticut, presented the American premiere of *The Changing Room* by David Storey.

theatre at the behest of the director Peter Hall to write *The Devils* (1961). Never truly popular until after the "breakthrough" of English drama in 1956, Whiting died before his talent had fully developed. Three of his plays, not up to *Penny* or *Devils*, were published posthumously—*No, Why?* (a one act, 1964), *Conditions of Agreement* (1965), and *The Gates of Summer* (1966).

On May 8, 1956, what is often referred to as the "breakthrough" occurred in English theatre when *Look Back in Anger*, by John Osborne (1929-), was produced at the Royal Court Theatre by the English Stage Company. Whether the change was totally due to the strong reaction accorded to Osborne's play, which dealt with new attitudes and reactions to England's traditional caste structure, is debatable. It probably was a combination of Osborne plus Whiting plus Fry plus a whole new social climate, developing since World War II, that conspired after 1956 to change the structure of the English theatre—but whatever the cause or causes, change it did.

Osborne, who had since 1948 been an actor with the Royal Court, went on to write *The Entertainer* in 1957, a powerful work centering around the broken-down music hall artiste, Archie Rice. In 1958 he finished *Epitaph for George Dillon*, and in 1959 *The World of Paul Slickey*. Neither of these last two works was totally successful, but his *Luther* (1961), again produced by the

English Stage Company, this time at the Théâtre des Nations in Paris, caused real theatrical excitement. In 1964 *Inadmissable Evidence* was a major success, but in the following year *A Patriot for Me* was refused a license by the Lord Chamberlain and had to be staged privately by Tony Richardson for members of the English Stage Society.

After 1956, by way of the English Stage Company, which had been established to encourage novelists and poets to enrich the moribund English theatre, a whole group of generally exciting playwrights began to work. The locus of important theatre shifted from the West End to the Royal Court and to Joan Littlewood's East End Theatre Workshop. Economically, and in percentage of audience, the West End theatres at first met the challenge of the "breakthrough," but in the 1960s the nationalized theatres (The National Theatre, the Royal Shakespeare Company, and, of course, the English Stage Company) and the burgeoning provincial repertory companies ended West End dominance.

The writers who helped end this domination are (besides Osborne): Arnold Wesker (1932-   ) whose "work" or "occupational" dramas, such as *The Kitchen* (1958), try to capture social truths about the total society in the limited arena of middle-class man working at his occupation; Shelagh Delaney

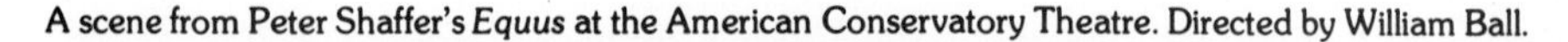

A scene from Peter Shaffer's *Equus* at the American Conservatory Theatre. Directed by William Ball.

(1939-), whose naturalistic *A Taste of Honey* (1958) chronicles the initiation of a young girl into an uncaring and often brutal urban environment; Brendan Behan (1923-65), whose *The Hostage* (1958) concentrates on a contemporary detachment about death; and even such an "old timer" as Graham Greene (1904-), who brought the simplistic social dogma of the 1930s into the 1950s with *The Living Room* (1953), *The Potting Shed* (1957), and *The Complaisant Lover* (1959). A number of other reasonably important writers, such as Bernard Kops (1928-), Henry Livings (1929-), Peter Shaffer (1926-), whose recent *Equus* may be the best play of recent times, and Robert Bolt (1924-) whose *A Man For All Seasons* (1960) has demonstrated remarkable staying power, have all made their mark on recent English drama.

However, the most important of these new playwrights appears to be Harold Pinter (1930-), an actor turned playwright. Pinter studied at the Central School in London and then spent nine years acting in Ireland and in provincial repertory. His first effort as a playwright was *The Room*, a one-act play that was produced in 1957 by the University of Bristol. *The Birthday Party* was Pinter's first full-length drama, a strange tale about the brutalization of a young man named Stanley, who may or may not be a pianist. In 1959 he completed *The Caretaker* and its success firmly established Pinter as one of the most important young English playwrights.

Pinter continued, throughout this period, to work in the short form, producing a series of outstanding one-act plays such as *No Man's Land, The Dumb Waiter* and *The Collection*. Finally, in 1965, he completed *The Homecoming*, a powerful, frightening, and yet comic drama which left him in artistic control of the English stage. A series of film scripts followed, and then *Old Times* (1970), which perhaps lacks some of the power of the earlier full-length dramas, and yet is still a cut above most other English stage fare.

ACTING

It is impossible to do justice to the contemporary British theatre without discussing the great actors that England has managed to produce. There have been a number of explanations as to why Britain has enjoyed so many fine performers during the twentieth century, but most come back ultimately to the British repertory system, which has proved to be one of the world's finest training grounds for the young actor.

One of the best performers in this outstanding group has been Dame Edith Evans (1888-1976), who made her acting debut as an amateur playing Cressida in an Elizabethan Stage Society production of *Troilus and Cressida* in 1912. It was not until 1924, however, that she attracted major public attention as Millamant in *The Way of the World*. During the 1925-26 season she was with the Old Vic, and in 1936 she returned to that company, playing a number of Shakespearian roles and gaining critical raves for her Lady Fidget in *The Country Wife*. She was outstanding as Lady Bracknell in *The Importance of Being Earnest* (1939), Katerina Ivanovna in *Crime and Punishment* (1946), Lady Wishfort in *The Way of the World* (1948), Countess Rosmarin in *The Dark is Light Enough* (1954), and Queen Katharine in *Henry VIII* (1958).

Maurice Herbert Evans also provided some of the English theatre's finest moments. Born in 1901, he enjoyed his first stage success as Lieutenant Raleigh in *Journey's End* (1928). He became a member of the Old Vic in 1934, acting in a variety of plays, including an outstanding production of *Hamlet*. In 1935 he came to America and remained, becoming an American citizen in 1941. In the United States he has received high critical acclaim as Romeo in *Romeo and Juliet* opposite Katharine Cornell, as Richard II, Hamlet, Falstaff, Malvolio, and Macbeth. He was also highly successful in the plays of Shaw, acting John Tanner in *Man and Superman*, Dick Dudgeon in *The Devil's Disciple*, King Magnus in *The Apple Cart*, and Captain Shotover in *Heartbreak House*.

Another fine actor of the century has been Sir John Gielgud (1904-) who, as the grand-nephew of Ellen Terry and the great-grandson of the famous Polish actress Madame Aszperger, appears to have come by his talent naturally. He made his debut at the Old Vic as the Herald in *Henry V* (1921), and in 1929-30 he returned to play such leading roles as Romeo, Richard II, Macbeth, and his finest role, Hamlet, which he repeated at the Lyceum in 1939 and subsequently at Elsinore in Denmark. During his outstanding career he has successfully essayed most major Shakespearian roles, as well as Mirabell in *Way of the World*, Joseph Surface in *The School for Scandal*, Vershinin in

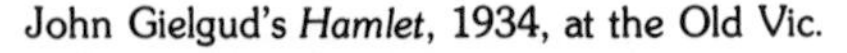
John Gielgud's *Hamlet*, 1934, at the Old Vic.

Three Sisters, Trigorin in *The Seagull*, and Gaev in *The Cherry Orchard*. Among the more contemporary plays in which he has starred are *The Lady's Not for Burning*, Coward's *Nude with Violin*, *The Potting Shed*, and Edward Albee's *Tiny Alice*, which even Gielgud's skill was unable to save.

One of the most underrated actors on the English Stage—perhaps because of his great success in films—has been Sir Alec Guinness (1914-). His first major triumph was as Sir Andrew Aguecheek in *Twelfth Night* (1937) at the Old Vic. He followed this with a modern-dress Hamlet directed by Tyrone Guthrie, and then repeated the role in his own Elizabethan-style production. He has since played such other Shakespearian roles as Richard III, and he includes, among his contemporary roles, Garcin in Sartre's *No Exit*, Henry Harcourt-Reilly in *The Cocktail Party*, T. E. Lawrence in Terence Rattigan's *Ross*, and Bérenger in *Exit the King*.

LAURENCE OLIVIER: Lord Laurence Olivier (1907-), English actor, producer, and first director of the National Theatre of Great Britain, is one of the best known and most highly admired actors of all time. Certainly one of the finest tributes to his skill and passion as a performer was made by Franco Zeffirelli, commenting on Olivier's creation in the role of Othello:

> *I was told that this was the last flourish of the romantic tradition in acting. It is nothing of the sort. It's an anthology of everything that has been discovered about acting in the last three centuries. It's grand and majestic, but it's also modern and realistic. I would call it a lesson for us all.*

In an interview with Kenneth Tynan, Olivier made a number of points regarding his attitudes toward and beliefs about the art and craft of acting. For Olivier, acting is, in essence, the art of persuasion, and the first person who must be persuaded is the actor himself—that is, he must be persuaded that there are aspects of the character within himself, and then he must use those aspects to create the character. To achieve this he must make ultimate use of observation and intuition. He must scavenge up every scrap of "human circumstance; observe it, find it, use it some time or another."

Just the reverse of those actors who create totally from the inside out, Olivier creates primarily from the outside in—which is heresy for the Actors' Studio supporters but has worked very well for such great (and dissimilar) actors as Olivier and Louis Calhern. Olivier describes his own process of creation in this way (referring specifically to developing his role as Shakespeare's Richard III): "I began to build up a character, a characterization. I'm afraid I work mostly from the outside in. I usually collect a lot of details, a lot of characteristics, and find a creature swimming about somewhere in the middle of them."

Once the "creature" is found, however, and identified, Olivier feels the absolute necessity of making use of stage techniques to create—to make physi-

Laurence Olivier, probably the greatest actor of the age, in *Henry IV* at the Old Vic.

cal—the creature for the audience, and every part of the actor is necessary to the act of creation. For Olivier,

> *it's a fusion of every single part of you that has to go into it. The mime actor doesn't need the voice; the film actor hardly needs the voice, hardly needs the body, except to use it as a marvelous physical specimen in such roles as demand that attribute. The stage actor certainly needs the voice, certainly needs all the vocal control, all the breath control, all the techniques of the voice, certainly needs all the miming power imaginable, certainly needs the hands, certainly needs the eyes—he needs them all.*

If Olivier has worked to accomplish anything in his illustrious career, one thing stands out, something that has little to do with the practice of acting but a great deal to do with the art of being—he has worked to make the art and craft of the actor not merely a part of the financial aspect of entertainment but a part of the life of the people. In that ambition he has achieved great success.

THE DIRECTOR

One of the major contributions made by the English theatre during this century has been in the area of directing, and the three major contributors have been Harley Granville-Barker, Tyrone Guthrie, and Peter Brook.

HARLEY GRANVILLE-BARKER: Harley Granville-Barker (1877-1946) was an actor, playwright, director, and critic during and after the Edwardian period of English drama. He brought new life to the stage and is considered by many to be the first of the modern producers. A contemporary of George Bernard Shaw, he is often given the credit for establishing Shaw as a dramatist. He tried to bring before the English audience of the nineteenth and early twentieth centuries plays with content as well as structure.

He was born in London to a mother who earned a living as a reciter and bird-mimic. Mrs. Barker's tours were managed by her husband, and so she was able to take Harley with her, teaching him to recite. He made his first public appearance in a play at the age of thirteen and began touring with different companies until he made his London debut in 1892 at the Comedy Theatre in *Poets and the Puppets.* Eventually he became associated with William Poel's Elizabethan Stage Society. It was while playing the part of Eugene in Shaw's *Candida* that the two men met and became fast friends.

Barker was a very bright, sensitive, and ambitious young man and from the beginning worked to branch out into other areas of the theatre. He became a director for the Stage Society and Court Theatre, and this position enabled him to work for the greatest change in drama. He brought back the best of the older drama and encouraged young playwrights to give the audiences plays with ideas.

If Granville-Barker's greatest contribution to theatre had to be singled out it would surely be his revolutionary approach to Shakespeare. Most of his critical works are on Shakespeare, and come directly out of his experience as a director. He wanted to make Shakespeare alive in the theatre. He was not concerned, as many were, with how Shakespeare had been staged in Elizabethan times; instead he sought ways that Shakespeare's works could be staged without distorting the plays. He did not agree with those who thought that the poetry was just an addition to the drama. Barker thought that the essence of the drama was its poetry. He felt that scenery was a distraction because the poetry was capable of creating far more intense pictures than all the technical capacity of modern staging. Shakespeare, he felt, used dialogue to paint a picture, and this makes scenery irrelevant, an intrusion, and distracting. He also quickened the delivery of the dialogue to help with the rhythm of the play. He attempted to capture the whole play through imagery, design, and theme.

In his *Prefaces to Shakespeare* (1927-1947), Barker offers advice to directors and actors who approach a production of a Shakespearian play. He believed that the plays should be performed as Shakespeare wrote them. "The blue pencil is a weapon with which few are to be trusted." Especially, the plays should not be bowdlerized or cleaned up. "Othello must call Desdemona a

A scene from Granville-Barker's production of *Twelfth Night*. Scene and costumes by Norman Wilkinson.

whore, and let those that do not like it leave the theatre." He warned producers that the soliloquy is a vital part of Shakespeare's stagecraft, which the playwright used as a means of bringing the audience into the closest possible contact with his characters' secret thoughts and passionate emotions. The most difficult and important task facing the modern production is keeping this intimacy of contact or the soliloquy will fail and lose its emotional impact.

As a director, Granville-Barker would begin by reading the play to the cast, seeking its sense rather than indicating characterizations. He would begin rehearsals without telling the actors any more about the characters than the stage directions, to see what the actors themselves first created. Then he would start forming them in the shape he wanted by using illustration and metaphor to stimulate the actors' own imaginations. He would, if necessary, demonstrate a rhythm or phrasing or emphasis, but he seldom gave an intonation. The fine polishing went on right up to the last rehearsal. He would give notes taken during the scene, but would never interrupt the flow of the scene. He was interested in and careful with such things as grouping, moves, scenery, and lighting, but he was only interested insofar as they affected the acting, to which everything else was subordinated.

His work as a playwright reflected his interest in the drama of ideas rather than drama as a superficial entertainment. In his plays he treated such problems as the double standard, caste distinction and class prejudice, and the "new" woman. He possessed the same questioning attitude and probing curiosity as Shaw. The only difference was that Barker was more realistic and depended more on understatement and restraint to achieve his dramatic effect.

Granville-Barker's *Prefaces to Shakespeare,* which represent a lifetime of study and experience in the theatre, are still studied by actors and directors who are looking for meaningful insights, creative approaches, and explanations of Shakespeare's poetry and language.

TYRONE GUTHRIE: Sir Tyrone Guthrie (1900-71) was born in Ireland. His first memory of the theatre was, as a child, seeing *Peter Pan* and *The Yeomen of the Guard.* He became infatuated with "star" performers such as Beatrice Boarer and Henry Lytton. This "infatuation" with star "quality" persisted throughout his career.

Guthrie was formally educated at Wellington and St. Johns College, Oxford, where he majored in history. It was at Oxford that he began to perform in plays, taking part in the University Dramatic Society's annual "Shakespearian."

The most important person to guide Guthrie in the early days of his theatrical career was James Fagan, director of the first Shakespearian play in which Guthrie was cast. Fagan invited Guthrie to join his university repertory theatre as an actor, but quickly shifted him to assistant stage manager because of his lack of acting talent. It was with Fagan and the repertory company that Guthrie, in a rather hit-and-miss fashion, "learned by doing" the rudiments of management, technical theatre, acting, and directing.

In 1924 Guthrie joined the British Broadcasting Company at Belfast, in charge of all programs other than music. He was responsible for choosing selections as well as the directing of radio plays. This increased his knowledge of dramatic technique and also provoked him to formulate his own opinions of theatre. Guthrie next worked as the director of the Scottish National Players in Glasgow, where he learned more about the subtleties of directing, not to mention how to keep a theatre from bankruptcy. Then, in 1928, Guthrie was hired as director by Terence Gray of the Festival Theatre at Cambridge. The company ran four seasons and it was during this period that Guthrie made the decision to work professionally as a director.

Before Guthrie's eventual employment at the Old Vic, he directed four more plays: In 1931, at the Westminster Theatre in London, James Bridie's *The Anatomist;* in 1932, at the Lyric Theatre, *Dangerous Corner;* in 1932, again at the Westminster Theatre, *Love's Labour's Lost;* and in 1933, at the Memorial Theatre in Stratford, *Richard II.*

Between 1933 and 1934 Guthrie was with the Old Vic, working closely with such stars as Flora Robson and Charles Laughton, and he learned much about theatrical management from Lilian Baylis, who was then the guiding light of the Old Vic. This was his real initiation into professional theatre. During this season he directed *Twelfth Night, The Cherry Orchard, Henry VIII,*

Measure for Measure, The Tempest, The Importance of Being Earnest, and *Macbeth.*

Guthrie then spent time traveling between London and Broadway. In 1938, after the death of Baylis, Guthrie assumed the position of administrator at the Old Vic and Sadler's Wells, and to his credit he was able to keep both theatres alive until the end of World War II.

Guthrie believed that "the only really creative function of the director is to be at rehearsal a highly receptive, concentrated, critical sounding board for the performance—an audience of one." He stated that the director goes through a process of "psychic evocation"—a process that consists of unconscious giving and receiving, from actor to director. "I don't shout or scream much, but I'm death on people who are late or slacking. Yes, I'm pretty nippy at times, like a sergeant major."

Perhaps the first rule of directing, for Guthrie, was that the director should never arrive at any stage of rehearsal with set decisions, but rather, should be open to several ways of doing things and should remain as flexible as possible.

In the prerehearsal period there are several steps that should be taken by a director. First, the script should be interpreted. Guthrie compared the stage director to a musical conductor, and even used such musical terminology as *crescendo* for directions throughout his scripts. He felt that performance is no more than an instrument of the director, and that the director should therefore be individual and follow his or her own interpretation of the play. The worst thing that a director can do is to play it safe.

As far as casting goes, Guthrie felt that directors should have a clear idea of what they want before they cast. Also, readings are a complete waste of time in that the good people usually do not do well whereas the pushy and the insensitive do. The actors are usually nervous at casting; thus, "their voices are upset, their muscles are tense, their diaphragms are quivery, and their throats are dry." Guthrie felt that the best way to cast a play was to see the actors in their own productions. That is not to say that he undervalued the casting process. In fact, he felt that casting could constitute nearly ninety percent of the director's task.

According to Guthrie, directors should come to the first rehearsal prepared to give specific movements, but as the play forms they must be willing to change their plans. They should work within an outline, but an outline that will allow flexibility. The movements should all be concerned with expression of ideas and not with the action. They should be concerned with the subtle "delineation of emotion by the way people are placed. It is more delicate than getting them into common sense positions."

Conferences with the leading actors and key personnel are important in order to exchange ideas about the "soul" of the play. The director, however, is always the leader. He or she should try, for example, to keep the designer from departing from the concept of the play through "doing his own thing." The director should not dictate, but should always be in charge. Thus, discussion during a rehearsal is bad in that it wastes the time of the minor actors. It should therefore be held in private before rehearsal.

Guthrie felt that the most important contribution of the director is establishing a creative atmosphere—that is, making the company feel as one. The director must create an atmosphere in which the actor is not afraid to experiment or do embarrassing things.

Probably Guthrie's most unique directing accomplishment was his modern-dress *Hamlet*, the opening production of the Tyrone Guthrie Theatre in Minneapolis, which he founded. Some of the comments that Guthrie made to his actors during the *Hamlet* rehearsals shed light on his directing process. "Take positions. We'll worry about how you get there later." Deeper into rehearsals, while reworking act I, scene 1, he pointed out that "you must act with your bodies and reactions to make up for the things we don't do with gauze and eerie lighting."

Guthrie rarely took time out before doing a scene to explain how he thought the scene should be played. He felt that in doing the scene the actors would get what he wanted from them. Also, he seldom spoke in analytical terms about the relationships of characters to each other. Rather, he felt that direction should be concerned with language and movement.

As for his direction of bit players and supernumeraries, Guthrie did not give everyone a specific movement to make, or even tell a player when to move; but everyone, through his explanations of the effect he wanted, was sure about what to do. That was achieved by having each individual on the stage find a variety of positions and then select the proper balance. That refusal to overdirect the minor roles probably grew out of Guthrie's feeling that there is nothing duller than seeing a bit-part actor move up to react and then move back to the same position.

Finally, Guthrie seemed to get more out of lines by using silence for emphasis. He felt that it is possible to illustrate action without telling actors what to do. He was specific to only a few people in an ensemble, encouraging the other members of the cast to create their own characters. It was through this method of group direction that he made his plays alive and fresh.

PETER BROOK: Peter Brook, born in London in 1925 and educated at Magdalen College, Oxford, where he founded the Oxford University Film Society, has staged plays at the Birmingham Repertory Theatre, at Stratford-on-Avon, in London, in New York, and on the continent. From 1962 to 1968 he was codirector of the Royal Shakespeare Company with Peter Hall and Michel Saint-Denis. American audiences have had the opportunity to see his productions of *The Little Hut, House of Flowers, The Visit, Irma la Douce, The Fighting Cock, King Lear, Marat/Sade, A Midsummer Night's Dream,* and recently *Candide.* Brook's films include *Marat/Sade* and *Lord of the Flies.*

In his book on dramatic art, *The Empty Space* (1969), Brook divides the whole of theatre into four groupings: the "deadly," the "holy," the "rough," and the "immediate." Deadly theatre, by Brook's definition, is the type seen most commonly linked to the critically and artistically despised commercial theatre. Brook feels that theatre is declining all over the world (a highly questionable judgment), mainly because theatre not only fails to elevate or instruct, it hardly even entertains. He compares today's deadly theatre to a jaded prostitute, and the theatre-going public to a customer who must pay far too much for too little pleasure.

> *The Deadly Theatre finds its deadly way into grand opera and tragedy, into the plays of Moliere and the plays of Brecht. Of course nowhere does the Deadly Theatre install itself so securely, so comfortably and so slyly as in the works of William Shakespeare.*

The deadly theatre approaches the classics with a set formula as to how they should be done, and this formula is essentially a repetition of the same style that has been badly used for decades. In fact, "style" is the one word that for Brook best describes the deadly theatre, since the deadly theatre has none. Such theatre may be avoided only by separating the eternal truths from the traditional and often superficial variations. The *deadly* theatre is not, however, *dead* theatre; it is alive and thriving all over the world, season after ongoing season. With this type of theatre, the basic question as to why theatre exists is never asked. If it were asked, even though it is rhetorical and basically unanswerable, deadly theatre would at long last die.

The holy theatre has been defined by Brook as being essentially, the invisible-made-visible. This definition or concept grows out of the notion that the stage is a place where the invisible can appear, made tangible through theatre's ability to penetrate surfaces and probe the realities that are hidden beneath. The holy theatre satisfies man's hunger for something beyond his daily existence, and it is this "something" that acts as a buffer against the often painful reality that exists outside the theatrical situation.

In holy theatre the ceremony comes first, followed by the structure that provides the dramatic framework which supports and contains the ceremony. For Brook this ceremony should be an ever-changing ritual that feeds our lives. Today, he feels, the theatre is just a watered-down imitation of old rituals that were once highly meaningful but have lost their significance in the toils of time. The holy theatre cannot consist of forgotten, meaningless ritual; it must be immediate, springing from man's spirit and soul as man celebrates some aspect of his life. The prophet for the holy theatre, Brook feels, was Antonin Artaud, who railed against the sterile theatre, promoting in its place a theatre that would work like the plague (by infection), by analogy, by magic; a theatre in which the play, the event itself, stands in place of the text. Brook also calls on Jerzy Grotowski in support of his search for holy theatre. He sees Grotowski as a visionary who believes that theatre cannot be an end in itself; who sees theatre as a vehicle, a means of self-study, and as the potential salvation of man. The leaders of world theatre must be made to realize that for theatre to survive a holy theatre must be achieved.

The rough theatre, for Brook, is the kind of theatre that is closest to the people. The rough theatre can function without style, since style can exist only if one has leisure to develop it, and the rough theatre is too immediate for leisure. Such theatre is an almost depressingly proletarian art form in which, for Brook, dirt provides its roughness and its edge; where filth and vulgarity are natural and obscenity is joyous. In this theatre the spectacle becomes socially liberating in the sense that, by its very nature, a theatre of the people is antiauthoritarian, antitraditional, antipomp, and antipretense. It is a theatre of noise and boisterous action. One of the few director-creators who achieved a rough theatre, according to Brook, was Meyerhold, the Russian genius whose theatre had the highest of aims—to return theatre to its original state.

Despite his wish not to look backward, Brook finds that the Elizabethan theatre is the most perfect example of the rough and the holy theatres joining together to create a statement. His thesis seems to be that we must find a way to move forward, which will lead us back to Shakespeare, since Shakespeare most perfectly combined the squalor of the ages with deep and metaphysical themes.

Under the catch title "The Immediate Theatre," Brook relates what is essentially his theatrical autobiography, the most important aspect of which is his belief that today's theatre, unlike the theatre of the nineteenth century, cannot attach itself to any one particular style. Today the world is moving at an ever-changing pace, and in all directions—backward, foreward, and sideways. And this movement can be basically good, not destructive, and it is not merely restlessness or fashion. At certain moments, as a result of fortunate decisions and honest effort, all comes together and the theatre of joy emerges—a theatre which combines the rough theatre and the holy theatre. But once that moment is gone it cannot be recaptured by slavish imitation, which will only allow the deadly theatre to creep back in. Instead, the search must begin anew for the fun of theatre, and when that is found the theatre of joy will again emerge.

SCENIC DESIGN

Perhaps the most influential scenic designer of this century (and the last few years of the previous century as well) was Gordon Craig. It is difficult to know where to place Craig, not only because he spanned the beginning of the century, but also because he operated in several fields—scenic design, directing, lighting, and theatre management.

GORDON CRAIG: Edward Gordon Craig (1872-1966) came naturally to the theatre. His mother was the celebrated actress Ellen Terry and his father was Edward William Godwin, an architect with a passion for the theatre. Craig loved the theatre all his life. He hated formal schooling and believed that the Lyceum Theatre was his real school and that the actor-manager, Henry Irving, was his real schoolmaster. He learned elocution in the Green Room and studied Irving onstage. At the Lyceum, where he remained for eight years, Craig gained a practical knowledge of stagecraft and became a fairly proficient actor. He grew restless and a bit distressed, however, when he realized that he was constantly comparing himself with Irving and that he could never be more than a fair imitation of that great actor.

As a result of this dissatisfaction Craig left the Lyceum and for the first time began to read seriously. He became interested in poetry, especially that of John Ruskin, whose antirealism helped turn his thinking away from the beliefs of the Lyceum and its preoccupation with realism. For the next three years

Gordon Craig's design for Electra. (From Craig's *On the Art of the Theatre*, London, 1911)

Craig read widely and began to formulate his aesthetic principles. He absorbed ideas from various people, often quite different. From William Blake came his fascination with symbols; from James Pryde he learned that art was not imitation but re-creation; Goethe suggested to him that the function of art was to express the inexpressible and that theatre must be visually symbolic; from Tolstoy came the notion that realistic theatre was the negation of art; and by way of Nietzsche he learned that all aesthetic activity implies a state of ecstasy.

It was Pryde, along with William Nicholson, who influenced Craig in one of his earliest artistic endeavors—woodcutting. Those two men (known as the Beggarstaff Brothers) so influenced Craig that his first carvings ended up as imitations. However, through concentration on his craft he learned not to waste time reproducing detail, to appreciate line and simplicity, and to be sparing with his resources. Also during this period, and certainly as a result of working with woodcutting, Craig developed his love for black and white as the central colors of all visual art. He found these colors to be the most essential, especially black, which he felt had roots in the deeper springs of nature itself.

By 1900 Craig was deeply involved in the fight against stage realism. He had studied in the art galleries of London, discovering the simplicity of the Italian architects and painters and the artistic importance of color and light as opposed to form. At the time Craig also read an article about the Roman theatre at Orange. The article described a huge wall, containing a central portal, that stood at the back of the stage. The wall emphasized vertical lines, its sculptured quality provided a strong contrast of light and shadowed areas, and it allowed the actors to be perceived in relationship to the simple, strong, architectural form.

Another idea that appealed to Craig was Wagner's music-drama, with its blend of music, poetry, and acting. Because Wagner advocated a new style of theatre architecture to accommodate his creations, Craig was compelled to develop some new forms himself. One of his projects had no boxes, no circles, a floor that sloped gently toward the stage, and scene changes masked by darkness and not covered up by a curtain. He also devised a small box at the back of the auditorium from which the director could run the show. He made no provisions for footlights; all lighting was from the side or above.

Craig was at last realizing the nature of art and the importance of both imagination and discipline. Art was not accidental; it had to come from conscious effort. For art, discipline was its life and anarchy its death. With these thoughts in mind, Craig became stage director at the Lyceum in 1899 for the production of Purcell's *Dido and Aeneas*. Staged in 1900, this production was the beginning of a movement in the production of poetic drama. In it Craig had all light coming from above, except for two spotlights at the back of the auditorium which could focus directly on the actors. Because he so much disliked the star system, Craig used mostly amateurs, and partly as a result of such casting it took him an unprecedented six months to complete the rehearsals for this production. In terms of set, he tried to work with the usual scenic painters but finally dismissed them, utilizing a purple-blue sky-cloth, no borders or wings, no customary landscaping, and minimal furniture. He tried to suggest mood, wanting the audience's imagination to run free, undaunted by detail.

In the production of *Bethlehem* no attempt was made to copy a stable because Craig wished to suggest the divine presence by the use of light. Instead of the traditional doll in the manger, a light shone from the depths of the crib, illuminating the faces of the actors gathered around the Virgin and Child. Never had this type of effect been used before.

As well as designing and directing, Craig was also writing. His first book, *The Art of the Theatre* (1905), met with tremendous enthusiasm in Europe. He wrote about what he was currently working on, made catalogues of his work, and eventually sold collections to libraries and institutions all over the world. In his first book, Craig surmised that until the status of the director was improved there could be no forward movement in theatre; the director had

Gordon Craig's grand conception for the Forum scene in *Julius Caesar*. (From Craig's *On the Art of the Theatre*, London, 1911)

to have complete control of every aspect of the production, for this was the only way to achieve artistic unity.

One of Craig's most famous ideas (infamous among actors) was his concept of the Über-marionette. Because he believed that actors were slaves to their emotions, he was looking for some method to ensure that intelligence remained the primary controlling factor for actors onstage. The answer seemed to be a superpuppet, with strings pulled by the director. Craig postulated that in order to give a good performance, actors had to be in complete control of their instincts so that their imagination and ability to create could lead them through their parts. If the actor lost control, his/her performance became a disjointed series of accidental scenes. Still seeking to achieve this, he also experimented with masks to dehumanize the actors, thereby making them conscious of their movements and gestures so that they would have to rely on their intelligence to re-create rather then reproduce.

At the same time that Craig was writing and theorizing he was also designing (and creating "plays") for the theatre of the future. *The Steps* was an outright dismissal of spoken drama and dramatic literature. It consisted of a series of scenes that were called "moods," each showing a flight of steps going across the stage with figures and light and dark patches appearing in different positions on them. It was the architectural fact of the steps themselves in which Craig was interested, and not what the actors were doing on them. The figures of the players might dominate the steps for a time, but eventually they would leave and the steps would remain. Actors (people) come and go, but art is eternal.

Imagining the stage floor as a chess board, Craig developed the idea of a stage with each square an elevator that would be able to raise and lower to any number of positions, thus providing an almost infinite variety of levels and playing areas. Along with this came his idea of using screens, equal in size to the squares on the floor and colored in monotones. The designer could employ them to create "places" on the stage, giving them color, shape, and animation through imaginative use of light. When Craig finally went to Moscow to produce *Hamlet* with Stanislavsky, he used his screens, which were unpainted

Program cover for the 1928 production of *Macbeth*, featuring a design sketch by Gordon Craig. The production was billed as being Gordon Craig's "first designment for the American theater."

canvas stretched over wooden frames. These screens were arranged to hint at streets and niches, when aided by the imagination of the spectator. Though the production was apparently not what the two men wanted—theirs was an uneasy collaboration at best—*Hamlet* was a success and the two great theatricians parted with at least mutual respect.

In 1913 Craig finally developed the school he had been wanting for so long—the Arena Goldoni. The school was to be set up in two successive operations. First should come the selection of fifteen to twenty salaried technicians who would learn Craig's theories and later act as his assistants. The second part of the operation would be the acceptance of twenty to thirty paying students. He had no intention of allowing his students to become parrots to his ideas. Rather, the school was to help them realize their powers of creative imagination by urging them to use their minds and fancies as a source of creation. Unfortunately the school lasted but a short time, forced to close by the problems created by World War I.

Unlike his contemporary, Appia, Craig put all elements of theatre on the same creative level, insisting that they all contribute to the total production. His major premise was that neither the script nor the acting alone constituted the art of theatre—that this lay in the whole production. It was toward this end that he worked until his death.

Ireland In the 1890s, in an Ireland still firmly under English rule, there was a remarkable upsurge of interest in literature and the arts. Temporarily frustrated in their struggle for political independence by the fall of the great nationalist leader Parnell, middle- and upper-class Irishmen turned for consolation and inspiration to the ancient heroic epics. It was only in the middle of the nineteenth century that these Gaelic sagas had been translated by a few curious professors as a scholarly exercise. Nationalistic politicians and journalists such as Thomas Davis, Gavan Duffy, and John Mitchell used these heroic epics to further their own cause. The sagas went unnoticed by the landlord class, seeming to them little more than progaganda. In 1878, Standish O'Grady, a brilliant Anglo-Irish writer and historian, published his *History of Ireland,* giving authenticity to the claims of the Irish nationalistic journalists. He also translated many of the sagas into colloquial English.

Folklorists like Douglas Hyde taught themselves the Irish language, still spoken by the peasantry along the western seacoast. They discovered, to their excitement, that the same epic stories were still part of the folk consciousness, along with a vernacular poetry composed and handed down by wandering bards. They also discovered that people whose first language was Gaelic spoke an uncommonly musical and vivid English, filled with rich Elizabethan phrases.

It was to the exceeding good fortune of the world that this wealth of poetic material was discovered by William Butler Yeats (1865-1939).

YEATS AND THE FOUNDING OF AN IRISH THEATRE

William Butler Yeats was born at Sandymount, Ireland, on June 13, 1865. Much of his early life was spent in London. His father, a gentleman of the landlord class and a trained lawyer who disliked the profession, spent much of his time in London, practicing as an artist. William did, however, spend many long holidays in Ireland with his family in Sligo on the Atlantic coast. He loved Ireland. He thought a great deal about Ireland. And, most important, he wrote about Ireland. His first anthologies, published in 1888, were definitely Irish: *Poems and Ballads of Young Ireland, Fairy and Folk Tales of the Irish Peasantry*, and *Stories From Carleton*.

Although his reputation in London literary circles was based on his lyric poetry, Yeats' interest in the dramatic form was strong. In the early 1890s, before he had any prospect of a theatre for its performance, he had written his first play, *The Countess Cathleen*, as an expression of his love for Maud Gonne (1866-1953), an Irish revolutionary. In 1894 he wrote *The Land of Heart's Desire* as a curtain raiser to Shaw's *Arms and the Man*. In 1886, his short drama, *Mosada*, appeared in the *Dublin University Review*. It was during this period that he conceived the idea to found a poetic theatre in Dublin. The thea-

Thomas Murphy's *The Morning After Optimism* at the Abbey Theatre, 1977.

tre he envisioned would be distinctly Irish and of the highest standard. It would express the real spirit of Ireland, the spirit which had been suppressed for centuries by the British. It would also counteract the vulgar, journalistic plays imported from England.

Yeats, along with many of his literary contemporaries, was disgusted with the conditions existing in the English theatre in the 1890s. To him the worst of artistic forms was the play about modern educated people. Though aware of only a portion of Ibsen's work, Yeats disdained his "drama of ideas" and the many imitations of the "problem" play that flooded the English stage. It saddened him to see Irish characters presented as farcical figures by the visiting English companies. And more than that, it enraged him that his own country, so steeped in rich legend and verbal beauty, should not have been allowed to develop its own native drama.

Armed with a faith in the Irishman's passion for oratory, Yeats set out to find the audience he needed. The material for his plays would come from the wealth of Irish legends—the pre-Christian heroic epics. He would restore the universal myths and give them to the people. He would acquaint the folk with chanted verse. By so doing, he would educate and reflect back to the Irish people their own historical beauty. He had no money, no company of actors, no theatre, and no plays except the two he had written. He only had his dream and the desire to realize that dream.

He proposed his plan for an Irish theatre to his friend and sometime patron, Lady Gregory (1863-1935). She was enthusiastic and drew Edward Martyn (1859-1923), a wealthy neighbor, into the plan. They called themselves the National Literary Society. In hopes of receiving financial support, they sent a letter to their friends, outlining their goals. They wanted to emphasize that their movement was not political in nature, and although it could not help but be nationalistic, its primary intention was to be artistic. The struggle to separate nationalism and art would be a constant one. Yeats was not aware at this moment what a bitter struggle it would be. He was intent on founding a theatre.

The replies to the letter were favorable. In 1899 the Irish Literary Theatre, as Yeats had named it, was born. Martyn agreed to assume all financial worries. They hired a Dublin hall, for the week beginning May 8, 1899, and set off to London to engage a company of actors. A friend of Martyn's, George Moore (1853-1933), agreed to help them with the staging of the two plays to be produced—Yeats' *The Countess Cathleen*, and Martyn's *The Heather Field*.

During rehearsals Martyn discovered a theological heresy in *The Countess Cathleen*, and on the advice of his confessor withdrew his support. It was at this early time in the history of the Irish dramatic movement that Yeats took on the role of strategist and fighter; a role that he was to sustain for many years. He sought an opinion in favor of the play from a leading Catholic theologian, Father Barry, and forced the performance through. He won the battle, but discovered that the attacks on his theatre—on moral, political, and nationalist grounds—were to be constantly renewed. That he would have to fight his own Irish people was an especially bitter revelation.

On the day of the first performance of the Irish Literary Society, *The Daily Nation*, a Dublin newspaper representing the views of sentimental nationalists, asked its readers to attend the performance of *The Countess Cath-*

leen, to "make emphatic judgement against these anti-Irish, anti-Catholic monstrosities." Yeats' response to this challenge was to bring in the British police to defend the players against violence. This act gave the nationalists what they were looking for—proof that Yeats was pro-British and anti-Irish. Yeats' attitude toward this brand of thinking was contemptuous.

Many of the London drama critics attended the first performance and all of them wrote favorably of the plays. The Dublin press was, in general, friendly. Yeats, pleased with his success in getting the dramatic movement underway despite the opposition, now devoted his energies to helping the theatre survive. He felt that the theatre must be recognized as "literary" if it was not to fall under the attacks of political and moral prejudice.

The second series of the Irish Literary Theatre opened at the Gaiety Theatre on February 19, 1900. The plays performed were: Alice Milligan's *The Last Feast of the Fianna;* Moore's adaptation of Martyn's *The Tale of a Town,* retitled *The Bending of the Bough;* and Moore's *Maeve.* All three were received with no opposition.

In the final series of performances, to please the Gaelic League, with which Yeats was in sympathy, the Irish Literary Theatre produced Douglas Hydes' (1860-1949) Gaelic play, *Casadh an t-Sugain* (*The Twisting of the Rope*). Yeats and Moore collaborated with some difficulty on a play derived from folk history, *Diarmuid and Grania.* The Gaelic League was delighted with Hyde's play, performed by amateurs from the League. *Diarmuid and Grania* was moderately well received. That it was acted by an English company was disappointing, both for the production's sake as well as the audience's.

A scene from the Abbey Theatre's 1976 production of Brian Friel's *Lovers.*

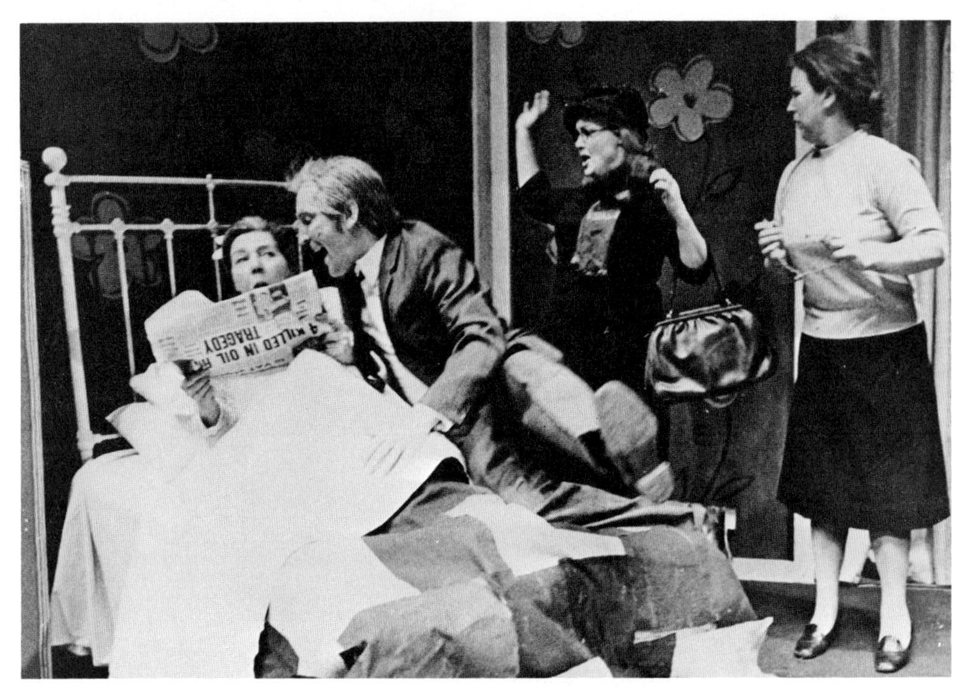

Collaboration was a considerable strain on the relationship between Yeats and Moore. Moore could not agree with Yeats that the play should be written in dialect nor that *Grania* should be portrayed as a peasant. After seeing the production of the play, however, both were in agreement about the necessity of building up a regular acting company. Moore thought it should be a stock company—British trained. Yeats preferred to look for an Irish company that would understand his objectives better. When A. E. (George Russell, 1867-1935) introduced Yeats to William and Frank Fay, organizers of an amateur group called the Ormonde Dramatic Society, Yeats was so impressed that he submitted his plays to them for production. At this point Moore withdrew from the Irish Literary Society.

Martyn had also withdrawn shortly before Moore, when he saw that his plays were not being performed. He had hoped that a more naturalistic theatre in the style of Ibsen would have developed, but Yeats' insistence on poetic drama based on heroic and folk material seemed to be holding sway.

The Irish Literary Theatre came to an end in 1901. It had served its purpose for Yeats. It had proved the possibility of a permanent national theatre in Dublin.

In April 1902, *Cathleen ni Houlihan,* a short patriotic play written by Yeats, was performed by an all-Irish cast, under the direction of the Fays, at St. Teresa's Temperance Hall in Dublin. The lead was played by Maud Gonne. The second play on the bill was *Dierdre,* written by A. E. and taken from the Irish legend. The plays were well received, and on the heels of this success the Irish National Theatre Society was formed. Yeats was elected president, Maud Gonne, A. E., and Douglas Hyde, vice-presidents, and W. G. Fay, stage manager. Nationalist dedication and political fervor ran high in this select company.

It was during his association with the Irish National Theatre Society that Yeats pulled further away from serving the cause of nationalism and became even more firmly committed to the service of art. When many of the company protested the production of John Millington Synge's *In the Shadow of the Glen,* and when the Irish press uniformly condemned the play as "a farcical libel on the character of Irish womanhood," Yeats saw clearly how the passion for nationalism could cloud one's vision of art.

Yeats, a seasoned veteran in the dramatic movement, was willing to forego his own creative development in the next several years and take on a new role of guardian. He defended the genius of Synge against the philistines. And he fought with untiring energy to "get the right for every man to see the world in his own way" admitted.

YEATS AND SYNGE

When Yeats first met John Millington Synge (1871-1909) in Paris in 1896, there was little he could see of the genius that Synge was to become. He advised him to give up Paris and go to the Aran Islands. Live there, he told Synge, as if you were one of the people themselves; "express a life that has never found expression." A few years later, when Yeats and Synge met again, he indicated that it was not creativity that he had expected from Synge, but scholarship. Yeats wrote that "he is really a most excellent man. . . . He works very hard and is learning Breton. He will be a very useful scholar." But, in 1903, when *In the Shadow of the Glen* and *Riders to the Sea* were read in Lady Gregory's drawing room, Yeats was to liken Synge to Sophocles and Aeschylus. This was the Irish genius which the dramatic movement had been seeking.

Yeats' praise of Synge was generous. On the reverse, there is very little written which expresses Synge's feelings about Yeats' genius. As Yeats says, "he hardly seemed aware of the existence of other writers. I never knew if he cared for a work of mine, but I do not remember that I had from him even a conventional compliment." Though there is little evidence of a close social relationship between them, there is much they have written which shows the deep respect and admiration they had for each other as creators.

Synge was impressed if not influenced by Yeats' early writings during 1902-1905. This was the period when Yeats was formulating and setting down principles of Irish poetic theatre, and Synge was in agreement with many of these principles.

As with Yeats, Synge was disillusioned with the naturalistic dramas of Ibsen, primarily for their lack of vitality. According to Joseph Wood Krutch, "Synge said that modern drama and all other forms of modern literature had ceased to be great or even true literature because modern literature had ceased to be at once True and Beautiful." Synge (and Yeats) felt that this was the inevitable consequence of destroying the folk roots of literature. It was important that the artist return to his country, and return to the spirit and imagination of the simple people of his own race. To draw one's themes and language from the folk spirit was to abandon the usually abstract questions—social, moral, and philosophical—that were so much a part of the modern drama of Europe.

It was in the people of Kerry and the Aran Islands that Yeats and Synge were to find their "next art." Yeats was drawn to these people because of the poetry in their language.

For both Yeats and Synge, the countryside was the place for the dramatist of the city to return to be renewed. Synge heard the poetry in the speech of the people, as Yeats did. He listened to the legends of the land as they had been carried down through the years into the life of today, but he saw something more than Yeats could have seen. He saw life itself. "On the stage one must have reality, one must have joy," Synge said in the preface to *The Playboy of the Western World.* "It is when we combine the ecstacy of a life, superb and wild, with the stoicism and simplicity of the realities that we achieve art." And the artist must record the harsh as well as gentle aspects of reality. Whereas Yeats looked for art in the peasant's history, Synge sought that art which is synonomous with the truth of the living peasant.

Though Yeats was a greater poet than Synge, Synge was the first to insist on the need to anchor poetry, no matter how ecstatic that poetry might be, in the common concerns of humanity. Synge wrote, in a letter to Yeats, " . . . for although exalted verse is the highest, it cannot keep its power unless there is essentially vital verse at the side of it." He was the first dramatist to set down truthfully the passion and splendor of folk life.

Both Yeats and Synge were firmly convinced that in any work of art, it was the artist's vision that was paramount, and it was the artist's personality that infused the work of art. Padraic Colum quotes Synge as saying that all his work was subjective and derived from his own moods. Yeats recognized the profundity of Synge's art, and it is a tribute to Yeats' greatness that he was willing to learn from him.

It was fortunate for the dramatic movement that Yeats was willing to defend Synge. The energy it would have sapped from Synge's creative life would have been intolerable. Synge was aware of how destructive the work of defense could be to an artist. However debilitating defense was to the artist, Yeats was too astute a man of the world not to realize that without defense art could be destroyed. This was the reason why he leaped so eagerly to the defense of Synge's *The Playboy of the Western World. The Playboy* became a principle; it was the answer to the political and religious attacks that had plagued the theatre for almost ten years.

Yeats had chosen his battleground well. *The Playboy* went into the tradition of the Abbey Theatre and changed the literary movement. It ended the interpretation of peasant life in terms of "crooning and faery" and supplanted these with violence and gusto; it encouraged writers to greater daring and the treatment of motifs that disturbed convention.

By 1911 it seemed as if Yeats' dreams of an Irish National Theatre had become a reality—Irish plays played by Irish actors before an Irish audience in a theatre which he owned and dominated. But there was one disturbing feature—the Irish dramatic movement was drifting away from Yeats' original conception of poetic drama.

Yeats had given his unlimited support to Synge when that creative genius was under fire, and it had turned the direction of the literary movement in a direction where Yeats could not and did not want to follow. But it was Yeats' courage that saved the dramatic movement in its finest hour.

SEAN O'CASEY—THE IRISH DRAMA COMES OF AGE

While the Irish drama was born in the movement under the guidance of Yeats and Synge, it remained for many years a nationalistic, provincial drama, known outside of Ireland only by a limited intelligentsia and a few theatre critics. It took the plays of Sean O'Casey (1880-1964) to make the Irish drama a truly international force.

O'Casey was born in the poor section of Dublin and grew to manhood in that city's slums. He received little formal education, but his intelligence was quick and questing and he rigorously applied himself to a program of self-improvement by way of constant reading. As a young man he held a number of jobs and became deeply involved in Ireland's growing movement toward independence. He joined the Sinn Fein, wrote some political tracts, and trained to take part in the Easter Rebellion of 1916.

The Shadow of a Gunman, produced at the Abbey Theatre in 1923, was O'Casey's first limited success. He followed it in 1924 with one of his best plays, *Juno and the Paycock*. These two plays established him as a major dramatist of more than limited national interests and concerns. However, because of his membership in the Sinn Fein and his near participation in the Easter Rebellion, many Irishmen expected O'Casey to continue to fight for Irish independence. Therefore, when *The Plough and the Stars* was produced in 1926 many Irish patriots came prepared to applaud. What they saw was a bitter attack on warfare generally and a cynical appraisal of the Irish patriotic movement that left them infuriated. There were battles at the theatre, with garbage thrown on the stage, and there were even riots in other areas of Dublin that were, apparently, provoked by the play.

Unhappy with the reception accorded *The Plough and the Stars*, sickened by the growing militancy of the nationalist writers and politicians, and disillusioned by the Irish religious restrictions, O'Casey left Ireland. He subsequently spent the largest part of his life in England, continuing to write plays but never again quite attaining the brilliance of *Gunman*, *Juno*, and *Plough*. Other major plays by O'Casey are *The Silver Tassie* (1929), *Within the Gates* (1934), *The Star Turns Red* (1940), *Red Roses for Me* (1943), *Purple Dust* (1945), *Cock-a-Doodle-Dandy* (1949), *The Bishop's Bonfire* (1955), and *The Night is Whispering* (later retitled *The Drums of Father Ned*, 1958). He also produced three volumes of autobiography: *I Knock at the Door*, *Pictures in the Hallway*, and *Drums Under the Window*.

As a dramatist, O'Casey worked in a variety of styles and forms—realism, expressionism, allegory, farce, and fantasy. The early realism

A scene from Sean O'Casey's *The Plough and the Stars* at the Abbey Theatre, 1976.

in which his best plays were written can be seen in *Juno and the Paycock*, which takes place in a small apartment in the slums of Dublin. Captain Jack Boyle, an exseaman and certainly never a captain, is a layabout who spends the largest part of his time (and whatever family money he can get his hands on) in the pubs with his friend Joxer Daly. The Captain's wife, Juno, through hard work and taking over unwillingly what she considers to be her husband's role of supervision, has managed to keep the family together. Boyle and Joxer, however, fail to understand what she is doing and consider her a nag and a tyrant.

Mary Boyle, the daughter, is having an affair with a local schoolteacher named Charles Bentham, who has written a will for Captain Boyle's cousin. When the cousin dies he leaves a substantial amount of money to the Captain, who celebrates by buying new furniture, overextending the family credit, and generally acting as if his own efforts were somehow responsible for this change in the family fortunes. This celebration is briefly interrupted by a neighbor's grief—Mrs. Tancred learns that her only son has been killed in the fight for independence and the funeral passes by under the Boyle's window. Mary becomes pregnant by Bentham, who deserts her and goes to England. It turns out that he failed to draw up the will in the proper manner and the Boyles, as a result, will get no money at all.

Johnny Boyle, the son, has been active in nationalistic activities. He has lost an arm and his hip has been damaged. When the Irish nationalists learn that Johnny betrayed Tancred, they come and kill Johnny in revenge. At last, in spite of Juno's heroic efforts, the family is destroyed. Juno, with Mary at her side, leaves Captain Boyle, the paycock, to drink and to his friend Joxer.

O'Casey's later affair with poetic, allegorical drama can be seen in *Within the Gates*. This play also displays the anticlerical bias that infused so much of his work. The action of the play all takes place within the gates of a public park. The main characters are a Poet (also known as the Dreamer), a Bishop, an Atheist, a Prostitute (also known as the Young Woman), and an Old Woman. The Young Woman is the child of the Old Woman and a theological student. The Young Woman was sent to a convent school and was eventually taken out by the Atheist, who was interested in her mother and who tried to convert the Young Woman to his beliefs, but without success. A series of incidents make the failure of the religious institutions apparent. A young Salvation Army Officer tries to interest the Young Woman in God, all the while seductively stroking her leg, and the Bishop steadfastly refuses to help her sort out her life. Eventually the Young Woman goes off with the Dreamer for a short period of love and song. She dies soon after dancing with the Dreamer.

Perhaps the strongest aspect of O'Casey's dramas, particularly in the later plays, is the beauty of his language. In the early, realistic dramas the language is complemented by the story. In these plays O'Casey used a tuneful, rhythmic, picturesque, and sometimes poetic prose that captured and extended the natural beauties of the Irish speech patterns. In the later plays, the symbolic and often allegorical fantasies, his language became even more poetic—perhaps too much so—and often too circuitous. In these late plays O'Casey seemed to take all his delight in the language itself, and sometimes gave too little reference to the narrative.

The first Dublin production of Sean O'Casey's *Cock-a-Doodle Dandy*, 1976, at the Abbey Theatre.

What O'Casey ultimately gave to the Irish drama, and indeed to the enduring drama of the world, was a brilliant style, beautiful dialogue, outstanding characterization, and a depth and breadth that took this drama out of the bounds of provincial nationalism and made it a drama for all people in all times.

THE TWENTIETH CENTURY IN AMERICA

At the turn of the century, American theatre was moving in two distinct and seemingly opposed directions. One direction was toward an organized commercialism and the other led directly toward a serious, artistic theatre.

In his production of *The Governor's Lady*, David Belasco put this exact replica of a Childs Restaurant onstage. (From *The Theatre*, 1912)

Immediately before the turn of the century the largest part of American theatre was the touring company—the road show. A few permanent regional theatres were scattered about the country, some of them boasting resident troupes, but New York was clearly the center of theatrical activity. Those theatres without resident troupes found it necessary to book all their shows out of New York, dealing with numerous producers.

This situation came neatly and unfortunately to an end in 1896 when Charles Frohman, Marc Klaw, Abraham Erlanger, and Al Hayman of New York, and Fred Zimmerman and Sam Nixon of Philadelphia banded together to form the Theatrical Syndicate. The Syndicate did not usually attempt to buy up, build, or in any way operate their own theatres. Instead they became an exclusive booking agency, getting control of major talent and then forcing theatre owners to book from them, or operate with inferior talent, or even to spend a large part of their season dark. They soon gained control of the major booking routes, which made touring financially impossible for the smaller, poorer troupes which could not then plan on finding bookings in major cities or towns a reasonable distance apart. Theatre owners or managers who attempted to hold out against the Syndicate were eliminated through pressure economics; in some extreme cases the Syndicate even built competing houses and supplied opposing shows at prices that forced the recalcitrant managers to knuckle under.

In spite of the pressure the Syndicate could bring to bear on a reluctant manager or producer, a few men did manage to hold out against them for awhile—notably James A. Herne, James O'Neill, and David Belasco—but eventually everyone except Mr. and Mrs. Harrison Fiske (the actress Minnie Maddern and her dramatist-editor husband) surrendered.

The stranglehold of the Syndicate began to loosen in 1900 when the Shubert brothers (Sam, Lee, and Jacob) leased a New York theatre, began putting on their own productions, and even established a rival theatre chain. Many

Samuel J. Hume, founder of Detroit's Arts and Crafts Theatre, designed this setting for Lord Dunsany's *The Tents of the Arabs.* (From Sheldon Cheney, *The Art Theatre*, New York, 1917)

managers, upset with the Syndicate's ruthless methods, defected to the Shuberts. This break in Syndicate power led directly to the formation of the National Theatre Owners Association, and by 1913 the power of the Syndicate was on the wane. In 1915 the death of Frohman, always the major force in the Syndicate, further weakened the organization, and by 1916 the period of the Syndicate was over.

The progress of American theatre toward a serious, artistic drama was not as clearly defined as the path toward commercialism, but progress was made. The plays of William Vaughn Moody were the opening wedge, along with a few of the plays of Clyde Fitch. The little theatre movement, sparked by interest in Ibsen and Shaw and what was going on in Europe, accelerated the movement. These were nonprofessional organizations and in most cases dedicated to promoting serious new American playwrights. The Toy Theatre, established in 1912 in Boston, was the first significant little theatre. It was followed by the Chicago Little Theatre, also in 1912; New York's Neighborhood Playhouse and Washington Square Players in 1915; the Provincetown Players in 1915; and the Detroit Arts and Crafts Theatre in 1916. These theatres, in the years immediately preceding World War I, led directly to the emergence of Eugene

O'Neill and a whole new generation of dedicated young American playwrights. Indeed, the period between 1896 and 1915 is in many ways the most important one in American theatre history.

Between World War I and World War II, American theatre underwent a virtual explosion. Fine new dramatists appeared. Theatre programs, such as George Pierce Baker's playwriting course at Harvard and his subsequent "47 Workshop" to produce plays written in his class, were established at colleges and universities throughout the country. Community theatres, nonprofessional and much like the little theatres but oriented more toward community entertainment and fulfillment, sprang up in cities and towns all across the country. And finally, the "new" stagecraft, imported from Europe just before World War I, began to flourish.

The new stagecraft really begins with Winthrop Ames (1871-1937) who had toured Europe to view continental theatrical production and who was so impressed with what he saw that, in 1912, he brought Max Reinhardt's production of *Sumurun* to New York. The excitement generated among young American designers by Reinhardt's production became apparent when, in 1915, the New York Stage Society, a private organization of theatre patrons, asked Harley Granville-Barker to direct a series of plays for the membership. For his production of Anatole France's *The Man Who Married a Dumb Wife,* Robert Edmond Jones was asked to design the settings. Jones, along with Lee Simonson and Sam Hume, had studied in Europe and become enamored of the new theatrical style.

ROBERT EDMOND JONES: It is virtually impossible to look at the American theatre during the years between 1915 and 1950 without coming across the work of Robert Edmond Jones (1887-1954). During these years the theatre abounds with examples and comments not only on his theories in design, but also on his philosophy of theatre as a totality. The brilliant, inventive and imaginative theatre that he helped to create can be seen in the settings of Jo Mielziner, in the plays of Arthur Miller, and in the acting of young theatre groups all across the country. He created a theatre that was symbolic, elegant, poetic, and eloquent—in these respects the exact opposite of the realistic theatre that surrounded him.

Robert Edmond Jones was born December 12, 1887, in Milton, New Hampshire, and grew up in an atmosphere of gentility, learning, and the Puritan ethic. He read books; he studied music; and he learned to draw and paint. He entered Harvard in 1906, graduating in 1910. As a boy he had read plays—Shakespeare in particular—but until he went to Harvard he had never seen a professional play, and it opened up a new world to him. He sought an education in drama, though he did not consider it as a career until he found he could combine his painting with theatre by way of stage design.

In 1913 Jones went to Europe, first to Florence and then on to Berlin, where he studied the work of Max Reinhardt. At the outbreak of World War I he returned to New York, where he soon was at work designing a set for the first production of the Washington Square Players. In 1915 he was selected by Harley Granville-Barker to design the set and costumes for his production of

Robert Edmond Jones' design for Shelly's *The Cenci*, which he planned to produce in the center of the audience, anticipating the revival of "theatre-in-the-round" or "arena" theatre.

The Man Who Married A Dumb Wife, which was the curtain raiser for Barker's production of *Androcles and the Lion*. Jones gave him a Reinhardt style set in black and white, with costumes in red, orange, and yellow. It was an auspicious beginning to a long and important career.

Over the next few years Jones designed several sets for Arthur Hopkins (1878-1950), worked regularly with the Provincetown Players and the Theatre Guild, and also did free-lance work. During this period he became closely associated with Eugene O'Neill, directing several of his plays and creating sets for *Desire Under the Elms*, *Mourning Becomes Electra*, and *The Iceman Cometh*. He was also a celebrated teacher, working with such talented students as Lee Simonson, Donald Oenslager, and Jo Mielziner. He designed a skeletal Tower of London for *Richard III*, a "mirrored confection" for Congreve's *Love for Love*, a water-color fantasy for Marc Connelly's *Green Pastures*, and a delicate gem for *Lute Song*, an adaptation of the ancient (c. 1350) Chinese play by Kao Ming.

Jones believed in teaching by example, in fusing his own personal sense of magic and excitement into his sets. In *Mourning Becomes Electra*, for example, following rough sketches by O'Neill, he used a brooding, neoclassic farmhouse to evoke the image of Greek tragedy. He designed sets reflecting his basic belief, by way of Appia, that the actor must be the central focus of theatre. For Jones it was the actor's representation of the author's words and actions that brought the play to life.

Theatre, Jones believed, existed in its magic and poetry, and thus he often went to Shakespeare to illustrate his theory. His sets were designed to evoke an image of a place, a feeling of the place, not to be the place itself. In Shakespeare he found the perfect example of this with an actor at the Globe providing all the setting necessary with the words, "In fair Verona where we lay our scene. . . ." Jones envisioned Hamlet standing on that same stage, looking out through the open roof at "this brave o'er hanging firmament, this majestical roof fretted with golden fire." "Golden fire" was the language Jones loved, and it gave him the image he needed to create a theatre that avoided the literal while pursuing the essential.

In lighting Jones found an infinitely usable tool for the creation of mood and emotion. Lighting, he felt, was the most primal of theatre mechanisms because it touches the animal in us, provoking our inherent fear of darkness while arousing our attraction to color. In *Richard III* and *Macbeth,* he made use of sharply defined light and shadow to highlight the hopes and fears of the characters. In *Love for Love* he used a bright, mirrored set, sparkling with light, to reflect the polished brilliance of Congreve's wit. He even looked forward to the day of mixed media productions, when film would be an integral part of lighting, enhancing the actor's characterization.

In costuming he believed in designing from the inside out, much as an actor designs a role. Starting with the basic personality, with the inner workings of the character, Jones believed, it is possible to work out toward a costume as rich in imagery as any aspect of the physical set.

Perhaps the most interesting thing about Jones was his ability to translate his vision into workable settings for such commonplace locales as a bar-

Robert Edmond Jones' design for the Theatre Guild production of Shakespeare's *Othello*. (From the souvenir program of the original production)

room or a New England farmhouse. Unfortunately, in terms of color usage, his renderings (reprinted in black and white) only hint at what audiences must have experienced. A critic described the barroom in *The Iceman Cometh* as "lustrous," and muted tones of the farmhouse in *Desire Under the Elms* reflected the harsh, yet beautiful, New England of Jones' youth.

The most impressive aspect of Jones' generalized but enthusiastic theory is that it worked, over and over again, and not only for Jones. His approach is still to be seen in today's theatre—in the cubic set of *Company* and in the mildly representational sets of *The Rothschilds*. His influence can be seen in sets which Arthur Miller demanded (and Jo Mielziner provided) for his plays, and in the concert staging of *Jesus Christ Superstar*.

For Jones the ultimate concept was *theatrical* as opposed to *realistic*. Certainly, as a concept this was not entirely new; while Jones was in college, Meyerhold was already assailing the detailed realism of Stanislavsky's sets, and many critics were fuming over what they called vulgar Belasco realism, or "Belascoism." When he completed his first design for the theatre, the "new stagecraft" was already an established fact, yet it took Jones to bring the theatre of symbolism and images to popular prominence in this country. Jones also contributed three major books to the theatre: *Continental Stagecraft* (1922) with Kenneth Macgowan, *Drawings for the Theatre* (1925), and a collection of his reflections on the theatrical arts titled *The Dramatic Imagination* (1941).

The new stagecraft was not a technical revolution; most of the technological necessities had been in use for a number of years. It was, rather, a visual revolution in which the by now traditional realistic approach was simplified, abstracted, and sometimes replaced with symbolic objects. After Jones, the major exponent of this approach was Norman Bel Geddes (1893-1958), who pioneered the concept of non-proscenium theatre. His design for Dante's *Divine Comedy*, an imaginative series of terraces (published in 1921 but never built) won him recognition from his fellow designers, and in 1923 his design for Reinhardt's production of *The Miracle* won the recognition of the rest of the theatrical world.

Like the Dante design, his 1930 plan for a theatre-in-the-round was never built. Then, in 1931, Bel Geddes designed a complex of steps and levels for a production of *Hamlet*. It was far in advance of its time and descendants of this design can still be seen today at theatres all over the country. He went on to design an experimental multiple setting for Sidney Kingsley's *Dead End* in 1935. The 1930s were the height of Bel Geddes' theatrical production, and for the rest of his career he concentrated on industrial design.

In more recent years the mantle of American scenic design was capably and even brilliantly worn by Jo Mielziner. He could hardly be described as a devotee of the new stagecraft, though he did study under Lee Simonson and Robert Edmond Jones. Neither could he be defined as strictly American or European in his approach. Indeed, he combined the best of all recent stagecraft into a style that was all his own and that has had great influence on the whole young generation of scenic designers.

Lee Simonson's design for *Hamlet*. The designs for this projected production called for a revolving stage which would keep turning to reveal new locations.

JO MIELZINER: Jo Mielziner (1901-76), one of the foremost theatrical designers of the past few decades, besides an impressive array of scenic designs for all segments of the performing arts, also made highly important contributions as a theatre architectural consultant, lecturer, and author. In spite of his enormous success as a designer, Mielziner sometimes tended to dwell on his frailness as a fallible human being in the world of art. He freely admitted his mistakes, and it is perhaps this openness that permitted him to speak so clearly and distinctly about his successes, with no touch of aggravating self-esteem, and with unusual clarity for an artist discussing his work.

Jo Mielziner was born in Paris in his father's Latin Quarter studio, and he grew up handling clay and paint and absorbing the artistic atmosphere of turn-of-the-century Paris. His father was Leo Mielziner, an artist who worked mainly in portraits. His mother, Ella Mielziner, was, during those early years, a correspondent for *Vogue*, covering the artistic life of Paris—theatre, music, and painting. She was an avid theatregoer, and Jo and his brother were exposed to the dramatic arts at an early age. In fact, it was at his mother's suggestion, during his apprenticeship as an artist, that Jo sought a position as theatrical scene painter. The Mielziners moved to the United States, where Jo attended the Pennsylvania Academy of Fine Arts. This education was helped along by a series of scholarships, and Jo eventually gave up all other studies to devote himself to art.

During the early years in America Jo's older brother, Kenneth, was having a degree of success in juvenile leads. He talked Jo into taking a job as an apprentice in the Bonstelle Stock Company in Detroit, where he worked in various positions such as actor and assistant stage manager. From Bonstelle, Mielziner went to the Theatre Guild in New York to continue his apprenticeship, eventually ending up as apprentice to Lee Simonson, and later to Robert Edmond Jones. Mielziner's first position on Broadway was as actor and stage manager for the Theatre Guild's production of Henri-René Lenormand's *The Failures* (*Les rates*) at the Garrick Theatre in 1923. Almost a year later he designed his first Broadway show, Ferenc Molnar's *The Guardsman* (*Atestör*), produced by the Theatre Guild and starring the Lunts. Following the success of this first production, Mielziner had an almost unbroken series of outstanding designs.

In all his written works, Mielziner demonstrated a deep concern for the beginning theatrical designer and tried patiently to let upcoming artists know

Jo Mielziner's 1935 design for Maxwell Anderson's *Winterset*.

about the pitfalls that they might encounter. Especially valuable in this sense is his warning about the six sins of omission that he himself committed during his early years as a designer.

The first sin was mistaking means for ends, which is to say, allowing egotism to rule instead of having proper concern for the unity of the production. Two of Mielziner's designs, for *That Awful Mrs. Eaton* and Arthur Schnitzler's *Anatol*, are examples of overstatement to a point of gaudiness. This not only distracted from the unity of the production but slowed scene changes, damaging the pacing and overall effect of the play.

The second sin was in turning to the theatre merely as a method of earning a living. Again, Mielziner's ego played a part in creating the problem. He enjoyed seeing his settings realized onstage and under lights, almost to the point of resenting the actors screening his creation from an admiring audience. It is always interesting to hear an artist confess to his faults, if only because so many people seem to think that all fine artists are great from the beginning, never failing, always growing in their art. Mielziner did indeed grow, but he also learned.

Sin number three was not learning early enough the importance of collaboration between the major creative artists. Theatre is at all times and in all ways a collaborative art, and Mielziner had to learn the full importance to the total theatrical production of the scenic designer, the lighting designer, the costume designer, the actors, and the director.

Sin number four was a failure to develop early the substantial critical ability necessary to get beneath the surface of the playwright's descriptions. When at last he began to read plays with deeper insight, he was able to put more into a setting than the mere requirements of the script embellished by his own ego.

The fifth sin of omission was a failure to recognize the need for collaboration, not only with the major designers but with the whole of the production company. Finally recognizing this necessity, Mielziner developed a concept in which the designers, producer, actors, composer, lyricist, choreographer, dancers, and so on, all work together like the spokes of a wheel. The hub of the wheel is the dramatist, and the rim of the wheel is the director, the one who sees to it that each spoke does its own share of the lifting and pulling on behalf of the dramatist. All the spokes of the wheel must work in unison to make a production a success.

Sin number six was the failure to recognize the complicated nature of the physical structure that houses drama. This last became an area of great interest to Mielziner, who in his later years became deeply involved in studies of the problems of designing theatre facilities. He designed many theatres and consulted on a number of others. His book on the subject, *The Shapes of Our Theatre* (1970), is a study of the history of theatre structure, containing fascinating ideas regarding solutions to problems that will be faced in the future. Besides covering the prerequisites of solid architectural planning of theatres, Mielziner also discusses many of the typical follies that can and have resulted in unworkable theatre structures, or stages that are extremely awkward to use. His book probes deeply into the problems that will likely face future theatres. How will they be designed? "No vital, truly contemporary theatre

Jo Mielziner's most famous setting, for *Death of a Salesman,* as it looked with the leaves projected over it.

can be conceived by traditional knowledge alone; on the other hand, the designer whose sole credo is 'innovation' is either dishonest in proclaiming unequivocal divorce from past tradition, or is apt to produce an ill-conceived theatre design." For Mielziner, the truly creative theatre architect will look to the past as well as to the future for solutions.

Jo Mielziner's contribution to theatre covered more than fifty years and included a collection of outstanding scenic designs that is almost unrivaled. In addition to his design contributions, he provided books, articles, and lectures covering the whole range of theatre's physical aspects. Finally, he worked diligently to improve the design of theatre facilities, ensuring that theatres to come will be more useful and more efficient in every way. Someday this last may be considered his greatest contribution.

As was true in stagecraft, European influence permeated American theatre throughout the 1920s, due mostly to a 1923-24 American tour by the Moscow Art Theatre. The interest provoked by the troupe's performance, especially its realistic acting techniques, was great, and the influence this touring company had on the developing American theatre was great. Even more important, however, was the decision of two of Stanislavsky's actors—Richard Boleslavsky (1889-1937) and Maria Ouspenskaya (1881-1949)—to remain in the United States and conduct the American Laboratory Theatre. They taught

Stanislavsky's system in a slightly modified version that was later popularized by Boleslavsky's book, *Acting, the First Six Lessons* (1933). Among their students were Stella Adler, Lee Strasberg, and Harold Clurman.

Periods rarely begin or end as neatly as the fussy historian would like, but the 1920s ended neatly in October 1929, with the stock market crash. The ensuing depression brought out the best and worst in theatre. In the beginning a number of experimental companies and schools sought to explore their art and the economic-sociological phenomenon of the depression. The best of these was clearly the Group Theatre, which Lee Strasberg (1901-), Cheryl Crawford (1902-), and Harold Clurman (1901-) began in 1931. The Group's approach was based on Stanislavsky's method, as modified first by Boleslavsky and then by the founders. With players such as Morris Carnovsky (1898-), Stella Adler (1904-), and Elia Kazan (1909-) it presented a series of outstanding plays by such young playwrights as William Saroyan, Maxwell Anderson, Paul Green, Sidney Kingsley, and especially Clifford Odets.

Other new and exciting theatre in the 1930s was presented by the membership of the Federal Theatre Project, begun in 1935 under the direction of

A scene from the Federal Theatre "Living Newspaper" production, *One-Third of a Nation.*

Hallie Flanagan Davis to ease unemployment in the theatrical area. The group was highly experimental and quite large, employing at one time nearly ten thousand theatre people. Today, it is primarily remembered for its creation of the "Living Newspaper" which sought, through interspersing vignettes with actual newspaper stories, to comment on the social-economic situation.

A near cousin to the Project was the "workers' theatre" movement. Begun in 1926 as the Worker's Drama League, it became, in 1932, the New Theatre League. Its success was limited, however, due to its members' insistence on doing only socialistic protest plays.

Near the end of the 1930s the most exciting happening was probably the formation of the Mercury Theatre in 1937 by Orson Welles (1915-) and John Houseman (1902-). Its first production was of Marc Blitzstein's *The Cradle Will Rock,* and its greatest success was *Julius Caesar,* which was done as a comment on the fascism growing so rapidly in Europe.

While the effects of the depression on theatre were undoubtedly great, in many ways the pattern of commercialism established in 1896 only grew stronger. The length of runs increased, largely because of economic necessity. The "pure entertainment" function of commercial theatre was exploited, mainly to keep theatre competitive with the motion picture. Partly as a result of this, one of the most purely American forms of theatre—the musical—began to develop great popularity. The musical revues of Florenz Ziegfeld, Earl Carroll, and George White became, in 1927, *Show Boat,* the first of the true musical dramas. During the 1930's, thirty-five musicals—mostly plays rather than revues—opened in New York, and some of them are memorable indeed: *Of Thee I Sing* (1931), *Face the Music* and *The Gay Divorcee* (1932), *Roberta* (1933), *Anything Goes* (1934), *Jumbo* and *Porgy and Bess* (1935), *On Your Toes* (1936), *Babes in Arms* (1937), *The Boys From Syracuse, Hellzapoppin',* and *Knickerbocker Holiday* (1938), and *Du Barry Was A Lady* (1939).

World War II exceeded its predecessor in every way, mocking the earlier slogan that World War I was the "war to end all wars." The United States, pulled into the conflict in 1941 by the attack on Pearl Harbor, mobilized all its resources, including the theatrical. Performers toured military installations for the USO, or toured the country to sell war bonds. It was a lean period for theatre, with only *Oklahoma* (1943) and *A Bell for Adano* (1944) moving outside of the traditional forms.

When the war ended the combination of motion pictures and, soon, rapidly expanding television, gave theatre its greatest challenge since the phenomenal growth of the motion picture industry in the 1930s. By 1948 there were 48 television stations, scattered between twenty-five cities, broadcasting to some seven hundred thousand home television sets. By 1958 there were 512 stations broadcasting to more than fifty million sets. By 1960 more than eighty-five percent of the people in the United States regularly watched television.

Interestingly, this did not destroy live theatre, though there were many prophets regularly predicting its demise. More and more theatre programs were developed at the colleges and universities. Community theatres, many of them serious, artistic ventures, sprang up in cities, towns, and small communities all over the country. Summer theatres, many of them in circuslike tents or in barns, began to proliferate. Major regional theatres developed in places that once had been regarded as unlikely spots for serious theatre—places such as Minneapolis-St. Paul, Tampa, and Houston. In New York, off-Broadway and even off-off-Broadway theatres began to draw substantial audiences for often exciting, experimental productions.

During the 1960s, largely because of the national schizophrenia brought on by the war in Vietnam, the theatre exploded into various new types of productions. There was antiwar drama, guerrilla theatre (addressing itself to literally hundreds of concerns), protest theatre (protesting almost everything), psycho-drama (which is in reality more a psychological tool than a viable form of theatre), experimental theatre of all kinds, theatre of the absurd, and (stronger than ever) the traditional drama.

More, perhaps, than any other theatre group in recent times, the group that calls itself the Living Theatre has influenced existing theatrical presentation—that is, it has explored new pathways, returned to poetic drama, and made possible new (or in some ways, old) language. In part this is because of the wide-ranging interests and the deep commitment to theatre of its founders, Julian Beck and Judith Malina. Also in part it is because of the energy and determination of the company to survive as an immediate viable theatrical entity. Founded in the late 1940s, the Living Theatre lasted until 1969 as a specific unit, and in a sense it still exists in the activities of the cells into which it has divided.

The Living Theatre became possible when Judith Malina (1926-   ), daughter of an orthodox rabbi who had fled Kiel, Germany, in 1928, met Julian Beck (1925-   ), son of a middle-class New York Jewish distributor of Volkswagen parts. This meeting in 1943 did not lead to action until 1946, when these two projected a temple for the nurturing of real music, poetic dance, painting, and a meaningful theatre that would combine all of these. The founders even composed that requisite of all revolutionary theatre, a manifesto, in which they defined their theatre as a method of encouraging poets to write plays by giving them a stage where such plays could be produced. This emphasis on poetic drama became a constant of the Living Theatre from its actual birth, in 1946, when they rented a basement, which they called the Wooster Stage, until they split up in 1969. The background of this project included the experiences of these two people in the depression of the 1930s, World War II and the concentration camps, the growing revolutionary movement, and a total commitment to art generally and to theatre as a holy of holies.

The Wooster Stage did not last long. The company was barely into the rehearsal of some Pound-Fenellosa versions of Noh plays when it was closed by the police, who were convinced that it was a front for a brothel. When they wrote Ezra Pound about their closure and the reason given, he responded by wondering how else a serious theatre could manage to support itself in New York. From 1948 to 1951 the Living Theatre stage was in the Beck-Malina apartment, where they tried to do poetic drama in a rather structured manner. They eventually did Lorca, Paul Goodman, Kenneth Rexroth, Gertrude Stein, Eliot, W. H. Auden, and William Carlos Williams, but the internal structure of the poetry itself, perhaps, denied the fluidity of staging that the Living Theatre was to accomplish later.

In 1951 they leased the Cherry Lane Theatre, and their first presentation was a series of short plays: *Ladies Voices*, by Gertrude Stein; *Childish Jokes*, by Paul Goodman; *He Who Says Yes and He Who Says No*, by Brecht; and *The Dialogue of the Mannikin and the Young Man*, by García Lorca. The first full-length production was another play by Stein, *Doctor Faustus Lights the Lights*. This interest in Stein grew largely out of an early commitment to form. Stein's work attracted Beck and Malina because it was revolutionary in terms of the word; it was part of a revolution that tried to revivify language and, along with this, to purify the basic structure and form of literature by getting rid of the platitudes and clichés and expanding the boundaries of meaning. Stein's plays and librettos try, often painfully, to dredge up metaphysical knowledge in the form of emotional and psychological associations, and in so doing she left almost totally to the director the physical actions that would fit the rhythms of her work.

The season at Cherry Lane began with verse plays, and the company eventually went on to such verse dramas as *Sweeney Agonistes*, by T. S. Eliot; *The Age of Anxiety*, by W. H. Auden; *The Idiot King*, by Claude Fredericks; *Phèdre* by Jean Racine; *The Cave at Machpelah*, by Paul Goodman; and *Women of Trachis*, adapted by Ezra Pound from Sophocles' play. In addition they did such "partial" verse drama as *Many loves*, by William Carlos Williams; *The Young Disciple*, by Paul Goodman; and *A Man Is a Man*, by Bertolt Brecht. Sometimes the dramas worked.

Technically, during its early period the Living Theatre tried a wide variety of stage effects. In *Beyond the Mountains*, by Kenneth Rexroth, they used many types of artifice, such as masks, dances to express inexpressible climaxes, plain costumes all black or white or gold, and sets consisting of large squares of cloth supported by ropes. For Goodman's *Faustina* they tried a symbolic set featuring hearts, livers, and other organs, and achieving a startling scenic effect when the architectural façade representing the civilization of Rome disappeared, leaving the stage bare of all trappings at the moment when Faustina speaks to the audience, reproaching them for not stepping in to halt the bloody action of the play. They tried *The Idiot King* in vague contemporary costume, and *Phèdre* very formally in seventeenth century costume on a stark white set glistening with the light that Racine speaks of throughout the script.

In terms of acting, they spoke Rexroth's ponderous, ornamented verse in a romantic, musical manner, and Goodman's spare verse in a manner that was strong, hard, and bold. They rehearsed Auden's *The Age of Anxiety* for over a year, trying through verbal technique and variation to break down the barriers created by the multiple meanings of the verse, searching for a style that would be clear and simple and yet preserve the several levels of the poetry. Racine's play was staged so formally in terms of movement that it was compared to a Japanese ballet, and for *The Cave at Machpelah* they combined various acting styles, from the formal style of a Corneille production to a realistic contemporary style.

Technically it was a period of broad experimentation that never satisfactorily resolved the basic problems inherent in handling verse drama. Ultimately, however, it led directly to the clean, simple, fluid style that characterized so much of the Living Theatre's later work.

Cherry Lane was closed by the fire department, and the company moved into a loft on One Hundredth Street, opening in 1954 with *The Age of Anxiety*. After nine major productions, spanning more than five years, the loft was closed by the building department. On July 15, 1959, the company opened the Fourteenth Street Theatre with what may be their greatest theatrical triumph, *The Connection*, by Jack Gelber. This theatre lasted until the production of Kenneth Brown's *The Brig*, in 1963, after (or during) which they were evicted by the landlord, and the building was occupied by the Internal Revenue Service.

Beck himself has pointed out that the work of the Living Theatre breaks up into three neat periods (to which should be added a fourth) that relate directly to the theatres occupied by the company. At the Cherry Lane they were making their initial statements and experimenting with their direction; at One Hundredth Street they were exploring techniques and learning their craft; at Fourteenth Street they were using what they had learned to "break through" the traditional limitations of theatre, moving from their early, formalistic notions toward something fluid and adaptable. In 1963 the Fourteenth Street Theatre closed and the Becks were tried for their tax debt and jailed for contempt of court, after which the company set off for the first of several tours of Europe, returning to the United States only to tour. It was on tour in Europe that the fourth phase of their work took form. In such creations as *Antigone*, *Mysteries*, and *Frankenstein* they developed a unitized flowing style that—in much the same manner as the Medieval drama of hundreds of years before—allowed them to handle time and space in all their dimensions.

In 1969 the Living Theatre split up into cells. Most of those cells have remained active, and Beck and Malina seem to be everywhere, turning up in New Haven one week and in San Francisco on the following week to demonstrate and discuss the achievements of Living Theatre with convening members of the American Theatre Association. It was a long pull for a small experimental theatre group, and before it split up the Living Theatre was one of the most exciting companies in the Western world. To some degree the revolution they sparked is still going on.

In 1963, by way of a series of experimental workshops, Joseph Chaikin initiated a program devoted to exploring new forms in theatre. Since that year the Open Theatre has been one of the most important of the little theatre groups, testing its theories and practices before semiprivate audiences in small New York and European theatres, until its demise, at the end of the 1967 season. Following its seminal role in creating two major productions (*America Hurrah* and *Viet Rock*), the Open Theatre began emerging as one of the best and most disciplined experimental companies in the United States. This reputation, besides the company's generally recognized excellence, owed much to the fact that its founder is both a philosopher and a moralist. Overwhelmed by the necessity to explore the fears and frustrations of life outside the theatre, much of Chaikin's work has developed an existential bias; for Chaikin it is behavior rather than ideas that provides insight and understanding.

Starting in 1959, Chaikin became one of the principal actors of the Living Theatre company, appearing in plays by Pirandello, Brecht, Gelber, Goodman, and William Carlos Williams. Thus, he learned from experience the demands that such drama can make, not only artistically but in terms of theatrical craftsmanship. Twice he started acting workshops within the Living Theatre company, but the continuing state of emergency attending the Living Theatre's early performances kept students away. Finally, with a group of Nola Chilton's exstudents, Chaikin found.the opportunity to explore innovative acting and staging techniques for nonnaturalistic materials.

Chaikin was definitely the moving force behind the Open Theatre, and it was his own personal popularity that drew the company and held it together. Throughout its existence, however, Chaikin maintained what one might call a diplomatic relationship with the company's internal affairs. Disliking personal politics, he avoided direct intervention in the various relations between actors and a workshop leader, or director, or writer. This pattern of nonintervention is important since it shaped philosophically the work of the troupe.

Participation in the workshop was not limited only to actors—playwrights, critics, and directors also took part. The roster of such participants indicates part of the reason for the company's success, including such people as directors Peter Feldman, Jacques Levy, and Roberta Sklar; writers Megan Terry, Jean-Claude van Itallie, and Michael Smith; and critics Gordon Rogoff and Richard Gilman.

Chaikin knew enough, or had learned enough from his stint with the Living Theatre, to start the theatrical exploratory work from where the Open Theatre actors "already were"—from the Method, which was based on Stainislavsky's principles, and from certain variations on the Method worked out by Nola Chilton (who had evolved certain exercises to help actors deal with nonnaturalistic materials). Chilton had used, for example, a principle of physical adjustment as an actor's "way-into-character" for absurdist plays. Her exercise, called "weapon people," provided a route of march into nonpsychological characterization by providing the actors with weapon images. This helped the performers to make physical adjustments to pure abstraction, and this physical adjustment principle seems to have led to Chaikin's "sound-and-movement" technique, which was the Open Theatre's basic unit of expression. The technique was a transmission of energy and a passing of kinetic material between two actors who come together and thereby create a dramatic event by inhabiting the same kinetic environment.

In the development of the Open Theatre's postnaturalistic theatre technique, sound-and-movement was the first step toward a series of exercises designed to promote in the actor the principle of seeking the essential physical expression of an emotion or attitude. In other words, the Open Theatre company sought to apply to acting technique the general principle that art is the image (rather than the result) of a process of investigation carried out by its creator. This was the basic concept of Chaikin's workshop research throughout the history of the company.

In addition to the exercises and techniques that Chaikin evolved in his workshop, the Open Theatre also borrowed freely from the techniques of other theorists on the art of acting, particularly Viola Spolin, Jerzy Grotowski, and Joseph Schlicter. It became a principle of the workshop that members would teach each other what they had learned elsewhere, and among the first things the company took up were Viola Spolin's theatre games, which Chaikin had encountered in the summer of 1963 while working with the Second City company in Chicago. The exercises included "Walking in Space," "Touching the Air," "Passing and Receiving," "Molding an Object," "Imaginary Objects," "Machines," "Focus," "Mirror Images," and "Transformation" (a radical change in the circumstances of a given improvisation, made by the actor's own improvising).

The basic strategy of Chaikin's work over the years was to make things visible in action. Thus, the workshop approached theatre not through talking but through doing. Discussion was minimal, and the emphasis was on improvising. By structuring the improvisations, Chaikin was able to structure the inquiry into the subject, and the result was always a scene that emerged from an inquiry conducted in totally theatrical terms. "The Odets Kitchen," for example, was an investigation of the reality behind (or perhaps below) surface behavior. Jean-Claude van Itallie, then a new writer and member of Chaikin's workshop, wrote a short naturalistic scene in which a mother, a father, and a daughter are stuck in their tiny New York apartment on a rainy day: the mother irons, the father watches television, and the daughter mopes. At first the three actors merely performed the script as written (labeled "the outside"). Then they began to explore the internal aspects of these characters through improvisation. Since these improvisations made use of the actors' intuitions it tapped their own internal reactions and processes and made available material that is difficult to reach by rational pathways. In the "outside" production of the script, Mother Odets might express satisfaction at finally getting the ironing done. This expression of relieved satisfaction did not necessarily take place, however, in the "inside" improvisation, where the actress might display pain (a burn from the hot iron) or intense frustration (from the monotony of ironing).

The Open Theatre, urged on by several of its supporters, rented the Sheridan Square Theatre for two performances in December 1963 and the Martinique Theatre for two performances the following April. The program for the performances contained the following explanation of the group and its purpose:

> *What you will see tonight is a phase of work of the Open Theatre. This group of actors, musicians, playwrights, and directors have come together out of a dissatisfaction with the established trend of the contemporary theatre. It is seeking a theatre for today. It is now exploring certain specific aspects of the stage not as a production group, but as a group trying to find its own voice. Statable tenets of this workshop: (1) to create a situation in which the actors can play together with a sensitivity to one another required of an ensemble, (2) to explore the specific powers that only the live theatre possesses, (3) to concentrate on a theatre of abstraction and illusion (as opposed to a theatre of behavioral or psychological motivation), (4) to discover ways in which the artist can find his expression without money as the determining factor.*

For the season of 1965-66, Ellen Stewart (of the Cafe LaMama) arranged for the troupe to appear at her theatre during one week of each month. As a result of her interest the Open Theatre was able to present its first full-length play developed improvisationally by a writer working with the troupe. *Viet Rock* was the first work to harness the frenetic energy of the early improvisations, and came directly out of the workshop that Megan Terry ran on Saturdays in 1965-66.

During the winter and spring of 1967, the Open Theatre came slowly to a stop, in large part because Chaikin felt the time had come to change direction—to explore America's internal problems of war, civil rights, and student dissension—and so the workshop closed at the end of the season. In the fall of 1967, however, Chaikin embarked on a path which led to a recognizable and interesting synthesis of the "inner-outer" duality in his production of the Open Theatre's first mature work of art—*The Serpent.*

The theatre of the 1970s seems to have retreated a bit from the violence and obscenity and uncontrolled experimentation of the 1960s. Emphasis is once again being given to the "word" in theatre—to the spoken language—and an emphasis on design has replaced the earlier demand for technical effects. Exactly where theatre is going is still undetermined, but it is alive, healthy, and clearly going somewhere.

TWENTIETH CENTURY AMERICAN DRAMA

In a very real sense, the twentieth century American drama begins with William Vaughn Moody (1869-1910), a poet, scholar, and playwright. Moody

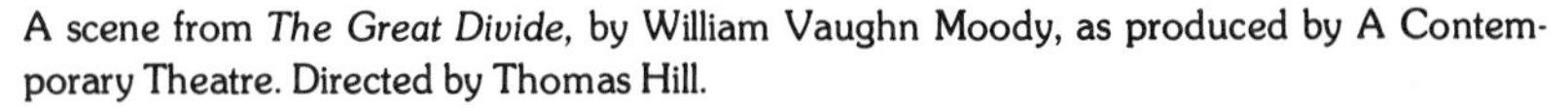

A scene from *The Great Divide,* by William Vaughn Moody, as produced by A Contemporary Theatre. Directed by Thomas Hill.

was born in Spencer, Indiana, and after a short stint of high school teaching he entered Harvard University in 1889. Completing his master's degree, he went on to teach English at the University of Chicago where, with Robert Lovett, he wrote *A History of English Literature* (1902), primarily in the hope that it would free him from academic drudgery. He almost completed a trilogy of poetic dramas: *Masque of Judgment* (1900); *The Fire-bringer* (1904); and *The Death of Eve* (which was never finished). These plays use, successively, Greek, Christian, and Hebraic mythology to explore man's relationship with God and, ultimately, to assert the impossibility of a division between man and his Creator. None of these verse dramas was ever produced.

It was in his prose plays, however, that Moody achieved real significance in terms of the American drama. *The Great Divide* (1906, under the title *A Sabine Woman*) and *The Faith Healer* (1909) were serious prose plays that departed from the traditions of their time to explore major aspects of American life. *The Great Divide* treated the conflict of values between the American east and west, and the necessity of achieving moral and spiritual unity. *The Faith Healer* dramatized the conflict between earthly and spiritual love, and celebrated the triumph of the spiritual over the merely biological.

Perhaps Moody's contribution can best be summed up in terms of the body of his work. He took an art form much abused and provided it with realism (to the best of his understanding and capability), depth, and sensitivity.

At the same time that Moody was attempting to make drama a more meaningful form, several other playwrights of lesser intellect but perhaps greater dramatic talent were also turning out some good plays. The best of these was probably Clyde Fitch (1865-1909), who was also the first American playwright to win wide recognition in Europe. Fitch wrote a total of fifty-five plays—thirty-three were original, and twenty-two were adaptations of novels or European plays.

Fitch was clearly the most popular playwright of the period. During the 1900-01 season he had four plays running concurrently in New York, and as a result of one of them, *Captain Jinks of the Horse Marines*, a young actress named Ethel Barrymore became a star.

The best of Fitch's early plays are probably *Nathan Hale* (1898) and *Barbara Frietchie* (1899), both based on characters out of American history. Among his best later works are *The Stubbornness of Geraldine* (1902), dealing with an American abroad, *The Girl with the Green Eyes* (1902), a study of jealousy, *The Truth* (1906), and *The Woman in the Case* (1909). Like Moody, Fitch was deeply interested in aspects of American life, but unlike Moody he bowed to the conventions of the day and included in his works a melodrama that seriously weakens them.

One of the most interesting and creatively long-lived of the early playwrights is Elmer Rice (really Reizenstein, 1892-1967), who studied and then practiced law and became a successful playwright at age twenty-two with a melodrama titled *On Trial* (1914). Dramatically it is a terrible play, but it is interesting because it introduced Rice to the stage and because it is the first American play to make use of what has since become a standard film technique—the flashback. After this initial production Rice had several fail-

American expressionism is evident in this production of Elmer Rice's *The Adding Machine*. Directed by Ron Dieb.

ures, and then in 1923 came *The Adding Machine*, an expressionistic indictment of the "machine age." The play had a limited run, was not popular, and received only guarded critical response. However, after some later revivals it was recognized as an important element in American theatre. In 1929 Rice's next play, *Street Scene*, won the Pulitzer Prize. It deals with life in the slums of early 1929 and the people who dwell in them.

The horrors of the Depression moved Rice to write *We, the People* (1930), and an early flirtation with Communism brought about *Between Two Worlds* (1934). Both plays failed and Rice swore to leave the stage, but not until he had impaled it on the dull horn of some rather bad satire in *Not For Children* (1935). In 1938 he returned to the stage with his production of *Flight to the West*, a passionate attack on Nazism. *A New Life* (1942) is insignificant, but in 1945, with *Dream Girl*, Rice finally managed to recapture his dramatic talent. In 1947 he revised *Street Scene* to fit music by Kurt Weill. His 1958 *Cue for Passion*, a bad psychological variation on *Hamlet*, has little merit.

In the year 1888 two of America's best dramatists were born—Eugene Gladstone O'Neill and Maxwell Anderson. Although he never attained the artistic stature of O'Neill, Anderson (1888-1959) went on to become one of America's most popular and respected playwrights. He graduated from the University of North Dakota in 1911, went on to try college teaching and newspaper reporting before, in 1923, having his first play produced—*White Desert*. The play was a theatrical failure, but it was written partly in verse and indicated the preoccupation with the poetic form that Anderson would display throughout his distinguished career. His one total departure from the poetic drama came in the following year when, with Laurence Stallings, he coauthored *What Price Glory?* It was a great popular success, dealing with the American soldier in battle during World War I with realism, sympathy, and humor. Two more plays written with Stallings failed to achieve the success of their first effort.

In 1927 Anderson finished *Saturday's Children*, a serious comedy about the effect of marriage on two young people. It was highly successful, partly because it has a serious statement to make, and the critical raves for its intellectual value perhaps misled Anderson, for he followed it in 1928 with *Gods of the Lightning*, a thesis play which also has a great deal to say, but which failed badly with both critics and audiences.

Following *Gypsy* (1929), an attempt at urban realism, Anderson completed a series of poetic historical dramas, the best of which are *Elizabeth the Queen* (1930), *Night over Taos* (1932), *Mary of Scotland* (1933), *Valley Forge* (1934), and *Wingless Victory* (1936). These plays were all commercially successful; the poetry is effective, and the style and tone are neatly adjusted to suit the topic and theme.

The best plays of his middle period are *High Tor* (1936), *The Masque of Kings* (1937), *Knickerbocker Holiday* (1938), and *Key Largo* (1939). *Winterset* (1935), which Anderson also wrote during this period, stands apart from the other works. It is his attempt to write a poetic tragic drama using the materials of American urban life in the 1930s, and while it is a noble attempt it somehow misses its mark.

The best plays of his later period are *The Eve of St. Mark* (1942), *Storm Operation* (1944), *Truckline Cafe* (1946), *Joan of Lorraine* (1946), *Anne of the Thousand Days* (1948), and *The Bad Seed* (1954).

EUGENE O'NEILL: Writing to Professor George Pierce Baker of Harvard in 1913, Eugene O'Neill (1888-1953) said simply, "I want to be an artist or nothing." His dedication to this goal never slackened and he allowed nothing to interfere with his steady progress toward becoming America's outstanding playwright. Even though most evaluations of O'Neill's stature as a dramatist are, all too often, merely reflections of individual preference, his impact on theatre cannot be denied. Perhaps this tendency toward an all too personal critical assessment grows out of the fact that O'Neill's plays always provoke strong emotional responses from audiences, and his work seemed constantly to fluctuate between high achievement and miserable failure. After the 1920 production of *Beyond the Horizon*, when O'Neill emerged as a major playwright, he received some of the most extravagant critical praise and contemtuous scorn ever directed toward a serious modern dramatist. Perhaps, too, this highly personal reaction of the critics to O'Neill's work is caused in part by O'Neill's own personal involvement in the material of his plays.

O'Neill once wrote "I don't think any real dramatic stuff is created out of the top of your head. . . . I have never written anything which did not come directly or indirectly from some event or impression of my own." Indeed, he had vast resources of personal events and impressions to draw upon—much of it filled with anguish and personal tragedy. In what may ultimately be considered his greatest play, *Long Day's Journey into Night* (written in 1941, produced in 1956), O'Neill portrays with remorseless honesty his own family. The characters in the play are called the Tyrones, but they are reasonably accurate pictures of O'Neill's parents, his brother, and himself. Like the elder Tyrone in the play, O'Neill's father became an embittered actor, filled with self-pity over his failure to fulfill his potential and attain greatness in his profession. O'Neill's elder brother died in 1923 of alcoholism, and Eugene himself was tormented by sickness and an inner frustration. His mother, a drug addict, finally entered a convent, overcame her addiction, and died in 1922.

O'Neill could not grow up in this kind of tragedy-ridden background and remain unscathed. For years he took refuge in alcohol, and throughout his life he suffered from a variety of illnesses. His extremely sensitive nature caused him to become so despondent that at times he even threatened suicide. After achieving fame as a dramatist he began to lash out at his children, primarily out of resentment at their interference with his privacy and his writing.

In 1909 O'Neil impulsively married Kathleen Jenkins, whom he later abandoned when she was pregnant. He did not meet their son, Eugene, Jr., until the boy was twelve years old. Eugene, Jr. commited suicide in 1950. O'Neill eventually disinherited his other two children, Shawn and Oona.

The program cover of the Theatre Guild's production of O'Neill's lone successful comedy, *Ah, Wilderness!*

The influence of O'Neill's personal life on his plays cannot be ignored. In his early work he drew on his experiences as a sailor. His days at Jimmy the Priest's, a waterfront saloon in New York, are reflected in the barroom scenes of *Anna Christie* (1920) and *The Iceman Cometh* (written in 1939, produced in 1946). *The Straw* (1921) is set in a sanatorium reminiscent of the one in which O'Neill was a patient during 1912 and 1913. At least part of the story of his brother James is found in *A Moon for the Misbegotten* (1947). O'Neill's memory of his father had a strong influence on the main character of *A Touch of the Poet* (1957).

In 1914 O'Neill enrolled in George Pierce Baker's playwriting course at Harvard. It was there that he learned dramatic theory and received encouragement from Baker to continue his writing. It was at this time that O'Neill's father financed the publication of *Thirst and Other One-Act Plays*. Some of these plays reflect O'Neill's early naturalism and his concern with man in conflict with nature. Shortly thereafter he became associated with the Provincetown Players, an experimental theatre dedicated to the development of a serious American drama. In 1916 this group put on *Bound East for Cardiff*, a drama depicting man's cruelty to his fellow man, though with a floridly romantic ending. It was O'Neill's first play to be acted. During his association with the Provincetown Players, O'Neill learned much about the creation of atmosphere and developed his technique for sharply-etched characterization.

In 1920, when O'Neill's *Beyond the Horizon* was produced, he won the Pulitzer Prize and almost immediate recognition as the leading American playwright of his generation. Like most of O'Neill's early plays, *Beyond the Horizon* is realistic in action and language. It is one of his longest plays and the symbolic arrangement of scenes is similar to the style Strindberg carried to an extreme in *Till Damaskus* (*The Road to Damascus*).

During the next five years O'Neill wrote an average of two plays per year. His prodigious writing created a problem for critics, who could not decide how to categorize O'Neill's work. While *Anna Christie* and *Beyond the Horizon* seemed to be the work of a realist, *The Emperor Jones* (1920) and *The Hairy Ape* (1922) seemed to mark O'Neill as an expressionist. Other of his plays bear the earmarks of naturalism and a personal mysticism.

The Emperor Jones gave audiences a new kind of theatre experience. Essentially, it is a dramatic monologue (a form that fascinated O'Neill throughout his career) which achieves power through its simple structure and elemental theme. All of the action except the introductory scene and the brief final scene takes place in the Great Forest. The play demonstrates one of the themes commonly found in O'Neill's plays—the soul in bondage to itself. Brutus Jones is driven by pride and the will to power. By the end of the play this instinct has pushed him to the point where he has no pride, and instead of being a powerful emperor he is reduced to a pitiful bundle of superstition.

Anna Christie won another Pulitzer Prize for O'Neill, although it suffers from obvious faults; because it was written sporadically, it lacks unity and cohesiveness. Also, in his attempt to project the "sincerity of life," O'Neill discovered that plot may indeed become the enemy of character. An even deeper problem with the play is O'Neill's indecision as to whose play it is to be, Anna's or Chris'. Anna herself is inconsistently drawn. She is first presented as a cynical prostitute, but at the appropriate moment she confesses to her lover and we find that she is now "pure" in soul. Finally, the ending of the play has been criticized for its mixed nature and "failure" as a tragedy.

Desire Under the Elms is one of the high points in O'Neill's career as a writer. The plot itself, as in other O'Neill plays, has echoes of his own background. The father, Ephraim Cabot, is a man incapable of showing love. The dramatic conflict which leads to the tragedy of *Desire* suggests O'Neill's divorce from his first wife and the rejection of their son. It is possible that his early guilt and fear of fatherhood are reflected in this play. O'Neill turns this story of adultery and infanticide into a modern Greek tragedy, where strong passions are exalted. The son rebels against the father and covets his stepmother, and the three characters are seen not as sick people but as human beings with passionate drives whose depth provides their justification.

The growth which O'Neill experienced in writing *The Great God Brown* (1926), *Strange Interlude* (1928), and *Mourning Becomes Electra* (1931), culminated in *The Iceman Cometh, Long Day's Journey into Night,* and *A Moon for the Misbegotten.* The action of these plays takes place in the year 1912, a crucial one in O'Neill's life as it ended in his commitment to a sanitorium because of tuberculosis. The plays are all clearly autobiographical, but their exact significance is unclear to any but O'Neill himself.

In his early plays, O'Neill portrayed the "quest" of his heroes for some "secret" of life. Their sufferings are dramatized and we are often shown how misfortune leads to a tragic recognition of their own nature, and sometimes to a kind of transcendence of that nature. For example, *Mourning Becomes Electra* concludes with the heroine's final recognition of her own evil. In these mature plays, however, the hero seems to be a spectator, rather than an active participant in the tragedy, and if there is a resolution it is that there is no final secret to be discovered.

The Iceman Cometh is a fascinating work due to its complexity and its several levels of meaning. The play, autobiographical in its setting, characterization, and theme, is set in a saloon that resembles Jimmy the Priest's, which O'Neill frequented in his younger days. The play is basically a comedy, but with strong tragic overtones that grow out of the removal of masks. That is, the characters momentarily glimpse the truth about themselves. Their discovery robs them of their dreams, and they must manage to put on their masks once again and regain their dreams or they will die.

After writing *Long Day's Journey into Night,* O'Neill noted that it should not be produced until after his death. When it finally was produced in 1956, it received immediate critical acclaim. The play is neither a drama of action nor violence. Rather than physical action, O'Neill portrays psychological action. We watch Mary Tyrone's journey from the real world in which she "smiles affectionately" at the beginning of the play to a world of drug addiction in which she merely "stares before her in a sad dream." In contrast, Edmund's psychological action is a journey toward personal knowledge and understanding motivated by conflicts with his father and brother. The father's journey is a tragic one, leading away from his earlier triumph. Alcoholic brother Jamie becomes steadily more cynical and hopeless. Eventually the play ends, not with hope but with Edmund's recognition of the truth that surrounds him.

Ben Gazzara appears as Erie Smith in Eugene O'Neill's *Hughie* at the Huntington Hartford Theatre, Los Angeles.

Eugene O'Neill's outstanding reputation is due in large part to his ability to approximate the Classical concept of tragedy. Following Aristotle's guidelines, O'Neill writes of men who are neither good nor evil, and who are defeated but not subdued by some internal force with which they are unable to cope. His dramas portray the psychological struggle of the hero to understand and thus control his psychological reality.

In his Nobel Prize address to the Swedish Academy, Sinclair Lewis perhaps best described O'Neill's contribution to American drama:

> *And had you chosen Eugene O'Neill, who has done nothing much in the American drama save to transform it utterly in ten or twelve years from a false world of neat and competent trickery into a world of splendor, fear, and greatness, you would have been reminded that he had done something far worse than scoffing, that he had seen life as something not to be neatly arranged in a study, but as terrifying, magnificent and often quite horrible, a thing akin to a tornado, an earthquake or a devastating fire.*

George S. Kaufman (1889-1961), born the year after O'Neill and Anderson, came to theatre by a circuitous route. He began in law school, dropped out to become a businessman, found that in business his only talent was as a stenographer, began composing humorous items for Franklin P. Adams' column in the New York *Evening Mail*, tried a column of his own and failed, became a theatre reporter for the Washington *Times*, and eventually became a drama editor. In 1918 his first play, *Someone in the House*, which he wrote with Larry Evans and Walter Percival, was produced. Kaufman went on to write one play by himself, but like the first work so many of his best were written with another party that he became known as the "great colloborator."

Dulcy (with Marc Connelly, 1921) makes use of a light-headed, cliché-mongering female that Kaufman originally created when he was writing for Adams' column. *Merton of the Movies* (with Connelly, 1922) was the first of the satires on Hollywood, and one that Kaufman himself would later exceed in *Once in a Lifetime* (with Moss Hart, 1930). *Beggar on Horseback* (with Connelly, 1924) examines the basic conflict between materialism and art. *The Royal Family* (with Edna Ferber, 1927) is a play about the theatre, especially the Drews and the Barrymores. He followed this with *Dinner at Eight* (with Ferber, 1932) and then another theatre piece, *Stage Door* (with Ferber, 1936), which tells of the experiences of a group of young actresses living in a rundown theatrical boarding house.

Of all Kaufman's collaborators, the most important was Moss Hart (1904-61). Together they wrote such brilliant comedies as *Once in a Lifetime*, *You Can't Take It with You* (1936), and *The Man Who Came to Dinner* (1939). On his own, Hart also completed a number of fine plays: *Face the Music* (1933), *Lady in the Dark* (1941), *Winged Victory* (1943), *Christopher Blake* (1946), *Light Up the Sky* (1948), and *The Climate of Eden* (1952). Unfortunately, his autobiography, *Act One* (1959), only covers Hart's career through the writing of *Once in a Lifetime*.

The middle 1920s, with such playwrights as O'Neill and Kaufman already working, was not a propitious time for a young playwright to begin his career, but in 1923 Philip Barry (1896-1949) had his first professional production with *You and I*. The play was moderately successful and so he followed it in 1924 with *The Youngest*, which failed rather badly. *In a Garden* (1925) was a delightful domestic comedy that did well with critics and audiences, as did *White Wings* (1926).

A scene from *The Royal Family*, by George S. Kaufman and Edna Ferber, with Eva LeGallienne and Rosemary Harris. Directed by Ellis Rabb.

With *John* (1927), a biblical drama, Barry tried to break away from the light, satiric comedy at which he excelled, but it failed and he went back to satiric comedy with *Paris Bound* (1927). A collaboration with Elmer Rice on *Cock Robin* (1928) also failed, and again Barry returned to comedy with one of his best works, *Holiday* (1928). Still trying to write "serious" drama, Barry turned out *Hotel Universe* (1930), a drama that attempts probing psychological insights, but that merely succeeds in boring audiences. *Tomorrow and Tomorrow* (1931) and *The Animal Kingdom* (1932) retrieved Barry's popularity, but *The Joyous Season* (1934), *Bright Star* (1935), and *Spring Dance* (1936) did little to enhance his reputation.

Here Come the Clowns (1938), an allegory of good and evil, and *The Philadelphia Story* (1939), his best comedy of manners, are probably Barry's finest works and plays for which he will be remembered.

In 1927 Robert E. Sherwood (1896-1955) joined this already outstanding group of playwrights with his production of *The Road to Rome*. He had begun working toward a theatrical career at an early age, writing his first plays while still in elementary school. Attending Harvard, he edited the *Lampoon* and joined the Hasty Pudding Club, where his play *Barnum Was Right* was produced in 1917. After serving in World War I in a Canadian regiment and being wounded, Sherwood returned to New York as an embittered pacifist. He wrote for *Vanity Fair, Life, Scribner's*, and the New York *Herald* until the success of his first play induced him to become a full-time playwright.

Sherwood's best work is in the field of light comedy, but he adopted several different styles and tones. *Reunion in Vienna* (1931) is a continental-style bedroom comedy, but he followed this with *The Petrified Forest* (1935), a powerful drama in which a sensitive, artistic intellectual is brutalized by a vicious gangster. The resistable rise of totalitarianism in Europe came under scrutiny in *Idiot's Delight* (1936), and then, in 1938, came the delightfully affirmative *Abe Lincoln in Illinois. There Shall Be No Night* (1940), written as the Nazi forces were overrunning Europe, is not Sherwood's best play, but the agony of the Finnish intellectual who decides to join the resistance and fight to the death makes it one of the most powerful.

More a product of the Depression than any other major playwright, Clifford Odets (1906-63) came out of the Group, where he struggled to create a serious theatre based on social commentary and Stanislavsky realism. His first play, a long one act titled *Waiting for Lefty* (1935), consisted of a series of vignettes describing how a number of workers had been converted to radicalism, and scenes of union meetings. When the play opened on Broadway, Odets added a second long one act, *Till the Day I Die* (1935), dealing with the underground anti-Nazi movement in Germany. In the same year his *Awake and Sing* looked at the causes and effects of the depression by focusing on the economic frustrations faced by an American-Jewish family. The play made Odets one of the most talked about playwrights in America; one people would watch and listen to as a spokesman for the Depression-bred radicalism.

Paradise Lost (1935) did not live up to Odets' reputation or his followers' expectations, but *Golden Boy* (1937) was an enormous success. This story of a young, sensitive, aspiring artist who is forced by the economic situation to give up music for professional boxing seemed to prove that Odets was indeed the playwright of the future. However, it proved to be a hollow expectation. *Rocket to the Moon* (1938), *Night Music* (1940), and *Clash by Night* (1941) all failed to achieve true dramatic distinction. *The Big Knife* (1949) managed to capture audiences with its rather heavy-handed melodramatics, and it was not until *The Country Girl* (1950) and *The Flowering Peach* (1954) that he once again achieved significant dramatic creativity.

One year before Odets burst upon the scene a publisher's reader, book reviewer, and publicist, who had been encouraged to write plays by the novelist Dashiell Hammett, made her appearance with a first play titled *The*

Clifford Odets' depression era drama, *Awake and Sing*. Directed by Alvin Keller.

Children's Hour (1934). Lillian Hellman (1905-   ) was born in New Orleans and grew up dividing her time between that city and New York. Her first play, based on a news story of an incident that happened in Scotland, and selected for her by Hammett, established her as a serious playwright. The play deals with the vicious pattern of destruction that occurs when a malicious child begins the false rumor that her two teachers are lesbians.

A careful and meticulous craftsman, Miss Hellman did not attempt to flood the stage with plays. In 1939 came *The Little Foxes*, the first of her two plays dealing with the rapacious Hubbard family. *Watch on the Rhine* appeared in 1941, a warning against the fascism that had already engulfed Europe; *The Searching Wind* (1944) continues the theme. *Another Part of the Forest* (1946) continued the story of the Hubbards, flashing back to their youth to show how they became the greedy, vicious characters they are. *The Autumn Garden* (1951) is a quiet, essentially Chekhovian play about a group of elderly vacationers who finally understand that they are unable to change what they have become. In 1956 she wrote the script for *Candide*, with music by Leonard Bernstein and lyrics by Richard Wilbur, and then went on to chronicle the possessive love of a sister for her brother in *Toys in the Attic* (1960). *My Mother, My Father and Me* (1963) is an unsuccessful adaptation of Burt Blechman's novel, *How Much?* It ran for only seventeen performances on Broadway.

In, but not of, the 1930s was William Saroyan (1908), who first attracted attention with his short stories and then went on to become a first-rate dramatist. His first play to be staged was a long one act titled *My Heart's in the Highlands* (1939), telling of a poet's battle to keep his integrity in this materialistic world. His next play, *The Time of Your Life,* also in 1939, won the Pulitzer Prize and the Drama Critics Circle Award for its affirmative but searching examination of a people's need for philosophical roots. *Love's Old Sweet Song* (1940) and *The Beautiful People* (1941) both continued Saroyan's theme of affirmation, but without the dramatic power of the earlier works. In *Hello Out There* (1942) he retreated to the one-act form, and *Get Away Old Man* (1943) is a pretentious work about a young writer in conflict with a Hollywood mogul. Saroyan has never seemed able to recapture the quality of his earlier works, though *The Cave Dwellers* (1957) comes close and *Sam the Highest Jumper of Them All* (1960) may yet catch on with directors and the public.

The Guthrie Theatre Company production of Tennessee Williams' *Cat on a Hot Tin Roof.* Directed by Stephen Kanee.

Thomas Lanier Williams (1911-   ) was born in Columbus, Mississippi, and much later adopted the nickname "Tennessee." His father, a traveling salesman, was away from home a great deal, and Williams' childhood, along with that of his sister Rose, tended to be rather traumatic—troubled by the father's absence and a series of illnesses suffered by both the children. Rose was slightly lame, withdrawn, and finally became a recluse. She was used by Williams as the model for Laura in *The Glass Menagerie*.

In 1931 Williams enrolled at the University of Missouri, where he began preparing himself for a career in writing, but lack of financial security soon forced him to withdraw and take the first in a long series of menial jobs which supported him until he finally completed his degree. He resumed his studies at Washington University in St. Louis, with financial help from his grandparents, and began the study of playwriting. In 1937 he entered the University of Iowa to continue his studies, and eventually he was awarded a bachelor of arts degree.

In December 1944 *The Glass Menagerie* opened in Chicago. It received immediate critical acclaim, and in March 1945 it opened in New York, where it ran for over five hundred fifty performances. Now assured of financial security, but perhaps unable to deal with his sudden and great success, Williams' life-style changed dramatically. He left the United States for Mexico to work on the play that eventually became *A Streetcar Named Desire*. His previous stay in the New Orleans French Quarter had provided him with the atmosphere that served him so brilliantly in this play. In 1947 *Streetcar* opened in New York to rave reviews and won for Williams both the Pulitzer Prize and the New York Drama Critics Circle Award.

Since the appearance of *The Glass Menagerie*, Williams has turned out a number of fine and not so fine plays. The best of these, besides *Streetcar*, are *Summer and Smoke* (1948), *The Rose Tattoo* (1950), *Cat on a Hot Tin Roof* (1954, which won Williams a second Pulitzer Prize), *Sweet Bird of Youth* (1959), *Suddenly Last Summer* (produced in 1959 on a double bill with *Something Unspoken*, under the collective title of *Garden District*), and *The Night of the Iguana* (1961).

After Williams, the strongest American playwright of the post-World War II period is Arthur Miller (1915-   ). Miller began his career as a dramatist at the University of Michigan where, as a student, he won three prizes for drama. One of these was the Theatre Guild National Award in 1937, which he shared with Tennessee Williams. After leaving the university he joined the Federal Theatre Project in the final phase of its existence. His first professionally produced play, *The Man Who Had All the Luck* (1944) lasted only five nights on Broadway, but his next work, *All My Sons* (1947), had a long run and won for Miller the Drama Critics Circle Award.

In 1949 Miller's *Death of a Salesman* opened on Broadway to great acclaim, winning the Drama Critics Circle Award and the Pulitzer Prize. This drama about the lack of any permanent, acceptable moral values in middle-class America, and featuring the disintegration and death of Willy Loman, seemed to be the first significant attempt at tragedy since Eugene O'Neill. In 1952 came *The Crucible*, a play about the Salem witch trials, which Miller had conceived back at the university. *A View from the Bridge* (1955) continued Miller's reputation as a writer unafraid to tackle major contemporary problems.

Miller's highly publicized marriage to film actress Marilyn Monroe finally ended in divorce, but it seemed to provide the subject matter for *After the Fall* in 1964. The play was not a success, but a more recent play, *The Price* (1968), has gone far in restoring Miller's prestige as one of the major playwrights of the second half of the century.

A production of Edward Albee's *Tiny Alice* at the Alley Theatre in Houston. Directed by Nina Vance.

William Inge (1913-1973) was primarily a playwright of the 1950s. As the 1950s opened Inge scored a major triumph with *Come Back, Little Sheba* (1950), and followed that with a Pulitzer Prize for *Picnic* (1953). *Bus Stop* followed in 1955, and *The Dark at the Top of the Stairs* in 1957. *A Loss of Roses* (1959) was Inge's first failure.

Since 1960 the work of Edward Albee (1928-   ) has excited theatregoers all over the world. His first play, a one act titled *The Zoo Story*, was first produced in German at the Schiller Theatre in West Berlin in 1959, and early in 1960 it had its American premier off-Broadway on the same bill with Beckett's *Krapp's Last Tape*. In April 1960 his second one act, *The Death of Bessie Smith*, also had its premiere in German, this time at the Schlosspark Theatre in West Berlin. *The Sandbox* (1960), is a very short play about the death of a sympathetic old woman, the only human member of an otherwise deadly dull family. *Fam and Yam*, still another short play and almost as dull as the family in *Sandbox*, also appeared in 1960 at Westport, Connecticut.

In 1961 one of Albee's best works, *The American Dream*, premiered at the York Playhouse. In it the once deadly family of *Sandbox* reappears, this time, however, to some purpose. The play is a powerful satire on life in the middle-American household, and the dialogue that came to nothing in *Sandbox* is, in this later work, a fine parody of American casual conversation.

Who's Afraid of Virginia Woolf?, Albee's first full-length play, opened on Broadway in 1962 and became a critical and box office success, running for nearly two years and winning the Drama Critics Circle Award and the Antoinette Perry Award. *Woolf* was, unfortunately, Albee's high point for many years. *The Ballad of the Sad Café*, an adaptation of Carson McCullers' novella, was Albee's next play to be produced (1963). It had been written before *Woolf*, but it has little of *Woolf's* dramatic power and lasted only four months.

In 1964 *Tiny Alice* premiered, with John Gielgud playing the lay brother. It puzzled critics and audiences alike, and lasted only five months before closing. *Malcolm* (1966), another adaptation, this time from a novel by James Purdy, was easily understandable in its antifeminism, but closed after only seven nights.

Albee's reputation had suffered drastically since *Woolf*, but *A Delicate Balance* (1966) partially restored it. The play is not nearly up to the level of the earlier success, but it played for four months, went on a successful tour, and won the Pulitzer Prize. It clearly did not deserve the award, and most critics felt that the Pulitzer committee was merely attempting to make up for refusing the award to *Woolf*, which clearly had deserved to win. *Everything in the Garden* (1967) was adapted by Albee from an English play by Giles Cooper. Again, it received only a tepid welcome from critics and audience and must be counted a failure.

Following *Garden*, Albee went back to his earlier style, writing two experimental one acts—*Box* and *Quotations from Chairman Mao Tse-tung* (1968). Neither play is up to *Zoo Story* or *American Dream*, but the recent success of *Seascape* (1974) perhaps proves that his experimental style is justified.

Lanford's Wilson's *THE HOT L BALTIMORE,* selected by the New York Drama Critics Circle as the outstanding American play in 1973, at the Mark Taper Forum, Los Angeles.

Perhaps the most seriously underrated playwright of the last thirty years is Neil Simon (1927-), whose string of hit comedies is almost unbelievable. Because these comedies make very few, if any, pretensions to depth or serious social comment, they have usually been avoided as serious works of theatrical art. And yet, several of Simon's plays are at least as significant in their commentary as anything by Plautus or Terence—two comic playwrights still venerated by critics and historians.

Simon began in 1961 with a mildly popular play, *Come Blow Your Horn,* but in 1963, with *Barefoot in the Park,* he established himself as a major comic writer. *The Odd Couple* (1965), *The Last of the Red Hot Lovers* (1970), *The Sunshine Boys* (1972), and *California Suite* (1976) have all had almost astonishing success, not only on stage, but in film and television adaptations.

Since the early 1960s the off-Broadway and regional theatre movement has resulted in productions for a number of young playwrights, but as yet very few have fulfilled what seemed to be their early promise. A few of these writers who have contributed plays of more than passing significance are: Paul Foster, *Tom Paine* (1968); Israel Horovitz, *The Indian Wants the Bronx* (1968); Terrence McNally, *Next* (1969); Rochelle Owens, *Futz* (1961); Robert Patrick, *Kennedy's Children* (1973); David Rabe, *The Basic Training of Pavlo Hummel* and *Sticks and Bones* (both 1971); Sam Shepard, *Chicago* (1965) and *The Tooth of Crime* (1973); and Lanford Wilson, *Hot L Baltimore* (1973).

A scene from Eric Bentley's *Are You Now or Have You Ever Been* at the Cleveland Playhouse, 1976.

THE DIRECTOR

In this century American theatre has been blessed with a number of fine directors—the names of David Belasco and Harold Clurman immediately come to mind. However, the best and most influential director of the twentieth century has almost certainly been Elia Kazan.

ELIA KAZAN: Elia Kazan (1909-   ) vitalized the Broadway stage for a period of more than twenty years. His repeated triumphs created a new awareness of the director's art, and by so doing increased its significance. His imprint on the plays of Tennessee Williams and Arthur Miller was so firm that playwright and director shared equal recognition. These playwrights' dramatic successes have often been attributed to the directorial techniques of Elia Kazan.

Kazan's theatrical career began in 1932 when he joined the Group Theatre as an assistant stage manager. With almost incredible speed he became one of its most dynamic leaders. His life with the Group Theatre led to a succession of directorial successes for a period of ten years on Broadway. Later, in his work at the Actors' Studio, he continued to develop further. So successful were his productions that he was appointed artistic head of the Repertory Theatre at the Lincoln Center in New York when it opened in 1964. However, early in its second season he quietly shed his codirectorship with Robert Whitehead and left the company. He has directed a few films since then, such as *America, America* and *The Arrangement,* but has never returned to the theatre.

Kazan's is a familiar though ironic success story. He was born in a poverty-ridden Greek suburb of Istanbul, Turkey, and was one of eight children. Luckily, his family made their way to the United States when he was five years old. He went to school in Manhattan and attended the Greek Orthodox Church. As his father's rug business began to prosper, they moved to New Rochelle.

When Kazan announced to his father that he would like to be an actor, his father's reply was "Go look in the mirror." Kazan's father wanted his son to enter the rug business, and did not share the boy's enthusiasm for the stage. After completing high school, Kazan entered Williams College, helping to pay his way by waiting on tables in a fraternity house. During the summer months he did odd jobs in a variety of New York theatres. He was graduated *cum laude* from Williams College and, against his father's wishes, he enrolled in the Yale University Drama School. In 1932 he married Molly Day Thatcher, who was also a Yale student.

Kazan was considered a poor actor at Yale and quit the program before long. One of his teachers introduced him to some members of the budding Group Theatre, and he joined them as an apprentice. Clifford Odets and Kazan became good friends, and Kazan acted in Odets' plays for eight years. He was

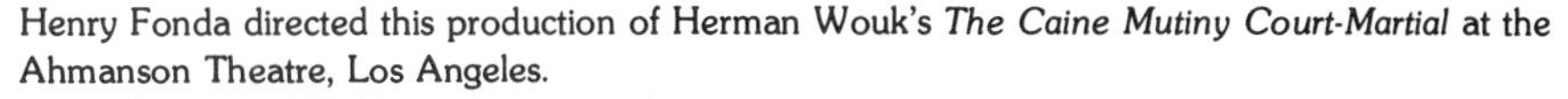
Henry Fonda directed this production of Herman Wouk's *The Caine Mutiny Court-Martial* at the Ahmanson Theatre, Los Angeles.

quite good in these roles and gave some memorable performances—in particular as the taxi driver in *Waiting for Lefty*. He played opposite Luther Adler in *Golden Boy*, with Sylvia Sidney in *The Gentle People*, and with Ingrid Bergman in *Liliom*.

Kazan's early efforts at directing were largely unsuccessful. His first success was *Café Crown*, and when the Group Theatre collapsed in 1941 Kazan was hired to direct the Thornton Wilder fantasy, *The Skin of Our Teeth*. Its merit was considered highly dubious by some who had seen the script, but Kazan undertook the task and along with it the preselected and formidable cast, including Frederic March, Florence Eldridge, and Tallulah Bankhead. It ran for 359 performances and won him the New York Drama Critics Circle Award for the best directing job of 1942. This began his twenty-year cycle of success—*Harriet* (1942), *One Touch of Venus* (1943), *Deep Are the Roots*, and many more. In 1947 the New York Drama Critics Circle voted *All My Sons*, written by Arthur Miller and directed by Kazan, as the best play produced that year. Later, he received the same award for Tennessee Williams' play, *A Streetcar Named Desire*, which established him as one of the most creative and dynamic directors in the American theatre.

Kazan gained recognition as a film director in 1947 when the New York Film Critics Circle selected him as the best director for his work in *Boomerang* and *A Gentlemen's Agreement*. The same critics also voted the latter film as the best of the year. He achieved his directorial "zenith" in film when he received the Motion Picture Academy Award (Oscar) for *A Gentlemen's Agreement*.

A script was never taken at face value by Kazan. Prior to embarking on a rehearsal schedule he lived with and studied the play carefully. He filled stenographic notebooks with random thoughts and ideas about the production, underlining the essential qualities of the play and catching them in a phrase. In this way he arrived at a keynote or a concept on which his production was based. With this unified concept he then cast the play, worked with his designer and staged his production. In some cases, he has even been instrumental in rewriting the script. No playwright working with Kazan sees his work produced exactly as he has written it. Both Arthur Miller and Tennessee Williams have allowed him to adjust their scripts to the staging conceived by Kazan and the designer Jo Mielziner. The playwrights were always pleased with the successful outcomes.

A Streetcar Named Desire was Kazan's most widely acclaimed directorial triumph. His approach capitalized on all of the play's vividness and inherent theatricality without letting it topple over into mere melodrama. With this play Kazan's technique and style as a director achieved its greatest effect.

Arthur Miller has commented on Kazan's directorial style as the search for an inner metaphor. He seeks to dramatize the metaphor in every human action. This is why his work has so much depth. His quest for metaphor explains the unique quality of his productions. Dramatizing metaphor requires a type of digression from realistic staging. This very digression is what enhances Kazan's work. Sometimes this technique was received negatively. Gordon Rogoff marked Kazan as the "master of one side of Americana—'exotica neurotica', the sub-hysterical, tense, limited view of life seen from a couch darkly."

Unfortunately, Kazan's short period at the Lincoln Center did not match his former brilliance. His opening play there was Arthur Miller's *After the Fall.* This play was suitable to Kazan's style and enjoyed a great deal of success. However, the beginning of the second season turned into disaster when he produced Thomas Middleton's *The Changeling*. Obviously Kazan's attempt at the classics was too bold a move for a man who had dealt solely with American realism. His inexperience with period drama was all too evident, and he was not allowed the time for experimentation that had marked his Group Theatre productions. It was all too commercial—there were too many bankers, industrialists, and administrators involved in the "high finance" of the long-awaited Lincoln Center. Kazan could not meet these commercial demands.

Kazan's directorial genius on the stage was matched by his success in motion pictures, but his films have suffered a decline in recent years. His early successes are his most memorable ones. *America, America* and *The Arrangement* cannot compete artistically with *A Tree Grows in Brooklyn* or *East of Eden*, not to mention *A Gentlemen's Agreement.* Nonetheless, Kazan's influence can never be dismissed; his work has created a new epoch in American theatre—one that is still influencing the theatre in our time. No one can think of Tennessee Williams or Arthur Miller without linking Kazan's name with theirs. No other director has held Broadway in such a firm grip for so long a period of time.

CRITICISM

A large part of the phenomenal success and enormous artistic achievement of twentieth century American theatre can be attributed to an excellent collection of theatre critics and scholars. They steadfastly refused to endorse mediocrity and they constantly clamored for artistic excellence and integrity. They established an outstanding list of theatrical ideals, and they insisted that actors and directors alike live up to or exceed these ideals. Perhaps at no other time in history has theatre been more influenced by its living critics.

STARK YOUNG: The formal education of the critic is always of interest and upon occasion has some import; this is particularly true in the case of Stark Young (1881-1963). He entered the University of Mississippi at fourteen, receiving his bachelor's degree in 1901, when he was twenty. From the University of Mississippi he went to Columbia, where he received a master's degree in English in 1902. From 1904 to 1907 he was employed as an instructor in English literature at the University of Mississippi. He was a professor of general literature from 1907 to 1915 at the University of Texas, and professor of English at Amherst College from 1915 to 1921. In 1921 he resigned to become a member of the editorial staff of the *New Republic*, a position he held until 1947 except for one year (1924-25) when he served as drama critic for the New York *Times*. Also, from 1921 to 1940 he served as associate editor of *Theatre Arts Monthly*. In addition to holding down these positions he was also writing, and by 1926 he had published three collections of dramatic criticism—*The Flower in Drama* (1923), *Glamour* (1925), *Theatre Practice* (1926)—and his first novel, *Heaven*

Trees (1926). Furthermore, before this same year he had completed an original translation of *Mandragola*, Macchiavelli's classic Italian comedy, and of Jean-François Regnard's *Le légataire universel* (*The Sole Heir*), from the standard repertory of the Comédie-Française.

The broad knowledge of general literature which his background indicates saved Young from the narrowness of outlook which often overtakes critics in such specialized fields as music, painting, and drama. In his early years he wrote plays of his own, both long and short, and in prose and verse. *The Saint* was produced by the Provincetown Players in 1924 and *The Colonnade* by the London Stage Society in 1926. He also gained some limited practical experience as a director, having directed Lenormand's *The Failures* for the Theatre Guild and O'Neill's *Welded* for a private producer.

Young had a special talent in his critical writing of doing away with unnecessary comment. Although upon occasion he might have seemed to be elaborate he was, in fact, a critic in the sense that his primary thrust was understanding and defining theatre. And he was a teacher in the purest sense. Within his collections of criticisms (*Glamour, The Flower in Drama, Immortal Shadows*) are many examples which illustrate his ability to describe theatrical phenomena in a manner appealing to both the general reader and the professional theatre worker. And he was able to make his judgments tactfully and justly.

Young's ability to analyze critically did not, however, result in scientific coldness or detachment. Indeed, his writing emphasized emotional quality. For instance, Young described Charlie Chaplin's clown as "foolish, pathetic, irrepressible, flickering, comical, lovable beyond all words," and coined such phrases as "sexless gallantry," and "tireless curiosity." He did not base his works on some kind of scientific foundation, but rather on the emotional impressions he received. His elaborate word imagery was merely an attempt to record his own and the audience's responses more fully and accurately.

A good starting point in determining Young's theories of acting and theatre in general would be examining his attitude about the developing concept of realism in acting. Although many people were, at this time, totally devoted to Stanislavsky's discoveries and the use and study of "the Method," Young held to a somewhat different point of view. Although Young did not discount the influence—or indeed the effectiveness—of the Moscow Art Theatre, he did resist the idea that realism is the equivalent of good acting. He asserted that when most people criticize actors they fail even to discuss acting at all. Instead their criticisms tend to be "a matter of mere impression and mutual personalities." Indeed, most lovers of the theatre do not think of acting fundamentally; instead they mostly discuss the exciting pleasure provided by "some radiant being there on the stage." They confuse "personal distinction" and "magnetism" with acting ability. It is understandable that this confusion exists since it is the actor that is employed as the medium; the actor's very presence creates the art. This individual magnetism on the part of the performer can be found, to some degree, in all the arts, but that quality is not the art. However, in acting particularly this quality is "part of the material" that is used, as is the voice, the body, and the mind.

John Steinbeck's *Of Mice and Men* at the Guthrie Theatre Company. Directed by Len Cariou.

Acting is *first* a craft. An actor who lacks personal magnetism or distinction can still be a good actor by knowing his craft. On the other hand, a person of great distinction, who "lacks a rounding in these essentials of acting, may be by temperament an artist but not yet an actor." Through his craft the actor translates life into his own terms and then adds that special quality which is his own as a creative artist.

In spite of all this, to conclude that Young was anti-realistic would be an error. He was very much against realism being equated with "good" acting, and he was totally against theatrical elements being abolished from the stage.

Stark Young had more specific ability and perception in terms of performance (and perhaps dramatic literature) than in any other area of theatre. He could describe the quality of movement, tempo, speed, level of execution, motivation, and illusion with a completeness and intelligibility that surpassed most other critics. And this critical perception was not just related to acting alone, but to all the other aspects of staging a play. For example, Young felt that a movement in and of itself is nothing. A gesture is a movement that "ensues from what came before and proceeds into what comes after." Duse did not, he pointed out, simply bow from her hips, but with every part of her body from her eyelids to her toes. In other words, the gesture must possess an unbroken flow as does a scene. "A moment approaches its most complete establishment, it arrives, but even as it arrives it is breaking down into what comes after." It is the rhythm toward and from itself that makes a movement alive. An entrance, like any other stage movement, must carry that quality of just having been some place, and with some place still to go.

On the subject of speed it was Young's opinion that all New York productions (read American) badly needed speeding up. Many scenes are, after all, merely dialogue statements, yet through great motivation (which the actor all too often feels is justified by intent) many American actors perform at a level of self-indulgence when it is not necessary and even when it is destructive to the playwright's intention.

Another aspect of dramatic creation is variety of tempo—all too often actors pick up their own tempo from the previous speech. This is particularly bad since each role has its own tempo, its own "time pattern. . . . What is true of visual design is true for the ear also: That every section of a play is a time-centre in itself, to which surrounding parts are related; all these centres in their turn are related to larger centres, and so on."

Young also found it worthwhile to comment on the difference between "obvious" and "inevitable." He stated that "a great moment is never obvious." After the moment is accomplished it becomes obvious in the sense that "the thing stands out as what we expected, as what would more or less naturally ensue." The inevitable, on the other hand, has the qualities of surprise and satisfaction at the same time. "The inevitable is like the sun on the wall; it is simple, complete too, but infinitely subtle, full of nuances, inexhaustible."

It has been emphasized that Young's contribution to theatre was not so much in resolving disputes as to whether this or that style was right or wrong, but in his ability to accurately describe the style chosen and then consider how well the choice worked. In his commentaries on the function of the director the same holds true. With changing times the functions have varied, and the ways in which the materials, literature, and the actors are utilized have also changed. However, because of his descriptive ability Young's theories still have interest today.

It must be realized, Young felt, that "the director has the same relation to the theatre that the orchestra conductor has to music." In other words, he uses the play in the same way as the conductor uses the score, and he uses the actors in the same way as the conductor uses the musicians. He creates a theatrical body to complete the idea he has derived from the play. Some directors, Young found, desert the play in an attempt to achieve "virtuosity," which means, essentially, using the materials of the play to express the director's own idea. A production becomes completely virtuoso when the main idea of the work and the mood are cast aside for the sake of expressing the director's personal idea. This, Young felt, is unfortunate, and the director who does it, who "distorts the play and forces it to ends not its own but his," is destructive not only to the individual play but to the art as well.

At the other end of the theatrical spectrum stands the director who translates as closely as possible into the theatrical medium that which he feels the playwright intended, eschewing all of his own ideas. Obviously the virtuoso director elects to do material suggesting ideas that he, himself, wants to express, but he cannot help being influenced, to some degree, by the materials.

Just as obviously the second director cannot help but insert some of himself into the materials he selects. Both directors, however, face major considerations that are extremely important in terms of the theatrical medium.

First of all, each director must consider in what ways he will use all of the elements—what balance and proportion he will strive to achieve. He must determine how he will utilize the play, the acting, the decor, and the stage movement to best express the idea. In directing a good play it is a combination of "the individual characterizations, the ensemble and the mutual exchange among the actors that must convey the idea." In a poor play, on the other hand, everything depends on the acting, "on the pathos and sentiment that the actors create." The director, then, must weigh time values and visual rhythm in the stage movement. He must "consider how much of the content of a theatre work will most fully appear in atmosphere and design, how much, that is, he will depend for his effects on the decor provided the play." In short, he must "see with his eyes" the perspective in which his production will take form.

Secondly, "within the nature of the play itself there is a problem for the director." He must see which aspects are subordinate to one another, what the main themes are, and determine the sequence of its parts. "*Othello,* for example, lives in its outline. The round pattern of the plot and of the leading characters is what expresses the idea, within this outline the shadings appear." Chekhov's plays need a "monotony of emphasis," whereas *Tartuffe* needs intense stress in the third quarter of the play. The director must also see the "relation of the lines and actions to the whole of the play."

Third, and finally, the director has to consider carefully his use of the actor, "for the actor is his cardinal medium." At one extreme the director lets the actor entirely alone. This might "freshen the acting by bringing into it more of the actor's own quality and way of creation." On the other hand, thirty actors in one scene, or even eight, could not be left to develop continuity or judge the ensemble effect. At the other extreme we have the director who gives his actors every bit of business, who spells out the interpretation and keeps a tight rein on every aspect of the entire production. This method might provide a "better chance for a regulated whole" as the actors develop into their roles, and there is less hit and miss in any area of coordination. However, the acting may (and almost certainly will) become mechanical and dry.

Stark Young died in 1963. To list his accomplishments, from reviews to critical essays to full-length critical works, would still not capture the whole of his contribution. He had not only a critical quality and attitude, but a defining gift that, more than anything else, makes up Young's contribution to theatre theory.

JOSEPH WOOD KRUTCH: The effect that Joseph Wood Krutch (1893-1970) has had on American drama during the last forty years is immense. For many years the resident drama critic of the *Nation* and, from 1925 to 1953, Brander Matthews Professor of Dramatic Literature at Columbia, Krutch was in an excellent position to influence the course that American drama would follow, and he did so in an impressive series of books: *Comedy and Conscience After the Restoration* (1924); *The Modern Temper* (1929); *The American Drama Since 1918* (1939); and *"Modernism" in Modern Drama* (1953).

Some critics and scholars, referring to Krutch, have attempted to link him to the naturalistic school of philosophy and, of course, criticism. However, in most cases he is identified as belonging to that group often called the Early Psychological Critics. For example, Walter Sutton, in *Modern American Criticism*, puts Krutch into this category. One of the reasons for assigning Krutch in this manner was his early work on Edgar Allan Poe (*Edgar Allan Poe: A Study in Genius*, 1926) in which, as Sutton perceptively points out, "Krutch isolates an early conflict as the key to Poe's life and writing. But this conflict, crippling as it was to Poe personally, was the enabling act that unlocked his peculiar genius and compelled its expression."

Although this book on Poe has become a standard critical work, Krutch later found some of his psychological concepts embarrassing.

> *What does surprise and now somewhat embarrasses me is that I seem to have been so taken by popular Freudianism as to all but equate neurosis and genius. . . . That neuroses are common while genius is rare is sufficient to suggest that the two are not identical. . . . It is easy enough to show that Shakespeare was Elizabethan, but such interpretative explanation leaves unanswered the question why all Elizabethans were not Shakespeare.*

The retreat from "popular Freudianism" implicit in the above passage signaled a return to more basic values that were founded, if not on the strictures of Aristotle, at least on the concepts he had gained from close study of both Greek and Elizabethan tragedy. This retreat had major import in terms of his dramatic criticism.

Probably the best known of Krutch's works, and certainly the most controversial, is *The Modern Temper*. It is a series of essays on the state of man as Krutch saw him during the decade of the twenties, and it seemed to be directed primarily at the attitudes, modes of living, and direction that life was taking during this time. The book was published just a few months before the stock market crash, which caused the almost immediate development of a whole new set of attitudes on life, attitudes which were markedly different from those of the early and even late twenties. However, despite its remarkably bad timing *The Modern Temper* had a strong impact in its own time and is still basic reading today. Although the book as a whole does not deal directly with drama, one chapter, "The Tragic Fallacy," is especially important for drama and has become the most discussed and most often reprinted chapter in the book.

To understand just what Krutch is saying in "The Tragic Fallacy" it is essential to remember that it is one essay in a series of essays; therefore an examination of the first chapter, which sets the stage for the rest of the book, is necessary. The first chapter begins: "It is one of Freud's quaint conceits that the child in his mother's womb is the happiest of living creatures. Into his consciousness no conflict has yet entered and the universe is as he wishes it to be." This chapter, titled "Love—Or the Life and Death of a Value," makes the point that science has tended to reduce life to a matter of mere biology. Krutch emphasizes his belief that "what had once been either a sin, a sacred mystery, or an aesthetic game was now a matter of biological function, and that while one might live for love either as a mystery or as a game, one could not very well live for it as merely nature's device for securing the survival of the species."

Act 1, scene 1, which serves as a prologue to *The Green Pastures*, from the 1931 Chicago production directed by the author, Marc Connelly, and designed by Robert Edmond Jones.

The point of all this is Krutch's belief that modern man has suffered a trauma in which he finds himself all alone in a universe that accords him very little importance. And yet, he feels, it is the nature of man to imagine a universe the way it should be, with himself at its center. This universe in which man finds himself is, thus, one in which the human spirit cannot be comfortable. Further, it is a universe that can only be revealed by modern knowledge and modern deduction.

> *That spirit breathes freely only in a universe where Value Judgments are of supreme importance. It needs to believe, for instance, that Right and Wrong are important and enduring realities, that Love is more than a biological function, that the human mind is capable of reason rather than merely of rationalization, and that it has the power to will and choose instead of being compelled to react in a fashion predetermined by its conditioning.*

Krutch believes that psychology, biology, and anthropology have conspired to convince modern man that none of the above beliefs is more than illusion, thus requiring either a surrender of our humanity and an adjustment to the real but alien world, or a life that becomes, in fact, a tragic existence in a world alien to our deepest needs.

"The Tragic Fallacy" is based on Krutch's deep-seated belief that the greatest tragic drama, that of Greece and Elizabethan England, for example, has always been associated with ages of confidence and a strong belief in the essential, indestructable greatness of man. The drama of such an age, Krutch said, "in order to produce its tonic effect . . . must exclaim when it contemplates [man's] refusal to be utterly defeated 'How like a God!' and it must find a new world 'brave' because it 'hath such creatures in it.' " Of course our world is not like that, as we have already found out; consequently since man has accepted defeat he is destined to be, even in art, more pitiful than tragic.

Krutch states flatly that "tragedies, in that only sense of the word which has any distinctive meaning, are no longer written in either the dramatic or any other form and the fact is not to be accounted for in any merely literary terms." It must, in fact, be accounted for in terms of the philosophy of the age, and the philosophies of the ages that produced great tragedy were God centered, as opposed to the modern age which is human centered.

> *Thus for the great ages tragedy is not an expression of despair, but the means by which they save themselves from it. It is a profession of faith, and a sort of religion; a way of looking at life by virtue of which it is robbed of its pain.*

Krutch did point out that "a tragic writer does not have to believe in God, but he must believe in Man"; that is, the belief must be that man is something more than animal—that he exceeds biology.

Not every age can achieve a faith which produces great tragedy. It is only at a certain stage of development of the progress toward a realistic intelligence that this faith can exist. A primitive society, or rather an unsophisticated culture, has its mythology, and the twenties were too sophisticated. What such a faith demands is an almost "adolescent belief in the nobility of man which marks a Sophocles or a Shakespeare."

Of the decade to (and about) which he was writing, Krutch said:

> *Distrusting its thought, despising its passions, realizing its impotent unimportance in the universe, it can tell itself no stories except those which make it still more acutely aware of its trivial miseries. When its heroes . . . are struck down it is not, like Oedipus, by the gods that they are struck but only, like Oswald Alving, by syphilis, for they know that the gods, even if they existed, would not trouble with them, and they cannot attribute to themselves in art an importance in which they do not believe.*

When, in 1956, Krutch was asked to write a brief preface to the paperback edition of *The Modern Temper*, he reevaluated his position in the original book and came to the conclusion that while his description of the origins of his *Temper* were as valid as ever, that the hopelessness he had felt in 1929 was no longer justified. Instead he postulated the "Minimal Man" who can be defined as a creature endowed with the following characteristics:

> *(1) The capacity to be at least sometimes "a thinking animal" who can, on occasion, reason rather than merely rationalize; (2) The ability sometimes to exercise some sort of will and choice which enable him on these occasions to resist conditions, traumas, and "the dialectic of matter"; (3) The power of making value judgments which are not always, inevitably, and no more than, a rationalization of the mores of his society. Or, to sum it all up, a man who cannot think as well as "react" is not a man at all.*

All in all, Krutch does come too close to home in his assessment of modern man's idea of his own worth and the effect of this idea on tragic drama. Whether tragic drama is impossible to achieve in our own age is a topic that is still being debated, and a measure of Krutch's influence can be seen in the fact that such recent theorists of tragedy as Arthur Miller still find it necessary to debate with a chapter of a book written in 1929.

GEORGE JEAN NATHAN: George Jean Nathan (1882-1958), began his critical career by writing for newspapers as a cub reporter, but he quickly tired of covering what he called "the dog bites man" stories. He soon left his first job, probably by request, since Nathan, the great dissenter, would in most cases champion the canine, while at the same time taking the dog to task for lack of taste. This sardonic streak did not serve Nathan well as a reporter for the more traditional journals, and he was forced to write for more liberal organs, specifically *Smart Set,* a magazine which featured another misanthropic social critic, H. L. Mencken.

Nathan and Mencken proved to be too much, even for the hardy readers of *Smart Set,* and so after many editorial battles they left the magazine to begin *The American Mercury.* Eventually this became a distinguished journal, sometimes given over to tilting at windmills, but often doing battle with real monsters.

Most of Nathan's usually penetrating critiques were written for the two above-mentioned magazines, along with *Esquire, Life,* and the *Saturday*

Los Endrogados, by Luis Valdez, performed by El Teatro Espiritu de Aztlan. Directed by Caesar Flores.

Review. Nathan eventually became the highest-paid theatre critic in America, a poor yardstick of success by his own judgment but a valid one nonetheless and one he was delighted to live up to.

Nathan eventually established a reputation as a sure judge and champion of young playwrights, having influenced and encouraged such talents as Sean O'Casey, Eugene O'Neill, Lord Dunsany, James Joyce, Aldous Huxley, Theodore Dreiser, and William Saroyan. In particular, O'Neill's first full-length play went a-begging until it was discovered by Nathan. It was because of his influence that *Beyond the Horizon* was produced, giving O'Neill his first major exposure.

Even prior to his sojourn in New York, Nathan had become an experienced man of the world. Born of wealthy parents in Indiana, he spent his summers abroad until entering Cornell. This exposure to the world outside of America later served him well in his writing and in the formulation of his critical judgment. Too, the foreign critics could not accuse him, as they did nearly all other American critics, of provincialism.

Throughout his life, Nathan regularly did battle with the theatrical equivalent of the gods on Olympus, particularly George Pierce Baker and William Archer. Baker always stressed dramatic structure as the backbone of a play. It was Nathan's belief that a play should be accepted if it works, with no regard for its structure. He also disagreed with Baker on the latter's pronouncement that a character must never be inconsistent. Nathan felt that real people rarely if ever conform; therefore, a stricter standard should not be demanded of stage characters.

William Archer was another prime target of Nathan's indignation. The basis of the disagreement was Archer's contention that a great play must necessarily have a message. Nathan thought this to be absolutely ridiculous. What, he asked, "is the nature of the 'message' of Huckleberry Finn, of the Iliad, of Michelangelo's sculpture, of a Brahms trio, . . . of the Grand Central Station? The message in each of these cases is simply, and nothing more than, this: that a great artist has achieved perfect form in his own domain of art. That is the only message that real art carries." To Nathan the worth of a play was measured in its emotional rather than its intellectual content. If one wanted ideas, one could easily turn to Kant or Hegel.

Along these lines, Nathan also took issue with Brooks Atkinson. Atkinson promoted the idea that the subject of a play was of paramount importance, and that all else derived from that. In response Nathan stated that "in judging a work of art, the choice of subject is a fact of relatively minor importance. The subject of one of Rembrandt's finest works of art is an old woman cleaning her fingernails. The subject of one of Bach's is a protest against the drinking of coffee."

In assessing the critical work of George Jean Nathan, it is necessary to not let his facile, chic arrogance detract from his real contributions. On the positive side, Nathan gave style, wit, and intelligence to American criticism. Through his writing and because of his power he helped to encourage what he considered to be the good in our theatre (such as O'Neill, Saroyan, and the off-Broadway movement) and to discourage what he sometimes wrongly considered to be the bad (such as Belasco, Augustus Thomas, and the star system).

He was, throughout his life, a crusader against puritanism, both on the part of the audience and the critics. In particular, he helped theatre to get away from the influence of William Winter, the reigning American critic prior to Nathan, who damned any play that did not live up to his moral values.

On the negative side, Nathan has been accused, justly, of an almost obsessive flippancy. True to his personal code, he took nothing seriously. He mocked everything, especially (and this was his saving grace) himself.

INTO THE FUTURE

Trying to predict—or even guess—the direction theatre will take during the closing years of this century is next to impossible. During the last two decades theatre all over the Western world has undergone major changes with a swiftess that is both unprecedented and bewildering. The social revolution of the 1960s, especially, had its effects on theatre, and the growth of the communications industry made these effects felt almost instantaneously. As a consequence, theatre went through a spasm of -isms, culminating in "absurdism," a catch-all title that managed somehow to include within its boundaries such varied movements as free theatre, open theatre, guerrilla theatre, people's theatre, and even theatre of the grotesque.

The 1960s came stumbling frantically to an end, and slowly the undisciplined experimentation of the decade gave way to a new emphasis on craft as well as art, on technique as well as emotion, on the word as well as the action. This retrenchment has been, on the whole, necessary and healthy. The new techniques developed during the 1960s are being applied systematically rather than haphazardly, and the new freedom to deal in any way with any topic is being exploited with care and precision and not used merely to bludgeon the audience.

What direction theatre will take in the next few years may be unpredictable, but it will certainly be exciting.

Index